Becoming Lili

Volume One
of
The Perennials Trilogy

Julia Blake

copyright ©Julia Blake 2017
All rights reserved

Sele Books
www.selebooks.com

This is a work of fiction. All characters and events in this publication, other than those in the public domain, are either a product of the author's imagination or are used in a fictitious manner. Any resemblance to actual persons, living or dead, or actual events is purely coincidental.

No part of this publication may be reproduced, distributed, or transmitted in any form or by any means, without the written permission of the author, except in the case of brief quotations embodied in critical reviews and certain other non-commercial uses permitted by copyright law.

For permission requests contact the author

www.juliablakeauthor.co.uk

ISBN 9781546386704

Becoming Lili is written in British English and has an estimated UK cinema rating of 18+
containing explicit sexual description
and mild language

Becoming Lili is an Authors Alike accredited book

Dedication

To my parents, as ever, thank you.
Oh, and Mum, Dad – please skip the sexy bits!

To all my Instagram family, you know who you are,
thanks for your support and for believing in me.

To Kim
Best Wishes
Julia Blake
x

Acknowledgements

So many people to say thank you to – firstly, to my editor and dear friend, Danielle Vinson, who had the daunting task of going through every single word of this novel – all 175,000 of them – and picking up any typos. Thank you, my dear, I promise to try and never write such a long book again!

Then there are my beta readers – Michelle Leigh Miller and Becky Wright, who very kindly gave up their time to painstakingly read the finished novel and alert me to any bits there weren't quite right. Both are talented authors, and you can find them at:

www.michelleleighmiller.com
www.beckywrightauthor.com

And a huge thanks to Becky Wright at the wonderful Platform House Publishing for all your help with formatting. Your patience, friendship, and support over the years have literally saved my life more times than I care to remember. Without you, I doubt I'd ever have got this writing lark off the ground.

Becky and the crew at Platform House Publishing are also responsible for the awesome cover, and for all your publishing needs why not contact them at:

www.platformhousepublishing.co.uk

Finally, I need to say a huge thank you to my daughter, Francesca. Thank you for helping your old mum with all the tech bits she didn't understand, and for patiently inserting all the illustrations and twiddly bits. I know how fiddly they were, and I am truly grateful you did them for me.

A Note for the Reader

Since the publication of The Book of Eve, readers have been begging for more. Whilst this is not a book about Eve and Scott – I feel their tale is done, sorry – this story is set in the lovely historical town of Bury St Edmunds, so many of the same locations will appear. Being set in the 1990's it won't feature any of the characters from Eve, or will it? Keep your eyes peeled, there might be the odd one or two scattered throughout!

As ever, I always appreciate comments, thoughts, or maybe even simple shout outs on Instagram @juliablakeauthor and Goodreads. And why not sign up to read my humorous blogs about life, parenthood and writing on "A Little Bit of Blake"

https://juliablakeauthor.home.blog/

Finally, there is my website for information about me, as well as background on all my books.

www.juliablakeauthor.co.uk

All the best
Julia Blake

Becoming Lili

Part One

Phyllis
1990~1996

Once ... there was an ugly duckling girl ...

Chapter One
"I feel so guilty I can't seem to like my own child."

First day of term. A new school year. The playground bulged with excited, noisy children all renewing old ties and resentments. In the car park, ancient buses heaved into pre-designated bays, disgorging more masses to add to the hoards.

Her hair was long and shapeless; its flatness plastered around her small head, the long fringe trailing in her eyes, making her peer anxiously from beneath its protective curtain. Its colour was called mousey by adults, shit brown by other children, and she hated it. Its stark difference to the bright curls and glossy bobs of other girls gave them another reason to mark her out as a target.

Although short, she was plump, another cause for anxiety. In a more innocent and forgiving age, it would have been called puppy fat, such a label giving hope the condition would be grown out of. But here, now, she was simply called fat pig, bloater, and pudding. Such terms gave no hope; only a failing sense of self-worth, and despair that things would never change.

Her eyes darted furtively as she made it as far as the playground without confrontation. Like an agent behind enemy lines, she kept her head down, trying to blend in, desperate to become invisible.

The bus ride to school had passed uneventfully, the other children too busy with news and events of the long summer holiday to bother with a small, brown ghost hunched miserably in the corner. There was plenty of time; a whole new school year stretched ahead, and she was having nightmares at the thought.

The boasting, bragging voices rose until the bus was a solid wall of sound. She sank deeper into herself, wearing her loneliness like a protective cloak. No one bothered to talk to her. She was the most despised girl in school, and as such was avoided by others, lest they were contaminated with the curse of her unpopularity. The only exception was when she was being bullied, then it was open season.

Phyllis. That was her. Named after her grandmother by a mother who couldn't be bothered to think of anything else. A mother who had been shocked to find herself pregnant with an unplanned, unwanted child. She spent the whole nine months in a state of denial, experiencing childbirth through a daze of drugs, then she gladly handed the baby over to a nanny, and scuttled with relief back into the arms of her passionately loved husband.

Phyllis loved her grandmother deeply. In the absence of any parental affection, she was the only source of loving concern she had ever known, but she wished she had another name, and that her mother had realised how important names are; how they label you to the rest of the world.

As Phyllis slunk furtively up the path, avoiding eye contact, gaze fixed determinedly on her feet, she wondered if things would be different this year. After all, they were older and more mature. With luck, her tormentors would have put aside such childish things and would leave her be.

A dim hope flickered. To be left alone was the most Phyllis ever allowed herself to dream about. Sometimes in her secret, most innermost thoughts, the notion of having a friend dared to form. During rare, wonderful dreams, she was surrounded by a gang of admiring and loving friends. She was the leader and was liked, perhaps even loved, but such fantasies were quickly dismissed.

Silly Philly couldn't have friends. It wasn't allowed. Even if there were those in school who didn't hate her, or felt sorry for the way she was treated, self-preservation meant they would never show their feelings. To do so could lead to them being treated the same way.

A group of older boys were congregated near the school's entrance. Only five minutes into the new term and already ties were off, sleeves rolled up and shirts pulled out, all desperately trying to break free from the depersonalisation of school uniform. Not realising that in their identical alterations of it, they were imposing another uniform of sorts upon themselves.

A snicker of laughter arose as Phyllis passed. Her heart thudded acknowledgement, but she kept on going. The older boys were not the ones she feared. They contented themselves with name-calling, the odd sarcastic comment, but nothing physical and nothing that truly hurt. No, the girls were the worst. Seeming to have a natural gift for inflicting pain, for knowing what to say or do to achieve maximum effect, Phyllis's female peers took bitchiness to new levels.

A teacher stood guard at the door and Phyllis's heart sank. Mr Jackson was well known for his quirky, idiosyncratic ways, and all the popular students clamoured to be in his class. Those were his favourites – his little coterie of hangers-on, who stroked his over-inflated ego, and made up, in part, for the fact that he was stuck in an over-crowded, rural middle school, instead of teaching in some posh private school, where he could impart knowledge into the grateful minds of rich students.

With slower pupils he barely contained his impatience, reducing to tears those who fumbled, fell behind, or didn't understand the first time. Phyllis was his special target. She dreaded his lessons, knowing she would be the butt of his sarcastic, biting wit, as he played up to his devoted followers.

She stopped and risked a glance up. His eyes were on her, sharp and cruel, cutting like a razor.

"And where do you think you're going, Phyllis?"

"Library, Sir."

"Surely, you've been at school long enough to know the rules, Phyllis. The bell hasn't rung, which means no one can enter its hallowed halls unless there are special circumstances. Are you a special circumstance, Phyllis?"

She felt the sullen expression on her face, could almost see herself through his eyes – a plain, unintelligent pudding of a girl, staring back at him through dead eyes, face devoid of all emotion under the unflattering, heavy fringe.

"No, Sir," she mumbled, hearing the barely suppressed laughter from the group of boys. Mr Jackson flicked a glance their way, relishing in his audience.

"No Phyllis, you certainly aren't a special circumstance. Now, run along."

"Yes, Sir." Phyllis turned despondently and ran straight into her worst nightmare. Five of them, arms linked, forming a solid barrier across the path with *her*, Michelle Rampling, in the middle. School femme fatale, thirteen, already in possession of a body ripe with promise, her well-developed curves and pouting blonde prettiness enough to give male teachers uneasy thoughts.

She eyed Phyllis with disdain, gaze flicking left and right to her cronies seemingly arranged in descending order of height and attractiveness, the better to showcase Michelle's rather obvious charms. To older, more experienced women, it was obvious that her ripe beauty would quickly fade into coarse flabbiness, but to Phyllis's twelve-year-old eyes, Michelle was the very epitome of female beauty. She was also the meanest bitch on the planet.

"Get out of our way, Silly Philly." Sharon Manners, chief henchman, and confidante cast a scathing look at Phyllis and glanced at Michelle, seeking approval for her opening salvo.

"Now, now girls," chided Mr Jackson mildly, cheeks flushing, as Michelle shot him a hormone-laden look which had him fiddling nervously with his tie.

"Hello, Mr Jackson," chorused the girls in unison, their clumsy attempts at flirtation even more effective for the allure of underage, forbidden fruit.

"Did you have a good holiday, Sir?" continued Michelle, pout more pronounced as she fixed her sooty-lashed, large blue eyes on his face. He swallowed, enjoying the attention, but realising the potential danger of the situation.

"Yes, yes, I did, thank you for asking, Michelle. Was your holiday good?"

"Oh, it was interesting, Sir."

"Interesting in what way, Michelle?"

"Well, let's say I learnt a little about life, Sir," Michelle cast a sly, sideways glance at her friends who all giggled self-consciously, before fixing her gaze once more upon the teacher.

"If you know what I mean, Sir."

Phyllis observed dispassionately how Mr Jackson seemed without a sarcastic or witty comeback. She marvelled that a few, carefully chosen words from a girl young enough to be his daughter, could render a grown man speechless. Michelle took a step forward, annoyed gaze flicking in Phyllis's direction.

"What you still doing here?" she demanded, and Sharon stepped up behind her.

"Yeah, Silly Philly, we told you to get out of our way."

"You really shouldn't call her that."

Phyllis looked up in surprise at the words uttered by Tanya Bryant. Thin and dark, she was the least attractive of the group, but the most dangerous. Her cruelly clever way with words, and readiness to let the others copy her perfect schoolwork, were all skills which had enabled her to bargain her way into the inner sanctum. Now Phyllis frowned as one of her most deadly enemies spoke in her defence.

"You shouldn't call her that," Tanya repeated, a spiteful, thin smile spreading across her face. "You should call her this," Tanya whispered in Michelle's ear and Michelle sniggered, promptly whispering it to Sharon and the others, who laughed nastily.

"You're right," said Michelle. "It was wrong of us to call you Silly Philly. We do apologise. No, Tanya's thought of a much better name." Phyllis's heart sank as she waited, head bowed, for the latest indignity to be heaped upon her.

"From now on," Michelle paused, glancing at the group of watching boys, then at the teacher to ensure that she was centre stage and that she had her audience's complete and undivided attention. "From now on, your name is Syphilis!"

The boys roared with approval, the name passed like a chant amongst them and out into the playground where it moved through the other groups of children like a Mexican wave. Soon the whole playground was abuzz, pointing her out to each other and laughing.

In despair, she turned to her teacher. Surely, he would act and stop this blood-sport. His mouth twitched with barely suppressed amusement, and Phyllis knew she'd receive no help from him.

The school bell rang, and the hordes rushed the door. Pushed and jostled, Phyllis's new name was jeered and catcalled in her face.

Someone barged into her, knocking her bag to the floor, and a laugh rippled through the masses.

Phyllis slowly retrieved her bag, and at a snail's pace made her way to registration, her hopes that this year would be different laying in shattered pieces at her feet. Older and more mature they might be, but she saw this merely meant the bullying would be subtler, more sophisticated, though no less painful to endure.

Is this it? Phyllis thought in despair. Is this my life - this misery, this hell? She longed for escape, but knew it to be an impossible dream, as far removed from reality as her secret hopes to have a friend one day ...

It was bitterly cold. A snowstorm had descended over the weekend, forcing Phyllis and her parents to endure two days cooped up together. Phyllis stayed in her room, only emerging for meals, using the tried and tested tactic of only speaking when spoken to. But even that hadn't protected her, as her mother's exasperated "Oh for heaven's sake, Phyllis, must you always be so sulky?" had proven.

It was Monday morning again. School again. Following such a tortuous weekend, Phyllis was almost pleased to be going back. Almost, but not quite. No matter how dire the weekend had been, nothing was as bad as the hell that was school.

It was snowing. Great fat, blobby snowflakes stuck to her eyelashes and fringe before melting in a sharp sting of cold on her face. As she trudged towards the bus stop, well wrapped up against the cold and wearing the new bobble hat her grandmother had knitted for her thirteenth birthday two weeks earlier, Phyllis braced herself for what was to come.

It started even before she'd crossed the road to join the other waiting children.

"Nice hat, Syphilis," called Tanya. "Which charity shop did you nick it from?"

The children hooted with laughter, and someone threw a snowball which struck her cheek with painful force. Phyllis had been touched when she unwrapped the hat, liking its bold primary colours, but saw now that her grandmother may as well have knitted the words, 'bully me', on it. She said nothing, bowed her head against the biting cold, the even more biting comments, and waited it out.

Time passed. The children became bored with such an unresponsive victim and turned their attention to how long they were expected to wait for the bus.

"They can't expect us to wait long," complained Tanya, shivering in her fashionable, thin coat. "It's frigging freezing out here."

There was a general chorus of agreement.

Phyllis listened, hope in her heart that maybe she would be able to go home, hide the offending hat at the bottom of a drawer, and never look at it again.

The door of the house adjacent to the bus stop opened and Mrs Andrews, Donna's mum, stuck her head out.

"Donna!" she called, "I've phoned the school. The bus is stuck in a snowdrift and won't make it today..."

Whatever else she may have said was lost in a great cheer, and the children began to quickly make their way home, thrilled with this unexpected gift of a day off school.

Phyllis picked her way across the icy street and quietly let herself back into her home. The house was on three levels, with the massive L-shaped lounge on the first floor. Phyllis took her boots and outerwear off and hung them neatly in the cloakroom.

Slowly, she made her way upstairs to let her parents know they would be forced to endure her presence for at least another day. Halfway up, she became aware of strange sounds emanating from the lounge – groaning, gasping, panting noises. Her steps slowed, and without understanding why, Phyllis crept silently up the last few stairs, peered cautiously through the bannisters.

The lounge door was open, and through it, Phyllis could see her father sitting on the sofa with her mother straddling him, silk dressing gown billowing out behind as she rose and fell onto his lap. Phyllis stared in fascination, knowing full well what they were doing. She understood about sex in a purely technical way but had never seen anyone doing it, not even on television.

"Oh yes." Her father's head lolled back. "Oh, Elizabeth, you're the best. I love you, oh my darling I love you!"

"I love you too." Her mother cried, before pulling his head back to hers and plundering his mouth with a deeply passionate kiss.

Phyllis knew she should leave; quietly creep away and come back later, but she was frozen to the spot with curiosity. Watching her parents' having sex was making her feel all jiggy inside – sort of hot and cold and confused – all at the same time.

Her parents' cries rose to a crescendo, and Phyllis knew some sort of climax was being reached. Gradually, their movements slowed, ceased, and her mother rested her head on her father's shoulder.

"That was amazing," he murmured. "I was beginning to think she'd never leave this morning. I kept thinking about you. What you were wearing under your robe, or rather, what you weren't wearing."

Her mother laughed, deep and husky. "Tell me, darling," she purred. "Do you think I'm a terrible mother? I've tried, heaven knows I've tried, but she's so, so..."

"Are you kidding? You're a fantastic mother. That girl has everything and she's never grateful."

"I know, but I feel so guilty I can't seem to like my own child."

"Well, let's face it." Her father broke off to kiss her mother. "She's a difficult child to like. Poor kid hasn't got a lot going for her, has she. No personality, unintelligent, and pug ugly to boot."

"Lionel," laughed her mother. "What an awful thing to say."

"I know," he chuckled. "But it's true, isn't it? The way she stares at you; that vacant expression whenever you try and have a conversation with her. You know it's lights on, no one home."

"Yes," her mother mused. "I must admit, I've sometimes wondered if, maybe, she should be tested to see if she's a special needs child, but she seems happy enough in her own little world. It's a shame she's not more attractive. I always feel that makes such a difference. After all, a lot of men positively encourage their women to be a little lacking in the brains department, so long as they're beautiful and have a good body. Poor Phyllis, I don't know what's to become of her."

"Why don't we leave this discussion for another day and relocate to the bedroom?" murmured her father, running his hands over his wife's body.

Phyllis fled, silently and speedily, back down the stairs, her mother's throaty laughter echoing in her ears. Pulling her boots and outdoor clothes back on, even the dreaded hat, she quietly opened the door and left the house.

Whilst she'd been inside the snowstorm had increased in ferocity. Phyllis could hardly see her hand in front of her face as she struggled down the eerily deserted village street. Her face was burning. There was a strange, nagging pain in her heart. Putting a hand up to her cheek, she was surprised to find tears, fresh and wet, the chill wind freezing them on her skin.

Why was she crying? Was anything she'd overheard a total surprise? Surely, she had known for years, all her life, that she was unloved, unwanted, unneeded? Still, it was a shock.

Deep down, tucked away in some long-abandoned corner of her heart, Phyllis had clung to the hope her parents did love her. That one day she'd get it right and find the key to making them happy and proud of her. Then they'd throw their hands up with joy at discovering what a treasure, what a jewel, their daughter was, and they'd love her, love her, love her ... the way she wanted, and needed, to be loved.

But now ... with her parents' cruel words ringing in her ears, their callous condemnation of their only child fresh in her memory, Phyllis knew that day would never come. Even if, by some miracle, her parents discovered they loved her, it was too late, because she, Phyllis, could no longer love them.

"I hate them!"

The words were ground out through teeth gritted against the pain. With them came a profound sense of relief. She didn't have to pretend to herself anymore. No longer would she lay awake planning ways to try and please her parents.

Aged thirteen years and two weeks, Phyllis severed forever the umbilical cord attaching her to her parents. It hurt, oh how it burnt; twisted at her insides, clawed at her bowels, and wracked her heart. To hear your own mother, say such things was unnatural. It went against everything. Mother's cherished and loved their daughters. They looked after them and were proud of them, no matter what.

As she trudged along despondently in the ever-deepening snow, Phyllis tried to mop the tears from her face, but without a tissue, she had to resort to using her gloves which soon became soggy and uncomfortable.

Where was she going anyway? Phyllis stopped and looked around. She had left the village far behind and was walking along the road which eventually led to town and her grandmother's house. It was over two miles away and the storm was worsening. Phyllis wasn't used to physical exercise but had no choice. She wasn't going back; nothing would induce her to go back and face her parents now. Apart from her grandmother, she had nobody else to turn to, and nowhere else to go.

Phyllis longed to be with her grandmother; to feel those warm, familiar arms about her; to sit in that cosy room in front of the fire with Mr Boots, her grandmother's cat, ensconced on her lap. To bask in her grandmother's approval, and to know that one person in the whole wide world loved her.

Thinking warm thoughts about her grandmother, Phyllis wiped the last of the tears from her face, braced her shoulders against the snow, and set off to make the long walk to the only place she'd ever thought of as home...

"Phyllis, oh my goodness! What on earth ...?" It was three hours later. Phyllis had finally reached her grandmother's house after the longest and most difficult walk of her life. Twice, she slipped over in fresh deep snow. The second time she had been tempted to simply lay there; let it all be over, to drift quietly into sleep and never need worry about anything again.

But the slow burn of hatred towards her parents, and the strong pull of her grandmother, had made her scramble to her feet to continue plodding along the deserted road.

Now she was here, at last, feeling her grandmother's love as she hurried Phyllis into the house, fussing over her.

"But how on earth did you get here?"

"Walked ..." Phyllis's teeth were chattering, the warmth of her grandmother's house making her nose run and her sinuses swell painfully.

"From school?"

"No, home."

"What? But why ..." Phyllis sneezed, and her grandmother decided to pursue the matter later. "Right," she said briskly. "Upstairs into a hot shower. I'll get you some warm clothes and a nice hot bowl of soup. Then you can tell me what happened."

Within an hour Phyllis was snug and cosy, wrapped in one of grandmother's nightgowns and woollen dressing gown, feet warm in a thick pair of socks propped up on the fender.

Her grandmother had hovered anxiously as Phyllis ate her way slowly through a large bowl of Scotch broth, and was now sitting opposite, a cup of tea in hand, waiting expectantly for Phyllis to explain.

"The school bus didn't come," said Phyllis. "So, I went home. They didn't hear me come in, and when I went upstairs, they were on the sofa ... they were, well, they were doing it ..." Phyllis broke off, and blushed into her soup.

"Do you mean they were making love?" her grandmother asked matter-of-factly.

Phyllis nodded, face on fire with embarrassment.

"Well," continued her grandmother slowly. "I'm sure it was a shock, but it's only natural, dear. After all, they are married, and obviously, love each other very much."

"I know that," said Phyllis quickly. "I do know about sex and stuff, Gran, we learnt it at school. It's not that, it's what they said ... afterwards ... Gran, do you think I'm a special needs child?"

Her grandmother's mouth set into a thin, tight line and her eyes went steely.

"Is that what they said about you?" she asked in a voice Phyllis had never heard her use before. She nodded, and her grandmother sighed.

"Tell me everything you heard, Phyllis, don't miss anything out, I want to know."

So, Phyllis told her, beginning with the bus stop, and ending with her long, cold walk. When she finished, her grandmother said nothing for a long time, merely handed her a tissue to wipe away her tears and patted her hand.

"What your parents said," she began slowly. "That was very cruel, very wrong of them, and I wish you hadn't heard it."

"I don't want to go back, Gran," Phyllis whispered, sniffling into her tissue.

"I can't say I blame you," replied her grandmother, sighing again. "I've let things be because I don't believe in interfering in the way people bring up their children; everyone has different ideas and standards. But enough is enough. It's time I put my foot down."

Phyllis stared with hope rising in her heart. "Do you mean I don't have to go back? I can stay here with you?"

"Yes, Phyllis, you can live here, if you want to."

"Oh, yes please," cried Phyllis, then her face fell. "But they'll never let me. They don't want me but won't want people to talk, and if I move here, people will."

"You leave your parents to me," replied her grandmother firmly. "You'll find they'll do as I say. Anyway, you sit and finish your tea, I've got to go and make a quick phone call to my solicitor."

"What about?"

"Oh, something I should have done a very long time ago. Nothing you need to worry about. Then I'm going to call your parents and have a little chat with them."

After that, life became a little sweeter for Phyllis. As she predicted, her parents objected, loudly and bitterly, to her grandmother's announcement that Phyllis was to live with her now. As soon as the roads cleared, they arrived, full of righteous indignation, demanding that Phyllis get in the car.

Her grandmother told Phyllis to wait upstairs whilst the adults had a 'little chat', before ordering her parents into the lounge. Waiting anxiously in her room, Phyllis listened to the raised voices booming through the floorboards and worried, gnawing in despair on her fingernails, hugging a purring Mr Boots to her chest.

"I'm not going back," she muttered. "I'm not, I'm not … They can't make me. Even if they do, I'll run away again."

There was silence, then the sound of the front door slamming. Rushing to the window, Phyllis peered out to see her parents marching to the car, her father's back stiff with outrage. He unlocked the car and got in as her mother went around to the passenger side and opened the door, glancing back up at the house as she did. Her eyes locked with Phyllis's. She glared – a cold, icy stare of contempt – before she got in the car, and they drove away.

Phyllis crept silently downstairs, unable to believe her frail grandmother had stood up to her parents and won. Going into the lounge, she found her grandmother slumped in her armchair. Phyllis thought how old and fragile she looked, and her heart constricted with fear. Rushing to her grandmother's chair, she dropped to her knees and buried her face in her lap.

"I'm sorry, Gran," she sobbed. "I'm so sorry."

"Sorry for what?" Her grandmother's hands smoothed her hair.

"For being so much trouble to everyone…"

"Now, you listen here my girl." Her grandmother tilted Phyllis's head back to look her in the eyes. "You're no trouble to me at all. I shall be delighted to have you living with me. We will take care of each other. You can start by pouring me a very small sherry. After all that, I think I need one."

Phyllis leapt to do her grandmother's bidding, carefully pouring the golden liquid into a small, cut-crystal glass, and carried it gingerly back, proud not a single drop was spilt. Her grandmother sipped delicately at the sherry, sighed with contentment, and settled back in the chair.

"There now," she said. "That's better."

"Gran," Phyllis sat carefully in the chair opposite. "Why do mother and father hate me?"

Her grandmother opened her mouth in denial, to pacify Phyllis with glib lies and reassurances, but something in the girl's eyes stopped her. So very young, she thought, too young to be faced with the reality of not being wanted by your parents.

"I don't know, Phyllis, I just don't know. I know they never wanted children, that you were a shock, but how they couldn't have lost their hearts to you when you were born, I don't know. You were such an adorable baby, with black spiky hair, chubby cheeks, and a happy little smile. When I first saw you in the hospital, I thought how beautiful you were. Although I must admit, I was very cross they named you after me."

"I don't mind," said Phyllis loyally. "It's a beautiful name."

"Bless you, dear. When I was young maybe, but times change, and whilst some names always remain popular and some go in and out of fashion, some shouldn't be resurrected and I'm afraid Phyllis is one of them. When you're older, maybe you could think about changing it to something that suits you better. You'll need to wait and see what name fits you best."

"You wouldn't mind?"

"Mind? Of course not, I'd say you were being clever. I always say if you don't like something about yourself, then change it."

"It's not always that easy, Gran. What about if you're ugly? That's not so easy to change."

Phyllis bowed her head away from her grandmother's keen gaze.

"Is that how you see yourself, Phyllis? Ugly?"

"It's all right, Gran, you don't have to be kind, I know I'm ugly."

"Phyllis Goodwin, I don't ever want to hear you speak like that again. You're still a child. You have so much time to grow and develop. You mark my words, one day you'll look in the mirror and wonder who that beautiful woman is."

"Really?"

Phyllis glowed with pleasure at such a thought and, for a moment, with her shining eyes and the sullen, haunted expression gone from her face, her grandmother caught a glimpse of the woman waiting within and it nearly took her breath away.

"Really, you wait, Phyllis, just you wait..."

"Gran, what was my grandfather like?" Phyllis's grandmother looked up, startled at the question which had come seemingly out of the blue. Phyllis was standing in front of the fireplace, gazing at the large black and white wedding photograph of her grandparents.

"Your grandfather?" Her eyes softened, and she held out a hand for the photograph. Carefully, Phyllis lifted it down and handed it to her, before settling on the rug at her grandmother's feet. "He was the most wonderful man I ever met. I wish you'd had the chance to know him properly, Phyllis. Do you have any memories of him?"

"Not many," Phyllis wrinkled her nose in memory. "I remember he seemed very big and tall. I remember him lifting me up and throwing me into the air."

"Well," her grandmother mused. "You were only five when he died, it's no wonder you don't remember him. But he loved you. He thought you were the prettiest thing he ever saw."

"What did he die of Gran? Heart attack, wasn't it?"

"That's right, I'll never forget it. One morning I was cooking breakfast and he said 'Phyllis, I don't feel so good.' The next moment he was gone." Her grandmother shook her head sadly, eyes misting at the memory. "I still miss him. There's not a day goes by I don't think about him."

"I'm sorry if I upset you, Gran, by asking about him."

"Why bless you, Phyllis. It should never hurt to be reminded of loved ones, even if they've left us. Now then, why don't you pop along to the chip shop and get us a nice fish supper, as it's Saturday night? You can even get yourself a coke if you like, and I might treat myself to a glass of sherry. There's £10 in my purse. Take that."

"All right," Phyllis scrambled to her feet. Chips for tea and coke, what a treat. As she let herself out of the house and ran lightly down the road, Phyllis thought she had never been so happy. It was early August, halfway through the summer holidays, and she had been living with her grandmother for eighteen months. The fact she no longer had to travel on the school bus was a major relief. She was still bullied viciously at school obviously – things hadn't improved that much – but somehow, having a warm, loving home to come back to, made it more bearable.

Phyllis never told her grandmother about the bullying. She didn't want to worry her and didn't see how telling would change anything. So, she struggled on alone, becoming more and more withdrawn and silent at school, living for the moment the bell would go and she could hurry home to her Gran.

Her relationship with her parents was now non-existent. In the beginning, her grandmother had invited them to tea on Sundays, in an attempt to mend bridges. After a few sessions of snide comments and wounding criticisms on her parents' side, and sullen noncommunication on Phyllis's, followed by floods of hysterical tears as soon as they left, she gave it up as a bad job.

Now as Phyllis queued and paid for their supper, carrying the warm, greasy parcel home, she was almost singing with happiness. No school for over a fortnight had dimmed the memory of its horrors. With still a month of holiday left, it was too soon to start fretting about the new term.

"Gran!" she called, as she let herself in. There was no answer. Phyllis placed the chips in the kitchen and crossed the hall to the lounge doorway. Her grandmother was sitting in the chair watching television; its high back was facing the door, so all Phyllis could see was her grandmother's hand, dangling down the side of the chair.

Phyllis smiled. Her grandmother was forever falling asleep in the chair, hotly denying she did any such thing, but now she'd caught her red-handed. Silently, Phyllis tiptoed across the floor, the giggle bubbling inside her. How typical of Gran to fall asleep in the ten short minutes she'd been gone.

Not asleep no – not with eyes so wide and staring, staring at nothing, the wedding picture clutched tightly in her still fingers. Phyllis cried out with the awful shock of it, before falling to her knees in front of her grandmother.

"Gran?"

Phyllis screwed her eyes up tight, in the hopes when she opened them again, her grandmother would sit up and laugh at her; would ask if she got cod or haddock, and was it time for sherry yet? But when she finally eased them open an eternity later, her grandmother was as before, those awful blank eyes looking straight through her.

"No-o-o!" Phyllis moaned the word out loud, rocking on her knees, clutching at her grandmother's skirt. "Please ... please don't leave me, Gran! What shall I do without you?"

Quickly, she crawled to the sideboard, pulled the telephone down, and with shaking fingers dialled 999.

"Ambulance," she answered through icy lips. "It's my Gran," she sobbed when connected with the controller. "I think ... I think she's dead..."

"It's all right, love," said the steady, warm voice at the other end of the line. "What's your address?"

Phyllis automatically recited it, hung up, and sat; her back against the sideboard, phone clutched to her chest. Waiting. Waiting in that still, silent room, the only sound was the ticking of the ornate clock on the mantelpiece and the buzzing of a large bluebottle against the windowpane.

Never taking her gaze off her grandmother's face, she wondered how the soul could flee the body so completely, leaving nothing there; no spark, no vestige of what had been. It was her grandmother, yet her warmth, her love, her compassion, her very essence was gone, leaving her face curiously blank, like a waxwork or a mannequin.

Phyllis crawled to her grandmother's body and carefully removed the wedding photo, returned it to its place of pride on the mantelpiece, and gently smoothed down her grandmother's skirt which had ridden up to show thin, knobbly knees.

Phyllis knew it was ridiculous; that her grandmother was beyond caring about such things now, but still she did it, knowing in life her grandmother would never have let strange men see her with her skirt all rucked up like that.

Then, slowly, Phyllis dialled again.

"Hello? Hello, Mother? It's Phyllis, I think you must come now … yes really … it's Gran. She's dead…"

Chapter Two

"You couldn't bear it that I had something to love."

Bereavement is a strange thing. It affects people differently. Some it simply demolishes, leaving them crying and railing at the injustice of a cruel, uncaring world.

Others have a delayed reaction, going through a period of calm whilst the practical side of death is dealt with, before falling apart once the final mourner has left, and the last crumbs of funereal cake have been swept away.

Then there are some whose grief turns inward. Unable to express themselves in an outward display of sorrow, emotions burrow and gnaw away at their very soul, until they permeate every fibre of their being, and they are saturated in sadness.

This was how it was for Phyllis.

Through a fog of numb, silent despair, she watched dispassionately as the paramedics arrived. They spoke softly and kindly to her as they examined her grandmother's body. The police were called. Nothing to worry about, they reassured her, merely standard procedure following an unexpected death.

Phyllis sat in the little-used dining room, hugging a purring Mr Boots to her chest, and waited. Waited to be told what was to become of her, although a small, scared part of her already knew with a sick dread of anticipation.

The police arrived at the same time as Phyllis's parents; her father was very practical, talking calmly and wisely to those in authority; her mother all loving concern and care, holding her hand whilst the grim realities of death were dealt with in the other room. Phyllis, knowing it was all a charade for the benefit of the audience, still drew a despairing kind of comfort from her mother's touch.

Left alone though, Phyllis quickly realised the past eighteen months might as well never have happened. The door closed behind the last policeman and her mother dropped her hand as if it were contaminated.

"Well," she said brusquely. "I suppose we'd better go. Collect a few things, we'll come back for the rest later. We're having a dinner party tonight and I need to get back to see to everything."

Phyllis stared at the obscenity of her mother's words.

"You're still having a dinner party even though your mother has just died?"

Her mother smiled a thin, mirthless smile, cold and compassionless.

"Well of course we're still having it. It's far too late to cancel. Besides, mother herself always said how important it is to never to let people down."

Phyllis gave up and silently went to do her mother's bidding. As she neatly folded jeans, underwear, and tops into a bag she looked around her bedroom. Her mother, she knew, would scoff at the faded, flowery wallpaper, and the chintzy curtains and bedcover. But Phyllis loved the room. Here she had experienced contentment for the first time, and a loving home life had been hers for a brief period.

Now it was gone, untimely snatched away. Phyllis wondered if it would have been better if it'd never happened at all. She'd had a taste of what life could be like when living with someone who genuinely loved her. It would be far harder now to go back to the way things had been before.

Slowly she carried her bag downstairs. Her mother was standing in the doorway of the kitchen looking in.

"What's this?" she asked.

"Fish and chips," Phyllis explained. "I'd got them for our tea."

"How awful," her mother shuddered. "Put them in the bin," she ordered. "We can't leave them there to stink the house out."

"Can't I take the fish out for Mr Boots?" asked Phyllis in despair, finding the thought of all that wasted food strangely upsetting.

"Who? Oh, mother's mangy cat. Very well if you must."

Silently, Phyllis unwrapped the greasy parcels, stomach heaving at the smell of cold fry, scraped the batter off the portions of fish and placed them in a small plastic container. The rest of the meal she rewrapped and threw in the dustbin outside.

Her mother watched, frown deepening, as Phyllis rinsed out the cat's water and food bowls, dried them carefully on kitchen towel, and placed them in a plastic bag along with cat biscuits, the container of fish, and a few tins of cat food.

"What do you think you're doing?" she said.

"Well, these are Mr Boots' things. He'll need them at … home," Phyllis stumbled over the word, then stared at her mother in consternation.

"He is coming back with us," she exclaimed, voice shrill with fear. "You can't leave him here."

"I don't see why not," her mother shrugged. "He's just a cat. We'll call in and feed him, or I'm sure maybe the neighbours would do it."

"No!" Somehow Phyllis found the strength to fight. "We're not leaving him here. If Mr Boots doesn't come with us, then I'm not going either."

"For heaven's sake, Phyllis," her mother exclaimed in exasperation. "It's just a cat. I don't see what all the fuss is about."

"We're not leaving him here."

Phyllis retreated into the familiar territory of sullen stubbornness, staring at her mother in mulish obstinacy.

"What on earth's all the shouting about?" Phyllis' father entered the room, his sharp expression conveying his annoyance.

"Phyllis is insisting we take that flea-bitten creature with us."

"He hasn't got fleas. We're not leaving him. He'd be unhappy and lonely. He might run away."

"Well, lock the cat flap so he can't."

"You can't do that, mother, he needs to go out to do his business."

"Can't you put a litter tray down or something?"

"I don't think that's a good idea, Elizabeth," Phyllis's father interrupted the verbal tennis match. "We don't want the property smelling of cat when it goes onto the market, do we?"

Phyllis stared at her parents in horror. "You're selling Gran's house?"

"What else are we supposed to do with it, Phyllis?" her mother's voice was edged with spite. "You surely didn't think you could go on living here alone, did you?"

She laughed at Phyllis's bleak expression.

"Silly girl ... you're only 14 and we're your legal guardians until you're 18 years old. After that, you can do as you please."

Phyllis's heart sank.

Four more years living with her parents.

She was right, it would have been better never to have left. This brief respite would make it that much harder to go back. She clutched the bag to her chest and glared morosely at her mother, who sighed in exasperation.

"Oh, for heaven's sake, Phyllis, we don't have time for this. Our guests arrive in two hours, and I still have to finish the canapés." At Phyllis's silence, she threw her hands up in despair. "All right, get the wretched creature, but he's your responsibility. I want nothing to do with it."

Phyllis nodded in agreement and hurried to catch Mr Boots and gently place him in his wicker carrying basket. She watched in dumb compliance as her father re-locked the back door, collected her bag, and ushered them all out to the car, carefully locking the front door behind him.

As she climbed into the back seat, cat basket beside her, Phyllis looked up at the tall, friendly house, wondering if she'd ever see it again.

Silently, her lips formed the word goodbye, and she placed a palm on the window as the car pulled away from the kerb, taking her away from the only home she'd ever known, and back to a life she had dared to think she'd escaped from.

No escape, no escape.

The refrain rattled around her brain. Phyllis could almost hear the prison door clanging shut, only this time it was far worse – she'd lost her only ally. She was truly alone, with no one to care whether she lived or died, was happy or unhappy. She was trapped with four more years of her sentence to endure until ... what?

Phyllis could see no further into the future than tomorrow and then tomorrow, days strung together stretching endlessly into an unknown horizon.

Phyllis thrust her fingers through the front of the cat basket, drawing comfort from Mr Boots as he licked them and purred throatily. Her heart lifted a little ... at least she still had one friend.

When they reached her parent's home, Phyllis took Mr Boots and escaped to the sanctuary of her old room. In her absence, it had been turned into a guest bedroom, and not one trace of her previous thirteen years of occupancy remained. Phyllis settled Mr Boots with a bowl of water and the unwanted cod, which he ate greedily, licking flakes from his whiskers.

Downstairs, Phyllis could hear the mingled conversation and laughter of her parents' dinner guests. Her mother had brusquely told her to make herself a plate of something and take it to her room, but Phyllis had declined, the mere thought of food making her stomach turn.

Now she lay fully clothed and wrapped in the duvet on the bed, feeling cold despite the relative warmth of the evening. Mr Boots, his supper complete, curled up in a marmalade ball of fur, warm against her chest.

Phyllis buried her face in his creamy, orange-spotted tummy, hearing his deep rumbling purr, as his paws flexed and contracted in a motionless dance of happiness.

Phyllis had opened her window so he could come and go as he pleased throughout the night. The garage roof was directly below, so he had an access route to the garden, and Phyllis hoped he was clever enough to find his way back to her room.

Phyllis looked at the bedroom clock.

Less than three hours ago, she had run down the road to the chip shop, happy and content, looking forward to a Saturday night treat of fish and chips and coke for tea. And now...

Phyllis thought again about her grandmother, her unseeing blank eyes, and felt a wave of almost crippling sorrow sweep through her. Turning onto her side, she hugged Mr Boots tightly until he squeaked in protest, then, despite it only being eight o'clock fell into a deep and dreamless, grief fuelled sleep.

The rest of the weekend passed in a blur of misery. If it hadn't been for the necessity of caring for Mr Boots and his loving, unquestioning companionship, Phyllis might very well have given in to the black wave of despair nibbling at the edges of her psyche.

Her parents' indifference to her grandmother's death wounded and shocked her, though on some level she was not surprised. Her mother's intense need for her father, and his for her, seemed to render them incapable of even basic human compassion for others.

Phyllis knew as well that any attachment her mother might have had to her mother had been severed forever when Phyllis had chosen her grandmother over her parents.

Phyllis was alone with her mother. There were things she wished to ask about the funeral and what was to happen to her. But her mother's mood was one of such brittle brightness, a thin veneer of busy efficiency barely masking the temper simmering beneath, that Phyllis was afraid to begin any conversation, least of all one guaranteed to ignite an explosive response.

Instead, she kept herself small and invisible, watching from corners as her mother stormed about the house in a fury of creative zeal. Phyllis had seen her mother like this before. Such extremes of mood were always the result of her mother attempting to finish, to round off as it were, her latest article or book.

Elizabeth Goodwin was a household name - Britain's answer to Martha Stewart. A familiar face on the covers of women's magazines across the land, Phyllis found it highly ironic her mother could write articles with such titles as 'Ten Steps to a Perfect Family Christmas', or 'Family Relations & How to Maintain Them' when her own family was so far from being perfect that even the flawless Elizabeth Goodwin was unable to fix it.

Now her mother was working on a feature for Woman magazine, on how to hold a sophisticated dinner party without becoming stressed. Moving around the kitchen with fixed concentration, she meticulously noted preparation and cooking times on a big planner. Organising an exact rota of when, and how, everything should be prepared, so that the less experienced hostess could merely follow Elizabeth Goodwin's plan, produce the perfect dinner party and be the envy of all her friends, basking in glory as they exclaimed, 'I don't know how you do it!'

Phyllis stayed out of her mother's way as much as possible, but thirst finally drove her to the kitchen. Quickly, silently, she took a glass from the cupboard and filled it from the tap. There was bottled water in the fridge, but as her mother was currently headfirst in there, muttering curses about butter which was meant to spread straight from the fridge but didn't, Phyllis decided tap water would do perfectly well.

She'd almost made her escape when her mother slammed the fridge door, spun around, and saw her. For a moment, a frown plucked at her mother's immaculately smooth brow, as if she was trying to remember who Phyllis was and what exactly she was doing in her kitchen, then her face cleared, and she almost smiled.

"Ah, Phyllis, just the person. Could you help me with something for a moment?"

"Me?" Phyllis was stunned. Her mother never asked her to help, least of all with anything to do with her precious culinary creations.

"Yes, you. Oh, do stop gawking, Phyllis, it's most unbecoming." Her mother slid a cookery book across the table at her. "Now, I'm making this sauce for the first time, and I need both hands free to gradually beat in the oil. Just read the next few steps aloud to me."

"I'm not sure," Phyllis picked up the book and looked at the recipe. "I'll probably get it all wrong."

"Don't be so ridiculous!" snapped her mother. "All you have to do is read out the next part of the recipe to me, there." One perfectly manicured nail jabbed at the page. "It's not exactly difficult, Phyllis. Now, do as I ask."

Phyllis sat down and stared at the book, head pounding, her mouth dry. The words moved and blurred on the page. She blinked, and they swam in front of her eyes, solid black hieroglyphs, meaningless and illegible. Frowning in concentration, she felt her mother's expectant eyes upon her.

"Well?"

Her mother's barked command panicked Phyllis even more and she knew she'd never be able to read the words now. Sometimes, if she was calm and quiet, reading was not exactly easy, no it was never that, but it was more manageable, and Phyllis had slowly limped her way through several books enjoying them for the escape they provided. But when she was under pressure, was anxious or scared, such as at school or now, reading became a nightmarish impossibility; words reassembling themselves on the page to become a freakish new language, totally incomprehensible.

Phyllis licked her lips, heart pounding in fear, sweat breaking out down her spine under her mother's cold, accusing glare.

"What's the matter? Why won't you read the recipe out? Honestly, Phyllis! I ask you to do one simple thing and you can't be bothered to do that."

"I'm sorry," stuttered Phyllis, misery constricting her throat. "I'm sorry, I can't…"

"What do you mean, you can't?" her mother's eyes narrowed. "Oh, my God!" she exclaimed. "You can't bloody read, can you?"

"I can!" Phyllis was stung by the assumption. "I can read, but sometimes the words don't look real. They don't make sense."

"Stop making excuses!" Her mother seemed outraged at the thought that any daughter of hers could be such a retard, such an intellectual non-entity.

"Get out of my kitchen," she snapped. "I don't want to look at you right now, Phyllis. Heaven only knows what your father's going to say about this! What on earth have you been doing at school all these years?"

Surviving! Phyllis wanted to scream at her mother. Slowly dying by degrees in a world of misery and loneliness, whilst you both live in your perfect bubble, not noticing, not caring I'm here and that I'm unhappy, so unhappy. But she said nothing, merely stared at her mother in sullen, uncommunicative silence, until her mother threw her hands up in a gesture of angry resignation.

"Just go, Phyllis."

Phyllis went, back to the sanctuary of her room, to the uncritical affection of Mr Boots. Curling herself into a ball on her bed she gently stroked his marmalade fur and praised his fat, sleek beauty. A contented grin spread across his face as she rubbed his chin, and his purrs rumbled through the room.

How can I take this? Phyllis wondered to herself. How much more can I stand? Phyllis knew this was her life now and could see no way out or chance of parole until she was eighteen. Even then it was doubtful she'd be able to leave.

Where could she go? With no money, no savings and no skills, Phyllis was realistic about her intense longing to one day have a little home of her own; somewhere she could be alone.

Softly, she whispered her secret dreams to Mr Boots ... confided in him her craving for a home, a place in which she felt safe. Maybe she could teach herself to cook. Maybe she could even have a TV. Phyllis's parents didn't like television. The only set in the house was ensconced in her father's study for occasional use if there was something on her parents believed worth watching.

Whilst living with her grandmother, Phyllis had fallen in love with television and had spent many a happy evening curled up on the sofa, gazing at the screen, transfixed by a medium so undemanding it needed no skills to use.

The day passed. Phyllis stayed in her room waiting for her father to come home. It had been mentioned at breakfast that Phyllis was to go with him that evening to her grandmother's house to collect the rest of her things. It was something to look forward to; a chance to go home, if only for a brief time.

Also, Phyllis was going to gather up all the cat food there was to bring back for Mr Boots. The small supply of food she'd originally brought back was nearly all gone, and she had no money to buy him anymore.

Finally, the day ended. Her father came home, collected Phyllis, and drove without speaking to the house. After unlocking the front door, her father seemed reluctant to enter the house, declaring he'd wait in the car, and she was not to be too long about it.

Phyllis pushed the door open and entered the familiar hall. At this time of day, sunlight flooded through the windows overlooking the garden at the back. A large, double-fronted Victorian detached villa, her grandmother often confessed the house was too big for her. But because it was the home her beloved husband had brought her to as a bride so many years before, she never considered moving out. Phyllis was glad her grandmother's last moments had been spent in the home she loved so much.

Quickly, Phyllis packed her things and loaded all the cat food she could find into a bag – enough for a couple of weeks at least. One last look around … how Phyllis loved this house. She wished she could simply lock the front door and stay here forever.

She hoped the next people to live here would have the time, money, and love to make it realise its full potential. Phyllis and her grandmother had often sat talking and drawing up plans and improvements for the house, but her grandmother's age and fear of upheaval meant they remained pure fantasies.

She hesitated in front of her grandparents' wedding picture, longing to take it, yet fearful if she did her mother would discover it. No, Phyllis shivered, the consequences didn't bear thinking about. It was best, no matter how much she desired it, to simply leave it be.

The journey back to her parents' house passed in silence, Phyllis sat alone with her thoughts, longing to get back to Mr Boots. He'd be hungry, wanting his dinner, and she planned to open the tin of cod and prawn flavoured food knowing it was his favourite.

They had been gone over an hour. Her mother was in the kitchen when the car pulled up in front of the house, and for a moment was silhouetted in the window, oblivious to their arrival.

Phyllis heard her father sigh. Stealing a glance at him, she caught the look of intense longing, love, and desire on his face and felt a sharp stab of jealousy. How she wished that one day someone would look at her that way, with such need and passion. Oh, how she longed to be the centre of somebody's universe.

They entered the house and went their separate ways – Phyllis up to her bedroom, and her father to the kitchen to be with his wife. Dumping her belongings on the floor to be sorted later, Phyllis was surprised not to be immediately greeted by a purring bundle of marmalade fur, noisily demanding to be fed.

"Mr Boots," she called softly. "Puss, puss." Frowning, she climbed onto her bed and peered out of the window; no sign of him in the garden.

Reluctantly, Phyllis went downstairs and entered the kitchen. Her parents immediately pulled apart. She could see traces of her mother's burgundy lipstick smeared on her father's mouth. Her mother's top button was undone, and Phyllis saw a glimpse of cream lace before her mother turned away to stir something on the stove.

The feeling of intruding, of being in their way, was almost too much to bear and Phyllis would have left immediately, were it not for her concern about Mr Boots.

"Mother, have you seen Mr Boots anywhere? Only, he's not in my room and it's time for his dinner."

Did she imagine it, or did a quick flash of guilt spark from her mother to her father? Phyllis felt something ... an intuition that danced its way up her spine. She heard the panic in her voice.

"Mother?"

Her mother didn't reply but glanced out the open back door, Phyllis followed her gaze, and saw to her horror, the cat basket wedged between the bins with its door open, his little tartan cushion half out on the ground. With a wordless cry, Phyllis rushed to the basket; it was empty but for a few tufts of ginger fur which clung to its wicker sides. In a fury, she turned to face them. They came to the back door, silently watching, a united front against her.

"Where is he? What have you done with him?"

Her mother shrugged, although her eyes wouldn't meet Phyllis's. "He was getting old; it was for the best. He'd never have been happy here. He would have missed your grandmother too much and pined away." She gave a careless laugh. "You wouldn't have wanted that to happen now, would you Phyllis?"

"He wasn't old," raged Phyllis. "He was only eight. That's not old. He could have lived another eight years, and he was settling in. He was eating, and he was happy with me. How could you kill him! You're a murderer. You murdered him!"

"Honestly, Phyllis, there's no need to be so melodramatic..."

"You're an evil murderer," interrupted Phyllis, tears welling.

"That's enough, Phyllis," ordered her father. "I won't have you talking to your mother like that. It had to be done. Your mother felt it would be kindest all round if it were done whilst you were out the way. She only had your best interests at heart."

"You knew?" demanded Phyllis, feeling sick to her stomach. "You knew! That's why you took me to Gran's house. You were both in on it, plotting to kill him. I hate you. I hate you both!"

"Phyllis!" barked her father. "Go to your room at once and don't come out until tomorrow. This behaviour is unforgivable. What on earth do you think you're doing, making such an exhibition? What will the neighbours think hearing you scream like that?"

"I don't care," sobbed Phyllis. "You killed Mr Boots. You knew how much he meant to me, and you killed him anyway."

She stopped, clarity drenching her in cold, hard understanding.

"That's why, isn't it? You knew how much I loved him, that he was all I had, so you took him away from me."

"Don't be ridiculous, Phyllis ..." began her mother.

"It's not ridiculous," replied Phyllis slowly. "It's the truth. You couldn't bear it that I had something to love."

She looked at her parents standing there, so together, so against her, and felt old and weary.

"It was punishment because I wanted to live with Gran and not you? That's what it was."

"No, of course, it wasn't," her father's voice was rich with indignant denial. Phyllis looked at her mother, saw the truth in her eyes, and despised her for it.

"I'll never forgive you," she stated quietly.

Something in her eyes, her bearing, silenced her parents and made them move aside without comment. They watched as she passed them, head held high, leaving the kitchen to go to her room.

Chapter Three
"Lying old bitch, she reneged on our deal!"

The day of her grandmother's funeral dawned fine and sunny. Following the wishes stated in her will, she was to be buried next to Phyllis's grandfather, and Phyllis felt comforted knowing that her grandmother wouldn't be alone ... that she had her husband with her.

No, it was only Phyllis who was alone now.

She ached for her grandmother, wishing she could be with her. To see her kindly, loving face, and be curled up on the floor at her feet, head on her lap, her grandmother's hand on her head.

The funeral was sparsely attended; a sprinkling of her parents' friends, her grandmother's neighbours, Mr and Mrs Jamison who had come to know and care for Phyllis during the eighteen months she lived next door to them. Bewildered by the speed of change, they were condescended to by her parents and did not stay long.

Mrs Jamison hugged Phyllis, sobbing a little over the loss of an old friend and neighbour. Mr Jamison patted her hand and told her to take care of herself. Phyllis watched them go with regret, knowing she'd probably never see them again.

Her grandmother's solicitor also attended; tall and elderly, Phyllis thought what a kind face he had. His demeanour was one of professional rectitude, and she was fascinated by his silver hair and twinkling blue eyes. She knew he'd been her grandmother's friend since before the War, and she had seen by the way her grandmother's eyes softened when she spoke about him, that possibly there had been something else there too ... a fondness, a regard, unspoken though treasured.

Phyllis tried to imagine having such a friend; someone who had been there when you were young, and who reminded you of those days when you were old.

After the funeral, a few of her parents' friends came back to the house. Phyllis watched, as these people who knew nothing about her grandmother, had never even met her, ate, and drank and talked and laughed. She resented them; resented the way that even at her funeral, her grandmother had been marginalised and pushed to one side by her parents.

Through it all, her grandmother's solicitor sat quietly watching, a small sherry clasped in his veined hand, a polite smile fixed on his face. Once he saw Phyllis peering cautiously at him from the corner of the room, and the smile became genuine. She felt its warmth and responded with a tiny smile that felt alien on her face.

Finally, it was over, and everyone left. The solicitor rose to his feet, and quietly but firmly, expressed his wish to read the last will and testament of the late Mrs Phyllis Mae Coulson. Her mother, somewhat taken aback at his insistence, asked rather sharply if it was necessary to 'go into all that now'.

The solicitor replied equally firmly, although politely, that it had been Mrs Coulson's wish that her will be read out to the family after the funeral. His words seemed to imply a vast extended family, in direct contrast to the reality of the three of them, and Phyllis wanted to giggle, as her mother's wishes were, for once, over-ridden, and the three of them were ushered to sit at the dining table.

The solicitor took his time settling into a chair at the head of the table, fussing with getting out the correct papers, and changing his glasses before he finally got down to the matter in hand.

"This is the last will and testament of Phyllis Mae Coulson dated the 19th of February 1991..."

"What?" Her mother's head snapped up, and she exchanged a quick, uneasy glance with her husband. "Mother made a new will last year. Why?"

Phyllis kept her head down. The date was a few days after she moved in with her grandmother. She remembered her grandmother phoning her solicitor the day Phyllis ran away from home.

"Mrs Coulson wanted to make a new will as she was dissatisfied with the contents of her previous one." The solicitor cast a quick, sideways glance at Phyllis. "She felt there were certain issues that needed to be addressed."

"Issues?" exclaimed Phyllis's mother. "I don't understand. It's all perfectly simple - as mother's next of kin, I inherit everything."

"Under the terms of the previous will, that was indeed the case," the solicitor paused, clearing his throat. "However, this will does differ substantially, in that Mrs Coulson has decided to bypass your claim to her estate completely."

Phyllis's father spoke for the first time. "What exactly are you trying to say?"

"Mrs Coulson felt you were financially secure in your own right, and that there was another member of the family who needed financial assistance more..."

"What?"

"Therefore, under the terms of the new will, your mother's estate goes in its entirety to her granddaughter, Phyllis Elizabeth Goodwin. Miss Goodwin is to inherit sole charge over all of Mrs Coulson's property and assets upon reaching her eighteenth birthday. The inheritance to be hers, absolutely, with no ties or binds in the form of trusts or conditions."

"What?" Her father's stunned reaction was mild compared to her mother's.

"No!" she howled, slapping her hand down on the table. "That's not ... why the conniving old ... no, that's not right, I was to get everything! That's what we agreed. She threatened to change her will if I didn't let Phyllis go and live with her. Lying old bitch, she reneged on our deal!"

"Mrs Goodwin!" The solicitor's shocked tones did little to halt the vitriolic outflow.

"I'll contest it!"

"You are, of course, within your rights to do so, but I wouldn't recommend it. Mrs Coulson insisted on having a complete medical examination before making the will. Her doctor has witnessed that she was of sound body and mind. I, myself, can witness that she was under no duress whatsoever to change her will, and she did so of her own volition. To contest the will would merely incur a great deal of financial outlay on your behalf, to no avail. The will is perfectly reasonable, legal and binding."

"You!" Her mother's bile now turned upon Phyllis. "This is all your doing, constantly running to mother with sob stories of being neglected and unloved. Lying and manipulating your way into her affections. You little viper. All these years we've raised you, and this is the thanks we get. Well, you can sign the estate over to us, that's all," her head snapped up to glare at the solicitor.

The solicitor sighed. "Miss Goodwin is within her rights to do whatever she pleases with the money. However, she does not legally become entitled to anything until she reaches her eighteenth birthday, and therefore is unable to sign the money over to you, or indeed anyone, until that day."

"Right," spat her mother. "Draw up the documents stating Phyllis will sign the estate over to us the moment she becomes eighteen, and that will be an end to it."

All through this exchange, the solicitor watched Phyllis carefully. For over fifty years, Richard Madison had been a friend of Phyllis Coulson. Could still remember as vividly as if it were yesterday, meeting the beautiful, vivacious nineteen-year-old. The pure joy of falling instantly in love with her, and the agony of discovering she was engaged to his best friend, Albert Coulson.

Throughout the years, the three had remained close friends. Richard had never married – his heart being irrevocably given to Phyllis. Following Albert's death, he hoped maybe Phyllis would look up and see Richard for the first time. See he loved her as truly, as passionately, as she had loved Albert. But it was no use. Phyllis's heart had been buried with Albert, and although she loved Richard deeply, it was as a brother, a friend, and with a sigh and a heart full of regrets, Richard had to be content with that.

He always acted as solicitor to Albert and Phyllis, giving them free advice on their minor legal requirements; assisting them when they purchased their house, advising Albert on how best to invest the money he inherited on the death of his parents and preparing both their wills. In return, he had been a part of their family, acting as godfather to their beloved daughter, Elizabeth.

Now, he looked sadly at his friends' child, trying to see in the vain, and selfish, cold-hearted woman sitting across the desk, some glimpse of the pretty little girl who'd run to greet him with a soggy handful of daisies and a lisped 'hello Uncle Wichard.'

He shook his head sadly. He could understand his friend's reluctance to bequeath anything to her grasping, greedy daughter, and her stuffed shirt of a husband, but had yet to understand what it was Phyllis saw in her namesake which had prompted her to leave everything to her.

Elizabeth Goodwin was demanding in a strident voice that the paperwork be drawn up now, this minute, so her daughter could agree to sign away her inheritance on her eighteenth birthday when Richard got what he was looking for.

If he hadn't been watching for it, he would have missed it. The girl, Phyllis, that sullen, plain lump of a girl, flashed her mother a look of pure unadulterated hatred, from eyes which gleamed with knowledge of exactly what it was her mother was trying to do to her. Richard came to a sudden decision and held up a hand to stem Elizabeth's bile laden diatribe.

"I wish to speak to Phyllis for a moment please … alone," he continued, as her parents showed no signs of moving. "Perhaps there's a room where we could converse privately?"

"I suppose you could use my study," Phyllis's father spoke for the first time, shaken by the afternoon's events. Not only the revelation of the changed will but by his wife's deranged outburst.

"Thank you so much," Richard replied getting to his feet. "Perhaps you could lead the way, my dear?" For the first time, he spoke directly to Phyllis. She raised her head to gaze at him, and the shock of looking into his old friend's eyes was almost overwhelming – their shape and that unusual deep brown colour. He always felt Phyllis's eyes were the most beautiful he had ever seen, and to find them now, reproduced in her granddaughter, was almost more than he could bear.

It brought home even more keenly that she was gone. He was the only one left. It made him determined to carry out his dear friend's last wishes to the letter; to befriend and champion her granddaughter, whom she thought so much of.

Phyllis silently led the way to her father's study, heart beating with thrilled anticipation. Gran had left her everything. Phyllis wasn't sure what everything entailed, but it might be enough to enable her to escape from her parents. The thought of freedom made her giddy, and she almost fell, rather than sat, on the chair which the kindly solicitor motioned her to.

"I thought it best," he began, "if we had a little chat away from ... well, distractions. It might be there are questions you wish to ask me, things you don't understand."

Phyllis sat and studied him, her eyes not giving away a single clue. Richard wondered what had happened to this child to make her so adept at disguising her feelings at such a young age.

"Do you have any questions, Phyllis? Anything at all you'd like to ask me?"

"Mr Madison," she began hesitantly, "could you tell me, what did Gran die of?"

"Do you mean you don't know?" Richard was startled. Whilst appearing young for her age, Phyllis was certainly old enough to have been told the truth.

"No," Phyllis shook her head. "All I know is I came home, and she was dead in the chair."

"Do you mean you're the one who found her?" Phyllis nodded. Richard felt a surge of anger at the callous disregard of her parents. "She died of something called an aneurysm, Phyllis, a sort of brain haemorrhage. I promise it would have been very quick. She wouldn't have known anything."

Phyllis nodded thoughtfully, and silence descended over the book-lined room.

"Tell me, Phyllis," Richard began, "do you want to sign your inheritance over to your mother?"

"No!" The answer shot back, firm, and strident. "It's mine. Gran wanted me to have it. She knew it was the only way I'd get free. It's mine, and she's not getting it."

"Why do you dislike your mother so much, Phyllis?"

"Because she hates me." The answer was shocking. "And because she murdered Mr Boots."

Richard felt a pang of regret, remembering the last time he visited Phyllis. Her large, marmalade, cushion cat had enthroned himself on his lap, purring like a traction engine for the entire duration of his stay, leaving a legacy of persistent orange hairs which had clung to his suit for days.

"Did Gran leave me a lot of money, Mr Madison?" Richard came back to the present to find the child peering at him. Unlike her mother, it was not greed he saw in her eyes, but rather an odd, somehow touching mix of desperate anticipation, fear, and optimism.

"Well," he began, wondering how well equipped she was to deal with the truth. "There's the money your grandfather left, and her inheritance from her parents. Your grandmother lived a frugal, quiet life and made wise investment choices, so her estate is quite considerable. After death duties, funeral expenses and one or two small bequests, it comes to over 2.5 million pounds ..." Phyllis's jaw dropped. "Plus, the house of course."

"The house?" Phyllis's eyes were as round as saucers. "Gran left me her house?"

"Yes, she did."

"Oh," breathed Phyllis. "I love that house, I thought I'd never see it again ... It's mine? Really, *really* mine?"

"Really, *really* yours, Phyllis," Richard smiled, comforted by the fact that Phyllis seemed indifferent to the amount of the bequest, instead focusing on her grandmother's home.

Phyllis's face clouded over. "No one can take it away from me, can they?" By "they", Richard knew she meant her mother, and hurried to reassure her.

"No, Phyllis, no one can take any of it away from you, not unless you want them to. Now then, we need to discuss a few practicalities. Obviously, nothing can happen until you are eighteen..."

"I wish I could have the money now," interrupted Phyllis, with a fierce longing.

"I'm sorry, Phyllis, those are the terms of the will. In truth, I don't think your grandmother ever thought she would die before you turned eighteen. However, as executor of your grandmother's will, I am empowered to make certain decisions on your behalf. I will, of course, continue to monitor your investments and advise you accordingly." Phyllis nodded, her eyes never leaving his face.

"Now, as to the house," Richard continued. "It's not a good idea for it to stand empty for the next four years. My advice would be to let the house out, the revenue from this could pay for maintaining the house, and any surplus would be added to your inheritance. What do you wish to do with the furniture? Are there any favourite pieces you wish placed in storage? Or would you prefer to simply sell everything, with the proceeds going to decorate and furnish the house to a level suitable to let?"

Phyllis considered, her cheeks flushed as she tried to assimilate everything that had happened that day, from burying her beloved grandmother, to discovering she was rich beyond her wildest dreams.

"I think," she began slowly. "I'd like to sell the furniture. Even Gran said it was too heavy and outdated. We used to make plans, Gran and I, about what we'd like to do to the house ..." her face clouded.

"I loved my Gran very much, Mr Madison," she stated. "You can't begin to understand what this means to me. She's given me a life. I only wish I could tell her how much I appreciate it."

"I'm sure she knows, Phyllis." Feeling absurdly moved by the moment, Richard busied himself writing notes on his pad. "So then, sell all the furniture. Is there anything you wish to keep?"

"The photos, all of them, and Gran's pearls. She always said they'd be mine one day, so I'd like to have them ... could you maybe look after them for me?"

"Of course, but you could have them now if you like."

"No, it's better if you keep them, I'm afraid they might get lost, or go missing somehow if they came into this house." Richard knew she was implying that her mother would take them and felt his heart constrict with sadness for her.

"Are you going to be all right, Phyllis?" he asked, impulsively.

"Yes," she replied, raising her head, and fixing him with a look which spoke of wisdom beyond her years. "I have to be, don't I? I have four years to wait before my life can begin, so that's what I have to do ... wait four years ..."

First day of term. A new school year. Feet dragging on the ground, Phyllis walked towards the bus stop. Somehow, she had managed to block from her mind that not only would she be returning to school as normal, but as she no longer lived in the town, she would have to catch the bus again.

She was dreading it. Whilst living with her grandmother, school had been as bad as ever, but at least she had someone to go home to. Now she had nothing. Less than nothing.

Since the reading of the will, and the revealing of its shocking contents, her mother had waged a silent war of attrition against Phyllis. Small, petty acts of spite were committed against her on an almost daily basis, and Phyllis could feel herself shrinking a little more every day. It was almost a relief to be going back to school, to escape the narrow confines of life within her parents' house.

Again, she found herself daring to hope things would be different. Surely everyone had grown up enough to find other things to occupy their time, rather than the continual bullying and harassment which she'd come to expect. She crossed the road, reluctantly walking towards the others.

Tanya Bryant was the first to spot her. "Yoh, look who's gracing us with her presence!"

The other children picked up on her cue, jeering and catcalling, Phyllis tucked her chin into her chest and continued walking. Maybe if she ignored them, they'd get bored with such sport. She noticed that not all the children were joining in, some were silently watching, not doing anything to stop it, but not participating either. Tanya Bryant was not so easily dissuaded though.

"Had to move back with darling mummy and daddy, did we? Poor little Syphilis, can't live with granny anymore, now she's popped her clogs!"

"Knock it off, Tanya, that's enough." It was one of the older boys who spoke. Looking up at the sudden silence, Phyllis saw uncomfortable looks on most of the children's faces, but Tanya and her cronies were now facing Phyllis, pushing, and jostling.

"Tell you what," shrieked Tanya, so entrenched in her own spite, she didn't realise she'd lost most of her audience. "If I had to live with Syphilis, I think my brains would explode too!"

In the sudden, shocked silence, even Tanya's friends stepped back in horror at her words. Phyllis's blood boiled. Her darling grandmother was dead. Mr Boots was dead. Her parents despised and neglected her. Worst of all, she had another four long years of suffering the surreal agony of being a millionaire, but still having to put up with crap from silly little non-entities like Tanya Bryant.

"Take it back," she snarled.

"What?" Tanya stepped away from the steely hatred of Phyllis's eyes.

"I said," growled Phyllis, "take it back. Take it back and say you're sorry!"

"No." Tanya flinched, but stood her ground, unable to back down and lose face. "It's true, her brains exploded cos she had to put up with a boring little shit like you."

Rage, white-hot and cleansing, flooded through Phyllis's body. She watched in disbelief as her fist appeared from nowhere and planted itself smack in the middle of Tanya's face. Almost in slow motion, Phyllis saw Tanya's nose explode in a bright shower of red drops, heard her howl of pain and disbelief, and saw the stunned expressions of shock on the faces of the others, before she turned and ran straight into the road.

With that same sense of distorted, slowed down time, she saw the car and knew with a portion of her brain that it was going to hit her. She saw her father's face, frozen with horror above his white clenched hands on the steering wheel and felt the impact; heard the snap of bone, the screams of children, saw tarmac rushing up to meet her.

For a brief, split second, she wondered at the absence of pain or fear, before her head connected with the road, and everything went black...

Chapter Four
"Hi honey, it's Lili!"

Her hands were shaking so much she couldn't get the key to work. Finally, it turned, and Phyllis let herself into the house, Her house. At 9:15, on the morning of her eighteenth birthday, Phyllis had left her parents' residence forever. She brought almost nothing with her – some toiletries, a few articles of clothing; from now on everything was to be fresh and new.

Phyllis had said nothing to her parents of her intentions; simply packed her few belongings the previous evening, and in the morning caught the 8:30am bus into town. A brief detour to Richard's office to collect the keys, then, at last, Phyllis was in the house she'd not seen, but which had filled her dreams for four years.

The last set of tenants had moved out the month previously, and Richard had arranged for it to be thoroughly spring cleaned from top to bottom. As Phyllis walked softly into the house, she could smell lemon polish. It seemed to fit her mood and she found herself smiling.

It felt good, Phyllis couldn't remember the last time she had any occasion to smile or laugh at anything, except maybe in the hospital when the nurses used to tell her jokes to cheer her up.

At the thought of her stay in hospital, Phyllis reflected that most people would feel being struck by your father's car would be the height of bad luck, yet it hadn't worked out that way.

Whilst Phyllis was lying in hospital with a broken arm, cracked ribs, a fractured jaw and concussion; questions were being asked about the incident.

The first few days after the accident, wild rumours and accusations spread like bushfire, children convincing each other through Chinese whispers that Phyllis was dying.

She was dead…

The police had been called in…

It was being considered manslaughter…

Shocked guilt followed.

Children told parents of the years of bullying and torment Phyllis had suffered.

Parents talked.

Children from the bus stop were referred to counsellors, who were told of the reason behind Phyllis Goodwin's inexplicable attack on Tanya Bryant, and subsequent flight into the road.

The headmaster was appraised, teachers were advised, social services called in.

Harsh accusations were made in the staff room. Mr Jackson handed in his notice and moved to a different school. Tanya Bryant was suspended. Children fell over themselves to point the finger; to escape being blamed for what had occurred.

The doctors told Phyllis she had been lucky. Her father was only going thirty miles an hour when she ran into his car, therefore the damage to her body was relatively minor. It was fixable. She was young and would heal as good as new.

In comparison to what might have happened, considering the speed cars usually went along the high street, yes, the doctors agreed, she'd been very lucky.

As Phyllis lay in plaster and in pain, she didn't feel particularly lucky but reflected it was better than being at home. The nurses fussed over her, and there was a television in the ward.

Richard Madison came to see her, elegant in his dark business suit. He brought her fat red grapes and beautiful yellow roses. Phyllis, who had never had flowers bought for her before, went pink with pleasure when the nurse bustled off to find a vase.

A social worker came to see Phyllis, asking questions, wanting explanations. Terrified of retribution, she stayed silent. The social worker went away to write her report of a child completely traumatised following long-term abuse by her peers.

This information leaked into the school and a collective sigh of relief was breathed at the news that Phyllis was refusing to name names.

Many children felt guilty at the role, no matter how small, they'd played in the whole affair. Tasting, perhaps for the first time, the bitter medicine of shame. Several teachers examined their conscience, reflecting they could have done something to stop things before they went too far.

A few felt they should look upon this as a wake-up call to the serious effects bullying could have, and lobbied to introduce revolutionary, anti-bullying tactics into the school.

Hitting his only child with his car had a profound effect on Phyllis's father. Traumatised by what had happened, his attitude towards Phyllis mellowed a little.

As he observed how stoically his daughter coped with her injuries and was informed by the school of exactly what she had suffered, he reflected on what could have happened if he'd been going a little faster, and Lionel Goodwin did a little soul searching.

The results of this were small but significant; he bought Phyllis a radio for her bedroom, now and again attempted a conversation with her and, more importantly, forced his wife to cease her campaign of guerrilla warfare against Phyllis.

So it was, when Phyllis left hospital, she returned to a home life that, although lacking in love and attention, was no longer an active war zone.

When she went back to school, she found her worst enemies gone, and the other children subdued and wary around her, affording her a grudging kind of respect for not being a sneak, even after the most severe provocation.

Nobody wanted to be her friend, things hadn't changed that much; but at least no one bullied her anymore, and that was as much as Phyllis had ever dared hope for.

The years that followed were strange ones for Phyllis. She seemed to exist in a kind of half-life; talking to no one except teachers and the occasional, stilted conversation with her father.

The bright spot of her life was the first Saturday of every month when she would take the bus into town and Richard would take her to lunch to update her on her financial matters and anything to do with the house.

Even though she didn't fully comprehend everything he said, Phyllis listened hard and later thought carefully about all he told her.

Phyllis's thoughts were now of Richard as she walked into the lounge, and the first thing she saw was a vase of beautiful yellow roses standing on the mantelpiece next to her grandparents' wedding photo, and a card welcoming her to her new home.

Slowly, with relish, Phyllis explored every inch of the house.

Every room needed to be examined, and it amazed her how much bigger the house seemed. In her memories, it had been smaller, darker, and she finally realised it was because her grandmother's dark furniture, the oppressive flock wallpaper, heavy velvet drapes and thick lace curtains, had all gone.

The house was now cream throughout, with minimum furnishings for the use of tenants.

Looking at the house through the eyes of an almost adult, Phyllis appreciated how big and potentially beautiful the house was. Built in 1840, when Britain was caught up in the excitement of having a young, ambitious queen on the throne, the house reflected the upward mobility of a newly created middle class.

Not as large as the townhouses of the country nobility, it was nonetheless several steps up from the terraced housing of the lower classes.

A large, rather lovely, stained-glass door opened into a bright and spacious hall, with an ornate staircase curving up and away at the end. The staircase then split in two, branching up to a landing that ringed the hallway in classic, white painted wood.

To the right of the front door were two reception rooms, both generously proportioned with high ceilings and fireplaces. The front room had a bay window looking onto the street, and the backroom had double glass doors leading into the large, unkempt garden.

To the left of the front door was another reception room, identical to the one on the opposite side in every respect. The room behind that was the kitchen, with a back door leading out into a jumble of outbuildings and then into the garden.

Up the rather grand flight of stairs and on the right, were two large bedrooms and an old-fashioned bathroom; on the left, three smaller rooms, all with reasonably high ceilings. The two largest rooms even had their original fireplaces.

Up yet another flight of less ornate stairs, the servants' quarters were tucked away in the attic – one large room, one smaller one, and a tiny box room which, in Phyllis's mind, cried out to be converted to a shower room.

It was a large house, and it was all hers. Phyllis's mind buzzed with plans and ideas; the fact that she could effectively spend whatever she wanted, do whatever she liked, making her feel dizzy.

Going into the kitchen, she discovered Richard had arranged for basic foodstuffs to be bought. In a daze of gratitude, she made herself a cup of tea and took it into the lounge to drink.

Sitting on the sofa, Phyllis listened to the silence all around, and wondered what she was going to do with the rest of her life.

A month later she was still wondering the same thing. After the initial relief and excitement at escaping her parent's house had faded, she realised she had no idea what to do.

Rather like a long-term prisoner, she was so institutionalised that it was hard for her mind to accept the world was now hers for the taking.

With no school or job to go to, Phyllis drifted through her days like a rudderless boat adrift in a vast expanse of ocean. Aimless and directionless, she filled her days with a mindless round of housework, shopping, television, and food. Food, especially, became her comfort and her joy.

When she lived with her parents, eating the nutritious, appetising, and superbly presented meals her mother cooked, Phyllis had taken food for granted.

It appeared on her plate.

She ate it in silence.

She never had to think about the reality of eating, of planning menus, shopping for ingredients, making sure all the components of a meal were ready at the same time. Having to do it herself dismayed and defeated her.

Finally, Phyllis gave up trying, instead filled her basket with comforting convenience food. Living in the town centre and not having a car meant Phyllis went shopping at least once a day, so was constantly exposed to temptingly easy and shockingly fattening foods.

After a month of such a diet, Phyllis was dismayed to discover that her clothes were beginning to feel tight, a worrying crop of spots had erupted on her face, her hair was greasier than ever, and indigestion and constipation were now her constant companions.

Phyllis worried about this but was clueless as to how to remedy it, seeking comfort from her fears in yet more food, which, of course, exacerbated the problem even further. It was further compounded by the sedentary lifestyle she was now living.

Phyllis had never been an active child. The horrors of PE, and being constantly picked last in games, had installed such a fear of sport in her, even the idea of joining a gym, or taking up any physical activity of any kind, was psychologically beyond her.

At least whilst she had lived with her parents, the low fat, low calorie, correctly balanced meals, and limited portions had kept her weight down. But now, with no one to advise or correct her eating habits, and easy access to an unlimited supply of highly addictive, pre-packaged food, Phyllis took the first steps on the path to obesity.

At her first lunch with Richard after leaving home, he was alarmed to notice the change in her appearance. The monthly lunches had begun as a duty to his old friend but quickly became a pleasure as Richard came to appreciate there was more to Phyllis than met the eye.

When, after a few meetings, he began to penetrate her barrier of mistrust, Richard discovered a sweet-natured and kind girl, thirsty for knowledge and experience.

The narrowness of her life had left her desperate for escape, and conversation over lunch had often been about what she would do upon receiving her inheritance.

Carefully, he questioned her on her new life, saddened at the pathetic list of activities she trotted out for his approval – shopping, housework, television?

Surely these were the preferences of the very old, not the choices of an eighteen-year-old who had the financial means to take the world by the throat and make it her own.

Gently, he suggested other pursuits – travel maybe, learn to drive, get a job? What about her plans to renovate the house?

Phyllis remained stubbornly opposed to changing the status quo though, and seeing her begin to retreat into mulish obstinacy, Richard changed the subject.

The day after her lunch with Richard, Phyllis awoke from ten hours of sleep in a restless, agitated mood. Unable to settle to anything on television, she looked around for something, anything to do.

Looking in the cupboards and freezer, Phyllis didn't fancy any of the food that was there, and more to give a purpose to yet another Sunday rather than from any real hunger decided to walk to Waitrose and treat herself to whatever she wanted for lunch.

The short walk made her breathless. Rather than carry a basket, she took a trolley, reminding herself to keep an eye on how much she put in it as it would all have to be carried home.

Briefly, she considered buying a car and learning how to drive, the thought causing her to break out in a cold sweat. She quickly dismissed the idea and concentrated on her shopping.

A big bag of salt and vinegar crisps, chocolate bars, a treacle tart, a large steak and kidney pie, oven chips, beans, ice cream, fizzy orange drink, jelly babies and pork pies; an eclectic mix of chemicals, fat, sugar, and salt was tossed randomly into the trolley.

Desperate to get home, shut the door, and eat herself into oblivion, Phyllis turned her trolley mid-aisle and saw her.

She wasn't tall, about Phyllis's height, but there any resemblance ended, and Phyllis froze to the spot, gazing in open-mouthed envy. Her back to Phyllis, she reached up to run her fingers along the bottles of olive oil, obviously searching for a particular one.

Her head was to one side, a mobile phone clamped between shoulder and ear. Phyllis blinked. She'd seen mobile phones before, of course, but never one so small. It practically disappeared into the girl's mane of shiny, chestnut, shoulder-length hair, which shone with all the glossy condition of a thoroughbred filly.

A short, snug, denim jacket in an eye-catching unusual lilac shade, barely skimmed the girl's waist. As she reached up, Phyllis caught a glimpse of red lace riding above the waistband of chocolate brown jeans, sitting so scandalously low on the girl's slim hips, Phyllis marvelled they didn't slide down.

Cut in a style Phyllis was unfamiliar with, the jeans suited the girl's petite stature perfectly as if designed with shorter women in mind. Phyllis's eyes travelled the length of those slim, shapely legs until they came to a pair of chocolate brown, leather ankle boots with spiky heels.

Phyllis was aware she was staring, that the girl could turn at any moment and catch her, but she couldn't help it. Something about her fascinated, drew Phyllis to her like a moth to a flame.

She wondered what her face was like, knowing instinctively it would be as stylish and beautiful as the rest of her. The girl was talking now, her voice quick and animated. Phyllis shamelessly eavesdropped.

"Hi honey, it's Lili. Yes, I'm in Waitrose now, I know, sorry, running a little late, but I've got the wine and champagne, the cream, baguettes, pate, brie, nibbles, and fresh fruit. Was there anything else you needed? Right, okay, thing is, they don't have the olive oil you needed to make the dressing."

The girl, Lili, tucked the phone under her other ear and began to search along the shelf, whilst Phyllis looked with naked curiosity into her trolley.

What seemed an endless array of bright, exotic fruits, some of which were unfamiliar to Phyllis, jostled alongside bottles of expensive-looking champagne and wine, pots and packages from the deli, and the large wedge of paper which was the Sunday Times. Phyllis looked at her own trolley, feeling sick at the comparison.

"Okay, yep, they've got that one, shall I get it instead?" A slim manicured hand plucked the desired bottle from the shelf. "Anything else? No, okay, I'm on my way now. Has everyone arrived? Oh, they're going to be so surprised, I can't wait to see their faces. Okay, bye, see you soon, love you."

The girl dropped the phone into her leather bag, which matched the boots perfectly.

Phyllis stepped forward, a strange, desperate, yearning welling up inside. She wished with a fierce longing she could be this girl; that she could be Lili.

The girl stiffened, olive oil still clutched in hand, shivered, and started to slowly turn.

In a wild and inexplicable panic, not wanting to be caught watching with such open avarice on her face, Phyllis abandoned her trolley and fled.

Barely knowing what she was doing, Phyllis walked to the beginning of the shop and grabbed another trolley. At the newspaper stand, she picked up a Sunday Times, then headed down the fruit and veg aisle. Still in a daze, she realised she had almost exactly reproduced the exotic, colourful fruit from Lili's trolley.

Sudden purpose ignited and Phyllis shopped as if possessed. A whole new world of miraculous food and drink opened before her, and it was greedily grabbed and thrown into the trolley – bags of brightly coloured salad leaves, stir fry vegetables, mixed peppers gleaming in their packets like edible traffic lights, fresh salad dressing, packets of herbs and bags of seeds and nuts.

Then Phyllis hit the deli, trying to look sophisticated as if she shopped there regularly. She hung back watching carefully, as shoppers took a little white number, waited their turn, and then picked what they wanted from the miraculous, confusing, amazing array laid out in colourful rows.

How had Phyllis missed all this wonderful food before? She had been to this shop dozens of times but had never seen this veritable feast of choice, all hers for the taking. Her turn came and she chose brie, pate, anchovies, and ham. Heart pounding, she picked at random things she felt sure Lili would choose.

Reaching the checkout, Phyllis was too mentally, emotionally, and physically drained to even wince at the bill. Never had she enjoyed shopping so much. She couldn't wait to get home and try everything, head spinning at the thought of so much choice.

As Phyllis handed over her new credit card to the cashier, she wondered how she was to get it all home, then spotted a telephone on the wall behind the tills with taxi numbers listed beside it.

What the hell, she thought wryly. It was turning out to be a day of new experiences, why not phone for a taxi for the very first time as well.

Chapter Five
"That's Boris, I'd say you've been picked."

That day was a turning point for Phyllis. That brief glimpse of a stranger, a snippet of overheard conversation, gave Phyllis's life purpose, a new direction. Without understanding why, or stopping to analyse it, Lili became her obsession; a benchmark against which Phyllis measured everything that happened in her life.

Healthy, beautiful food became a mission for Phyllis. What sort of meals would Lili have? In search of ideas, Phyllis ventured to unknown territory – the library. With a pounding heart, she obtained a library card and trawled the shelves, her initial panic at the sea of words abating, as she realised that she didn't have to read any of them unless she chose to. Nobody was going to force her or stand over her and criticise if she stumbled or made mistakes.

Such freedom was liberating. Phyllis spent the whole morning simply looking; picking books at random and perusing them, putting them back; wandering around the non-fiction department, gazing in wonder at all the books, so many books, on every subject you could think of. Finally, she discovered the cookery book section and chose a selection of books which she carried to a table.

Some she discarded immediately as being too complicated, too wordy. Others she put to one side to have a closer look at, ending up with a pile of half a dozen books which seemed to meet all her requirements; not too many words, and plenty of colourful pictures showing her step by step what she had to do. For some reason, Phyllis mostly chose books on Mediterranean and Italian cookery, with one on stir-fries and another on pulses, beans, and lentils.

Instinctively, she felt sure this was the kind of food Lili liked best. In her imagination she could see her, standing by a stove, casually concocting some simple but stylish dish, a glass of red wine in one hand, laughing and chatting to the myriad of friends gathered around her. Lili would always be the centre of any social circle, Phyllis felt she would be the arranger, the planner, the one at the very heart of her gang of friends.

With a thrill of anticipation, Phyllis carried the books home, eager to explore this wonderful, colourful, culinary world spread before her.

Of course, it wasn't all plain sailing. She had disasters alongside her triumphs. The time she didn't understand the difference between a bulb and a clove of garlic and ended up producing something inedible, which made her sweat garlic for three days. The recipes she simply misread and put too much or too little of some vital ingredient in, leaving her wondering why the results looked nothing like the picture in the book.

But she persevered, slowly beginning to develop a feel, an instinct for food preparation, so if her eyes told her to add a tablespoon of something, yet her gut feeling was this was too much, she could return to the recipe, painstakingly re-read it, and correct herself before making a mistake.

It became a game for Phyllis – how many colours could she achieve on her plate in one meal. Without planning to, without being aware of what was happening, Phyllis began to lose weight drastically, to become so much healthier and fitter, her mind more alert, as a combination of good, healthy food and more reading forced her brain to work for perhaps the first time in her life.

Phyllis began getting up earlier instead of sleeping her life away, aimlessly drifting through days. She found places to go, and things to do. Twice a week there was a market in the centre of town, and Phyllis would get up early to buy her produce fresh, having planned her meals and carefully written herself a list.

The town in which Phyllis lived was a lovely market town in the centre of Suffolk. Rich in culture and history, it offered a myriad of historical experiences, guided tours, and informative walks through the town and abbey remains in the beautiful gardens. Phyllis tried them all, learning more about the place in which she lived in a few weeks than she had in the previous eighteen years.

She even ventured to the hairdresser her grandmother had used. A small, single person salon, it catered mostly to the blue rinse brigade and was ill-equipped to deal with an eighteen-year-old's needs. Still, they trimmed her fringe and cut away the split ends, so her hair swished over her shoulders in a plain, mousy parody of Lili's gorgeous, chestnut mane.

As Phyllis stared at her reflection in the mirror, she longed with a burning desire to be like Lili, to be slim and beautiful, but above all, Phyllis craved Lili's confidence, her poise and self-assuredness. Sadly, she remembered her grandmother's words, wondering if she would ever look in the mirror and see an attractive woman.

Phyllis constantly hoped to see Lili again. Everywhere she went she scanned people's faces, looking for that familiar, glossy sweep of hair. Whenever she shopped in Waitrose, she would turn into each aisle, heart thudding with optimism, only to be disappointed.

Sometimes she thought she felt her presence and would turn sharply, only to find no one there.

Once, she thought she saw her on the street ahead, walking arm in arm with a girl with long blonde hair, laughing and chatting, slim hips swaying as they turned into a different street. By the time Phyllis hurried to the corner, they'd gone, and even though Phyllis walked slowly down the street, peering into every shop and café, she could see no sign of them.

Her time was occupied with so many new activities, it was with surprise Phyllis realised a whole month had passed, and it was time for lunch with Richard. Dressing in the morning, she realised her best skirt and blouse felt looser, and she had to find a safety pin to stop the skirt from sliding down.

Phyllis looked at her reflection as she slowly pulled a brush through her hair. What she saw was a definite improvement; the spots had thankfully gone, and the new cut was tidier, the fringe no longer trailing in her eyes like bindweed. Yet Phyllis had no idea what to do with her hair once she washed it. Not even owning a hairdryer meant it dried flat and shapeless, plastering itself around her head in a very unflattering manner.

Phyllis laid down the brush, remembering Lili's gorgeous mane, and how the light had bounced off the myriad of rich tonal colours as she'd run slim fingers casually through her hair. Phyllis wondered how hair could be made to look so beautiful. Perhaps, she thought, some people were lucky enough to be born with lovely hair, whilst others … she looked again at her dull hair and sighed.

Phyllis was a few moments late arriving at the restaurant, and Richard was already there and seated at their normal table when she breathlessly rushed in.

"Sorry," she exclaimed, pulling off her coat and giving it to the hovering waiter. "Mineral water, please," she requested.

As she settled into her chair, Richard stared in surprised delight. She looked different – not just the obvious changes, the clear complexion, the drastic weight loss – but something in her very manner seemed changed. She seemed more confident, more alert. There was a glow about her, a renewed sense of purpose. The waiter brought her mineral water. Richard reflected this too was new, Phyllis's usual drink of choice being coke.

Gazing at their menus, he wondered if Phyllis would go for her traditional choice of steak and chips, but this time she did seem to be studying the menu intently, staying silent when Richard announced his intention to have Dover sole. When the waiter came to take their orders, she asked about the specials, listened attentively as he listed them, before choosing the Mediterranean pasta bake with salad. Seeing Richard's surprised look, she smiled.

"I've been trying new foods; I got bored with always having the same old things, so I've been experimenting a bit."

"I'm delighted to hear it," replied Richard. "Now then," he paused to take a sip of his Chardonnay, "tell me what else you've been up to since we last met?"

As their lunches were served and they began to eat, Phyllis talked. She told of trips to the library, of meals she'd cooked, both successful and otherwise; of her new habit of reading the Sunday Times and how much she was enjoying it; of guided tours around the town, funny walks around the abbey ruins and old churchyard, with the guides dressed up as a monk and a gravedigger, respectively. Phyllis had a good eye for detail, more than once making Richard laugh with sharply witty descriptions.

"I've got a surprise for you." Phyllis cleared her throat and looked at Richard a little shyly. "I've thought a lot about what you said and you're right, I do need to move on with my life, and that's why I've booked myself onto a driving course."

Richard was astonished but delighted and pressed for more information. Phyllis, thrilled by his reaction, gladly told how it had been a spur of the moment thing. She had seen the advertisement in the local paper for an intensive two-week driving course at the end of which you took your test. She told him how she cut the article out, stuck it on the fridge, and thought about it for a week, before finally plucking up the courage to phone and book herself a place on the next available course, which was starting on Monday. She was excited about it, of course, but nervous. Really, *really,* nervous.

"You'll be fine," Richard reassured her. "And of course, once you've passed your test, you'll be able to buy yourself a little car, and then you'll have the freedom to go wherever you please."

"Yes, I suppose, the thing is …" Phyllis broke off, fiddling with her coffee spoon. "The thing is, Richard, I'm worried about running out of money. I've spent a lot, and what I wanted to ask was, well, is it okay to spend some money on silly things like driving lessons and cars?"

"Oh, my dear," Richard smiled at Phyllis's naïve anxieties. "Since your grandmother's death, your money has been busy working for you. It's not just sitting in a bank somewhere. No, some of it has been invested, shares have been bought. Your original inheritance has increased quite substantially and is gaining interest every day. So, you see, Phyllis, so long as you don't go mad and start buying private planes and football teams, it would be almost impossible for you to run out of money and, trust me, I would intervene long before that. Don't worry about it. Enjoy the money; buy what you think you need; what you think you'd like. After all, that's why your grandmother left it to you with no strings attached. She trusted you to be grown up enough to deal with it."

For a moment, Phyllis didn't respond, merely sat with her eyes fixed on her coffee cup. Then she glanced up and smiled. Richard thought to himself what an attractive girl she could be. With a little effort and some feminine touches, Phyllis could be someone who demanded attention. Already, her face had the potential for beauty. Now the fat had begun to drop away, exposing her bone structure, he could see flashes of his old friend's youthful loveliness struggling to escape from a teenager's sullen expression. A little more weight lost, a little more confidence gained, a decent hairdo, maybe some make-up and some animation to her features, and Phyllis would be a woman to be reckoned with.

When they parted, Richard couldn't help but wonder what changes another month would bring or had Phyllis reached a plateau of personal achievement. Having come this far, would she be able to take herself any further? Or would the effort prove too much? He hoped not, and as he kissed her on the cheek and wished her luck, it was not only the driving course he was referring to.

Confidence was a funny thing, reflected Phyllis, gazing in stunned wonder at the certificate in her hand. A few short weeks ago she'd been a timid and introverted teenager; her emotional, personal, and social development stunted by exceptional circumstances. She lacked the self-confidence to even attempt any of the activities a normal girl her age would take in her stride. Then, she saw Lili.

That brief glimpse of how it was possible to be had somehow kick-started her life, giving her the confidence to try new foods, join the library, explore her native town, and become more aware of the outside world; to struggle to break free of the insular bubble in which she was trapped.

It was like those long and complicated rows of dominoes, she mused. With one tap on the first domino, thousands were knocked down. Lili had unwittingly administered that first tap that had led to this. She looked at the certificate in her hand and couldn't help the smug smile of self-satisfaction. She had passed. Two long, terrifying, exhausting, stimulating weeks later, she, Phyllis Goodwin, had passed her driving test.

Phyllis wished with all her heart she had someone to share it with; someone to understand how important it was. After a lifetime of being conditioned to believe she was a failure, too incompetent to ever achieve anything, she'd finally done something worthwhile … something to be proud of.

She propped the certificate on the mantelpiece. It didn't matter. Even the lack of friendship in her life couldn't detract from the glory of this moment.

Two days later, Phyllis decided to address this need for companionship and phoned the local cats' home. Her mind was made up – she was going to get a kitten. The thought of it was enough to make her feel breathless with thrilled anticipation. A kitten. Someone to love and fuss over.

Paying a visit to the pet shop, Phyllis could hardly contain her excitement as she bought a carrying basket, pet bean bag, food and water bowls, litter tray, litter, and an assortment of cat toys. Her kitten, her cat, she wondered whether it would be a little boy or a girl, and what colour its coat and eyes would be.

Taking a taxi to the cats' home that afternoon, Phyllis was determined to get her own car soon. It was too inconvenient having to walk everywhere or rely on public transport. She paid the fare, arranged with the driver to come back in an hour, then rang the bell, heart thudding in anticipation.

After what seemed an age, an elderly woman let her in, explaining they were short-staffed, and that she'd been in the middle of feeding. Barely pausing for breath, she led Phyllis through another gate into a large, enclosed garden roofed with wire, and ringed with various sheds and shelters.

Phyllis gasped. Cats were everywhere – draped on every surface, feeding from bowls heaped with food, playing rough and tumble on the ground, curled up asleep in assorted beds and baskets.

"You're lucky," explained the woman. "We currently have lots of kittens in. Shall I leave you to have a look around, see if any of the kittens pick you?"

"Pick me?" queried Phyllis.

"That's right," replied the woman and smiled. "That's the way it usually works. Your cat will choose you. It may not be the one you thought you wanted, but it will be the right cat for you."

Not knowing what to do, Phyllis wandered around the enclosure, stopping to pet every kitten she saw, waiting to see if one chose her. They were all so sweet; little bundles of fur with pipe cleaner tails and squeaky meows; she loved and wanted them all, but wasn't drawn to one, nor did one seem drawn to her. Sighing, Phyllis stepped back, smiling at the antics of a group of black and white kittens as they played pounce and chase at her feet.

Something swiped her across the side of the head from behind. Phyllis jumped and swung around to come face to face with the ugliest cat she'd ever seen. Large and corpulent, he stretched out on a shelf at shoulder height, gently batting at her face with a softly sheathed paw.

"Sorry, boy," she said softly. "But you're not what I'm looking for." Phyllis didn't know how she knew he was a boy, but the large chunky head, the stocky thickset body, and the jagged scar streaked over one eye gave the cat a masculine appearance.

He seemed affable enough though, and Phyllis reached up to give him a friendly stroke, before returning to the seemingly impossible task of finding her kitten. As she did, the strangest thing happened.

The cat gently patted her hand down onto the shelf, then laid its big ugly head in her palm and stared at her.

Phyllis stared back, noting the unusual, beautiful, pale green colour of his eyes, the ragged ear bent over at the tip giving the cat a jaunty, devil-may-care, appearance. She moved closer, looking deeper, mesmerised.

Dropping one eye in a slow and deliberate wink, the cat got up, stretched, then delicately stepped from the shelf onto Phyllis's shoulder. Phyllis automatically held him, heard deep, rumbling purrs as he settled comfortably into her embrace, licking gently at her neck. Stunned, Phyllis looked at the woman who smiled knowingly.

"That's Boris," she said. "I'd say you've been picked."

That night, as Phyllis settled in bed, her hand felt down the cover for the warmth and bulk of Boris. As she heard his purrs start up, sounding like some ancient, petrol-driven lawnmower, she smiled in happiness and drifted off to sleep.

The first Saturday in May arrived. Once again, Phyllis dressed carefully for lunch with Richard, surprised at how quickly time had passed since their last meeting. She was looking forward to seeing Richard; had much to tell him about her experiences learning to drive and, of course, acquiring Boris.

Thinking about him brought a smile to Phyllis's lips. She cast an affectionate look where he lay, sprawled in an ungainly heap in a patch of sunlight on her bed. Since the arrival of Boris in her life, Phyllis had had much to laugh about and was thankful such a character had chosen her to live with.

At times, the cat seemed almost to talk as he fussed and grumbled, displaying such attitude and personality, Phyllis wondered why he'd ended up alone and unwanted in a cats' home. The similarity of his situation and her childhood formed a bond between them, and Phyllis could hardly remember what life had been like before Boris.

Slipping into her best skirt and blouse, Phyllis noticed the skirt was so loose it needed a safety pin on each hip to hold it up, and the blouse bagged over her reduced breasts. She frowned, shuddering at the thought she might have to go shopping.

Phyllis hated clothes shopping. Too insecure to venture into fashionable clothes shops, Phyllis tended to shop in Marks & Spencer or one of the smaller shops designed for older women. As a result, her clothes were all far too old for her, and now she'd lost over two stone in weight, they were all far too big, enveloping her slim frame, making her look odd – a child dressing up in her mother's clothes.

Once again, she was late getting to the restaurant. Richard was already seated, sipping at his habitual glass of wine, when Phyllis was shown to his table. His first thoughts were a mixture of delight that she'd lost yet more weight and looked better for it, mingled with dismay at the ugly clothes she was still dressing in.

However, keeping his thoughts to himself, he merely expressed his congratulations at her breathless imparting of the news she'd passed her driving test, listening with amused patience as she filled almost the whole of the lunch with tales of Boris. As obsessed as any new parent, she chatted on about his character, his looks, the funny things he'd done in the two weeks since she'd got him.

"So," enquired Richard when Phyllis finally fell silent and was toying with her dessert. "What's next Phyllis? Do you have any thoughts or plans for the future?"

"Well," began Phyllis, glancing at him shyly and nibbling at her lower lip. "I was thinking, maybe I should try and get a job..."

"An excellent idea." Richard enthused heartily.

"The thing is," continued Phyllis. "I don't know what sort of job I could get. I mean, I've no qualifications, no experience, I can't type or use a computer. What sort of job could I possibly do? I suppose there's always shop work, but I don't fancy that, although I don't know what I do want to do. Oh, it's all so confusing."

"I think," replied Richard slowly, "it doesn't matter what job you get. Maybe it's more important to gain experience; an understanding of what it means to be in paid employment. After all, you don't have to stay in the job long if you don't like it, just long enough to get a feel for working. You have an advantage over most girls your age, Phyllis. You're financially secure, so can take your time finding the right career for you."

"I know," agreed Phyllis. "It's not so much the doing of a job that concerns me, it's more the getting of one. I've never applied for a job before, so I don't know how to go about it. I don't have a typewriter, couldn't use it even if I had one, and my handwriting is so awful nobody would give my letter a second glance."

"So, go to a typing agency," suggested Richard. "I know there are a couple in town. Why don't you take along any job advertisements that catch your eye and let them type the letters?"

Phyllis put down her coffee cup and stared at him. "I never thought about that," she murmured. "That's brilliant, I'll try. Who knows? Maybe by next month, I might have found myself a job."

"Phyllis," began Richard. "I'm sure you can do anything you put your mind to. I'm so proud of you, of all you've achieved."

He lifted his coffee cup to her in a silent toast, whilst Phyllis beamed with red-faced joy at his encouraging words.

The idea of a job stayed with Phyllis the whole of the following week, alternatively filling her with hopeful anticipation and dread. By Friday, the day the local paper came out, she had managed to convince herself she'd look in the employment pages, but that it would be a complete waste of time because there'd be no jobs advertised which would be even vaguely suitable.

To her surprise, there were four, all for office juniors, which she felt she might be able to do. Carefully cutting them out, Phyllis walked to the typing agency which had also advertised itself in the local paper. Heart in mouth, she found the agency housed in a large, newly built, yellow brick building down one of the side roads off the main town centre. She hesitated outside for a moment, pulled all her courage together, and walked in.

Inside, she found a large attractive office housing a variety of computers, and other assorted office equipment which Phyllis could only guess the function of. A pair of young girls were busily typing at two of the workstations, one engrossed in copying from a pile of papers. Every now and then she would stop typing to squint at the handwritten pages, before resuming her fast, staccato tapping of the keys. The other girl appeared to be wearing headphones, as Phyllis gazed in fascination, she saw she was working a foot pedal under the desk and realised this must be audio typing. Phyllis watched in awe as the girl, eyes fixed on the screen in front of her, never once looked down at her fingers flying over the keyboard.

"Can I help you?" Phyllis turned in shock to the woman now standing behind her holding a full coffee pot. She raised amused eyebrows as Phyllis gaped in silence. "Can I help you?"

"Um, yes, please," Phyllis fumbled with her bag, reddened as it fell to the ground, the clasp giving way and the contents spilling all over the floor. "Oh no!" she exclaimed, dropping to her knees to pick everything up.

The woman put the coffee pot down and knelt to help her. "Don't you hate it when that happens?" she said cheerily, her voice warm and kind. "Now then," she continued when all Phyllis's belongings were safely stowed back in her bag, "what can I do to help?"

"I was wondering, um, if you could please type some letters for me applying for these jobs?" Desperately, Phyllis pushed the cuttings at the woman, who looked at the four advertisements ringed in red.

"Not a problem," she said. "If you don't mind waiting, I've got a spare ten minutes. I could do them for you now."

"Thank you," stuttered Phyllis, unable to believe how easy it was.

"Help yourself to coffee," continued the woman, waving a hand towards the small seating area in the corner of the office. "There are magazines and papers there too."

Thanking her, Phyllis sat on a small grey sofa and picked up the local paper from the top of the pile. Turning to the employment section, she once again scanned its pages, reading laboriously in her head the four she'd picked out. Rustling over the page, idly glancing through the part-time listings, she saw it.

'Wanted. Reliable Girl Friday!' read the ad. 'Must be hardworking and dependable, computer skills useful but not essential as on the job training will be given. Hours Tuesday to Thursday, 10:00am to 4:00pm.' Phyllis frowned; she'd not considered working part-time before, but why not? As Richard had said, the important thing was to gain experience.

"Excuse me," she called, and the woman looked up from her keyboard, a friendly enquiring smile on her face. "Could you possibly do one more letter for me?"

Twenty minutes later, having signed the letters and watched as the woman expertly inserted them into crisp, white envelopes, Phyllis paid over what seemed an absurdly low sum for such skilled work, also paying for five first-class stamps. Thanking the woman, she walked to the nearest post box and posted them, her hands clammy and her heart beating with hopeful expectation.

The next day was Saturday. Wandering about the market crowded with busy shoppers, Phyllis enjoyed the sense of purpose it gave her to be selecting fresh produce for the coming week; buying cheese and butter off the open-sided van, talking to the fresh fish seller about what was good that week. With her shy, but friendly manner, and readiness to stop and chat, Phyllis was popular with the stallholders she regularly visited.

Sunday morning dawned, a beautiful and breezy spring day. Feeling a need for fresh air and exercise, Phyllis packed a flask of coffee and some bacon sandwiches, meandering down to the Abbey Gardens for an impromptu picnic breakfast. Chatting to the elderly lady on the bench next to her, watching children as they raced and shrieked in the play area, looking around the beds of blooming flowers, Phyllis had a very pleasant morning before drifting home, buying a paper on the way.

Back home, she brewed more coffee and spread the paper out on the lounge floor, its mass surprising her as it did every week. Mug in hand, she sprawled belly down on the floor, slowly and carefully reading the home section. Her favourite, she loved it when an article had before and after pictures and would stare intently at what had been done to completely transform a wreck into a home, then look around her house and sigh. Apart from buying a few kitchen utensils, Phyllis had done nothing to improve her home. It was still as it was when she'd moved in.

It wasn't that Phyllis didn't want to change the house ... she didn't know how to. The thought of trying to find builders and decorators to transform into reality her vision of how the house should look, daunted her. Too afraid to take that step, Phyllis lived with the house as it was. After all, it was warm and clean, the furniture was basic to meet the needs of tenants, but it was adequate for her.

Today, as usual, Phyllis slowly and laboriously worked her way through the pages, stumbling over words, carefully running her finger under each line of print, reading and re-reading until she felt confident, she understood every single word.

The centre spread was a focus on a young, successful interior designer, currently taking London by storm. Phyllis's lips parted on a small sigh of pleasure, as she minutely scrutinised the pictures of his work. Yes, this was precisely how she envisaged her house being – this beautiful and clever mix of old and new.

Her heart gave a skip of excitement as she read the designer's quote – that he 'believed in working with the character and features of the rooms he was asked to design' and 'there was nothing he enjoyed more than breathing life and character back into tired and life worn properties.'

With rising exhilaration, Phyllis looked around the room. Tired and life worn – it exactly described her house. Maybe, this was the way forward … the answer to her prayers. An interior designer, but not any old one, Phyllis searched the blurry print for the designer's name. She wanted this one. She wanted Conrad Stevens.

Phyllis allowed the daydream to rush over her like a spring tide. She would write to him, hire him to completely renovate the house. After all, she had money, so why not? He'd be her guide, her mentor. He would transform this house into the home of her dreams.

Then doubt and paranoia grabbed her throat in a stranglehold. She couldn't contact him, she couldn't. He probably only ever designed for posh society people in London. There was no way such a famous designer would ever come to the middle of Suffolk to help her renovate her house. No, it was unthinkable.

Quickly, Phyllis turned the page, her mind retreating into its locked room of low self-esteem and confidence, the idea dismissed and forgotten. Then it hit her like a thunderbolt between the eyes. Next came the gardening section, and as she turned the page, she saw it – a full-page, colour picture of a lily.

Phyllis dropped the paper, started back in shock, staring at the pristine, classic beauty of its long, slim green stem, the creamy-white throat of its flower. It was a sign, an omen, the thoughts flashing through her befuddled brain. It had to be.

Slowly, she turned back a page – Conrad Stevens. It gave his name, but not his address. Where could she find his address? Phyllis's mind was made up. After such a blatant prod from the gods, she had no choice. She would write to him. She had to.

With trembling hands, she cut out the picture of the lily and stuck it on the fridge door. She decided the best course of action would be the library. Perhaps she could find Conrad Stevens's business address in the London Yellow Pages. She doubted it would be that easy, but it was as good a place as any to start.

Much to Phyllis's surprise, it did turn out to be that easy, and two hours later she was staring at the final, hand-written letter it had taken her many attempts to get right.

Dear Mr Stevens,

I saw your article in the Sunday Times and very much liked the pictures and what you said. I now own my grandmother's house and would very much appreciate it if you could please give me a quote for completely renovating it.

The house is a large Victorian villa and could be lovely, but it is as you said in the article, tired and life worn. I love my home but don't know how to make it as I see it in my dreams. Please help me. I know that your fees are probably quite high, but I would like to say that I have the money to pay whatever it costs to make my home beautiful.

Yours faithfully,
Phyllis Goodwin

Phyllis stared at the letter. Mentally drained by the effort of writing it, the words slipped and danced all over the page. Knowing there were probably spelling mistakes, but unable to see them and feeling her confidence faltering, Phyllis quickly addressed the envelope in block capitals, found a stamp in the back of her purse, and set out for home, determined to post it in the first post box she saw.

Later that evening, cooking dinner, she stared at the picture of the lily. Perhaps it was an omen; a portent that her life was finally about to begin. Phyllis trembled with anticipation before sharply reining in her imagination. Maybe it was, and maybe it wasn't. It was too late to think about it now.

Phyllis smiled a little with quiet pride at what she had achieved. Even if she never heard back from any of them, the fact remained she had applied for five jobs and had written to a nationally acclaimed interior designer. She'd done something to try and break free of her narrow, confined life. It felt good.

Chapter Six
"How soon could you start, Phyllis?"

For the next two days Phyllis watched for the postman with all the intensity of Boris watching a mousehole, disappointed when, if he did deign to stop at her front door, the only thing he pushed through the letterbox was junk mail.

Finally, on Wednesday, she received replies from two of the full-time positions she applied for. They were sorry; she had been unsuccessful in her application and was not to be considered for the position. However, they would keep her details on file for further reference, wishing her every success in her future career.

Even Phyllis, with her limited knowledge of the ways of the world, recognised a definite rejection when she read one and didn't hold out much hope of ever hearing from either company again.

The next day another pair of rejections came through, plunging Phyllis into a trough of dejection, her self-confidence, which had been struggling to assert itself the past few weeks, lying in smashed shards all around her.

It was completely pointless even trying again, she decided sulkily. Who was ever going to offer her a job? With no experience, no qualifications and a complete lack of life skills, hell, even she wouldn't want to employ her.

Friday dawned, a whole week since she sent out the letters. Phyllis barely stirred in her slumber when she heard the rattle of the letterbox.

No, she was staying right where she was, warm and cosy. Boris sprawled next to her, flat on his back, legs akimbo, advertising his wares to the whole world and snoring like a traction engine.

When Phyllis finally stumbled downstairs, stupid, and confused from too much sleep, it took her a few moments to understand the significance of the contents of the plain white envelope.

It was a reply from the fifth application, the part-time one for a Girl Friday.

No, not a reply, it was an invitation to attend an interview that afternoon at their offices in town. Phyllis sat down heavily in a chair in stunned surprise.

They wanted to see her.

They wanted to interview her!

After the moment of pure joy came the terror.

Oh hell, what was she going to wear? Running through the options in her wardrobe, Phyllis realised with a sinking heart that she had no choice...

She was going to have to brave the shops and buy something new.

Dorothy Evans prided herself on being an excellent judge of character. She always claimed within five minutes of meeting someone, that their personality would be an open book to her. Indeed, this skill had proved invaluable in her chosen career of running the largest employment agency in the area.

The ability to speedily sum up the strengths and weaknesses of a candidate enabled her to place them unerringly in the correct position, with an almost one hundred percent success rate.

The girl sitting opposite was proving the exception. She was young; painfully so, Dorothy knew the girl had turned eighteen a few months previously, yet she seemed younger, possessing a naivete and innocence rare, if not extinct, in modern eighteen-year-olds.

Dorothy sensed the girl was inexperienced, not only in employment terms but also when it came to life.

Phyllis shifted uncomfortably in her chair under the silent, intense scrutiny of the woman sitting behind the large, black ash desk. Nervously, she smoothed her new skirt purchased only that morning from Marks & Spencer.

Once again, Phyllis had completely bypassed the items on sale for girls her age, instead heading unerringly into the section of the shop usually the exclusive domain of women over fifty.

Seeing the neat, calf-length black skirt, she grabbed it off the rail with an audible sigh of relief, although much to her surprise, she had to go down to a size ten before it fitted correctly.

A classic black skirt, she reasoned, who could go wrong with that? Team it with a white blouse and maybe she'd stop feeling so out of place. But she didn't.

Wilting before the keen-eyed gaze of the employment agency proprietor, Phyllis became achingly aware of the fact this woman must be over forty, yet the beautifully tailored, burnt orange trouser suit with its long-line, sleek jacket, was fashionable and youthful, cleverly cut to enhance her still trim figure, the warm colour bouncing light up into the woman's sharp, clever face.

The neat skirt and white polyester blouse which had looked okay in the shop felt all wrong. Phyllis squirmed with acute discomfort, seeing herself through the older woman's eyes – a frumpy, plain, unintelligent girl.

What on earth was she thinking? Believing maybe, just maybe, she could be like other girls and get a job, any job, even a silly little part-time one like this?

Phyllis sharply reined in her self-doubts, struggling to concentrate as the woman talked, explaining about the job.

"I own this agency," the woman was saying. "We're an employment agency, placing people in permanent and temporary positions. It's interesting, although hard work. You need to develop a feel for people's personalities and abilities, so the right applicant can be placed in the right position. However, that needn't concern you. I currently employ five seniors responsible for interviewing and placing candidates. We also have two full-time secretaries who take care of the admin side of things, then there's Alex on reception, whom you've already met. She deals primarily with telephone and reception work, although helps out the secretaries if we're busy."

Phyllis thought about the snotty blonde who eyed her up and down with all the arrogant dismissal of a beautiful twenty-five-year-old, before asking her politely to take a seat and ringing to let Ms Evans know she was there.

Phyllis had sat on the hard, grey modular seating, pretending to flick through a fashion magazine, feeling the usual panic welling up, as the other girl's curious gaze wandered over her with barely disguised amusement.

Ms Evans was still explaining about the job, so Phyllis quickly tuned back in. "We need an office junior. A sort of Girl Friday, to do all the other things we simply don't have the time to do."

"What sort of things?" Phyllis, at last, found her voice.

"Well, duties vary from the mundane such as watering the plants and making coffee, to the more exciting like photocopying, running errands, and answering the phone. That's another reason why we need someone, Alex is getting married and will be on her honeymoon for three weeks. Of course, we're all going to share her work between us, but having an extra person around will be very useful."

Phyllis nodded, her brain whirling.

Photocopying?

Answering the phone?

Could she do those things? Was she capable?

Phyllis had never been trusted to do anything before. Responsibility was alien to her, and her palms went damp at the thought.

"Now," Ms Evans continued, "you're probably wondering about the hours. Monday is a quiet day; workloads haven't had a chance to pile up. We've discovered through experience, that the busiest day of the week is Tuesday, when temps have had a day in a new placement, sometimes deciding one day was enough and not turning up the next," she paused, smiling grimly.

"Likewise, Friday is a quiet day; any problems have been sorted and everyone's winding down for the weekend. We work through lunch collectively, as a company, taking our lunch hour at four and going home. Lunchtimes are busy. People tend to phone or call in through their lunch breaks, and we need the full capacity of staff to deal with them. Of course, we don't expect you to work all day without a break or something to eat. You're free to help yourself to refreshments whenever you want. Most of us eat at our desks and one of your jobs is the sandwich run. Are you following me so far?"

Again, Phyllis merely nodded.

Dorothy found herself wondering what was going on behind that flat, blank façade. But the truth was, Phyllis's application had been the only one they'd received in two weeks of advertising. The position of office junior was one only the young would even consider applying for, and what youngster can afford to live on a part-time wage?

Dorothy sighed, studying the girl in front of her. So very young, dressed like a granny, and saddled with the name Phyllis. Still, she didn't have many other options.

"How soon could you start, Phyllis?" she enquired.

"You mean, you're offering me the job?" Phyllis stuttered, shock tripping her tongue, freezing her brain.

"Yes," continued Ms Evans. "Maybe we could consider a three-month trial period to see how you get along, and look at making it permanent after that?"

"All right," agreed Phyllis breathlessly, and beamed a wide smile of sheer delighted exuberance.

Dorothy Evans gasped to herself, in an instant completely revising her original opinion of Phyllis as a plain, frumpy little mouse of a girl.

'Why,' she thought in surprise, 'she's stunning, absolutely stunning. Or rather, she could be.'

"Thank you."

Phyllis was still stammering, unable to believe she'd managed to get a job. She couldn't wait to tell Richard.

"Will it be convenient to start next Tuesday, Phyllis?"

"Yes ... of course, that will be fine..."

"Right then, we'll see you at ten o'clock next Tuesday. I hope you'll be very happy here, Phyllis. It's a fun, but hard-working office, and I'm sure you'll fit in very well."

Phyllis smiled again, feeling an almost desperate eagerness to prove to this stylish, kindly woman that her faith was not misplaced. That she, Phyllis Goodwin, was more than capable of doing the job and would become a valuable and essential member of the team.

Although, a still, quiet voice inside was already sounding a note of caution; that it was all too good to be true.

That something would inevitably go wrong.

Three weeks later, Phyllis was in despair. Being in paid employment was not turning out to be at all what she expected. For a start, there was the sheer logistical nightmare of being up and at work by ten every morning.

Phyllis had got out of the habit of working to a schedule; of having to be up early. At first, she found it incredibly hard and was late two out of the first three mornings.

This, it was made quite plain by the sarcastic comments of her colleagues, was completely unacceptable.

So, Phyllis bought herself a very loud alarm clock, making sure it was set sufficiently early to allow plenty of time to get ready and walk the short ten minutes to the office.

Then there was the physical exhaustion.

Completely unused to labour of any sort, Phyllis passed the first fortnight in a haze of total fatigue, exacerbated by mental tiredness brought on by having to constantly think.

Buckling under the combined strains of physical, mental, and emotional meltdown, Phyllis stumbled through her tasks half asleep, temples throbbing with unbearable tension, longing for four o'clock when she could stagger home and collapse into bed.

Everyone at the office was very kind to her, seeming to sense it was all new and she was trying her best.

Even Alex, the blonde beauty on reception whom Phyllis had been so intimidated by, was always ready to offer advice and assistance, yet Phyllis imagined censure in their looks.

She knew if she didn't get to grips with it soon, she wouldn't even make it to the end of the three-month trial period. She'd be asked to leave long before then.

Phyllis couldn't explain, not even to herself, why it was so important to make a success of this, her first job. After all, it wasn't as if she needed the wages which, given their pitiful nature, was probably just as well.

Phyllis desperately wanted to fit in; to be accepted as an essential member of the team; to prove to herself she was as good as other people, that she could do something right.

At night, when she lay in bed on the brink of slipping into the soothing anaesthetic of deep sleep, she worried if she proved incapable of holding down a silly, little, part-time office job, nothing else that followed in her life would have any meaning. That she would fail at everything she attempted thereafter.

Her thoughts would wander to Lili.

She would imagine what career Lili had because that's what she'd have … not a mere job but a career. Something meaningful and worthwhile, and she'd be good at it.

Then Phyllis would squeeze her eyes tightly shut as bitter tears of failure welled up, soaking her cheeks and pillow.

Gradually though, Phyllis got used to the work and the early starts. The increased physical activity, the fact she was literally on her feet all day, meant she lost yet more weight, and even her new size ten skirt started to bag over her hips.

The walk to work, running errands around town, trips to the post office, the sandwich run out in the fresh air every day, meant her sluggish blood was stirred for the first time.

She started to gain colour in her cheeks, a spring in her step, and her habitual sullen, hangdog expression was replaced with an intense look of concentration, as she desperately tried to get her head around all the intricacies of her new duties.

Most of the jobs Phyllis could manage without a problem. Not unintelligent, once shown how the coffee machine worked and where everything was, it was only a matter of learning everyone's preferences when it came to frequency and choice of refreshments.

Keeping the office tidy and watering the plants was also not very taxing, Phyllis enjoyed looking after the plants so much she bought some for her own home, loving their fresh green appearance, and simple, undemanding needs.

Of all her duties, she enjoyed most those that took her out of the office. It gave her a sense of purpose and pride to hand-deliver packages and letters, to queue up in the post office to get the franking machine topped up and send off parcels.

Even making the sandwich run every day was something to be looked forward to. After all, no one could think she was purchasing all that food for herself; she must be buying it for work colleagues.

Photocopying gave her a few nightmares, but, after she managed to jam it three times in one day, Beth, one of the secretaries, spent half an hour kindly and patiently explaining all the machines quirks and foibles until Phyllis felt ready to take exams on photocopying, so confident was she with the machine.

No, most of Phyllis's duties were manageable, even enjoyable, except one...

Filing.

Phyllis hated filing with a passion.

Panicking at the rows of letters on the files, her heart would sink, as they blurred and merged in front of her confused eyes, performing a complicated little dance, rendering them unreadable.

Barely managing to keep up with it, Phyllis went home each evening convinced she'd misfiled everything, and that tomorrow someone would look for a file that was not there.

When this occurred, as it did several times in those early fraught weeks, everyone was very kind to Phyllis, reassuring her she'd get the hang of it and not to worry.

Everyone made mistakes.

But Phyllis did worry; her worry escalating until it consumed almost every waking moment, even invading her restless, uneasy dreams.

Filing grew in her mind to become her nemesis – the one thing Phyllis knew would be the cause of her downfall and would be the reason why, at the end of the trial period, they would ask her to go.

Sometimes when Alex was not busy, she'd lend a hand. Phyllis envied her methodical quickness, watching as she checked names and numbers with such ease that Phyllis felt even more dispirited, almost wishing she hadn't helped at all.

As she filed, Alex would chatter non-stop about her forthcoming wedding – the dresses, her honeymoon and most of all about her fiancé, Simon.

Listening to the incessant flow of girlie small talk, Phyllis wondered if she'd ever be in the same position as Alex, but then would catch sight of them, side by side, in the smoked glass partition, and would sigh wistfully at the comparison.

All too quickly, the first Saturday in June rolled around, and Phyllis dressed for lunch with Richard.

She was looking forward to it.

Total exhaustion every evening had curtailed Phyllis's more adventurous excursions into food preparation.

Meals consisted of stir-fries and salads, speedily cooked and consumed before she stumbled into bed, so Phyllis was anticipating an excellent lunch.

Maybe this time, she'd even try a glass of wine with it.

Pulling on her black trousers, which Phyllis had bought two weeks earlier after realising this was all the women at work seemed to wear, teaming it with a simple, pale pink, V-necked jumper, she looked at her reflection in the mirror and sighed a little over what she saw.

Her appearance had improved, there was no doubt about that, but it was not enough.

Unable to see the potential lurking beneath the surface, she had gone as far as she could by herself. She needed help to take that small extra step into beauty.

Wandering into the kitchen to check the door was locked, Phyllis's eyes were drawn to the picture of the lily stuck to the fridge.

No answer had been forthcoming from the renowned Mr Stevens, and Phyllis winced as she imagined his reaction to her badly spelt letter.

Laughter, she thought ruefully, had probably been his reaction.

For once, Phyllis arrived at the restaurant ahead of Richard and took advantage of his absence to carefully read the menu. So many lovely things to eat, it was difficult to choose.

In the end, she committed the pan-fried monkfish to memory and was innocently sipping water, menus folded in front of her when Richard was shown to her table.

"Phyllis, my dear," he exclaimed, kissing her on the cheek. "You look lovelier every time we meet."

Phyllis flushed with pleasure. Even though she took his words to be polite small talk, they were still nice to hear.

"Now, tell me," he continued, "what have you been up to since last month? Is there any news on the job front?"

"Yes, there is," stated Phyllis shyly. "I did it. I got a job."

"Really? That's marvellous news. You must tell me all about it."

"I'm working as an office junior for the Evans Employment Agency..."

"We use them sometimes, they're very good. I know Dorothy Evans is thought very highly of."

"It's only part-time, but it's quite nice. It gives me time to do other things. Also, I'm finding it very tiring, so it was a relief, especially in the first week, that it wasn't full-time."

"Well done, Phyllis. I'm so proud of you!"

Richard leaned back in his chair, beaming at her with delight, and Phyllis felt herself glow in his approval. All her life she had longed for her parents to be proud of her, to make her feel as if she were special and worthwhile, but she'd been a constant disappointment to them, not measuring up to their impossibly high standards.

Phyllis had sometimes wondered what it would feel like to hear someone say those simple words ... 'I'm proud of you'. Now Richard had said them.

As Phyllis looked into the kind eyes of the man she'd come to regard as being so much more than simply her solicitor, warmth welled up inside and her eyes filled with tears.

"Oh, my goodness, Phyllis, what's wrong?"

"Nothing," Phyllis dabbed at her eyes with the snowy white napkin. "It's just, no one's ever been proud of me before. My parents, they ..."

She broke off as the waiter approached their table.

Quickly, Richard scanned the menu before selecting the rack of lamb with a glass of Merlot; Phyllis pretended to be reading the menu for a few moments, before ordering her pre-selected choice of the monkfish and asking for a glass of house white, deciding it was probably the safest option.

As they waited for their meals, Phyllis chatted to Richard about her new job, the people she worked with and the duties she had to perform, although glossing over her intense hatred of filing, concentrating instead on all the things she most enjoyed doing.

About the letter to Conrad Stevens, Phyllis stayed silent, preferring to not admit what a ridiculous fool she'd been.

"Well," interjected Richard when she paused for breath. "I can't begin to tell you how pleased I am, Phyllis, I think it's remarkable, all you've achieved in a few months."

He smiled at her shy delight, noting again how much of an improvement there'd been in Phyllis's appearance since last month.

More weight had been lost, and Richard frowned slightly at the sight of angular collarbones jutting through the thin wool of her sweater, as Phyllis put her elbows on the table and lifted her glass to her lips.

"How's the wine?" he asked.

Phyllis nodded and smiled, unwilling to admit it tasted like cat's pee to her uneducated palate.

Richard watched as she ate her fish with obvious enjoyment; and thought how like her grandmother she was … the shape of her eyes, the way she held her head, that long slim neck and soft brown hair.

Now all the excess fat she'd been carrying for years had been shed, Phyllis's cheekbones had emerged, high and defined. They gave her face a slightly Russian appearance, which was added to by her small up-tilted nose and sharply pointed chin.

It was an arresting face, but completely devoid as it was of make-up, and with hair which dragged her expression down, draining the colour from her skin, it needed enhancing and defining to achieve its full potential.

As they waited for their coffees, Phyllis gave Richard a small, quick smile.

"I'm supposed to be going to a nightclub next Thursday," she began, hesitantly. "But I'm not sure I want to go."

"Who are you going with?"

"The girls from work. It's Alex's hen night, she's getting married the following week and she's issued orders we're all to go on her hen night. There's a meal, then we're going to the local nightclub."

"How wonderful," exclaimed Richard. "It sounds like great fun," he added firmly, seeing Phyllis's unconvinced expression. "Are all the other women at work going?"

"Yes, even Ms Evans, although she said she wouldn't stay too long at the club."

"Well then Phyllis, you can't not go, Alex would be very disappointed. It would look odd if everyone else went and you didn't. You'd feel dreadfully left out."

Phyllis was doubtful whether Alex would even notice if she were there or not, but she did see his point about feeling left out.

"Maybe you're right," she agreed slowly. "Perhaps I could go, then leave when Ms Evans does."

She sipped unthinkingly at her wine, barely stopping the shudder of disgust as the acrid, paint stripper flavour slipped over her unprepared tonsils.

"You might surprise yourself, Phyllis," Richard smiled as their coffees were placed before them.

"You might enjoy it."

Chapter Seven
"My name's Amy. Amy Sinclair. What's yours?"

Richard was wrong, thought Phyllis miserably; she was not enjoying herself. Squashed beside Beth, she watched in unvoiced envy Alex and her group of friends leaping and wiggling on the crowded floor and reflected on how she had secretly been hoping for so much more from this evening.

It started reasonably well. Arriving at the restaurant ten minutes too early, Phyllis loitered nervously outside until Ms Evans, Beth, and a couple of the others arrived. Tagging on behind, she followed them into the hot, noisy Chinese restaurant.

Phyllis had never had Chinese food before. To her relief, a huge assortment of dishes that had been pre-booked was placed on warming trays down the centre of the long table, leaving the girls to help themselves to whatever they wanted. Phyllis ended up sitting next to Beth. The kind-natured, older woman had already taken Phyllis under her wing in the office, and Phyllis was more than happy to let Beth explain what each dish was. Phyllis enjoyed most of the food, although found some of it quite cloying and greasy compared to the lightweight, nutritious meals she'd become accustomed to.

Wine arrived on the table in a steady, never-ending stream, and Phyllis sipped slowly at hers; at first, amazed how the others threw the drinks back with so little effort; then alarmed, as she saw how loud and coarse their behaviour was becoming. Finally, at about eleven, Alex declared she was ready to hit the club, scrambling somewhat shakily to her feet, clutching her bag of presents comprising mostly of sex toys and flimsy bits of underwear.

She adjusted her veil, which Phyllis blushed to see had tampons and condoms pinned all over it and led the way out of the restaurant.

After a raucous, but mercifully brief, rampage through town, they arrived at the club. Phyllis hung back with Ms Evans, Beth, and one or two of the other more senior women, as Alex and the others traded ribald comments with the doormen, and men, waiting in the queue.

No one seemed to bat an eyelid when Alex, spurred on by her chanting, laughing friends, had a long kiss with one of them, although Phyllis couldn't help feeling concerned about the appropriateness of the bride behaving like that. But, as nobody else was concerned, she decided to say nothing.

Once inside, things quickly got worse. Phyllis hadn't known what to expect, but it certainly hadn't been this hot, dark, noisy, crowded, heaving mass. It throbbed and pulsed with vibrant energy to a seemingly never-ending cacophony, that in no way resembled any kind of music Phyllis had ever heard before.

Nervously drinking the water Beth got for her, acutely conscious of how wrong her outfit of black work trousers and short-sleeved blouse was, Phyllis was only too happy to shrink down at a table with Beth and wonder how long she would have to stay before it would be okay to leave.

Alex and her friends loudly called for more drinks, then threw themselves onto the dance floor with shrieks of delight. Watching their long, colt-like legs flashing and moving in their uniform of black lycra tights, and short silky skirts, she squirmed deeper into the darkness of the booth, praying for salvation.

Several glasses of water later, Phyllis had to pluck up the courage to ask where the loos were, and self-consciously fight her way through the crowd, all the time wishing she were at home, curled up asleep in her bed, Boris wheezing and snoring beside her.

Apologising, pushing her way through noisy, flirting, laughing groups of beautiful people, she was acutely aware how frumpy her clothes were, that her hair hung around her face like a pair of old curtains, of how her face must pale into insignificance beside the expertly painted and powdered complexions of the women who pushed past, mostly in packs, although occasionally a lone female would stride by, confident and assured.

At last, she found the right door and entered another kind of hell, where groups of girls were clustered around mirrors, shrieking with laughter, performing all sorts of mysterious feminine tasks with brushes, lipstick, and mascara.

Waiting in the queue, Phyllis watched in fascination as one girl poked a pencil into her eyes and, with a steady hand, drew a black line on her inner lids to transform herself into a doe-eyed Egyptian beauty, whilst another whisked her hair up into a complicated double knot on the back of her head and liberally sprayed from a miniature tin of hairspray, causing shrieks of outrage and disgust from the girls behind.

Phyllis listened in silent, wide-eyed wonder, as girls openly chatted to each other about how drunk they were, who they were hoping to get off with, and did anyone have any change for the Durex machine. Finally, she reached the head of the queue and escaped into the temporary sanctuary of a cubicle.

Weeing quickly, Phyllis sat for a moment, unwilling to go out, and gradually became aware of strange noises coming from the next-door cubicle. Reluctantly eavesdropping, she realised someone was being violently and loudly, sick. On and on the retching sounds went, until Phyllis's kind heart could bear it no longer.

"Are you okay?" she timidly asked, the only answer was more gagging and gasping, and a muffled groan. Flushing the loo, Phyllis exited, looking in concern at the other girls crowded in the small, overheated room. Gesturing towards the next cubicle, she asked.

"Do you think she's okay in there?"

"Don't know," one of the girls applying lipstick shrugged. "She's been in there for ages. Poor cow. Shouldn't think there's anything left to come up." Now seriously worried, Phyllis tapped on the cubicle door.

"Hello," she called. "Are you all right in there? Do you need any help?" There was silence, then another groan. Gently, Phyllis pushed at the door. To her surprise, it was unlocked. "Hello," she called again. "I'm coming in. Is that okay?"

The only reply was a soft wordless whimper, which Phyllis took to be assent. Cautiously she pushed the door open, squeezing into the small cubicle, past the motionless figure knelt in prostrate subjugation before the loo. Trying not to look at what was splattered around the bowl, Phyllis crouched beside the girl and gently touched her on the shoulder.

"Are you okay?" she asked again. Slowly, the girl glanced up. Phyllis caught a quick glimpse of tear-filled blue eyes, and an ashen trembling face, before once again she heaved and retched in utter misery. Holding back the impossibly long, baby blonde hair and softly rubbing her back, Phyllis wondered if it was possible to bring up internal organs and if she should ask someone to fetch help.

Finally, an eternity later, the worst seemed to be over, nothing more was coming up. The violent spasms abated, then stopped. The girl seemed to regain her senses, shuddering at the evidence of her illness. Turning to Phyllis, she registered her presence for the first time and burst into noisy, uncontrollable sobs.

Desperately pulling reams of paper off the roll, Phyllis mopped the girl's face, uttering soothing platitudes to calm and reassure her.

Eventually, the sobs stopped, and Phyllis felt confident enough to help the girl to her feet. Thankfully, she flushed the loo, led the girl out of the cubicle and over to a basin, where she helped her to wash her hands.

"Here," said a dark-haired, painted beauty beside her, handing her a small packet of lemon fresh wipes. "Clean her face with this, it'll help neutralise the smell." Gratefully, Phyllis took the wipes, tenderly dabbing at the girl's swollen, vomit-flecked cheeks, lips, and chin. Like a child or a doll, the girl stood listlessly and submitted to Phyllis's ministrations.

"Have you got a brush?" asked another girl. "Only, I always feel better if I brush my hair after tossing. It always seems to get so tangled." There was a chorus of agreements from the others.

Looking around, Phyllis noted the expressions of concern on the other girls' faces, girls whom she had previously dismissed as arrogant and bitchy.

"I don't have a brush," she admitted. "Do you have one we could borrow?"

"Sure," said the girl, producing a small plastic one from the depths of her bag. "Run it under the tap," she advised. "It'll make it easier to get through the tangles."

Following her advice, Phyllis carefully brushed out the girl's long, fine hair, amazed at its pale, straw-like colour, and silky softness. The girl looked down at her hands, clenching and unclenching around the edge of the countertop.

"Thank you," she whispered. "I'm sorry, I'm so sorry."

"That's what I do," said another girl. "Every time I puke, I end up apologising to the world. You should put some blusher on," she advised. "You look like a ghost." Phyllis shrugged helplessly. The girl sighed, then held out a blusher compact to the blonde-haired girl who stared at it weakly, as if she had no idea what to do with it.

"Turn around," ordered the girl, who then briskly swept two broad strokes of subtle colour over the girl's cheekbones.

"I've got some lip gloss," offered another, and proffered a small, round pot. "Dip your finger in it and run it over her lips. It's great cos it's not too obvious."

In amazement, Phyllis stepped back, watching as several girls efficiently and sympathetically powdered, primped, and painted until the little washed-out spirit looked human again. The sense of camaraderie touched and astonished her. The degree of compassion and caring being shown by total strangers brought a lump to her throat, making her vow to never judge people by their appearances.

One of the girls turned to Phyllis and handed her some gum. "Now," she said, briskly and knowledgeably, "take your friend to sit on the steps by the coat check. It's quieter and not so smoky. Get her some water, still water, and make sure it's not from the fridge. You don't want it cold or else it'll make her sick again." There was a chorus of agreements and nods from the others.

"Get her to sip it slowly, then take her home. And maybe your friend shouldn't drink so much next time."

"Oh, but she's not my ..." began Phyllis, only to feel the blonde girl's hand creep, small and cold into her own. "Okay," she finished. "I'll make sure she doesn't, and thank you, all of you, for your help."

Quickly, Phyllis led the girl unresistingly from the ladies to the coat check, where she gently propped her against the wall.

"Stay here," she cautioned. "I'll get some water. I'll be as quick as I can."

"Is your friend not feeling so good?" enquired the coat check girl sympathetically.

"No," Phyllis shook her head, smiling at her. "She's had too much to drink."

"It happens," the girl shrugged, and laughed. "Least, it happens to me. It's okay, you go and get her some water; I'll keep an eye on her for you."

"Thank you," Phyllis replied gratefully and fought her way back through the crowds to the bar. Returning, she found the girl still sitting exactly where she'd left her, head buried in her hands.

She looked up at Phyllis's approach, who was relieved to see she appeared more alert, more aware of her surroundings and that the ghastly greenish tint to her skin had faded.

"Here," said Phyllis kneeling beside her and passing her a bottle of water. "Sip it slowly. You don't want to be sick again."

Thankfully, with shaking hands, the girl sipped, swigging water around her mouth to get rid of the acrid taste. Nodding her thanks to Phyllis, she took another sip, the bottle banging against her teeth. Gently, Phyllis helped her to hold it steady so she could drink some more. They sat, without speaking, for what felt like ages, Phyllis painstakingly feeding her baby sips of water, noting with relief how the colour was gradually returning to her face, and her eyes were beginning to lose that glassy stare.

"Thank you so much," she finally murmured. "You've been so kind. I don't know what I'd have done without you."

"Are you here alone?" Phyllis asked in concern.

"No," the girl shook her head, a look of despair on her face. "I was here with friends. At least, I thought they were friends. These girls I work with ... they asked me out with them but at the last minute said they couldn't. They didn't have the money for taxi fare in and out of town; they live in a village. So, I arranged for my brother and me to pick them up and take them home again. He wasn't pleased about it, I don't think he minded bringing us here, it was the taking them home at two in the morning he wasn't too impressed with. But I was so desperate, I begged him. In the end, he agreed to please me. I so wanted them to be my friends, you see..."

Phyllis did see, squeezing the girl's hand in sympathy.

"But, when we got here," the girl continued sadly. "I soon realised I'd been used to get a lift. They didn't want to know me and left me sitting in the corner. So, I told them I was going to phone Kevin, that's my brother, to come and pick me up. I was angry, mostly at myself for being such a fool. I think they saw their hopes of a lift vanishing, because they told me not to be silly, and started ordering drinks. I'm not used to drinking; the odd glass of wine now and again, but nothing much else, it wasn't long before I started to feel ill. I told them I didn't want any more, but they laughed, took money from my purse, and bought more drinks, I don't know what, cocktails of some kind I think, they were all mixed up. After a while, I went hot and cold all over, knew I was going to be sick. I begged them to help me, but they walked away and left me hanging onto the bar. The man behind it told me to go to the ladies. I think he was afraid I was going to be sick on the floor. Somehow, I made it there, and that's where you found me." She paused, looking dejectedly at Phyllis.

"I'm sorry," she continued mournfully. "I'm so sorry you got dragged into all this. You must think I'm stupid."

"No, I don't," replied Phyllis, patting her hand. "I don't think you're stupid, but I do think those girls are evil. They're certainly not your friends, and I wouldn't waste any more of my time on them. A friend would never treat you like that. Real friends care about each other and look out for one another."

"I wouldn't know," the girl's eyes blurred over. "I haven't got any friends, except my brother, but he's family, so doesn't count, and he's not a girl, so it's not the same, and he's older, so tends to think I'm a bit silly most of the time," she sighed.

"I suppose I should phone him, I don't want to stay here anymore, I want to go home," the last word came out on a wobble, and Phyllis could see she was fighting back tears. "But they took all my money. I haven't even got 10p for the phone."

"Here," Phyllis took her purse out, passing 10p over. "Go and call your brother. You need to get home and go to bed."

"Thank you," the girl gratefully took the coin, and scrambled shakily to her feet. Phyllis watched as she stumbled to the payphone and dialled a number.

"Hi," she said softly, endeavouring to sound lucid. "Can you come and get me? Yes, already. No, we won't be giving them a lift." Phyllis watched the girl's face harden. "They're making their own way home."

She gently replaced the handset, walked unsteadily back to Phyllis, and thankfully slid down the wall to sit next to her. Her head lolled sideways as she looked at Phyllis, eyes crossing with the effort of trying to stay coherent.

"Oh, I feel terrible," she murmured, pressing the heel of her hand into her forehead. "All this, and I still didn't end up with a friend at the end of it."

"Yes, you did," Phyllis took a deep breath. "I'm your friend."

The girl slowly took her hand away from her face, looked steadily at Phyllis, then smiled a slow, sweet smile.

"My name's Amy, Amy Sinclair. What's yours?"

"It's ..." Phyllis hesitated, heart beating fast. Before her was an opportunity, could she ... should she take it? "It's Lili," she finally said firmly. "Lili Goodwin."

"Hi Lili," said Amy and offered her a hand. "It's nice to meet you. I only wish the circumstances hadn't been quite so disgusting."

"That's okay," Phyllis smiled, shaking the proffered hand. "It's nice to meet you too."

Amy pulled her hand away and scrabbled futilely in her bag.

"Do you have paper, a pen?" she enquired, desperately probing the four corners of her postage size handbag, sending keys, purse and lipstick flying.

"No," Phyllis shook her head. She looked over to the coat check girl who was reading a magazine. "Excuse me," she called. The girl looked up and smiled.

"How's your friend feeling now?" she asked in genuine concern.

"She's much better. Could we possibly have some paper and a pen, please?"

"Sure," remarked the girl good-naturedly, passing over a ballpoint and a coat check slip. Quickly, Phyllis ripped the paper in half, wrote her name and telephone number on one of the pieces, passed it to Amy who stored it in her bag, before she too scribbled her name and a number on the other half and gave it to Phyllis, who carefully tucked it inside her purse.

"I suppose I'd better go outside and wait for Kevin," said Amy, carefully pulling herself up. Once upright, she swayed and Phyllis grabbed at her, holding her steady. "I don't feel so good, Lili," mumbled Amy, pressing a hand to her lips.

"Come on," said Phyllis. "Let's get outside. Maybe fresh air will help." Reclaiming their jackets, she gently helped Amy into hers. Gingerly, they made their way down the long flight of steps, past the bored, gum-chewing expressions of the bouncers, and out onto the pavement. Far from improving things though, the fresh air served only to push Amy further into incoherency.

"You've been a good Samaritan, Lili," she slurred, clutching at Phyllis's arm, feet shuffling as she attempted to stay upright.

"It was nothing," said Phyllis, trying to hold her up, and praying she wouldn't be sick again. She desperately hoped her brother would turn up soon before they both ended up a tangled heap on the floor.

At that moment, a blue car screeched to a halt beside them, and a tall, blond man jumped out.

"Amy!" he called. Amy looked up and gave him a stupid, hiccupping grin.

"Hi, Kevin," she slurred.

"What's the matter with her?" he demanded; head whipping round to fix an accusing glare on Phyllis, as Amy lurched forward, sprawling headfirst into her brother's arms.

"Had a little drink," she confided in a loud whisper. "Don't think it agreed with me," she concluded with a drunken giggle.

Her brother's lip curled in disgust. "Jeez, you stink of booze," he exclaimed, turning on Phyllis in a rage. "How could you let her get like this? You knew she wasn't used to drinking, yet you let her get like this. I mean, look at her. Look at the state of her!"

"Now wait a minute ..." Stung by the unfairness of his words, Phyllis tried to defend herself, but he simply shrugged her off with an abrupt dismissive gesture.

"I don't want to hear your excuses," he snapped. "And I don't want you anywhere near my sister again, do you hear? Leave her alone. She's too young and innocent to hang around with the likes of you. I should never have agreed to it."

"What!" Phyllis's hackles rose in response to this chauvinistic tirade. "I would think," she began, in tight-lipped fury, "that your sister is old enough to make up her own mind about who she can and can't see, you don't have the right to..."

"I have every right," he cut her off in mid-flow, eyes flashing dangerously. Some distant part of Phyllis's brain registered how attractive he was; how much Amy resembled him with those Nordic, blond, good looks. "Not only is she my younger sister – she lives with me. Reasons to be concerned about when she goes out clubbing for the very first time and comes home paralytic!"

"I'm not," protested Amy resentfully, pulling herself up to her full height, glaring at her brother with righteous indignation, the effect of which was somewhat spoilt when she stumbled back, banging onto the bonnet of his car with a bump and a giggle.

"Oh, Christ!" Kevin's eyes rolled heavenwards. Grabbing his sister by the arm, he dragged her round to the passenger side and stuffed her in, snapping closed her seat belt, and slamming the door on her drunken protests. Stalking back to the driver's side, he cast Phyllis such a look of arrogant contempt and dismissal, it had her shaking with outrage and dismay at the unfairness of it all.

She'd done nothing wrong. She had tried to help; had thought maybe ... finally, she'd found a friend. Then this egotistical, unreasonable, chauvinistic pig of a man had jumped to conclusions, assumed the worst, and levelled hurtful, unjust accusations at her.

"I haven't done anything," she began desperately. He jumped into the car and slammed the door. "Wait," she screamed as he revved the motor, but he levelled her a look of such disdain she quaked and fell silent before it, watching in mortified silence as he drove off into the night.

Phyllis stood alone on the pavement, hearing the muffled thump, thump of the nightclub music, and feeling the amused, seen-it-all-before expressions of the bouncers. Finally, she sighed, stuffed her hands into her pockets, and set out to walk the ten minutes home; knowing it was probably stupid to do so on her own, but unable to summon up the energy to care.

Chapter Eight
"Talk about a face only a mother could love."

The next day, Friday, Phyllis didn't have work so stayed in bed, seething over the previous evening's events. Arrogant pig, she thought, teeth clenched in fury. How dare he accuse her like that? Who the hell did he think he was?

Then regret welled at the memory of Amy's sad face commenting on her lack of friends. What a wasted opportunity, she mused unhappily – for them both.

Unable to bear wallowing in her self-pity anymore and driven to distraction by Boris's constant demands for breakfast, Phyllis rolled out of bed, got washed and dressed, and wandered downstairs in search of diversion.

After feeding Boris, she moodily ate a bowl of cereal, washed up her meagre breakfast things, made a pot of coffee, and drifted listlessly about the ground floor.

Pulling out the business section of last week's Sunday Times, Phyllis tried to read, but her attention kept wandering, the effort required to make the letters form legible words too much for the state of mind she was in.

Eventually, she gave it up as a bad job and sat back, fighting tears, going over everything that had happened the night before, and thinking of all the things she should have said, but hadn't.

Unexpectedly, the doorbell rang, shocking her with its alien, intrusive tone. Phyllis jumped, heart pounding. Who on earth would be calling on her on a Friday morning? She rose, hovering indecisively, before crossing the hall and opening the front door.

On the step was the oddest-looking man. He was short and stocky, with cropped dark hair framing a slightly plump, almost cherubic face with a pair of twinkling, pale blue eyes.

His clothes were undoubtedly the most outrageous and stylish Phyllis had ever seen on a man. Dark blue trousers, topped with a pale pink, open-necked shirt and an elegantly cut waistcoat matching the trousers.

A pink handkerchief poked out of his waistcoat breast pocket, a lightweight cream, and dark blue, pinstriped linen jacket completing the foppish, Edwardian look.

At his feet stood a black leather holdall which shouted expensive, beautifully matching the man's shoes. In his hand, he clutched a black leather wallet, and Phyllis saw a taxi idling at the kerb.

The man looked at her expectantly. Phyllis's jaw dropped, as she gaped in stunned, speechless shock. A frown flittered across the man's face as they studied each other; then he spoke.

"Is your mother here?" His voice was high and light, its softly rounded tones speaking of old money and a good education.

"My mother?" stuttered Phyllis, instantly defensive.

"Yes, Phyllis Goodwin?"

"Well ... that's me," Phyllis replied, hesitantly.

"You're Phyllis Goodwin?" The man's surprise was evident. Phyllis blushed as he studied her intently, before bursting into a sunbeam smile, which crinkled his cheeks up and made his eyes practically disappear. Phyllis pictured those little naked cherubs who appear on birthday cards and had a sudden urge to giggle.

"But of course, you are," the man declared emphatically, holding out a plump, well-groomed hand. "I'm Conrad Stevens. You wrote to me."

"Oh," cried Phyllis in amazed delight, and shook the proffered hand. Although soft textured, the handshake was firm, and she found herself returning his infectious grin, instinctively liking him.

"Please, come in," she continued, stepping back to allow him access. "I'm sorry, it's so unexpected, I didn't think I'd get an answer."

Conrad waved to the taxi, a dismissive gesture, before following her into the hall.

"I know, I know ... normally, I wouldn't be able to even consider taking on a new client, but the Cunningham's have decided to get divorced rather than remodel. Do you know Robert and Davina Cunningham? No? What a pity. Such a lovely couple, or rather they were." He dropped his bag at his feet.

"So, that left me with a simply huge gap in my schedule, and I was exhausted from doing up Bunty Smythe's country house – dreadful woman, looks like a horse and suffers from chronic bad taste. Then I read your letter, which simply spoke to me, it really did, and I realised you were practically next door to friends of mine who've moved here. So, I decided to treat myself to a little break, visit Robert and Annaliese, and give them a few tips on doing up this simply ravishing Hall they've bought. Not that Annaliese needs my advice. That woman was born with style."

All this was delivered so rapidly, without Conrad feeling the necessity for air, that Phyllis was dazed, not knowing how to respond.

"Love the house!" he exclaimed, looking around the hallway. "Is that fresh coffee I smell?" he demanded, fixing Phyllis with an almost accusing glare.

"Y-yes," she stuttered, unsure whether to apologise or offer him some. "Would you like a cup?"

"Sweetie!" Conrad clutched a hand theatrically to his chest. "Does the Pope have a predilection for wafting around in white nighties?" Phyllis blinked in total incomprehension. Did that mean yes or no?

Conrad sighed and patted her gently on the cheek. "I see we have some work to do," he said. "Now, lead me to the coffee, and after I've fed my caffeine addiction, I want to roam and wander all over this gorgeous house; and then you can tell me all about it."

"All about what?" Phyllis asked hesitantly.

"Why sweetie," replied Conrad, blinking at her with the innocence of a fox caught red-handed in the chicken run, "all about you! It's one of my criteria for taking on a client, I must know you better than you know yourself. After all, if I don't know what's inside your soul, how can I be expected to create the perfect home for you?"

"I suppose," replied Phyllis, feeling a lot like Alice did after she'd tumbled down the rabbit hole. "It's this way," she continued, and led him into the kitchen, thankful she'd washed up her breakfast things so at least it was all clean and tidy.

Conrad paused in the doorway, and looked around the cramped dark room, at the kitchen units he estimated to be circa the 1960s, the electric cooker standing in glorious isolation against one wall, the faded linoleum, blank white walls, and plain pine table and chairs.

"Hmm," he mused. "I see why you need me – this is dreadful, Phyllis – may I call you Phyllis? It's funny, I've never had a client called Phyllis before. Such an old-fashioned name, not one you hear nowadays. Why are you called Phyllis?"

"After my grandmother..."

"Ah yes, the one whose house this was. Tell me, what work has the house had done to it?"

"Erm, a new roof four years ago, complete new central heating system and re-wiring. There were double-glazed windows installed then too, so it's not in too bad a..."

"It's a blank canvas!" declared Conrad. "A perfect blank canvas. Hopefully, there are some architectural features left. Please tell me you have fireplaces?"

"Five, although the..."

"Fantastic! How much land is there out the back?"

"The garden is about two hundred feet long and..."

"Superb! So, we can extend into it if necessary?"

"Well yes, but will it be necessary? I mean, it's quite a big house already, and I..."

"Picture it, sweetie!" cried Conrad, throwing his arms wide. "Completely gut this drab little rat hole of a kitchen and take this down," he thumped the outside wall.

He rushed to the back door, dragging Phyllis with him, opening it, and pulling her through the lean-to and out into the garden.

"Remove all these sheds," he waved his hands expansively at the jumble of outbuildings. "Construct a simply divine, double-height conservatory, flowing into the garden through gorgeous double, doors at the end. We'll find you a fabulous, long, wooden table, and have the kitchen completely open plan, so when your guests are sitting at the table, you can chat to them whilst cooking. Oh, can't you just see it?"

And Phyllis could, she really could.

Staring at him in awe, she could smell the food she was cooking for her mythical guests; taste the wine she was drinking. Watching Conrad gesticulate and prance, she felt a rising tide of excitement and flashed him an exhilarated smile that made the breath catch in his throat.

"Why sweetie," he exclaimed in surprise. "I have a feeling the house is not the only blank canvas around here."

"What do you mean?" stammered Phyllis.

"Never mind," he replied with a twinkle. "Let's have some coffee. You show me the rest, and then we can talk."

Over the next hour, Phyllis had her mind turned inside out with the thoughts, ideas, impressions, and suggestions Conrad bounced at her, and off her, as he dashed around the house, up and down the stairs, in and out of every room, Phyllis jogging breathlessly in his wake, trying to keep up both physically and mentally.

Fuelled by an entire pot of coffee, there seemed no end to his creative vision, Phyllis marvelled at his ability to pluck inspiration from thin air, creating pictures of how it could look; pictures so vivid, so alive, Phyllis could see them too.

Finally, they collapsed on opposite sofas in the lounge, breathless with laughter, united in delighted anticipation at the vision of classic though contemporary, stylish though comfortable, they'd created.

"It's going to be beautiful!" declared Conrad, throwing wide his arms in an all-encompassing gesture. "Absolutely beautiful! Oh, what a joy it's going to be to work with someone on my wavelength, who won't insist on having plastic, life-size Labradors either side of the front door!"

"No!" exclaimed Phyllis in horror, then, "Bunty Smythe?" she guessed.

"Oh, that woman!" cried Conrad, hand to forehead in pure Sarah Bernhard style. "Now then," he jumped up like a deranged jack-in-the-box, fixing Phyllis with his gargoyle-like twinkling gaze. "More coffee, I think, then we need to talk about you."

"There's not very much to talk about," protested Phyllis, following him into the kitchen.

"You let me be the judge of that," retorted Conrad, opening the fridge and taking out milk. "For a start, you can explain the significance of this?" he tapped the newspaper cutting of the lily, raising his eyebrows at Phyllis.

"Does it have to have any significance at all?" Phyllis asked defensively. "Couldn't I have it there because I like lilies?"

"Maybe," agreed Conrad, spooning fresh coffee into the pot. "But I don't think so; I noticed the way you looked at it, almost as if you were drawing inspiration from it."

Seeing Phyllis hesitate, he shrugged and laughed.

"You may as well tell me, sweetie, I'll get it out of you in the end."

Phyllis looked at the picture, her expression changing to one of intense yearning.

"It's there," she began hesitantly, "because it's me, or rather it's what I want to be, I want to become Lili."

"You want to become a flower?" asked Conrad in confusion.

"No, not a flower, I want to become her, Lili."

"Oh, I see," breathed Conrad. "Lili's a person?"

"Yes."

"Someone, you admire?"

"Yes."

"Someone you want to be like.

"More than anything."

"And the picture's here to remind you?"

"That's right," agreed Phyllis, pleased he understood so quickly. "Every time I look at the picture, it makes me think of her."

"So, who is she?"

"Lili," replied Phyllis, confused.

"Yes, but who is Lili? What do you know about her?"

"Nothing, I've only ever seen her once briefly, in the supermarket, and even then, I never saw her face." She paused, looking at Conrad in despair.

"I know it's completely crazy, but she's my inspiration. Because of her, I changed my eating habits, lost all that weight, found the courage to pass my driving test, and get a job. I'm sorry," she added. "You must think I'm mad."

"Not at all, sweetie," Conrad denied. "I'm intrigued, I want you to sit down and tell me everything, absolutely everything."

"I don't know if I can," replied Phyllis. "I simply wouldn't know where to start."

"Well, to steal a phrase from one of the greatest films ever made, let's start at the very beginning, it's a very good place to start."

At Phyllis's blank stare, Conrad threw up his hands in despair. "The Sound of Music."

"Sorry," Phyllis shook her head. "I've never seen it."

"Where have you been all your life, sweetie? Mars?"

"I may as well have been," replied Phyllis bitterly, tears pricking her eyes.

"Now I *am* intrigued," replied Conrad. "Come, let's sit, drink coffee, and you can start at the very beginning with Chapter One, I am born…"

"I'm sorry," sniffed Phyllis. "Is that another film?" and wondered why Conrad burst out laughing.

Two hours later, Phyllis leant back on the sofa and wiped tears away from her cheeks. Emotionally drained, she had begun with Chapter One, I am born, and had finished with the events of the previous evening.

Conrad proved to be an exceptional listener. With a few insightful questions, he'd extracted information Phyllis would normally never have dreamt of sharing with anyone.

Conrad sighed and fixed her with a sympathetic gaze.

"Poor little duckling!" he exclaimed. "It's amazing. Your mother is *the* Elizabeth Goodwin? What a bitch! You know, now I come to think of it, I always did think she was a little, well, how shall I put it, chintzy. All that dependence on napkins folded just so. Well, I certainly won't recommend her to any of my clients again!"

Phyllis blinked, taken aback at his instant championing of her, and his open condemnation of her mother. "Tell me, sweetie," Conrad continued, "do you see much of your parents now?"

"No," Phyllis sniffed and shook her head. "I haven't seen them since I left home."

"Do you mean to tell me," exclaimed Conrad, outraged on her behalf, "that their daughter walked out on the morning of her eighteenth birthday, and they haven't even checked you're okay?" Phyllis slowly shook her head again.

Conrad huffed with disbelief. "You are better off without them, sweetie. I hate to say it, but you are." He paused, a wicked gleam entering his eye.

"Tell me, this Kevin, Amy's brother … was he very good looking?"

"I suppose he was," replied Phyllis, confused. "Why?"

"Oh, no reason," Conrad dismissed the subject with an airy wave of his hand. "I was curious, that's all …"

He broke off as a loud thump from the kitchen announced the arrival of Boris through the cat flap.

"What on earth was that?" he asked.

"Oh, Boris," replied Phyllis.

"Boris?" queried Conrad, then stared as the animal in question sauntered nonchalantly into the lounge, leapt onto the sofa beside Conrad, settled his not insubstantial rear on a cushion beside him, and proceeded to fix Conrad with a gaze of such naked curiosity that Conrad snorted with laughter.

"Well," he commented dryly. "You're a big ugly brute aren't you. Talk about a face only a mother could love."

Almost as if responding to the insult, Boris dropped one eye in a long, lazy wink, and Conrad started back with surprise.

"He winked at me," he spluttered. "Your cat winked at me."

"I know," Phyllis giggled. "I think he's got something wrong with his eye. He sometimes does that, it's so funny."

Conrad put out a hand, rubbing at one of Boris's mangled ears. Immediately, deep, rumbling purrs resounded from Boris's chest as he pushed his big ugly head into Conrad's palm, before settling down, face turned lovingly up to him.

"What a character," remarked Conrad. "So, sweetie, what are you going to do next?"

"Do?" faltered Phyllis. "About what?"

"Well, about Amy and you. What's the next step in your quest to becoming Lili?"

"I ... I don't know," Phyllis looked doubtful. "What do you think I should do?"

"Hmm," mused Conrad. "That's a tricky one. I think..."

Whatever he'd been about to say was interrupted by the ringing of the phone. Phyllis started, staring at it with such consternation that Conrad was amused.

"Who do you think that could be?" she murmured in alarm.

"Well, answer it and find out," he retorted.

Hesitantly, Phyllis picked up the receiver.

"Hello?" she ventured slowly, for some reason her heart knocking against her ribs, her breath catching in her lungs.

"Hello, Lili?"

Phyllis's eyes bulged in shock. She sent Conrad such a look of sheer panic he sat bolt upright on the sofa, leaning towards her in concern.

"Hello?" The voice was young, female, high and nervous. "Hello, Lili? It's Amy."

"Amy?" at last Phyllis found her voice.

"Yes, we met last night in the club."

"Of course, Amy, how are you today?" Seeing Conrad making hand gestures of excitement at her, Phyllis smiled at him.

"Well, I felt awful this morning. It was so bad I had to have a day off work, but I'm feeling better now."

"That's good," replied Phyllis.

"Anyway, I wanted to thank you so much for all you did for me last night, and to apologise."

"Apologise? What for?"

"For the unbelievable rudeness of my brother. He was worried about me. He thought you were one of the girls I told you about, and that you'd got me in that state. Of course, as soon as I could think straight this morning, I told him what had happened, and he feels awful about it. So, I was wondering if you'd like to come for dinner tonight, so he can apologise to you in person."

"Dinner? Tonight?"

Phyllis felt her tongue stick to the roof of her mouth, looking at Conrad in panic, her whole face one big question mark. Firmly, he shook his head, pointing to himself.

"Umm, I can't do tonight, Amy, I have a friend around."

"Well, maybe tomorrow night?" Phyllis heard the hope in Amy's voice and found herself automatically responding to it.

"Tomorrow?" she looked to Conrad for guidance. Once again, he shook his head, pointed to himself.

"No, I'm sorry," she continued slowly. "My friend's staying for a few days."

"Oh, okay," Phyllis heard the note of rejection in the young girl's voice, her assumption she was being given the brush off. She turned pleading eyes to Conrad as he began mouthing something to her.

"I could do next weekend," she offered, trying to decipher Conrad's inaudible whispers and frantic hand signals.

"Ok," Amy brightened down the line. "That would be great. Say Saturday, 7:30? I'll give you our address."

"Umm," Phyllis gestured at Conrad who scrabbled in his pocket, producing a rather lovely steel ballpoint pen and small, leather-bound notebook.

Quickly, Phyllis copied down the details, repeated them back to Amy, agreed how lovely it would be to see her again and that she was looking forward to it.

She hung up, staring wide-eyed at Conrad as he beamed at her in delight.

"Oh sweetie!" he breathed. "Oh, how exciting. It begins!"

"What begins? Conrad, I don't understand. What just happened? Why ...?"

Phyllis broke off confused, unable to understand why she felt weepy, and more than a little cross.

"Why did you make me say no? She might not have asked me again!"

"But she did." Conrad was unable to wipe the grin from his face.

"But she might not have done."

Phyllis felt a flash of temper at the thought. Conrad jumped to his feet, taking both her hands, and pulling Phyllis abruptly to hers. Spinning her around, he pointed to her reflection in the mirror over the fireplace.

"Look," he exclaimed. "Look at your reflection and tell me what you see."

"Myself," ventured Phyllis uncertainly.

"Exactly," he cried, looking at her expectantly, eyebrows raised as if enough had been said.

"Conrad," Phyllis whined, "I don't understand."

"All right," he sighed. "Let's put it another way. What, or rather who, don't you see?" Phyllis shook her head in confusion, knowing he was trying to make her comprehend something, unable to grasp what.

"Lili," he exclaimed. "Do you see Lili when you look in the mirror? From what you've told me about her, I certainly don't."

"Well, no ... but ..." Phyllis winced at her image, as far removed from Lili as it was possible to get.

"It's a golden opportunity," continued Conrad. "A chance to establish yourself as Lili with these people. Because I'm betting, they don't remember what you look like, Amy because she was too pissed, and Kevin because he was too angry. Don't you get it? Don't you understand, Phyllis? This is it! This is how you become Lili."

Phyllis stared in rising excitement, his words sinking in. "You're right," she murmured.

"Of course, I'm right," Conrad exclaimed impatiently. "That's why I made you postpone her for a week. We're going to need that week to transform you..."

"Transform me?"

"Into Lili."

"Oh," breathed Phyllis. "You said we, does that mean...?"

"You're not getting rid of me, sweetie, not when things are getting exciting. Could you bear to have a house guest for a few days?"

"Oh, yes," cried Phyllis in happy relief. "If you could help me, Conrad, it would be so wonderful. I don't think I can do it alone."

"You don't have to," he replied with a twinkle. "Let me call Matthew and explain I'll be staying a few days longer."

"Matthew?"

"My partner," explained Conrad.

"I didn't realise you had a business partner," said Phyllis naively. "I thought it was just you."

"Oh sweetie," sighed Conrad. "I only hope you never completely lose your innocence. It is rather sweet. No, Matthew is my life partner, my better half." At Phyllis's look of incomprehension, he smiled. "My boyfriend," he finished bluntly.

"Oh," squeaked Phyllis. To her horror, her face flamed red as she understood what Conrad was trying to tell her. "I see," she said.

Conrad laughed at her discomfort. "Does it shock you?" he asked curiously. "Make you feel differently about me?"

Phyllis stopped to consider the question; to think about how his disclosure had made her feel. Frowning slightly, she examined her innermost thoughts, before turning a full and frank smile upon him.

"No," she answered firmly. "It doesn't shock me at all. Should it?"

"Some people it would," Conrad replied, wryly. "I'm glad you're not one of them."

"I don't see why it should make any difference," said Phyllis determinedly. "After all, people are people. Surely, we should only judge others by their actions, and by the way they treat us, not by whether they prefer men or women?"

"Quite right," said Conrad, patting her hand. "You've got to come and visit us in London, Phyllis, or maybe I should call you Lili. We'd have such fun, and I know Matthew will adore you."

"What's he like?" asked Phyllis curiously.

"Matthew? Oh, he's my rock, my soul mate; he keeps me grounded; stops me from taking myself too seriously and believing all the nonsense they write about me in magazines. Without Matthew, my life would be one long round of empty parties and shallow friends, I'd have burnt out years ago."

"It must be nice," began Phyllis slowly, "to have someone like that in your life."

"You will, one day," stated Conrad confidently. "After all, how old are you Phyllis?"

"Eighteen."

"So very young," he sighed. "Oh, to be eighteen again." He frowned. "Actually, I wouldn't want to be eighteen again, I'm far happier being thirty, rich, and successful."

"What happens next?" Phyllis asked hesitantly, half afraid to hear the answer.

"You leave that to me," twinkled Conrad. "Trust me … we're going to have the best fun ever."

Fun. Much later that evening, when Phyllis was alone in bed, she thought about the whole concept of fun, realising she'd had no idea what fun was. Oh, she could have given the dictionary definition, but if asked what it felt like to have fun, she'd have been unable to answer. Now she could.

One evening in Conrad's company had opened Phyllis's eyes to what life could be; how interesting and funny other people were; how much enjoyment there was in spending an evening with someone who made you laugh so hard, speech became impossible.

They cooked an Italian meal, Phyllis learning more about food in one evening, than she had in four months. A keen and extremely competent cook, firmly believing in the maxim the first bite was with the eye, Conrad showed Phyllis how a simple plate of pasta could become so much more when eaten by flickering candlelight, with soft music playing in the background, and in the presence of another whose company you found intensely enjoyable.

With cries of delight, he discovered her untouched wine rack, muttering phrases such as 'well rounded' and 'full of interesting oaked fruits' which had gone straight over Phyllis's head. He opened a bottle of red and left it on the side to breathe whilst they prepared dinner.

Phyllis eyed it with trepidation, wondering if she had the nerve to tell Conrad she'd far rather have a glass of water. Much to her surprise, her first nervous mouthful revealed a whole array of wonderful, warming, fruity flavours, which burst onto her cautious taste buds.

She glowed with pleasure, not only at the unexpected deliciousness of the wine but at the whole experience of eating an Italian meal and drinking red wine with a friend.

It made her feel sophisticated and grown-up. The wine relaxed and soothed her, to the point she had trouble dealing with all the unfamiliar and warming emotions swirling around inside, making her sigh with contentment.

After dinner, Conrad devised a complicated plan of action, involving appointments to be made, and shopping to be done.

Phyllis listened intently, heard nothing, happy to put her complete trust in him and let him do with her what he will.

"What days did you say you worked?"

"Huh?"

Conrad's question broke into Phyllis's blissful musings, and she stared at him, blinking in the dim candlelight.

"What days next week will you be at work?"

Patiently, Conrad repeated his query. A smile played over his mouth as he watched emotions flicker across her face. Such expressive features, he mused.

It was plain this evening, simple though it had been, marked a turning point in Phyllis's life.

He had opened a window into her narrow dark existence; had let the sunlight of possibilities flood in. He felt a glow of selflessness, of a good deed well-done settle upon him, and his fondness for Phyllis grew.

"Umm, Tuesday, Wednesday, and Thursday," Phyllis replied, dragging her mind back to more mundane things such as work.

"That works well," commented Conrad. "It gives us three days to lay the groundwork for your metamorphosis. Then, whilst you're at work, I can get on with the job I came to do, namely, planning how this simply divine house of yours can be transformed. Then, we have next Friday for the real fun to take place."

Metamorphosis.

Phyllis said the word quietly to herself, liking the way it sounded. It made her feel like a caterpillar imprisoned in its cocoon, waiting for the right moment to burst upon an unsuspecting world in all her brilliant butterfly beauty.

At eleven, Conrad packed her off to bed, even though Phyllis wanted to stay up late talking in the candlelight. No, they had a busy day tomorrow and would be making an early start. Phyllis would need at least eight hours of quality beauty sleep.

Thinking eight hours wouldn't be enough to achieve such a goal, Phyllis trotted off obediently to bed, where she was quite surprised to fall instantly into a deep and happy sleep, courtesy of emotional fatigue and half a bottle of wine.

Chapter Nine

"My young friend needs to be measured for a bra."

Next morning, Phyllis was awoken early by the smell of rich, full-flavoured coffee, as Conrad breezed into her room without knocking, waved a mug under her nose, and plonked it down on her bedside cabinet, exclaiming on his way out.

"Wakey, wakey, sleeping beauty. The bathroom's all yours, I've fed Boris the Bold, breakfast in twenty." The door snapped shut, leaving Phyllis blinking stupidly, wondering what time it was, and why she had a nagging headache behind her eyes.

An hour later they left the house. It was nine, ridiculously early as far as Phyllis was concerned, and she shivered crossly in the chilly breeze. Unable to understand why she was so out of sorts, Phyllis stomped in silence, leading Conrad towards town and the market that was busy even this early.

Conrad kept casting sly sideways glances at her until finally, Phyllis could bear his knowing smirks no longer. "What?" she snapped, stopping dead, turning to glare at him accusingly.

"Nothing, sweetie," he retorted, eyes wide, the very picture of innocence. "Feeling a little under the weather, are we? Have an ickle bit of a headache?"

"Yes." So surprised at his perception, she forgot to be cross.

"It's a proud moment," Conrad clasped his hand to his chest. "My baby girl, all grown up and having her first little hangover."

"Am I?" Phyllis stared, a big grin spreading across her face. "Am I really?" It was ridiculous, but it seemed so grown up. Having listened to others at work display their hangovers with the bravado of returning war veterans, to experience one of her own felt somehow liberating. They resumed walking, Phyllis's mood now jubilant, and Conrad smiled at her transparent, smug satisfaction.

"Oi," he poked her in the ribs. "Don't get carried away. Drinking's something we'll have a little chat about. Yes, it's fun, it's something you should be able to handle and enjoy, but there' are rules and limits, and you need to discover what those are, otherwise, you'll end up doing damage to yourself."

Phyllis hung her head, nibbled her lip, cast a cheeky sideways glance at him from under her lashes and grinned "Yes, Mum."

"Behave yourself," Conrad huffed in mock exasperation. "We have a lot to do. Right ..." they reached the market square, which on Wednesdays and Saturdays heaved with rows of brightly coloured market stalls selling a wide range of produce, traders' voices drawling loudly in the bright June morning.

"How lovely!" exclaimed Conrad, looking round with rapt attention. "What an absolutely sweet little town. But first thing's first, please tell me there's a Marks & Spencer?"

"There," Phyllis pointed where the familiar logo could be spotted. "But ..." she began, disappointed their first port of call was not one of those frighteningly mysterious fashion shops other girls her age gravitated to like moths to a flame. "Aren't their clothes a little old-fashioned, I thought..."

"Sweetie, we're not going there to buy clothes. Well, not unless we see something that's absolutely you. No, when you build a house what must you always do first?" At Phyllis's blank stare he sighed. "Foundations; you have to make sure the foundations are good, so that's where we're going to start. Come on." He strode off through the crowds, leaving Phyllis to trot after him in confusion.

Bustling through the double doors, Conrad ignored the escalator and scampered up the stairs, two at a time, like a goat scaling the Alps, not stopping until they'd reached their destination. Catching up, Phyllis struggled to regain her breath.

"Foundations?" she managed to gasp. Conrad opened his arms wide and gestured to the racks around them.

"Underwear," he exclaimed.

"Oh," he heard the disappointment in her voice.

"You'll soon change your mind," he grinned. "Now then, first of all..." He looked around, searching for something. "Ah yes," he exclaimed. "Come on." Once again, Phyllis was staring at his retreating back. She sighed in weary resignation, hurrying after him as he approached a matronly woman wearing the store's uniform, busy refilling a rack with packets of tights.

"Excuse me," the woman looked up and smiled.

"Yes sir?"

"My young friend needs to be measured for a bra, and then we need to completely re-stock her lingerie drawer."

"Conrad ..." Phyllis began in shocked outrage.

"Certainly," said the woman, smiling at Phyllis. "Come into the changing rooms, dear, we'll see what size you need." Before Phyllis could say another word, she was hustled into a changing room, jacket and blouse were stripped from her, and the woman expertly applied a tape measure around her chest.

"34B," she announced. "That's a nice size," she reassured her. "Not too big, not too small."

"Oh," replied Phyllis, not sure how she was supposed to respond. "Thank you very much," she finished lamely.

"You're welcome, dear," smiled the woman. "Now, pop your things back on, I think your … umm friend… is waiting outside to help you buy underwear."

Phyllis felt the question mark in the woman's eyes, was embarrassed at her assumptions, then thought about Lili. If she were Lili, she wouldn't give a damn what people thought. No, she'd revel in making them wonder, and in shocking them.

"Thank you," Phyllis smiled directly into the woman's eyes, and shook her hair back. Leaving the cubicle, she went in search of Conrad, a small smile playing on her lips. Maybe underwear shopping was going to be fun after all.

An hour later, Phyllis staggered out of the store in a state of shock, £250! She had spent £250, and it all fitted in two carrier bags. She'd bought underwear, piles of it, nightwear, a new robe, and packets and packets of the ubiquitous black lycra tights she'd seen all the other girls wearing.

As Phyllis thought about the underwear she'd bought, her mouth went dry with delight. Leaving the changing room, she reached for her normal packets of white cotton briefs and bras, but Conrad had cried in outrage and smacked her hand away.

"No!" he exclaimed in horror. "Please do not even contemplate such boring, middle class, middle-aged things. No," he continued, plucking a beautiful jade silk bra and brief set off the nearest rack. "This is the sort of thing you should wear – lovely, gorgeous, and most importantly, the bra should always match the briefs."

"But Conrad," protested Phyllis. "No one sees my underwear except me, so what does it matter?"

"Sweetie," sighed Conrad, "it matters. Aren't you the most important person there is? Besides, knowing you're wearing nice underwear does something to a woman's confidence. Trust me, I know. Now then … Oohh, look at that simply gorgeous rose pink set with the little rosebud in the cleavage.

Phyllis gave up, watching in stunned disbelief as the pile of underwear grew in her basket, their colours combining to form a glorious bouquet of silk and lace. Her interest and excitement grew as she fingered their soft prettiness and tried to imagine wearing them. Maybe Conrad was right. If imagining wearing them was lifting her spirits, how would she feel when they were on her body, lace softly caressing and touching her. Phyllis swallowed, glanced wildly around, cheeks flaming, before hurrying over to where Conrad was rhapsodising about a purple corset.

"Where next?" demanded Phyllis, excited. She'd bought all the foundation one girl could possibly need. Surely, it was now time to buy some actual clothes.

"Boots," replied Conrad, setting off at speed through the crowds.

"The Chemists?" asked Phyllis in disbelief, shifting bags to a more comfortable position, and hurrying after him. "I don't understand," she gasped, catching up as he strode through the shop's double doors and grabbed a basket. "What do we need to buy from here?"

"Well, for starters," Conrad exclaimed, flicking a hand through her lifeless locks, "a hairdryer and some decent hair care products."

"Oh, but …" Conrad was already off down the aisle on his latest mission.

When one basket was filled, he merely grabbed another, Phyllis staring in dismayed confusion at the jumble of products being tossed into them. Conrad threw explanations over his shoulder, which did little to enlighten Phyllis, wide-eyed in wonder at the growing mountain of things Conrad assured her no girl could be without.

Hairdryer, shampoo, conditioner, styling products, cleanser, toner, moisturiser – a girl must follow a rigorous facial cleansing routine daily, he assured her. He stopped, spinning to face her with such a stern expression Phyllis quaked. She must never, he intoned fiercely, ever, go to bed without taking her make-up off.

"I don't care how tired or how drunk you are, missy," he insisted, all but wagging his finger at her. "You cleanse, tone, and moisturise, night and morning. Understand?"

"Yes Conrad," it seemed simplest to agree. The scavenger hunt through the shop went on – a manicure kit, eyebrow tweezers, eyelash curlers, cotton wool balls, soft cosmetic tissues in a range of pastel tones, body lotions and shower gels, make-up – so much make-up. Phyllis who had never worn make-up before in her life stared with greedy glee at all the beautifully mysterious packages and pots Conrad piled into the basket with careless abandon.

The final bill of £200 shocked her less than the previous one, and Phyllis wondered if she was becoming used to spending such vast amounts. Staggering under the weight of her bags, Phyllis dashed after Conrad, wondering if she dared ask where they were going.

"Ah," he exclaimed in delight. "A music store. Just what we're looking for."

"Is it?" asked Phyllis, looking in disbelief at the scarily unfamiliar shop. It was one she passed many times but had never summoned up the courage to enter, the trendily dressed shop staff being enough to put her off. Now, she followed Conrad as he confidently strode through the shop, plucking CDs seemingly at random from the racks, and tossing them into a basket.

"Umm, Conrad," Phyllis finally found the courage and the breath to speak up, "why do I need so many CDs? I mean, I'm not sure I even like modern music."

"No," Conrad spun on his heel to face her. "That's the problem. There's a big wide world of music out there, sweetie, and Britain is playing a huge part in shaping it. Tell me, Phyllis, have you heard of Oasis? Pulp? Blur? What's number one right now?"

"I don't know," Phyllis hung her head in shame.

"Well, you're eighteen, you should know," Conrad's expression softened as he took in her crestfallen face. "Lili would know," he continued gently. "She would know, understand, and enjoy all the marvellous music that's around right now."

"You're right," Phyllis took a deep breath, looking him in the eyes. "You're right, she would. What do you think I should buy?"

Twenty minutes later, Phyllis walked out of the shop the proud owner of over a dozen CDs. "Tonight sweetie, after dinner, we'll listen to some of these and then ..."

"Conrad."

"Yes?"

"I don't have a CD player." Conrad stopped dead in the street, glared crossly at a large, elderly lady as she ploughed into the back of him, and pulled Phyllis to one side out of the throning crowds.

"What do you mean, you don't have a CD player?

"I mean, I don't have a CD player."

Stifling a curse, Conrad thought rapidly, turned on his heel, and plunged into the crowd. Phyllis began to question his retreating back, realised the futility of it, and simply followed as he strode through the milling shoppers, not looking left or right, not checking to see if she was following him either.

Phyllis trailed breathlessly as they entered a small electrical store located halfway down the high street, near Marks & Spencer. He must have noticed it earlier, she realised in amazement; noticed it and filed it away for future reference.

Forty minutes later, Phyllis was the proud owner of a state-of-the-art stereo system. Listening in total incomprehension, she let Conrad deal with it all, nodding when her opinion was asked, not understanding a word of what the salesman – call me Colin – said. Young, desperately keen for the commission such a large sale would net him, he even allowed Conrad to gently bully him into delivering the system on his way home from work that evening.

Satisfied with the morning's work, Conrad stepped from the shop, paused, looking up and down the crowded street. Phyllis despondently hefted bags into a more comfortable position. She wondered, with a sinking heart, where he'd be dragging her off to next. Conrad glanced down, expression softening as he took in the exhaustion and shell shock etched on her face.

"Come on, sweetie," he said gently, taking half the bags from her. "Let's go home, dump this lot, then I'm taking you to lunch." Brightening at the thought of shedding her load and at the prospect of being fed, Phyllis smiled back, trying not to think of how much money she'd spent that morning.

Half an hour later, they were seated at a small, cosy, table for two in a newly opened, fashionably popular restaurant tucked away down a side street, which Conrad had found using some sort of instinctive homing device.

Perusing the menu, sipping a glass of Perrier, Conrad raised his eyebrows at Phyllis as she squirmed self-consciously on her chair, partly a reaction to the subtle sophistication of their surroundings, partly because when they returned home to drop off the bags, Conrad rummaged in one, pulled out a flesh-coloured plain bra and briefs set, and ordered her upstairs to put them on. No explanation forthcoming, Phyllis, not liking to ask, had simply complied.

"How are you feeling, sweetie?"

"I'm fine," replied Phyllis, managing to return his smile. Satisfied, he bent his attention to his menu, leaving Phyllis to stare at hers in dismay. Calm down, she ordered herself sternly, as words began their usual slide from legibility into chaos. Unfamiliar with the restaurant, she couldn't even begin to guess what might be listed on the menu, and stole unobtrusive glances at the other diners, hoping to extract clues from what was on their plates.

Conrad sighed in happy dilemma. "What a surprisingly sophisticated menu," he muttered. "It's difficult to decide…"

"Hmm," agreed Phyllis, thankfully. "Isn't it?" Inspiration struck. Folding her menu, she picked up her water glass and flashed him a big smile. "I can't decide either," she declared. "Why don't you choose something for me? Pick whatever you think Lili might like."

"What fun!" declared Conrad, eyes sparkling at her challenge. "Now then," he muttered, scanning the menu. "What would Lili choose?"

Phyllis sighed with relief, gratefully sipped her water, and watched with quiet envy as Conrad speed read the whole menu. As if she'd been watching for some invisible signal, the waitress appeared at their table as Conrad appeared to come to a decision, and Phyllis observed in awed silence as he assertively flipped out requests to the waitress, so sure of himself, so confident and poised. In a way, he reminded Phyllis of Lili – that self-assuredness – that sense of being so comfortable in his own skin.

Conrad gave the waitress their menus, and a smile so laden with charm, she flushed and scurried off to the kitchen with their order.

"So," Conrad leaned back, surveying Phyllis over the top of his glass, "how do you feel this morning went?"

"I don't know," Phyllis sipped nervously. "We certainly spent a lot."

"It was necessary, trust me, sweetie. It's what an average teenager would have spent by the time she reached eighteen, but it would've been spread out over years. Unfortunately, you've had to spend it all in one day, so it feels somewhat excessive. Believe me, you'll soon understand everything we bought today is essential. You'll wonder how you ever lived without decent skin and hair care products, make up, and a hairdryer, I still can't believe you've managed all this time without that."

"I let it dry naturally," Phyllis shrugged. "When you've got hair as awful as mine, there's no point in bothering too much with it."

"Sweetie," exclaimed Conrad in exasperation, "the only reason your hair is so awful is because you've never bothered too much with it. Just you wait. A decent cut and colour, a few lessons on blow drying ... your hair won't know what's hit it."

Phyllis privately doubted that but was too polite to say. Instead, she watched as the waitress brought wine, expertly uncorked it, and poured a little into Conrad's glass. She hovered expectantly as he tasted, nodding his approval. Deftly, the girl filled their glasses, placed the bottle in a cooler, flashed them a quick, shy smile, and hurried off to fetch their starters.

Phyllis tentatively picked up her wine, previous experience with white wine having left a sour taste in her mouth, she was hesitant to try it again. Under Conrad's expectant gaze, she took a deep breath, and sipped at the chilled, straw-coloured liquid, feeling beads of cold condensation on her fingers. Letting the wine wash over her taste buds, Phyllis turned delighted eyes up to Conrad's laughing ones, taking another sip to make sure.

"It's lovely," she exclaimed, surprise evident in her voice.

"Oh sweetie," Conrad laughed. "Your face. You looked like I'd given you arsenic to drink instead of a rather lovely little Chardonnay."

"I've had white wine before," explained Phyllis, "but it didn't taste anything like this. No, this is nice." She took another sip, then set the glass down as the waitress bustled over to them with the starters. Frowning, she watched as a warm goat's cheese tartlet with mixed leaf garnish, and raspberry vinegar dressing was placed before Conrad, and before her was placed a large bowlful of...

"Mussels?" she queried, dismayed gaze going from the gleaming, garlic-drenched shells, each with a slimy, still alive looking occupant, up to Conrad's face, which was the picture of innocence. "Mussels? I'm not sure, Conrad, I've never ... I don't think I can..."

"Up until yesterday you didn't think you liked wine, and you didn't think you enjoyed shopping. The world is full of new experiences, Phyllis, each one to be approached with an open mind and a determination to give it a fair trial. After all, what's the worst that could happen here?"

"I could hate them."

"Yes, you could. Then we'd swap, and I'd eat those simply yummy-looking mussels, and you'd have this nice, safe, cheese tartlet."

"Oh ..." Put like that, Phyllis realised she had no other option than to try the disgusting looking things, reluctantly scraping one out of its shell. The fact it clung to its former home with an almost bulldog-like tenacity didn't lessen her unwillingness to put it in her mouth. But Conrad's words, his innocent smirk, and the knowledge that Lili wouldn't hesitate to thoroughly enjoy a plateful of mussels made her sigh with reluctant determination, close her eyes, and pop the whole mollusc into her mouth.

Slowly, she chewed, trying to analyse the flavours. It was nowhere near as bad as her imagination had led her to believe. It tasted of the sea, and the garlic sauce it was cooked in. Phyllis opened her eyes, looked at Conrad.

"It's not too bad," she conceded, forking up another, thoughtfully chewing it. "It's quite nice."

"Sure, you don't want to swap?"

"No," Phyllis scooped up another mussel. "These are nice," realising to her surprise the further down the bowl she ate, the more she was enjoying them. Conrad smiled, touched his wine glass to hers, and commenced eating his starter.

An hour later, Phyllis leant back and let out a great sigh of contentment. The main course of Thai green chicken curry with lemongrass and saffron rice, which Conrad had chosen for her, had been equally delicious, although her mouth was now tingling with the heat of unfamiliar spices.

Sipping cautiously at hot coffee, she looked curiously at Conrad, reflecting how strange it was she'd only known him for twenty-four hours, yet liked and trusted him more than anyone else in her life, apart from Richard, although her relationship with him was on a completely different footing. The thought of the staid, dignified Richard taking her underwear shopping made her want to giggle.

"Drink up, sweetie," Conrad glanced at his watch. "We need to get a move on. There's still so much to do."

"What?" queried Phyllis, enjoying the feeling of euphoria and lethargy induced by a large, midday meal, and two glasses of wine.

"Oh, now comes the fun part," Conrad grinned wolfishly at her. "Why do you think I made you change your underwear? We're going clothes shopping," he smiled at her look of panic. "Don't worry, I'll be with you, and I promise you're going to love it."

Phyllis wasn't so sure, but decided she'd come too far to back out now...

Chapter Ten
"It's simple, just think of the Spice Girls."

Topshop, on a Saturday afternoon. Chewing the gum Conrad had whisked out of his pocket to help lessen the impact of garlic and curry laden breath, Phyllis followed him shyly into the store and her preconceived idea of hell.

Teenagers and young women browsed through racks, greeting each other with cries of tribal recognition, exchanged dirt and gossip, while desperately trying to find the perfect outfit which would magically attract the one guy fate intended them to meet.

Feeling insecure, and dreadfully out of place, Phyllis slunk quietly into the shop behind him. Subconsciously, her body language reverted to that she'd used at school – blend in, act inconspicuously, don't do anything which will draw the enemy's attention.

Displaying no such qualms, Conrad strode in as if he owned the place, attracting ample attention in the form of sidelong glances, even openly curious full-on stares. Ignoring them all, he began rummaging through clothes rails, stopping now and then to examine an item more closely, before either sweeping it off and tossing it over one arm, or discarding it and moving on to the next.

Phyllis watched in thrilled anticipation as the pile of clothes grew, until Conrad decided they had enough to be making a start with and led the way to the changing room.

"Five items only," declared the girl on the door. Conrad tutted in annoyance, before moodily selecting five items which he transferred to Phyllis, all but bodily pushing her through the door into the communal changing area.

Clutching clothes to her chest, Phyllis shot Conrad a despairing look of panic before sidling into the changing room. Inside, girls were in various stages of undress, pulling clothes off hangers, wiggling into them, chatting, and laughing with each other.

Some, like Phyllis, seemed ill at ease with their bodies and struggled to try clothes on without exposing an inch more flesh than possible. Others, the little Miss Perfects, strutted around the changing room in their underwear, showing off their flawless bodies to enviously watching, usually less well endowed, friends.

Hanging the clothes up, Phyllis hesitated, unsure which to try first, before unbuttoning her blouse and reaching for a pretty flower sprigged t-shirt Conrad had selected to go under a blue, pinstripe, mini pinafore dress. Once it was safely on, she wiggled into the dress, smoothed it down, zipped it up, and pulled her trousers off.

Gazing in the mirror, she could see it fitted but was uncertain whether it looked good on her or not. As her reflection stared miserably back, Phyllis thought how wrong Conrad had been; she wasn't having a ball, and this was not fun.

"Sweetie, what on earth are you doing in there?" Conrad's voice broke into her thoughts. Phyllis looked up, cheeks flaming, as the girls around her giggled. Dropping her mortified gaze to the ground, Phyllis made no reply, hoping he'd either shut up or go away.

"Phyllis?"

Still, she didn't reply. The other girls looked around in interest, wondering which of them was being summoned.

"Oh, for heaven's sake, this is impossible! Cover your eyes, girls, I'm coming in!"

There was a commotion at the entrance to the changing room and to Phyllis's absolute and complete horror Conrad strode in, followed by an incensed, twittering member of staff.

"Sir! This is the ladies changing room, you can't go in there! Sir!" Shrieks and shouts, as girls dived into tops, clutching clothes in a desperate attempt to cover underwear. Without sparing a glance for the chaos he'd caused, Conrad marched over to Phyllis, frozen to the spot in utter mortification.

"There you are, sweetie. Right, let's have a look at you."

"Sir!" the assistant tugged ineffectually at his sleeve. "Please leave now, or else I'll get the manageress."

Conrad flicked an annoyed glance her way. "Yes, do, please get her, I need to have a word with her anyway about this absurd, five items only rule."

The assistant gaped at him like a trout out of water, glanced wildly around as if seeking help, before turning tail and fleeing the room.

"What on earth do you think you're doing?"

One of the girls gathered her wits enough to aggressively challenge Conrad. She stepped closer, backed up by her friends, and Phyllis closed her eyes in a dismayed flashback to school; to the countless times, she'd been beaten down by girls like this, perfect and pretty, confident in their popularity and out to get the freakish misfit.

"Sweetie," in his campest voice, Conrad turned to face the angry, petulant, young woman. "Are you planning on buying that? Because it's wrong, simply all wrong..."

"That's none of your business," snapped the girl. She paused, glanced down at the top straining to cover her ample assets. "What's wrong with it?" she continued curiously.

"Well, for a start, it's too tight and it's so making the wrong statement unless you want to make the statement you charge by the hour." The girl's mouth gaped in a soundless expression of outrage, as Conrad blithely continued, "It's also completely wrong for your shape and body type."

"Body type?" asked another girl in interest. "What do you mean, body type?"

"My dear, there are five different body types which all women fit into. The trick is to know which body type you are, so you can choose which clothes will suit and enhance your look."

"So, how do you find out which body type you are?" enquired Miss tight t-shirt. There was a murmur of interest from others, several crowding around Conrad.

"It's simple, think of the Spice Girls," Conrad flashed them all an innocent grin. "I take it you *have* all heard of the Spice Girls?"

"Too right, Girl Power." There was a ripple of laughter.

"The five body types are classic, romantic, sporty, outrageous, and gamine. So, Posh Spice is classic, Baby Spice is romantic, and so on."

"Oh, I get it," breathed one girl in excitement. "Sporty Spice will be, well, sporty, Scary Spice is outrageous, and Ginger Spice is gamine," she paused, wrinkling her nose. "But what's gamine?"

"It's a term used to describe a woman who's petite and has neat, well-defined, features, someone who's almost a classic, but they have a quirky twist," Conrad explained patiently. "Think Audrey Hepburn or Meg Ryan," he added helpfully.

"Hey Lucy, that's you exactly," cried one girl to her small, dark-haired friend, who was standing there clad in nothing but a mini skirt, and a red lacy bra.

Lucy nodded, turning to Conrad in excitement. "So, if I'm a gamine body type, what sort of clothes should I wear?"

"Go for neat, well-tailored things that fit you extremely well, the fit is the key for gamine body types, but then accessorise with well-co-ordinated and interesting accessories. For example," Conrad looked around the changing room before snatching a dress off a nearby peg. "Put this on," he ordered, handing it to her.

Phyllis and the others watched in silent interest, as the girl put the dress on and turned to look in the mirror. The dress was a simple, sleeveless, little cotton summer dress, black with tiny white polka dots, a tie belt, and an interesting cutaway mandarin collar.

Lips pursed, Conrad stepped back, thoughtfully surveyed her, whilst everyone seemed to hold their breath.

"Accessories!" he declared grandly, and the girls scattered to obey, offering up jewellery, scarves, bags, and sunglasses. Taking his pick, Conrad pulled Lisa's long, dark hair back and tied it with a white, silky scarf, clipped large, round, white earrings to her lobes, pushed several white enamel bangles onto one arm and slipped dark glasses onto her nose.

"Red lipstick," he snapped his fingers. Girls rummaged in bags, and various tubes were proffered. Conrad glanced at them, chose one, and applied it carefully. "Now," he stated, standing beside Lisa as they looked in the mirror. "You see..."

The girls looked, a collective sigh of awe was breathed, and Phyllis was astounded at the difference. A normal, averagely pretty girl had been transformed into a film star, all pouting lips, and oversized shades. As Lisa posed and primped in the mirror, the other girls crowded around Conrad, asking excited questions, begging him to help them discover their body types.

Suddenly, the curtain to the changing room was yanked back, and an angry-looking young woman strode in.

"Sir, I'm going to have to ask you to leave," she demanded, looking surprised as a united groan of dismay echoed around the room.

"No." "We want him to stay." "He can't go yet he's going to tell me my body type."

Conrad held up a hand. Silence fell. He smiled disarmingly at the manageress. "What's your name?" he purred.

The manageress looked taken aback. "Jennifer ... but that's not..."

"Listen, Jennifer, what a very pretty name by the way. My client here ..." Phyllis blushed as Conrad waved a languid hand in her direction, and a dozen pairs of interested eyes swivelled to gaze with envy and speculation.

"My client here is going to spend an obscene amount of money in your shop, so I'm afraid we will have to insist your absurd five items only rule be bent slightly."

"That's not the issue here," demanded the manageress, her eyes never leaving Conrad's placidly smiling face. "This is the ladies changing room. You're a man. You're not allowed in here!"

"Trust me," drawled Conrad. "The virtue of all these simply divine ladies is completely safe with me." There was a knowing snigger at his words, and the girls ranged themselves with Conrad, glaring almost hostilely at the manageress.

"That's still not the point," a note of despair had crept into her voice, as the manageress seemed to sense she was losing the battle.

"Why don't we put it to the vote?" suggested Conrad. "All those in favour of me staying, to offer advice and help to any girlie who wants it, put your hand up."

A unanimous sea of hands shot up. Conrad looked at the manageress in raised eyebrow victory. She looked around, exasperated, and threw up her hands in defeat.

"All right, all right," she mumbled. "If everybody's happy with that."

A ragged cheer erupted. Conrad bestowed the beaming smile of a magnanimous winner upon the hapless manageress.

"Just how obscene an amount will she be spending?" she muttered to him.

"Oh, positively pornographic," he reassured her, slipped an arm around her shoulders, and spun her to face the others. "Now then, girls," he began in the tone of a teacher addressing his class. "What body type do we think the lovely Jennifer is?"

"Classic!" came a chorus of voices, and Conrad beamed in delight.

After that, clothes shopping was fun. Clustering round Conrad like wasps round a honey pot, the girls clamoured and begged for fashion advice, and tips on how to dress.

Cheerfully, gleefully, he gave it; all the while making Phyllis work her way through an ever-growing pile of clothes and accessories; some he discarded, whilst others he tossed to a waiting assistant to be placed behind the till.

An impromptu lesson on posture and walking turned into a catwalk fashion show, spilling out of the changing room into the main store. It drew girls in from the street outside, initially to gape in astonishment, then become interested, finally to join in.

Girls pranced and posed for bewildered boyfriends, each other, but mostly for themselves, enjoying this all too brief escape from the real world, the touch of outrageous glamour, which Conrad had brought to otherwise normal lives.

Phyllis found herself caught up in the giddy excitement of the moment, singing along to the infectiously catchy music played at full blast over the music system. She sang tunelessly to the Spice Girls, their signature tune, helpless with shared laughter, as the others strutted and danced in outfits selected by Conrad.

The suspicious frown on the face of the long-suffering manageress quickly turned to a smile of avaricious delight as the girls shopped, oh my, how they shopped.

Trying on complete outfits which Conrad put together for them, posing for friends, seeing how good they looked, swept up in the feel-good moment, they bought armfuls of clothes and accessories, the tills constantly sounding out their song of retail. And Topshop, Bury St Edmunds, looked set to have its most successful day on record.

Two hours later, and nearly £400 poorer, Phyllis stumbled out of the shop in Conrad's wake, clutching numerous carrier bags to her chest, aware she was wearing a dazed, rabbit-caught-in-headlights, expression.

Going into sensory overload, Phyllis was unsure how much more she could take, although Conrad was showing no signs of even slowing down, let alone stopping.

"Shoes!" he declared, turning right into a trendy, over-priced shoe shop. Phyllis groaned and followed, staggering as she struggled to manoeuvre the bulky Topshop bags through the narrow door.

Finally, the never-ending day ended; shops were closing, and Conrad declared himself satisfied with the day's haul. Besides, he reminded her, they had to be home by six because that was when call-me-Colin was delivering her new stereo.

Trailing home, fingers numb from bag handles cutting off circulation, Phyllis wondered if her arms would ever snap back into their sockets. Her back ached incessantly from the sheer weight of all her shopping. Seemingly unaffected by his load, Conrad led the way, chattering non-stop about the day's events. Phyllis stared at his upright, smug back with a glare of almost loathing.

Letting them into the house with a sigh of relief, Phyllis nearly fell over the pile of bags from the morning's shopping session, gave a small whimper of dismay at the mountains and mountains of stuff she now owned. Giving her an understanding, albeit slightly patronising smile, Conrad patted her arm.

"Never mind, Sweetie. Why don't you go and run yourself a deep, hot bath with some of that fabulous new Calvin Klein bubble bath we bought today, and I'll bring you up a nice cold drink."

"But what about call-me-Colin, the stereo man?"

"I'll deal with him; you go on up. Poor sweetie, you look absolutely pooped."

"Well," Phyllis sighed, "it's been a very long day."

"But a fun one?" asked Conrad, anxiously. "Please tell me you've enjoyed at least some of it?"

Phyllis considered ... She thought about the face of the woman in Marks & Spencer, her assumption Conrad was her lover; remembered roaming the aisles with Conrad, listening to him philosophise on life, the universe, and the purpose of lipstick; the different tastes and textures of their lunch, and how sophisticated she'd felt sitting with a friend, drinking wine, in the middle of the day, in a smart restaurant.

Finally, she remembered the giddy, madcap excitement of their shopping extravaganza in Topshop. How exhilarating it had felt to be swept up in a collective, unforgettable experience. A small smile tugged at her mouth, and she looked sideways at Conrad.

"Well ..." she conceded.

His smile broadened into a grin. "I knew it," he exclaimed in triumph. "I knew you'd love it. I knew that buried beneath all those layers of repression – a shopaholic was simply dying to get out."

"I'll say," muttered Phyllis, wincing as she thought of the hundreds of pounds, she had spent in one day. "Heaven only knows what Richard's going to say."

"From what you've told me of him, he'll be delighted," Conrad shrugged off her concerns and began to collect up the bags of shopping. "Now go, have your bath, and relax, this evening's going to be a chill-out session. Nothing more strenuous than listening to music, I promise."

Laying in a sinfully deep bath, luxurious bubbles tickling her nose, breathing deeply of their satisfyingly expensive aroma, Phyllis let out a gusty sigh of pleasure, felt herself begin to relax and unwind, easing out aching muscles and sore feet, stresses of the rollercoaster day already receding.

A brief knock at the door and Conrad barged in, tumblers of chilled white wine in hand. Phyllis gulped in panicked embarrassment, looked down frantically at her naked body, before realising it was so covered in bubbles, he would need x-ray vision to penetrate its frothy covering.

"Here we go," he said, handing her a tumbler of chilled white wine. "Just what the doctor ordered – a very hot bath and a very cold glass of wine."

"Thank you," murmured Phyllis, oddly thrilled at the decadence of it all. Conrad flipped down the loo lid and sat, sipping with obvious pleasure at his wine.

"I must say, sweetie," he began. "You've certainly got an impressive collection of wine down there, considering you must have put it together completely by chance."

"Well," Phyllis stopped and blushed. "I did follow some advice I heard on TV."

"Oh?" asked Conrad in interest. "What advice was that?"

"Well," Phyllis's embarrassed flush deepened. "I once saw a comedian, I can't remember which one, who said you were pretty sure of getting a good wine if it was over five quid and didn't have a picture on the label."

Conrad threw his head back and roared with laughter. "Oh sweetie," he finally gasped, wiping his eyes. "Promise me you won't change, even when you've become Lili and are simply gorgeous and everything, promise me you'll keep that innocent sense of humour. It's so wonderful, so much a part of who you are, it would be a shame if you ever lost it."

"All right," Phyllis smiled shyly at him. "I promise."

The doorbell sounded. "That'll be call-me-Colin, the stereo man," remarked Conrad, taking another gulp of his wine. "I'll go and see to him. You take your time and come down when you're ready."

An hour later, Phyllis wandered downstairs in a haze of pleasure. After her bath, she spent a very pleasant twenty minutes putting away all her new clothes, shoes, and accessories; her hands stroking and caressing their newness. Enjoying the deep thrill of possessiveness, it gave her to see the rows of beautiful clothes hanging in her wardrobe, knowing they were hers to wear whenever she wanted. For a moment, she toyed with the idea of putting on a new outfit but felt strangely shy about it, so instead pulled on her comfortable old jeans and a sloppy t-shirt.

In the lounge, she found Conrad sprawled on the floor, tie pulled off, shirt sleeves rolled up, deep in the instruction booklet of the new stereo system, the almost empty bottle of wine by his side indicating she had some catching up to do.

"How's it going?" she asked, beginning to scoop up the various bits of plastic, cardboard and polystyrene packaging that were littered all over the floor.

"Okay," he murmured distractedly, flashing her an excited grin, happy as a child with a new toy. "What a great system," he declared. "Trust me, sweetie, you won't go far wrong with this stereo."

"Good," said Phyllis, picking up the last piece of cardboard, chucking the whole lot in the large box the stereo had been delivered in. Kicking it behind the sofa, she wandered over to where he sat, topped up her empty glass with the remaining dregs of wine, pulling a rueful face as she did so.

"Sorry," Conrad glanced up. "Is it a dead soldier? I'll go and open another bottle, I did put one in the fridge, or we could switch to red if you like."

"Don't mind," she shrugged. "What's for dinner?"

"Thought we could order a pizza or something if that's okay with you."

"Okay," again Phyllis shrugged, feeling oddly anticlimactic and strangely out of sorts. After all the excitement of the day, it seemed such a let-down to be merely sitting there, looking at her new stereo, and contemplating ordering a pizza for dinner.

"Won't be long now," Conrad commented mildly, barely glancing in her direction.

"Pardon?"

"I said, it won't be long now."

"Won't be long before what?"

"Before even the idea of staying home on a Saturday night will be completely alien to you," Phyllis made a wordless sound of enquiry. Once again, Conrad flashed a little boy grin. "No, you'll be too busy going out with your friends clubbing and having fun."

"I don't think so," Phyllis smiled doubtfully at the thought.

"Well, you've got to think so, otherwise what's been the point of today? Life is there for the taking, sweetie. You've got to get up off your backside, get out there, and grab it with both hands. Now, let's order pizza, open another bottle of wine and then we'll have a look at your new CDs."

Chapter Eleven
"And of course, you'll be doing it all in high heels."

Next morning, Phyllis awoke to a somewhat larger hangover and the enticing aroma of brewing coffee and frying bacon. Rolling over in bed she rubbed at her forehead, squinting blearily at the hands on her alarm clock, trying to make sense of it all. When her eyes finally deigned to open enough to make out the time, she was rather surprised to see it was nearly eleven.

Scrambling hastily out of bed – astonished Conrad had let her sleep so late – she pulled on her new robe, used the bathroom, and hurried downstairs, bare feet padding soundlessly on the faded carpet in the hall, to arrive breathlessly in the kitchen doorway as Conrad turned from pouring steaming hot coffee into two mugs.

"Morning," she exclaimed, wincing as he jumped back in shock and clutched theatrically at his chest. "Sorry."

"That's quite all right, sweetie," he replied, dabbing at the coffee stains on the work surface. "I enjoy starting my Sunday with a heart attack." Grinning, Phyllis slid into a seat, gratefully accepting the coffee he offered her, sniffing appreciatively at the smell of bacon.

"So," she asked, taking a tentative sip of the scalding hot coffee, watching as he expertly sliced bread. "What are we doing today?"

"Today," began Conrad, slapping butter onto the bread with gusto, "we are going to be working on your posture, and how you walk..."

"Doesn't sound too difficult," muttered Phyllis.

"And dance..."

"Dance?"

"And of course, you'll be doing it all in high heels."

"What? Conrad, you can't be serious?"

"Oh yes, I am, deadly serious. We need to get you out of those ugly flats, into something a little more flattering and feminine. After all, you wouldn't want all those simply gorgeous shoes you bought yesterday to rot in the wardrobe, would you?"

"Well, no..."

"Exactly, so today you'll get used to wearing them. By the time you go to bed tonight I want you to be proficient in walking, running, and dancing in every single pair of your new shoes."

With a sinking heart, Phyllis realised he was right, he *was* deadly serious, and her feet ached thinking about it.

The day started reasonably well. Conrad watched her sit, stand, and walk. Then he made her put on various pairs of shoes and do it all over again. On and on he went, making her walk upstairs, come back down, run up and down the garden path – heaven only knew what Mr and Mrs Jamison had thought of that!

He put on music and made her dance, Phyllis cringed at the look on his face at her first clumsy attempts. Patiently, he danced with her, showing her how to hold herself, how to move, what to do with her arms and hands.

For a man, he was incredibly light on his feet, and Phyllis watched in envious awe as he danced around the cleared lounge, making it look so easy and so natural.

The best part of the whole experience had been the music. As she listened to the same songs, over, and over again, Phyllis started to enjoy them and began to pick up the words. Concentrating fiercely on what her feet were doing as she tried to get it right under Conrad's eagle-eyed stare, she couldn't help singing along.

Feeling, at last, she might be getting somewhere, she glanced up at Conrad in triumph, her feet tangled, she tripped, and ended up in a sprawled heap on the carpet, rubbing at her sore backside, glaring furiously at him as he laughed like a drain.

But, gradually, she began to find her natural rhythm. Slowly she stopped obsessing about what her feet were doing and started to feel the music.

The track ended, and Conrad skipped to the stereo, frantically jumping tracks until he found the song he wanted. It was one they hadn't played before. Phyllis waited, heart thumping, for the lyrics to begin, only to realise there weren't any.

The music swelled, grew, entered her body. Throbbing and pulsing, her heart hammering in time to the beat, almost unconsciously, she began to move.

Swaying and shaking, she closed her eyes to better experience how the music was making her feel. She tossed her head from side to side, enjoying the swish of hair across her face, the dizzying sensation it gave her to dance without seeing.

All too quickly, the track ended. Phyllis came back into her body, opened her eyes, and stared blindly at Conrad leaning against the wall watching. Slowly he nodded, his eyes never leaving hers.

"That's it," he said simply. "You've got it."

"What was that?" she gasped, heart still pounding with the thrill and exhilaration of totally immersing herself in music for the first time in her life.

"It's a style of music called trance," he explained. "It's very popular, so it's good you enjoy it and dance so well to it. Now then," his brisk words snapped her completely back into the present. "Let's try something else."

By the time Conrad was finally satisfied, Phyllis had progressed from feeling like her feet had been put through a meat mincer, to feeling as if they'd been amputated at the ankles.

With a groan, she flopped onto the sofa, gratefully pulled off the offending shoes, and tossed them halfway across the floor. Moaning and mumbling she rested one foot gently in her hands, trying to massage the life back into her poor cramped toes.

Conrad entered the lounge. Tutting in disapproval, he bent to pick up her shoes from where they'd fallen and placed them neatly by the sofa. Phyllis cast him an evil look, toying with the pleasant fantasy of throwing them at him. As if reading her thoughts, Conrad sat next to her, picked up her other foot and began to expertly massage it.

"So," he said with a wicked grin. "Hasn't today been fun?"

"Fun?"

Phyllis swivelled her head to stare at him in open-mouthed disbelief.

"Fun?" she repeated, voice rising incredulously. "Umm, let me think … no!"

"Oh sweetie," Conrad retorted, his tone one of mock hurt. "You do disappoint me. Why not?"

"Shopping is fun. Going for lunch is fun. Listening to music is fun. Undergoing brutal foot torture by a crazed tyrant and ending up with ten screaming blisters where my toes used to be, is not fun."

Conrad simply smiled and gently patted her foot.

"You did well, Phyllis, you really did. I think you're a natural. You have a good, easy rhythm. Your dancing reflects the music, and most importantly, when you're dancing, you look like you're enjoying it."

Phyllis felt her heart swell with pride at his words and ducked her head away, ashamed of the easy blush she felt burning her cheeks.

"I do enjoy it," she mumbled. "At least, I enjoy the music, and I guess I did enjoy the dancing. I don't enjoy the fact my feet feel like they've been stepped on by a giant in hobnail boots."

"You'll get used to the shoes," he reassured her. "Pretty soon, you'll look back on today and wonder what all the fuss was about. Now, what do you want for dinner?"

They decided on pasta again, making it together, and moving about the cramped kitchen in perfect synchronicity.

As Conrad blended a delicious tomato and basil sauce, Phyllis washed and sliced a salad, a bottle of red wine standing on the side to breathe and thought how well Conrad had fitted into her life; how well she had fitted into his.

After dinner, Conrad lined up a row of miniatures he had insisted on buying from the off-licence the day before, together with a variety of different mixers.

They sat facing each other across the rows of Lilliputian bottles, Conrad fixing Phyllis with a stern look.

"Now then," he began. "It's time we had that talk about booze. It's fun to drink, it's fun to get sloshed, it is not fun to get falling-down drunk. It is not fun to have no control over yourself, and it is not fun to be sick from drink."

Phyllis remembered how Amy had suffered and nodded her head in agreement.

"I am going to impart to you Uncle Conrad's rules for safe and successful drinking." Phyllis raised her eyebrows and Conrad wagged a finger in mock admonition.

"Don't look at me in that tone of voice, young lady," he retorted. "This is serious. Rule one: never drink on an empty stomach. If you do, the alcohol will go straight into your bloodstream and you will get seriously pissed, seriously quickly.

Rule two: try to dilute the drinks. Have water or fruit juice in-between, never mind if you think it looks boring or a bit sad. It's better than having to end the evening early because you got drunk.

Rule three: don't mix your drinks. Find a drink you like and stick to it. If you absolutely must have cocktails, make sure you follow rules one and two.

Rule four: if you begin to feel drunk, i.e., room spin, out of body experience, or vurps…"

"Vurps?" asked Phyllis in confusion, trying not to laugh at the saintly expression Conrad was wearing whilst delivering his sermon.

"Vurps, vomit burps …"

"Oh yuck!"

"Yes, oh yuck, very oh yuck, and a forerunner to being sick, which is so not attractive. Now, have you got all that?"

"Absolutely. Never drink on an empty stomach, drink plenty of water, don't mix my drinks, and stop when I feel I've had enough."

"Good. Now then, let's find your drink." Solemnly Conrad opened the first bottle. "This is whisky; not usually a ladies' drink, but you never know."

He splashed a little in a glass and handed it to Phyllis. One sniff of its pungent odour was enough to put her off, but remembering his words about trying things, she tentatively sipped it.

"Oh gross, yuck, yuck."

Hurriedly spitting it into the bowl thoughtfully provided by Conrad, Phyllis grabbed her glass of water and washed her mouth out, desperate to get rid of the taste.

"Okay, not whisky then. Next gin, mixed with the usual tonic, although it can be drunk with other things." The gin went the same way as the whisky and Conrad shook his head sadly.

"That's a shame, nothing better than a nice gin and tonic. Oh well, vodka next. We'll try it with orange, seeing as how you found the tonic too bitter."

The vodka and orange was better. As Phyllis sipped cautiously at the mix, leery of trying it after the previous mouth curdling experiences, she found the sweetness of the orange, and the almost undetectable, underlying tang of the vodka, quite pleasant. In fact, very pleasant.

"I like this one," she declared, hanging onto the glass, and taking another sip. "It's much better than those other yucky things." With a toss of her head, she dismissed them, cradling her drink possessively in her hand.

"Good, here, try it with coke," sloshing the rest of the bottle into a glass, Conrad added some coke, and slid it across the table to her. Phyllis tentatively tried it, rewarding him with a dazzling smile.

"Yes, I like this one too."

"Well, there we go, vodka is your drink. Remember what I told you – drinking can be fun and is a very sociable thing to do with your friends, but there's nothing in the world more ugly or pitiful than a woman who's had too much to drink. Also, you need to think about your liver and other internal organs. Too much booze is a big no-no as far as they're concerned."

"Okay, I'll remember …" Phyllis paused, glanced up shyly at Conrad. "Thank you," she said simply.

"What for?" he asked, pouring a miniature brandy into his glass.

"For tonight and today, yesterday, the shopping, the music, the mussels … well, thank you for everything."

"You're welcome," he patted her hand, obviously touched. "I am having the best time ever. I feel like I'm Pygmalion and you're my Eliza Doolittle."

"Who?" asked Phyllis innocently. "Isn't he the one who talked to the animals?"

Conrad threw up his hands in exasperation and was about to launch into his usual tirade when he spotted the sly smile lurking around her mouth, the mischievous twinkle in her eyes.

"Why you little …" he exclaimed. "You know exactly what I mean."

"Yes," Phyllis laughed joyfully at having finally got her own back. "My Fair Lady was Gran's favourite film; I must have watched it a dozen times with her."

"Your Gran was a woman of great taste. Now then," Conrad glanced at his watch, "I'll make a quick call to Matthew, then, what say we relax in front of the telly and finish up our drinks. I'll have the rest; it seems a shame to waste them."

"All of them?"

Phyllis looked at the colourful array of unopened miniatures. "You're going to drink all of them? What about rule three, never mix your drinks?"

"Absolutely right, sweetie, so I'm not going to have mixers with any of them…"

After the excitement and activity of the weekend, Monday was a quiet and pleasant day. Following a late breakfast, they wandered into town and Conrad took her shopping for clothes for work, helping her select a capsule wardrobe of neat little mini-skirts, a variety of mix-and-match tops, together with a pair of black, square-toed shoes which were comfortable, and after her day of torture in heels measuring three inches and higher, felt low with their paltry two-inch chunky heels.

Phyllis wasn't sure she had the guts to wear a mini skirt to work, but Conrad insisted she was eighteen, a size eight, and had fantastic legs. If she didn't wear them now, whilst she was young and gorgeous, when was she going to wear them? Besides, teamed with thick black tights, her new shoes and a neat little top, they didn't look tarty. Instead, they looked somehow innocent and youthful. Smiling at her reflection in the mirror, Phyllis was forced to admit, once again, Conrad was right.

Afterwards, they went shopping in Waitrose for food for the rest of the week, and Phyllis showed Conrad the exact spot where she had seen Lili.

"And you've never seen her again?" Conrad asked gazing at the rows of olive oil with as much reverence as a believer would bestow on the last known site of the Holy Grail.

"Not for sure, I thought I did once, walking ahead of me with a girl with long, blonde hair, but she vanished before I could catch up with them."

They wandered home, laden with goodies, and that night, after dinner, for fun, they pushed back the sofas in the lounge, and Conrad taught her the Macarena.

Going back to work the following morning was quite a wrench. Even though Phyllis would only be gone a few hours and knew Conrad would be working whilst she was absent, it still felt strange, leaving the house without him. It also felt odd pulling on her old work clothes. Having psyched herself to wearing her new office outfits, Phyllis found it hard to understand why Conrad insisted she wait until the following week to launch Lili on her unsuspecting work colleagues.

Wait, he advised her, until the transformation is complete. There's no point, he continued, wearing fabulous new clothes when her hair still looked such a mess.

Grudgingly conceding the point, Phyllis slouched off to work in a bad mood, which was not improved by Alex, hyped up on pre-wedding anxieties, gradually getting on everybody's nerves. In the end, Ms Evans sent Alex home early with strict instructions to get a good night's sleep and stop worrying about everything.

The next two days followed a similar pattern – breakfast with Conrad then off to work, to listen to Alex's worries and soothe them as best she could. Then home, dinner with Conrad, followed by an evening of planning, TV, music, or chat. Phyllis didn't dare admit to herself how much she was going to miss him when he left.

Thursday afternoon she returned home to be greeted by Conrad's announcement that, in her absence, he had emptied her room of all her old clothes and taken them to the local charity shop. Not sure how she felt about this, Phyllis was trying to think what to say, when Conrad took her by the hand and led her into the kitchen.

"Now then," he began, whisking a bottle of champagne out of the fridge, and opening it with a dexterity that had Phyllis smiling in awe.

"As this is our last night together…"

"Is it?" interrupted Phyllis in dismay.

"I'm afraid so, sweetie, I simply must go back to London late tomorrow…"

"Must you?"

"Yes, I'm sorry, I must. Don't worry. We have one more day tomorrow and, my word, is it going to be a busy one."

"Why?" stammered Phyllis, taking a sip of champagne, discovering it fizzed up her nose in a not unpleasant manner. "What are we doing tomorrow?"

"You, my dear girl," retorted Conrad, "have appointments all day, so we're going to have an early dinner and night. But first, I want to take you on a tour."

"A tour? A tour of what?"

"Of your home, or rather of your home as it's going to be … we'll start in the hall. Bring your champagne, you're probably going to need it…"

During the next hour, Phyllis discovered what Conrad had been doing over the past three days, as he led her from room to room, excitedly showing her his plans, and making her see his vision with the aid of beautifully drawn sketches and mood boards.

Explaining, describing, drawing pictures in the air, he took her with him into her home of the future, until she could see it, feel the texture of the fabrics; visualise it enough to know it was everything she had ever dreamed of and more.

Even his scheme to knock the large reception rooms through to make one large space, with the bay window at one end and doors onto the garden at the other, brought a smile to her face as he talked her through the idea.

"Don't demolish the central wall completely; leave a slight lip all around and then install fabulous wooden folding doors…"

"What for?"

"So, you'll have the choice of two smaller cosier rooms, or one big, open-plan space. Each half of the room will have its own separate identity, but both rooms will work together as a whole." Gesturing towards the fireplace he continued.

"I see a fabulous piece of modern art hanging above each fireplace; a pair of pictures which, again, work well separately, but make sense when viewed together."

"Where will I find…"

"You leave that to me, sweetie, I have a young artist in mind. He's unknown, but I think I can safely guarantee, anything of his will turn out to be a very wise investment." He paused, expectantly. "So, what do you think?"

"I think," Phyllis began slowly, "that you're a genius, I love it. I love it all. When can it be done?"

"We need planning permission for the conservatory, and I may have to source local builders as my normal contractors might not be prepared to travel so far out of London. I won't lie to you, sweetie, it's going to take time, and it's going to take money to make all of this come true."

"I have plenty of both," replied Phyllis, finishing her champagne. "I want everything you've planned. If that means I must wait longer and pay extra to get it, that's what I'll do. I trust you."

Conrad smiled, enveloping her in a big, brotherly hug.

"Bless you, Phyllis," he said, sounding suspiciously close to tears. "Bless you."

Chapter Twelve
"Don't worry, I haven't killed a client yet."

Although Conrad had said they would be making an early start; Phyllis hadn't realised how early he meant and was grumpily unprepared for being unceremoniously yanked from her slumber before seven the next morning.

Yawning and muttering, she sulkily staggered downstairs for breakfast, annoyed to find Conrad already showered, dressed and in an infuriatingly chipper mood.

"Why are you so full of beans?" she demanded irritably, deliberately stabbing the butter knife into the jam pot to annoy him.

"Because my sweet," he smacked her hand away, handing her a clean knife. "Today is the day it all comes together. As we say in the trade, this is – reveal – day."

"Huh? What's going to be revealed?"

"You are sweetie. This morning you are merely Phyllis. I guarantee by the time I leave at five this afternoon, you will be ..." he paused for effect. "Lili!"

"What?" Phyllis stared at him; her grumpiness forgotten. "Really?"

"Trust me," Conrad twinkled. "Now, be a good girl and eat your toast up, or we'll be late."

Late for what he didn't say.

When they left the house, Phyllis still had no idea where exactly they were rushing to. She was none the wiser ten minutes later when Conrad led her to a large, ornate building which they entered through double glass doors, where an immaculately maintained blonde, in a neat, pink overall, perched at a reception desk.

"Good morning," she cooed. "Can I help you?"

"Miss Goodwin, for her eight o'clock with Susie."

"Certainly, Sir, please take a seat, Susie will be right with you."

Dazzled by the blonde's high-wattage smile, confused as to where she was, what was to happen to her and who Susie was, Phyllis hissed at Conrad.

"Where are we?"

"Beauty salon," Conrad hissed back. He idly picked up a magazine and began flicking through it.

A beauty salon? Phyllis looked around curiously. Behind the reception desk, a corridor snaked its way towards the back of the building. Several cream doors led off it and Phyllis wondered exactly what went on behind them.

Catching the blonde's eye, she was subjected to another million-dollar smile, and hastily followed Conrad's example with the latest edition of Vogue. She knew of the existence of beauty salons, of course, her mother had regularly attended one, but was vague as to what occurred inside one.

The double doors swished open. A very well-preserved woman in her fifties strode confidently over to the desk.

"Mrs Ashman, I have an 8:15 with Monique."

"Certainly, Mrs Ashman," the blonde simpered. "Please take a seat, Monique will be right with you." The woman turned to the sofa, smiled at Phyllis, and settled herself next to Conrad.

There was a clack of kitten heels, a rustle of pink nylon, and a diminutive brunette sashayed into reception. Exchanging a brief word with the receptionist she headed over, beaming a smile of exuberant welcome. Susie, Phyllis presumed.

"Good morning," she positively purred. "I'm Susie. If you'd like to go into consulting room one, I'll be right with you."

"Oh, right, okay," stuttered Phyllis, darting a look of panic at Conrad.

"Go on, sweetie, I'll be just out here." He rose and watched, as reluctantly, fearfully, Phyllis got up, slowly crossed reception, and went through the first door. Reaching out a hand, he stopped Susie.

"It's her first-ever wax," he quietly murmured. "You might want to start with the worst if you know what I mean."

Susie's pert eyebrows rose in understanding. She nodded obediently, before passing through the door which shut fast behind her. Sitting back on the sofa, Conrad felt Mrs Ashman's curious eyes on him.

"Her first time?" she enquired.

"Yes," he nodded.

"What's she in for?"

"Facial, manicure, pedicure, eyebrow wax, and full body wax."

"Ouch," exclaimed the woman in sympathy. "Does she know?" At Conrad's head shake, her lips pursed in a smirk. "You're going to be popular," she observed wryly.

Five minutes later, they exchanged amused glances at a barely muffled shriek of outraged pain which echoed into reception. Conrad sank behind his magazine, shaking his head with suppressed laughter.

The woman was right, he was going to be popular.

Half an hour later Phyllis staggered out, swaddled in an oversize, pink, towelling robe, and clutching a canvas bag containing her clothes. Slowly, painfully, she hobbled over to Conrad and raised a shaking hand to point accusingly at him.

"You ..." she spluttered. "You ... she..."

"Oh sweetie," he sympathised, trying not to laugh at her shocked expression.

"I've had boiling wax poured everywhere – and I mean *everywhere* – and all my hairs ripped out. She even did my eyebrows, look." Phyllis pushed her fringe back, and Conrad looked with interest at the newly shaped and defined brows.

"That's much better," he enthused.

"I didn't know you could get your eyebrows waxed," Phyllis exclaimed, flopping next to him on the sofa. "Why did they need to be done?"

"Are you serious, sweetie? I mean, I know the Gallagher boys are big right now, but the mono-brow look for women was over in the last ice age."

"Miss Goodwin," Phyllis looked up in dread as Susie's pretty face popped around the corner. "We're ready for you in consulting room three if you'd like to follow me."

"No," Phyllis turned on Conrad in panic. "No more, please, no more."

"Relax," he chuckled, helping her to her feet, "the worst is over. From now on it's all going to be nice and painless, I promise."

Two hours later, Phyllis drifted from the salon on cloud nine, dreamily admiring her beautiful hands and nails, painted for the first time. She wiggled her feet inside her shoes, relishing their new softness, and the fact her toenails were now painted the same pretty, shell pink colour as her fingernails.

"Feeling good?" enquired Conrad, smirking at her languid expression.

"Hmm, oh yes," agreed Phyllis. "That facial was amazing; so relaxing, my skin feels so soft and smooth." After a brief examination, Susie had declared her skin was in quite good condition, but it did seem dry with a few blocked pores. What cleansing routine did she use? Phyllis had stuttered at this, unwilling to admit it was soap and water.

The manicure and pedicure had also been very pleasant. Phyllis had learnt a lot from closely watching everything Susie had done to transform rough, nail-bitten hands, into smooth, classy looking ones fit for a queen or Lili.

"Where are we going now?" Phyllis came back down to earth to realise they weren't heading home but instead were bound for the town.

"Hairdressers," came Conrad's short reply.

"This isn't the way to my hairdressers..." she began.

"It is," replied Conrad. "Because this is now your hairdresser." He stopped at the doors of a very trendy salon in the town square, one which Phyllis would never in a million years have thought about going into.

"Here, but I don't know, Conrad..."

"Trust me, sweetie," he commanded, ushering her in. "We have an appointment booked with Kay," he explained to the young girl at the desk.

"Certainly," she said briskly. "Have a seat. I'll let Kay know you're here."

Numbly, Phyllis sat on another sofa and picked up another magazine, this one on hairstyles. Flicking through pages of outrageous, outlandish, and plain ridiculous styles, some of which defied the laws of gravity, Phyllis felt the old panic grow.

"Conrad," she whispered frantically. "I'm not sure about this."

"Trust me," he ordered again, looking her in the eyes. "We're so close now, Phyllis, we're on the home straight. A few more hours and it'll all be over, but you've got to relax and trust me."

"Okay," Phyllis swallowed hard, and nodded. "I trust you. I do. I'm a bit ... scared, that's all."

"Nothing to be scared of," said a voice. Phyllis looked up, startled, to see a tall, dark-haired woman standing in front of them, dressed from head to toe in black, the only colour being large, gold hoop earrings, and a slash of bright red lipstick. "I'm Kay," she said, giving Phyllis a friendly, reassuring smile. "Don't worry, I haven't killed a client yet."

"She's never had a proper haircut," explained Conrad.

"So, I can see," retorted Kay. She sat on the coffee table in front of them, lifted a hand to Phyllis's hair, ran her fingers through it, and held up a hank for inspection.

"Condition's not bad," she grudgingly conceded. "But there's no style or definition, and the colour's flat. What did you have in mind?" She addressed Conrad as if she instinctively surmised who was making the decisions.

"Well," mused Conrad. "I was thinking we should add depth and colour, and it needs a completely new style, something to emphasise her cheekbones. Much as I loathe copycat cuts, I was thinking she could carry off a Rachel."

"Hmm," Kay's eyes narrowed thoughtfully. "I think you're right, though maybe not quite so elaborate; something a little easier to maintain herself. No point doing a fancy cut that ends up a dog's dinner when she tries to do it at home."

"True," conceded Conrad.

"What's a Rachel cut?" Phyllis by now was tired, and a little cross at being spoken about as if she were not there.

"What's a Rachel cut?" exclaimed Kay in amazed disbelief. "Rachel off Friends, of course. Where have you been the last two years, down a well?"

"Something like that," agreed Conrad smoothly. "Shall we get started? She has a make-up appointment at three."

This was the first Phyllis had heard about it and she turned excited eyes to Conrad, but before she could comment, was swathed in a cape, and handed over to a junior to be washed and conditioned.

Thoroughly relaxed by the unfamiliar experience of someone else washing her hair, Phyllis sat in the chair, looking at herself in the large, brightly lit mirror. With her hair combed off her face, she saw what Conrad meant about her eyebrows, and wondered why she never realised how her straggly thick brows closed her face in, giving her a perpetually sulky expression. Now, they looked sophisticated and were clearly defined into glossy arches. Phyllis decided regular visits to the salon would be essential to maintain them. At least having those waxed hadn't hurt, not like ... Phyllis shifted uncomfortably, remembering where else had been waxed.

"Coffee?" enquired Kay, pulling across a trolley laden with medieval torture devices.

"Please," replied Phyllis gratefully, and the little junior scampered off into the back room. Looking in the mirror, she saw Conrad watching with interest as Kay carefully combed all the tangles out of her hair.

Over the next two hours, Phyllis was initiated into the mysterious world of hair, watching in dumbstruck wonder, as Kay wrapped her hair in dozens of bits of tinfoil, and painted reddish, gloopy stuff all over her head.

Once she was satisfied the colour had taken, Phyllis was led to the sinks and her hair washed. Back in the chair, Kay examined the colour with a pleased expression, before whisking out her scissors and attacking her hair with a casual speed which alarmed Phyllis somewhat, until she reasoned to herself Kay must know what she was doing.

Finally, Kay painstakingly blow-dried her hair using a large round brush, patiently stopping occasionally to show Phyllis exactly what she was doing. A last fuss with the scissors, a spritz of shiner, a cloud of hairspray later, and it was done. Kay stepped back and Phyllis saw herself properly for the first time.

It was beautiful.

Her hair was beautiful, glossy, and gleaming with a myriad of tonal autumnal colours. It swept in a gorgeous, silky curtain down to her shoulders, still straight but magically fuller and thicker, with an offset parting which allowed a long strand to casually sweep over her eyes, drawing attention to newly found cheekbones.

Phyllis gulped, cautiously putting a hand up to feel its silky glamour and watched as her mirror image stared and stared at the glory that was her hair. Eyes blurred, she turned a tearfully appreciative gaze on Kay, who was smiling at her reaction.

"Thank you so much," she whispered. "I love it … it's so, so…"

Kay's expression softened, and she gently dropped a hand onto Phyllis's shoulder. "You're welcome," she said, almost gruffly. "I must admit, it's turned out better than I hoped. Poker straight hair is so in right now, and whereas most girls are having to use straightening irons, your hair is so naturally straight it fell into place."

Phyllis managed a watery smile at the irony of her detested, line straight hair turning out to be an asset. Conrad cleared his throat, Phyllis glanced up to catch him dabbing surreptitiously at his eyes.

"You look amazing, sweetie, but we're not done yet."

Hastily, Kay brushed the excess hairs from Phyllis's neck and shoulders and pressed her card into her hand. "Come back for regular trims," she advised. "The colour will need maintaining. Keep an eye on it and make an appointment when you start to get root regrowth."

"I will," Phyllis promised fervently. "And thank you again."

Hurrying from the salon, Phyllis could feel her hair bouncing and moving. Look at me, she wanted to shout. Look at my hair. Isn't it gorgeous? Isn't it just like Lili's?

Luckily, the store where she was booked for a make-up session was close. They were right on time as they rushed through the doors and up to the cosmetics counter, where a trim, middle-aged brunette in a red suit was waiting for them.

Already on a high following her beauty treatments and the triumph of her new haircut, Phyllis was more than willing to put herself into the hands of another expert and learn as much as she could about the wonderful and mysterious world of make-up.

It was very pleasant, she discovered, to feel the woman's soft, knowledgeable hands as they patted and stroked, brushing lotions and potions onto her freshly pliant skin, all the while demonstrating and explaining to Phyllis what went where, how much to apply, and what colours would work best for her skin.

"You have amazing eyes," murmured the woman quietly. "They're a lovely, warm, brown colour, but when you look closely, you can see all sorts of green flecks in them." Phyllis had never noticed but was quite prepared to take her word on it.

Afterwards, the woman held a small hand mirror up, and Phyllis peered at the painted stranger looking back at her. Unable to see more than a portion of her face at any one time, Phyllis felt a vague disappointment that she didn't feel more different.

Leaving the store, clutching a bag of free samples and a ludicrously expensive bottle of foundation, Phyllis felt almost anticlimactic. She didn't know how she'd expected to feel, but surely should be experiencing some emotion.

"Where now?" she wearily asked Conrad.

"Home," he replied simply, glancing at his watch. "We have time to do the reveal, have some sandwiches and then I need to be off to catch my train."

Phyllis nodded, trailing drearily after him, tears pricking her eyes at the thought that soon Conrad would be gone. She'd be alone again.

Reaching home, Conrad wouldn't let her look in the mirror, instead hustled her to her room, where he rifled through her clothes, frowning in concentration.

Phyllis watched with interest as he picked out a short, wrap-around skirt made of some sort of silky material. Barely skimming mid-thigh, it was black with a scattering of silver roses across it. This he teamed with a thin knit, black, sleeveless, polo neck jumper.

"Put these on," he ordered. "Be careful not to ruin your hair or make-up."

Crossing to the chest, he pulled out matching black underwear and tights, tossed them on the bed, then picked out a pair of fashionable black shoes with square chunky heels.

"Yell when you're ready." He left the room, and Phyllis hurried to obey, calling out to Conrad five minutes later.

Shyly, she waited for approval, desperate to look in a mirror. He studied her, lips pursed, fussed with her hair, removed a smudge of mascara, and stepped back with a strangely serious expression.

"My work here is complete," he said gently. "Go take a look."

Nervously, she brushed past him and stopped, strangely reluctant to look, because at that point she would finally find out if Gran had been right. Was there a beautiful woman inside? Could she possibly become Lili, or was she doomed to forever be Phyllis?

Swallowing hard, mouth dry, heart thumping wildly against her ribs, she gasped, shut her eyes, then turned to the full-length mirror hanging on the landing wall.

"Open your eyes, sweetie."

Conrad's voice was ripe with amusement. Slowly, slowly, she allowed her eyelids to flutter up and saw herself, properly, for the first time.

She saw a girl, no, a young woman, fashionably slim, the slinky skirt clinging to size eight hips, fitting in all the right places. The thin black jumper with its high neckline, cut-away sleeves, and cropped waistline showed smooth flat flesh whenever she lifted her arms, a bewitching blend of decency and tantalising tease.

Long, traffic-stopping, lycra-clad legs seemed to go on forever; slender ankles and small shapely feet encased in chunky shoes emphasising the delicacy of the rest of her.

The hair was a triumph. Glossy and glamorous, it caressed her bare shoulders, shimmering in the afternoon sun pouring through the window, glowing with vitality.

The face ...

Phyllis took a step forward in disbelief. Was that her face? Surely not. The woman in the mirror was – not pretty, that was too tame a word to describe the exotic Slavic vision who stared back at her – no, she was ... she was...

"I'm beautiful," she murmured, dazed, and confused.

"Of course, you are," reassured Conrad, contemplating her reflection. "I never doubted it for a minute. Now," he paused, looked at her and then at her mirror image.

"When you look in the mirror, who do you see?"

"Me," Phyllis was bewildered by his question.

"No, who do you see?" he repeated urgently.

"Lili ..." she whispered. "I see Lili ... I've become Lili."

Becoming Lili

Part Two

Lili
1996~2004

Never has an ugly duckling,
turned into such a beautiful swan...

Chapter Thirteen
"Our parents were killed in a house fire two years ago."

Now that Conrad had left her, she danced alone; her reflection in the full-length mirror reassuring of her new beauty until she felt drunk on it. Long legs flashing under short skirt, she was magnificent in her abandon. Feral, like a young, wild animal, lost in the pleasure of the moment. On her bed lay a colourful pinwheel of brand-new clothes – frighteningly fashionable, intensely desirable, they were beautiful in their newness, and they were hers, all hers.

Retreating from the silence that descended after Conrad left, she dragged the stereo into the hall to relieve her loneliness. Inevitably, it wasn't long before the sedate try-on session turned into a fashion show, with her the only model. She pranced and preened, as the music throbbed, brand new stereo speakers stretched as far upstairs as they could go, volume on full, bass button down.

Parched, she charged breathlessly to the kitchen, dragged coke from the fridge, and splashed it into a tumbler. Almost without thinking, she added vodka to the coke, then took both bottles up with her, and carried on dancing.

The music was in her soul; oh, how she loved it. How could she have ever thought she didn't like modern music? It was a revelation. It was the truth. Britpop ruled. She watched herself in the mirror, marvelling at this beautiful stranger; the wildly tossed hair, the attractive face with arresting contours and angles; the slim supple body and long coltish legs, knowing if she had seen someone like her walking down the street, she'd have stared with awe and envy.

"You're beautiful!" she told her reflection, plastering a kiss on those perfectly pouting lips.

The world whirled, and she grabbed the door frame. Her head thumped – a tide of acrid-tasting bile rushing into the back of her throat. Hand to mouth, she stumbled to the bathroom. Falling to her knees in front of the loo she retched, again and again, sobbing with disgust. Finally, wrung out and exhausted, she staggered to the bedroom and clung to the door. When the bed circled back around, she pushed all her new clothes off to land in a heap on the floor, crawled under the duvet and fell into a deep, drink-induced slumber.

A car alarm shrilled, jerking her out of a black hole of drunken sleep. Grunting, Lili rolled over, staring blearily at bright sunlight pouring through partially drawn curtains. Painfully raising her head, she wiped at her mouth, discovering sour-tasting dribble crusted in the corners. Struggling to sit, Lili discovered something else. All the little headaches she'd had over the week of Conrad's visit were nothing compared to the mother of all hangovers she was suffering from now. Her brain lurched, rattled, and pushed alarmingly on the inside of her skull as if trying to escape. Her eyeballs were gritty. Sometime during the night they'd been removed, rolled in a bucket of sand, and reinserted. Groaning, Lili rubbed at them and looked with dismay at her mascara encrusted fingers. She'd gone to bed without taking her make-up off. Conrad was going to kill her.

Swinging her legs over the side of the bed, Lili bent to retrieve her slippers, and her brain slammed violently into the back of her eyeballs, wringing a moan of agony from a Sahara dry mouth. She slumped on the floor, waited for the world to calm down and stop throbbing, then spied all her new clothes lying in a dishevelled heap on the floor, and groaned again. What exactly had she done last night? Patchy memories, vague images of drunken dancing, but none of how she'd got to bed.

Moving from the bedroom with all the speed and agility of a ninety-year-old up from a hip operation, Lili stopped short at the sight of the tumbler of drink standing on the floor, and the opened plastic bottle leaning crazily against the bannister. Thirstily, she grasped the bottle and swigged desperately at the remaining coke, the flat liquid with its lukewarm, metallic taste seeming to soothe and ease her poor, churning guts.

Confronted with her lipstick kiss mark on the mirror, she pulled a face at the vision of loveliness in the glass; face grimed with old make-up, mascara rubbed from her eyes almost meeting smudged up lipstick. Foundation had rubbed dirty marks on her face, and deep folds marred her right cheek where she'd slept too soundly on a creased pillowcase. Under the stale make-up, her skin was yellow and sallow, her eyes bloodshot and puffy, and her hair, her gorgeous hair, stuck up all over like porcupine quills.

Realising she had finally revived from her seemingly never-ending coma; Boris bounded upstairs and attacked her legs. Piteously mewing and complaining, he wound around her shins, his tale a heart-rending one of abandonment and starvation. In danger of tripping over him, Lili pushed him away, sat on the top step, and tried to summon the energy to begin the descent.

"You've no idea how bad I feel," she groaned. Boris bent his tattered head, sniffed with disdain at the discarded glass on the floor, and cast her a look of outraged disgust.

"Okay, okay, I know," she muttered. "I think I broke every single one of Conrad's rules, and boy, am I suffering for it now. Well, it's taught me a lesson – never again!"

Stumbling downstairs, Lili shakily fed an ecstatic Boris, gagging at the ripe smell of cat food. She filled a pint mug with water and climbed wearily back up to the bathroom. Carefully, she tied her hair back, thoroughly cleansed her face until not a single scrap of make-up remained, then scrubbed at her teeth until they bled. Finally, she rubbed in some of the ludicrously expensive skin food Conrad had insisted she buy, feeling her dehydrated skin suck it in gratefully.

Hanging up all her beautiful new clothes, she tutted in annoyed self-condemnation at the cat's hairs clinging to them, thinking with grim amusement that at least Boris had appreciated the new cat bed she'd provided him with. Crawling into bed, Lili set her alarm for three o'clock. That left plenty of time to get ready to go to Amy's. A thrill of happy anticipation shivered through her stomach. Snuggling under the covers with a groan, she instantly fell asleep.

Opening her eyes moments before the alarm sounded, she was relieved to feel a painful death was no longer imminent. Sitting up, blinking at the clock, she switched off the alarm before it could ring and hastily scrambled into the bathroom where she peed forever, then examined her face critically in the mirror. Thankfully, it wasn't too bad. At least her colour was back to normal. With the resilience of youth, the water she'd drunk, and the four hours of sleep, she looked ok.

She pulled a paddle brush tentatively through her hair. To her relief, it fell back into the cut, swishing gorgeously around her shoulders, shining luxuriously. That was good, that was very good. Kay had warned her to make sure she had plenty of time when she attempted to do the hair herself for the first time. Lili had already earmarked Monday as hair experimentation day.

Carefully, Lili put the stereo back to rights and pushed it into the lounge. It had been a very stupid thing to do. Her new, expensive stereo system might have been damaged. But it had been fun having music upstairs, the carefree dancing. Maybe she'd go back and see call-me-Colin and buy a portable CD player as well. After all, why not? She could afford it, and she wasn't afraid to spend money now.

Her stomach rumbled, demanding food. Reasoning she wouldn't be eating for at least another four hours, Lili decided it would be wise to feed the last vestiges of her hangover. Several slices of toast and a large glass of orange juice later, she felt restored, rejuvenated, and renewed, small pinpricks of excited anticipation creeping up her spine at the thought of the evening ahead.

Speeding across town in a taxi, shaking with nerves, damp palms clutching a bag in which two bottles of wine were clanking, Lili plucked nervously at the skirt of the denim, mini pinafore dress she had teamed with a raspberry and white striped polo shirt. The mirror had reassured her that she looked gorgeous, but now she wasn't sure. Perhaps she should get the taxi driver to turn around, take her back, and wait while she changed. No, don't be stupid. There was no time. She'd be late. She looked fine...

Arriving at the address Amy had given her, Lili found it was a block of rather seedy-looking flats on a disreputable council estate, on the wrong side of town. Nervously, she paid the taxi driver and began to look for the right number, heels clacking up concrete stairs which smelt of urine and things decaying.

Pausing outside number thirteen, which boasted a newly painted door and a cheery welcome mat, Lili had one last fuss with her hair and skirt, then knocked tentatively on its flat blue surface.

There was a moment's silence, a sense of movement behind the door, then it flew open and there was Amy, laughing, talking, and so pleased to see her. Lili was astonished at how genuinely pleased to see her she was. Lili was swept inside on a tide of excited girlish chat, which carried them down the narrow hallway and into a spacious living area. Bright and cheerful, it presented a warming first impression, and Lili saw the large space was divided into well-defined areas. A compact, but efficiently useable kitchen was tucked up one end, a round pine table and four chairs dividing it from the rest of the room, which was taken up by a very pleasant seating area with double doors opening onto a small balcony.

Lili exclaimed with pleasure at the confusing, eclectic crowd of plants that jostled for room in the confined space, and a tall figure stepped into the room from the balcony, the watering can in his hand still dripping.

"Hello, Lili," said Kevin, and Lili was tongue-tied with shyness.

"Hi," she managed to stammer, wondering how she could have forgotten how good-looking Amy's brother was.

"It's all right," Amy laughed, misunderstanding the reason for Lili's hesitation. "He's sorry for being so horrible to you last week and has promised to behave himself.

Looking at them, both so fair and attractive, Lili saw the family resemblance, wondering what it would be like to have a brother. She held out the bag.

"Wine," she said, shaking off nerves, determined to get this right. "I didn't know what we were eating, so brought red and white."

"Thank you," said Amy, taking the bag. "You didn't have to, but thank you, it's kind of you. Oh, it's cold," she exclaimed, taking out the white and handing it to Kevin.

Reluctantly agreeing to his sister's demands they invite this girl, Lili, to dinner, Kevin had tried to remember what she looked like, but it had been late and dark, and he'd been so entrenched in angry assumptions, his only memory was of large, deep brown eyes, round with shocked indignation.

Amy drew Lili onto the balcony to see the plants, and Kevin had to stop himself from staring at this exotic, fascinating creature recently arrived amongst them. The coldness of the bottle drew his attention. His eyebrows rose as he recognised it as a good quality chardonnay, one he knew would retail at around ten pounds a bottle. An unexpected treat, and far superior to the local supermarket's bargain bucket brand currently chilling in the fridge. A quick look at the red showed it to be of equal value to the white. Mouth quirking with an ironic smile, Kevin reached for the corkscrew to open both. Perhaps the evening was not going to be such a loss after all.

Not knowing what to expect, Lili soon discovered Amy was an excellent cook, the crab soufflé starter melting in her mouth.

"This is amazing," she exclaimed. "Thanks," she continued, as Kevin topped up her wine glass. "Where did you learn to cook like this?"

"From Mum," replied Amy, taking a small sip of wine, screwing her nose up in obvious delight at the taste. "Mmm, that's lovely," she said, taking a bigger mouthful.

"Is your mum a professional cook or something?" Lili asked, finishing her last mouthful with a sigh of satisfaction. At the sudden silence, she looked up, saw Kevin and Amy glance at each other, then Amy looked down at her plate, biting her lip.

"Mum *was* a great cook," Amy began carefully.

"Was?" Lili asked shakily, and with a sick foreboding knew what was coming next.

Kevin placed a hand over his sister's. "Our parents were killed in a house fire two years ago," he stated flatly, looking Lili straight in the eye.

Lili briefly closed her eyes in mortified horror. "I'm so sorry," she whispered, dismayed at committing such a blunder. Hadn't she known, somehow, she'd spoil it? Her first time out and already it was ruined. "I really am sorry."

"Hey, Lili, it's okay," Kevin placed his other hand over hers. She felt the shock of contact, the warmth of his skin covering hers. Face aflame, she raised large, worried eyes to his kindly concerned ones.

"You didn't know," he continued. "How could you? So please, don't worry about it."

"No, honestly Lili," Amy too could see how upset she was, seeking to console and placate. "It doesn't upset us to talk about it. It's been two years. We're ..." she paused, exchanging a glance with her brother. "We're okay about it now," she stated firmly.

Seeing the stricken look still on Lili's face, she hurried to change the subject. "So, tell us a bit more about you, Lili. Where do you live? What job do you have?"

Realising what Amy was trying to do, Kevin rose and began clearing the plates, stacking them haphazardly by the sink, listening with interest as Lili told Amy where she lived, and that she worked in an employment agency. It was strange, he thought. She was forthcoming about her house, her job, her cat, and her love of music, but strangely reticent about everything else. Lili volunteered no information about her family or childhood at all, seemingly diverting the conversation away from such subjects. Musing maybe she was simply being tactful following her faux pas, he carried the bottle of red wine to the table and deftly took over the conversation so Amy could dish up the delicious smelling coq au vin.

"I love your name," Amy remarked, handing Lili a plate of sublime smelling food. "Please, help yourself to vegetables. Lili – it's a lovely name. Is it short for something? Elizabeth, maybe?"

Lili's heart clutched with fear.

Did they know? How could they have guessed? What's in a name? Only a label, a front, a brand, it declared to the world who and what you were. No, no, it was okay, relax, breathe. Look at her face. It was an innocent comment, nothing to it.

"No, it's Lili," she replied, voice a study in casualness. "It's not short for anything. I'm just ... Lili." She forced herself to smile, sip her wine, and try her food.

The evening wore on; the food was superb, the wine flowed, the atmosphere mellowed. Lili finally relaxed. This was good. This was better than good. She listened, enjoying the ebb and flow of conversation, the easy, good-natured banter between Kevin and Amy. Envy, quiet and wistful, stirred at their closeness. As a child, she had longed for a sibling, someone to share her loneliness with.

Kevin too was enjoying the evening. Not only was Lili beautiful; she was good company – sincere and amusing in a dry, understated way. Seeing his sister blossom in her presence, and laughing out loud, Kevin couldn't help but feel warmly towards Lili.

The past two years had been hard for the Sinclair's. Losing their parents had been a devastating blow. For a long time, Kevin blamed himself. If he'd still been living at home, maybe things would have been different. Instead, he'd been at a horticultural college pursuing his dream of becoming a landscape designer. When the police came to tell him of his parent's death, and that his sister was in hospital, he had no concept his world had, quite literally, collapsed.

Alone at twenty, with a sixteen-year-old sister to look after and precious little money, Kevin put aside his hopes and desires. Taking the first job he could find working for an insurance firm, he watched and worried as Amy, struggling with her own demons, sat her GCSEs at his insistence, and completely stuffed the lot.

It transpired that his parents had not been very efficient when it came to life insurance and pensions. Once debts and funeral expenses had been met, there was barely enough left to pay a deposit on a two-bedroom flat, in a part of town Kevin had previously never spared a thought to, much less ever imagined he'd wind up living in.

Trying to cope with his grief and disappointment, Kevin still had to deal with a moody and uncooperative teenager. Cutting contact with all her friends, who were busily taking up places at universities, Amy had morosely taken a lowly paid, office junior job.

Kevin had silently witnessed her slide into depression, until her youth, natural high spirits, and friendly personality began to finally reassert themselves. That was why, despite his misgivings, he agreed to take her and her so-called friends to the nightclub last week, and why he'd gone along with her plan to invite Lili to dinner.

Watching her face glow in the candlelight, hearing her delighted giggles, Kevin thought how long it had been since he'd seen his sister happy. For that alone, he thanked Lili.

After dinner, they moved to the sofa with coffee, shivering in the breeze from the open balcony doors. Kevin got up to close them, the girls laughing as a palm frond flopped in the way, and he fought to keep it out whilst trying to shut the doors.

"I don't think I've ever seen so many plants in such a small area," exclaimed Lili. "Who's got the green fingers?"

"Oh, that's Kevin," laughed Amy. "Not me. I even manage to kill spider plants. No, Kevin's amazing with plants and things, that's what he was training to be a landscape gardener, before ..." her voice trailed away, and the brightness left her eyes.

Hastening to fill the silence, Lili said the first thing that came into her mind. "Well, maybe you could come and sort my garden out. It's a right mess. I know absolutely nothing about gardening, so don't even know where to start."

"Really?" asked Kevin with interest. "How big is it?"

"Oh, about thirty-foot wide, and about two hundred feet long," replied Lili vaguely.

"Is it south, or north-facing?" Kevin's eyes lit up.

"Don't know," replied Lili. "The sun sets on the back of the house if that's any help."

Kevin nodded, "I'd certainly be happy to look at it for you; maybe give you some ideas."

"That would be great," agreed Lili, glancing at her watch. "I guess maybe I should be phoning for a taxi. It's getting late."

"Oh, no, must you go?" Amy's disappointed voice was touching. It warmed and reassured Lili. She must have got it right. She must have managed to fool them. "When can I see you again?" she continued. Lili smiled at her, thinking how pretty Amy was with her long blonde hair, clear blue eyes, and pale skin.

"What are you doing next Saturday?"

"Nothing," Amy shook her head, eyes hopeful.

"Well," Lili took a deep breath, "why don't we go clubbing?"

"I don't know," Amy's face looked doubtful. "I'm not sure if I'm cut out for clubbing, not after what happened last time…"

"You'd be with me," replied Lili, assuming a false air of confidence. "I'd make sure you were okay. It'll be fun. I live so close to the town centre you could come to mine to get ready. You could even stay the night if you wanted."

"Ok," Amy brightened, turning to Kevin. "Could you drop me off at Lili's next Saturday?"

"Of course," he replied. "But I'm not sure I like the idea of you girls walking home alone late at night," he continued with a frown.

"Oh, we'll be all right …" began Amy.

"Come with us," interrupted Lili.

"Pardon?"

"Come with us," she repeated, her excitement growing. "Why not? It'll be fun. We can eat at mine first, then walk uptown, have a drink, and hit the club." Seeing the doubtful look on his face, she pressed the idea home. "Afterwards, we can walk back to mine. No one will dare attack us if you're with us, and you can both stay the night."

"But Lili," began Amy in surprise. "Do you have enough space?"

"Oh yes," retorted Lili airily. "Plenty of space."

"I don't …" began Kevin, Lili could sense he was about to say no.

"Then, in the morning," she continued desperately, needing him to say yes if this was to work, "you could look at the garden, see what you think."

"Please, Kevin …" pleaded Amy.

"Well, all right," he conceded. "Anything to please you."

But, as the two girls excitedly began to make plans, he was forced to admit the reason he'd capitulated had more to do with the plea he'd seen in Lili's eyes, than the one he'd seen in his sister's.

Chapter Fourteen
"Does mother even know you're here?"

Life, thought Lili in surprise, was good. It was better than good. She was happy, really, happy, for the first time in her life. Thank you, Conrad, she thought humbly, thank you. It was the following Saturday – seven days later – and it was true, Conrad had completely transformed her existence.

Sunday had been a very pleasant day; Lili had scrubbed and cleaned the house from top to bottom, trying to imagine how it would look through Kevin and Amy's eyes – Kevin and Amy, her friends. Lili kept stopping to hug herself with joy.

She had friends; friends who were coming to stay for the weekend. They were going to go out and have fun together, her and her friends. She would get this right; she would make it work.

Paying special attention to the spare rooms, Lili picked out the two nicest ones for the brother and sister, planning to take a trip up to town on Monday to buy all new bedding, and any other accessories she saw to cheer up their rooms.

Amy phoned in the afternoon to chat and make plans, both girls revelling in the novelty of an hour spent exchanging girl talk. It was agreed Lili would try to get Amy an appointment with Kay, Amy breathlessly excited at the thought of going to such a trendily intimidating hair salon.

They would go shopping, they decided, have lunch, and afterwards would go back to Lili's, play music, and lazily get ready. Kevin would arrive at six, then they would eat, exactly what would be decided on the day. The three of them would then go for a drink, before hitting the club.

Later, Lili phoned Conrad, giving him a full and animated report on the previous evening. Listening to his familiar, dearly loved voice, so full of enthusiasm and interest, Lili felt again how keenly she missed him.

Monday afternoon had been designated hair experimentation time. With a sense of nervous anticipation, Lili stepped into the shower with the whole range of expensive hair care products she'd bought. Taking her time, religiously following Kay's instructions, she was relieved when the hair fell back into the excellent cut, looking almost as good as before.

After dinner, Lili laid out her clothes ready for work and picked out which make-up she intended to use. It was strange how quickly she had become used to wearing it, to seeing her face with its mask of paint and powder. When she took it off in the evening, it was almost as if a stranger was looking back at her from the mirror.

Tuesday arrived – Phyllis's first day as Lili at work. As she walked nervously into the office, Lili wondered how her work colleagues would react to the new her. Alex was still away on honeymoon, so Beth – who was covering reception – was the first Lili saw.

"Can I help ... good lord! Phyllis, is that you? What on earth happened? You look amazing. You look like a completely different person." Lili beamed as Beth jumped up and walked around her, delighted eyes examining her with shock and astonishment.

"I decided to change my look, so I had a haircut and did a little shopping."

"Had a haircut?" Beth shook her head in amazement. "Honey, you have got to tell me where you go. Wait until everyone else sees you."

The reaction of the others had been equally satisfying, their delighted surprise gratifying, as she enjoyed being the centre of admiring attention for the first time.

Damien, one of the seniors, even cornered her in the kitchen to ask if she'd like to go to The Tavern with him on Saturday. There's a live group playing, he said casually. He'd heard them before, and they were good. If she liked, he could pick her up, say at seven?

Naively, Lili flashed him a dazzling smile of gratitude, charmingly replied she would have loved to, but unfortunately was already going out with friends. In her innocence, not realising she'd turned down her first-ever date.

There was only one low point in the week. With Alex away, Lili was left to struggle with the filing on her own. She hadn't realised how much she had come to depend on the other girl's assistance.

It didn't help that everyone else was having to juggle their work to try and cover. The seniors were too busy to do more than answer their phones, Beth and Maggie, the typists, did what they could, but were working to full capacity, so the brunt of the work was on Lili.

Spending time on reception, endlessly answering calls, jogging from copier to coffee machine and back again, rushing about on numerous errands, Lili didn't have time to think about filing, let alone do any. It began to stockpile alarmingly, and it was a relief to bung it all in a cupboard, shut the door and go home Thursday afternoon with the pleasures of the weekend to look forward to.

Friday passed in a pleasant blur of shopping, making sure the guest rooms were perfect, phoning Conrad, and doing her nails. Still not very good at this, Lili decided to do them Friday, rather than risk looking as if she didn't know what she was doing in front of Amy.

Saturday, Lili woke early, excitement rousing her before the alarm. Hastily, she washed, carefully applied makeup, and brushed her hair. Wandering into her bedroom, she stood before the wardrobe in a patch of sunlight, trying to decide what to wear.

Amy was arriving at 10:30 and Lili wanted to go to the market and buy lots of flowers, mostly to cheer up the somewhat dated décor, but also because she felt Amy and Kevin would appreciate the simple, homey touch of having fresh flowers in their rooms.

Kevin ... Lili paused halfway through pulling on a summery mini dress. She never imagined it would be possible to have a male friend, but why not? It felt nice; sort of how it must feel to have a brother.

Although only eight when Lili left the house, the sun was already warm, promising another lovely day. Lili felt like bursting into song, as she hurried to the flower stall and had first pick of the brightly coloured blooms.

Returning home, mind already occupied with which flowers should go where, she almost walked into the tall, slightly stooped figure standing on her front doorstep, hand raised, caught in the act of pressing the doorbell.

"Dad?" Lionel Goodwin jumped and turned. The sun blazing into his eyes, he peered at the young woman behind him. Framed in a halo of flowers, she seemed a vision, an angel, crowned with a nimbus of bright, shining light, and he gaped, unable to comprehend what he was seeing.

"Dad?" the vision spoke again. He blinked, and the angel resolved into his daughter, but not as he remembered her. No, this beautiful, confident woman frowning at him in enquiry, was a world away from the plain, downtrodden, mouse of a girl he'd seen five short months earlier.

"Oh, is it you? Umm yes, good, I'm glad I caught you. I wanted ... that is, I felt it was probably best if I saw you, rather than ..." His voice trailed away uncertainly, her expression was almost annoyed, and he could have sworn she glanced at her watch.

"Could I come in, please? I think we need to talk?"

She hesitated, almost as if trying to think of an excuse to send him away, finally sighed, opening the front door, and ushering him in.

"Take a seat," Lili waved her father in the direction of the lounge, heart pounding at his presence. "I'll put these in the kitchen."

Filling the sink with water and dumping in her armfuls of flowers, Lili wondered why he was there, and whether she should offer coffee. Once more, she glanced at her watch, 9:30; Amy would be here in an hour. No, Lili decided, she'd offer him nothing; he could say his piece and go.

Drawing her resolve around her, Lili entered the lounge and sat opposite him, smoothing her skirt over her knees. She caught a glimpse in his eyes of how shocked he was by her changed appearance. The knowledge of her newly found beauty gave her confidence. Straightening her spine, she leant back, gaze cool and level on her father's face.

"How have you been? You look well, I..."

"What do you want Dad? Why are you here?" Startled by her bluntness, Lionel paused, uncertainty clouding his eyes. The daughter he knew would never have dared to interrupt him. No, she'd have waited, head bowed, sullen expression fixed until he'd finished talking, then would have mumbled some inane comment, before escaping back to her room.

"I wondered how you were. If you were all right. After all, you left so abruptly..."

"I left five months ago, Dad," she dared to interrupt him again. "If you were concerned, why has it taken you so long to check I'm okay?"

"Well, I ... that is we, your mother and I..."

"Does mother even know you're here?"

"No," her father bowed his head, uncomfortably, then raised his eyes to meet Lili's. She thought she saw a glimpse of something, perhaps shame, in them. "No," he continued. "She doesn't know I'm here. I thought it best all-round not to rock the boat, as it were."

"So, why are you here, Dad?"

"To let you know we've sold the house and are moving out of the area."

"Where are you moving to?"

"New Zealand."

"Oh, I see," Lili paused, examining her feelings, curious as to what impact her father's news had on her. To her relief, she felt nothing beyond idle curiosity. "Well, I suppose that could be defined as moving out of the area," she said, seeing her father's mouth twitch slightly at her coolly dry comment. "Am I allowed to ask why?"

"I've been offered a position at a top university there, and your mother is keen to break into television down under." Indeed, Lionel had been surprised how readily his wife agreed to the move until he heard rumours of a personality clash between Elizabeth Goodwin and the new head of programming at the BBC. A rumour that claimed in the backlash of a diva-like temper tantrum, her proposed series had been cancelled.

"I felt you deserved to know," he finished lamely, remembering with bitterness the scene between him and his wife when he tentatively suggested they couldn't relocate to another hemisphere and not bother to inform their only child.

Shocked by the viciousness his wife had displayed upon the subject of their estranged daughter, Lionel let the matter drop, not wishing to bear the brunt of his wife's increasingly volatile mood swings. However, later that night, his conscience had troubled him, demanding for once he did not obey his wife's dictate.

Considering the problem, he finally decided that for the continuance of his reasonably peaceful existence, it was probably best if he paid a discreet visit to his daughter whilst his wife was away on a book signing tour.

So, here he was, sitting opposite this glamorous stranger who bore his daughter's name and carried hints of his wife and dead mother-in-law's genes in her face, being subjected to a disinterested, indifferent stare. Fiddling with his tie, Lionel felt his discomfort grow, until, finally, he could bear it no longer.

"I'm sorry," he said.

Lili raised startled eyes to meet his shamefaced ones. "Sorry for what, exactly?" she replied.

"Well, that maybe you didn't have such an easy time of it during your childhood. Your mother and I, we … well, we never wanted children. It was a shock to us when you arrived. We didn't know what to do, how to treat you …" his voice trailed away as his daughter gave him a look of such cold and utter contempt, it choked the words in his throat.

"I don't know how to answer that," Lili replied slowly, a cold, hard knot of anger growing inside her. "Didn't have an easy time during childhood? No, you're right, I did not have an easy time during childhood." Sarcasm dripped from her words, and she had the pleasure of seeing her father wince. "Do you have any concept of what it was like for me? I was bullied, tortured, abused at school, and you did nothing to stop it."

"We didn't know…"

"Well, you should have known," Lili shouted at him. "I am your daughter, yet you treated me with less respect than you would a total stranger. You've no idea how I suffered; how much I longed for your attention, for a few crumbs of the love you had for each other."

"I'm sorry, we…"

"No!" Lili held up a hand in sharp denial. Her father abruptly ceased talking. "Enough," she continued. "You've said enough. Whatever you think you can offer me, it's too little, too late. I'd like you to go now, please, I have friends coming for the weekend, and have things I need to do."

"Oh, yes, of course, I …" Lili felt a strangely satisfying burst of pleasure watching her father flush and bluster, at a loss for words, reeling from the impact of her speech.

Rising, Lili led the way to the front door and opened it, leaving her father in no doubt as to her wishes. Red-faced and silent, he reached in his pocket for a card, which he pressed into her hands.

"This is our new address in New Zealand," he explained sombrely. "Should you need us … me … for any reason," Lili looked at the card for a moment, before nodding once and slipping it into the pocket of her dress.

"And I know you probably don't believe me, and I can't say I blame you, but I am sorry." He left, walking steadily down the path.

Lili watched him go, not sure if she should rip the card into a thousand bits – or call him back. Sorry at the chance her father had had which he'd let slip through his fingers, allowing his life and his heart to be controlled by the selfish coldness of another.

The club was hot and sticky, sluggish air conditioning struggling to cope with warm weather, and the sheer volume of people packed into its dim, cavern-like interior. The dance floor heaved with a wildness of bodies, twisting, and moving to the thumping, pulsing rhythms, blasted out at eardrum piercing level by the resident DJ. All around, people laughed, drank, chatted, and flirted.

It was dark and smoky, crowded, and sweaty, and they loved it like that.

So far, the day had been a success beyond Lili's wildest dreams. After the shock of her father's visit, Lili quickly put the flowers into various vases, angrily stabbing their stems into hasty arrangements. Furiously, she went over in her mind his unsatisfactory, fumbled apology, as if trying to make up for eighteen years of neglect. No, she decided, thrusting a rose into an already overfull vase, and scratching her finger in the process, let them go to New Zealand. The further away, the better. She didn't, wouldn't care.

By the time Kevin dropped Amy off, Lili had calmed down, wiped away her angry tears and fixed her make-up, determined nothing was going to spoil the weekend. Bubbling over with excitement, Amy waved goodbye to her brother and followed Lili into the house, carrying two overnight bags, and holding up a hanger bearing Kevin's shirt and trousers.

Breathlessly, she explained Kevin had gone to some famous garden and would be back by six. Here were his clothes; could she possibly hang them up so as not to crease them? Eyes popping in wonder at the size of the house, Amy followed Lili upstairs, exclaiming with pleasure at the rooms Lili had allocated for them.

"What an amazing house, Lili!" she cried. "Do you live here with your parents?"

"No," replied Lili, carefully. "They moved to New Zealand for my dad's job," she explained casually, reasoning to herself it was, more-or-less, the truth.

"You lucky thing," remarked Amy. "Having the whole house to yourself; it's fantastic." Lili merely smiled, watching as Amy quickly and efficiently put her own and Kevin's things away.

"Look," confided Amy, opening her purse and showing Lili a wad of notes. "Look what Kevin gave me – £100! Wasn't that great of him?

He said he's been saving some money, and that he wanted me to have a good time today; to have a nice lunch and buy myself something to wear tonight. Don't I have the greatest brother?"

Lili agreed warmly, yes, she did indeed have the greatest brother, feeling wistful, gentle envy at Amy's glowing happiness over Kevin's thoughtful generosity.

Rushing uptown, the girls barely made it to the hairdressers in time for Amy's appointment. Lili watched with interested pleasure as Kay snipped off dead ends, thinned and feathered Amy's fringe, then blow-dried her hair into a gleaming, golden mass, which shone and rippled down to mid-spine.

Speechless with wonder over her hair, Amy raised no objections when Lili whisked her into Boots for a free make-up session, where the beautifully made-up consultant explained about skin tones and colourings, showing Amy how to maximise her big, baby blue eyes, and enhance the peachiness of her skin. Wandering the aisles, the girls selected a few items of make-up to start building up Amy's cosmetics box. Mindful of the difference in their financial status, Lili tactfully restrained herself from buying anything, contenting herself with helping Amy.

Then, they went to lunch, Lili confidently leading the way to the restaurant where she ate with Conrad a fortnight previously. Pretending absorption in her menu, she listened closely to Amy rhapsodising about the choices, before picking something that sounded good.

As they ate, Lili learnt about food appreciation, experiencing all the different tastes and textures of their meals through Amy's knowledgeable eyes, she was humbled at how little she knew.

"How come you're such a good cook, are so obviously passionate about food and yet you work in an office? Why aren't you a chef or something?" Some of the pleasure faded from Amy's eyes, and she fiddled with her fork for a moment, before giving Lili a small, tight smile.

"I wanted to go into catering," she explained. "I had a place at catering college lined up, but that was before..."

"Before?"

"Before Mum and Dad died," she paused and took a deep breath. "It took me a long time to get over it, I had to pass my GCSEs to take up the place, and when I completely failed the whole lot, it didn't leave me with a lot of other options."

"I see," replied Lili slowly. "I'm sorry for bringing it up."

"No, that's okay," Amy was quick to reassure. "I have to start talking about it; to being okay with the way my life is now. Kevin's been amazing. He gave up his dream to look after us, yet I've never heard him complain once."

"He doesn't seem the type to complain," agreed Lili.

"No, he's not, that's why I was so pleased you insisted he come tonight, Lili. It was so great of you. He seldom goes out. He doesn't have any friends, and although he hasn't said anything, I think he's lonely. Well, he must be, stuck in that tiny flat with his baby sister for company. It'll be good for him to get out and do something different, something fun."

"It'll be good for all of us," said Lili firmly.

Spending the afternoon buying outfits for the evening, Lili found herself liking Amy more and more. Her sense of humour, although touchingly innocent and childlike, was also bubbly and infectious. It brought gaiety and lightness to the shopping trip, making it the fun, female sharing experience Lili had hoped it would be.

Suitably shopped out, the girls wandered home at five, looking forward to the female rite-of-passage of getting ready, putting on loud music and opening the vodka. Kevin turned up at six to find his sister and her friend, flushed and giggly, their girlish high spirits bringing a smile to his normally serious face, as they took him all over the house on a tour which led, finally and inevitably, into the garden.

Looking at the barely concealed hunger on his face, Amy realised, for the first time, exactly what her brother had lost; what their parents' deaths had taken from him.

Silently, she slipped a small hand in his as they stood outside, listening as Lili talked them through the changes to be made to the kitchen, and the new conservatory. Getting excited about the plans, Kevin asked professional questions, nodding at Lili's answers, before waving the girls away and wandering off to explore the garden.

Racing back into the house, the girls took an armful of CDs upstairs, switched on Lili's new ghetto blaster, and proceeded to indulge in the time-honoured occupation enjoyed by women throughout the ages – that of making themselves beautiful.

Returning from the garden, Kevin scratched Boris under the chin when he came mumbling and complaining around his legs. Searching in cupboards, Kevin located the cat food and spooned some into the cat's bowl, smiling as the corpulent animal dived in with all the dignity of one who'd been deprived of food for days, if not weeks.

Wandering upstairs, wincing at the noise coming from Lili's room, he contemplated knocking but decided against it. Instead, he went to his room, noticing little Lili touches everywhere. Fresh flowers, a bottle of mineral water and a glass, the stack of thick, fluffy towels in the middle of the bed. Grabbing one, he decided to make use of the empty bathroom, assuming when the girls were hungry, they would emerge, and a food decision would be made.

The pizza had been ordered, delivered, and consumed; large, hot, and spicy, dripping with every topping known to man, and quite a few only a woman would consider.

The girls rushed back upstairs to change from the robes they had eaten in, delaying getting dressed – partly for the practical reason of not wanting to get pizza on their new clothes – partly for the unspoken, subconscious motive of wishing to make a grand entrance, all decked out in their newly acquired finery.

Listening with amusement to the squeals and laughter coming from upstairs, Kevin felt his spirit's lift. Not one for nightclubs, he hadn't been to one since college, when he used to occasionally hit the clubs with his mates if funds allowed. He had never been to the local club, time and circumstances conspiring to ensure it never happened. He found himself looking forward to the evening; to spending social time with his sister away from the confines of the flat; and, he was forced to admit, to spending more time with Lili, getting to know her better.

She fascinated him. Not just her physical beauty, although, of course, that had impacted on him with all the force of a meteor, but her personality; her quirky, somewhat off-beat, sense of humour; the way she seemed ever so slightly out of tune with reality. Quite why he found this so attractive, he didn't understand, but, without a doubt, he was attracted to Lili. Very attracted.

A clatter on the stairs alerted him to the girls' arrival, and he looked at the door with interest as they positioned themselves, waiting for his reaction. He felt the breath catch in his chest as he silently gazed at them, hardly able to believe the blonde babe posing coyly, fresh, and gorgeous in a pale blue, ruffled mini dress, was his little sister Amy. In his male ignorance, Kevin only knew she had done something different to her hair; that the skilfully applied cosmetics made her look somehow more mature and more beautiful, her large blue eyes enhanced by clever use of shadow and mascara.

Turning his attention to Lili, his eyes popped at the tight-fitting, halter neck, black mini dress she was not quite wearing, its starkness relieved by a heavy gold collar clasped around her neck, its chunkiness emphasising the angular jut of an almost too thin collarbone.

To match the dress, Lili's make up was Egyptian based, her dark eyes defined with black eyeliner, already generous lips plump with shiny, red gloss, glistening and pouting, inviting any red-blooded male in the vicinity to imagine what it would be like to sample them.

Kevin – a red-blooded male – felt his mouth go dry at the thought, becoming aware of the girls giggling at his slack-jawed, stunned reaction, and waiting for his comments.

"You look stunning," he began slowly. "Absolutely stunning, both of you. I'll be fighting the men off you with a stick all night."

"Don't bother on my behalf," giggled Amy. "What about you Lili?"

"Oh, I don't think anyone's going to be after me," Lili replied, airily. "Besides," she continued, almost fiercely. "I'm going to have fun, not to get chatted up. It always seems when people get romantically involved with each other, everything is ruined. No, I want to enjoy myself and stay single." Looking at her with a sinking heart, Kevin realised she meant every word.

Walking uptown, hearing the thump of music blaring from every pub they passed, Lili felt the throbbing pulse of the town. It was Saturday night. All around them massed young people, like them, dressed to kill and out for sport. Lili felt gloriously and wonderfully alive, and for the first time in her life, felt young.

"Where are we going?" Amy asked in trepidation.

"We could try The Tavern. They've got live music tonight," Lili replied knowledgeably, silently thanking her lucky stars she at least knew where the pub was, as she walked past it every day on her way to work.

The others agreed, following as she pushed open the door, leading the way into the pub's smoky, dark interior. Long and narrow, with red walls and dark wooden furniture, the pub felt comfortingly womblike and was already packed with early evening drinkers, tanking up before moving on.

As they entered, the band were setting up. Random chords and notes being played on drums and electric guitars added to the atmosphere, making Lili's heart miss a beat with excitement.

Fighting their way to the bar, they got served reasonably quickly, it not occurring to either of the girls that they gained the barman's attention a lot quicker than the group of young men who'd been there before them. Clutching drinks, they managed to find a tiny table crammed in a corner opposite the band and squeezed around it, knees knocking companionably together.

Kevin surreptitiously watched the way Lili looked around, almost as if she'd never been inside a pub before; and thought again what a fascinating bundle of contradictions she was. She sipped her drink, looked up and caught him studying her. For a moment, their eyes locked, and he saw something, unease perhaps, flicker deep within hers, before she flashed him a friendly grin.

The band started, and they quickly realised why they'd managed to get a table this close to them. In the confined space, the volume was such that normal conversation was nigh on impossible but, Lili realised, it didn't matter.

Damien had been right; the band were good. A homespun version of Oasis or Blur, the archetypical Britpop group, which was so in right now, they sang their songs of modern urban love and angst, the crowd cheering them lustily after each one.

Eventually, after an hour, a group decision was reached to abandon the pub and move on. Clattering down the street, Amy chatted excitedly about how good the band had been, and how she was now deaf in one ear. Laughing, they joined the end of the queue to get into the club.

Inside was the same as last time, but completely different, or maybe she was different. The crowds of people were no longer intimidating, merely exciting. The throbbing, pounding music was familiar, and Lili felt her body start to move in time, feet itching to dance.

"Oh, I love this one!" she exclaimed, grabbed Amy's hand, and dragged her, laughing and unresisting, onto the dance floor.

How weird, she thought, her first time on a dance floor, but it felt like she'd come home. Moving together in well-synchronised harmony, unaware of what a vivid and contrasting picture they made, Amy so blonde and Lili so dark, they danced and sang together, strobe lights making their movements jerky and unreal.

At the song's end, they went in search of Kevin and found him leaning on the railing at the edge of the dance floor, fresh drinks lined up before him. With thirsty cries, they grasped them, their young, supple bodies swaying in time to the music. Positioning themselves on either side of Kevin, they sang and flirted with him, completely caught up in the giddy, exciting atmosphere.

The DJ announced the next song, *Wonderwall,* and a cheer arose. As the familiar music began, the whole club as one lifted their voices and sang. Strangers sang heartily to each other, the whole room swayed. Lili marvelled at the way such a simple thing as a phenomenally popular song, could unify a group of people into a coherent entity, thrilled at the collective experience.

The song's final haunting notes trailed out, another cheer erupted, then people jolted back into reality and the moment was over, leaving Lili, Amy, and Kevin blinking at each other in the dim lighting.

"That was wonderful," exclaimed Amy, turning to Kevin with a teasing smile. "How come you knew all the words? I thought you never listened to modern music?"

"I think I'd have to be living on Mars not to know that one," retorted Kevin dryly.

"I need the loo," stated Amy, draining her drink.

"I'll come with you if you like," replied Lili.

"No, that's okay, finish your drink, won't be long," she pushed confidently through the crowd.

Watching her go, Kevin turned to Lili with a smile. "She's having a great time. You're all she's talked about this week. It's been Lili this and Lili that, and how wonderful she thinks you are."

"Amy's great," replied Lili, shifting uncomfortably under Kevin's direct stare. "Oh," she cried as the next song started. "I love this one." Putting her glass down, Lili's body twitched in time to the music, as the unmistakable sound of the trance song she'd learnt to dance to under Conrad's expert tutelage, burst onto her eardrums.

"It's no good," she exclaimed. "I have to dance, sorry."

Leaving Kevin's side without a backward glance, she fought her way onto the dance floor and carved out a small space for herself near the DJ. As before, the music swelled; grew inside her heart, and she felt herself being sucked inside it. More intensely than at home, the music beat up from the floor, through her feet and into her head, strobe lighting and clouds of dry ice puffing up beside her, all adding to the exhilarating, out-of-body experience.

Vaguely aware of others dancing around her, their actions made jerky by the strobe, Lili felt her body being possessed by the soul of the music. Suddenly, Kevin was there, dancing with her, and Lili's eyes widened with pleasure as she realised what a good dancer he was. Unconsciously, she moved closer, body mirroring his until they seemed to move as two halves of a whole. The next moment, Amy was back, and the circle expanded to include her.

After that, Kevin was rarely allowed off the dance floor. Now the girls knew he could dance, he was dragged back on time and time again. Picking up her cue from Amy, Lili adopted a sisterly attitude towards Kevin, which both thrilled and dismayed him.

He wanted Lili to feel relaxed and comfortable around him but was also wise enough to know the further into the mates' zone she put him, the less likely she was to ever consider him as anything other than a friend.

Chapter Fifteen

"You don't have to buy me dinner as some kind of bribe."

Three days later, Lili realised she was in trouble – big trouble. The backlog of filing had reached mammoth proportions, threatening to spill out of the cupboard into which she had stuffed it. Her panic grew hourly, as she waited for somebody to look for a file that wasn't there.

Desperately trying to keep on top of her normal work, plus her share of Alex's jobs, Lili barely had time to reflect on the irony of an employment agency that didn't bother to take on a temp when someone was away.

Frantically stuffing a sandwich down her throat as she stood over the photocopier, her brain skittered around the problem, trying to see a solution – a way out of the mess. Briefly, she considered asking Beth for help, thought of the mounds of paperwork and files all haphazardly abandoned in the cupboard and shuddered. No, she'd left it too late to ask for help now.

If only she could have some quiet time to herself – space to calmly sort through it all – she'd be okay. Once it was up to date, she would make sure she kept on top of it and ask for help if it ever got too much again.

Her thoughts went back a step ... some quiet time to herself ... was it possible? Excitedly, she examined the plan from all angles. The office closed at four; Ms Evans was quite adamant about that. No one stayed late. No one worked overtime.

Lili once asked Beth why such a rule was applied, and Beth had smiled knowledgeably, Ms Evans liked keeping a firm hand on things, she explained. No one else but her had keys to the building, and, as she went home at four, that meant everyone else did as well. But why, pursued Lili, did she go home so early?

Beth's smile changed to one of female understanding and told Lili about Ms Evans finding love late in life; the husband who worked from home, the baby born last year, all valid reasons why Dorothy Evans firmly locked the doors at four and turned her thoughts homeward.

How could she manage to be left in the building? More importantly, how could she get out again? Being left in was not so difficult. In the confusion of everyone leaving, Lili was sure she could hide in the toilets until everyone was gone.

As for the getting out part, Lili shook her head. They were on the ground floor; she'd crawl out of a window if she needed to. Her excitement grew as she made her plans. It could work – it had to.

Over the past few weeks, her job had become important to her, and Lili was desperate enough to try anything, no matter how crazy, to make sure she kept it.

The first thing that struck her when she finally plucked up the courage to emerge from the toilets, was the quiet. Normally, the office was a constant hive of activity, phones ringing, printers clattering, people shouting to each other, but now ... the place was silent, eerily so. Lili shivered, aware of how much trouble she'd be in if caught. Quickly turning her mind away from such thoughts, she hurried to the cupboard and began pulling out files.

An hour later, her heart rate had slowed, and she was beginning to see results. What had been a random collection of paperwork was slowly gaining some semblance of order.

Carefully assembling the work into alphabetical piles, Lili saw there was more work here than she could get through in one evening; and realised with a sinking heart that she would probably have to do the same thing tomorrow night, maybe even the night after.

A sudden bang in reception had her scuttling under a desk in heart-stopping panic. It had sounded like the front door slamming, but it couldn't be, could it? No one came back to the office after they closed; no one, but Ms Evans, had the key.

Ms Evans.

Lili's eyes widened in panic, it had to be Ms Evans. Perhaps she'd forgotten something and come back, or maybe tonight was the one night she'd decided to work late. Whatever the reason, she'd see the files all over the floor, couldn't miss them, and then she'd find Lili, and then ... and then...

From her position under the desk, Lili watched in fear as a pair of blue jeans walked into the room. Frayed sneakers stopped inches away from her nose and turned, as their owner surveyed the room.

"What the fuck?"

Not Ms Evans, definitely not Ms Evans, Lili froze in self-preservation. A burglar? Her eyes squeezed shut in fear.

"How the bloody hell am I supposed to hoover with this crap all over the floor?"

The voice was female, annoyed, with a broad Essex accent. Of course, the cleaner. If she'd thought about it properly, she would have remembered the offices were cleaned every evening.

"You might as well come out," there was rough amusement in the voice. Lili's eyes snapped open to find an upside-down face peering at her.

"Come on," she repeated. "Out you come."

Feeling foolish and a little alarmed, Lili crawled out, sheepishly getting to her feet. "Hello," she muttered nervously, risking a quick smile as she and the cleaner surveyed each other curiously.

Lili saw a girl a couple of years older than her and taller by a few inches. Her long, jet black, straight hair was pulled into a ponytail – slanted eyes, and a slightly flattened nose all clues to Chinese blood in her heritage, yet for all that, she looked English too.

Lili thought she was one of the most exotically beautiful people she had ever seen.

"Well?" the girl's foot was tapping in annoyance, the look she was giving Lili far from friendly. "Who are you, and what the fuck are you doing here?"

"I'm Lili, I work here, I had to do some overtime. I'm sorry, I forgot you'd be in, I'll move my files out the way."

"Too damn right you will," snapped the girl, her eyes narrowed to suspicious slits. "Overtime?" she repeated. "No one does overtime in this office, no one." The eyes narrowed even more. "Does Ms Evans know you're here?"

"Of course," replied Lili airily.

"Right, I'll phone her at home and check, shall I?"

"All right," said Lili, displaying a confidence she was far from feeling.

The girl pulled a slip of paper from her pocket, picked up the nearest phone and began to dial. She dialled two numbers before Lili's nerve cracked and she leapt forward, slamming her hand down on the disconnect button.

"No, please don't ... all right, I'll tell you the truth." Slowly the girl lowered the handset and raised her eyebrows. "I'm the office junior, well I'm on a trial period, and I love working here but Alex, that's the receptionist, is away on honeymoon and I've been trying to do her work as well as my own and I'm managing, that is, I'm managing most of it, but the filing's got a little out of hand..."

The girl snorted as she surveyed the piles on the floor. Desperately, Lili swallowed and continued.

"I don't get the time to catch up during the day, so I thought if I had some quiet time in the evening, I'd get it all done. No one would ever know, and I'd keep my job."

"I see," The girl paused, looked at Lili with a friendlier gaze, then shook her head. "I'm sorry," she said, "but you can't stay here. If Ms Evans were to find out I'd be sacked, and I can't afford to lose my job, I need the money."

"I'm sorry."

Lili felt instant shame for putting her in such a position. After all, to Lili, it was just a job. She didn't need the money. Whilst she would be very sorry to lose it, she wouldn't be plunged into financial ruin, whereas this girl...

"I'm sorry," she said again. "I didn't realise, didn't think ... I'll pick all this stuff up and go." She turned towards the depressingly high piles of paperwork.

The girl's expression softened.

"Wait," she said. Lili turned, face hopeful. "How much trouble will you be in if you don't get this lot ..." she gestured towards the heaps, "sorted?"

"I'm not sure," Lili shrugged, not wanting to force the girl into an awkward position. "I won't be offered the job when my trial period ends, but that's okay, there are other jobs."

"Yeah, but ..." the other girl sighed. "Okay," she said. "You can stay while I'm here." She eyed the floor doubtfully. "You've got about an hour before I need to hoover. Reckon you can get it finished in that time?"

Ruefully, Lili shook her head. The girl sighed again, pressing fingers to her forehead in exasperation.

"How many nights?" she demanded. "How many nights until you're straight?"

"Three," replied Lili confidently.

"Three," repeated the cleaner. "Okay, three nights. If you get caught, you take all the blame."

"Absolutely," Lili agreed joyfully. "What's your name?" she added as the cleaner turned to go.

"Lindy," she replied. "Lindy Smith."

"Thank you, Lindy," said Lili with a smile. "I'm..."

"Lili," finished Lindy. "I know, you said earlier."

Working as quickly as she could, one eye on the clock, Lili managed to clear about a quarter of the piles, relieved a proportion of the paperwork was back in its correct place.

Five minutes before Lindy was due in, Lili managed to heap the remaining files back into the cupboard, not a random mess this time, but carefully constructed alphabetical piles, ready to be pulled out the next night.

The steady drone of the hoover, which had provided a backdrop to her work for the last twenty minutes, grew louder as Lindy pushed her way through the door into the main office, and acknowledged, with a nod and a grin, the now clear floor.

Hopping onto a chair, raising her feet off the floor, Lili watched as Lindy expertly pushed the nozzle between and under the desks until the floor was completely clear. Switching off the machine, Lindy coiled the flex around its handle and looked at Lili.

"You ready to go."

It wasn't so much a question as a statement. Lili nodded, and stood up, following Lindy down the corridor, where she stored the hoover in the cupboard and took down a shabby backpack off the coat rack.

"Right," she said, jingling keys in her hand. "I'll see you tomorrow then..."

"Lindy," Lili interrupted, a sudden thought exploding in her mind.

"Yeah?"

"Have you eaten yet?"

"No, I'll have something when I get home," Lindy looked enquiringly at her. "Why?"

"It's just, well, neither have I, and I was wondering if I could buy you a drink and some dinner, that is, if you'd like to, as a way of saying thank you."

"Okay," replied Lindy easily, then looked down at herself and smiled. "So long as it's nowhere too posh, I'm not exactly dressed for anywhere classy."

"Fine," agreed Lili hastily. "The pub around the corner looks nice, and it does food."

"Okay," agreed Lindy again then shook her head. "You don't have to do this you know, Lili. We've agreed to three nights. You don't have to buy me dinner as some sort of bribe."

"I'm not," denied Lili, her voice ringing with outrage. "I want to buy you dinner as a way of saying thank you and because, well, because it's nice to go out with friends."

Lindy's face went still. Lili remembered hearing somewhere the expression 'inscrutable Chinese', and for a moment knew exactly what it meant. Then Lindy seemed to relax, her lips curved upwards in a smile.

"Right," she agreed, pulling her backpack on. "It's nice going out with friends."

That evening set the pattern for the next two. By the time Saturday morning came around, and Lili was once again dressing for lunch with Richard, she felt nothing but satisfaction at what had been achieved in one short week.

Completely up to date with the filing, Lili was determined to never get into such a mess again, promising herself she would ask for help rather than let the paperwork pile up.

Chatting to Amy several times on the phone that week, Lili felt their connection was growing stronger all the time, and she had spent the previous evening at Amy and Kevin's eating takeaway Chinese and playing a painfully long game of Monopoly.

Conrad phoned, eager to let her know he had found the artwork for her reception rooms. With excitement, Lili agreed to travel to London the following Friday morning to stay for a long weekend. She also took great delight in filling Conrad in on every detail of her new friend, Lindy.

Each evening, once Lindy had completed her work and Lili had chipped away at a bit more filing, the girls had gone to eat at the local pub.

Seemingly reluctant to give too much of herself away, it wasn't until Thursday evening that the relaxed atmosphere, the two pints of cider she'd had, and Lili's openly friendly nature worked their magic on Lindy, and she opened up, and talked, really talked, telling Lili about her life, and letting her see her true personality.

Twenty years old, Lindy had lived in Romford most of her life. Daughter of a teenage, single mother, she'd had a hard beginning, her mother possessing neither the money nor the intelligence to give her daughter the nice things in life.

What about your father, Lili enquired, Lindy shrugged, he was oriental, only that much could be certain; her mother had been working the streets at the time; a young, desperate runaway.

Lindy limped through school, leaving as soon as she could to work in a local factory. It was there she met Wayne, the young, upwardly mobile factory manager. Cheerfully admitting to Lili that she hadn't loved him, sixteen-year-old Lindy had seen him as an escape route; a way out of the sticky clutches of the inner-city council estate, where she lived with her mother in a damp and dingy one-bedroom flat.

Determined not to end up like her mother, a brainless though amiable lush who went through men the way other women did tights, Lindy played a dangerous game of wait-and-tease with Wayne, until out of his head with barely suppressed lust, he would have promised anything in return for her spreading her legs.

Things finally came to a head when Wayne was offered a job managing a factory in Bury St Edmunds. Reluctant to move, he was urged into it by Lindy who saw it as the perfect ticket out. Not just for her, she added, for him too.

Wayne succumbed. Claiming Lindy was his fiancée, they moved to a small but cheerful flat near the factory in Bury. As he had fulfilled his side of the bargain, Lindy knew she had no option but to uphold her end of the deal.

One cold and frosty night in early January the deed was done, Lindy's virginity lost in a brief ten minutes of testosterone-fuelled activity. She was sixteen years old. As she blotted up her blood with a tissue, the snores of the sated Wayne echoing off the windows, Lindy had lain there wondering what on earth all the fuss was about.

The relationship had limped on for the rest of that year until one night – disillusioned, frustrated, and angry – Wayne hit her. Not hard, not really, Lindy hastened to add, seeing Lili's eyes widen in horror. It was more a smack of despair.

You see, she added, he wanted so much more than Lindy could give him. Whilst sex had made Wayne keener on her, it had the opposite effect on Lindy. Her indifference to him in bed, her scant tolerance of him out of it, all serving to drive the poor man to respond the only way he knew how.

It had been with a sense of relief that Lindy had taken her meagre belongings and moved out. She'd had almost a year to plan for it; had known of its inevitability from the start.

Her various cleaning jobs paid reasonably well, and Wayne had always been generous with handing over housekeeping money, so she never had to dip into her wages. Lindy had enough in her bank account to put down a month's deposit and move into a little place of her own.

It's not much, she explained, a studio flat, but it was hers. Maybe one day she'd be able to afford something better. In the meantime, she was young and strong, had jobs, a place of her own and money in the bank.

The one thing she didn't have was friends. Leaving the few she called mates far behind her in Romford, Lindy had never had the time or inclination to seek out new ones. This lack of human contact bothered her, but she never realised how much until Lili asked her to go to dinner as friends.

Studying the younger girl, Lindy wondered how someone so gorgeous could have such an untouched air about her. Seemingly unaware of the appreciative male gazes that came her way in the pub, Lili had sat, all eyes and ears, listening to Lindy's story, concentrating in a way Lindy found deeply flattering.

She was a virgin, of that Lindy was certain, observing the twin spots of colour which appeared on her cheekbones when Lindy casually spoke of her lost innocence, traded in for a roof over her head and a new way of life. Yet, Lindy sensed no condemnation or judgement in Lili's gaze and liked her even more for it.

Despite there being less than two years between them, Lindy felt centuries older than Lili, as if she had experienced and lived through things the younger girl could only dimly guess at, making her feel oddly protective towards her.

During their meal on Thursday evening, they traded addresses and phone numbers, agreeing to stay in touch; to be friends. Lili spoke to Lindy of her other two friends, Amy, and Kevin, confident she would like them.

Lindy didn't share her certainty. Painfully aware of her background and accent, she listened enviously to Lili's soft, well-rounded voice, which spoke of class and position; of an upbringing completely alien to hers.

Observing Lili's pretty manners, good quality clothes, obviously expensive haircut, and neat, nicely painted nails as they curved around her wine glass, Lindy looked down at her scruffy work clothes, bitten nails, and pint glass.

Desperate for a fag, but not wanting to in front of Lili who was clearly a non-smoker, Lindy wished to be like her; so poised and confident. Surely, any friends of Lili's would look down their noses at such a social non-entity.

When they finally parted that evening and went their separate ways, it was with very different emotions. Lili practically skipped home – pleased it was Thursday and the start of another exciting weekend – and thrilled at the gaining of another friend.

Lindy let herself into the flat, her place. So perfect before, now small, and shabby. Reaching for her fags, she hesitated, one held to her mouth, then abruptly crumpled them in anger and unceremoniously tossed them in the bin.

Hell, she would make Lili's snooty friends like her, and if it meant pretending to be something she wasn't, so what. Lindy was a born survivor and a natural actress. The truth was, now the bright light of Lili was in her life, Lindy was determined to do whatever it took to keep it there.

For once, Richard was a couple of minutes late getting to the restaurant. As he made his way to their normal table, he was surprised to see a strange young woman sitting there. Glancing around to see if Phyllis had been seated elsewhere, he hesitated, unsure.

The woman lifted her head and smiled.

"Hello, Richard."

"I beg your pardon, do I ... oh, good heavens, Phyllis, is that you?"

The young woman nodded shyly. Richard sat heavily in the chair opposite, unable to take his eyes off the beautiful stranger smiling in obvious delight.

Looking closer, he could still see her behind the glamorous and sophisticated façade and thought for the first time how much she resembled her grandmother, as she had been when they first met, all those years ago.

"My word, what happened to you? You look amazing?"

"I know," replied Lili, and he realised the changes weren't merely superficial surface ones. She seemed stronger, more confident. There was poise and a maturity to her that had been lacking before.

"Oh Richard," she exclaimed, reaching across, and taking his hand. "I've had the most wonderful month and have so much to tell you."

"Can I get you something to drink, Sir?" Richard glanced up at the waiter, then across at her flushed and excited face.

"Yes," he reached the decision easily. "Champagne," he ordered, smiling at her gasp of delighted agreement. "We're celebrating."

"Certainly, Sir," responded the waiter, with a smile.

"Now then," Richard leant forward in anticipation. "Tell me everything, and I mean everything."

Two hours later, pausing only to order and eat their meals, Lili pushed her coffee cup away, as she finished telling Richard of her new friend, Lindy, and the very pleasant evening she had spent with Amy and Kevin the night before.

"Well," exclaimed Richard, and shook his head in wonder. "Well," he said again, unsure how to respond, or what to say. "Is that what I should call you now, Lili?"

"I would prefer it," Lili responded with a blush. "That is if you don't mind."

"Mind? Of course, I don't mind. After all, it's up to you what you wish to be called. And do you know I think it suits you, the new you that is. The way you look now, your old name wouldn't have done at all. So, you're off to London to stay with this Conrad fellow?"

"Yes, yes, I am," agreed Lili, smiling at the expression on his face. "Don't worry about me, Richard, I'll be quite all right, Conrad and Matthew will look after me."

Secretly wondering if that was not precisely what he was worried about, Richard wisely stayed silent and decided to change the subject.

"I have some news of my own Phyl... umm, Lili."

"Oh? What's that?"

"Well, I'm not getting any younger and I've decided to retire." At Lili's alarmed face he smiled, patting her hand. "Don't worry, I feel personally attached to your case so I'm going to suggest your financial affairs be taken care of by a young man I know. He's only a junior within the firm he works for, but he's got a good head on his shoulders, and I'm confident will take care of you more than adequately."

"Oh, I see," Lili bit her lip anxiously. "It's just, I've come to depend on you, Richard, I'm not sure I want to deal with anyone else. Who is this man anyway? What's his name?"

"Martin Madison."

"Madison? Oh, any relation?"

"Yes, he's my great-nephew."

"And he's a solicitor too?"

Lili relaxed slightly, Richard's great-nephew. Well then, surely, she'd be able to trust him.

"No, he's a financial advisor, but I feel that's what you need, Lili. Someone with modern ideas and the know-how to build up your portfolio so your money works for you."

"Okay," Lili slowly nodded her head. "If you feel that's what I should do, maybe you could get him to call me next week."

"Of course," Richard paused, sipping at his coffee.

"Richard?"

"Yes?"

"Does this mean we'll no longer meet for lunch?"

"Of course not, my dear, not unless you no longer wish to. I look forward to these lunches and consider them more than just business. I feel, and hope you do too, that you've become much more than a client. We're friends, and as such can carry on meeting for lunch whenever we want to."

"Yes," replied Lili firmly. "We're friends. To friendship," she said and raised her coffee cup to his in a smiling toast as the waiter moved in to clear their table.

Chapter Sixteen

"It makes me feel cold, and alone, and a little scared."

As the train began to move Lili's heart clutched with nervous excitement, and she desperately tried to maintain a blasé and sophisticated expression.

It was Friday morning, and Lili had boarded a train to take her to London, Kings Cross; further than she had ever been in her life. She had to change at Cambridge. Prickles of anxiety were already dancing along her spine at the possibility of getting it wrong; of boarding the wrong train.

Calm down, she ordered herself, picking up her magazine. It had been a stimulating and packed week, and Lili leant her head back against the seat as she thought about all that had happened.

They'd gone clubbing again Saturday, Lili was fearful the evening couldn't possibly match up to the previous week, but it had been fun. Afterwards, they'd hit the local kebab shop with other hyped-up clubbers, all sharing the feeling that even though it was two in the morning, it was far too early to go to bed.

Walking home through the still, dark streets, eating chips smothered with mayonnaise, the girls squealing with disgust at the kebab Kevin had bought, Lili wondered if life could get any better.

Once again, Amy and Kevin stayed the night, the three of them not surfacing until the sun was vertical. They wandered around the house in various stages of undress and hangover, a collective decision made to not go very far, or do too much.

They cooked breakfast, taking blankets out into the overgrown garden to laze around on, drinking mugs of strong coffee and freshly squeezed orange juice, and eating massive bacon and egg baps, yolk oozing between their fingers like warm sunshine.

They dozed and lazed, coming to terms with hangovers, Kevin muttering ideas and suggestions for Lili's garden until finally she pulled herself up from her prone position on the blanket and flicked juice at his bare chest.

"Stop telling me about it," she laughed. "I'll never be able to remember all those instructions, let alone carry them out. Why don't you do it?"

Kevin stopped laughing and shaded his eyes from the sun. Seriously, he stared into her dancing eyes, noticing for the first time the green flecks that sparkled in their deep brown depths.

"What do you mean?" he asked, heart thudding with hope.

"I mean," repeated Lili. "I want to employ you to do my garden."

"But ..." he stuttered. "I never finished college. I'm not qualified."

"So?" Lili demanded. "You don't need a piece of paper to be able to garden, for heaven's sake. I'd pay you and everything. I wouldn't expect you to do it for nothing. You must charge me a fair price, and of course, I'd pay for all the materials. Look upon it as your first commission," she continued. "After all, you've got to start somewhere if you want to be a landscape designer."

A silence fell over the garden.

Twisting round to look at him, Lili saw the truth of things in his eyes.

"You've given up, haven't you?" she said slowly. "Your dream of becoming a landscape designer. You've let it go."

"What else could I do?" demanded Kevin, slightly shamefaced. "I had to get a job to support us."

"Yes, *then* you did, but are you telling me you're happy to be stuck in an office for the rest of your life? I've seen how your eyes light up when you talk about plants and gardens; the way you look when you're making plans for my garden. It's as natural to you as breathing and as necessary. You can't give it up, Kevin, you simply can't."

"Well, what do you suggest?" Kevin asked, half hopeful, half annoyed.

"Make a start with my garden. Create the perfect garden for me. Then, on the back of that, try to get other commissions. I don't mind if you use me as a reference, and prospective clients can come and look at the amazing garden you've created for me."

"How can you be so confident it's going to be amazing?"

"Because I know you," replied Lili, touching his face in a casually friendly manner that had his heart rate accelerating, and his eyes closing briefly with a longing so fierce, it scared him. "I know you won't rest until it's perfect."

Thinking of that Sunday afternoon as the train picked up speed, Lili's lips curved in a small, secret smile of satisfaction, as she remembered how Kevin's enthusiasm had fired.

Sending her scuttling into the house for paper, pencil, tape measure and string, he had both girls writing down measurements, holding the tape, as he strode, paced, and measured.

Reduced to helpless fits of laughter at the intense look on his face, both Amy and Lili refused to take him seriously, clowning around, and driving him to annoyance, then to reluctant humour.

Realising the futility of trying to achieve anything, Kevin put away his makeshift tools, making plans to come back with proper equipment the following weekend whilst Lili was away.

Lili had also seen Lindy twice the following week, inviting her to dinner Monday, then going bowling for the first time in her life on Thursday evening, excited at the prospect of introducing Lindy to Kevin and Amy.

A frown pulled at Lili's face as she thought about the two occasions. The dinner on Monday had gone reasonably well. Lindy, stiff and awkward to begin with, had been overawed by the house, and the simple yet elegant pasta meal Lili had prepared, although she relaxed as the evening wore on, and the wine flowed.

Bowling on Thursday though, Lili's frown deepened, hadn't gone as she planned, or hoped. Apart from the fact she'd been completely useless, her ball ending in the gutter nine times out of ten, the atmosphere had been strained; not relaxed and friendly in the way Lili had come to expect.

No, it hadn't been good at all.

Lili bit her lip as she thought about it, forced to admit it had been Lindy who'd caused the friction. Unable to relax with the others, and admit her preconceived notions were wrong, Lindy had become increasingly curt and abrupt, Amy, in particular, bearing the brunt of Lindy's insecurities.

Jealous of the easy friendship between the blonde girl and Lili, listening to the three of them talking together, their accents sounding to Lindy so upper class and posh, Lindy tried to overcompensate but ended up being brash and obnoxious.

Several times Lili's heart sank as Lindy trampled on feelings, making inappropriate and crass comments. Yes, she reflected, the evening had been a strain. It had been a relief when they said goodbye and went their separate ways.

So now here she was, on a train, early on a sunny Friday morning, rattling her way to London, and Conrad. Looking out the window with interest, Lili wondered what the weekend ahead held in store. Her curiosity rising at the thought of "her" artwork Conrad claimed to have found.

Deeply mysterious about it, all he had said was it was "very Lili" and would be drawn no more.

Cambridge came and went. To her relief, finding the right platform was a simple matter of asking a porter, and following his instructions. Once settled on the train Lili relaxed, relieved there were no more stops or changes until Kings Cross, where Conrad and Matthew would be waiting for her.

"Lili!" Stepping off the train at Kings Cross, Lili experienced a heart-stopping moment of panic as she looked around for Conrad. His call had her face breaking out into a dazzling smile of relief, as she dropped her bag and threw herself into his arms.

"Look at you!" exclaimed Conrad, returning her hug with gusto. "Just look at you, sweetie. You look fabulous, simply fabulous." Turning he gestured to a tall, dark man watching the proceedings with a gentle smile on his face.

"This is Matthew," explained Conrad, and Lili's hand was grasped in a firm handshake of greeting, as she breathlessly stuttered out a hello.

Quite what Lili had been expecting, she wasn't sure; maybe subconsciously had formed a picture in her mind of another Conrad, outrageous and over-confident.

Certainly, the tall, slim, blue-suited man with a kindly face, and dark amused eyes, was something of a surprise, and Lili instinctively warmed towards him. He looked, she decided, like a benevolent banker, if such a thing were possible.

"It's very nice to finally meet you, Lili," he said, voice rich with warmth and humour. "Conrad has told me much about you."

"It's nice to meet you too," Lili replied.

Matthew smiled then glanced at his watch. "I have to go. I have a meeting at eleven. Welcome to London, Lili. I'll see you later this evening."

"Thank you." Lili saw Matthew touch Conrad's arm; a look, a moment, passed between them. Lili sighed at the love and commitment she sensed. Watching Matthew push his way through the crowd, tall and sober, Conrad turned to Lili with a big smile.

"Isn't he a honey?"

"He certainly seems very nice," agreed Lili, smiling at Conrad's choice of words.

"Right then," Conrad picked up Lili's bag, dancing his way towards the taxi rank. "Let's go."

"Go?" enquired Lili, adopting her usual jog to keep up with Conrad. "Go where?"

"First stop, home, to dump this lot. You can freshen up, then lunch. We've got an appointment to view your artwork at two. After that, I thought a little shopping, then home for a quiet family dinner."

"Sounds great," panted Lili. "Conrad, wait ..." she gasped, trying to keep up in heels.

He laughed, threw her bag in the back of a taxi, then threw her in after it.

Following a quick tour of Conrad and Matthew's stylishly beautiful apartment, Conrad whisked Lili off to a trendily bohemian café in Covent Garden, where they enjoyed a light lunch and a bottle of wine.

Suitably mellowed, Lili blithely climbed into yet another taxi with Conrad and sat back as the taxi trundled away from the city centre, travelling miles along thronging, crowded streets, Lili gaping in fascination at the vast diversity of colour, dress and ethnic origins of the people passing by.

Finally, they arrived at a huge, derelict warehouse. Much to Lili's surprise, this was where Conrad instructed the driver to stop. Crunching over broken glass and other assorted, less salubrious rubbish, Lili's misgivings grew, and she cast a worried look at Conrad's back as he nimbly picked his way through the debris.

Turning, he caught sight of her face, laughing at the doubtful expression. "Relax, sweetie," he ordered brightly. "Trust me."

"I do," Lili muttered, gingerly negotiating around a pile of dank, blackened rags flapping in the breeze like beached guillemots in an oil slick. Laughing, Conrad led her into the building and up never-ending concrete stairs. Finally, they reached the top, and Conrad pounded on a pair of metal doors – so rusty and begrimed – Lili wondered at the merest possibility of them ever opening.

Long moments passed. Conrad seemed almost at the point of pounding again, when, with a teeth-clenching scrape and a wail, the doors were wrenched back. There stood one of the most beautiful men Lili had ever seen.

He was tall; well over six feet, Lili tipped her head back to gaze in wonder at his carved, handsome face; gorgeous even with the annoyed scowl it was currently sporting; his piercing blue eyes and long, dark hair scraped back in a ponytail. Wearing only ragged denim cut-offs and a paint-splattered t-shirt, he was wiping his hands on a grimy cloth from which the richly pungent smell of turps was issuing.

"Conrad?" The man's face lit up in a stunning smile. Lili's heart jumped; a purely female, knee-jerk reaction to his pin-up, good looks. "What are you doing here?"

"We had an appointment," explained Conrad patiently.

"Thought that was Friday?" He-man frowned.

"Greg," Conrad sighed in exasperation. "This is Friday."

"Oh," Greg stopped, considered, then shrugged.

"Lili…"

"Huh?" Lili couldn't take her eyes off the artist. He was so … so … male!

"Lili," Conrad smirked knowingly at the dazed look on her face, and Lili forcibly snapped her attention back to him, an embarrassed flush warming her cheeks. "Greg, this is Lili, the young lady I was telling you about, who's looking to buy some artwork for her beautiful home."

"Hi, Lili." Blue eyes turned towards her; his mouth curved in a lazy, devastating smile. "I would offer to shake hands but ..." he turned paint-splattered palms over ruefully. "It's nice to meet you."

"Nice to meet you too," stammered Lili, as they entered.

Light and space; the almost overwhelming impressions crowded into Lili's brain. The area was massive – half of one whole floor of the warehouse was rented by Greg as a combined studio and living space. Lili stumbled in behind the men, eyes shooting off in different directions, desperately trying to assimilate and make sense of the information being fed to her senses.

Paintings were everywhere – five and six deep leaning crazily against walls, smaller ones stacked randomly in storage boxes – everywhere the smell of paint and turps pervaded, making Lili's head spin.

Light flooded through the vast windows, but Lili shivered. The room was chilly, despite the warm July sunshine outside. She wondered if there was any heating in the room, and how cold it would get in the depths of winter.

A makeshift screen partially closed off one corner of the room. Behind it, Lili could make out an unmade bed, duvet heaped as if he had literally crawled out of it, and immediately started working. Looking at the faint bloom of stubble on his face, the dark hair hastily pulled back, Lili assumed that was what Greg had done.

The men were still talking. Hastily, Lili tried to pull her attention back to what they were saying but was irresistibly drawn to the beauty displayed so casually, all around. To Lili's relief, Greg's style of painting was both accessible, and understandable. She had been concerned at Conrad's description of him as a modern artist and steeled herself to be confronted with almost anything, deeply relieved to find she liked what she could see.

Drawn to a fabulous seascape, Lili's eyes almost feasted on the magnificent, storm-tossed beauty of the steel grey waves which crashed and clawed at the towering cliffs, a full moon barely visible through wind-whipped clouds.

"Do you like it?" Lili jumped, so engrossed in the picture she'd not heard Greg approach, turning dazed eyes up to meet his amused, though curious, ones.

"No," she replied slowly. "I don't ..." Seeing the wounded surprise on his face, she hurried to try and explain herself. "Like is too tame a word for it. How can you say you like something like this ...?" She gestured towards the picture, shivered, rubbing at arms gone to gooseflesh. "No," she continued. "I don't 'like' it, but I can feel it. It makes me feel cold and alone, and a little scared."

Greg's expression softened, and he nodded.

"Good," he said. "That's what it's supposed to do. Now ..." he continued, "those are the paintings Conrad thought you might like, over there, each side of the window." He gestured to the far wall.

Slowly, Lili walked towards the pair of canvases. As her eyes focused on the paintings, she gasped, turning startled eyes to Conrad.

They weren't as large as some of the others, both approximately five feet square, and Lili could see they would fit precisely above the fireplaces in her reception rooms. She blinked at the colour pouring from them; they were perfect, just perfect. She decided no matter how much they cost, she had to have them.

The paintings were of lilies; beautiful, pristine, arum lilies. One showed a tall, elegant, glass vase of lilies. It stood in a room that faded into the background, the flowers dominating the picture. Beyond the vase, doors opened onto a garden. It was possible to see cool shadiness spilling through double doors onto the floor behind the round table, on which the vase of lilies stood. The greens and creams of the garden reflected in the long, supple stems, and creamy throats of the lilies.

The other painting was of the same vase of lilies but painted as if standing in the garden, looking through the doors at the lilies within the dark interior. All around the periphery of the painting, foliage and creamy flowers tumbled over weathered, stone walls, and ancient red brick paving, yet the eye was irresistibly drawn through the doors to the lilies; a bright, burning blaze of light in an otherwise dim room.

Lili stared, understanding what Conrad meant when he'd spoken of two paintings that could be viewed separately, but would also work together. Conrad cleared his throat. Lili turned, still lost in the magic of the paintings, eyes wide and unfocused. She nodded. Conrad's face cleared. Turning to Greg, he clapped a hand on his shoulder.

"I think we can consider them sold," he exclaimed, and Greg smiled in agreement. "Shall we go and negotiate the price?"

"There's no room for manoeuvre on the price," snapped Greg.

"Greg, Greg," tutted Conrad. "There's always room to manoeuvre on the price." Chuckling, he led Greg to where a battered desk and two chairs stood. Uncaring and unconcerned, Lili drifted back to her paintings, daydreaming about the day her house would be finished, and they would take pride of place in her lounge.

Business concluded to the satisfaction of all, Greg opened a bottle of wine to celebrate and found another chair for Lili. Perched gingerly on a rickety wooden stool with one leg shorter than the others, and an alarming habit of listing to the left, Lili clutched her grimy mug of gut-rot Spanish red, listening as they talked.

"You coming to Daisy's 21st tomorrow?" Greg enquired.

Conrad nodded, taking a delicate sip of wine, and shuddering at the taste. "Of course, wouldn't miss it for the world, I spoke to Miss Daisy only yesterday to reconfirm it was okay to bring Lili."

"Who's Daisy?" Lili enquired nervously; a trifle concerned at the thought of crashing some strange girl's 21st birthday.

"Greg's baby sister," explained Conrad. "The sweetest girl that ever lived. You're going to love her. Who else is going?" he enquired, risking another sip of wine.

"Miriam and Robert, my elder sister and her husband," he explained to Lili with a smile, topping up her mug. "Sid and the usual crowd," he continued. "Oh, and Jake and his wife are over from the States on honeymoon."

"Ah yes, the delightful Vivienne?" There was an edge to Conrad's voice Lili had never heard before.

"The one and only," Greg confirmed, lips tightening perceptibly.

"So," Conrad drawled slowly. "He married her then?"

"Oh yes, he married her."

Conrad and Greg exchanged a look, which Lili couldn't even begin to understand, although she was aware of the tension, sharp and tangible, which crackled between the two men.

"Who is Jake?" she finally asked, and the tension dissolved.

"Jake's my cousin from America," explained Greg. "Our grandfathers were brothers and left Poland to make their fortunes in America, but only Jake's made it that far. Mine fell in love with a London girl and settled here, but the families stayed in close touch, Jake's more like a brother than a cousin. He got married last week. He and his wife are in Europe on their honeymoon. Well, let's say, they're in the cities which offer good shopping."

Uncomfortable with the disapproval in his voice, Lili changed the subject. "Where's the party being held?" she asked, finding that the wine seemed to improve the further down the mug she got.

"At my parent's house," Greg replied, throwing back his wine as if it were water. "What are you going as?" he enquired. Lili turned bewildered eyes onto Conrad.

"Going as? I don't know, I mean, I didn't ... is it fancy-dress or something?"

"Or something," agreed Greg with a wry grin, pouring the last of the wine into his mug. "My darling sister got the crackbrained notion it would be great fun to have a themed fancy-dress party."

"Themed?" stuttered Lili, now seriously worried.

"Yes, themed. Iconic figures if you please. Completely daft, but it is her 21st so the rest of us had to play along."

"Conrad?"

"Don't panic, sweetie," Conrad waved his hands in a conciliatory gesture. "You have a costume. It's all sorted."

"But ... but, what am I going as?"

"You'll see," twinkled Conrad. "Trust me," he added as Lili's mouth opened to comment further. "You'll look amazing." He drained his wine, then jumped to his feet. "Come on, sweetie," he exclaimed. "Let's go shopping. Greg, we'll see you tomorrow. Wrap those pictures carefully, and I'll arrange payment and collection."

"Okay," Greg got lazily to his feet, shooting Lili a conspiratorial grin which set her heart rate speeding, and her blood pressure spiking. "I'll see you at the party, Lili, whatever you end up going as."

"Thank you for the pictures. Goodbye," Lili barely had time to utter the words before Conrad was bustling her out the door, down the tedious stairs to the end of the road, where they managed to catch a taxi to Oxford Street.

By the time they got home, and Lili could remove her shoes, her poor brain was throbbing as much as her mangled toes. Going shopping in a small provincial town, she realised, was nothing compared to shopping on Oxford Street.

The noise, the crowds, the push, and shove of people; the roar of sirens, motorbikes, and road works. Feeling naïve and a little lost, Lili had clung to Conrad, following him like a lamb to the slaughter. Refusing to be drawn any further about her outfit for the party, he had acceded to her desire to buy Daisy a birthday present.

Browsing, Lili's eye was drawn to a charming necklace comprised of yellow and white enamel daisies, on a pretty, silver chain. Tentatively asking Conrad's opinion was reassured by his enthusiastic agreement that Daisy would love it. Watching whilst it was gift-wrapped, Lili wondered about her mysterious costume.

"Here you go, sweetie," Conrad handed Lili a glass of water which she thankfully gulped at. The long, hot day, the wine and the heat and dust of London had all conspired to leave Lili battling dehydration and the first stirrings of a headache.

Pursing his lips in sympathy, Conrad looked at Lili sprawled in exhaustion on the sofa, face strained and fatigued. Mentally thanking Matthew for insisting Friday be a quiet 'at home' evening, Conrad hurried to fetch tea and biscuits.

An hour later, Lili revived enough to bring up the subject of her costume again. "But you must tell me what I'm going as, Conrad. Surely, I need to try it on. What about if it doesn't fit?" she pleaded.

"All right," Conrad threw up his hands in surrender. "Stay here," he ordered. "I'll lay the costume on your bed." Lili squeaked with anticipation, and Conrad hurried from the room. A moment later, she heard all manner of mysterious rustlings and banging, then Conrad appeared in the doorway, looking inordinately pleased with himself, grinning all over his cherub-like face.

"You can go and look now," he announced. Lili jumped up and shot past him into her bedroom.

Lying in the middle of the bed were a few scraps of clothing, and what looked like a large gun. Edging closer, Lili saw it *was* a gun in a leather holster, with straps intended to tie around her waist and thigh. Puzzled, she poked at the rest of the costume – sand coloured, skimpy shorts, a pale blue vest top, stout-looking boots, a buff backpack, a pair of round sunglasses, and a padded bra! What on earth?

"Conrad?" Frowning, she picked up the gun and the bra, holding them up questioningly towards him. "Who am I going as?" she asked, and he smiled at her puzzled face.

"You, my dear," he said, "are going as Lara Croft."

"Who?"

"Oh no," Conrad's face took on a pained expression. "Please don't tell me you've never heard of Lara Croft?" At Lili's head shake, he sighed. "Come with me," he said, practically dragging her into the lounge. "Prepare to learn," he stated.

When Matthew returned home from work an hour later, it was to find Lili staring at the screen in addicted, horrified fascination, as Lara hurtled off a cliff to land in a mangled, twisted heap at the bottom. Raising his eyebrows at her howl of disbelief, he took off his jacket, settled down beside her on the sofa, and hit replay on the console.

"How many times have you killed her?" he asked casually.

"Five," mumbled Lili through gritted teeth. "I've drowned her, had her pecked to death by birds, savaged by dogs, impaled on a spike, and now I've broken every bone in her body." Turning she flashed him a sudden smile. "It's brilliant fun."

"Ah yes," Matthew agreed mildly. "You have to have a seriously warped sense of humour not to enjoy killing Lara. Had a good day?"

"Hmm," responded Lili, eyes flickering on the screen as Lara once again scaled the castle walls. "I bought two pictures," she continued.

"The lilies?"

"Yes."

"Good, Conrad was convinced they were right for you."

"They are." A companionable silence settled. Lili reflected how odd it was she'd never met Matthew before today, but already felt so comfortable with him.

Conrad popped out of the kitchen. "Oh good," he exclaimed, handing them both glasses of ice-cold, white wine. "I thought I heard you come in. Dinner in ten." And he popped back out again.

"Ten minutes hey," said Matthew, taking a sip of wine and smiling at Lili. "Shall we have another go at killing Lara then?"

Chapter Seventeen

"I believe the little lady asked you to let her go."

London, Lili decided the next day, was a wonderful but terrifying place. After a quiet evening playing Tomb Raider and chatting with Conrad and Matthew, she went to bed in the beautiful guest room, and slept deeply and peacefully, only waking when Conrad banged on her door the next morning.

Rested and refreshed, Lili felt ready for anything, and Conrad decided they would play tourist – jumping on and off the tube, paying whirlwind visits to Trafalgar Square, the Tower, Westminster Abbey, and Big Ben.

Following a late lunch, they returned to the flat at three, and Conrad insisted Lili take a nap, claiming as the party would be an all-night one, it would be a good idea for her to get some rest.

As reluctant as a toddler, Lili baulked at the idea, but much to her surprise had fallen instantly into a deep, energising sleep, waking some three hours later in time to get ready for the party.

After her shower, Conrad instructed her not to blow dry her hair as normal. Instead, he combed it through and scraped it back in a tight, French plait dead-straight down her spine. Wriggling into her costume, Lili had grave misgivings about how she would look in such an un-sexy, mannish costume.

Leaving her room in search of a full-length mirror and assistance in tying on her gun, she ran into Conrad, and her jaw dropped.

"Conrad! What ... I mean, who on earth are you supposed to be?"

Conrad preened, turning to show off his beautiful costume. A wig of glossy brown curls cascaded onto black velvet, frock-coated shoulders. Glimpses of white lace teased at throat and wrists; an elegant waistcoat of black silk was adorned with the gold chain of a beautiful fob watch. Tight cream breeches were tucked into shiny black boots, which matched his shiny black top hat.

"Beau Brummell," he replied, sighing at her blank look. "Really, Lili, you must brush up on your history. He was a famous leader of London society in the late seventeen hundreds. He was second only to the Prince of Wales as a trendsetter."

"Oh," replied Lili, her head spinning. "Well, whoever he was, you look fantastic." Grinning cheekily, she added, "And I love the boots." Conrad pursed his lips and gave her a look.

"Can you help me with my gun?" Wisely changing the subject, she held out the gun, and Conrad quickly tied the straps around her waist and thigh.

"You look great, sweetie," he stated. "But we need to get your make-up done. In here," he ordered bossily, hustling her back into her bedroom. He pushed her down onto the dressing table stool and picked his way fussily through her cosmetics.

Enjoying the feeling of being made up, Lili sat patiently as Conrad expertly applied a layer of foundation, brushed colour along her cheekbones, then seemed to spend a lot of time on her eye make-up. After applying, blotting, and re-applying a thick coat of deep plum lipstick, he picked out a gold eye pencil, and to Lili's surprise, applied a spot of gold colour to the centre of her lower lip.

"There you go," he exclaimed. "You look stunning."

Lili tried to look around him in the mirror. Grabbing her hands, Conrad pulled her up and out the door. Leading her down the hallway, he stopped in front of the full-length mirror and positioned her so she could look at her whole costume for the first time.

Her eyes widened in shock.

Un-sexy?

Mannish?

Oh no, her costume was far from being any of those things. The skimpy shorts made her legs look like they went on forever, and Lili silently thanked her lucky stars that all the sunbathing in the garden had left her with a deep, and healthy-looking tan. The padded bra created ripe curves, all showcased nicely under the barely-there vest top, the straps of the backpack emphasising her newly acquired breasts even more.

The gun tapped against her thigh as she posed in front of the mirror, and Lili smiled at her glamorously dangerous image, then leaned closer to examine her face. The stark hairstyle pushed her angular cheekbones even further into prominence, highlighted by Conrad's clever use of blusher.

Her eyes, outlined with black pencil, glittered with female allure and power, and as for her lips! The deep shiny plum colour made her lips twice as plump and luscious; the spot of gold colour gave her a pout, which even Lili could see was undeniably sexy.

"Well?" Lili smiled at the impatience in Conrad's voice, her mirror image pouting.

"I love it," she replied, and he grinned in relief.

"What's Matthew going as?" she asked, whipping her gun out, watching her kick-ass sexy reflection go through its moves.

"Richard the Lionheart," a voice said behind them.

Lili turned to see Matthew leaning against the wall watching her antics with an amused expression.

"Wow, you look great," exclaimed Lili, taking in his medieval apparel, complete with a white surcoat emblazoned with the crusaders cross, crown, and low-slung sword belt sporting a very realistic looking sword.

"Ready to go?" he enquired.

Lili re-holstered her gun and nodded enthusiastically. "You bet."

To Lili's surprise, instead of taking a taxi, Matthew led the way down to an underground car park where they all piled into a stylishly expensive Ford Mondeo.

"Matthew doesn't tend to drink at parties," explained Conrad. "And it beats trying to get us lot into a taxi. What with guns and swords, I'm not sure any self-respecting taxi driver would take us."

"Why don't you drink at parties, Matthew?" enquired Lili curiously.

"I think it's because I like to stay in control of myself," he replied. "Besides, if I got as drunk as her ladyship here, who do you think would look after him?"

Lili laughed at Conrad's outraged splutter, settled back in her comfortable seat, and watched with interest as the streets sped past.

Half an hour later, Matthew turned into a quiet, leafy avenue, where large, grand-looking, detached houses lined the roadside, all set back behind imposing hedges and walls. Lili could tell this was where people possessing both class, and money lived.

Slowing the car, Matthew indicated right and pulled into the sweeping driveway of the biggest house on the avenue. Sprawling, made of mellow red brick, it wouldn't have looked out of place in the heart of the Cotswold countryside, lazing under the brilliant golden rays of early evening sunshine.

Entering through the open door, Lili heard party sounds from deep within the house, the muffled thump of music, laughter, and the clinking of glasses.

Glancing around as they passed through a grand hallway big enough to fit the entire ground floor of her house into, she was aware of beautiful antique furniture, ornate mirrors, and imposing artwork, which made her think of Greg, wondering if he was there yet and what he was dressed as. Her sturdy boots clunk clunked on the black and white floor tiles, and severe nerves rattled up her spine, making her gasp for air.

Reaching the end of the hallway, Conrad pushed open a large pair of double doors, and the noise reached out, embracing, and pulling them into the party. The room was large, with a row of open glass doors down the left side of the room, presumably opening onto a garden.

There was a small, raised stage at the far end of the room, where a professional-looking band were playing mellow, pre-dancing music.

There were clusters of tables and chairs, twinkling lights, streamers, balloons, and banks of flowers.

The room was already crowded with people dressed in a bewildering array of costumes, some so obvious, such as Elvis and Spiderman, that even Lili recognised them, but mostly she couldn't even begin to guess whom they were meant to be.

"Conrad!"

Looking around, Lili saw a girl detach herself from a group of people and rush over to them as fast as her full, billowing skirts would allow. Daisy, Lili presumed, and watched curiously as the birthday girl arrived, slightly breathless, in front of them.

She saw a girl looking only about sixteen, even though Lili knew her to be 21. Her hair was dark like Greg's, dressed high on her head in a confection of curls that bounced and tumbled over bare shoulders. Only a scant inch or so taller than Lili, her well-rounded body was squeezed into an ornate and bejewelled gown of rustling blue silk. It was trimmed with frothy lace which flounced at the hems of elbow-length sleeves and framed an ample, well-raised bosom, that heaved following her minor exertion.

"Conrad," Daisy breathed again, and Conrad stepped forward, gathering her into a tight hug which lifted her off her tiny, jewelled feet, and made her squeal for mercy.

"Happy Birthday, darling Daisy," he exclaimed. Setting her back down he held her at arms-length and examined her from head to toe.

"No, don't tell me, let me guess," he commanded. "Marie Antoinette?"

"That's right," laughed Daisy, then clutched at her side. "Bloody corset," she grimaced. "I think Miriam was a bit too enthusiastic when she laced me into it, I can hardly breathe."

"Well," replied Conrad, eyeing her somewhat ample assets with a lecherous leer. "It certainly did the job! I've never seen you looking so ... perky before."

"Don't be rude," replied Daisy primly, lips twitching into a perfect cupid's bow of a smile, which suited her sweet, heart-shaped face to perfection, making her resemble an enchantingly pretty elf.

"Hello Matthew," she cried, accepting his kiss. "What a fantastic King Richard you make! And you must be Lili," she cried, turning to Lili enthusiastically.

"Yes," smiled Lili, warming instantly to Daisy's vivacious charm. "Happy Birthday and thank you so much for inviting me to your party." She handed Daisy the gift-wrapped necklace.

"Ooh," Daisy's blue eyes, so like Greg's, rounded with delight. "A present. Thank you, you shouldn't have." With evident excitement, she ripped the pretty wrapping off, squealing with pleasure at the necklace inside.

"Oh, how perfectly lovely," she exclaimed in obvious delight. "I love it. Thank you, Lili, it's perfect."

"You're welcome, I'm glad you like it," replied Lili with relief.

"I love it, absolutely love it," enthused Daisy, gazing at Lili with dancing eyes. "And I love your outfit too," she added. "Isn't Tomb Raider the greatest thing? You make such a great Lara. There's no way I'd show my bum and thighs off in shorts like that, but you've got such a fantastic figure they look good on you."

"Thank you."

Taken aback by such wholehearted compliments, Lili was unsure how to respond, and was relieved when Daisy turned her attention to Conrad.

"And you, Conrad, who have you come as?"

"Beau Brummell."

"How appropriate," commented Daisy dryly. She spun around and clasped Lili's hand. "Later, the band are going to play some great dance music. Do you like to dance Lili? I hope so, I do and it's my birthday, so tonight everyone has to dance."

"I love dancing," Lili reassured her.

"Where's Guy?" enquired Conrad, and Daisy blushed prettily, a dimple appearing in each cheek.

"Oh, he's around somewhere. I better go and find him. Loads of the guests are his friends anyway, so he can jolly well help me meet and greet. Catch you later, Lili. Don't forget, you promised to dance." And she was gone, dancing across the room in a swirl of lace and blue silk, leaving Lili breathless, as if she were the one wearing the corset.

An hour later, drink in hand, Lili was having the time of her life. Conrad had tried to stick close and introduce her around but kept being ambushed by various groups, so Lili had been left to her own devices. Daunted at first by this, she soon came to realise there was a strange kind of freedom in being the mysterious, glamorous stranger. Nobody knew anything about her, she could just be Lili.

Conrad had chosen her costume wisely. Having prior knowledge of the guest list, he'd known Lili would be one of the youngest and had let her youth and vitality shine through with a simple, though striking, outfit. The stark masculinity of her clothes, vividly counteracted with the pert breasts, long shapely legs, and her face, with its exotically female contours and full-lipped pout.

Her natural shyness and uncertainty with the situation came across as cool aloofness, and people, particularly men, clamoured to be near her. Surrounded by Conrad and Matthew's friends, an intriguing smile flirting with her mouth, Lili was an instant hit.

"It's a shame there are no games," exclaimed Sid, toying with his Freddie Mercury moustache. Conrad had introduced Lili to Sid, explaining he was a designer currently clawing his way up the slippery slide of the fashion world.

"Games?" enquired another. "What sort of games did you have in mind, Sid?" A knowing chuckle rippled through the group.

Sid gave an exaggerated sigh. "Get your minds out of the gutter, please, boys," he exclaimed. "There's a lady present," he bowed courteously to Lili. She smiled back, put at ease by the camp flirting and teasing which so reminded her of Conrad in one of his outrageous moods.

"No," Sid continued. "I mean real games like I used to play at parties when I was a kid. You know … pass the parcel, musical chairs, that sort of thing. I used to love playing games and I was good at them. Well, I used to win a lot."

"Don't you mean you used to cheat a lot?" enquired another dryly. A shout of laughter erupted, and Sid placed his hands on his hips in mock outrage, as the others joined in, offering suggestions as to what kind of games were the most fun or best icebreakers.

"I don't know what you mean," he stated, then turned to Lili. "What about you, Lili?" he asked. "What game do you think would be a good icebreaker?"

Lili stared at him blankly. She'd never been to a party before and certainly hadn't played any games. Desperately, her mind raced as she tried to think of a game, any game, then remembered one she had seen advertised on TV.

"Twister?" she tentatively offered. There was a split second of silence before the whole group exploded into delighted laughter.

"That's a good one," cried Sid in delight. "Ooh, I know, even better, naked Twister!" There was a roar of delight from the others, and Sid hugged Lili, "Oh Lili," he exclaimed. "You kill me, you really do. You're so funny."

"Lili?"

Lili turned to find Daisy behind her, face flushed with excitement, eyes dancing with joyful expectation.

"Daisy, Daisy, give me your answer do," sang Sid, whisking Daisy into his arms and twirling her around. "I'm half crazy, all for the love of you."

"Behave yourself, Sid." Giggling, Daisy extracted herself from Sid's grasp. "Whatever would Jeremy think if he saw you flirting with me?"

"It would do him good," retorted Sid. "He might start to appreciate me a bit more." Daisy's face sobered, and she patted Sid on the arm sympathetically.

"Oh Sid," she exclaimed. "Is he still not treating you right?" At Sid's philosophical shrug, she gave him a quick hug. "Call me next week," she ordered. "We'll do lunch. You can tell me all about it. Now, I'm afraid I'm going to steal Lili, I want her to meet Mummy and Daddy, and Guy."

Tucking her arm through Lili's, Daisy led her away amidst a sea of protests and goodbyes. Waving to Sid and the others over her shoulder, Lili glanced down at their costumes, her lips twitching at the contrast. Daisy's, the ultimate in femininity and her own, the total antithesis.

"Who is Jeremy?" she asked, as they pushed their way across the crowded room.

"Sid's partner," Daisy explained. "He's a complete and utter bastard and treats poor Sid appallingly. It's such a shame; Sid's an absolute sweetheart. He doesn't deserve to be treated so badly."

"Why does he stay with him?" Lili asked curiously.

"He loves him," Daisy stated simply, stopping before a group of three people. The older couple, dressed as Queen Elizabeth I and Sir Walter Raleigh, were clearly Daisy and Greg's parents, their piercing blue eyes having been inherited from their father. He was appraising Lili in a manner that left no doubt he'd been fond of the ladies in his younger years. The long dark hair was a legacy from their mother, and Lili hoped she looked as good as Daisy's mother did when she was in her sixties.

"Mum, Dad," began Daisy, pulling Lili forward, "this is Lili. She's a friend of Conrad's. Isn't her costume great?"

"It certainly is," leered Mr Kolinsky.

"Daddy," drawled Daisy. "Ignore him," she added to Lili. "He's the most dreadful perv; I don't know why Mummy puts up with him."

"I sometimes wonder that myself," her mother replied, with an amused smile. "Hello Lili," she turned her attention to Lili, who smiled in response to the interested warmth on Mrs Kolinsky's face. "I hope you're enjoying the party," she continued.

"Oh, yes," replied Lili. "It's wonderful."

"Should be," muttered Mr Kolinsky, "amount it's costing me."

"Has your brother turned up yet?" Ignoring her husband, Mrs Kolinsky smiled brightly at Daisy.

"No, not yet. I expect he got caught up in his latest work and forgot what the time was. You know what Greg's like."

"Unfortunately, I do," her mother sighed.

"Aren't you going to introduce us, Daisy?"

All through the exchange with Daisy's parents, Lili had felt the eyes of the third member of the group as they swept over every square inch of her body. Trying not to shudder, she watched Daisy cross to him and slip her arm around his waist.

"Sorry, sorry," she laughed up at him, eyes clearly showing the feelings in her heart. "Lili, this is my boyfriend, Guy Bellingham. Guy this is my new friend Lili. She's come from Suffolk to buy some of Greg's art and come to my party."

"Has she now?" drawled Guy, extending a languid hand to Lili, smiling directly into her eyes. "Which part of Suffolk?" he enquired.

"Bury St Edmunds."

"Oh, I know it. Near Newmarket, isn't it?"

"Yes, that's right."

"Charming part of the country."

"I like it."

Guy nodded – his eyes thoughtful. He was good-looking, Lili thought, in a safe, upper-class kind of way. Even though he couldn't compete with Greg for sheer masculine presence, he was attractive, and it was clear from the adoring, almost slavish look Daisy was bestowing on him, that she thought he was perfect.

A sudden commotion had all turning to see Greg striding through the crowd, which parted at his approach like Moses and the Red Sea. Dressed as a rakishly handsome Dick Turpin, he arrived with a flourish of his cloak, and a devil-may-care smile that set many a female heart aflutter, Lili's included.

"Happy birthday, brat," he said and deposited a large wicker basket at Daisy's feet. With evident excitement and no thought to her dress, she dropped to her knees, quickly undid the catch, and flipped back the lid.

"Oh, oh, what an absolute darling, how sweet!" cried Daisy in delight, pulling out of the basket the cutest, sleepiest looking spaniel puppy Lili had ever seen. With soft fluffy ears, an absurd little tail which was busy wagging with joy and a much-chewed red bow tied to its collar, Daisy's birthday present was as appealing as its giver.

"Greg, thank you, thank you!" Climbing unsteadily to her knees, Daisy gave him a one-armed hug as the puppy squirmed in her clasp. "He's beautiful, I love him."

"He, is actually, she," replied Greg in amusement.

"Oh, look at her Lili, isn't she the cutest little thing?" Daisy held the puppy out to Lili, who felt her heart-melting as she looked into those sad, dark eyes.

"She's gorgeous," she replied, then frowned. "But why's she covered in pink stuff?"

Daisy looked closer at the puppy and realised it was true. The puppy had streaks of pink smeared over the top of her little head, and down one cheek.

"Greg?" she queried. "Why is my puppy covered with pink paint?"

"Oh, there must have been some magenta paint still on my hands when I was putting her in the basket," he explained with a sheepish grin. "Sorry."

"Magenta, of course," breathed Daisy. "That's what I'll call her, Magenta, Maggie for short. Oh, I've got to go and show her to everyone. Catch you later Lili."

Dragging Guy behind her, Daisy danced away. Mr and Mrs Kolinsky drifted off as well, leaving Lili and Greg standing alone together.

"Hello again, Lili," Greg grinned, as he quite openly ogled her. "Or should I say, Lara? I must say, I do like your outfit."

Lili blushed. Suddenly her shorts seemed too skimpy, and her vest top too tight as it strained to contain her artificially inflated breasts. Completely out of her depth, she took a deep breath, before giving Greg a shy, sweet smile.

"Th-thank you," she stuttered. "I like yours too. It suits you."

"Dick Turpin, dastardly scourge of the highway at your service, milady," Greg theatrically swirled his cloak and bowed. "Is Jake here yet?"

"I don't know," Lili replied uncertainly. "I don't know what he looks like."

"I don't see him," Greg muttered, his height allowing him to scan over the heads of the crowd. "Or the trollop."

"I beg your pardon?"

Surely, she'd misheard.

Greg flashed an innocent smile, shook his head, as a decision seemed to be reached by the band, who launched into a spirited rendition of a pop song.

Immediately, the partygoers, who'd been steadily tanking themselves up with free booze, perked up and invaded the dance floor. With a whoop and a shriek, Sid and co arrived behind Lili, grabbed her by the arms, and carried her onto the dance floor. Laughing, fighting off their attempts to steal her gun, Lili settled down to the serious business of dancing and having fun.

Later, exhausted, Lili staggered over to where Conrad was sitting eating French bread smeared liberally with brie.

"Having fun?" he enquired between mouthfuls.

"Uh-huh," Lili gasped, collapsing onto a chair beside him and pouring herself a glass of water from the jug in the middle of the table. Pinching a grape off Conrad's plate, Lili flexed her feet within her sturdy boots. Used to heels, it felt strange to be wearing such heavy footwear for dancing.

A sudden drum roll had them both looking up in surprise as the music stopped, the lights came up, and Guy walked onto the stage and took the mike off the lead singer. Curious mutters arose from the revellers, as he leant forward to speak into the mike.

"Erm, ladies and gentlemen if I could have a few moments of your time, please. Firstly, I'd like to thank you all for coming to Daisy's 21st birthday party. I think you'll agree with me it's a simply marvellous occasion."

A cheer arose at his words. From where Lili was sitting, she could see Daisy's parents. They too looked surprised at what was happening, and, possibly, a little put out that Guy had taken upon himself the task that surely should have been performed by them.

"If the lovely Daisy could come up here please," Guy continued. "I have my birthday present to give to her."

There was a stirring, a muttering in the crowd and Daisy was there, still clutching Maggie, a bemused expression on her face as she carefully climbed onto the stage.

A fleeting look of annoyance passed over Guy's face. Taking the puppy from her, he passed it to the lead singer, then to the delight of the crowd went down on one knee before Daisy. She flushed bright red and clutched her hand to her heart, as he opened a small ring box and showed her the contents.

"Daisy Kolinsky, would you do me the great honour of becoming my wife?"

"Yes."

There was no hesitation over Daisy's reply, sure and swift it flew straight from her heart and her lips. Jumping to his feet, Guy slipped the ring onto her finger, gathered her up in his arms and kissed her, thoroughly and soundly, to thunderous applause and cries of congratulations.

Caught up in the atmosphere, wildly clapping and cheering herself, Lili saw Conrad's sombre, unsmiling face, before he turned on his heel and left the room.

"Conrad?" Lili caught up with him by the front door. "Conrad, what's wrong?"

"Nothing," he replied, shaking his head. "It's me being silly. It's ... oh like I said, it's nothing."

"It's obviously something," Lili persisted. Behind them, the band launched into a spontaneous chorus of *Congratulations*. Sighing, Conrad walked out the front door, crunching on gravel as he headed around the side of the house towards the gardens. Not knowing what else to do, Lili followed him. Finally, Conrad stopped and turned.

"Tell me, Lili," he began, "what did you think of Guy?"

"I don't know," Lili shrugged. "He seemed all right. I didn't have time to ... I don't know ... form an opinion. Why?" Conrad didn't reply, merely sighed again. Lili narrowed her eyes thoughtfully. "You don't like him, do you?" she said.

"No," he agreed. "I don't like him very much."

"But why?" breathed Lili. "He seemed okay, and Daisy's crazy about him."

"He's not good enough for her," confided Conrad. "I've known Daisy nearly all of her life. She's the sweetest, dearest, kindest girl alive, and one of the most malleable."

"What do you mean, malleable?"

"Daisy allows herself to be controlled by others. She never seems to fight for what she wants. Instead, she's always happy to go with the flow and fall in with what everybody else wants to do."

"And that's a bad thing?" Lili was confused.

"It could be," Conrad replied. "She and Guy have been together since she was sixteen years old. She's never had another boyfriend or has ever had any friends; other than the ones he graciously allows her to have. Being ten years older than her, he controls almost every aspect of her life, and has done for the past six years."

"But if she loves him, why would she want anybody else?"

Lili could see where Conrad was coming from but felt compelled to defend Daisy and her choice.

"All I'm saying is – she's never had the chance to experience life outside her narrow little world. Daisy will go straight from her father's house to her husband's bed, with no time in between to discover who she is, and what she wants from life."

"Maybe what she wants is to be Guy's wife," Lili suggested, shivering in the cooling evening air. Whilst they'd been inside dusk had fallen like a soft, shadowy blanket, cloaking the extensive gardens with a mysterious cloudy haze.

"And another thing." Now Conrad was on his soapbox, he seemed reluctant to get off it. "He asks her to marry him, here, tonight, at her 21st birthday party. Why?"

"He thought it would be romantic," Lili offered the explanation tentatively.

"Or, more likely, thought he'd save himself the expense of buying a 21st birthday present, and an engagement ring. That by asking her in such a way, her party would become the engagement party, and he'd save himself some money there too."

"Well, maybe he's hard up for cash," retorted Lili.

"Lili," Conrad looked at her pityingly, "Guy's family owns half of Buckinghamshire. Trust me, they're not short of a bob or two. No, the man's careful with money to the point of being mean."

Not knowing how to respond to that, Lili said nothing.

"I know you probably think I'm being unreasonable and perhaps you're right," Conrad sighed. "It's just ... I don't think he'll make her happy."

"It's her decision, Conrad," Lili said softly. "You can't live other people's lives for them. They must be free to make their own choices. Make their own mistakes too."

"When did you get to be so wise?" Conrad chuckled.

"I had a good teacher," Lili retorted.

"I suppose we better get back to the party," he continued. "Offer our sincere congratulations and all that," he brightened. "You never know, they may open more champagne. Coming?"

"I think I'll take a quick look around the garden before it gets too dark to see," Lili replied.

"Well, don't be too long."

"I won't be. Save me a glass of champagne."

Conrad vanished into the gloom, and Lili wandered about in a strangely retrospective mood, thinking about what he said – wondering about choices, about love. Perhaps Conrad was right. Then she remembered the expression on Daisy's face when Guy proposed, how happy they both looked, and thought maybe he was wrong.

Finally, Lili glanced up, realising she'd wandered so far, she could no longer see the twinkling party lights. It was now so dark she could hardly make out her hand in front of her face. Shivering, she decided to retrace her steps and re-join the party.

Reaching the corner of the house, Lili saw a young man leaning against the wall, forehead resting on the red bricks, arms braced as if to take his weight. Recognising him as one of Guy's friends, Lili stopped and gently touched his arm.

"Are you okay?" she asked in concern.

The man turned his head to look at her, eyes glassy and unfocused, and Lili realised with distaste that he was plastered.

"Fuck," he mumbled, his gaze darkening with undisguised lust. "It's Lara Croft, come to save me. Hello gorgeous."

Lili stepped back, moved to pass him, but a hand, surprisingly strong considering his inebriation, shot out and grabbed her wrist.

"Let me go, please," Lili ordered, trying to keep her voice calm, even though her heart was racing with sudden panic. "I want to get back to the party."

"What's the rush, darling," he leered, tightening his grip on her wrist until she winced with pain. "We could have our own little party right here."

"No, we couldn't," Lili replied, struggling to release her wrist. "I said, let me go."

"Aw, come on," he pleaded, pushing her back against the wall. Gripping her other wrist, he nuzzled drunkenly at her neck. "You know you don't mean it."

"I do," Lili gasped. "Let me go!" she begged, fear in her voice.

"Make me," he whispered in her ear. His alcohol-foul breath was hot on her face, and she turned her head to avoid the kiss he was trying to give her.

"I believe the little lady asked you to let her go," a voice drawled. Staggering around, the drunk peered uncertainly into the dusk as a match flared, a cigarette was lit, and a cowboy sauntered out of the gloom.

"Who the fuck are you?" Lili's would-be seducer demanded.

"I'm the guy who's telling you to take your hands off the lady," replied the cowboy. Lili squinted in the darkness, trying to see her rescuer more clearly as he stepped closer, inhaling on his cigarette, eyes narrowed dangerously at the drunk.

He was tall and rangy, with long muscular legs clad in tight-fitting jeans. A pale blue shirt, and chocolate-coloured leather waistcoat, barely contained his broad chest as he inhaled on his cigarette, its tip lighting up the night like a mini distress flare.

Raising her eyes, Lili's gaze was drawn irresistibly to his face. Lean, hard, tough, dangerous – words flew through her brain in a frenzied attempt to apply a label to the tanned, uncompromisingly male features that swam before her confused stare.

Strangely familiar, piercing blue eyes met hers in a coolly level look, and Lili was vaguely aware of tousled hair which caressed the collar of his long black coat. A Stetson, dark and sinister, sat atop his head casting shadows over his face.

"You still haven't let the little lady go." Either he was American or could pull off the best Yankee drawl Lili had ever heard.

"Oh, fuck off and get your own screw," the drunk retorted, turning his attentions onto Lili, pushing her violently back against the wall and bending to nuzzle her cleavage.

It happened so fast.

One moment Lili was trying to fight the drunk off, the next he was lying on the floor groaning, clutching his stomach, as the cowboy stepped back and inhaled calmly on his cigarette.

"Ma'am," he touched his hat politely in her direction, before disappearing once more into the gloom.

By the time Lili gathered her startled wits together and rushed after him, he'd gone; vanished somewhere into the darkness of the night, leaving her breathless, with a wildly beating heart that felt strangely full of hope.

Picking her way gingerly around the drunk now busily vomiting into the bushes, Lili hurried back to the party and found Conrad sitting at a table, four glasses of champagne before him, looking anxiously towards the door.

"There you are," he exclaimed. "I was about to send out search and rescue."

"Sorry," Lili replied, picking up one of the glasses and taking a sip. Strangely reluctant to relate to him her experiences in the garden, especially the bizarre maelstrom of emotions the encounter with a certain rugged cowboy had whipped up inside her, Lili smiled at him over the rim of her champagne flute, gulping at the sparkly bubbles which seemed to match her mood.

Feeling giddy with anticipation, her eyes scanned the crowd of happy revellers, hopefully searching, until abruptly, thrillingly, she saw him again across the room.

His piercing blue eyes focused on her face, and he smiled right at her; a long, lazy grin that sent shivers racing down her spine. Touching the brim of his hat to her again, he bent to talk to a woman by his side.

Tall, curvy, blonde, and incredibly beautiful, she was dressed as Marilyn Monroe. She turned amused, cat-like eyes in Lili's direction.

Lili hated her on sight.

Her ripe, womanly body which made Lili's own feel childlike and androgynous, was pressed possessively into the cowboy as he slung an easy arm around her waist.

"Conrad," said Lili, dropping her eyes away from the smugly perfect couple.

"Yes?"

"Who's that man, over there, the one dressed as a cowboy. He looks … familiar."

"Well, he should," replied Conrad, following her gaze. "That's Jake, Daisy and Greg's cousin. There's a strong family resemblance, around the eyes mostly."

"And the woman beside him?" Lili asked with a sinking heart, already knowing the answer, but having to hear him say it.

"The pneumatic blonde?" Conrad's gaze turned steely. "That's Vivienne, his blushing bride, and the biggest bitch that ever drew breath."

Chapter Eighteen
"Lili? You were jealous of Lili?"

Why did it hurt? Lili's mind demanded logically. He saved you from an unpleasant situation, that's all. Why did it hurt to discover he was married? A newlywed, on honeymoon with his beautiful bride? Because it did hurt, deep within; a strange, forlorn ache; a nagging, unsettled pain the like of which Lili had never felt before.

Married, he was married, so there was an end to it.

It didn't matter that during those brief seconds when he looked deep into her eyes, Lili felt he was gazing right into her soul. All her secrets were stripped bare before him, exposing her inner self, vulnerable and needy. That he could somehow sense the desperate longing buried within for someone to love and cherish her.

Firmly reprimanding herself to get a grip, and not be so melodramatic, Lili looked up as Daisy rushed over, flaunting her ring in delighted glee.

"There you are," she exclaimed brightly. "Look, isn't it gorgeous?" Lili and Conrad dutifully examined its sparkle and made appropriate noises.

"I'm so happy, I could burst," cried Daisy. "And Jake and Vivienne have arrived. You must come and meet them, Lili."

Before Lili could think of an excuse, Daisy grasped her hand and dragged her reluctantly across the dance floor. Lili barely had time to compose her features into a neutral expression before they arrived in front of the stunningly sexy couple.

Close up, Lili realised Vivienne was older than she first thought. From a distance, she looked not much older than Daisy, but now Lili could see Vivienne was probably in her late twenties. It didn't change the fact she was one of the most beautiful women Lili had ever seen.

Her stunning, platinum blonde hair, was artfully arranged in a style mirroring the late screen goddess; her white, halter-neck dress an exact copy of that worn by Marilyn in The Seven Year Itch – a film Lili had watched with her grandmother many years before.

Large, pale blue eyes narrowed as they rested on Lili. With an amused expression, her gaze flicked over Lili's body, before dismissing her.

As for Jake, Lili's breath caught in her throat. Sexy, arrogant, and attractive as hell. He wasn't classically handsome like Greg, there was a little too much roughness in his face.

He had that lean, dangerous look which screamed a warning to all womankind – here is one big, gorgeous, male package of trouble. Take him on at your peril.

Jake smiled at Lili; a long, lazy grin, plainly showing his appreciation of her as a woman. Yet his arm stayed firmly round his wife's waist. Lili saw his eyes immediately go back to feast on her with a fiercely possessive gaze and knew he was completely and utterly infatuated with his bride.

"Jake," exclaimed Daisy, "you finally got here. Look." Proudly, she held out her left hand to display her engagement ring.

"You missed it. Guy proposed up on stage in front of all these people."

"Hey, congratulations short stuff."

Jake's affection for Daisy was obvious as he relinquished his hold on Vivienne to give her a wholehearted bear hug.

"Yes, congratulations, Daisy," drawled Vivienne, husky Southern Belle accent conjuring up images of mint juleps, rustling silk dresses, and cotton plantations.

"May I see the ring? Why I do declare, isn't that the sweetest little thing. I wonder if maybe I should have chosen a small stone like that, instead of letting Jake talk me into having such a large diamond."

She flashed her ring finger on which a monstrous boulder weighed her delicate hand down.

Daisy's face fell.

Lili felt a spurt of anger towards the older woman, Conrad was right. She *was* a bitch. With a few, effectively chosen words, she had completely spoilt Daisy's pleasure in her engagement ring and had done it with such syrupy expertise that Jake, ignorant male he was, stood smiling, blithely unaware of the poisoned arrow his wife had let fly in Daisy's direction.

"Won't you introduce us, Daisy?"

The faintest touch of reprimand in Vivienne's tone had Daisy flushing again. Lili slipped an arm through hers in silent solidarity.

"Of course," stuttered Daisy. "This is my new friend Lili. Lili, this is my cousin Jake Kolinsky and his wife, Vivienne."

"Lili?" Vivienne enquired, with exaggerated politeness. "Is that short for anything?"

"No, just Lili," Lili lifted her chin, looking Vivienne straight in the eye. "I prefer small things."

The slight widening, then narrowing, of those baby blue eyes, indicated Vivienne had received and understood the message.

"Hi there, Lili."

Jake's large warm hand clasped Lili's in a brief shake of greeting, sending tingles of sensation shooting through her.

"I know you're Marilyn Monroe, Vivienne," continued Daisy. "But who have you come as, Jake? Billy the Kid?"

"Could be," Jake shrugged. "Or Wild Bill Hickock, Butch Cassidy, Wyatt Earp; the Wild West is full of iconic figures. You ladies pick whichever one you want." He turned to Lili with a devastatingly sexy smile. "I've been trying to figure out who you've come as?"

"She's Lara," said Daisy. "Lara Croft," she elaborated further at Jake's look of incomprehension.

"Sorry," he shook his head. "Still none the wiser."

"Lara Croft from Tomb Raider," declared Daisy exasperated. "Oh Jake," she exclaimed, impatiently, "it's only the greatest computer game ever."

"Some of us don't have time for children's games," drawled Vivienne.

"Jake!"

Greg's cry of pleased recognition was timely. Lili's mouth had fallen open in a disbelieving gape at the unbelievable rudeness, and sheer bitchery of the woman and a scathing comment had arisen in her throat.

At Greg's arrival, however, she wisely swallowed it down, watching in amusement as the two most handsome men in the room embraced, and enthusiastically back slapped, plainly delighted to see each other.

"Greg …"

At Vivienne's honeyed voice, Greg stiffened, stepped back, the friendly light in his eyes being replaced by a look of guarded hostility.

"Vivienne."

His voice was polite, too polite Lili thought, observing him with interest. Her position as an outsider allowed her to detect the tiniest nuances in his body language, which left no doubt he detested this woman.

"Congratulations on your marriage," he continued blandly. "It's a shame you felt the need to marry so quickly. I know the whole family were disappointed to miss the wedding."

"Well, you know what it's like when you're in love," simpered Vivienne slipping a territorial arm around Jake's waist and shooting Greg an intense, venom-laden look from under her lashes.

"I mean, one minute we were in Vegas, having fun, with marriage the absolute last thing on our minds, the next we were in the chapel saying I do," she purred.

"Still not quite sure how it happened," confided Jake with a laugh.

But Lili, looking at those slanted cat's eyes watching for Greg's reaction with a strange, indescribable expression, had a pretty good idea of what had occurred.

"But, what about you, Greg," continued Jake good-naturedly. "How's it going? Sold any more pictures yet?"

"Sold two yesterday."

Greg was studiously ignoring Vivienne. Slipping an arm around Daisy's shoulders, pulling her close, he seemed determined to maintain a whole conversation with Jake, as if he didn't wish to acknowledge Vivienne's presence at all.

"Hey, that's great," exclaimed Jake. "To anyone we know?"

"To Lili here."

Greg nodded a head in Lili's direction, bestowing a warm, blue smile upon her now blushing features.

"He's pretty good, isn't he?"

Lili felt her blush deepen as another pair of Kolinsky piercing blue eyes were turned in her direction.

"Yes," she stuttered. "I think he's wonderful, in fact…"

"Jake, get me some champagne."

Bored with a conversation not revolving around her, Vivienne interrupted so gracefully, only Lili was aware of her mouth still open in mid-sentence.

"Sure thing, honey," Jake glanced apologetically at the others. "We only just got here, so I guess we better get something to drink and say hi to your folks. We'll catch up with you all later. Happy birthday again, Daisy."

With a final smile in their direction, Jake allowed his wife to lead him away, Vivienne shooting an amused, condescending glance in Lili's direction, which had her own eyes narrowing in dislike.

"Well," Greg exhaled slowly. "I never thought I'd see the day Jake Kolinsky let himself be led about by the balls by that vain and manipulative, two-faced bitch."

"Greg!" Daisy exclaimed in shocked laughter. "You shouldn't talk about her like that. After all, she is his wife."

"Aw come on, Daisy," teased Greg. "Don't defend her. You don't like her either."

"No, no I don't," Daisy replied in a sober tone. "I'm afraid she's going to hurt him because even though I don't think she loves him; I know Jake's completely obsessed with her. Sooner or later, he'll discover the truth about her, and it will devastate him."

"How did they meet?" Lili asked curiously.

"On the set of *Enemy Unknown*," replied Daisy, as if that answered Lili's question.

"I'm sorry, where?"

"Jake's film, Vivienne was in it, and Jake was on set advising on the screenplay." She saw Lili's blank look of total incomprehension. "You have no idea who Jake is, do you, Lili?"

"No, sorry, should I?"

"Well, it's true he writes under a pen name, but it's no secret. Jake's a writer. He writes under the name of Jack Cole. You must have heard of him, Lili, even if you've never read any of his books."

"Oh!" Lili exclaimed in shock. It was true, she hadn't read any of his books, but even she with her limited knowledge of novels had heard of the famous American novelist. His intense thrillers of political intrigue and international espionage were major bestsellers, spawning a host of box office smash hits and placing his hero, Cain Roberts, on a par with James Bond or Indiana Jones.

"I see," she finished weakly, feeling silly she hadn't known; hadn't realised. "So, Vivienne's an actress?" she continued.

"Well, she was a model," explained Daisy. "But she's been trying to break into acting and was cast in the role of Melinda Myers. She's the bad guy's woman. At least you think she is, but it turns out she's FBI and dies saving Cain's life. It's a great film – one of Jake's best. So, Vivienne was on set and Jake was there too. He always maintains artistic control over the screenplay. They met, and that was that..."

"Yeah," Greg interrupted cynically. "She took one look at Jake, the dollar bills flashed in her eyes, and she decided to hook herself a good-looking, wealthy husband."

"You *really* don't like her, do you?" laughed Lili.

"No," Greg agreed with complete candour. "I don't. Now then, can I interest you lovely ladies in escorting me to the dance floor?" He bowed deeply, flourishing his cloak, and held out an arm to each of them. The two girls giggled, allowing him to lead them onto the dance floor.

Midnight came and went with the party showing no signs of stopping or even slowing down.

Feeling the effects of too much alcohol, Lili switched to water and went in search of food. Finding Conrad at the buffet, she was only too happy to sit quietly between him and Matthew at their crowded table, munching hungrily on delicious canapés and tiny, mouth-watering sandwiches, watching the dancing, and smiling at the drunken antics of people out to have a good time.

Through a gap in the crowd, she saw Daisy and Greg sitting together at a nearby table, Daisy's head lolling on Greg's shoulder, Maggie the puppy sprawled sleepily across their laps.

As Lili watched an older woman and man, both carrying sleeping children, stopped at their table and spoke to them. There was enough of a resemblance for Lili to deduce this must be Miriam, their older sister, with her husband and children.

Swigging down the last of his champagne, Greg nodded and got to his feet, pulling Daisy up with him. Kissing his older sister on the cheek, he relieved her of a sleeping child and followed his brother-in-law.

Miriam slipped an arm around Daisy's waist and spoke to her, rubbing at Maggie's ears. Daisy nodded, her eyes animated, and said something back, although Lili was too far away to hear what. Still with arms around each other, the sisters crossed the floor to where their parents were sitting.

Idly swinging her gaze back to their now abandoned table, Lili saw, or rather thought she saw, something odd. Greg had drained his champagne glass, yet it was full again, brimming with sparkling, effervescent bubbles.

Lili blinked.

There were no waiters at the party, the revellers collecting their drinks from one of four free bars dotted around the house. So how had the glass been filled?

Lifting her eyes, Lili caught a flash of white through the crowd, and saw Vivienne press close to her husband, topping his glass from a bottle of champagne.

"Lili?"

Pulled away from her musings, Lili looked up to find Daisy smiling expectantly. Energy sparked from her, and it was clear she'd got her second wind.

"You promised to dance with me," she exclaimed, pulling Lili to her feet. With a groan, Lili stuffed the last of her sandwich in her mouth and staggered onto the dance floor, the incident with the champagne glass forgotten.

They danced for hours, Sid and co discovering them with cries of joy, clowning around, making noise, and performing complicated and silly dance steps. Soon, a large group of excited youngsters dominated the dance floor, older partygoers deciding to either call it a night or sit back and rest.

Guy joined them on the dance floor. A wooden, unimaginative dancer; his ornate Napoleon outfit was the perfect foil to Daisy's fussy Marie Antoinette costume.

Watching them together, seeing Daisy's happiness, the way their hands and eyes sought each other, Lili decided Conrad was wrong. Guy loved Daisy, every bit as much as she loved him.

Even if he was a little controlling, well, that was only to be expected given the differences in their ages. As Daisy gained maturity and confidence, any disparity between them would surely vanish.

The husky voice of the statuesque lead singer continued to belt out popular songs. Lili glanced up at the stage, thinking how beautiful the woman was with her long black hair and shapely figure, and what an amazing voice she had.

"They're good, aren't they?" Daisy cried. At Lili's enthusiastic nod, she continued, "We've decided to book them for the wedding. You'll come, won't you, Lili?"

"Of course," beamed Lili. "If I can. When's it to be?"

Daisy and Guy exchanged a look and a quick kiss. "We don't want to wait too long, so we're thinking of June 1997."

"I'd love to come," promised Lili, smiling with pleasure. Guy whisked Daisy away, and Lili was grabbed by Sid, drawn into a dance, laughing as he clasped her in his arms and bent her backwards in a parody of a Fred and Ginger routine.

Staggering off the dance floor later, Daisy and Lili leant against each other in a state of total collapse, Guy looking on in amusement, gulping thirstily at the water he fetched them from the bar.

"Have you seen Vivienne?"

At Jake's question, they shook their heads. "No, sorry old boy," replied Guy, his clipped, public schoolboy accent a direct contrast to Jake's more casual American drawl. "Have you lost her?"

"Oh, she's here somewhere," he replied, his relaxed tone belied by the worry in his eyes.

The frenzied song ended, and Daisy groaned, resting her head against Lili's arm.

"I don't think I can dance anymore," she whimpered. "My feet hurt too much."

"Why don't we slow things down," murmured the singer's husky tones. "We'll be taking a break in about ten minutes, but before we do, let's have some smooth numbers to grab your partners and hold on to. We'll kick off with a personal favourite of mine and take a trip back to 1979."

The music started, rich and slow; it rolled languidly through an introduction before the singer began to sing.

"There she is."

Following Daisy's pointing finger, they all looked and saw Vivienne, white dress glowing like a beacon, being led onto the dance floor by a darkly handsome pirate. As they watched, she moved easily into his arms and they began to dance, bodies flowing effortlessly into the sensual, sexual rhythm of the song.

"Who's that?" Jake's voice was casual, but glancing up at him, Lili saw the edge of jealousy as it flashed in his eyes.

"It's Adam, he's one of Conrad's friends."

"Oh, he's gay," the relief in his voice was obvious. Lili saw the look that passed between Daisy and Guy.

"No, he's ..." Daisy hesitated, unwilling to speak. "Not gay." Apologetically, she laid a sympathetic hand on his arm. "They're dancing, Jake, that's all, just dancing. You should dance too."

"Right, dancing ..."

Jake pulled his attention away from the couple with an effort, focusing his gaze on Daisy.

"Will you dance with me?" he asked, a note of desperation in his voice.

"Oh no you don't," Guy broke in before Daisy could answer. "I've been waiting all night for a chance to smooch with my fiancée. Now they're finally playing something slow, it's me she's going to be smooching with, not you." Daisy's face melted, and she turned loving eyes up to Guy. "Sorry old boy," he added, leading Daisy onto the dance floor.

"Sorry, Jake," Daisy called back. "Why not dance with Lili?"

Awkwardness fell over the moment. Lili cringed at his obvious reluctance, silently cursing Daisy. Jake looked across the crowded dance floor as his wife threw her head back, laughed at something her partner said, coyly shaking her head, and tracing a finger seductively down his cheek. He swung her around, and they were hidden from sight behind a press of entwined couples.

"Come on."

Jake made his mind up. Grabbing Lili's hand, he led her onto the floor and pulled her into his arms, her body fitting naturally into his. Smoothly, proficiently, he swept her into the dance. Lili felt her heart stutter at the unfamiliar sensations welling and bubbling deep inside.

The song was one she wasn't familiar with; the sultry rhythm coaxing her body to sway tantalisingly close to Jake's. Trying to focus on anything other than the feel of his tall, muscular body, Lili desperately concentrated on the words.

... something about her needing him tonight, about showing him a sunset if he'd stay with her till dawn...

Jake's hand slid slowly down her spine until it rested easily in the small of her back, his other hand clasping hers. Lili imagined his heart pulsing through her palm, finding an echo deep within her chest.

Being so much taller than her, Lili's head was resting on his chest, and she had to fight the urge to simply nestle in; to rest her cheek against his heart and wish the rest of the world away.

... the husky tones of the singer implored her lover to stop playing games with her heart, to stay with her till dawn...

Taking a deep, steadying breath, Lili inhaled a lungful of Jake; his smell, his essence, some sort of masculine spicy aftershave, a faint whiff of cigarettes, and under it all, him; his aroma, male and haunting.

It seeped into and saturated her senses until Lili knew she'd be able to tell him apart from all other men by the scent of him.

Her knees trembled.

His large, capable hands automatically steadied and controlled her, his grip tightening on her back. Lili waged an internal war against her newly awakened female instincts; her body almost screaming its insistence that here, now, she'd found her mate, the one she'd been looking for all her life. The search was over. He was here, holding her, this man, the man, her man.

... she needed him, wanted him, needed him to stay with her till dawn...

No, no, no!

Logic fought back, slapping down emotions until they quivered in surrender. He's married, at least ten years older than you, and married. He's rich and successful and lives on a different continent.

He's married, Married, MARRIED.

Lili's eyes snapped open as she felt Jake's body stiffen, his arms go rigid, breath leaving his body in a gasp of disbelief. Looking up, she saw he was gazing across the room, eyes narrowed, mouth a grim line of displeasure.

Following his line of vision, Lili saw Vivienne and her partner were no longer visible and Jake's head snapped back, eyes scanning the room, his height an asset in searching for his errant wife.

Feeling superfluous and embarrassed, Lili too found her eyes roving the crowd, searching for a flash of a white dress, a glimpse of platinum hair. But all she found was Greg leaning against the wall, his eyes wide and fixed on the spot where Vivienne had been.

Greg shook his head as if to clear it, rubbed at his eyes, and seemed to stagger. Then he too merged into the crowd, pushing between swaying couples until he exited the room through a side door, melting away into the darkness of the night.

"I'm sorry ..." Jake released her, stepped back, anguish visible on his face. "I'm sorry," he said again. "I can't ... I have to ... I'm sorry, Lili ..." and he left her, forcing his way through revellers until they swallowed him up and she could see him no longer.

He left her, standing in mortified misery in the centre of the dance floor, whilst the last notes of the song rang mockingly in her ears.

... if he stayed, she'd show him a sunrise, he just had to stay with her till dawn...

Unable to face anyone; unable to understand what had happened; unable to accept the emotions which had been unleashed, Lili ran. Off the dance floor, into the hall and up the stairs. Avoiding the pleasant sitting room which had been designated a quiet area, she silently stepped over the rope barrier bearing the sign, *private, family only,* and crept up another half flight of stairs.

Knocking quietly on the first door she came to, she waited, heart thumping, for a response. Not getting any, she gently eased the door open and slipped inside.

Lili found herself in a pretty bedroom. A bedside lamp had been left on, and she could see by its dim glow a dressing table piled high with presents, including her daisy chain necklace. This, and the heap of young feminine clothing on the bed, told Lili she'd found Daisy's room.

Breathing a little easier for her trespass, knowing Daisy wouldn't mind, Lili crossed the room to the open, full-length windows, hoping for some air.

Long, flower-sprigged muslin moved in the slight breeze. As she parted their billowy lengths, she realised the double windows were doors opening onto a charming balcony with ornate, wrought iron balustrades. Stepping into the welcoming balm of the summer night, Lili felt tears shudder up from inside.

Why was she crying? She was being ridiculous. She meant nothing to Jake; less than nothing. To be upset because he left her flat in the middle of the floor to go and find his wife, well, that was plain silly.

Gripping the edge of the railing, Lili felt a tear run down her face and sharply told herself to pull herself together. Taking a deep breath, she looked over the edge of the balcony, curious as to which part of the garden it overlooked.

Below was a small, enclosed courtyard garden, a pretty fountain splashing merrily at its heart. In the dim glow of moonlight and the light spilling through open doors below, Lili saw raised beds brimming with sweetly scented herbs and flowers. Two curved benches with high, decorative backs faced each other over the fountain, and a narrow archway led off into the darkness, presumably into the rest of the garden.

Breathing deeply of the still, healing night, Lili pulled back at a sudden movement below. Someone entered the garden from the house. Peeking over, Lili saw Greg.

Staggering, he crossed to one of the benches and shakily sat down. Elbows resting on knees, he dropped his head into his hands and rubbed at his temples, as if trying to dislodge a headache.

Lili frowned, was he drunk? She wondered if she should speak to him, ask if he was okay, but was reluctant to do so, bearing in mind she was currently trespassing.

More footsteps, a flash of white, then Vivienne sashayed into the garden, her body slow and purposeful. She crossed to Greg, hands-on-hips, surveying his bent head in amusement.

"Well, well," she drawled. "What have we got here?"

"Vivienne?" Greg raised bleary eyes to survey her in tired resignation. "What do you want? I've nothing to say to you."

"Really?" Vivienne's voice dripped honey. Lili felt acute discomfort at her role as an unwilling eavesdropper yet didn't move. Telling herself they would hear if she did, she stayed where she was, rooted to the spot with fascinated horror.

"That's funny, Greg. I remember a time when you had plenty to say to me. Whatever happened to your promises to love me forever? Isn't it truly amazing how short a time forever turned out to be?"

Lili's eyes widened with shock. Vivienne and Greg?

"That was before I realised how big a bitch you are, Vivienne, that you're incapable of loving anyone but yourself."

"Well now, I seem to recall I gave you plenty of my love, Greg," Vivienne ran her fingers seductively through his long hair, gripped, and jerked his head back. "Do you need reminding? Have you forgotten that week in Mexico?"

Bending her head, she fastened her scarlet painted lips onto his in a passionate, all-embracing kiss, which made Lili's face flame, and her heart race. For a moment, it seemed Greg was responding, kissing her back, then his hands gripped her arms tightly, and slowly, painfully, he pushed her away. Rising to his feet, he released her, wiping at his mouth with a shudder.

"You're my cousin's wife," he spat the words, disgust, and loathing mingling with naked lust on his face. "If you loved me, Vivienne, it sure as hell didn't take you long to get over it. How long was it? Two, three months? Why did you choose him, Vivienne? Was it to get back at me? Or purely because he's got so much more money than me?"

Vivienne shrugged. A languidly sensual move, it served the purpose of drawing attention to her magnificent breasts. Greg's eyes flicked down.

He swallowed and looked away, a flush of angry desire washing over his face as Vivienne stepped forward, lightly trailing fingers down his chest.

"You want me, Greg..."

"I don't!"

"Don't deny it, don't try to fight it. You want me ... and I want you. Nothing must change. We'll have to be discreet, that's all."

"Discreet?" Greg stared at her disbelievingly. "Jake's like a brother to me. For better or worse, you're his wife. You're strictly off-limits, Vivienne, I would never do that to Jake, never!"

"Oh, I think you will."

Her fingers continued their butterfly-light descent down his body, skimming the loose, white shirt of his highwayman costume, before brushing the front of his cream breeches.

"Never!" Angrily, Greg slapped her hand away.

Giving a low, sultry laugh, Vivienne took his hand and slipped it into her dress. Pouting, she placed her hand over his, moving his fingers against her nipple. Feeling it stiffen and flex beneath his unwilling fingers, her warm, braless flesh teasing and tantalising, Greg groaned, his resolve slipping.

"No."

Teeth gritted, he wrenched his hand away from her magnolia scented skin, away from curves he knew too well, looking with revulsion into the face of the woman who, for a brief time, he had thought himself in love with.

"Perhaps you need another drink, Greg," breathed Vivienne. "Maybe some more champagne?"

Greg stared at her in dawning comprehension.

"You filled my glass up earlier," he said slowly. "And before that, it was filled, and I didn't know who by. It was you, wasn't it?"

"Just being friendly," shrugged Vivienne. "After all, we're family. Why Greg, you're surely not accusing me of trying to get you drunk? On two little glasses of champagne?"

"No, not drunk."

Greg's eyes narrowed he wiped at his clammy forehead, trying to focus.

"Not drunk ... you bitch," he exclaimed. "What the fuck was in the drink?"

"I don't know what you're talking about ..." Vivienne's words were choked off, as Greg gripped her shoulders and shook her hard, anger blazing from his eyes.

"Don't fuck with me, Vivienne, and don't try to manipulate me. You and me, that's over. It was over the day I turned up at your place unexpectedly and found you in bed with someone else. You're a lying, scheming bitch and I wish I'd never met you. If Jake knew the truth about you, about us..."

"Are you going to tell him, Greg?" Vivienne laughed, a low, husky laugh that chilled the blood in Lili's veins. "Because if you do, I'll deny it. In the end, it'll all come down to whose word he believes, and we both know it won't be yours."

"No."

With a gesture of disgust, Greg released her and stepped away, mouth twisting with revulsion.

"I'm not going to say anything. I won't risk Jake cutting himself off from his family because one day when he sees what you are, what an evil, manipulative, whoring bitch you are, he's going to need them around him."

"You'll wait a long time for that day, Greg, trust me."

With a snort of disbelief, Greg walked away, back rigid with anger.

"Oh, and Greg," Vivienne's voice halted him, her soft tones rippling through the balmy night air. "When you're lying in your cold, lonely bed, think about what you turned down, what you could've had. Then think about me with Jake."

"Vivienne?"

Jake's call from another part of the garden reached them. With a muffled curse, Greg stepped through the archway, vanishing into the shadowy garden beyond. Vivienne casually adjusted her dress, posing herself neatly on the bench, seconds before Jake stepped out into the garden.

"Where the hell have you been?" he demanded, voice rough with ill-concealed relief at finding her alone.

"Here," she mused. "By myself, in the night, thinking..."

"I thought you'd gone off with that guy."

"What guy?" Vivienne raised innocent blue eyes.

"Adam, the guy you were dancing with."

"Why would I go anywhere with him?" her voice was soft with naïve surprise. "He asked me to dance, I agreed, and we talked about America. He has family over there. Then I saw you all over that girl, that Lili creature everyone's fawning over..."

Above, Lili stiffened with resentment.

"Lili? You were jealous of Lili?"

At Vivienne's downturned expression and trembling bottom lip, Jake moved to her, clasping her hands, and pulling her to her feet.

"Is that why you ran off?" he demanded.

"I'm sorry."

My word, she's good Lili thought, as Vivienne's blue eyes brimmed with tears.

"I'm sorry," Vivienne continued, dabbing with a fluttery gesture at her eyes. "I guess I got jealous, I love you so much, and to see you dancing with her, draped all over her ... I couldn't stand it."

"But she's nothing to me, I swear it, Vivi, nothing." Shaking her head, her hand held to her mouth in abject misery, Vivienne pushed past him.

"Vivi, wait!" Jake reached for her. Spinning her around to face him, he pulled her close, large arms enfolding her into his chest.

"How can you believe I'd look at anybody else when I'm married to you," he whispered hoarsely. "And at Lili of all people. I only met her tonight. I mean, she seems a perfectly nice girl, but I need a woman, and not just any woman, I need you Vivi, only you."

"Promise?" she murmured. Long, scarlet tipped nails raking his hair, she pulled his head to hers.

"Promise," he muttered, lips closing onto hers.

As the couple below entwined in a deeply intimate kiss, Lili knew she should move, take that step back into the bedroom, but her feet seemed frozen to the spot.

Wiping a hand across her face, Lili found it wet with tears.

Grief for Greg, and the pain he'd been through at the hands of that woman; grief for Jake, for the pain he had yet to come; her own grief, at the total shattering of love's first tentative stirrings.

Softly murmuring words of love, Vivienne pulled Jake's head down to her breast, pushing aside the material of her dress, and offering him one coral tipped nipple, rather as a mother would offer a sweet to a fractious child.

His mouth fastened greedily onto her flesh, and she moaned, arching her back, pressing against his rugged, straining body, throwing her head back so Lili could see the slim, white column of her throat.

Suddenly, she opened her eyes, and stared upwards, straight into Lili's horrified gaze.

Time froze.

For an instant, their eyes locked.

Then, a slow knowing smile spread across Vivienne's perfect face.

"Oh honey," she moaned, her regard never leaving Lili's face. "Make love to me, make love to me here, now …"

She raised her brows in a gesture of challenge, almost daring Lili to stay and watch.

Lili's gasp of horror was drowned out by Vivienne's triumphant, breathless laugh, as Jake took her at her word, pushing her against the wall of the house.

Heart shuddering with shock, Lili finally moved back into the pretty bedroom, its innocent pink, and white frills a shocking backdrop to the unmistakable sounds of the hasty and violent coupling taking place below.

Chapter Nineteen
"He's one of us now. We'll take care of him."

A month later the image of Vivienne's cruelly, triumphant smile still burnt within Lili's mind, as did bittersweet memories of Jake. During the day when she was busy at work or out having fun with her friends, Lili pushed thoughts of him to the back of her mind. But when she was alone, or in the stillest, quietest moments of the night, she remembered, and mourned for what might have been.

It was a busy month. Alex returned from honeymoon, tanned, relaxed, and more than a little put out to find she had been usurped as office babe by Lili. Especially as married Alex was now off the market, whereas Lili was still young, free, and single. But, being a good-natured girl, Alex soon put aside her feelings of pique in favour of awe at the miraculous transformation performed in her absence.

Richard retired, and Lili was contacted by his great-nephew, Martin Madison. An appointment had been made for the following week, and Lili had duly gone to his office not knowing what to expect.

What she found was a young man, barely four years older than herself, but carrying the demeanour and cares of a man twice his age. As Lili sat on an uncomfortable chair on the other side of his desk, listening as he talked at her about stocks and shares, savings plans, portfolios and pensions, her mind wandered.

Mentally, she took away his boring blue suit and replaced it with young, fashionable clothes, such as the ones Kevin wore. Martin's soft brown hair was nice, she decided but needed a more youthful cut; something with a bit of attitude, some edge.

Pulling her mind back, she smiled. "It all sounds very good. So why don't you do what needs to be done, and I'm sure that'll be fine."

"But don't you want to decide for yourself?" Martin seemed staggered at her blasé attitude.

"Umm," Lili considered his question. "No," she decided, smiling at him again. "I trust you completely to do the right thing." Looking at her shining, friendly eyes, Martin decided right there and then, no account would ever receive as much attention as Lili's.

"Who's the pretty girl?"

"What?" Dragging his mind back to the present, Martin followed Lili's gaze to a framed photo of a fashionably pretty girl in her early twenties standing on the corner of his desk.

"Oh, that's Debbie, my fiancée," he explained.

"She's very pretty," replied Lili, looking with interest at the photo. "When's the wedding?"

"It's very soon. The second Saturday in August to be precise."

"Well, congratulations. I hope the weather holds and you have a wonderful day.

"Thank you very much. Now, if I could draw your attention back to your pension options…"

Lili lifted her face to the sunshine, warm on her cheeks and bare shoulders, thinking how lucky Martin and his fiancée were. It was the second Saturday in August, and the weather was perfect. Warm but not scorching, with the slightest of breezes to cool wedding guests, but not destroy hats and hairstyles.

Slipping an arm through Kevin's, she smiled at him as they followed Amy and Lindy across the crowded market square. He grinned back, sharing a silent joke as they watched the two girls stop by the hat stall, and begin trying on hats, laughing at some of the more outrageous ones.

That was something else that had changed during the month, Lili reflected – Lindy's relationship with Kevin and Amy. Upon her return from London, they went clubbing together, but once again, the evening had been soured by Lindy's defensive, hostile attitude, and her dislike of anyone having Lili's attention but herself.

Reluctantly concluding that her dream of them all hanging out as a group of friends was simply not going to happen, Lili tried once more, hoping a quiet simple meal out would help them to bond; but it wasn't to be.

Feeling hopelessly outclassed and out of place in the quietly sophisticated restaurant, Lindy had drunk too much and become noisily belligerent, causing even mild-mannered, easy-going Kevin to glare at her with barely concealed dislike.

Eventually, Lili had given up. As they split the bill and paid, she decided never again would she subject her friends to Lindy's hostility. From now on, she thought sadly, she would see her friends apart. With a heavy heart, she followed the others to where Kevin had left his car. Being mid-week, therefore a work night, everyone was going back to their own homes and weren't staying at Lili's, as had become the tradition at weekends.

Feeling the beginnings of a headache behind her eyes, Lili climbed into the back with Lindy, sitting in silence as Kevin skilfully manoeuvred out of the tight parking space and set off across town.

To Lili's surprise, instead of taking her home first which would have been the logical thing to do, Kevin turned left to drive to the estate where Lindy lived. Opening her mouth to comment on this, Lili quietly closed it again, realising Kevin was dropping Lindy off first because he wanted to get rid of her. She also had a strong suspicion he was going to have words with her about Lindy.

Sighing in weary resignation, not looking forward to having to defend Lindy's behaviour, Lili felt Lindy turn to look at her in the darkness, sensing the anxiety which seemed to hover in the air between them. On an impulse, she took Lindy's hand and gently held it. For a moment, Lindy's hand lay inert and still, then she squeezed fiercely as if she could feel Lili slipping away from her. Was aware she was forcing Lili to make a choice but was terrified of what that choice would be.

Pulling up outside the block of flats where Lindy lived, Lili felt Kevin and Amy's silent relief.

"Well, bye, then," said Lindy, hesitantly. "I'll see you around maybe."

"Bye," replied Kevin briefly, Amy said nothing, merely turned in her seat, and half-smiled a farewell.

"Bye, Lili," Lili heard the despair in the older girl's voice and felt her heart constrict in sympathy.

"Take care, Lindy," she replied. "I'll call you tomorrow."

Lindy brightened at her words, slammed the door shut, and set off towards the block. As they watched her approach the front lobby, a police car parked a little further down the road, switched its headlights on.

"What's going on?" exclaimed Kevin, as two policemen climbed out of the car, walked briskly up the path and intercepted Lindy before she could reach the door.

"I don't know," replied Lili bemused. "But I'm going to find out." Quickly, she scrambled from the car, walking to where the two policemen were talking intently to Lindy.

"Lindy," she said. "Is everything okay?"

Lindy looked up, her face in the fluorescent glare from the nearby streetlight bleached chalk white. In that instant, Lili felt everything English in Lindy's face had drained away, leaving her Asian features standing out in stark contrast.

"Oh Lindy," Lili cried. "What is it? What's happened?"

"Mum's dead," Lindy mumbled the words through clenched lips.

Lili gasped, instinctively putting her arms around the older girl. Lindy stood, rigid and unyielding, then seemed to let go and sagged against her. Lili felt shudders sweep through Lindy's body as if she were fighting the tears. Lili looked over Lindy's shoulder at the policemen.

"Is it true?" she asked. "What happened?"

"Perhaps Miss Smith would like to go indoors," suggested one of them. "A cup of tea might be a good idea. Could you stay with her?" he asked. "I don't think she should be alone right now."

"Yes, yes of course," Lili stroked Lindy's hair back from her face. "Lindy," she said slowly, almost as if talking to someone with limited knowledge of English, "I'm going to tell the others what's happened, then I'll come up with you. After we've spoken to the police, you're coming home with me. We'll pack what you need and get a taxi back to mine."

Lindy nodded, her eyes wide and unfocused. Gently, Lili untangled herself and hurried to the car. At her approach, Amy wound her window down in alarm.

"What's happened? What's the matter?"

"Lindy's mum has died."

"What, how?"

"I don't know. The police haven't told us yet. I'm going to go up to Lindy's flat with them, make tea or something, then I'm taking Lindy back to mine. She shouldn't be on her own. You go, I'll call you tomorrow."

Amy and Kevin glanced at each other. As if a silent message had passed between them, they took off their seatbelts and got out of the car. Kevin sauntered around and took Lili's arm.

"We'll wait," he said.

"Oh, but that's not necessary ..." began Lili.

"We'll wait," he declared firmly. "Then, when you're ready, we'll drop you both off at yours."

"And I'll make the tea," decided Amy, "so you can stay with Lindy."

"Thank you," said Lili, gratefully.

Once squeezed into Lindy's minuscule flat, Amy busied herself in the tiny kitchen, whilst Kevin melted unobtrusively into the background. Lili and Lindy sat on the sofa, Lili with her arm around Lindy, and the policemen told them the sad, rather sordid tale of the demise of Lindy's mother at the desperately young age of 36.

As deaths go, it was rather a pathetic one, but perhaps was in keeping with a life that had been altogether pointless and pitiable. Running away at 16 from an abusive stepfather, Lindy's mother had hit the streets, turning to begging and prostitution to make ends meet. Unintelligent and naïve, she inevitably ended up pregnant from one of the faceless, meaningless, twenty-quid-a-go fucks. Nine months later casually delivered a beautiful, healthy baby girl, who narrowed the paternal candidates down considerably with her distinctly Chinese features.

Moved into a small, one-bedroom flat by Social Services, Lindy was raised in good-natured squalor, her mother loving her in an offhand, careless way, rather as one would love a puppy or a kitten. Supplementing her benefits with one live-in male protector after another, Lindy had grown up witnessing her mother's dependence on external sources – be it alcohol, drugs, or men – seeming unable, or unwilling, to even consider the possibility of being responsible for her own life.

When Lindy also left home at a very young age, albeit under better circumstances than her mother's, she had known she would never go back, that she would somehow make a better job of life than her mother had.

With mixed emotions of affection, pity, and contempt, Lindy sent money to her mother whenever she could spare it. In the three years since she only returned once – a fleeting day trip on the train, not even wanting to stay one night in case that life somehow sucked her back in.

And now, her mother was dead. From the evidence, the police had been able to piece together, and disinterested statements from neighbours, they told Lindy of her mother's latest 'boyfriend'. A hulking great brute of a man who seemed to have a mysteriously never-ending source of cash. He happily supplied her mother with all the fags and booze she wanted, in return for the right to call her flat and body his own.

The neighbours all agreed he seemed all right, leastways they hadn't heard any shouting from the flat, and Lindy's mother had never been seen sporting the 'I walked into a door' bruises so prevalent amongst women living at that level of life.

As to what had happened that night, nobody was sure. All the police could state with certainty, was there had been an emergency call for an ambulance made by a male with fear in his voice, from a phone box two streets away from where Lindy's mother lived. Giving the flat's address, he told them to hurry. Someone was in trouble and needed urgent medical help.

Arriving at the scene, paramedics found Lindy's mother unconscious, a syringe crushed beneath her body. Rushed to hospital, she'd been pronounced dead on arrival. Official verdict – death from a heroin overdose. Unofficial verdict – death from neglect.

Listening to the policeman's solemn, even tones, fingers clasped around the mug of hot sweet tea Amy had pressed into her hands, Lindy's teeth chattered against the rim, tea burning her mouth as she sipped unwillingly at the hot liquid. Feeling guilty because she felt no sorrow, other than an acute awareness of what a waste her mother's life had been, Lindy vowed fiercely, silently, she'd be different, she would amount to something, would be someone. When she died, she'd leave more behind than a daughter untouched to the point of indifference at her demise.

When the police had left, Lili helped Lindy pack up a few belongings. Silently, sympathetically, Kevin had driven them home. Upon reaching Lili's, Amy had climbed from the car and gently hugged Lindy, patting her with sensitive compassion. All her brashness gone, Lindy hugged Amy back, whispering her thanks for the young girl's concern.

The funeral was to be held in Romford. When Kevin and Amy learnt of the date, they both took the day off work and Kevin drove them all down to attend the hasty, and pitifully attended interment.

In wonder at their unspoken, united support, Lindy asked...

"Why are you being so good to me?"

"Because you're a friend," they'd replied simply.

Back at Lili's that night, alone in the guest room officially designated as hers, Lindy sobbed for the first time since learning of her mother's death. The cold walls around her heart which had opened a chink to admit Lili, finally crumbled as she learnt the true meaning of friendship.

Now, walking across the marketplace on a sunny August Saturday, the warmth of Kevin's arm through hers, and laughing at the antics of Lindy and Amy at the hat stall, Lili felt an encompassing sensation of contentment well up inside as she enjoyed her friends' company, feeling secure and loved within her little group.

The only fly in the ointment as far as she could see was with three girls and only one man the group was a little uneven, and Lili worried that Kevin would grow bored of all-female company.

"I need a drink," Kevin announced, looking at his watch. "Let's go to the pub." A chorus of agreements arose.

Entering the cool dimness of The Tavern, Lili blinked, waiting for her eyes to adjust. Already crowded, they managed to get a table by the open front doors, settling down to kill a couple of hours in the company of each other and alcohol.

Three drinks later, it was Lili's round. Dutifully, she gathered up their empty glasses and went to the bar which spanned the entire length of the pub. Setting them down on its polished oak surface, she caught the eye of Dylan the barman, so-called because of his aged hippie appearance, and uncanny likeness to the permanently stoned rabbit of the same name in the Magic Roundabout.

He nodded to indicate he'd seen her, and Lili swung onto a barstool to wait until he finished filling the complicated order the noisy group further down the bar were placing. Leaning on the bar, her gaze idly swept over the rest of the pub, spotting a few familiar faces that were regular fixtures. Abruptly, she stiffened, eyes going back to a gap in the crowd at the far end of the bar, telling herself she must be mistaken and craning her neck to see through the press of bodies. Surely it couldn't be...

Quickly, Lili slithered off the stool and pushed her way to the back of the pub, excusing herself as she moved through the crowd of young men, gaining a few whistles, complimentary comments, and flirtatious offers as she did. Flashing non-committal smiles, Lili squeezed through and saw to her stunned amazement it was him.

"Martin?" she exclaimed. "What are you doing here?"

The young man slumped morosely over his pint, looked up with an uncomprehending gaze. Not recognising her, he bent his head to stare into the dregs of his drink, as if seeking answers to the mysteries of the universe within its amber depths.

Undeterred, Lili slid into the seat opposite, reaching over to touch his hand. He raised his head and stared at her. This time, recognition stirred sluggishly in pain-filled eyes.

"Oh," he said slowly. "Hi, Lili."

"What are you doing here, Martin?" Lili persisted. "You're supposed to be in a church somewhere getting married," realising he was wearing full, traditional wedding garb complete with a top hat, which was sitting on the seat beside him.

"What happened?" she asked slowly.

"She dumped me," Martin replied flatly. "Jilted me at the altar."

"Oh, my God," breathed Lili in horror. "Why?"

"Because she's in love with someone else and has been for ages, I mean, how great is that?"

"Martin, I'm so sorry..."

"It gets worse. Want to know who the other guy is?"

"Only if you want to tell me," replied Lili slowly.

"It's Derek," he stated. "My best friend and best man, or rather, ex-best friend and ex-best man."

"Oh Martin, I don't know what to say."

"My best friend... I mean, how fucking clichéd is that? Couldn't she have been a bit more original? Cookery classes!" he exclaimed.

Lili blinked in surprise. "I beg your pardon?"

"Cookery classes. It's where she told me she was, every Tuesday and Thursday. Told me she wanted to learn to cook so she could make great meals for me when we were married. Christ, what a bloody fool I was to swallow that. Ha! Get it? Swallow that?"

Lili saw the dumb misery in his eyes and her heart turned over in sympathy. On an impulse, she moved to sit beside him, placing the hat on the table. Putting an arm around him, she held him tight and whispered.

"I'm so sorry. What a horrible, horrible thing to happen. How did you find out?"

"I'm stood at the church like a right lemon, waiting for my bride, wondering where the hell Derek's disappeared to, when Debbie's dad comes in white as a sheet, looking like he wants to kill someone. He tells me, in front of everyone, Derek had come to the house demanding to speak to Debs. Next thing, she's ripping off her wedding dress and Derek's grabbing her suitcase. She tells them the wedding's off, she's in love with Derek. Debbie's mum asks her what she's talking about. How can she possibly be in love with Derek when she's due to marry me in 20 minutes?"

"And what did Debbie say?" Lili felt shudders running through his body, and knew by the wetness on her neck, he was sobbing.

"She says to tell me she's really, *really* sorry. She tried to fight against it, they both had, but at the end of the day, she couldn't go through with a wedding doomed to end in divorce, because she no longer ... loved me!"

"Ssh," soothed Lili, rocking him slightly in her arms. "It's okay, you let it all out."

"They've gone on our honeymoon!" he exclaimed.

"What?" Lili stared in outrage. "They've done what?"

"Gone on our honeymoon. Two weeks in Jamaica – which I paid for."

"But that's ... that's ..." Lili struggled for a word to describe how appalled she was.

"When he finished telling me, Debbie's dad stood there. You could've heard a pin drop in that church. Then he put a hand on my shoulder and said, I'm sorry son, I'm so sorry. He looked so old, so beaten, and I could see how upset he was by what she'd done. They were all looking at me, staring; all those people, our families, our friends ... I couldn't stand it, so I walked down the aisle alone ..." his mouth twitched with bitter humour at the memory.

"Nobody followed me, I think they were too shocked and, I don't know, maybe they thought I needed to be on my own. I walked out of the church and kept walking. I walked into town, ending up here. I needed a drink, but all the money I had was some change in my pocket for the collection, enough to buy a pint. I suppose I should go home, but don't want to, I don't know what to do, Lili," he looked at her in despair.

"Well, I do," Lili replied firmly. "You wait here whilst I order some drinks, then you're coming to sit with me and my friends."

"I don't know," Martin replied doubtfully. "I'm not very good company right now."

"That doesn't matter," Lili said. "You shouldn't be on your own. Sometimes it's better to be with strangers than with family at a time like this. Now, you wait here, I'll buy drinks and tell them about you, then I'll come and get you. What would you like to drink?"

"But I haven't got any money..."

"That doesn't matter, I have," Lili said, grinning wryly at him. "You, of all people, know I can afford to stand you a few drinks."

Martin nodded, a reluctant smile breaking out on his face.

"Okay," he said, looking more cheerful. "So long as your friends don't mind."

"They won't. You wait here, I'll be back. Oh, what are you drinking?"

"Pint of Abbot."

"Okay," Lili walked back to the bar and waited until Dylan sauntered over. Taking her order, he raised an eyebrow in Martin's direction.

"What's the story there?" he asked curiously.

"His fiancée jilted him," Lili replied quietly.

"Ouch," Dylan's face wrinkled in sympathy. "When was the wedding?"

"Today."

"Poor bastard," Dylan replied, waving away her money. "This round is on the house." Thanking him, Lili collected up the drinks and took them back to the others, who looked at her in surprise.

"Where on earth have you been?" Lindy asked. "We were about to send out search and rescue."

"A friend of mine's here and he's in big trouble." Quickly, Lili sat down and told them everything. When she finished, there was silence around the table and Lili saw expressions of concern and sympathy on their faces, the compassion shining in Amy's eyes.

"That poor man," she said slowly. "That poor, poor man. What an awful experience to go through."

"The thing is," began Lili nervously, "I was kind of wondering if it'd be okay if he came and sat with us. Only, he's got nowhere else to go and I don't think he should be alone right now."

"Of course, absolutely, not a problem," the refrain of agreements rang out, and Lili beamed with relief.

"Thank you," she said gratefully. "I'll go and get him."

Leading Martin to the table, Lili saw her friends waiting as if viewing them through Martin's eyes. Amy, small and fragile, hauntingly pretty with long, blonde hair caught up behind her ears in two long bunches flowing almost to mid-waist. Lindy, confident and strong, her darkly foreign good looks enough to make her stand out in any crowd. And then there was Kevin, tall and rugged, tousled blond hair bleached pale by exposure to the sun, framing a tanned and handsome face, his eyes warm with sympathy as Lili and Martin reached their table.

"Everyone, this is Martin. Martin, this is Amy, Lindy and Kevin."

"Hi, Martin." Amid the chorus of greetings, Martin flushed slightly and sat quickly in the chair which Kevin thoughtfully pulled up for him.

"So, Martin," Lindy, as usual, wasted no time cutting straight to the chase. "Lili told us what your bitch of a fiancée has done."

"Yes, well," said Martin, plainly unsure how to respond.

"Want me to kill her for you?"

Leaning forward in deadly seriousness, Lindy looked into his eyes, a ghost of a smile passing over her face at the shock on his.

Martin hesitantly returned her smile. "If you wouldn't mind," he replied. "That would be great."

"Sure, no problem," replied Lindy cheerfully. "How do you want it done?"

"I'm a great believer in the old head in a gas oven method," chipped in Kevin. "It's quick and easy, leaves no mess to clear up."

"Nah," Lindy rejected the suggestion. "It's too quick, too easy. For a crime of this magnitude, a more painful end is required."

"What do you suggest then?" enquired Martin, getting into the spirit of things.

"Well," Lindy considered with her head on one side. "Personally, I favour disembowelling. Okay, it's a little messy, but it sure is fun, and certainly gets the point across how pissed off you are."

"True, true," Martin nodded his head seriously.

"Just going to the loo," Lili murmured slipping out of her seat, leaving them fiercely debating the merits of hanging versus drowning. Quickly, she headed in the direction of the ladies situated at the top of a long flight of stairs, reached through a doorway to the right of the bar. Luckily, the payphone was also at the top of the stairs.

Searching through her bag for her address book, Lili fished out some change and dialled Richard's home number. It barely rang before the phone was snatched up.

"Hello?" Richard's voice was alarmed and fearful.

"Richard, it's Lili, I..."

"Oh, Lili," the disappointment in his voice was evident. "I thought you were ... never mind. I'm sorry, Lili, I can't talk now, we're in the middle of a family crisis."

"I know," Lili replied. "It's all right, I've found him. He's here, Martin I mean, he's with me."

"What? He's with you? But ... where are you, Lili?"

"We're in the pub. We came in for a drink, my friends and I, and that's when I found Martin. He was sitting at a table, nursing a pint. He told me what happened. Oh, Richard, it's awful."

"I know," Richard sighed, his voice sounding old and tired. "Is he all right, Lili?"

"Not really," she replied quietly. "Would you be?"

"No," Richard sighed again. "I suppose I wouldn't. Thank you for calling, Lili, his parents are frantic with worry. If you keep him there, I'll send his father to pick him up. Which pub did you say you were in?"

"The thing is," Lili broke in quickly. "The thing is, he doesn't want to go home, not yet. He doesn't want to face everyone and go over and over it all. I think he wants to put it to one side, for tonight anyway. There'll be plenty of time to talk about it later. For now, he needs to step back from it."

"What are you suggesting, Lili?" Richard sounded thoughtful as if her words had struck a chord.

"He's with us, Richard, we'll look after him. Tell his parents not to worry, he's in good hands. I wanted to let you know he's okay, not busy killing himself or something, and that he's with us."

"All right, Lili, we'll play it your way. But will you promise me he'll phone his parents tomorrow morning? They're very worried about him."

"Yes, I'll make sure he calls them, but please tell them not to worry. He's one of us now. We'll take care of him."

Hanging up the phone, Lili thought about what she'd said, realising it was true. Martin was one of them now. It was funny ... only that afternoon she'd been concerned because Kevin was the only guy in the group and now, here was Martin.

She went downstairs, saw the jukebox standing to one side and was unable to resist its shiny chrome and red surface. Lili had a love/hate relationship with the jukebox. She loved that she could choose whatever music she wanted to listen to but hated it because the writing on the labels was so small, and they whizzed past her eyes so fast, most of the time Lili ended up choosing songs at random, without a clue as to what she'd picked.

It had become a standing joke amongst the pub regulars that Lili believed the jukebox possessed. It played songs she hadn't picked, couldn't possibly have picked, because no one with any degree of coolness would have chosen that song.

Pushing in her pound coin, Lili wrinkled her brow in concentration, trying to make out the tiny letters on the playlists. Determined not to end up picking something by the Dooleys, as had happened last time, she stared at the titles as the letters performed their usual little dance.

Distracted by an outburst of noisy laughter from a group in the corner, Lili lost the plot completely and ended up pushing buttons haphazardly, heart sinking as she realised, she had no idea what she'd chosen.

Making her way back to the table, she slid into her seat and sipped her drink. The conversation had moved on from 101 ways to kill your cheating fiancée, to which beers went best with curry.

"I've been to the jukebox," she announced, rather in the way, someone would tell of a pilgrimage to a sacred site.

"Oh no," the collective moan rang round the table. Martin looked surprised.

"What did you choose, Lili?" demanded Lindy. "Oh please, don't let it be Frank Sinatra again."

Lili shrugged sheepishly, and Kevin sighed in despair. "Lili has a problem with the jukebox," he explained to Martin, "in that she's completely unable to grasp the simple concept of reading the label before you subject the rest of the pub to the song."

"It's not my fault," Lili protested laughing. "I can't help it if that jukebox is possessed by the devil." There was a click as the first record dropped into place. To Lili's horror, and Martin's amusement, the squeaky voice of Leo Sayer informed everyone they had a cute way of walking.

"Lili!" groaned half the pub…

A couple of drinks later, Martin's emotions had naturally evolved from stunned disbelief, through grief, and had now entered the bitterly belligerent stage.

"Bitch," he exclaimed, swigging aggressively from his pint. There was a murmur of agreement. Amy, looking concerned at the direction the conversation was taking, exchanged an apprehensive glance with Lili. "Cookery lessons, ha!" This was a by-now-familiar refrain as Martin constantly harked back to it, seeming to view it the single most damning aspect of his ex-fiancée's perfidy.

Lili glanced at her watch, noted it was nearly half-past four. Her action triggered a reflexive movement from the others; there was a general bustle of finishing drinks and gathering up belongings.

"What?" Martin too gulped down the last of his beer. "What's happening? Where are we going now?"

"Back to mine," Lili informed him, "to get ready."

"Ready?" he asked in confusion. "Ready for what?"

"Clubbing!" the girls chorused, and Kevin grinned.

"Want to come, mate?" he casually enquired. Lili could have kissed him for the easy, good-natured way he had accepted Martin into the group.

"Are you sure?" Martin's face was a mixture of doubt and hope, as if he wanted to, but was unsure it was appropriate to be out having fun after what had happened.

"Well," Kevin considered, "much as I enjoy having my own private harem…"

"Oi!" objected Lindy, poking him in the ribs.

"It'd be great having another bloke along to even things up," Kevin finished, rubbing at his ribs, and shooting Lindy an evil look. "Sorry Lindy love," he drawled. "You may think you're one of the boys, but you just don't cut it."

"Hey!"

"Well, if you're sure …" Martin began hesitantly.

"Of course, we're sure," Amy reassured him gently. "You shouldn't be alone tonight, I mean, it must be healthier to be out amongst people, rather than sitting alone brooding about it."

Martin nodded, a sudden thought hitting him.

"My parents! I hadn't thought ... they'll be worried, I must call them." He looked around desperately as if expecting a phone to miraculously appear.

"It's okay," Lili reassured him. "I phoned Richard ages ago, told him you're with us and that you'll call your parents in the morning."

"Oh," Martin stared at her, at a loss. "Thank you," he eventually murmured. "But I suppose I'd better go home tonight," he continued, reluctantly.

"Not unless you want to," Lili stated briskly. "Everyone always stays at mine on Saturdays. There's plenty of room, and you're more than welcome."

"Oh," he said again.

"Lili's is the greatest place to stay," Kevin informed him with a grin. "She has the coolest toys."

"Okay," replied Martin, brightening a little at Kevin's friendly comment, then looked down at himself and his face fell.

"But I can't," he stated. "I mean, I don't have anything to wear, I don't want to go clubbing in top hat and tails."

"Could he borrow some of your stuff?" Amy asked Kevin.

"Well, I don't mind," he replied, "but it would all drown him, no disrespect mate," he continued to Martin. "We're built differently."

Lili studied them ... it was true. Whilst Kevin's build was very young farmer, Martin's was more, young conservative.

"And anyway," continued Kevin. "Whilst I don't have a problem with lending you shower gel and deodorant, I do draw the line at you borrowing my toothbrush and underwear," he exchanged a wry grin with Martin, and both men shuddered.

"There are some rules," Kevin stated firmly, "men do not break."

"Oh, stop," drawled Lindy in disgust. "What do you think you are, some kind of secret society?"

"Have no fear, Cinderella," laughed Lili. "You shall go to the ball. Come on."

"Where are we going?" Martin asked, scrambling to his feet, following as they all traipsed out of the pub to stand blinking in the bright sunshine. It was always a shock leaving The Tavern. Its dimly lit, cave-like interior, making it easy to forget sunlight still existed a few feet away.

"TopMan," replied Lili. "It's only half four, we've got enough time..."

"Time for what?" asked Martin in confusion.

"Time ..." began Lili, looking conspiratorially at Lindy and Amy, "for a makeover," they chanted and laughed at the look on his face.

Grinning, Kevin clapped a friendly hand on his shoulder. "Give in and go with the flow, mate," he advised. "You'll end up doing what they want anyway, so you may as well save your breath."

An hour later, they were back at Lili's laden with shopping bags. The girls were breathless with laughter, although Martin still seemed in shock. After being hustled, protesting, into the changing rooms, armfuls of clothes being ferried in and out by an obliging, grinning Kevin, the girls hovering impatiently outside, Martin had emerged suitably clad for a night out on the town, looking uncertainly down at his new apparel. Lindy had let out a long whistle of appreciation which had Martin reddening and looking helplessly at the others.

"You look wonderful," reassured Amy softly. Going even redder, Martin ducked back into the changing rooms to try on some casual chinos and t-shirts.

After Lili paid for the selected clothes and underwear, Martin promising to pay her back, they paid a quick visit to Boots to buy basic toiletries. Glancing at Martin out of the corner of her eye, Lili couldn't help thinking how attractive he looked in the stone-coloured chinos and khaki t-shirt; so much better than the awful, middle-aged suit he'd been wearing the first time she'd met him.

"What are we eating?" she enquired, flopping down on the sofa.

"Pizza," stated Lindy firmly, Amy nodding in agreement.

"We always have pizza," groaned Kevin. "For once, can't we have something else? I'm starving. I fancy a big, sod-off burger with all the trimmings and half the potato crop of Suffolk as chips. What do you want Lili?"

"I don't mind," Lili replied. "Anything is good. I'm hungry too."

"Pizza then," crowed Lindy. "Three against one, so that's settled."

"Wait a minute," demanded Kevin. "What do you fancy Martin?"

"Umm," Martin thought about it. "Well, right about now I should be dining on champagne, prawn cocktail, chicken supreme and tropical Pavlova. But as there's been a change in plan, I think a monster burger and chips sounds good."

Amy's expression softened at his words, and when Lindy's mouth opened to argue further, she laid a cautionary hand on her arm.

"Then that's exactly what you'll have," she stated.

Kevin straightened and smirked. "I feel there's been a power shift," he stated. "The testosterone levels have risen, and man no longer stands alone." He ducked to avoid the cushions thrown at him with force by all three girls...

After huge portions of greasy burgers bursting at the seams with onions, bacon, cheese slices, and barbecue sauce, together with glistening mountains of ketchup-drenched chips had been ordered, delivered, and consumed, the girls disappeared upstairs with CDs and vodka to begin the arduous task of transforming themselves.

Kevin collected up the greasy wrappings, followed by Martin, placing them in the bin outside the back door. Staring at the garden for a moment, already seeing in his mind's eye how it could be, he started as Martin quietly spoke.

"It seems hard to believe I should now be at my wedding reception."

Kevin turned to look at him. Martin's eyes were fixed on some point in the garden, his expression unreadable, his mouth set fast. Kevin sighed, wishing Amy or Lili were there. Not even good with his own emotions, he was adrift when it came to dealing with other peoples.

"I'm sorry," he said. Martin's eyes refocused, he shrugged and smiled a wan smile of resignation.

"It's strange," he said. "I've been with Debs for four years; lived with her for two, been engaged for one. This is the woman I was planning on spending the rest of my life with, but now, when I think about her, what she did, I feel nothing for her at all, just anger and hurt pride. Maybe ..." he swallowed, thinking the unthinkable.

"Maybe it's for the best, what's happened. I mean, if I can be here stuffing my face with chips, looking forward to going clubbing with strangers, rather than sitting at home wracked with grief, doesn't it suggest perhaps I didn't love her either? That even though I can't agree with the way she did it, perhaps Debs showed more honesty and courage than me in calling the wedding off?"

Kevin stuffed his hands in his pockets, rocking back on his heels, unsure of what to say, or how to respond to Martin's unexpected words. Turning, he finally looked at the other man, and in that silent non-verbal way that men communicate, and women can't understand, both decided the other was a decent bloke and had the potential to be a good mate.

"Yeah," Kevin agreed eventually, "perhaps." Both men nodded, turning to survey the garden, stances a mirror image of each other, feet planted solidly, hands in pockets, lips pursed, brows furrowed in deep thought.

"Look at that fat cat," Martin exclaimed, breaking the profound, manly, pondering-the-mysteries-of-the-universe silence. Kevin followed Martin's gaze, smiling as Boris sauntered casually up the garden, big ugly face turned skywards to the swifts swooping and chattering, so tantalisingly close.

"That's Boris," he said. "Lili's cat," he elucidated further.

"Really?" Martin surveyed Boris for a moment as he rolled over in the dirt in a most undignified fashion, exposing his corpulent paunch to the world. "Surprising," he muttered. "I would have thought Lili's cat would have been something sleek and sophisticated, like a Siamese or something like that, I mean, Lili's so ... well, so..."

"Quite." Kevin agreed dryly, turning his head to cast Martin a long, level gaze, stating louder than any spoken word, 'hands-off, don't even think about it'. Martin's eyes widened slightly. He swallowed and nodded, message received and understood.

The portly feline rolled over, recognising Kevin as someone who knew how to handle a tin opener and trotted across hopefully, fawning shamelessly over Kevin's legs as he knelt and scratched behind the cat's ears.

"Boris is another of Lili's lame ducks," continued Kevin.

"Lame ducks?" Martin frowned.

"Lili collects strays," explained Kevin. "Boris, Lindy, you, Amy and myself … we're all strays, misfits, broken biscuits in some way. Lili unites us all into something much more. I mean, other than this Derek prick, do you have any other friends?"

Martin considered the question for a moment. Reluctantly, and almost shamefacedly, he shook his head.

"No," he agreed. "We saw lots of people, but they were all Debbie's friends, not mine. I doubt if I'll ever see any of them again. I wouldn't be surprised if most of them didn't already know about Debbie and Derek, I'm sure the girls did anyway."

"We didn't have any friends either," said Kevin. "Because of … well, things that have happened, neither Amy nor I had any real friends at all until we met Lili, and then through her, Lindy."

"Yeah, Lindy," Martin grimaced. "She seems … feisty?"

"Oh, she's that all right," laughed Kevin. "But don't let the tough shell fool you. Underneath, she was as desperate and needy as the rest of us. No friends, drifting through life. Until Lili, that is."

From an upstairs window floated the sound of girlish laughter. Glancing up at the sound, Martin caught Kevin's eye and smiled.

"Sounds like they're having fun," he stated.

"Yeah, it's what Lili likes best – being with friends and having fun. It's odd … in a way Lili seems older than us all, as if she's been through something that's scarred her, made her wary of people. Yet, in other ways she's as innocent as a child; naïve and trusting, as if she's experiencing life for the very first time. It's that fascinating mix of naivete and sophistication that makes her so special, so wonderful…"

Kevin broke off, aware of Martin's quizzical expression. Flushing slightly, he cleared his throat, turning his gaze back to the garden.

"So, what happens now?" Taking pity on him, Martin changed the subject, breaking the awkward silence which had descended on them both. "What's the routine?"

"Well, as soon as the bathroom's clear we mount a raid on it. Then, because the girls still won't be ready, we have a go on the PlayStation."

"PlayStation?" exclaimed Martin excitedly. "Lili's got PlayStation?"

"And tons of games. Told you Lili's is the coolest place to play."

An hour later, exactly as Kevin had predicted, he and Martin were sprawled on the sofa engrossed in a game on the PlayStation. Both were freshly showered, shaved, and changed, the different brands of shower gel, deodorant, and aftershave lingering in the air in a not unpleasant manner.

Frowning in concentration as Kevin's car overtook him on a hairpin bend, Martin sensed movement at the door. Taking his eyes off the controls, he stared at the visions posing in the doorway.

He already knew the three girls were pretty in their individual ways. Lindy, the archetypical, male fantasy of a doe-eyed, far eastern woman. Amy, a blonde doll, whose fragile prettiness stirred protective feelings in the male breast. Lili, whose striking features, and friendly nature were naturally appealing. They were girls no man would ever be ashamed to be seen with.

But now ... who was this trio of beauties? This stunning collection of women with legs that went on forever; women whom any man would kill to call his own. They smiled knowingly at his slack-jawed, wide-eyed reaction, posing for his benefit.

Lindy was an exotic feast in black and fuchsia, bobbed black hair clipped up at the sides to expose a long, swan-like neck, eyes seductively outlined in black. Amy was a vision in ice blue, long, blonde mane rippling down her back, large blue eyes made enormous with clever use of eye shadow. And Lili, whose slender body was encased in scarlet, her pouting, Slavic features making his heart rate trip and his palms go clammy.

"Shit," was all he could think to say. Kevin smiled in sympathy.

"I tell you, mate," he said, casually running Martin's car off the road to explode in a dazzling fireball. "Mere women go up those stairs, fucking goddesses come down..."

The club was hot and steamy; crowded with hordes of beautiful people all out to lose themselves, if only for one night, in collective, mindless pleasure. Singletons roamed the club, searching for prey, its strobe-lit dance floor a modern-day mating market as people eyed, assessed, discarded, and connected in ageless, timeless ritual.

Lili and her friends conquered the dance floor, making it their own. Determined not to let Martin brood, the girls bullied him onto the floor. Ignoring his protestations of two left feet, they flirted and danced with him, forcing him to move. They acted up to him until his body relaxed and began to flow with the pulsing, throbbing beat, and he was the envy of every red-blooded male, having three such highly desirable females dancing with him.

Alcohol flowed, spirits soared, hearts raced, and bodies sweated in the sensual, stifling, sticky atmosphere. Feeling the room cartwheel around her, Lili wisely switched to water, seeing that Amy and Lindy had done the same.

Something seemed to enter them that night. An almost frantic, desperate desire to be wild and reckless, set their hearts pumping and pulses spiking. At last, Lili headed for a chair, determined to sit at least one dance out. She stopped in her tracks as the familiar strains of her favourite trance track juddered from the speakers.

Spinning around, she caught the DJs eye. He grinned, saluted her, and gestured towards the floor. Grabbing Amy and Lindy by the hands, she dragged them, protesting, back the way they'd come. As usual, the music swallowed her whole, its beat throbbing up through the floor, through her feet, into her brain, until her whole body was the music and she simply existed in that moment.

When the track finished and she opened her eyes, it was to find Martin staring at her in stunned awe, whilst the others grinned at his amazement. Dropping an arm around her in a friendly hug, Kevin smiled at her flushed, dazed expression.

"Was it good for you too, honey?" he drawled.

Later, gulping water thirstily, Lili fended off questions from an over-excited Martin.

"Jeez, Lili," he exclaimed. "Where'd you learn to dance like that? That was amazing, I've never seen anything like it. It was like the music was inside you." Lili squirmed, embarrassed by his admiration and the considering look in his eye; a look which hinted he might be prepared to forget about his erstwhile fiancée if a certain brown-eyed, dark-haired maiden gave him the green light.

"Oh listen," she gasped thankfully, as the next song began. "I love this one." Grabbing his hand, she tugged him onto the floor, snagging Lindy and Amy on the way.

A classic rock anthem – they all knew the words. The dance floor erupted with men playing air guitars to the introduction, and women acting out the lyrics. As one, the masses swung into the chorus.

Lili looked around frantically for Kevin; they should all be together for this one. For some reason, it was important all her gang were there, around her. Suddenly, he was beside her, warm blue eyes smiling as he picked up the beat. Voices raised, they hoarsely belted out the words of the classic Bon Jovi track of sticking together through hard times, coming together in an anthem of hope and despair. Joined at the hands, they raised their arms as one, singing with all their hearts.

Feeling the warmth of her friends' hands, Lili felt her heart would burst from happiness. So many years alone, so many years praying, longing, and wishing for friends, now she had them – four of the best friends in the world.

It was good. It was better than good, more than she had ever dreamed possible. Laughing wildly as the song ended, she dragged them all into a group hug; her gang, her friends…

Chapter Twenty

"I can't say I blame you, sweetie. He is rather gorgeous."

The day before Daisy's wedding dawned bright and clear, the sun peeking coyly over the horizon, promising a day of balmy, blissful heat. The weather forecast for the rest of the weekend was equally optimistic.

Picking her way gingerly around piles of assorted building debris littering the hall, Lili placed her overnight case near the front door and hung her wedding outfit in its protective bag on the lounge door. She held onto the pretty pink hatbox, not wanting to risk getting it dirty.

Surveying the state of the hall, thinking about the state of the house in general, Lili sighed. Renovation work on the house had been an ongoing concern for almost a year now. Although Conrad assured her the end was in sight, a few short weeks away, Lili wondered if things would ever be finished; ever be straight.

It had been an interesting year – the best of Lili's life despite the random acts of mass destruction as her beautiful old home was given a facelift. The biggest project by far was the gutting of the kitchen and the building of the conservatory.

Lili remembered Christmas plans having to undergo a radical, last-minute change, as an unexpected delay in the delivery of her kitchen meant the gang had to spend Christmas Day in Kevin and Amy's cramped flat, instead of in the more spacious surroundings of Lili's house.

Lili smiled, recalling Martin's disgust at his parents' insistence he spend Christmas Day with his family, not with his friends. So, on the actual day, it had been the four original gang members of Lili, Kevin, Amy, and Lindy, bumping knees around the tiny table, gorging on the fantastic feast prepared by a flushed Amy.

Boxing Day had been spent together though and in Lili's house. The problem of having no cooking facilities was negated by having a massive buffet and firing up the new gas barbecue in the big, empty space which was to eventually be Lili's dream kitchen and conservatory.

Thinking of how the kitchen looked now, Lili couldn't help the smile of possessive wonder which spread over her face. It was without a doubt, the most beautiful thing she'd ever seen. Sleek, futuristic looking, pale wooden cabinets, with a gleaming slab of granite worktop, the price of which had made Lili gulp, until she saw it in situ, instantly falling in love with its coolly perfect, midnight blue surface, the twinkling sparkles of silver deep within its heart. At Amy's suggestion, slabs of marble and oak were inset into the granite, providing perfect surfaces for chopping and making pastry. These slabs could then be removed and washed with ease.

Almost complete, the kitchen was awaiting the delivery of a massive refectory table that Conrad had found for her. Already, an eclectic assortment of wooden chairs stood in the conservatory, waiting for the parties and dinners Lili had planned.

The rest of the house was also in its penultimate stage, and it was possible to see glimpses of how it would be. After the construction of the conservatory, the biggest job had been taking down the wall between the two reception rooms. Lili had no concept of how much dust would be released when the old lathe and plaster wall was dismantled, or how far this dust would travel. Despite sealing the doors to both rooms with plastic sheeting, clouds of the pervasive substance had billowed throughout the house, settling everywhere there was a surface, even penetrating through cupboard doors, so all Lili's clothes acquired a fine coating of the pale, powdery matter.

Outside, things had been as chaotic, with Kevin taking the garden back to bare bones, before skilfully, patiently, reassembling it into an elegant and beautiful haven, complete with a perfectly situated summer house boasting an electrical supply to run a small fridge and music system. There was a shady, wooded area at the bottom, an ideal retreat on hot summer days, and a large area spanning the entire width of the house paved in gorgeous, old, red bricks which a specialist company had artfully laid in a traditional herringbone pattern.

The garden had been expensive, but Lili considered it worth every penny. Already, the scene of many parties, Lili would wander out there early in the morning, coffee in hand, to look at all the beautiful, and to her eyes, unknown plants. She felt the garden suited her, marvelling at Kevin's talent, especially as he only had weekends, evenings, and the odd bank holiday to perform this miracle.

On a personal level, the year had found the group of friends bonding tightly into a strong, close-knit entity. It hadn't all been plain sailing; there had been minor disagreements, personality clashes, and misunderstandings. But, overall, it had been a magical year for Lili, as she learnt the true pleasure of spending large amounts of time with people she cared deeply for.

Amy had blossomed from a pretty, but shy, teenager, into a beautiful and outgoing young woman, her interest in food and cooking expanding into an all-consuming passion. Encouraged by the others, Amy attended several cookery courses of increasingly higher levels of expertise until, on the last one, the tutor exclaimed there was no more she could be taught. She was a natural who cooked on instinct; a pinch of this, a dash of that. She was, he declared, that rarest of creatures ... a born chef.

Kevin, too, had changed over the year. Working on Lili's garden had reawakened his love of all things gardening, and he felt even more keenly all that he had lost on the death of his parents. Physically, he'd changed too. Doing most of the labour himself to keep costs down, his muscles had strengthened and grown until his already rugged physique became one that made women take a second look; his blond, good looks heightened by the tan achieved through so much time spent outside.

But one thing had not changed; the intense, at times almost painful, love he felt for Lili. Spending time with her, working with her in the garden, watching her face glowing with happiness, Kevin knew he was falling even deeper in love, and that there was nothing he wouldn't do for her.

Yet, Lili was oblivious to his feelings. To her, Kevin was a dearly beloved friend; an integral, essential part of her group of much-loved friends. She marvelled at his skills, valued his friendship, and appreciated his rock steady, constant good nature.

Kevin knew if he tried to take their relationship onto the next level, he ran the risk of damaging their friendship; that such an action could splinter their little band. The risks were simply too great, so Kevin never even hinted to Lili of his true feelings. Only his sister, Amy, guessed his regard for Lili went deeper than that of a mere friend, though she never spoke of it to him. Martin too, sometimes, remembered the unspoken warning Kevin had shot his way that first day, yet, as time went by, he wondered if maybe he'd misunderstood, or that Kevin had been joking.

It had been a difficult year for Martin. After his drastic introduction into the gang, he suffered an understandable backlash of negative emotions over his cancelled wedding. Moods swinging widely from relief at his escape to blinding rage, to weepy regret, made Martin a complex person to be friends with, but the group stuck with him. Understanding his intensely conflicting emotions, they patiently listened to his grievances, sympathised with his anguish, and agreed with his rants.

Gradually though, Martin came through the experience, emerging on the other side, happier than he had ever been in his life. So much so, that on bumping into Debbie and Derek in the club six months later, Martin had been able to calmly address them, before joining his friends on the dance floor, where they were the undisputed rulers; body language so in tune, they seemed to move as five parts of the same creature.

Watching her handsome, somehow changed, ex-fiancé with his group of glamorous friends, did Debbie glance at her plump and downright ordinary new husband and wonder? Possibly, but Martin no longer cared. As far as he was concerned, Debbie jilting him was the best thing that could have happened. Because of that one selfish action, he met Lili and her friends, now his friends and life had never been sweeter.

Perhaps the biggest change had occurred in Lindy. Never shaking off her feeling of insecurity, Lindy buried it deep within, fearful of lashing out at her friends in a rash moment of inverse snobbery. Painfully aware her upbringing was reflected in her attitudes and accent, Lindy quietly set about re-inventing herself.

Taking Lili and Amy as role models, she began to take an interest in food and wine, and to care about her appearance; to understand even though she was, in her words 'just a cleaner', that was no reason why her hair shouldn't always be freshly washed, and her face made up.

Gradually, partly through spending so much time with her friends, partly through a conscious effort on her part, her accent softened and changed, losing its harsh abrasiveness to become more rounded; her vocabulary extending as the walls of Lindy's hitherto narrow world expanded in all directions.

Listening to Lili enthuse about her friendship with Conrad, Lindy had bitten back her instinctive reaction, instead vowing to reserve judgement. Upon finally meeting Conrad, Lindy realised labels were unfair and dangerous things to apply to people. As she saw through his outrageous exterior, to the good and loyal heart beating within, she felt ashamed of her ugly preconceptions.

During the year, various others had come and gone within the group. Attempting to cure himself of Lili, Kevin tried dating other women. No relationship ever lasted longer than a few weeks, and he finally admitted to himself that until the situation with Lili was resolved, it was unfair to use innocent women as poor substitutes.

Martin, too, had a few dalliances, but his newfound freedom and unfamiliar status as handsome, carefree, bachelor boy, was not one he was willing to relinquish. Women came and went, but ultimately all seemed to demand he make a choice – spend less time with his friends, and more with them. As far as Martin was concerned, this was the easiest decision in the world to make. With a mixture of amusement and concern, the group watched as Martin cut a swathe through the female population, earning a reputation as a love 'em and leave 'em, Casanova.

Lindy was more discreet over her affairs. As all her emotional and companionship needs were met by the group, that left sexual needs. Falling into an affair with a client's husband, Lindy kept it a secret from the others, sensing they would disapprove of such a sordidly illicit, pointless relationship.

The affair lasted three months, Lindy discovering there was a lot more to sex than she previously thought, and only ending when Lindy turned up to clean as normal and discovered her client sobbing. She confided in Lindy with an almost desperate need to talk, about how she was convinced her husband was having an affair, and how devastated and scared she was. If he left her, what would become of her and their three, small children?

Feeling cheap and dirty, Lindy ended the affair. After that, she made sure her few, purely sexual flings, were with partners as emotionally unencumbered as she.

On a professional level, things were distinctly looking up for Lindy in that she was now an employer. After Christmas, Martin casually mentioned his cousin was looking for a little job that could be fitted in around the school run to earn her some pin money. He remembered Lindy complaining she had more jobs than she could handle and wondered if she'd be prepared to pass one of her jobs on to his cousin. Shrugging, Lindy agreed, only to look astonished when Lili interrupted.

"No, don't pass one of your jobs along," she ordered.

"Why not?" Lindy enquired in surprise, and the others looked up in interest.

"Don't simply pass it on. Tell her she can work for you, and charge your client your normal rate," Lindy, being a hard-working, honest cleaner, commanded quite high rates. "Pay Martin's cousin a bit less, then you keep the difference."

The others gaped at such a stunningly simple scheme, and thus it was that Smiths Cleaning Company was created. From humble beginnings, it expanded almost overnight, primarily by word of mouth, until now Lindy had four women working for her, and was looking for more to deal with her ever-growing client list.

Amy was the only member of the group to have a serious relationship during the year and was the only member to have her heart broken. Meeting Darren in the club one Saturday night, Amy had been instantly attracted to his dark good looks and nonchalant attitude. Falling hard and fast, Amy had proved a naively easy conquest, losing her virginity to him a short month later, and confiding in Lili and Lindy she was convinced he was 'the one'; that her love was returned absolutely.

Lili was doubtful, Lindy downright cynical, having come across Darren's type before. But, in the face of Amy's shining happiness, both kept their counsel, watching with a doomed sense of the inevitable as, with a hundred small acts of petty spite and selfishness, he slowly broke Amy's trusting heart. He finally dumped her in the middle of the club, snarling accusations at her whining and whinging, leaving Lindy and Lili to pick up the pieces of a broken Amy, whilst the men made it plain if Darren valued his pretty face, and wanted to keep it intact, he better leave – now.

A month later, Lili sat on the bathroom floor with Amy, watching with heart-stopping fear for a blue line that never appeared; relief at not having to pay an even higher price for being gullible causing her late period to arrive that evening.

All in all, Lili mused, clutching her hatbox to her chest, it had been an eventful year. Now, she was excited about Daisy's wedding and was looking forward to it, especially as it would be the first wedding she had ever attended.

During the year, Lili had made several trips to London to stay with Conrad, always making the effort to see Daisy whilst she was there. In turn, Daisy had come to stay with Lili on several occasions.

The first time she came alone, and spent an uproarious weekend with the group, being absorbed naturally into it as if she had always been a member. The second time, Guy came too. He seemed surprised to find that two good-looking men formed part of Lili's circle, and Lili noticed with amusement that Daisy was not allowed to visit alone again.

In the beginning, Lili hoped for news of Jake, desperate to hear even snippets of information about him. She bought his books, painstakingly reading her way through them, enjoying the fast-paced, action led plots, and relishing the feeling of being close to Jake.

But, even the most intense first crush needs sustenance to build on. Jake and Vivienne left England soon after Daisy's party and hadn't, to Lili's knowledge, been back. Gradually, those intense feelings faded. Lili almost forgot what it had felt like to look into his piercing blue eyes; how his strong arms had held her close when they'd danced.

Lili knew Jake would be present at Daisy's wedding. Curiously, she examined her feelings, wondering how she felt at the prospect of seeing him. Thankfully, she concluded she felt nothing. He had been a pleasant, if slightly embarrassing interlude, that was all. About Vivienne, Lili's feelings were less benign. That memory still stung, and she had no desire to renew acquaintance with the older woman.

And so, the year turned; Christmas and New Year had come and gone, the happiest Lili had ever known, birthdays had been celebrated, including her nineteenth. She thought of the stark difference between it, and her eighteenth. It seemed aeons ago, a plain mouse of a girl had left her parents' house forever and caught the bus to a new life. Now, it was a year later, the weekend of Daisy's wedding, and Lili waited for the man who was to give her a lift with mixed feelings of trepidation, and anticipation.

The wedding was to be held at Hixley Hall, home of the Bellingham's, deep in the heart of Buckinghamshire, and the problem of how to get there had consumed Lili's thoughts for weeks. Train connections being a logistical nightmare and still without a car, Lili decided to travel to London, then drive down with Conrad and Matthew. But a week ago, Daisy had phoned in great excitement.

One of Guy's university friends lived close to Lili, in the village of Felsham to be precise. Was that close? Lili agreed, yes, it was close, and Daisy informed her in an eager gush she'd spoken to Johnny – that was his name, Johnny Gedding. He was driving down Friday and had agreed to give Lili a lift. Wasn't that great news?

Unsure if it was or wasn't, Lili had no option but to accept the offer with good grace. So now she stood, ready far too early through fear of keeping this unknown Johnny waiting, nerves making her jiggle and constantly feel she needed to wee.

Half an hour past the time when he should have picked her up, Lili was beginning to panic. Wondering if she'd misheard the time, or perhaps he'd forgotten her, she hovered anxiously in the hall, trying to decide whether to call Daisy or not. Finally, she decided to have a wee first, her bladder by this point threatening to overflow, then give Daisy a quick call to double-check the time.

Leaving the bathroom a few moments later, she cursed as she heard the impatient knock at the door. Peering out the landing window, she saw a red sports car of some kind parked at the kerb and knew her lift had arrived.

Picking up her hatbox, she rushed downstairs and threw the front door open to reveal a young man in his mid-twenties, handsome in a nonchalantly rich way, his well-cut clothes screaming class, and possessing the natural polish that being born wealthy seems to impart. He looked down as she opened the door, pulling dark shades further down his nose.

"You're Lili?" he asked, peering in disbelief at her over the top of the sunglasses.

"Yes," she answered, slightly peeved.

"Well," he replied slowly. "I must say, you're not at all what I was expecting."

"Oh?" snapped Lili brusquely. "And what, precisely, were you expecting?"

"I was told to pick up a family friend called Lily, I assumed you'd be an elderly spinster relative who kept cats and smelt of mothballs."

"Sorry to disappoint you," Lili almost snarled.

"Believe me, sweetheart," he removed his shades and leant against the door, raking her body with an intensely appraising stare, before raising a brow in approval. "I'm far from being disappointed."

He smiled a long, lazy smile. It was as if the sun had come out from behind a cloud. Lili gulped; her sarcastic retort forgotten. A treacherous flush flaming her cheeks, Lili ducked her head, fumbling for her case.

"Umm, well, I guess we'd better get going," she mumbled, "as we're leaving almost an hour later than planned."

"Are we?" Johnny enquired, casually plucking her case from her clumsy hands. "This everything?" he asked. Lili picked up her handbag from the hall table, preparing to shut the front door.

"Yes," she replied, glad her back was to him as she carefully locked the door. Kevin would be around that evening to work on the garden and feed Boris, but still, she took a few moments checking the door was secure, wanting time to compose herself before facing his knowing, amused expression.

He led the way to where the sleek, scarlet machine crouched like some predatory animal stalking its prey. Sliding her case into the small boot next to his own, more masculine looking, overnight bag, he manoeuvred the hatbox carefully on the shelf-like, back seat, then took her outfit from her, hanging it up in the back, and motioned to the car as if waving her into a carriage.

"Shall we go?" he enquired. Lili heard the barely concealed amusement in his voice as if he knew how intensely uncomfortable, he was making her and was enjoying it.

"Thank you," she murmured, scrambling into the low-slung, passenger seat.

To Lili's surprise, the trip passed very pleasantly. Johnny made a witty, interesting companion, and was an extremely competent, albeit fast, driver. Whilst he expertly handled the high-performance vehicle, music played on the stereo and they talked, mostly about inconsequential matters such as music and films they liked, but also about more intimate, personal subjects. Lili learnt Johnny was twenty-four and still lived with his parents. When she expressed surprise at this, he shrugged lazily, blaming it on a gap year, four years at university, and a complete disinterest in applying himself to anything even remotely resembling a career.

From his accent, and his casual disregard for earning a living, Lili deduced Johnny's parents were wealthy; not comfortably well-off as her own had been, but seriously wealthy. Not having the motivation of needing to work to live, Lili sensed he was drifting aimlessly through life, seeking the next thrill – the next diversion.

They stopped halfway for petrol and coffee when Lili discovered something else about Johnny – he was a charmer. Something about his upper-class, supremely confident, and diffident attitude, had women falling over themselves for him. All women. From the teenage petrol pump assistant, and the motherly soul who served them coffee, to the elderly lady in the queue, whose tray Johnny gallantly carried to a table. Young and old, he charmed them all.

Initially, Lili wondered if it was an act, but after watching him she decided it was more an innate part of his personality. Johnny simply liked and admired women, all women, from all age groups, and all walks of life. That he would be as courteous to a humble pensioner as he would to the grandest duchess in the land, perhaps more so.

She also realised why he looked so familiar as he made his way to the serving hatch to smilingly request a second cup of coffee. He ran a hand nonchalantly through his floppy fringe and the penny dropped. Amy's favourite film was Four Weddings and a Funeral, and Lili had watched it with her on several occasions, Johnny bore a striking resemblance to Hugh Grant, in attitude as well as looks.

Climbing back into the car once more, Lili felt relaxed enough to enquire about his friendship with Guy.

"Guy?" he replied, "Bloke's a prick, can't stand him."

"What?" Lili spluttered in shock. "But why are you going to his wedding, then?"

"Well, I like Daisy. She's all right. Far too nice to be marrying him. Besides, there's going to be lots of free booze and food, and anyway, it's something to do."

Lili sat speechless, not sure what response to make, and Johnny pulled a face. "Oh dear, have I shocked you?" he mocked. "Don't worry, Lili. Guy doesn't like me any more than I like him."

"So, why are you invited then?" enquired Lili curiously.

"He's a snob," shrugged Johnny. "His family may have lived at Hixley Hall for three generations, but mine have lived at Felsham Hall since 1068. Guy may have gone to his father's university at Oxford, but my family founded one of the universities over four hundred years ago. Guy latched onto me once he realised who I was, who my family was, and I've been trying to shake him off ever since. He seems to think claiming friendship with me will give him a leg up the old boy network. What he hasn't grasped is I don't give a shit about all that stuff."

"Oh, I see," replied Lili, brain racing as she compared this new information about Guy, with what Conrad had said about him at Daisy's party last year, drawing uncomfortable conclusions about Daisy's future happiness.

"So, why is he marrying Daisy then?" she asked, voice etched with concern.

"She's rich," again Johnny shrugged. "At least her family is, which I suppose to Guy amounts to the same thing."

"But he loves her, doesn't he?" At the worry in her voice, Johnny glanced across, face softening.

"Of course, he does," he replied heartily. "Who couldn't love Daisy?" Lili slowly nodded, relieved when the subject was changed, and the rest of the journey passed without it being raised again.

Reaching Hixley Hall, Lili's jaw dropped at the ostentatious size of the place. It had been bought by Guy's grandfather for a pittance after the war, the previous owners having been forced to sell due to the combined tragedies of loss of family fortune, and all three heirs in the trenches of France. Guy's own family's fortunes had been mysteriously created through the war by dubious, black-market dealings. Three generations later, the Bellingham's rubbed shoulders with the elite and ignored their less than salubrious past.

Now, the latest son and heir was getting married, and the Hall was dressed for the occasion. A team of gardeners had been working around the clock to ensure the grounds looked their absolute best. The Hall itself was a bower of sweet-smelling pink roses and ornamental daisies, and every one of its twenty-two bedrooms had been scrubbed and polished for the wedding party.

Lili and Johnny, as non-family members, were staying in the local inn situated outside the magnificent double gates to the Hall's equally imposing driveway. As they turned into the inn's car park, Lili saw it was already crammed with an impressive array of expensive, high-performance cars, and remembered Daisy telling her the whole inn had been hired to accommodate guests.

Checking in, Lili and Johnny found they'd been issued rooms on opposite sides of the hallway on the second floor. "Oh good," leered Johnny. "That means I can creep across after lights out."

Pleasantly surprised by her charming room with its single brass bedstead, and a cosy, though well-equipped, bathroom, Lili hastily unpacked, freshened up, and slipped into a full length, black halter-neck dress, complete with matching heels and sparkly jewellery.

There was a grand welcoming dinner that night, and Daisy had warned her to wear full evening dress. A bus was being sent to collect all the guests from the inn and ferry them safely up the long driveway. Heavens forbid any guest had to walk, even though it was a perfect summer's evening.

Slightly breathless from her quick turnaround, unsure what time the bus was coming, and afraid of keeping everyone waiting, Lili threw open her bedroom door to find Johnny standing outside, hand raised to knock. They both jumped, though Johnny quickly recovered, his eyes showing his appreciation for her appearance.

"Hey, sexy," he drawled.

Lili blushed. "Is this okay?" she asked in concern. "I wasn't sure what would be acceptable …" Her voice trailed away. Miserably aware she sounded naïve and gauche; Lili busied herself collecting up her black, satin clutch bag.

"Don't worry," reassured Johnny. "You look stunning."

"Well, so do you," replied Lili. It was true, the traditional tux suiting Johnny as if he wore it every day. He held out an arm.

"My lady," he drawled. "Your carriage awaits. May I escort you downstairs?"

Any fears Lili had about the suitability of her dress were quickly dispelled upon arriving at the hall. As the guests mingled and chatted, Lili looked for Conrad and Matthew, relieved Johnny seemed happy to stay by her side.

"I don't see them," she murmured, anxiously crowd scanning.

"Your friends?" enquired Johnny, adroitly acquiring two glasses of champagne from a passing waitress. "You'll be lucky to spot them in this crush."

"So many people," observed Lili, wincing as a rather portly man stepped on her foot. "Are they all coming to the wedding?"

"Oh probably," Johnny replied cheerfully, looking around at the great and beautiful greeting each other with braying cries of recognition, all the while quaffing champagne as if it was water.

"Come with me," he exclaimed. Taking her hand, he led her to the far wall where an exquisite tapestry depicting a medieval hunting scene hung in faded splendour. Casting a quick glance around, Johnny deftly moved aside a corner of the tapestry to reveal a concealed, narrow staircase. Hastily hustling Lili through, he followed, allowing the tapestry to drop behind them.

"Up here," he stated, squeezing past Lili, and making no attempt to hide how much he enjoyed it. "It's the old minstrels' gallery where musicians would sit and play during balls and parties. You should be able to spot your friends from up here."

Reaching the top of the stairs, treading carefully in long skirt and heels, Lili found herself standing in a wooden box enclosed on three sides, and opening out over the noisy throng below.

"How did you know it was here?" she asked, looking around her in interest.

"Oh, I spent a couple of holidays with Guy," replied Johnny with a grin, "before, I realised he's such a social climber it's a wonder he doesn't have permanent vertigo. I wouldn't go too close to the edge," he cautioned. "It might not be entirely safe."

Carefully edging forward until she had a bird's eye view over the large baroque hall, Lili watched the swirls and movements of the people below. Intently searching, she didn't find Conrad or Matthew; instead, she found Jake.

Her heart gave an involuntary judder, the breath catching in her lungs, and Lili wondered why she was so surprised to see him. After all, hadn't she known he was coming? Hadn't she been told by Daisy that Jake and Vivienne were flying over from America especially for the wedding? So, why was it such a shock? Why did it seem all the noise and chatter of the two hundred or so other guests faded away into insignificance as she gazed hungrily at him?

He stood on the edge of the crowd, magnificently male in a well-cut tuxedo, eyes lazily scanning the crowd. As Lili stared, he took a glass of champagne from a passing waiter, sipped idly at it, seeming relaxed, and completely at ease. Forgetting all about Conrad and Matthew, forgetting even about Johnny standing next to her, Lili felt a tsunami of emotions rush over her.

How could she have ever thought for one moment she had forgotten him; that he meant nothing to her and was just a silly, harmless crush felt by an emotionally immature teenager. No, this intensity, this invasion of sensation, was much more than a simple crush. She stiffened as his head came up and his eyes perused the crowd, almost as if he could feel her gaze upon him.

Knowing he'd never spot her up in the gallery, she nevertheless took a slight, involuntary step back, gasping as that piercing blue regard swung upwards, moving over her hiding place, before passing onto the other guests.

"You okay?" Johnny's quiet words dragged her sharply back to the present, and she shot him a reassuring smile.

"Of course, I can't see them anywhere though."

"They might be in one of the other rooms," he replied seeming to accept her words at face value. But his dark eyes never left hers, as if seeking an answer there.

"No, no," Lili exclaimed. "There they are." She pointed as Conrad and Matthew entered the hall, resplendent in their tuxedos, stopping to exchange pleasantries with Mr and Mrs Kolinsky and another older couple, whom Lili assumed to be Guy's parents.

Discreetly slipping out from behind the tapestry, her eyes were unerringly drawn to where she'd seen Jake, but, almost to her relief, he was no longer there. Not sure how to handle the various thoughts and emotions bubbling up inside if he did speak to her, Lili was terrified of making a fool of herself in front of him.

Lili pushed her way through the elegant guests, followed by Johnny, towards Conrad and Matthew, progress impeded as Johnny greeted and was greeted, by almost everyone in their path.

"Do you know everyone?" she grumbled.

"What can I say?" he shrugged modestly. "I'm a popular guy."

Finally, they reached them, Conrad's face lighting up at her approach. "Lili," he exclaimed, swinging her up in a hug. "Look at you, just look at you. You're stunning!"

Blushing with pleasure, she hugged Matthew, turned to introduce Johnny, but it wasn't necessary. Of course, he already knew them.

"Where's Daisy?" Lili asked. "Has anyone seen her?"

"Oh, she's around somewhere," replied Conrad vaguely. "No doubt you'll see her at dinner, speaking of which …" he gestured, drawing their attention to ornate double doors being flung open. They moved to join the rest of the crowd filtering into the massive dining room.

"I wonder if I can bribe the staff to make sure I'm on your table," Johnny muttered to Lili, slipping an arm possessively around her waist. Lili caught the knowing glance between Conrad and Matthew, wanting to tell them how wrong they were. Johnny was a sweetheart. She was confident he would become a good friend but compared to Jake, he seemed so young – just a boy.

Giving him a non-committal smile, she wandered with the others up to the doors, where a bevvy of waiters and waitresses were busily making sure all guests were directed to the right table.

Passing through the doors, giving her name to the young waiter, Lili let her eyes wander over the shining beauty of the great dining hall. At least twenty round tables were dotted about, eight gilt chairs placed neatly around each one. Every table was covered with a snowy white, damask tablecloth. Beautifully perfect centrepieces of pink roses and white daisies stood on each table, whilst swags of the same flowers caught up the tablecloths at strategic points.

Along the top of the hall ran a long table where the main wedding party were seated. Following Conrad and Matthew to their table, she caught sight of Daisy, stunning in a midnight blue evening gown, talking to Guy by her side. At the table were also both sets of parents, Miriam and Greg, a pair of young brunettes whom Lili assumed were bridesmaids, and two young men talking animatedly to each other – best man, usher? Lili didn't know. Then there was Jake.

He sat at the end of the table. He seemed apart from the others, not talking to them, his eyes intently watching. Following his gaze, Lili saw Vivienne sitting at one of the tables, a stunning, gold evening gown slipping off one shoulder, as she smouldered and laughed with the group of young men clustered around her.

Looking back at Jake, Lili saw his eyes narrow, and his face harden. He reached inside his breast pocket, feeling for something, but his hand came out empty, and he drummed his fingers impatiently on the tablecloth.

"Earth calling Lili," Lili dragged her gaze back to her companions; flustered as she realised Conrad had been trying to attract her attention for several moments.

"Sorry," she mumbled. "I was … umm, looking at everyone."

"I know precisely what you were looking at," retorted Conrad, "though I can't say I blame you, sweetie. He is rather gorgeous." Lili stared at him in horror. Had she been so transparent? Had Conrad been able to read so clearly the emotions deep within her heart?

"Who?" enquired Johnny with interest.

"Oh, a certain young artist called Greg," continued Conrad. "Lili met him last year, and let's just say, was rather smitten with him."

"Greg?" Relief swamped her. She gave a mischievously teasing smile. "Hmm," she drawled. "He is rather pretty."

"Naughty girl," chided Conrad, and grinned.

"I don't see anything special about him," commented Johnny sulkily, and everyone at the table laughed.

Finally, the mammoth task of seating everyone was done. In a way, Lili supposed this rehearsal dinner was a good idea. At least tomorrow everyone would know exactly where his or her seat was, and the wedding reception would be able to flow unimpeded.

At their table of eight, besides Lili, Johnny, Conrad, and Matthew were a pair of young, pretty, blonde identical twins. Bright and bubbly, they were Daisy's cousins and thought Johnny the wittiest man they had ever met. An air of gaiety was soon established, as Camilla and Louisa giggled and flirted outrageously with Johnny. Also, at their table, to Lili's delight, were Sid and his partner, Jeremy.

Sid had fallen upon Lili with delighted cries of recognition, yet she couldn't help but notice that once his initial excitement at seeing her again had subsided, he seemed vastly changed from the exuberant, outrageously camp person of last year. Now, he appeared subdued, his behaviour almost restrained. Lili observed the way he constantly deferred to Jeremy and wondered.

Remembering what Daisy had told her about Jeremy, she discreetly watched, drawing her own, unfavourable, conclusions. There was no doubt he was handsome, yet his eyes were cold. When he smiled it was fixed, lacking any degree of warmth or humour. Urbane and charming, he spent most of the meal talking to someone at the next table, whom he clearly felt was of more importance than the flotsam and jetsam at his own.

Instinctively, Lili disliked and distrusted him. Seeing the unhappiness in Sid's eyes, the way his hands shook as he lifted his glass, her initial aversion to Jeremy deepened into an out and out loathing. She decided she would attempt to speak to Sid privately, to check he was all right. Used to being deeply unhappy and alone herself, Lili was extra sensitive to others in the same plight.

Other than her concerns over Sid, the meal was an extremely pleasant one, Lili, too, succumbing to Johnny's charms. His shameless flirting and wicked sense of humour had the whole table in fits of laughter, and Lili enjoyed herself immensely. The food was excellent, the wine superb, and the company, apart from sour-faced Jeremy, witty and entertaining.

"We're so glad we're at your table," confided Louisa with a smile; at least, Lili thought it was Louisa. "You're fun. All the other tables are full of the most boring old stiffs."

Looking around, Lili realised she was right; they were the youngest and liveliest table in the room. She wondered why Daisy had so few friends. Surely, someone as sweet and friendly as Daisy should be inundated with companions. She remembered Conrad's words about Daisy only being allowed friends Guy deemed proper.

When the meal was over, Mr Bellingham rose and gave a short speech welcoming everyone and hoping they had all enjoyed their dinner. A great cheer went up at this point. He then made everyone laugh with his reminder to the 'riff-raff' staying at the pub, that the bus would be ready to take them back at precisely midnight. He apologised for it being an early night, but as it was the wedding tomorrow, he felt it prudent if everyone got to bed early.

"Does it have to be your own bed?" Johnny enquired innocently. There was a good-humoured roar of laughter.

Wandering back into the hall with the others, Lili found whilst they'd been at dinner a string quartet had set up in one corner of the room. Waiters and waitresses once again circulated offering champagne, and there was a free bar in the billiard room serving wine, spirits, and soft drinks.

In the large and comfortable lounge which had been designated a quiet sitting area, a pretty waitress was dispensing tea, coffee, and hot chocolate. Feeling she'd had enough alcohol for the moment, Lili decided to get herself a hot chocolate, eyes widening at the cream and chocolate shaving laden concoction she was handed.

"Good lord," was Johnny's comment, when she returned carefully carrying the tall mug. "Are you going to eat all that?" he enquired innocently, eyeing it covetously.

"Yes, I am," retorted Lili, smacking his hand away with her spoon, as he tried to purloin the chocolate wafer which had come with it.

"Wow," exclaimed the twins. "We're going to get one of those. See you later Lili."

Taking a sip, the chocolate under the copious amounts of cream was delicious but red hot, and Lili choked and spluttered as it scalded a path down the wrong way.

"Steady on," laughed Johnny, enthusiastically thumping her on the back.

"Hello, Lili."

Red-faced, eyes streaming, coughing, and spluttering, Lili looked up. There, stood Greg looking worried, and, horror of horrors, Jake looking amused.

"Oh, hi," she managed before a fresh coughing fit made her turn away in despair.

"Are you okay?" Greg asked in concern.

"Hmm," she gasped, gratefully accepting Johnny's handkerchief. Dabbing her eyes, she had a vision of how she must look, and fought frantically to pull herself together.

"Hi Greg, Jake," she replied, as casually as she could. "Nice to see you again."

"You too, Lili," replied Greg warmly. "Hey Johnny," he continued, "good to see you. Still intent on making a career out of being a rich brat?"

"Absolutely," retorted Johnny. "And you? Still slapping paint on a canvas and calling it art?"

"Yep, actually managed to sell another one last week."

"Hey cool, how many is that sold now? Two, including the one you conned me into buying?"

"Four actually," retorted Greg, grinning at the good-humoured banter.

"Oh? Who else did you sucker into thinking you're the next Van Gogh?"

"Lili bought two."

"Now, what'd you go and do a thing like that for?" enquired Johnny.

"Well, why did you buy one?" laughed Lili.

"Oh, I felt he needed encouraging," shrugged Johnny, smiling wickedly. "Plus, I have more money than brain cells." All through this exchange, Lili was painfully aware of Jake standing silently behind Greg. His eyes constantly searched, and Lili knew he was looking for Vivienne.

"Johnny, this is my cousin Jake Kolinsky." The two men shook hands.

"Hi, Jack Cole, right? Love the books."

"Thanks,"

"Jake this is Johnny Gedding, the future Lord Felsham."

"Lord, no shit?" enquired Jake casually. He felt inside his pocket, again his hand coming out empty.

"Lord?" squeaked Lili. "Really?"

"Well, not until the old man pops it, and I don't think either of us is in a rush for that to happen. I think the thought of me inheriting the title is enough to keep him alive forever."

Jake smiled with the others, yet Lili noticed the smile didn't reach his eyes. Once again, his gaze passed over the room.

"I better go," he said. "There are people I need to say hello to. It was nice to see you again, Lili, you too Johnny." And just like that, he was gone.

"What's eating him?" enquired Johnny.

"Oh, he's probably gone to find his wife, Vivienne," explained Greg, with an apologetic shrug. "She tends to be a little elusive at parties – if you know what I mean – and she's made him give up smoking, so he's a little tetchy."

"Why has she made him give up smoking?" enquired Lili.

"They've been trying for a baby, unsuccessfully, so Vivienne went on a change for conception course thing. She was told smoking can affect fertility, so the cigarettes had to go. Well, suppose I'd better circulate, brother of the bride and all that. See you later, guys."

Lili watched him go – stopping to exchange a brief word with Conrad and Matthew as he passed them on their way back from the bar, bearing three whiskeys.

"I must say," remarked Conrad, handing one to Johnny. "They breed them gorgeous in the Kolinsky family. What's the matter with you, Lili?"

"Oh, some hot chocolate went down the wrong way."

"I'll say it did," retorted Conrad with a grin. "It's all over your face." Squeaking in dismay, Lili thrust her hot chocolate into Johnny's hands, and shot off in search of the ladies…

Wasn't that sodding typical, Lili thought, giving a moan of despair in the mirror. There she was, trying to make a good impression, wanting Jake to see her as a beautiful, sophisticated woman, and look at her. Scarlet lipstick smeared everywhere, mascara smudged halfway down her face, and to top it all, a cream moustache.

With a weary sigh, Lili pulled out her make-up bag and began emergency repairs. Why, oh why, couldn't he have seen her earlier when she was looking halfway decent? Lili had no doubt Vivienne would never look anything less than stunning. She could have wept at the contrast between them.

She froze, lipstick halfway to her mouth. What on earth was she thinking? Nothing had changed since last year. Jake was still a married man, was still older than her, and still didn't know she existed. This stupid crush was pointless, futile, and nothing could ever come of it. The best thing she could do was forget about him.

Talking sternly to herself, Lili repaired the damage to her face and forcefully stuffed everything back into her bag. That's what she would do, forget about Mr Jake Kolinsky, with his rugged good looks and oh so gorgeous blue eyes. He was nothing to her and never would be, so she might as well get over it now.

"Lili."

The door to the ladies flew open, and with a rustle of blue silk, Daisy rushed in, throwing her arms around Lili.

"There you are. I've been looking all over for you. Tell me, what do you think of Johnny?"

"He seems very nice," replied Lili, slightly taken aback at such a direct question.

"So," continued Daisy archly. "Am I a good friend or am I a good friend? It was my idea to get Johnny to give you a lift and to have him on your table at dinner. I can't believe it never occurred to me earlier, especially as he lives so close to you."

"Huh?" Lili stared at Daisy baffled, then the penny dropped. "Daisy, you're not playing cupid's apprentice by any chance?"

"No! Okay, maybe a little bit. But, truthfully Lili, what do you think of him?"

"As I said, he seems very nice."
"That's it? Very nice? Don't you think he's handsome?"
"I suppose so."
"He's very charming, isn't he?"
"Yes, he is."
"He's rich too."
"Hmm, I know."
"He'll be Lord Felsham someday."
"Really?"
"Oh, Lili!" Daisy almost stamped her foot with exasperation.
"I'm sorry," laughed Lili. "But what do you want me to say? That we've fallen madly in love and want to pick out curtains? We only met today. As I said, he seems very nice and I hope we can be friends, but I don't think he's my type."
"So, what is your type?"
"Oh, I don't know," replied Lili casually, an image of blue eyes and tousled blond hair flashing through her mind. "I don't think I've met my type yet. So," she continued, changing the subject, "tell me about tomorrow. Is everything ready?"
"God, I hope so," laughed Daisy. "It's too late now if it isn't. No, the only tiny worry is Guy's cousin Amelia, she's one of the bridesmaids. She phoned earlier to say she wasn't feeling well. She's going to take a couple of aspirin, have an early night and drive down in the morning. I'm a bit worried she won't make it in time."
"Don't worry, I'm sure everything will be fine," soothed Lili, slipping an arm through Daisy's and leading her out of the ladies.
"Oh, I'm not worried, not really. It's just if she doesn't make it, I'll only have three bridesmaids and it'll ruin the whole look to have an odd number."
"It's not going to happen, so forget about it. Enjoy your last night as a single girl."
"Oh Lili, just think … by this time tomorrow I'll be Mrs Guy Bellingham. I can't wait, I love him so much. I can't wait to begin the rest of our lives together."
Lili smiled at Daisy's excited face and shining eyes, wondering as they joined the others, if she would ever feel that kind of love, and pushed away the fleeting thought of Jake before it could take hold.

Chapter Twenty-One

"You can't help someone who doesn't want to be helped."

The remainder of the evening passed pleasantly, although, at one point, Lili noticed Sid and Jeremy having an altercation. As she watched, concerned, Jeremy walked away, a sneer marring his perfect features. At the look of utter devastation on Sid's face, Lili gave a little gasp and made to go to him.

"Don't." At Conrad's single command, Lili looked up in surprise. "Don't Lili," he said again. "This is something Sid has to sort out for himself. You can't help someone who doesn't want to be helped."

"But he looks so sad," replied Lili softly, watching Sid rush desperately after Jeremy. There was a brief exchange of words, Sid's body language pleading, Jeremy's dismissive before Jeremy vanished through one of the doors into the garden, Sid trailing uncertainly behind.

"And he'll stay sad," responded Conrad, "until he finds the courage to admit he's made a mistake; that Jeremy's not the one."

At the stroke of midnight, the music stopped, and Mr Bellingham thanked everyone for coming, informing them the bus was awaiting all guests staying at the inn.

There was a disappointed murmur, a general sense of being sent to bed early as the evening was getting interesting, but gradually people started to drift in separate directions, either towards the front door or up the grand staircase.

Lili wished Conrad and Matthew good night. As very old family friends they were staying at the Hall. As she queued with the others to board the vintage 1930s bus which had been hired and decorated for ferrying guests, Johnny sidled up and whispered in her ear.

"Distract the driver. Ask what time he's picking us up tomorrow or something."

"What?"

"Just do it," he hissed and lifted her onto the step.

"Umm, what time are you picking us up tomorrow?" Lili asked. The driver blinked owlishly at her from behind thick, black-framed glasses, and Lili felt Johnny's back pressing against hers as he helped others onto the bus.

"Wedding is at midday," the driver replied. "I'll be outside the pub at eleven-thirty, leaving at twenty to twelve. So, don't be late, otherwise, you'll be walking."

"Thank you," replied Lili, wondering if the distraction had served Johnny's purpose, whatever that was. From the depths of the backseat, his head emerged, a quick thumbs-up flashing her way.

"Thank you," she said again, making her way down the aisle towards the back, eyes narrowing as she passed Jeremy sitting by himself. Of Sid, there was no sign, and Lili wondered where he was.

Reaching the back, she was astonished to discover the identical blonde heads of Camilla and Louisa hiding in the corner.

"What are you two doing here?" she exclaimed.

"Ssh!" urged Johnny, tugging her down into the seat.

"I thought you were staying at the Hall," she whispered.

"We are," giggled Camilla, or was it, Louisa? "But we don't want to go to bed yet, so Johnny smuggled us onto the bus so we can all have a drink together back at the pub."

"Oh, did he now?" said Lili. "Will the bar still be open?"

"Don't worry," replied Johnny airily. "I know the owner. He'll stay open for us."

"Do you know everyone in the world?" Lili enquired, amused, despite herself.

"Not quite," replied Johnny. He took her hand, kissed the palm, and held it over his heart. "But now I know you, my world is complete, and I can stop searching."

"Ahh, that's so sweet," cooed the twins.

"Oh please," drawled Lili, then remembered one of Lindy's favourite sayings. "Dry that one out and you could fertilise the lawn with it."

"Why Lili, I'm hurt you doubt my sincerity," retorted Johnny innocently.

"So, after we've all had this nice little drink," Lili continued, shooting Johnny a look, "how are the girls getting back to the hall? I presume you don't intend them to walk?"

"No, of course not," Johnny waved his hands dismissively. "Don't worry. I'll run these charming young ladies' home in my car. It's a Ferrari you know," he confided to the twins with a wink, who looked at each other and dissolved into fits of giggles.

Upon reaching the inn, Johnny gallantly escorted them into the bar and settled them around the embers of a dying log fire. Gratefully, Lili moved towards its fading heat. Despite the warmth of the June day, this late at night, it had turned distinctly chilly, and all three girls shivered in their flimsy evening wear.

A moment later, Johnny returned, followed by a stooped, slightly weather-beaten man, who looked to be in his late sixties but was probably a great deal younger.

"This is Mick. He owns the pub," Johnny casually introduced the landlord with a wave of his hand. "Mick, these delightful young ladies are Lili, Camilla, and Louisa."

"Johnny says you want drinks," Mick was obviously a man of few words. At their chorus of agreement, he nodded and ducked behind the bar.

"Right then," looking inordinately pleased with himself, Johnny turned to the others. "What does everyone fancy, champagne?" The twins burst into giggles again.

"Yes please," they chorused, and Lili shrugged.

An hour later, Lili had had enough. It had been fun, at first, watching Johnny gently flirt with Camilla and Louisa; teasing them and making jokes about not being able to tell them apart; but, as the hands on the clock crept past one, she yawned and thought longingly of bed. Catching her eye, Camilla smiled sympathetically.

"I know how you feel," she said. "I think it's time we were going. After all, Lou, we don't want big eye bags tomorrow."

"It's tomorrow already," replied Louisa, glancing up at the oversized clock on the wall, and stifling a yawn herself.

"It's not tomorrow until you've been to bed," Johnny commented flippantly. "And if that's where you delightful ladies feel you need to be, then your carriage awaits." Turning to Lili, he again pressed a kiss to her hand. "Please don't go up until I get back," he urged. "I won't be long."

"Well ..." began Lili, reluctantly.

"Please," he wheedled.

"Okay," she agreed, saying her goodbyes to the twins as they finished their drinks and headed for the door. Snuggling back in her comfortable, velvet-upholstered wing chair, Lili stared deep into the flickering heart of the fire which Mick had revitalised for them, thinking about the day, and everything that had happened.

The outer door to the pub banged. Lili jumped in her chair. Had she nodded off? Surely that wasn't Johnny back already? It felt like they'd only just left. Footsteps sounded in the passage, and Lili sat upright, blinking sleepily.

"That was quick ..."

The words died on her lips as Jake prowled into the room. Lili stared, all thoughts of sleep chased from her mind, as her body instantly and completely jerked alert.

"J-Jake," she stuttered in shock. "What are you doing here?"

"What'd you want?" Mick appeared like an aged jack-in-the-box.

"Whisky, on the rocks," Jake snapped brusquely, waiting with barely concealed impatience as Mick painstaking got down a tumbler, wiped it clean with a cloth, ladled in ice, and filled it from the optic. Handing it over, he almost had his fingers removed as Jake snatched the glass, and downed the drink in one, long gulp.

"Another. Make it a double this time," ordered Jake, handing the glass back. Lili watched with silent concern as Mick shrugged, refilling the glass with amber-coloured liquid. Jake turned from the bar, drink in hand, his eyes locking with Lili's.

"Lili," he mumbled, almost sheepishly, looking around the bar in surprise. "You here alone?" he enquired. "Where's your boyfriend?"

"Who?"

Lili was having trouble concentrating, her mind was in a whirl, questions and doubts swirling around. Why was he here, now, alone? And where was Vivienne?

"Your boyfriend," he repeated impatiently. "Lord whatever."

"Do you mean Johnny? Oh, he's not my boyfriend..."

Jake shrugged, sat down in the chair opposite, stretching his long legs towards the fire. He sipped from his drink, sighed, and placed it on the table. Again, his hands wandered to his pocket, looking for cigarettes Lili realised.

"Honestly, Johnny and I, we're friends, that's all ..."

It seemed desperately important to Lili that she convince him there was no one in her life.

"I mean, we only met today. I don't have a boyfriend."

"Why not?" Jake fixed a piercing gaze on her, and Lili felt heat fan her cheekbones.

"I don't know," she murmured. "I guess I haven't met the right person ... or ... rather, I have but they're unobtainable." She stopped, horrified at her words.

"Tough break," said Jake sympathetically, and Lili shrugged, hoping he'd let the subject drop. "Strange things, relationships," he said.

Lili stared blankly, unsure how to respond, but he didn't seem to expect an answer. Instead, he gazed morosely into his whisky, as if an answer could be found within its depths.

"The first year of marriage is the hardest, right?" he glanced up at Lili, his expression almost begging her to agree with him.

"So, I've heard," she murmured.

"It was always going to be tough," he continued, more to himself than Lili, as if thoughts pounding through his mind were being voiced aloud.

"We both have demanding careers, and we're both used to being alone," his head snapped up to look at Lili. "Compromises have to be made, right?"

"I guess so ..." she replied slowly.

"So why," he drained his glass, gestured to Mick to fetch another. "Why does it always feel like I'm the one making them?"

Lili shook her head, heart thumping at the confusion and unhappiness she glimpsed deep within his eyes.

"Is everything okay with you," she took a deep breath, continued, "and Vivienne?"

"Oh, yeah, it's just ..." Wearily he rubbed a hand over his eyes. "This whole baby business has got us both on edge, that's all. Vivi's got to go for tests when we get back. She's finding it hard to accept there may be something wrong with her, some reason why she can't conceive. Hell, I keep telling her it doesn't matter, it could be me that's the problem. Even if they find we can't have kids, so what?"

"You could always adopt," suggested Lili tentatively.

"I said that tonight, but Vivi went ape," he smiled ruefully. "We had a huge fight. That's how come I ended up here, I needed a drink, but the Hall's shut up and everyone's been sent to bed like naughty school kids, so I figured the bar here might still be open."

"Johnny's friends with the landlord," explained Lili. "He kept the bar open for us."

"Oh, where's Johnny now then? Gone to bed?"

"No, he took Camilla and Louisa back to the Hall."

"The giggling twins, what were they doing here?"

"The same as you."

Jake nodded thoughtfully, sipping at his drink, gaze wandering to the glowing embers of the fire. A companionable silence settled over the room, and Lili felt a great wave of tiredness roll over her. Closing her eyes, she snuggled further into the chair.

"You look beat," Jake's quiet words made her jump. Her eyes flew open. "Why don't you go on up. Busy day tomorrow for everyone."

"I know, but I promised Johnny I'd wait until he got back," she frowned at the clock. "He should have been back ages ago."

"Maybe he got side-tracked," suggested Jake.

"With the twins?" asked Lili dryly. "More than likely."

At that moment, the outer door to the pub banged again, and Johnny entered the room, half leading, half carrying Sid.

"Sid?" Lili exclaimed, jumping to her feet. "What happened? What's the matter?"

"I found him outside the Hall," Johnny explained, helping Sid to a chair by the fire.

"I didn't realise how late it was. I missed the bus and didn't know what to do."

Sid was shivering like a whipped puppy, and Lili instinctively took his hands in hers, chafing them to try and warm him up.

"It was so dark, Lili, I didn't fancy walking all that way on my own. I've never been so pleased to see anyone as I was to see Johnny. Thank you," he looked up at Johnny gratefully.

"That's all right, mate," Johnny dismissed his thanks. "Glad to be of service."

"But how come you missed the bus?" Lili asked.

Sid's face crumpled. "Jeremy finished with me tonight," he stuttered, "and I couldn't face everyone, I felt such a fool and I didn't want to make a fuss at Daisy's wedding."

"Oh Sid," sympathised Lili. "I'm so sorry, I knew something was up when I saw you two arguing. And at dinner, he was so ... so..."

"Shitty to you," finished Johnny helpfully. Lili shot him a look. "Sorry," he muttered. "How about a drink everyone? I know I need one, and I'm sure Sid does."

"Thanks, another whisky," replied Jake.

"No, thank you," murmured Lili, still crouched by Sid's side.

"Sid?"

"Oh, I don't know, maybe a brandy. That's good for shock, isn't it?" he appealed to Lili, and she couldn't help having the sneaking suspicion maybe Sid was enjoying, just a little, being the centre of attention and having so much fuss lavished on him.

Drinks were distributed by a taciturn Mick, showing no surprise at the sudden arrival of Sid in the bar. Lili eased herself up onto the chair next to Sid's, still holding his hand, watching with motherly concern as he gulped at his drink, coughing as its fiery contents burnt its way down.

"Better?" she asked.

"A little," sniffed Sid, and clutched at her hand. "Take my mind off it," he begged her. "Please, Lili, distract me. Talk to me about something else."

"Like what?"

"I don't know, anything," he declared dramatically. "Tell me what you're wearing tomorrow. Tell me about your dress."

"Well," began Lili self-consciously, aware the eyes of all three men were upon her. "It's really nice. It's a shift dress made of gorgeous lilac silk with cream lace straps and trim. It's a little daring..."

"Good," interrupted Johnny, leering at her.

"It's a little daring," continued Lili, shooting Johnny a shut-up look, "because it's quite short, and the back simply doesn't exist at all. There's a matching jacket to wear at the actual wedding, which I can take off later at the reception."

"Fabulous," breathed Sid. "It sounds fabulous. And your hat?"

"Oh, the hat," grinned Lili. "The hat is enormous..."

"Trust me, it is," confirmed Johnny. "I had to try and fit it in the Ferrari."

"It's made of lilac silk covered with cream daisies and has a huge lacy bow on one side."

"Oh Lili, I can't wait to see it. You'll look divine, simply divine," Sid seemed to have momentarily forgotten about Jeremy, and Lili smiled at his excitement.

"I love it," she said. "It's the most beautiful dress I've ever owned, and I can't wait to wear it. Speaking of which," she glanced up at the clock again. "I'm sorry, you'll have to excuse me. It's gone two and I need my beauty sleep."

"Sleep." Sid's face crumpled again. "How can I sleep in the same room as him? How can I bear it? He said he's not going to the wedding, he'll be off first thing, but he's up there now. How can I face him? What shall I do?"

"I tell you what," said Johnny, good-naturedly. "My room has twin beds. Why don't you bunk down with me tonight?"

"You mean it?" Sid stared at Johnny with gratitude. "Oh, thank you, you've saved my life."

"Look, I'll even come up to your room if you like, help get your stuff. He won't dare make a scene if I'm there."

Sid spluttered his thanks, stumbled out of his chair, and made to follow Johnny. At the door Johnny paused, turning to Lili.

"We won't be long. Wait for me. As soon as I've helped Sid get his stuff and shown him to my room, I'll come down and get you."

"I'll come with you now," said Lili, and made to get up.

"No, don't," Johnny glanced over to where Sid was loitering in the door and dropped his voice. "Stay here in case there's ... trouble."

"Want me to come with you?" enquired Jake.

"No, that's fine, I don't think he'll make a fuss, but just in case, I'd rather you waited here, Lili."

"All right," agreed Lili reluctantly, watching as he and Sid left the bar. "Poor Sid," she sighed, unthinkingly taking a sip of Sid's brandy, and wincing at the taste.

"Like I said," drawled Jake. "Strange things, relationships."

Lili smiled in agreement. There was silence for a moment as they both sat, deep within their thoughts, then Jake cleared his throat.

"Thank you, Lili..."

"What for?" she asked in surprise.

"For earlier, for listening ... I don't have anyone I can talk to, hell, I'm a man. We're supposed to go to our caves and grunt, right?"

"Something like that," Lili smiled.

"But it felt okay, talking to you. You're a good listener, Lili. So, thank you."

"You're welcome," replied Lili solemnly, feeling a deep, inner warmth as he gave her a friendly grin.

The moment stretched.

Then they both jumped as the phone behind the bar rang. Mick answered it with a grumble, grunted an affirmative and hung up. Jerking a thumb upwards, he said to Lili.

"You're wanted, room 14."

"Who by?" Lili asked, startled.

"Himself," was the monosyllabic reply, from which Lili assumed he meant Johnny.

She turned worried eyes to Jake. "What do you suppose has happened?" she asked, feeling a slight frisson of alarm.

"Don't know," Jake stood up. "But I'm coming with you."

Too grateful to refuse, Lili followed him as they left the bar, and went upstairs to the guest rooms where the door of number 14 stood ajar. As they entered, Lili couldn't hold back her gasp of dismay. The room looked as if a small, localised hurricane had paid it a visit and tossed clothes and belongings everywhere.

Johnny looked up at their entry, gesturing helplessly towards the mess, and towards Sid, crouched on the floor, his back to them, attention fixed on something in his hands.

"You been burgled?" Jake asked in concern, looking around at the scene of total devastation.

"No," replied Johnny through gritted teeth. "Sid's ex decided not to wait till morning. He left Sid a little going away gift."

"Jeremy did this?" Lili gasped, looking around in horror.

Jake let out a low whistle. "Hell, hath no fury ..." he muttered.

"Sid, darling," Lili crouched down in front of Sid. "I'm so sorry."

"He smashed it," Sid interrupted. "He smashed it, Lili!"

"Smashed what?" Lili asked gently. Sid opened his hands to show her a beautiful gold fob watch, or rather what was left of it.

"It was my grandfather's," he explained. "It was all I had left of him. He knew, knew how important it was to me, yet he smashed it up. Why?"

His eyes were those of a hurt and bewildered child, and Lili felt tears well at his pain.

"I don't know," she murmured, stroking his hair. "I don't know why."

"He's done this before," continued Sid. "Not quite on this scale, but he's done this before. He'll deliberately pick a fight, trash my things, and storm off. Then a few days later he comes back saying he's sorry, that it won't happen again, but it always does, and I always take him back. I'm so weak, Lili, so bloody weak. I always take him back. I fall for it every time even though I know..."

His voice trailed off.

He looked at the twisted and mangled watch, then back to Lili. Seeming to find solace in her quiet, steady gaze, he took a deep breath and said quietly.

"He doesn't love me at all, does he?"

"No," Lili shook her head sadly. "When you love someone, Sid, you don't hurt them. You'd rather die than do anything to cause them pain, and you'd never, ever destroy something they love."

Jake cleared his throat. Lili glanced up and for a moment their gazes locked, then his eyes turned away as if unable to bear the emotion he saw in hers.

"The thing is," Johnny broke in, "dear Jeremy wasn't happy with smashing the watch and messing up the room. Unfortunately, he also took revenge on Sid's clothes."

Lili looked closer at the devastation. All around were bits of shredded underwear, and shirts minus their sleeves. A beautiful, pearly grey suit lay sprawled, its jacket slashed and ripped, the trousers missing both legs. Horrified, she looked at Johnny.

"His wedding suit, oh no! Sid, what are you going to do?"

"Not go of course," replied Sid. "I've only got the clothes I'm wearing."

"Could you not wear them?" Lili asked innocently.

All three men exchange pained looks.

"It's a tux, Lili," Johnny explained patiently. "He can't wear a tuxedo to a wedding. This isn't Vegas." Lili's eyes shot once more to Jake, who shuffled his feet, looking faintly embarrassed.

"Do you have anything he could borrow?" she asked.

"No," Johnny shook his head regretfully. "I have a spare shirt you're more than welcome to borrow, but I only brought one suit with me."

"Me too," said Jake. "And anyway, anything I had would be too large." It was true; Sid being slim and wiry meant anything he borrowed off Jake would drown him. Lili closed her eyes in despair.

"Think," she muttered. "There must be something we can do."

"It's all right," Sid reassured her bravely. "I won't go."

"No," snapped Lili and Johnny simultaneously.

"That's not an option," continued Lili. "Don't worry," she patted Sid reassuringly on the hand. "We'll think of something."

"Ok, here's an idea," declared Johnny, stuffing his hands in his trouser pockets, and rocking back on his heels. "Aylesbury's only twenty minutes away. It must have a gent's outfitters. How about if you and I get up early tomorrow morning, Sid, and make sure we're waiting on the doorstep when they open? We can have you re-kitted top to toe, and still be back in time to catch the bus."

"You'd do that for me?"

Sid gazed at Johnny almost in tears again, the light of hero-worship shining in his eyes. Johnny cleared his throat, looking desperately at Lili.

"That's okay," he mumbled gruffly. "Right, that's sorted, I think maybe we should all get some sleep, I'll go and see if I can borrow a local directory or something off Mick."

"There you go, Sid," Lili gave Sid a quick hug. "Told you we'd think of something."

"Oh Lili, you're the best. Do you know, I almost wish I wasn't gay so that you could be my girlfriend."

"Why thank you, Sid," Lili laughed in delight. "That's the nicest thing anyone's ever said to me."

"And as for Johnny, hmm, he's definitely straight, isn't he?" Sid asked innocently.

"Definitely," replied Lili firmly.

A speculative gleam came into Sid's eyes. "Pity," he mused, setting off down the corridor after Johnny.

Jake and Lili glanced at each other and burst out laughing.

"Poor Johnny," spluttered Lili. "Do you think we should warn him?"

"Nah," drawled Jake. "Let him fight his own battles. What room are you in?" he continued. "I'll walk you to your door."

Mindful of the other sleeping guests, neither spoke as Jake escorted Lili to her room. Lili paused, key in the lock, unsure of protocol – if she should invite him in or not.

"Goodnight," she eventually whispered.

"Goodnight, Lili," he whispered. "I'll see you tomorrow." His face loomed large, a warm, friendly kiss brushed across Lili's cheek, making her eyes go huge with shock.

"Oh, and Lili…"

"Hmm?"

"I look forward to seeing you in your dress."

He left, a dark shadow disappearing down the hall. Hands shaking, Lili unlocked her door and sidled in. Quietly closing it behind her, she slid down to the floor, a quaking, shivering heap.

Well, she thought in bewilderment, he knows I exist now…

After her nocturnal adventures, Lili feared she wouldn't sleep, but much to her surprise the moment her head hit the pillow, complete exhaustion claimed her, and she sank like a stone into a deep and satisfying slumber.

Johnny and Sid knocked on her door at 8:30am, wondering if she wanted to come to Aylesbury with them. One look at the incredulous expression on her face had them backing away, promising to see her when they returned.

Stumbling back to bed, Lili fell asleep again. Waking an hour later, she decided she should get up to begin the pleasurable task of making herself beautiful.

An hour later, Lili was sitting in the restaurant; showered, hair washed and styled and basic make-up complete, relaxing in a simple cotton dress as she sipped her coffee with pleasure. She decided to slip back to her room at about eleven to change into her wedding outfit and complete her make-up.

Idly, she wondered where the others were, and if they managed to get Sid some new clothes. She hoped so. Lili knew how fond of Sid Daisy was, and how upset she'd be if he couldn't attend her wedding.

A sudden commotion at the door had Lili looking up in stunned surprise, as Greg and Jake, each immaculately attired in morning suits with pale blue waistcoats, burst into the restaurant and rushed over to her, both talking at once.

"Lili, thank heavens we've found you. You must come with us. There's an emergency up at the Hall, Daisy needs you!"

"What are you talking about? Emergency? What's happened?"

"No time, you have to come now."

Before Lili could open her mouth to utter another word, Jake hustled her out of her chair and hurried her to the door. "But ... but, the others, they'll wonder where I am..."

"Mick," Greg bellowed through the kitchen door, to the amusement of the other guests. A grunt came in reply.

"Tell Johnny, Lili's already gone to the Hall." There was a further grunt, Greg grabbed Lili's other arm, and almost bodily carried her out of the pub.

"Wait, what's going on? What emergency ..."

Ignoring her pleas for enlightenment, Greg threw her in the back of the car and jumped in after her. Jake leapt into the driver's seat, gunned the engine, and was off before Greg had time to slam his door.

The drive to the Hall took only moments, Jake screeching to a halt with a spurt of gravel. Still in shock, Lili simply gave in, allowing them to hurry her up endless flights of broad, sweeping stairs, along miles of corridor, until finally, they arrived, panting, at a pair of white double doors slightly ajar.

Behind them, Lili heard pitiful weeping and the low drone of a soothing voice. Knocking briefly, Greg swept the doors open, pulling Lili into the room with him.

"We did it. We got her. She's here."

Concerned, Lili took in the scene. A large, beautifully proportioned bedroom; Daisy sitting at the dressing table in a cream slip, sobbing helplessly, Mrs Kolinsky kneeling beside her, hair in curlers, patting her on the shoulder. The two brunettes from last night, clad in violent pink bridesmaids' dresses, huddled together, expressions of distress etched on their faces.

Miriam paced the room, her expression one of exasperation; and lurking uncomfortably a trim blonde in a white overall clutching a make-up brush, and a man who was obviously the hairdresser.

"Daisy?" Lili cried, rushing over to her. "What is it? What's happened?"

"Oh, Lili," sobbed Daisy, raising a woebegone and swollen face to her. "Something terrible has happened, the worst thing..."

"What? Oh, Daisy darling, what on earth has happened?"

"Guy's cousin, Amelia … she's got chicken pox!" howled Daisy.

"Is that it?" demanded Greg. "Is that why you had us go tearing off to practically kidnap Lili? You're a bridesmaid short?"

"Jeez," chimed in Jake. "Is that all? I thought it was something serious."

"All!" raged Daisy, rising from her stool like an Amazonian warrior. "Something serious? This is bloody serious!" She advanced on the two men who backed away, twin expressions of trepidation on their faces.

"Now calm down Daisy," said Greg, holding out his hands as if to ward her off. "It's not like it's the end of the world…"

"Not the end of the world!"

The whole room quaked at the transformation of the sweet, mild-mannered Daisy into a demented, wild-eyed harridan.

"Not the end of YOUR world maybe! I've only been planning this wedding for a year, but that doesn't matter, oh no! It doesn't matter that my photos will be unbalanced because there are only three bridesmaids, and that the seating plan will be out at dinner. Of course, none of that matters, because, as the great Greg Kolinsky who knows FUCK ALL about weddings has said, IT'S NOT THE END OF THE WORLD!"

With a great cry, Daisy turned into Lili and proceeded to sob vast, hysterical tears into her neck. Over her head, Lili looked in concern at the two men who were ashen-faced at Daisy's distress.

"Just go," she advised quietly. "We'll sort it, but I think you should go now."

Greg and Jake didn't need telling twice. With expressions of relief, they fled from the room, banging the doors shut behind them.

"Ssh, it's okay Daisy, it's okay," soothed Lili, unpeeling Daisy's vice-like grip from around her neck and leading her back to the dressing table.

Mrs Kolinsky shot a look of despair at Lili, as she eased Daisy back onto the stool and brushed the hair away from her face, wincing at the devastation the heavy crying jag had wrought on Daisy's pretty, pixie face.

"L-Lili …" stuttered Daisy, wiping frantically at her eyes and nose with a disintegrating tissue. "Would you … I mean, I wondered … why I sent the boys to fetch you … would you consider being my bridesmaid?"

"Me?" Lili stared at Daisy in surprise, who peered hopefully back. "Of course, I will, if it'll help."

"Oh Lili," gulped Daisy, throwing her arms around her neck and hugging her. "Thank you, thank you so much." An air of relief swept over the room.

"Thank you, Lili," Mrs Kolinsky's thanks were heartfelt. Over by the window, Miriam rolled her eyes, assuming command.

"Right, that's settled," she declared. "Okay, Daisy, go with Janine, and see if she can sort your face out."

Obediently, Daisy trailed into the adjoining bathroom with the white-clad Janine.

"Mother," snapped Miriam, her mother almost jumped to attention, "you go with Maxwell. He'll finish your hair, then, when he's done you, he can attempt to rescue Daisy's hair."

With a flutter and a flurry, Mrs Kolinsky and the hairdresser scuttled from the room. Miriam turned her steely gaze on the bridesmaids. "You two, help me get Lili into Amelia's dress." She frowned. "There may be a slight problem though."

"Problem?" asked Lili, wiggling out of her dress. "What problem?"

"Oh, the problem Amelia is a good four inches taller than you and about four stone heavier, that's all," Miriam stated flatly, as she and the two bridesmaids dropped a voluminous, tent-like mass of bilious, pink taffeta over Lili's head.

Fighting her way out of its encompassing, suffocating folds, Lili held out a foot of bodice which wasn't even coming close to touching, turning panicky eyes to Miriam.

"It's massive," she whispered, not wanting Daisy in the next room to hear. "What are we going do?"

Miriam considered, lips pursed, as the bridesmaids fussed with the dress, pulling it this way and that to no avail. Lili looked like a little girl dressing up in her mother's clothes. Miriam sighed and reached a decision.

"There's nothing else for it," she decided. "Come with me, Lili, we'll have to make it fit. You two," she swung her attention back to the bridesmaids. "Go find my mother and tell her the problem. Tell her I've taken Lili to my room, that I'll need the largest pair of scissors she's got, a needle, and a reel of pink cotton. Hurry!"

With squeaks, the bridesmaids dashed from the room, and Miriam helped Lili gather up the dress so she could at least walk. Trailing in Miriam's wake, trying not to trip over, Lili came face to face with Greg and Jake, still lurking worriedly outside the door.

"Lili," cried Greg then stopped, face comical as he looked her up and down. "What on earth are you wearing?"

"I'm on emergency bridesmaid duty," she giggled, holding out the dress so they could see the scale of the problem. "Problem is – the dress is a teensy tiny bit too big."

"Umm, yes," agreed Greg, lips twitching. "What the hell is Guy's cousin. A sumo wrestler or something? Jeez, Lili, you can't wear that. What are you going to do?"

"Miriam has a cunning plan," confided Lili. "It involves cotton, a needle, and a very large pair of scissors. Should I be afraid?"

"Of my sister wielding a big pair of scissors?" Greg asked in horror. "Too right you should, I still haven't recovered from the haircut she gave me when I was three."

"Lili." Miriam was impatiently waiting. "You two," she rounded onto Greg and Jake, who snapped to attention. "Find Guy, the best man, and that other usher. Get to the church, there'll be guests to seat. Lili, come with me." She marched off down the hall.

"Oops, got to go, wish me luck." Lili wobbled off down the hallway in pursuit, desperately trying to maintain some shred of dignity and not fall flat on her face. She smiled, as behind her she heard Greg give a half laugh and a comment.

"Good old Lili, she's such a trooper."

Jake made no reply, and if Lili had looked back, she would have seen that neither was he laughing. Instead, his face was serious, a frown pulling his forehead as he watched her sashay down the hall, looking even worse from behind.

Moments after they reached the sanctuary of Miriam's room, the bridesmaids burst in, complete with a sewing kit, and brandishing the biggest pair of dressmaking scissors Lili had ever seen.

"Mrs Kolinsky is doing her own hair and has sent Maxwell to fix up Daisy's," they announced breathlessly. "She said when you've finished with Lili's dress, take her back to Daisy's room so her hair and make-up can be done."

Miriam made Lili release the dress so the full scale of the problem could be assessed. Catching sight of herself for the first time in the full-length mirror in the corner of the room, Lili gulped, bit her lip.

She looked hideous.

Not only was the dress about four sizes too big for her, but its colour of bright pink was not entirely flattering. Lili thought wistfully of her beautiful lilac and cream mini dress hanging in her room at the inn, and a pang of regret pierced her.

"Hmm," Miriam considered. "The biggest problem is the width on the bodice. Well, nothing for it." With a confidence Lili sincerely hoped wasn't for show, Miriam picked up the scissors and cut two broad panels out of the back of the dress, down the length of the zip to the waistband.

"You've cut the zip out," gasped one of the bridesmaids. "How will she do it up?"

"Be quiet," snapped Miriam, squinting, and threading a needle with bright pink cotton. "Hold very still, Lili," she commanded. "I'm going to have to sew you into the dress. There's no time to do anything else."

Hardly daring to breathe, Lili froze to the spot as Miriam proficiently joined the two cut edges with beautifully precise stitches, almost instantly transforming the bodice so it moulded to Lili's body and pushed up her small, neat breasts. From the waist up, at least, the dress looked a hundred times better than it had.

Snipping off the cotton, Miriam turned her attention to the length. Making Lili climb carefully onto a chair, she quickly and efficiently hemmed all the way around, so the dress whispered on the ground.

"Good thing you're wearing flats," commented Miriam. "One slip of a heel and the whole lot would be ripped out. Be careful getting in and out of the car and you'll be fine. There," helping Lili down, she moved her to the mirror. "What do you think?"

"It looks amazing, thank you," gasped Lili in heartfelt relief.

The dress was still slightly bunched around the waist, and nothing could alter the fact the colour didn't suit but compared to what it had looked like before, it was a vast improvement.

"Take her to Daisy's room," ordered Miriam crisply, "whilst I get dressed. We need to hurry. Only another fifteen minutes and the cars will be here."

Quickly, Lili and the bridesmaids, whom Lili learnt were Guy's sisters and were called Vanessa and Lavinia, dashed back along the corridor to find a radiantly beautiful Daisy, as far removed from the sodden wreck of a girl Lili had last seen as it was possible to get, being helped into her wedding gown by her mother.

Before Lili could comment, she was whisked over to the dressing table by Janine, who expertly swept blusher along her cheekbones, applied shadow to her lids, mascara to her lashes, and colour to her lips.

Feeling she was on a conveyor belt, Lili was hustled across the room to Maxwell the hairstylist, who sprayed, backcombed, and caught her hair up high off her face with a beautiful slide, decorated with the official wedding flowers of pink roses and white daisies.

"Are we all ready?" fussed Mrs Kolinsky.

Lili turned, only to be stunned into silence by her first proper look at Daisy in all her wedding finery.

The gown was perfect, made of soft, creamy satin, with a tight bodice that showcased Daisy's slightly Rubenesque proportions perfectly. Sparkly bugle beads formed a scatter of tiny daisies across the whole dress, and puffy, lacy sleeves skimmed Daisy's shoulders, exposing her rounded, feminine curves.

A graceful headdress of roses and daisies formed a pretty crown around Daisy's head, and a delicate veil frothed and billowed, cascading in creamy white folds onto the ground behind her.

Mrs Kolinsky dabbed at her eyes, and Daisy reached out a hand to take her mothers in a loving handclasp. As Lili watched, she felt a bitter lump in her throat. Even if she ever got married herself, there would be no emotional mother and daughter moment for her.

Bouquets were swiftly handed out, a stunning concoction of trailing pink roses, white daisies, ivy, and baby's breath, all threaded with pink and white ribbons for Daisy, and scaled-down versions for the bridesmaids.

A discreet knock came at the door, and Mr Kolinsky's worried voice sounded through the wood.

"Is everything all right in there? The cars are here. We need to go."

"Come on, girls," Mrs Kolinsky pulled herself together, hurried the bridesmaids out of the room, pausing at the door to gently touch a hand to her husband's face.

"She's ready," she said softly.

A look passed between them; a look which spoke of the combined joy and anguish of their last baby, their little girl, flying the nest.

Outside, Miriam was waiting impatiently, immaculately attired in her dress. Daisy had her wish of four matching bridesmaids.

"At last," Miriam exclaimed. "Come on, the cars are waiting."

Gripped by sudden terror, Lili merely nodded, following the others down the broad flight of stairs, holding her skirts up high, terrified of falling. Clutching her bouquet to her chest, she trailed uncertainly out to the cars, climbing into the back of the vintage Daimler next to Miriam.

"Now don't worry about a thing, Lili," Miriam comforted. "It's all pretty straightforward, traditional format and everything, like any normal wedding."

"Umm, I suppose now's not a good time to tell you I've never been to a wedding before," confided Lili nervously.

"What?" Miriam stared at her in disbelief, casting her eyes skywards. "Okay, don't worry," she ordered. "Stick with me and you'll be fine."

The actual wedding ceremony passed in a blur. Lili was pushed into place next to Miriam. Anxiously measuring her steps to the older woman's, they followed Daisy down the aisle to where Guy and the other groomsmen were waiting.

Listening to the ancient and beautiful words of the marriage ceremony, Lili watched in quiet envy while Daisy breathlessly made her vows, her pretty face glowing with love as she placed her heart and happiness, into Guy's hands.

Experiencing a moment of panic when the bridal party paired off for the walk back down the aisle, Lili hesitated, unsure, then Jake was there, solemnly offering her his arm, smiling as she slipped hers through his with obvious relief.

The photographs lasted forever, and Lili's face froze in a permanent smile as picture after picture was taken. Through the crowd she caught glimpses of the others, noticing with relief Sid clad in a rather smart, dark blue suit.

Then there was the greeting line-up to survive, where interminable numbers of guests, all in identical suits, flowery outfits, and big hats, shook her hand. But, through it all, Jake and Greg flanked her, having designated themselves her official guardians, offering support and encouragement.

Finally, her official duties were over, and they were all seated at the top table, enjoying a superb four-course meal, which Lili tucked into with gusto. She hadn't had time for breakfast that morning, so consequently was now famished.

The meal finished, champagne was served, speeches were made, and toasts offered up. Guy traditionally thanked the bridesmaids, sending a conspiratorial wink in Lili's direction.

After the last speech, Mr Bellingham rose to his feet to thank them all for coming, informing everyone there was to be dancing in the great hall, but the first dance was reserved solely for the main wedding party.

"What happens now?" muttered Lili to Greg, under cover of the general scraping of chairs.

"Well, we all have a designated dance partner for the first song. Traditionally, the bride and groom are supposed to dance alone, but given Guy's two left feet it was decided to camouflage them with the rest of us. So, Daisy's dancing with Guy, the parents' swap partners, Miriam, as matron of honour, is dancing with the best man..."

"Aren't I the lucky one," muttered Miriam. Lili giggled. To her horror, she recognised Guy's best man as her molester from the party. Luckily, his gaze had passed over her with complete lack of recognition, and Lili later learnt he was engaged to Guy's sister, Vanessa.

"I'm dancing with one of Guy's sisters," Greg continued. "I forget which one, and Harry, the other usher, gets the other one, so that means you're dancing with..."

"Me," interrupted Jake, grinning at Lili. "So long as that's okay?"

"Oh, yes, yes of course," stammered Lili, feeling all fluttery and female.

Taking her new husband's hand, Daisy led the way from the dining hall, the other members of the bridal party lining up behind them. Lili and Jake were last. As Lili swept by on Jake's arm, she caught a glimpse of Vivienne, face like thunder under a large, stunning black and white hat.

Entering the hall, Lili saw Guy and Daisy had re-hired the group who had performed so superbly at Daisy's party. The lead singer, her black hair now shorn to a spiky cap, stepped up to the microphone.

In a deep husky voice, she welcomed everyone to the wedding reception of the new Mr and Mrs Bellingham, informing them the first song was by special request of the bride and groom. It meant a lot to them, as it was the first song they had danced to after the groom had proposed.

With a feeling of inevitability, Lili heard the instantly recognisable opening bars of music as Jake pulled her easily into his arms, and the whole bridal party danced with varying degrees of competence.

If I close my eyes, Lili thought, I could almost be back a year ago, dancing with the same man to the same piece of music…

… she still needed him tonight, still wanted to show him a sunset, still wanted him to stay with her till dawn…

But it wasn't the same.

Then, Jake's eyes had constantly roamed the crowd, searching for his bride, his arms hadn't encircled her quite so firmly, and surely his grasp hadn't been quite so tight. Lili took a deep breath, the smell of Jake once again filling her lungs; that at least hadn't changed.

Neither had her reaction to him.

Her heart still pounded, and her blood still raced. Feeling the colour graze her cheeks, Lili turned shy eyes up to meet his steady, blue gaze, unaware of how attractive a picture she made; her dark eyes almost deep enough for a man to drown in, her cheeks flushed, and her full bottom lip trembling.

Something in Jake's face changed, became almost tender. Was it only Lili's imagination, or did his grip tighten ever so slightly?

"Well now," he drawled softly. "You're quite a girl, aren't you, Lili?"

"What do you mean?"

"What you did for Daisy today."

"Oh, it was nothing."

"No, it was something. I know how much you were looking forward to wearing your dress, and instead, you got lumbered with a pink marquee."

"Daisy's a friend. A silly dress can't compete with that."

"You mean it, don't you?" Jake looked at Lili as if something important had occurred to him. "A lot of women wouldn't have let that influence them; I know some who would rather lose the friend than be caught dead in an unflattering dress."

"Well, that's plain silly," Lili retorted forcefully. "Besides, once Miriam worked her magic, the dress didn't turn out so bad."

"Still, it's not the dress you planned to wear, but you wore it out of love. That made it beautiful, makes you beautiful."

Lili stared at Jake, as the song crashed into its powerful guitar instrumental section, and he swung her back in a low dip, which had the crowd applauding good-naturedly.

They danced the rest of the song in silence, Lili desperately trying to understand and assimilate what he had said. Jake too seemed lost in his thoughts.

Lili was almost relieved when the singer belted out the final notes of the song and a round of applause was given to the bride and groom.

Other guests began to crowd onto the floor. Lili and Jake stood, gazing levelly at each other. Jake smiled and raised her hand to his mouth.

"As I said, you're one hell of a girl, Lili," and he pressed a warm kiss to her palm.

"Jake!"

Vivienne's shrill tones broke into the moment. Jake turned to greet his wife, and Lili took the opportunity to slip soundlessly away into the crowd...

An hour later, Lili was sitting with her friends when Daisy came bustling over. "Lili darling," she exclaimed, enfolding Lili into a satiny embrace. Lili smelt the sweet aroma of her perfume, the faint scent of the flowers in her hair.

"I haven't had a chance to thank you properly for what you did, and I wondered if you'd perform one more bridesmaid duty for me."

At Lili's look of enquiry, she continued.

"Could you come and help me take my veil off? I'm fed up with it. The damned thing keeps being trodden on."

"Of course," laughed Lili, allowing Daisy to pull her out of her seat, up the main stairs, and along the corridor to Daisy's bedroom. To her surprise, Miriam was already there brandishing a pair of scissors. Lili cast her an anxious look, as Daisy took down a hanger from the back of the door.

"Ta da," she exclaimed. Lili gasped; it was her dress.

"You've performed over and above the call of duty today," Daisy explained. "And now I want you to change into your lovely dress and enjoy the rest of the reception."

"Oh, oh," cried Lili. "Thank you! Not that I haven't enjoyed being your bridesmaid," she added hastily. "But..."

"But you want to wear your pretty dress, and that's quite understandable," finished Miriam gruffly. "Turn around, let's cut you out of that monstrosity."

Twenty minutes later, feeling gorgeous in her wonderful dress, Lili walked downstairs, arm in arm with Daisy.

"But I don't understand. How did my dress get here?"

"Greg and Jake went back to the inn about half an hour ago, and persuaded Mick to open your door so they could get it for you."

"How did you know about it?" Lili was curious. There hadn't been the time that morning to discuss it with Daisy, and she certainly hadn't mentioned it to anyone else.

"Oh, well, you have Jake to thank for it."

"Jake?"

"Yes. He's the one who insisted you should at least wear your dress for the reception. It was all his idea..."

Whatever else Daisy had been about to say was cut short by Guy bounding up the stairs to meet them.

"There you are, darling," he exclaimed. "Sorry Lili, afraid I'm going to steal her away. There are some people we still have to talk to."

"Catch up with you later, Lili," and Daisy left her standing on the stairs, Jake's name hovering questioningly on her lips.

Jake? It had been Jake's idea to get her dress.

Searching the crowd, Lili found him easily. The band was playing a slow, melodious ballad and he was dancing with his wife. Vivienne's back was to her, and Jake was watching Lili over her head, smiling in approval.

As their eyes met, Lili silently formed the words *thank you*. He dipped his head in reply, the warmth in his eyes making her heart miss a beat.

As if sensing their silent communion, Vivienne turned. Lili was subjected to a long, cold stare before Vivienne pulled Jake's head down to hers and planted a possessive, passionate kiss on his lips.

Lili dropped her eyes, finished descending the stairs, an inevitable, weary sadness arising within her, as she acknowledged the one thing that she wanted most in the world, was the one thing she simply couldn't have.

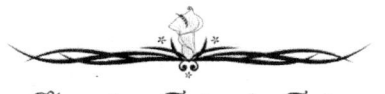

Chapter Twenty-Two
"Why did Johnny call you Lili?"

Was she in love? A month later Lili was still asking herself the same question. Never having been in love before, it was difficult to know for sure. It was true, she thought about Jake continuously; longing to see him again. He invaded her dreams almost nightly, causing her to awaken, breathless and yearning with an intense throbbing need for something – she didn't know what. But was that love?

One evening, when she and Martin were alone in the kitchen, she said, "You know all about music don't you, Martin?"

"It's a hobby of mine, why?"

"Oh, I heard a song and liked it, but don't know what it is."

"Well, how does it go?"

Self-consciously, Lili shakily sang a few lines, and Martin's face registered instant recognition.

"Oh, that's easy. That's *Stay with Me till Dawn* by Judy Tzuke."

"How would I go about getting a copy?" Lili asked tentatively.

"Tell you what, I'll see if I can track it down for you, I may not be able to get the original vinyl single, only the whole album..."

"That wouldn't matter," interrupted Lili quickly.

"Okay," Martin replied good-naturedly. "I'll see what I can do."

A week later he handed her a CD. Refusing to take payment for it, he flushed with pleasure that he had been able to do something for Lili for a change.

Thanking him, Lili tucked it away, not wanting to listen to it in front of the others. Later, alone, she played it over and over, closing her eyes, and reliving the memories through the music.

Johnny was an instant hit with everyone within the group, except Lindy. Something about his easy charm, wealth, good looks, and lazy, devil-may-care attitude to life seemed to rub the hard-working Lindy up the wrong way.

He was friendly and gentle with Amy, good mates with Kevin and Martin, and flirted outrageously with Lili, but it seemed everything he did or said was a red rag to Lindy. Initially shocked by her hostile reception of him, Johnny simply turned up the charm, convinced there wasn't a woman alive who could resist him, but Lindy merely shot him down in flames at each, and every, opportunity.

Finally, Johnny resorted to insults himself; the sheer inventiveness and scale of the verbal abuse between them escalating until Lili worried it could rip the gang apart.

However, she soon realised everyone else found it vastly amusing. Even Johnny and Lindy seemed to relish the merry war they were waging, deriving intense enjoyment from thinking up even more outrageous indignities to heap on each other.

Johnny injected fresh new ideas into the group. Under his influence, the gang spread their wings and tried new experiences; piling into cars and setting off for the coast; jumping on a train and visiting places of interest; and driving to Ipswich to try their hand at the latest craze sweeping the country – Laserquest.

Everyone enjoyed strapping on big guns, crawling around a huge warehouse, and shooting at anything that moved, pounding rock music assaulting their eardrums. Afterwards, looking at the printouts to see who'd shot who and where, Lindy commented dryly, "Hey, Lord Snot, you shot me in the back eighteen times. What kind of a person does that tell us you are?"

Johnny casually replied, "A silent one?" Grinning as Lindy scowled, and the others fell about laughing.

One fine sunny Sunday, it was decided to pack a picnic, and visit the extensive and beautiful grounds of Felsham Hall, Johnny offering to give them a guided tour of the areas not usually open to the public.

Walking around the fabulous, breathtakingly beautiful grounds, even Lindy was silent with awe that Johnny called this magnificence, home. His parents, Lord and Lady Felsham, wandered down to meet them, curious to make the acquaintance of their son's new friends.

Relieved to discover a group of attractive, friendly, young people, with pleasant manners and an understandable sense of humour, they happily accepted glasses of wine and settled down on the picnic rug with the group.

Watching the way Johnny casually interacted with his parents, the obvious, easy affection that existed between them, Lili sighed with envy, thinking how lucky Johnny was and that he truly seemed to have a charmed life.

As Johnny introduced the group to his parents, Kevin was surprised to be individually singled out for a special mention. "This is Kevin, the one I was telling you about," was Johnny's somewhat cryptic comment. Kevin looked alarmed, and Lady Felsham's eyes narrowed thoughtfully.

"Johnny tells me you're a marvel with gardens and all things green?" she enquired in her quintessentially English, somewhat gruff, upper-class accent. "Got a small project in hand. Perhaps you could draw up a few ideas and give me a quote for doing the work?" At Kevin's enthusiastic agreement, she nodded, pleased.

"Good, give me a ring and we'll arrange for you to come and take a look."

A week later, to Kevin's stunned disbelief, he had been hired by Lady Felsham to create a new section of garden out of an abandoned patch of wilderness where the old stable used to stand. It was Kevin's first commission, besides Lili's garden, and for weeks his mood swung between euphoria and chronic fits of self-doubt.

The group were excited by Kevin's big break. Lili, especially, was thankful to Johnny. Guessing it was his championing of his friend that had persuaded his mother to give Kevin an interview, but also knowing, ultimately, that it was Kevin's knowledge and confidence in his ability to carry out the task, which convinced her to hire him.

Lili wondered if she had never met Jake would she have been tempted by Johnny's not so subtle attempts to seduce her. Whether she would have fallen for his charm and boyish good looks, or whether she'd have resisted, reluctant to become another notch on his bedpost.

But, when she compared him to Jake, Johnny faded away to nothing in her mind and all she could think about was whether she would ever see Jake again.

Casual questions put to Daisy during a phone call on her return from her honeymoon, solicited the information that Jake and Vivienne had returned to the States with no plans to visit the UK for the foreseeable future. Lili silently grieved.

From a professional point of view, things seemed to be generally on the up for the group. Kevin was busy drawing up plans and having consultations with Lady Felsham every spare moment he could.

Lindy now had six women working for her and was finding that paperwork and interviewing potential clients and employees was taking up more and more of her time. She still did some cleaning herself, mostly for her original clients, but gradually found herself assuming more of a managerial role.

Lili had a slight promotion at work. Alex left to have a baby and Lili, with the encouragement of the group, applied for and achieved her position as receptionist. Although her duties were similar, it was a more responsible position commanding a higher salary, and meant Lili had more contact with clients; something that initially worried her but now formed the most enjoyable part of her job.

Martin had also been working hard to achieve a much longed-for promotion. Not fully convinced he stood a chance, he nevertheless gave it his best shot, taking the view if he didn't achieve this one all the preparation would stand him in good stead for the next. Much to the group's delight, he was successful and smoothly made the transition from Junior to Senior Financial Assistant.

That left Amy and Johnny.

The least ambitious of the group, Amy loathed her job working in an office full of spiteful, older girls, yet without experience or qualifications could see no way out of her predicament. Quietly, she watched the others achieve promotions and create their own businesses, her generous heart overjoyed that her friends were satisfied and happy in their chosen careers.

Most of all, she shared her brother's happiness in finally fulfilling his long-held dream. Always ready to look over plans, and sit patiently whilst he expanded on his ideas, it never occurred to Amy to be jealous or envious, it simply not being in her nature.

One Friday evening, they were gathered at Lili's to have a barbecue. The men were busy bonding around the flames outside, and Lili and Amy were in the kitchen preparing the food.

Happy because she was doing what she loved best, namely cooking for her friends, Amy chatted merrily as she basted, seasoned, and chopped. Lindy was running late as she had a cleaning job that afternoon.

The door banged, and Lindy rushed into the kitchen, Lili glanced up in surprise at her somewhat precipitous entry as Lindy marched straight up to Amy, an air of self-importance hovering over her.

"I've got good news for you," Lindy burst out.

"For me?" The blonde girl looked a little alarmed.

"Yes, Adele, that's the client I've been to, is having an important dinner party a week tomorrow and her caterer has let her down badly, something about a mixed booking. So anyway, I've told her you can do it."

"What?" Amy cried in shock. "You told her what?"

"I've told her you can do it."

Lindy paused, obviously waiting for Amy to fall upon her neck with grateful cries of thanks. When Amy simply stared at her, Lindy shuffled her feet awkwardly, shooting a despairing glance at Lili.

"Well then," Amy calmly picked up her knife and continued to slice peppers, "you'll have to tell her that I can't, won't you."

"What? Why? I thought you'd jump at the chance to cater a proper dinner party. I mean, you cook for us all the time and it's always fantastic. I told Adele you're the best cook I know."

"I see," Amy laid down the knife and turned to face Lindy. "Because I occasionally cook for my friends, that makes me qualified to tackle a sophisticated dinner party for … how many people?"

"Ten," mumbled Lindy looking sheepish.

"Ten? Ten people?" Amy huffed in exasperation. "Good lord, Lindy, what were you thinking of? I can't do that."

"Well, I don't see why not," the sheepish expression had been replaced by one of mulish obstinacy. "You cook for us six. It's only four more people."

"Yes, but you're my friends," retorted Amy. "It doesn't matter if something goes wrong because you're my friends, and you're not paying for it to be perfect."

"But your cooking is always perfect," insisted Lindy.

"That's not the point," Amy snapped, her temper rising.

"Then what is the point?" Lili enquired quietly. Both girls looked at her. "Amy, it was sweet of Lindy to have the confidence in your abilities to recommend you to her client ..." She held up her hand as Amy's mouth opened.

"However," she stated, shooting a firm look at Lindy, "it might have been better if she'd run the idea past you first. But what's done is done. Amy, why don't you go and see this lady and talk to her. Find out what she wants, then decide if it's something you could do."

"But Lili, ten people?"

"As Lindy says, it's only four more than you're used to cooking for, and we'd all help, you know we would. Even the boys can chop and slice if necessary..."

"I can't do it," Amy's face was an agony of indecision. "It's not fair to even raise this woman's hopes, I simply can't do it!"

"Maybe not," replied Lili. "But you won't know until you try."

There was a long silence in the kitchen as Amy considered Lili's words, then she sighed, and Lili knew she'd won, Lindy punched the air with glee.

"Yes!" she exclaimed. "I'll phone Adele and tell her you'll be along to see her tomorrow morning."

"Tomorrow?" interrupted Amy desperately. "Lili, I'm not..."

"You need to see her as soon as possible," Lili replied firmly. "Then, if you decide the job's too much for you, it will give her time to find someone else." Reluctantly Amy nodded, and Lindy dashed off to make the call.

The next day, the group watched in silent support as Amy, dressed in a little black suit borrowed from Lili, and clutching a professional-looking notepad and chrome pen borrowed from Martin, climbed into Kevin's car, and went to her interview with Adele.

An hour later she was back, dancing on air, brimming over with excitement, as thoughts and ideas spilt out of her in all directions.

"You're right, Lindy," she exclaimed. "Adele is lovely. She told me what snobs her husband's colleagues' wives are, and how she always feels they're looking down their noses at her. I felt so sorry for her and so angry with them, I couldn't help myself. We started talking about food and planning menus and before I knew what was happening, I'd agreed to do it. Oh my, I've agreed to do it!"

The excitement drained out of her, and she sagged as the full impact of the monumental task she'd undertaken hit her with all the force of a hurricane. The others hurried to reassure as self-doubt crept onto Amy's face.

For the next week, a state of panic gripped the group as they were all swept up into the whirlwind that was Amy. Using Lili's kitchen, as the one at the flat was too small, Amy sample cooked, tested, tasted, rejected, and settled on a simple yet stylish four-course meal, wisely deciding to let the food speak for itself. Trays of complicated canapés and superb desserts, which could be made in advance, would leave no guest in any doubt as to the proficiency of the chef.

Saturday came. Her house gleaming from Lindy's ministrations, Adele let the group in, excitement evident in her round, homely face, as she watched various trays, containers, and plates being carried into her spacious and fully equipped kitchen.

The guests would not be arriving until seven, but Amy wanted plenty of time to lay the table and prepare as much of the meal in advance as she could.

Exuding a professionalism that Lili knew she was far from feeling, Amy reassured Adele that everything was under control, and she was not to worry. She could go to the hairdresser and beautician, secure in the knowledge everything would be fine.

And everything was fine.

Like a fish returned to its natural habitat, once in the kitchen, Amy assumed a mantle of maturity and responsibility belying her years, and Lili watched in proud amazement as, like a general marshalling her troops, she whizzed around the kitchen in a frenzy of controlled adrenalin.

Lili and Lindy, clad in neat black skirts and cream blouses, waited at table, Johnny served as wine waiter, and Kevin and Martin drew the short straw of kitchen duty.

Working well together as a team, they collectively held their breath as course after delicious-looking course was carried to the table, all the plates coming back scraped clean. The few minor hitches thankfully happened backstage.

Later that evening, the last guests having left after lavishing praise and thanks upon Adele and her husband for such a sumptuous dinner, Adele hurried into the kitchen where Amy and her crew were busily clearing down the kitchen and loading the cars with the now empty platters and containers.

"Thank you!" she exclaimed, clasping Amy to her in a grateful hug. "Thank you so much, it was wonderful. It was all wonderful. Thank you … all of you," she added, looking around at the relieved, beaming smiles on the group's faces.

"Yes, thank you," her husband said entering the kitchen, his rotund face carrying an expression of heartfelt relief and gratitude the evening had gone so well. That for once his wife, who, like himself, came from humble beginnings, had been able to hold her head high in the presence of his colleagues' more highly bred wives.

"Here you go, I believe this was the agreed amount." He pressed an envelope into Amy's palm, and she flushed with pride. "You might want to count it," he continued.

"No, no, that's fine," Amy stuffed the envelope into her bag.

"And here's a little bonus."

Amy looked at the second envelope in shock. "But I can't accept this ..." she began, flustered.

"Yes, you can," stated Adele determinedly. "You've all worked so hard. This is a little something to share amongst you. And rest assured Amy, we'll certainly be using you again. You need to get some cards because I'm sure the others will be calling me to get your name and number." Amy looked close to tears and Adele patted her sympathetically on the hand.

"Thank you," she said again simply. "You did a superb job, Amy."

Upon reaching home and opening the second envelope, the group were stunned to discover it contained a further £100, which, despite their protests, Amy insisted on scrupulously dividing between them.

And then there was Johnny. Sometimes Lili despaired he would ever be anything but the perennial playboy rushing about in his sports car – disappearing for days on end to go racing at Ascot; yachting at Cowes or shooting in Scotland.

He fitted so seamlessly into her group, sometimes Lili forgot about his other life, his other friends; people like him who had too much money and time on their hands.

He would phone to cancel a date because he was off on another jolly, and Lili knew when he returned, he'd be moody and hyperactive, like a toddler who's gorged on too many e-numbers. He would then whip the group up into some spontaneous adventure, persuading them to take a trip to London or catch the ferry to France.

Lili had to remind him the rest of the group had limited time and funds. It annoyed them when he casually made plans for the whole group involving outlays of cash, and days off work.

Lili firmly vetoed his suggestion that he simply pay for everyone, knowing the others would never accept Johnny's charity, however well-intentioned, and some, particularly Lindy, would take offence.

One afternoon, Lili was at reception when the double doors swung open, and Johnny sauntered in. Lili had actively discouraged her friends from contacting her at work due to the problem of her colleagues knowing her by a different name. Taken aback, Lili stared at him as he grinned, perching on the corner of her desk.

"Johnny," she exclaimed. "What are you doing here?"

"I'm bored," he moaned, "I wondered if you fancied doing food and a film tonight?"

"Okay," she smiled. "I finish in twenty minutes. Do you want me to meet you?"

Before he could reply, there was a clack of heels and Ms Evans entered the reception. "Good heavens," she stopped and stared. "Johnny? What are you doing here?"

"Hello, Dorothy," Johnny hopped down from the desk, and to Lili's intense surprise gave a flustered Ms Evans a hearty kiss on each cheek. "How are Jonathon and that adorable little baby of yours?"

"Oh, not so little. She's due to start pre-school in a week."

"No, is it that long since I last saw you?"

"Must be, I haven't seen you since Jackie and Ralph's wedding, and Jemima was only four months old then."

They gave a collective sigh as if mourning the passage of time. Lili made a conscious effort to close her mouth which had gaped open with shock. It was true – Johnny really did know everyone.

"But why are you here?" Ms Evans asked. "Surely, you're not looking for a job?"

"I don't think so," retorted Johnny with a grin. "No, I came to see if your gorgeous receptionist fancied going to the pictures."

"Oh, do you two know each other then?"

"Yes, Lili's a friend of Daisy Kolinsky, or rather Daisy Bellingham as she is now. We met at the wedding last June. I was rather surprised you weren't there, Dorothy?"

"We were double-booked," explained Ms Evans with a grimace. "My niece got married the same day. Shame, I'd have much rather gone to Daisy's wedding, I heard it was a good bash." She turned to Lili. "Well, what are you waiting for, off you go."

"But ... but ..." stuttered Lili. "It's not four yet."

"Oh, I think we can turn a blind eye this once, don't you think so, Johnny?"

"Absolutely," agreed Johnny, hustling Lili out of her seat, picking up her bag and pulling her towards the door. "Thanks, Dorothy. Give a big kiss to baby for me and say hi to Jonathon. I'll mention to mother I've seen you. Perhaps you could all come over one day."

"That would be super. Bye Johnny, nice to have seen you again."

"And you. Come on Lili. If we're quick, we can catch the four o'clock showing."

The next day, Ms Evans made no mention of the incident until the afternoon when Lili took in her tea, glancing up as Lili placed it on her desk.

"I didn't realise you were friends of the Gedding's?"

"Yes, well, Johnny mostly, but of course, I've met his parents. One of my friends, Kevin Sinclair, is a landscape gardener. He's been hired by Lady Gedding to do some work for her, so we've been over there a few times to hold tape measures and things."

"Has he now?" Ms Evans eyes grew thoughtful. "Well, our garden desperately needs something doing to it. Perhaps you could get your friend to give me a call?"

"Of course," Lili smiled. When Ms Evans eyes dropped to the file on her desk, she turned to go.

"Why did Johnny call you Lili?"

Lili froze, hand on the door, and slowly turned to meet Ms Evans enquiring eyes.

"Well," Lili took a deep breath, "that's what everyone calls me outside of work. All my friends I mean."

"I see," Ms Evans paused, took a sip of tea, her well made-up nose wrinkling at its heat. "It's a pretty name," she finally said. "I can understand why you prefer it."

From then on, Ms Evans called her Lili. Where she led, the others quickly followed, until soon no one was calling her anything else.

For this, Lili felt a profound sense of gratitude towards Johnny, knowing it was Ms Evans innate snobbery that made her want to emulate him.

If the future Lord Gedding knew her as Lili, then so would she.

The last Saturday in August arrived, bright and clear. It was Martin's birthday, and a celebratory barbecue had been planned. Giving the house a quick tidy, Lili was grateful the renovation work was now complete, and the builders had finally left.

Although the results made all the mess and noise worth it, Lili was relieved it was over, and her home, her beautiful home, was at last hers again.

And it was beautiful.

Entering the hallway through the renovated door with its superb glass panels, you were dazzled by the ageless impact of black and white tiled floor, cherry red stair carpet and original brass stair rods, now polished and gleaming.

Side tables of gleaming cherrywood faced each other across the tiled expanse. On each stood a stylish, etched glass vase, which Lili kept filled with Arum lilies, their elegant green stems, and perfect creamy throats, making a coolly contemporary statement.

To the left of the front door was the dining room. Here, Conrad had gone to town, creating an elegant, warm room with rich, burgundy walls, thick cream carpet and full-length, cream curtains. Again, the furniture was gleaming cherry, and Lili loved the opulence of the long antique table with its twisted legs and matching chairs, all re-upholstered to match the curtains. Normally seating ten, cunning extra panels hidden inside meant it could expand to seat fourteen, maybe more at a push.

Across the hall was the lounge. Conrad's plan to create a flexible space that could be two smaller rooms, or one vast space worked incredibly well.

So far, Lili had left the beautiful wooden doors folded back, but could already imagine when the colder weather arrived, it would be nice to create a smaller, more cosy room.

Greg's pictures had been installed. Hanging in splendour above each fireplace, they immediately drew the eye. Lili loved them, loved everything about the room, and could hardly believe she lived in such an incredibly beautiful house.

The most radical change was at the back of the house, with the demolition of the old kitchen and the building of the conservatory. It was, perhaps, Lili's favourite room in the house. She loved the way it felt to cook in the superb kitchen, especially with the double doors open onto the magnificent garden Kevin had created for her.

Upstairs, the changes continued with the creation of an amazing master suite for Lili, with a private bathroom and walk-in wardrobe, complete with a full-length mirror and revolving shoe rack, which could hold enough pairs to satisfy even the most avid shoe collector.

Next to Lili's bedroom was a large guest room with a king-size bed and private bathroom. Lili saved this room for couples; for when Conrad and Matthew, or Guy and Daisy came to stay.

Across the hall were two further rooms and a generous bathroom.

These rooms were Amy's and Lindy's, both decorated following lengthy consultations with the pair as to what they would prefer. Accordingly, Amy's room was a bower of femininity. Pink and pretty, its brass bedstead with flower-sprigged cover and matching curtains, perfectly complimented Amy's romantic personality.

Lindy's room was a total contrast. Plain cream walls set off caramel tones in the soft furnishings, and her bed was stylish with caramel leather head and footboards.

In the attic, Conrad had agreed with Lili's idea and the box room had been turned into a sleek shower room, the whole floor having been handed over to the three men; their domain whenever they stayed at Lili's.

The bathroom reflected this in that no female touches were to be found in there at all. Stark, stylish, and uncompromisingly male; no flowers ever made their way up the stairs, no girlie detritus ever cluttered its surfaces. Apart from cleaning it, Lili left it alone.

Kevin and Martin shared the larger attic room. Lili had offered one of them the guest room downstairs, but they decided against being stranded in the middle of the exclusively female floor. They'd rather stay in the male domain, even if it did mean sharing a room, so accordingly, Lili bought two small double beds.

The other, smaller attic room was Johnny's. He seemed to be the one who stayed the most at Lili's. Still living with parents, Johnny often stayed over mid-week; the others invariably having work the next day. Johnny, free from the shackles of paid employment could, and did, treat every night like Saturday night.

It was late afternoon – delicious, barbecued food had been consumed, candles blown out, cake cut and presents opened. Now, Kevin sat watching a haphazard game of rounders. Run out by Johnny, he observed lazily as the others shrieked, made up rules, and cheated in the warm rays of the late afternoon sun.

Amy finished putting food away, then wandered over to sit next to him. Glass of wine in hand, she topped up his glass, carefully placing the bottle down on the herringbone bricks, warm under her small, bare feet.

"Who's winning?" she murmured, shading her eyes from the sun.

"I don't think anyone knows," Kevin replied, shaking his head in amusement as Lindy threatened to insert her bat so far up Johnny's arse, he'd be picking splinters out of his tongue if he didn't stop fart-arsing about and bowl her a decent shot.

For a while they sat, brother and sister, watching their friends hard at play. Lindy finally had a shot she liked and smashed it down the garden, only to howl in disbelief as Lili, by some freak chance, caught it, jumping up and down in excitement.

"Out!" she bellowed.

"Yes!" screamed Johnny in triumph.

Picking Lili up, he kissed her on the mouth. Amy, by pure coincidence, happened to be looking at Kevin's face. The split second of agony she glimpsed there enough to make her gasp.

"Oh darling," she sighed. "Do you love her so very much?"

For a long moment, Kevin didn't reply, then simply shrugged, and gave a jerky nod. Amy laid her head on his shoulder, hugging him in silent sympathy...

Next morning, Lili woke later than usual, feeling the hangover settle like a heavy, constricting fog. They had all drunk more than usual, perhaps because it was Martin's birthday, perhaps because it was almost the end of summer. Autumn was approaching and long, lazy days in the garden were coming to an end.

Going to the kitchen in search of coffee and aspirin, Lili was surprised to find it empty. Usually, at least one person would be up making coffee, scavenging for breakfast, bits of the newspaper lying all over the table.

Hearing a voice in the lounge, she padded curiously to the door and peered in. She was taken aback to find the rest of the gang in there, huddled on sofas, staring with morbid fascination at the TV, the light from its screen flickering over pale faces in the gloom cast by still drawn curtains.

"What's going on?" she asked, unease creeping down her spine.

They looked at her, the faces of the three men set and solemn, Amy's face wet with recently shed tears. Even Lindy, stolid Lindy who seldom showed emotion, wore an expression of grim disbelief.

"Oh Lili," whispered Amy. "Diana's dead…"

Later … weeks, months later … Lili tried to analyse the intense, irrational madness of grief that swept the nation, maybe even the world, following the death of Diana.

She spoke to Amy about it, trying to understand the strong, emotional backlash which had occurred, making grown men cry in the street, and millions of people traipse to London to bring flowers to her funeral.

"I didn't know her. We had nothing in common, our lives were poles apart, yet I sobbed at her funeral and every time I heard that wretched Elton John record on the radio it would start me off again. Why? Why did it affect me, all of us, so much?"

"She was so beautiful," murmured Amy. "So beautiful, and so rich, but all her beauty and riches weren't enough to save her. And if she couldn't be saved, then what hope is there for the rest of us?"

Chapter Twenty-Three
"I own this club; I can let whoever I want in."

"Poxy bloody machine!" Lili raised her eyebrows in amused surprise. Although the curse had been muttered, she still heard it from her position one row away from the photocopier. Curiously, she eased a book silently off the shelf and peered through the gap. She saw a man; Lili guessed him to be in his mid-thirties, tall and powerfully built.

Short, cropped hair hugged his well-shaped head like a helmet, and broad shoulders shrugged in an exasperated gesture of impatience.

He was attractive, she thought – if you liked men who looked like they belonged in a boxing ring. Although at that moment, his rugged features were wearing an expression of infuriated frustration.

They were in the library; Lili to get some new cookery books, and the strange man apparently to use the photocopier. Although from the curses and evil looks, he was currently heaping upon the unfortunate machine, he wasn't having a lot of luck with it.

As Lili watched he ran a hand over his head, glared at the machine, and her lips twitched at the colourfully inventive threats the poor photocopier was now subjected to.

His head swung up, his eyes locking with hers through the books. Lili took an involuntary step back.

"Hello," he grinned, seemingly unabashed she had overheard him threatening to give the copier a re-programming with a hammer.

"Hi," mumbled Lili, hastily dropping her eyes back to the books.

"Listen, sorry, but I don't suppose you know how this damn thing works do you?"

Cautiously, Lili edged her way around the bookshelves. The man flashed a hopeful smile, and she saw his eyes were an unusual, pale green colour. For some reason, he reminded her of Boris. Maybe it was the chunky, thickset body, the strong, almost ugly, but still attractive face, or perhaps it was the kindness in his eyes.

Whatever it was, Lili relaxed, looking at the photocopier with interest.

"Well, that depends. What are you trying to do?"

"I've got some plans for a conservatory my architect sent me. I'm trying to make a copy of them, but all that keeps coming out is blank paper."

His accent reminded her of Lindy's, or rather how Lindy's used to be, before two years of exposure to the others softened the Essex edge from her voice.

"The problem is the plans are so faint, the copier can't see them. That's why the copies are coming out blank," Lili glanced knowledgeably at the plans.

"So how do I get around that?"

"You have to override the default setting."

"Huh?"

From the expression on his face, it was plain Lili might as well have spoken in Mandarin. Lili stepped up to the machine.

"Here, I'll show you, it's quite easy. Press this button until it goes to the darkest dot, put your plans under again. Sometimes it helps if you press on the cover while it's copying."

"Why? What does that do?"

"I'm not too sure, I think it squashes the original down on the glass so perhaps the copier can see it better." Lili crowed with triumph as the machine spat out a perfectly legible copy. "Here we go. How many copies do you need?"

"Two of each page, thanks, I'd never have got the damn thing working myself."

"That's okay, glad I could help," Lili turned to go, but his voice pulled her back.

"I'm Tom, by the way, Tom Mackenzie."

"Oh, Lili … Lili Goodwin," Lili shook the proffered hand, her own being swallowed up in a hand that looked like it could crush concrete without a second thought.

"Nice to meet you, Lili. Don't suppose I can buy you coffee as a thank you?"

Lili hesitated. It being a Friday morning, she'd no place to go or anything pressing to do yet was cautious of spending time with this strange man.

Then he grinned. Once again, the resemblance to Boris was uncanny; that hopeful friendliness that made her smile in return and agree.

They sat in the library's coffee shop and talked. Lili learnt Tom and his elderly mother had recently moved into the area, and then the conversation moved onto a wide range of topics. Tom seemed to have an almost encyclopaedic knowledge of every subject under the sun, although his confessed passion was music. As this was an interest Lili also shared, they found their conversation centred around the music world.

When Tom looked at his watch, and with evident reluctance said he had to go, Lili felt a genuine pang of regret. Much to her surprise, she had enjoyed talking to him, feeling her viewpoints and opinions stretched by the broad and far-reaching conversation.

"Do you come to the library often?" she enquired casually, not sure how one went about asking a man if you could see him again.

"Not really," he replied. "I only came in today because the copier at work is broken, and I haven't got one at home yet."

"Oh," said Lili. "I see. So, I guess I'll see you around then?"

"Probably. Thanks for helping, Lili, much appreciated. Now, I've got to run, I'm meeting the architect in half an hour." As abruptly as he'd entered her life, he left.

Mentally shrugging her shoulders, Lili slowly pulled her jacket on, checked out the two books she had selected, and grimaced as she left the shelter of the library, the full force of the late August downpour catching her unprepared and without an umbrella.

Once home, she made tea and sat at the kitchen table, turning the pages of her new books, her mind wandering back to the previous weekend when the whole group had hired a van and helped Kevin and Amy move.

Lili smiled, thinking about the beautiful, four-bedroom cottage on the outskirts of town her friends had bought; the main attraction for Kevin, the half-acre of untouched land that came with it.

What an amazing year it had been for them both.

True to her word, Adele had used Amy again, wholeheartedly recommending her to all her friends. Amy began to find herself in demand to cater for dinner parties, birthdays, anniversaries, even the odd, small-scale wedding. Over Christmas the rest of the group had hardly seen her, she'd been so busy.

Finally, in April, Amy had taken a deep breath, handed in her notice at work, and become a full-time caterer, supplementing her freelance work by offering cover to local restaurants when their chefs were absent.

The Sinclair's had fallen in love with the cottage in June, deciding between them they were solvent enough to buy it. Yet, Amy had insisted it was Kevin's name on the deeds.

Lili suspected the cottage was merely a stepping-stone for Amy and that soon, perhaps in another year, she'd be earning enough to buy a home of her own.

If Amy's star was in the ascendant, Kevin's had gone stratospheric.

Upon completion of the stunningly beautiful garden for Lady Felsham, the local paper had run a story on its grand opening, with a picture of Kevin as the designer.

Then, a month later, the home and garden section of the Sunday Times ran a feature on stately homes which were modernising themselves, yet still retaining the period feel. The new, contemporary, medieval-style knot garden at Felsham Hall was a perfect illustration of this, and once again a picture of Kevin appeared.

Local radio then contacted Kevin, persuading him to do a live interview on the morning breakfast show, with a mini phone-in where listeners could call and discuss their gardening problems with local garden designer, Kevin Sinclair.

The show had been a surprising success, and Kevin had been invited back a further two times before the local television channel caught up with him.

Now, Kevin was a local celebrity. His first television series which aired Wednesday evenings on Anglia television had stunned even its producers with its instant success.

Maybe it was his quietly knowledgeable air or his passion for gardening that shone through the screen into people's homes inspiring them to take an interest in their own little plots. Maybe it was that he was a local lad, born and bred, or maybe it was the fact he was, as one TV critic put it, 'drop dead gorgeous' and 'made gardening sexy'.

It was undeniably true that when Kevin Sinclair smiled his slow, genuine, warm smile directly into the camera, ran his fingers through tousled blond hair and recommended planting trailing pelargonium in hanging baskets, women nearly trampled each other in their rush to buy. By the end of the weekend, there wouldn't be a single pelargonium left in any garden centre anywhere in East Anglia.

Kevin made gardening fun by dragging the crew out from behind the camera and making them get their hands dirty. Once, the soundman made fun of Kevin's threadbare jumper, enquiring where he'd got it. To Kevin's reply, his mother had knitted it for him, the soundman unwittingly commented she needed to make him another, as this one was falling apart.

Kevin had smiled, a sadly ironic smile, informing the region that regrettably, his mother was dead. From then on, the postman groaned under the weight of hand-knitted jumpers sent to the television centre.

Stunned by the almost overnight fame he achieved, Kevin stayed completely grounded and committed to his friends. As far as he was concerned nothing very much had changed, except he'd been able to give up his despised job as an insurance salesman and was being paid to do exactly what he loved the most. The fact he was being paid an awful lot of money didn't go to his head either.

Convinced it couldn't last, Kevin saved and invested as much money as he could. He also worked hard at the private landscape design side of his career, knowing if the television cameras went away, he could still earn enough to live very comfortably.

Fan mail began to arrive at the studio; a trickle at first, which gradually became a flood, until he could no longer cope with it by himself. It fell into two categories – genuine enquiries from keen gardeners; these Kevin tried to answer personally – and letters from obviously lonely women who saw him as the answer to their prayers; these were handled by a secretary, adept at sending back a carefully worded reply with a standard autographed photo.

These letters made Kevin, who genuinely had no idea why women were making such a fuss over him, feel distinctly uncomfortable that anyone could think such things about him, let alone commit them to paper.

No, nothing had changed. There were still only three women in Kevin's life.

Amy – his sister.

Lindy – his friend.

Lili – his love.

Not that Lili had any inkling of the ever constant, unwavering depth of feeling Kevin had for her.

Drinking her hot tea with pleasure, Lili's smile deepened as her thoughts moved to Johnny, for he too had travelled a long way in a very short space of time.

From playboy to businessman in a year. Not bad going she mused, feeling a flash of pride as she reflected on how hard he worked, and how it had all started so innocuously...

Martin was issued a laptop by work and carried it home with pride. Still relatively rare, the rest of the gang watched with awe as Martin played with it, all except Johnny. He was engrossed in the Racing Post, picking out a sure thing for the 2:30 at Newmarket, paying no attention to Martin's attempts to retrieve a lost file.

At Martin's fifth cry of 'oh bugger it' however, Johnny threw down his paper with a huff of exasperation, strode over to the laptop, and with a few keystrokes brought the file back up on the screen, leaving Martin and the others staring at him open-mouthed.

"How ... what? What did you do? Where was it?" stammered Martin, slightly miffed at the ease with which Johnny had handled his new toy.

"You'd archived it by mistake," was Johnny's offhand reply. "It's a common mistake, easy to correct if you know how."

"Oh," replied Martin, looking dubiously at the small flickering screen. "Do you know about computers then?" he asked.

"A bit," the casualness of reply left Lili feeling it was probably an understatement.

"Well," Martin joked. "I wish you'd come into work and teach us. We've had all new computers installed, and none of us has the faintest idea how they work."

"Okay," Johnny shrugged, dismissing it from his mind.

But Martin didn't forget, excitedly telling his superior about the IT expert he knew who could come in and train them all, for a fee of course. Interested and impressed, his boss made Johnny an offer which had even the jaded future Lord raising an eyebrow and, more as a favour to Martin, Johnny spent a week giving expert tuition and one-on-one training.

At the end, Johnny was surprised to find he'd rather enjoyed himself, had a cheque in his pocket for a substantial sum of money, and the basis of a new career.

Martin's superior recommended him to a colleague, who hired Johnny to help his staff get to grips with their new technology, and so it had begun. Mostly spread by recommendation, Johnny had been launched on a career as a freelance IT consultant, a job which suited him perfectly.

Due to the flexibility of his hours, he could, if he chose, take time off to jaunt around the world. Although, as time passed and his business grew, Johnny found intense satisfaction in earning his own money, being respected for something, and the wild excursions became almost a thing of the past.

His parents were delighted, despairing of their son ever settling down to a steady career. The fact he had successfully built up a solid business so quickly impressed them mightily, despite the fact they didn't fully understand precisely what it was he did.

A small, but to Johnny intensely satisfying, benefit of building a successful career practically overnight, was that it pissed Lindy off. One of her main weapons against him had been, as she put it, his work-shy, lazy-arse attitude to life.

Seeing her face as he casually mentioned the fees he commanded, Johnny couldn't help but laugh, even though Lindy was gradually building her cleaning business up into a good, solid career.

Yes, Lili decided, tipping the dregs of her tea down the sink, and placing the cup in the dishwasher, all in all, life was good.

It was Saturday night. The group were out, determined to party. Lindy's birthday, Kevin and Amy's new home, the fact it was the first time they'd been clubbing for a couple of weeks, there didn't have to be a particular reason … being together, being young and having money in their pocket, were grounds for celebration.

Walking towards the club a chill breeze sprang up, making the girls shiver in thin dresses, and Lili hoped the queue was not too long. Rounding the corner they let out a collective groan at the tailback of shivering clubbers wrapping arms around scantily clad bodies, as an unseasonably cold snap caught everyone unprepared.

Resigning themselves to a long wait, Lili and her friends walked past the club's entrance to join the back of the queue.

"Oi, Lili!"

Surprised, Lili's face lit up as she recognised one of the door staff, looking very masculine in a dinner jacket. Tom grinned as she joyfully acknowledged his greeting.

"Tom, hi, I didn't know you worked here."

"Only started last week. You lot coming in?"

Lili pulled a face at the queue. "Well, eventually. See you in about an hour, I think."

"Don't be daft, in you come."

"Are you sure?" Lili asked as the queue grumbled unhappily.

"Yeah, sure, come on in. You don't want to stand out here, it's bloody freezing."

"Thanks, Tom." Gratefully the rest of the group followed Lili into the club. "Tom, these are my friends. This is Amy, Lindy, Kevin, Martin, and Johnny. Everyone this is Tom. We met yesterday in the library." The group chorused their hellos.

"Lili here stopped me from committing GBH on the photocopier ... no, no, you put your money away," Tom interrupted himself. "Donna, you put Lili and her mates on my guest list."

A bored Donna shrugged, shifted gum to the other cheek, and scribbled something in a book.

"Thanks, Tom."

One and all the group expressed their gratitude, and Lili felt Lindy and Amy's questioning eyes fix intensely on her. Tom patted her on the arm.

"You go on in. Once the rush has cleared, I'll come and see you."

Entering the club, the music tugged at them, and Lili felt her body start to throb in time to the beat. Lindy fished a £10 note out of her bag and passed it to Kevin.

"First round on me," she stated. "We'll have the usual. Bogs now," she ordered, fixing Lili with a meaningful stare. "You have some explaining to do." Amy nodded in agreement. Leaving the bemused men behind, they hustled Lili into the ladies.

"Now," Lindy demanded, "where on earth did you meet such a hunk, and why did you not inform us about him immediately?"

"Who? What hunk?"

"What hunk? Mr Why don't you walk straight on in and oh don't worry about paying, that's what hunk?"

"Oh, Tom. Is he a hunk, do we think?"

"Duh, yeah ..." Lindy rolled her eyes at Amy, who nodded enthusiastically.

"He's not my type," she said. "But he is gorgeous, in a sort of older, rough, dangerous kind of way. So, is there something you feel you ought to tell us, Lili?"

"No," Lili laughed. "Tom seems nice. We met yesterday in the library..."

"I so need to start reading more," muttered Lindy. "I had no idea you could pick up men like him in the library."

"I didn't pick him up," protested Lili. "He's not my type. He's a friend, that's all. Besides, he's far too old for me."

"Yeah, yeah," drawled Lindy sarcastically. "Pull the other one."

"I mean it," stated Lili firmly. "He's just a friend…"

Of all the friendships Lili formed, her one with Tom was perhaps the most unusual. Superficially, it seemed they had little in common. Older than her by fifteen years, part of a world completely alien to Lili's, still they became firm friends, finding pleasure in each other's company.

Tom took Lili to meet his mother, Muriel, a pragmatic, down to earth lady in her late sixties, who took life in her stride and had unshakeable faith in her son.

Lili was touched by Tom's concern for his mother, realising the only reason Muriel lived alone in a delightful little garden flat in the town centre was because she wanted to. Several times, Tom attempted to persuade his mother to move into the seventeenth-century farmhouse he had bought outside Bury, but each time she gently refused.

One day, Tom happened to mention how his mother loved to go shopping and to lunch, but he didn't always have the time, and anyway, the thought of Tom escorting his mother into a ladies' boutique was enough to make Lili smile. Quietly, she offered to take his mother one Friday, and it quickly became a regular occurrence.

Muriel enjoyed the company of this beautiful, yet modest, youthful, yet sensible young woman whom her son thought so much of. She observed with satisfaction the way Tom's eyes would soften when he saw her, how his expression grew wistful when talking about Lili, and her mother's heart nursed a secret hope.

But Lili carried such an untouched air about her, Muriel felt sure if there was a man in the world who could ignite the flames within Lili, it wasn't Tom.

On Lili's part, Muriel reminded her so much of her grandmother it was a bittersweet experience spending time with her. Muriel's sharply observant wit and dryly caustic tongue made Lili smile. When they went shopping together or had lunch, Lili knew people assumed she was Muriel's granddaughter, and her heart ached.

Accepted as an honorary member of the group by the others, Tom always let them queue jump to get into the club and would never let them pay.

Learning Lili was finally buying a car, he insisted on going with her – the car dealers quickly changing their minds about which cars to show to Lili once they realised, she was Tom's friend.

One Saturday, the group turned up at the club as usual to find no sign of Tom. Assuming maybe he was on holiday or sick, they queued and paid in the normal way, too grateful for all the times Tom had eased their way in to grumble at his absence.

They'd not been in the club long when Lili felt a large hand fall on her shoulder. Turning, she saw Tom, face as black as thunder, standing behind her.

"Sorry, Lili," he said, his mouth grim. "I was busy and the new girl on the door didn't know you. Here."

To Lili's surprise, he pushed their entry money into her hand.

"We don't mind paying to get in, Tom," exclaimed Lili. "We're so grateful you let us in for free, but don't expect it."

"Do you seriously think I'd charge you or your friends, Lili? Not after all you do for Mum." He shook his head emphatically. "No, as long as I have a say in it, you'll never pay to enter this club."

"Thank you," stuttered Lili, taken aback at his vehemence. "But we don't want to get you in any trouble with your boss."

"My boss?" Tom stared at her, an incredulous smile spreading across his face. "But ... I thought you knew Lili?"

"Knew what?" Lili asked.

"I am the boss," he laughed. "I own this club. I can let whoever I want in."

"Oh," said Lili, feeling a bit stupid. "Tom," she called as he turned to go. "That's not why I do it, you know," she lifted her hand with the money still clasped in it. "This isn't why I go and see Muriel."

"I know it's not," replied Tom. "I know that's not the kind of person you are, and that's why I ..." he stopped.

To Lili's astonishment a flush swept over his strong face, he mumbled something, turned, and fled, leaving Lili staring in baffled surprise.

"Oh dear," drawled Lindy behind her sarcastically. "Is that another one biting the dust then?"

"What?"

Lili turned, as Lindy and Amy exchanged grins, bursting into a spontaneous chorus of the classic song by Queen.

"What are you talking about?" demanded Lili, and Amy laughed.

"You really don't know, do you?"

"Know what?"

"That every man you meet falls in love with you."

"They don't!"

"Oh, yes they do," chimed in Lindy. "But don't worry about it. You do that ice queen, we can be friends thing, that you do so well, and they soon get over it."

"So, you reckon that Tom..."

"Is completely and utterly head over heels in love with you? Oh yes."

"No, that's crazy, you're wrong. He can't be!"

"Why?" asked Lindy, curiously. "Do you think you're so unlovable?"

"No, it's not that, it's just … well, I'm not the sort of person men fall in love with."

As the two girls hooted with derision at this statement, Lili silently amended it in her head; at least, the man I want to fall in love with me hasn't.

Later that evening, when they finally staggered back to Lili's after the usual riotous evening, it was to discover a message on the answerphone from Daisy.

Greg had been asked to exhibit his paintings in a small gallery in London in two weeks. It was last minute because he was a replacement for an artist who'd had a temperamental fit and pulled out. He was very nervous, and Daisy wondered if Lili would like to attend the opening night to offer moral support.

Chapter Twenty-Four
"Would you call me a friend, Lili?"

Using her key to let herself into Conrad and Matthew's apartment, Lili reflected how much she had grown up since that first trip to London two years before when she spent the entire journey worrying about getting on the wrong train.

Now a veteran of many visits, whilst Lili couldn't say she particularly liked London – all the noise and people still bothered her somewhat – at least she had absolutely no qualms about travelling from the station to the apartment by herself.

It was Friday.

Greg's exhibition was to be held that evening. As requested, Lili was attending to offer moral support. Conrad and Matthew were also going but had prior work commitments for the day, so Conrad had sent Lili a key, instructing her to make herself at home, saying that he'd be back as soon as possible.

Lili didn't mind. It had been a long week. She was tired and a bit relieved at the prospect of a few hours' solitude. Besides, if she had to spend time alone anywhere, Conrad's apartment was as good a place as any. She had brought Jake's latest novel with her, intending to relax on the spectacular roof terrace and struggle her way through it.

At least that was the plan, but she found herself unable to concentrate, distracted by the amazing view over the London rooftops, balmy in the warmth of an Indian summer, and by a vague sense of expectation jittering at her nerves.

Giving it up as a bad job, she leant against the railing staring out across the city, wondering how Greg was doing, imagining he was probably involved in last-minute preparations and panicking.

It amazed her that someone so talented could have doubts about their ability. Lili had brought her chequebook; she wanted more of Greg's work, at least three more pictures.

She knew Daisy and Conrad also intended to buy, so that would be a good start for Greg.

The entry phone buzzed making her jump with surprise. Staring uncertainly at the intercom, it buzzed impatiently again. Anxiously, she pressed the button.

"Yes?" her voice was husky with nerves.

There was a brief pause, then a voice.

"Conrad? It's Jake, can I come up?"

Jake?

Lili stared at the intercom as if it was an unexploded bomb.

Jake?

What on earth was he doing here? Speaking to Daisy, she'd enquired casually if he and Vivienne were coming, but had been told that they, unfortunately, couldn't make it at such short notice.

"Hello? Conrad?"

The voice was impatient. Lili was unable to speak. In despair she pressed the door release button, knowing in two minutes, possibly less, Jake would be ringing the doorbell.

Two minutes.

It's amazing what a woman can achieve in two minutes, Lili shot into her room, ripped a brush through her hair, gargled mouthwash, shakily applied eyeliner and lipstick, and dabbed perfume on her pressure points.

The doorbell rang.

She dropped the bottle, spilling half the contents over the dressing table. Muttering curses, she frantically grabbed tissues and mopped up the sweet-smelling spillage. Bugger, she thought, the room smells like a tart's boudoir.

As she hurried down the hall, the bell rang again and she paused, hand on heart, taking a deep, shaky breath to attempt to pull herself together before opening it. Jake turned as the door opened, surprise flashing onto his face.

"Lili? What are you doing here? Where's Conrad?"

"Conrad's at work," she explained. "And I'm here for Greg's exhibition."

"Oh right, the exhibition."

He seemed distracted. Lili noticed lines of stress around his mouth, shadows under his eyes, and the fact he'd lost weight.

"I'd forgotten about that," he looked disappointed.

"Why don't you come in?" she asked, hurriedly opening the door wider. Jake hesitated, shrugged, and entered.

Heart pounding, Lili led the way back into the vast open-plan room slathered in light from the wall of windows opening onto the terrace.

"I was about to make coffee," she lied breathlessly. "Would you like some?"

"Sure," Jake shrugged. "Why not."

"Make yourself at home," she said casually. "I won't be a moment." Escaping to the kitchen, she stood, dazed with shock, before clumsily putting the kettle on.

Coming back five minutes later, carefully carrying a tray of coffee and biscuits, Lili found Jake on the terrace leaning on the railing, staring moodily out across the city.

Quietly, she placed the tray on the table, hovering uncertainly, unsure whether to speak or not, then finally crossing over to lean on the railing next to him.

"What time will Conrad be back?"

Jake turned to look at her. Once again, Lili saw the sadness on his face.

She wanted to comfort, but simply said, "I'm not sure, in time to get ready for the exhibition."

Jake nodded, rubbed a hand across his face, and smiled down at her. Lili felt her heart do its usual somersault. What was it about him that affected her so? It had been a year since they last met, yet she loved him.

The realisation came, sudden and sharp – no more doubts or hesitation – she loved him.

So, that was that.

Dropping her eyes, unwilling for him to read the raw emotion she could feel within them, Lili missed the softening of his expression as he looked at her.

"Little Lili," he said.

She heard the amused fondness in his tone and her hackles rose. What wouldn't she give to hear him say her name with love and need, not address her the way you would a child? She raised a brow in enquiry, and he placed a hand over hers.

"Have you come all this way to support Greg?"

"It's a big deal for him," Lili stated waspishly. "His first exhibition, of course, I wanted to be here for him. Greg's a friend."

"And you'd do anything for your friends, right Lili?"

"I guess," Lili was unsure where the conversation was leading.

"Would you call me a friend, Lili?"

"Of course," she replied, her eyes never leaving his.

"Well, I need all the friends I can get right now, so that's good," was his rather strange answer.

Lili blinked in concern. "Is everything okay, Jake? Why are you here? Not for the exhibition, you'd forgotten about that, so why have you come to England? Is Vivienne with you?"

"No, she's … back in the States," Jake paused, frowning. "What the hell," he shrugged. "I may as well tell you, it'll be common knowledge soon enough, Vivienne and I … we've separated."

"Separated?"

Swift joy pierced her heart, and Lili ducked her head away from his gaze, not wanting to betray her feelings of jubilation.

"I'm so sorry, Jake," she managed to say in a calm, sympathetic voice. "Do you want to talk about it?"

"There's not much to talk about." Jake turned his back on the view. "I'm sorry, could I have some coffee? It was a long flight, and my body clock is totally out of whack. I need caffeine to get it going again."

"Of course," murmured Lili.

Jake sat as she busied herself pouring two cups of hot, fragrant coffee, pushing one across the table towards him. Quietly mumbling thanks, Jake took a gulp, briefly closing his eyes in appreciation.

"That's better," he stated, putting the cup down on the table. "Tell me something," he began, turning to face Lili. "What did you think of Vivienne, Lili?"

"Well … I didn't know her, so I couldn't … that is, we barely exchanged more than a dozen words so …" Lili's voice trailed away under his coolly level gaze.

"You didn't like her, did you, Lili?"

"Well, I wouldn't say that …" Lili floundered, out of her depth.

"It's okay, I don't want to put you in an awkward position." He sighed. "The truth is, Lili, nobody seems to like Vivienne. She has no friends. Oh, there are people she sees regularly, we go to their parties, they come to ours, we lunch together, but, after a while, I realised Vivienne has no feelings for them. She's close to no one except me, and lately, I've wondered how well I know her."

Lili sat, silent and attentive, listening to every word, large solemn eyes fixed on Jake, her coffee forgotten.

"This whole baby thing has been kind of tough too, Vivi had all the tests and they found nothing wrong with her, so I guess the problem is me. She hasn't said anything, but I know she blames me. Sometimes I see her look at me if we see a baby on the street or TV, and I can feel her eyes accusing me … it makes me feel, oh hell, it makes me feel a complete failure as a man."

"That's untrue and unfair." Lili broke in hotly. "You're a human being, not a sperm machine. Your sole function on this earth is not simply to impregnate someone." She broke off, cheeks flaming with embarrassment at her own words.

"See what I mean?" Jake gave an ironic laugh. "You're always protecting your friends, Lili. No, I'm afraid it's true. In that department, I've let Vivi down. The one thing she wanted is the one thing I can't give her."

"Is that why you separated?"

Lili shook her head in confusion, having problems equating the Vivienne she knew and despised, with the desperately maternal woman Jake was describing.

"Because you can't have children?"

"No," Jake drank more coffee, shaking his head. "If that were the only problem, we'd get over it somehow. No, it's more than that. She's changed. She's not the woman I fell in love with. Maybe everyone was right. Maybe we did get married too quickly. Perhaps we should have waited and got to know each other better, but at the time it seemed the right thing to do. I had no doubts. Perhaps I should have."

Lili bit her lip, unwilling to comment, instead pouring him more coffee, and pushing the plate of biscuits towards him.

"She's hard to live with," Jake confided.

The floodgates were opening, and Lili sensed his relief at the offloading of his burden.

"I mean, hell, I'm no picnic to live with either, but with Vivienne, everything has to go her way or the highway. There's no room at all for compromise in her world," he paused, sipping gratefully at his fresh coffee.

"She's intensely ambitious; I honestly think her career is the most important thing in the world to her. I know acting's a tough game, perhaps actors do have to be single-minded, a little ruthless maybe, but the things I've heard Vivienne say, the things I've watched her do to secure a role or make sure someone else doesn't … well, it goes beyond professional rivalry," he shook his head.

"There was a young actress, new in town, naïve. She was up for a part Vivi wanted. She probably wouldn't have got it, hell, Vivi's good, she has solid experience behind her. *Enemy Unknown* was a box office smash. It was doubtful the studio would have gone with an unknown, but Vivi wanted to make sure. So, she planted enough particularly vicious rumours about a drug dependency in the right ears. The actress was dropped. It's unlikely she'll ever be given another role in Hollywood."

"But that's awful," Lili burst out, unable to believe what Jake was telling her. "Are you sure it's true? I mean, how did you find out?"

"Vivienne told me," Jake confided with a wry grin. "She thought it funny, seemed to think I'd be impressed with her cunning, her cleverness. When she realised, I was sickened by what she had done, she turned on the tears, claiming she'd done it out of fear of growing old. That unless you've made a name for yourself by the time you hit thirty, you're washed up in Hollywood. She was very convincing. Not so long ago she would have fooled me, the tears, the lies, but this time – I saw right through them, saw through her act – and I didn't like what I saw underneath."

Lili rubbed at her arms, her flesh chilling in reaction to his words, Jake glanced at her, and Lili's heart almost broke at the sadness on his face.

"There were other things, small things, that at the time didn't register, but later, thinking back, added together to make a person I wasn't sure I wanted to be with. I confronted her, tried to talk to her, desperate to see if we could salvage our marriage, but she turned on me, I've never seen her so angry. The things she said, the words that came out of her mouth, they …"

He stopped, looking directly at Lili.

"My marriage is over," he stated simply.

"I'm sorry," replied Lili quietly in genuine sympathy.

Whilst she felt nothing but relief that Jake was no longer with Vivienne, she empathised with his pain and wished she could ease it somehow.

"She's moving out this weekend. I needed to be somewhere else, so without stopping to think, I came here and checked into a hotel. I know I could stay with the family, but don't think I'm up to coping with all the sympathy yet. Once here, I didn't know where to go or who to see first. I don't know why I chose Conrad, maybe because I've known him so long, he's almost family, yet he's not. I knew he wouldn't judge or give me advice, so I came here and instead found you." He paused and smiled.

"I found you," he continued quietly. "My little friend Lili, with the big eyes and even bigger heart. Little Lili who loves her friends and is good at listening. Maybe I'm glad Conrad was out after all."

Lili's lip trembled, desperately ridiculous words of love and longing choking her. She held them back. Now was not the time to make declarations of undying love. He had only just left his wife; the wound was raw and painful. He was still grieving over his failed marriage.

"Would you like to go for a walk with me?"

"I'm sorry?" Lili dragged her confused mind back.

"It's a lovely day. It would be nice to get out, so I was wondering, would you like to go for a walk with me?"

"Yes," Lili stuttered. "Yes please, I'd love to..."

Meandering down Kensington high street, the low, bright autumn sun dazzling her eyes, Lili kept catching sight of them in shop windows, walking slowly and easily together, arms nearly touching, Jake so tall and masculine by comparison she appeared fragile, almost ethereal.

It felt surreal, dreamlike, and Lili savoured each sensation, the light breeze tickling strands of hair across her cheek. The sounds of the city faded into obscurity as she stole sideways glances at the tall, dearly beloved stranger who strode so confidently by her side.

They paused with the crowd to cross the road, and a forward surge jostled Lili almost off the kerb. With a murmur of concern, Jake caught her hand. Somehow, upon reaching the other side, he failed to let go of it again.

In unspoken agreement, they wandered into Hyde Park, its cool greenness a welcome relief from the hurried frenzy of the streets. There was an easy, companionable silence between them, and the notion occurred fleetingly to Lili if her life were to end right then, she'd be content, being with Jake in this shady oasis, his palm warm and strong against hers, feeling the throb of potential.

They spent an hour in the park; walking, sitting on a bench, people-watching, their conversation light and inconsequential. Yet, in those brief exchanges, Lili felt the weight of unspoken possibilities, and her heart ballooned with all the love for this man she had been holding in, not allowing herself to feel.

He looked at her, smiled, stood, and held out his hand. Silently, Lili placed her palm against his, their fingers laced together, and a bond, intangible and unbreakable, was formed. In a moment of sudden, blinding clarity, Lili knew there could be no other for her. Not now, not ever.

"Do you know how easy it is to be with you," he murmured. "I don't think I've ever met anyone so undemanding, so unassuming, not like …"

He broke off, face darkening. Lili knew his thoughts had returned to Vivienne, and a little of the shine rubbed off the day.

They had lunch in a small, friendly, Italian restaurant, where they sat by the open window eating pasta, drinking rich, blood-red wine, watching the vast diversity of souls that make up the streets of London pass by.

The food was good, and the wine was excellent. But when she finished, Lili couldn't have told you what had been on her plate.

They sipped coffee, a reluctance hovering between them. Lili knew it was late. Soon he'd suggest heading back.

Part of her wished this moment could be suspended in time forever; another part fretted impatiently to move on, to get over this necessary caution given the newness of his separation.

She yearned to be so much more to him than a friend and occasional confidant. His little Lili ached to be his lover. Heat fired her face at the wild thoughts burning as she sat, calmly drinking coffee.

"Will you go to the exhibition tonight?" she casually enquired.

"The exhibition?" Jake looked thoughtful. "I'm not sure …" he began hesitantly.

"I think you should go," Lili interrupted smoothly. "It's Greg's big break. It would mean a lot to him if you were there."

She paused, a look sliding onto her face, brazen, arch, and pure woman. Her fingers inched across to lightly connect with his.

"It would mean a lot to me if you were there," she finished.

Jake swallowed.

Lili saw a look flash into his eyes; an acknowledgement of her as a woman, sexual and desirable. She gloried in her newly discovered feminine powers.

"Perhaps you're right," he murmured, looking slightly stunned.

"Besides," continued Lili airily, as if nothing monumental had occurred between them, "if you don't go and Greg learns you were in London, he'd be dreadfully hurt."

"There is that," Jake muttered, smiling at her. "Okay, I'll go."

"Good," declared Lili coolly, as if the outcome had never been in any doubt. Looking around the restaurant, she caught sight of the clock. It was almost four. "I suppose we should think about going."

Relaxed after his promise to see her again tonight, Lili was now impatient to move time on; to get back to the apartment, pamper and indulge; to make herself beautiful for this evening – for him.

Jake nodded, signalling for the bill.

The protective bubble encasing them, keeping the rest of the world at bay, burst with an almost audible pop, and real-life gushed in.

He walked her home, where they hesitated, unsure how to say goodbye. They were friends, but both knew a line had been crossed. That their relationship hovered uncertainly in no-mans-land.

"Do you want to come in?" Lili asked finally.

Jake considered, shaking his head.

"Best not," he said, with evident reluctance. "I'd better get back to my hotel and grab some sleep before tonight. The time difference is catching up with me."

Lili nodded, noting the dark shadows under his eyes, the tiredness which dragged at his face. Unthinkingly, she put a hand on his cheek, feeling the prick of stubble under her palm as she lightly stroked down his jawline.

Jake caught her hand in his with a fierce, almost predatory look, and Lili gasped as her heart knocked against the back of her throat.

"Not yet," he murmured.

Lili's brows drew together questioningly.

"Not yet," he said again. "I'm not saying no, Lili, I'm saying not yet."

Was it obvious? Would everyone be able to see the difference? Standing in front of the mirror, Lili looked wonderingly in the glass at the strange woman she saw.

Nearly three hours of preparation lay behind her, evident in the sweep of painstakingly blown dry hair, the perfection of an artfully made-up face, the shine of glossy nails, and smooth, flawless skin.

But it went deeper than mere surface adornment.

Slowly, Lili ran her hands down her silk-clad body, intently watching the woman in the mirror as her lips parted on a breath of newly awakened, sexual awareness, pupils dilating until her eyes turned black with impenetrable fathoms of desire.

She glowed with love; was saturated with anticipatory craving. It surrounded her with an almost palpable aura of want and need.

Tonight …

Tonight ... Hopes and wishes accumulated over two long years would finally reach their climax.

Lili watched, transfixed, an unfamiliar hunger growling in the pit of her belly, as the mirror image woman fleetingly trailed her palms over small, neat breasts leaving nipples solid and aching.

Unbearably aroused, Lili shifted uncomfortably, smoothing the silky material of her evening gown over slender hips.

"Lili? Are you nearly ready to go?"

The bang on her door and Conrad's voice, shocked her into the real world, a frustrated gasp slipping from her lips. She breathed deeply to calm and steady herself.

"Just a minute," she called, surprised by the ordinariness of her voice, glancing back at her reflection with satisfaction.

"Oh yes," she whispered. "Tonight..."

Arriving at the gallery, Lili was pleased for Greg that it was already crowded. Dreamily following Conrad and Matthew forging a path through the masses, a tiny smile of satisfaction played across her face, and many a pair of male eyes were irresistibly drawn to the darkly beautiful woman who sparkled with a secret, inner happiness.

Jake wasn't there yet.

Lili could feel his absence like a black, empty hole. It didn't matter. Anticipating his presence was sending chills up her spine as she pictured his expression when faced with her newly found womanhood.

He didn't stand a chance.

Despite his protests, Lili knew tonight she was irresistible. Tonight, he would have to acknowledge the attraction that snapped and tugged them ever closer together.

She drifted through the crowd. Someone pressed a glass of champagne into her hand. She drank deeply of its brilliant effervescence, the bubbles matching her mood as sheer exhilaration took possession of her willing body.

An hour later the smile was slipping. There was no sign of Jake, and Lili feared he might still be asleep. Quietly, she slipped through a door marked staff only, hoping to find a telephone.

She knew which hotel he was staying at. If Jake had changed his mind about coming to the exhibition, then she would call a taxi and go to him.

Walking lightly down a carpeted corridor, Lili heard voices raised in angry, bitter confrontation.

Getting closer, realising it was Greg and Daisy, she paused outside the door, hesitated, then turned to go, unwilling to eavesdrop on her friends.

One step was taken before Jake's name dragged her back.

"You can't blame Jake."

Daisy's voice was calm, although Lili heard the conciliatory, almost pleading note beneath her cool tone.

"Can't I?" By contrast, Greg's was sharp and angry.

"You're not married, Greg, you don't understand how hard it can be. When two people vow to stay together forever, compromises, even sacrifices have to be made."

"That's bull, Daisy. How can you possibly tell me you approve?"

"I didn't say I approved, I said I understood. There's a difference."

"Okay, so you claim to understand why's he gone back, why he couldn't even have waited one more day, why he's not fucking well here? You explain it to me then. Because I don't get it. He turns up alone, unexpected. I've left her, he says. That's great. We all applaud him because none of us..."

Greg's voice rose as he hammered his point home.

"None of us like her. She's a bitch, she hasn't made him happy, it's long past the time he should cut his losses and walk away. But then, not half an hour later, he gets a call from her, and off he trots to the airport like a good little boy to catch the first flight to the States, and you expect me to be okay with that?"

He'd gone?

Back to Vivienne?

Greg and Daisy were still talking, but Lili no longer heard. Her hands flew to her mouth, her heart pounding in her ears.

He'd gone back to Vivienne!

She froze, eyes wide and unseeing.

He'd gone.

No, he couldn't have...

He wouldn't have...

She'd thought, after today...

She'd been so sure, so certain...

But he'd gone?

No, it wasn't true, it couldn't be...

Yet – he'd gone...

Choking back sobs, Lili fled, fumbling with the handle of a door marked private, slipping into a darkened room. Shutting the door, she dropped bonelessly to the floor, biting at her hands to muffle her primal groans.

Gasping with pain, she rocked and clutched at her hair.

No, No, NO!

She ground the word out, tasting the acrid sting of bile in her throat, as the champagne so gaily consumed earlier regurgitated itself in a wave of rancid despair and disbelief, and Lili curled into an amoebic ball on the floor, her world disintegrating into shards of bitter disillusionment.

"Did you hear something?" Daisy broke into Greg's rant, her head cocked towards the door, brows knitting in a frown.

"No, and don't change the subject."

"I'm not."

Puzzled, Daisy pushed the door open, peering down the semi-lit, empty hallway.

"That's odd," she murmured. "I could have sworn I..."

"What the hell do you suggest we do about Jake?"

"Nothing."

Daisy looked at Greg's face, flushed with anger, and her expression softened.

"Look," she began, her tone soothing. "I know you're disappointed he's not here, but he's trying to save his marriage, and whatever you feel about Vivienne, that's important." Daisy paused, laying a hand on Greg's arm.

"Try not to take it personally. You know under normal circumstances Jake would have been here, but he had an opportunity to make things right with his wife, and if there's a chance, even a tiny one, of mending a broken relationship, then he had to take that it."

Greg sighed and shook his head, expression unconvinced.

"Marriage is so hard," Daisy continued. "You think it will be easy. You love each other, right? But it's not easy, it's difficult. It's all about compromise, putting aside your own needs to make your partner happy, and about, maybe, I don't know, not being selfish, not thinking about yourself anymore, instead thinking as a couple, a team..."

Daisy's voice trailed away as she became aware of Greg's concerned stare. Uneasily, she shrugged.

His expression became gentle, an older brother confronting a much-loved, baby sister.

"Daisy," he paused, plainly uncomfortable, uncertain how to begin, what to say. "Are you okay? I mean, is everything all right with you and Guy?"

"Yeah, sure, of course, absolutely, why shouldn't it be."

Daisy paused; aware she was protesting too much. Helplessly, she gestured with her hands. Greg moved closer, drawing her near, enfolding her in his arms, shocked at the scalding tears which fell.

"It's just ... it's just..."

"Ssh," soothed Greg. "It's okay, you can tell me. What's wrong?" voice roughening, he looked searchingly into her face.

"Is he treating you okay? Because if he isn't..."

"No, no, nothing like that," Daisy was quick to reassure, dabbing at her eyes. "It's hard, that's all, the first year of marriage. It's so hard."

Unconsciously, she echoed Jake's words to Lili.

Stepping back, she flashed Greg a quick, bright smile.

"Look at us," she exclaimed. "What are we doing? The most important night of your life and we're skulking in a back room arguing about someone who's not even here."

"Daisy?" Greg looked untrusting of her sudden mood change.

"We need to get back out there," determined Daisy, taking her brother's hand in her own and clasping it tightly.

"You should be out there, meeting and greeting. Come on. Let's go and get horribly drunk on all that free champagne and sell some pictures."

"Okay." Greg smiled in resignation as Daisy tucked her arm through his and led him towards the door. "If you're sure that you're all right?"

Together, they walked down the corridor, little suspecting as they passed the last door on the left that a human heart was breaking, silently and completely, behind it.

Chapter Twenty-Five
"I'm afraid I'm an all or nothing kind of guy."

Security and independence. Lindy Smith had craved them ever since she had been old enough to understand the concepts. Now, clasping the keys to her new home for the first time, it felt good, very good.

Lindy was the last of the group to buy her own property. Even Johnny had finally moved out of Felsham Hall a couple of months earlier into an attractive, seventeenth-century cottage in a small village outside town. Lindy had been surprised by his choice, convinced he'd have gone for a sleek, sophisticated bachelor pad, rather than a period property, that for all its charms needed a great deal of work.

She could have afforded a mortgage earlier, her cleaning company was doing phenomenally well, yet Lindy hesitated. Her innate caution of over-committing held her back until she had a substantial deposit saved and had no more excuses for not moving out of the rented flat she'd lived in since arriving in Bury.

Taking her time selecting her new home, Lindy had finally fallen in love with a Victorian semi tucked away at the end of a quiet street, five minutes from the town centre.

It wasn't massive; it originally had three bedrooms, one having been converted into a generous bathroom, but there was a spacious open-plan kitchen, dining and living room, and a new, tasteful conservatory which swallowed up most of the garden leaving a secluded courtyard, ample for her, given Lindy's dislike of gardening.

Owning her own home gave her a fiercely possessive thrill. Occupying her own space full of beautiful new things brought an emotional lump to her throat, as she reflected on how far she'd come, mainly, she insisted, due to Lili and the rest of the group.

Deeply loyal to her friends, Lindy relied on them to meet all her emotional and social needs and was the only member with no friends outside their tightly-knit group. She loved them all, though Lili had perhaps the tightest hold on her heart. She even cared for Johnny but would rather have had her tongue ripped out than admit it.

Lindy's attitude to Johnny had mellowed slightly, watching with grudging admiration as he formed a business with nothing but his skills, but she still felt a deep, unacknowledged envy of someone who'd had life handed to him on a platter, this envy manifesting itself as insults and sarcasm which he expertly fielded back. If Lindy was brutally honest with herself, she rather enjoyed these skirmishes.

It was Johnny that Lindy was thinking of now, as she drove along quiet country lanes towards his house on a Wednesday afternoon at the end of September.

The whole group had congregated at her house the previous evening for a housewarming party, but it was not until the following morning she realised he had left his Filofax behind. Knowing how important it was to him, Lindy had tried calling him at various stages throughout the day, each time getting the engaged tone.

Realising this probably meant he was on the internet, she finally threw the diary onto the front seat of her newly purchased car, jumped in, and pointed it in the direction of his home. Muttering curses about thick shit men who'd forget their own heads, she expertly manoeuvred the vehicle around twisty lanes whose verges dripped with blackberries, hoping Johnny's latest squeeze, the delightful Laura, wouldn't be there.

Johnny's love life was a source of constant amusement to the rest of the group. Lindy's sarcastic comment – that the milk in her fridge lasted longer than his relationships – was almost an accurate one. Johnny's choice of woman tended to run to trust fund babies with chest sizes bigger than their IQs, and insipid, though amiable, personalities.

However, his latest conquest, Laura, was different.

The daughter of a stud owner in Newmarket, Laura was clever, manipulative, and shrewd. She set her sights on Johnny as being suitable husband material and pursued that objective with a single-mindedness Lindy could have found admirable, even amusing, if Laura hadn't been an utter snob, treating Lindy like some grubby-faced scullery maid who belonged strictly below stairs.

The rest of the group were treated with varying degrees of civility. To Lili, Laura was sycophantic, realising early on how much Johnny adored her, knowing it was in her own best interests to remain on friendly terms.

She flirted with Kevin, enjoying being seen with a celebrity, no matter how low-key. She completely ignored Martin and Amy, considering them unworthy of her attention.

That left Lindy, whom Laura despised, never missing an opportunity to belittle or mock her, subtly ridiculing her accent and occupation, yet doing it in such a way that Lindy was unable to defend herself. She was left fuming with rage, tied up in knots by the other girl's cutting witticisms.

Johnny had been seeing Laura for almost a month now, and Lindy prayed she'd soon go the way of all the others.

Arriving at the cottage ten minutes later, Lindy's heart sank as she recognised Laura's silver convertible nuzzled against Johnny's red Ferrari. For a moment she considered driving away again, then straightened her spine in anger.

No, she would not be scared off by this woman. She would simply ring the doorbell, give Johnny back his Filofax, say a polite hello to Laura and leave.

Her resolve firm, Lindy walked to the door. To her surprise, it was ajar. She entered the cottage uncertainly, her call of greeting swallowed up by the roar of the coffee grinder in the kitchen. Lindy smelt the rich, enticing aroma of freshly ground beans as she made her way down the hall.

"But why don't you want to have everyone over tonight?"

Johnny's voice was petulant, and Lindy froze to the spot outside the partially open kitchen door, not wanting to interrupt a domestic.

"I don't want to," Laura snapped, and Lindy heard a clack of heels on the floor.

"Why not?" Johnny persisted. "I need a better reason than that. They're my friends, my best friends, but you never seem to want to spend any time with them."

"You want a reason? I'll give you a reason. I don't like them. There, is that good enough for you?"

"What?" Johnny sounded stunned. "You don't like them? But why not?"

"Lili's all right. At least she leads an interesting life. I mean, she's always off to London and knows some of the same people I do. Kevin's a sweetheart, he's doing something with his life. Martin and Amy, well, they're boring little non-entities who'll never amount to anything. As for Lindy..."

"What about Lindy?"

Johnny's voice was flat, toneless, although Lindy detected a hard edge to it, and couldn't help thinking if she'd been Laura she would have known to shut up at that point and apologise, laugh it off, change the subject. But perhaps Laura wasn't as tuned in to Johnny as she thought she was and ploughed on regardless.

"Do I need to spell it out?" drawled Laura, her upper-class accent scraping down Lindy's spine like a fingernail down a blackboard. "I mean, honestly, I don't know why you waste your time with any of them, but Lindy is so far below you in terms of class, intelligence, manners, financial status, you name it, she's your inferior on about every level. And as for that accent..."

"Lindy doesn't have an accent."

Johnny's voice remained mild. Part of Lindy wanted him to leap to her defence, but then, she reminded herself, why should he? Why should he defend a girl who had done nothing but snipe at him ever since they'd met? Still, it hurt to hear him take it so calmly. Unnoticed, his Filofax slipped out of numb fingers.

"Oh please," demanded Laura. "You can take the girl out of Romford, but you can't take Romford out of the girl. I mean, look what she does. She's a cleaner, for heaven's sake. Need I say more?"

"No," Johnny replied. "You don't need to say any more. I think you've said quite enough."

"What?"

The shock in Laura's voice almost brought a smile to Lindy's face; almost, but not quite. The hot, tight, sick feeling in her chest prevented that.

"I think you should leave now."

Johnny's voice was still, calm, uncaring and for a wild instant, Lindy had the irrational thought it pained her more than Laura's spite that he wasn't angrier on her behalf; that he didn't shout at Laura, demanding an apology.

"Leave? But ... but why?"

"Because I don't want to see you anymore," replied Johnny mildly.

"Because of that common little tramp?" demanded Laura hotly. "Because that's all she is, you know, the brat of a prostitute who's probably turning tricks herself. Is that why you're so keen to defend her? Are you screwing her as well? Christ, if you are, perhaps the others are too? Is that it? Is she the group whore?"

"That's enough," Johnny's voice finally snapped. "I said I wanted you to leave, and I meant it."

"Oh, don't worry," Laura's voice was shrill with outrage. "I wouldn't stay another minute anyway, not and be insulted like this!"

She slammed through the kitchen door, almost sending Lindy flying, eyes widening at seeing her there.

"You!" she hissed. "Heard enough, did you?"

Lindy made no reply, merely narrowed her eyes, and stared at Laura, who struggled to regain her composure.

"You little bitch! Do you seriously think he'll ever be interested in you? Johnny being friends with scum like you is laughable enough, but if you seriously think..."

"Laura!"

Johnny's voice snapped between them, and Laura backed away, hatred flashing from her eyes as she trembled under Lindy's unwavering, inscrutable gaze.

"Just you wait," she threatened. "I'll see you ruined, I'll..."

"Get out of my house, Laura."

With a final, dramatic sob, Laura turned and fled. A moment later they heard the roar of a high-performance engine and the protesting squeal of brakes. Johnny turned to Lindy, his face pale.

"Lindy," he began. "I'm so sorry. I had no idea what a bitch she was. If I'd known, I'd never have ... how much did you hear?"

"Enough," Lindy ground the word out through gritted teeth.

"Lindy," he put out a hand to her, and Lindy's control snapped. Screaming in seething fury, she slapped it away.

"You bastard!" she growled, lashing out in wild, reckless rage, as years of suppressed insecurities boiled over. Sobs erupting from her chest, she lashed out in blind, uncontrollable anger.

"Hey!" Johnny cried, trying to avoid her flailing fists. "Cut it out Lindy," he demanded, wincing as her small fist connected with his cheek. Desperately, he grabbed both her wrists, holding them high above her head as she raged and thrashed in his grasp.

Beyond reason, beyond thought, Lindy brought her knee up between his legs. Johnny twisted to avoid the blow, sandwiching her against the wall in a frantic attempt to calm her.

Trapped by his tall, surprisingly strong frame, Lindy snarled at him, breasts heaving against his chest as she fought to get free.

"Calm down," he ordered, but Lindy still struggled. Johnny, his anger rising, shoved her back, feeling her taut softness along the full length of his body.

Looking down into her beautiful face alight with passionate anger, Johnny realised something; something so basic, so obvious, he wondered how he could have been so blind.

Obeying the urge, he bent his head, claiming her lips in a kiss. Brief, but intense, it rocked him back on his heels. He dropped her wrists in horror, as her eyes went wide and blank with shock.

"Fuck, Lindy, I don't know what ... I'm sorry, I didn't mean to ... you can hit me again if you like," he offered desperately.

Lindy stared at him for a heartbeat, then stepped forward, fisted her hands in his hair, yanked his head painfully down to hers, and plundered his mouth in a savage kiss of territorial possession.

Heat, intense and primal, flared between them. Johnny's own hands instinctively clutched at her shoulders, dragging her closer. The kiss went on and on, mouths demanding and taking, bodies straining, hands exploring.

Shit! Lindy?

Truth exploded in his brain. The motive behind the hostility which had simmered between them for the past year was revealed – want, need, lust, it had many names, but only one inevitable conclusion.

Ripping his mouth away, he tugged the soft linen jacket from her body to reveal the silky t-shirt straining over swollen breasts. He bent, mouth closing with brutal intensity over an already rigid nipple, biting and suckling through the thin material, his other hand impatiently wrenching the t-shirt from her jeans, snaking up to cup its throbbing twin.

Lindy cried out, her mind retreating from the awful glory of his touch, leaving her body free to take what it wanted, what it had needed for over a year.

This man!

Here, now.

Desperately, her hands pulled and ripped at his shirt, buttons scattering at her impatience, as she pushed it over his broad shoulders, groaning with desire at the sight of toned, male flesh, its perfectly sculptured planes and angles demanding her touch.

Frantically, he fumbled at buttons and zips, clumsy with need, yanking her jeans down, slipping trembling fingers between her thighs to find her hot and ready; slick flesh scalding, as he rubbed at the small, swollen nub of her womanhood.

Again, she cried out, hoarse and guttural. He felt muscles spasm over his hand, then pulse in glorious wetness which made his throat constrict with male triumph.

"Now," she growled, in turn ripping open his jeans. "Oh, now!" she moaned. "Now, please, now!"

Desperately, she fought to release him from the restricting, confining denim, barely getting them down to his knees before she was pulling them both roughly to the floor. Unbelievably aroused, Johnny struggled to pull Lindy's jeans down far enough to allow him access, his body shuddering as she closed a fist around him.

Finally, he wrenched one leg free of her jeans, ripping off her shoe in the process, rolling to position himself between her thighs, feeling the heat and excruciating pleasure as she rubbed the engorged head of his penis between her swollen, hungry lips.

Plunging into fiery depths, he heard her yell of disbelieving need, a growl of satisfaction ripped from his own throat. Muscles clamped, vice-like, around him. Pulling almost all the way out, he paused, taking them both to the limit before thrusting back in, right up to the hilt, grinding against her in a timeless, ageless dance.

Lindy bucked up off the floor, nails scoring unfelt and unnoticed rents down his back, her breathing ragged and uneven, head thrashing from side to side, long hair a black, writhing pool on the cream hall carpet.

Her fingers grabbed hanks of his hair; mouths meeting in an explosive kiss of feral need. Johnny felt the give of fabric as he simply ripped her t-shirt down the front, pulled down her surprisingly feminine bra, and feasted on her womanly curves.

Lindy pushed, rolling them over to straddle him, flushed and triumphant. Johnny gazed in stunned admiration as she rode him like some Amazonian warrior queen, supple body arching under his caresses.

Pure sensation took over; conscious thought fled. Johnny's body reared up to meet hers. Heart pumping, breath quickening, knowing he was on the verge of orgasm, he could do nothing to stop it and could tell from the rapid pulsing of Lindy's muscles along his shaft, the agonised cries erupting from her throat, that she was there with him, their frenzied mating dance racing towards its inevitable climax.

Time slowed, bodies stilled for one crucial second, then the wave crashed over them. Twin orgasms, painful in their intensity, ignited. Johnny felt his hot seed explode up into her body, felt the answering throb of her powerful climatic surges, milking him dry, wringing an agonised groan from a parched mouth.

Lindy collapsed onto his chest. They lay, racing heartbeat to racing heartbeat, before she rolled over to lie, breathless and spent, on the floor beside him, ragged gasps echoing in the darkening hallway. Clothes hanging, ripped, and tangled, bodies sweating and exhausted.

Slowly, the ability to think returned to Johnny. He became aware of the sting of air on his shoulders. Looking up, he realised the front door was wide open. Groaning from the effort, he crawled over and pushed it shut. Lindy dragged herself to a sitting position, clutching shredded and crumpled clothing, eyes round with disbelief. Johnny surveyed the scene, a grin spreading across his face.

"Well," he declared, evident satisfaction in his voice, "that was ... surprising." He reached a hand to Lindy, only to jerk in shock as she slapped it down, scuttling crab-like away from him, angrily attempting to climb back into her clothing.

"Hey," he exclaimed. "What was that for?"

"You ... you bastard!" Lindy spat the words in barely suppressed anger.

"Technically incorrect," he retorted. "Both parents safely married long before I was even thought of, thank you very much. Now, suppose you tell me what the hell your beef is, apart from me that is," he leered.

"Don't be so fucking crude," Lindy snapped.

"Okay, okay," soothed Johnny. "Don't get your knickers in a twist," he paused, looking around. "By the way, what did happen to your knickers?"

Lindy growled, but Johnny merely smiled, sliding down the wall to sit next to her, watching in amusement. Muttering curses, she located her knickers and hastily pulled them on, yanking up jeans which she had helped pull down only minutes earlier. Her shredded t-shirt she held up in disbelief, turning an accusing gaze onto Johnny, who shrugged sheepishly. Lindy sighed in exasperation, angrily pulled on her jacket, buttoning it up over her bra.

"Where are you going?" Johnny's smile faded as Lindy slipped on her shoes and headed, tight-lipped, to the door. "Wait," he jumped up, hurriedly tugging up his jeans, and intercepting her as she reached it. "Where are you going?" he demanded again, gazing at her in consternation.

"Home," she snapped. "Get out of my way."

"Home? But you can't bugger off home. Not now. Not after this..."

"Watch me," she retorted, pulling at his hand. "Let me out," she snarled.

"Lindy, for fuck's sake, we need to talk..."

"There's nothing to talk about."

"Nothing to ...? Well, for a start, we need to talk about what the hell happened here. We need to talk about us."

"There is no us. All that happened here was purely physical. We had an itch, we scratched it, end of story."

"How can you say that?" Johnny's face registered incredulity, the hurt in his eyes making Lindy swallow and turn away. "Lindy, what happened was amazing ..." he paused, gently touching her face. "I had no idea I felt this way about you. That you..."

"That I what?" Fire flashed from eyes that snapped up to stare, hard and accusing, into his. "Look, don't read more into this than there is. We had sex. It was good." At his raised brows, she paused, flushed. "Okay, very good. I had a nice orgasm, thank you very much, but that's it."

"That's it?" Johnny shook his head in disbelief. "I don't believe you,"

"That's it," insisted Lindy. "What more do you want from me? Vows of undying love? Plans to go and pick out curtains?"

"No," retorted Johnny. "But some simple emotion, hell, even some common courtesy might be nice. Not wham, bam, thank you, man."

"Oh, you don't like it when the shoe is on the other foot," taunted Lindy. "All those women I've seen parade through your life ... are you trying to tell me you were in love with every single one?"

"Of course not. I've never been in love before ..." Under Lindy's steely glare, Johnny's words died in his throat. "I didn't love them," he repeated firmly. "But neither did I make them feel like cheap, disposable shags."

"I'm sorry," Lindy had the grace to look ashamed. "You're my friend. I never meant for this to happen, never imagined for a second it could. Now it has, it's ... awkward, I don't know what to do, what to say."

"Well," Johnny considered, head on one side, then smiled a lazy grin. It made her heart stumble in her chest, a pulse flare in her groin. "I could open us a bottle of wine, and we can discuss, like the good friends we are, exactly what happens next."

"Okay, a glass of wine," her eyes narrowed, as his face brightened. "But I'm warning you, Gedding, you even think about getting soppy on me and I'm out the door."

"Don't worry, Smith," he paused, "The only person getting soppy around here is you." He laughed at her scowl.

"One glass of wine," she repeated, stomping into the kitchen behind him. "Just one, then I'm going home..."

Fresh, slightly chilly air blew in through the open window cooling the exhausted lovers as they lay, limp and sated, on the bed. Slowly, Johnny traced a gentle finger down Lindy's side, over her hip, marvelling at the creamy perfection of taut skin; the concave of her stomach, and those slender, gorgeous thighs, which only moments earlier had been wrapped tightly around his hips, urging him on, until blinding satisfaction had simultaneously claimed them.

They never even finished that glass of wine. Intensely aware of her presence, Johnny uncorked the bottle, poured ruby-red wine into fragile stemmed glasses, silently handing one to her, a thrill shocking him at their brief touch of fingers as she quietly took the glass. They sipped slowly, eyes never leaving the other's face.

Johnny felt the heat rising; was stunned he could want her again so soon. He was reluctant to speak, unwilling to shatter the atmosphere of erotic longing welling up all around, so intense, so keen, he could smell it. He could almost taste her sharp womanly flavour in his mouth. Need curdled in his belly, and he ached with desire for her.

Watching her over the rim of his glass, his heightened awareness noted fingers that slightly shook; the tip of a tongue constantly flicking over dry lips; the flush on her cheeks, and the flash of dilating pupils as she glanced nervously up at him.

It was enough.

He knew she felt it too ... that ache, that yearning. Swiftly he crossed the kitchen, set her glass down, and gently cupped her face in his hands.

"No ..." her protest was half-hearted, insincere.

He ignored it and bent his head, gently, softly, tasting and teasing. Different from before, less urgent, less punishing, the kiss was that of a lover – exploring, arousing. Johnny's lips insistently demanded a response. Slowly, reluctantly, Lindy gave it.

"Do you know how good you taste?" he murmured, hands stroking softly down the slim column of her throat to lightly caress agonisingly sensitive breasts.

"Tell me," she whispered back, gasping as his long, clever fingers slowly undid her jacket buttons and grazed the lilac lace of her bra.

"Like cream, but spiced, heat and softness all rolled into one exciting taste." His head dipped and sampled, feasting on rosy firm flesh. Her head fell back, a sigh of pure pleasure forcing itself through lips swollen from his gently arousing kiss.

His arms encircled and lifted. Lindy looked around, dazed and bewildered, as he carried her from the kitchen and started up the narrow, winding stairs.

"What ... where ...?" she murmured, hearing his soft answering chuckle.

"I'm taking my lover to bed; I don't want any more carpet burns on my arse."

"Hmm," she agreed, nibbling his neck. "It is a rather nice arse."

Johnny reached the top of the stairs, pushed open the door, and gently laid her on the antique brass bed which creaked companionably when he crawled onto it beside her, quietly beginning to undress them.

They loved twice more, each time awakening a deeper need; a wanting, a yearning to touch, explore, and possess. Never had Johnny felt this way with anyone before. He marvelled it was with Lindy, this woman with whom he had battled royally for so long. Lying beside her, unable to stop touching and caressing, he tenderly trailed his fingers over her waist, her hip, admiring her perfection.

She stirred, turned her head to silently gaze at him from those almond-shaped eyes. It hit him then. He loved her; had always loved her, had fought against it, knowing with hindsight there was a glorious inevitability to it – they were meant to be together. His heart sang with rightness. She was here. He was complete.

"Lindy ..." he murmured, wanting to say the words, to hear her say them back. She breathed in – his heart stopped, and anticipation flooded. His eyes narrowed with love, then widened with shock, as she lightly pushed him away, swinging her legs out of bed.

"Where are you going?" he asked, pulling himself up on the bed.

"Home, it's late." The indifference of her reply cut him to the quick.

"Home? But ... but I thought you'd stay the night. Stay with me, I'll even cook you breakfast in the morning." He heard the pleading in his voice and despised himself for it.

"Stay?"

Lindy turned, startled, to gaze at him, dropping her eyes from the raw emotion she read in his face.

"I can't stay," she mumbled, turning away, reaching for underwear, her back rigid.

"What's wrong?"

Despair made his voice harsh, and Lindy cast him a quick, tight look before getting up to pull on jeans.

"Nothing, I need to go home."

"But what about us?"

"I told you before, there is no us," Lindy sighed in exasperation. "This was a mistake," she stated flatly. "I should have left after the first time, before you..."

"Before I what?" Johnny demanded hotly. "I didn't exactly rape you, you know!"

"No, no, of course not" Lindy retreated from the painful anger in his eyes. "It's like I said before, we had an itch, we scratched it."

"Lady," drawled Johnny lightly, trying to rein his temper in. "We scratched it three times. That sure was some itch."

Lindy flushed. Whether from anger, guilt, or remembered desire he couldn't tell. It pained him she could be so casual, so uncaring. She opened her mouth to speak, then turned away. Locating shoes, she pulled them on, stamping her feet into them with exaggerated movements as if spinning out the moment, delaying the time when she would have to look at him again and see the eagerness in his eyes; the hope she would have to crush, once and for all.

"Johnny," her voice gentled.

She reached out a hand and softly stroked his arm. He winced, jerking the sheet up to cover his body, feeling vulnerable in his nakedness faced with her fully clothed practicality, and her slightly patronising adult to child tone.

"It would never work, you know," she swallowed nervously at the look in his eyes. "Us. I love you as a friend, I admire you as a human being. And now ..." she paused, uncomfortably. His eyes never left her face; his expression hooded and unreadable.

"And now," she pressed on regardless. "I desire you as a lover. I can't lie to you. The things you did, the way you make me feel ... I've never experienced anything like it before, I want you Johnny, but it can only ever be physical."

"Why?" the single word hung between them.

Lindy pulled her hand away. "Because I'm incapable of feeling love. There's something wrong with me, inside ... Oh, I love my friends, and as I said, I love you as a friend, but I have this fault. This flaw. It means I can never be *in* love with you or anyone."

He wanted to object, to protest, to scoff even at the absurdity of her words, but something stopped him. Maybe the conviction in her voice or the sadness in her eyes, something made him hold back, realising whatever the reality was behind her bizarre statement, Lindy believed wholeheartedly in it and that made it the truth.

"So, what do you suggest?"

Deliberately keeping his voice light, he was rewarded with a flash of relief, of gratitude, in her eyes.

"I don't know," she replied slowly. "Of course, it would be better all-round if things went back to the way they were, if we left it at this, but..."

"But ...?" he repeated, trailing a hand up her thigh. He heard the quick intake of breath, felt her skin tense beneath his touch, and knew relief that in this, at least, he was not alone. That this powerful, aching need he had for her was reciprocated.

"But I'm not sure, now it has happened, whether things could ever be the same between us," Lindy paused and gazed steadily at him. "I want you," she continued, and his heart twisted at the honesty burning in her face.

"So, help me, it's selfish, I know, and you have every right to turn away from me, but I want you. I won't lie to you ... there have been other men, men I've used to satisfy a basic, physical need. But this – the way we are together, the way you make me feel – it's like I've been dying of thirst all my life and never even knew it."

"Okay," Johnny's heart flipped over with love, but he kept his voice light, relaxed, one friend addressing another. "We'll try it your way, Lindy, for a while. Lovers, yet no intimacy. Sex with no strings. We'll be friends who fuck."

"Hmm," she winced away from his crudity, his deliberately cruel summing up, then nodded sadly. "I guess I deserved that," she observed with a wry smile.

"What do we tell the others?"

"We don't."

Her instant reflex took them both by surprise.

"We tell them nothing," Lindy continued more calmly. "What's the point? They'd never understand. It would be awkward and embarrassing for everyone. Besides, there's no need. This ... whatever it is, will burn itself out soon."

"And if it doesn't?"

"It will," Lindy stated firmly. "It's physical, so without any kind of emotional foundation, it won't last. It can't ..." She glanced at the old-fashioned alarm clock standing on the bedside cabinet. "It's late, I have to go." Johnny felt a twinge of hope at the shred of reluctance he thought he detected in her voice yet said nothing.

Lindy leant forward and kissed him, hard and firm, her lips already achingly familiar against his. Briefly, his eyes closed in a moment of agonised despair before he once again cloaked his feelings behind a mask of indifference.

Long after she had gone, and the roar of her car's engine had faded away into the velvety darkness pressing against the bedroom windows, he sat, silent and immobile, before sighing and running a weary hand through his hair.

"We'll see, Lindy," he muttered, his eyes sad. "We'll see..."

And so, it began ... the affair that wasn't. For three months Johnny bided his time; hid his true feelings from Lindy, the group, the world; waiting and hoping for her to realise, to understand, how right they were together, and that by denying her true feelings she was stifling something good, pure, and honest.

Lindy, Lindy, Lindy.

She consumed his thoughts, his waking moments, his erotic restless dreams. When he was with her, he was filled with the glory of her presence. When they were apart, Johnny ached and yearned with an intensity that scared him.

He had never been in love before; he knew that now. All the brief, silly infatuations of the past could be viewed dispassionately as being exactly that – brief and silly. Even the strong feelings he had for Lili paled into insignificance beside the all-encompassing, all-demanding need he had for Lindy.

Slowly, as she relaxed with him and took at face value his apparent acceptance of the situation, she cautiously opened the door to her past; to a childhood so devoid of love and affection, his heart broke for her. He longed to spoil and pamper her to make up a little for the dreadful aloneness and disregard she'd suffered.

He held back, knowing even the slightest indication of his true feelings would have her slamming the door shut and running scared. Then he'd be without even the merest crumbs of her, which was all she grudgingly afforded him now.

The sex continued to be stunning, awesome in its power and intensity. Sometimes Johnny felt they shared an addiction ... a crazy, insatiable, obsession. One which made them take outrageous risks, such as having wild, reckless sex in his kitchen whilst the rest of the group, blissfully unaware, watched a film in the lounge. In the beginning, the thrill of the secrecy, the spontaneous nature of their relationship, was almost enough.

Almost, but not quite.

Christmas came and with it a sort of epiphany for Johnny in that he finally accepted that what Lindy offered was not enough. He wanted and needed so much more. Spending Christmas Day at Lili's, watching the others opening their thoughtful gifts to and from each other, he'd felt apart, detached, as if he existed on a different plane.

Carefully, he spent the day studying Lindy. Unaware of his silent scrutiny, she interacted with their friends and never betrayed, not by word or thought, that Johnny was any different from the rest.

It hurt.

Johnny knew things could no longer stay as they were. He could no longer wait for Lindy to discover she loved him, for he was in no doubt she did. It showed in her eyes when they were together, and in a hundred small, but telling clues his greedy eyes gratefully noticed.

After New Year had been celebrated in usual, riotous fashion, Johnny seemed to retreat inwards. Lindy wondered whether the relationship was approaching the burn-out she had predicted.

Telling herself she should be grateful it was, nevertheless, she panicked she'd soon be without him. That they would go back to being purely platonic friends and she ached at the thought.

One evening, a few days after New Year, they lay together in Johnny's bed. Somehow, they always seemed to end up there, as if Lindy were afraid if they were at hers, she would lack the strength to make him leave afterwards.

The sex had been as explosive as ever, although Lindy was convinced that she felt a certain coolness from Johnny, noticing he pulled away afterwards when usually he clung to her, desperate to maintain intimacy for as long as possible. Sighing she sat up, preparing herself to dress and leave for drive the ten-minute drive home; ten minutes which seemed to take longer every time she left him like this.

"Please, don't go."

The command took her by surprise, and she stiffened. The bedclothes rustled behind her in the dimly lit room and a hand, firm and masculine, gripped her arm.

"Please, Lindy, don't go. Stay with me tonight."

She heard the appeal in his voice and something else. There seemed almost an air of finality in his tone as if he were giving her one last chance.

She hesitated.

If Johnny had remained silent at that point, had given her the choice to make alone, who knows ... she may have chosen differently. But he didn't, he spoke again. This time his voice was demanding, and Lindy instinctively pulled away.

"I have something to tell you, Lindy, and I know you probably don't want to hear it, but I can't go on like this."

"So, you're finishing with me," she forced herself to shrug, casual and dismissive. "Oh well, we had a good run, nearly four months, not bad…"

"Lindy."

"Told you I was right about not telling the others…"

"Lindy."

"Think how awkward it'd be if they knew. Whereas now, we can…"

"Lindy!"

At the sharpness in his voice, she fell silent, eyes twisting to meet his, registering his anguish and hopeful despair. Clumsily, he fumbled in a bedside drawer, pulling out a small, square box. She stared at it, shocked and numb.

"Lindy, I love you," Johnny faltered before her blank stillness, forcing himself to go on. "I love you. I want us to be a proper couple, be together every day. I want everyone to know about us, I'm fed up with the lies and the sneaking about as if we're doing something wrong. It's not wrong, I love you. I think you love me, and I want to declare that love to the world."

He snapped open the ring box to show her the gleam of ruby and gold within. Her eyes flew from it to him, and back again.

"I should be kneeling," he gave a half-laugh. "This wasn't how I planned it at all, but here goes. Lindy Smith," he held out the ring to her like an offering. "I love you, so very much, please will you marry me?"

Silence exploded in the room.

Lindy, eyes hard and disbelieving, shrank away from the stunningly beautiful ring as if it were a venomous snake. The thought flashed through her head it was exactly the kind of ring she would have chosen for herself, different from bland diamond engagement rings, its flame-coloured stone burning like an ember.

It triggered the further realisation that Johnny had searched long and hard to find just the right ring for her; that he knew her perhaps better than she did herself.

For a moment, she wavered. Then old fears, old uncertainties reared up and her head slowly shook. She saw the light of hope fade in his eyes, the tentative beginnings of his smile wither and die, as the hand holding the box slowly, but inexorably, drew back.

"No," she whispered. "I'm so sorry, but no … I can't…"

"Why?" he snapped. "For god's sake, Lindy, explain to me why?"

"I told you," she retorted. "I can't love you, not that way. My childhood…"

"What about your childhood?" Finally, Johnny was tired of it all; of constantly walking on eggshells and obeying her rules; tired of her denial of the plain, simple, truth. "You had a crap childhood, so what? I understand, but lots of people come from poverty. That doesn't mean they have to turn away from love all their life."

"It wasn't just the poverty, although how you can sit there, Lord Felsham," he winced at the heavy sarcasm in her voice, "and claim to understand. You, a person who's never known a day's want in his entire life. How dare you claim to fucking understand what it's like, what having less than nothing can do to a person!"

"I'm sorry," he said quietly. "You're right, of course, I can't understand, not really, what it was like. But I do understand we love each other, and that there's no reason why we can't be together…"

"Was your mother a prostitute?" her brutally stark question burst into the room.

"No, of course not, but…"

"Mine was. Oh, not a full time one, she didn't have the looks or the brains to do it properly and make a decent living out of it. Her prostitution was the casual £20 a fuck type. When she got caught with me, she started bringing clients home, only she didn't call them clients, she called them uncles," Lindy paused, swallowing.

At the look on her face, Johnny reached out, but Lindy pulled back, unwilling, and unable to accept his comfort.

"Some stayed a few days, some even stuck around for longer, but they were all the same … bunging mum money so they could live with her and screw her. By the time I was five, I must've had a dozen uncles at least. I remember once, I was about ten – old enough to understand what was going on, too young to have to deal with such a thing – I begged her to stop, pleaded with her if she loved me at all to at least try to find a different way, but do you know what she told me?" Her eyes flicked up, hard and demanding. Johnny shook his head, mesmerised by her words.

"I'm sorry babe, but I love them, I can't live without a man in the house, and I know it's not worked out so good in the past, but maybe next time ... That's what she always said. Maybe next time it'll be true love. Yeah, well, guess what true love got her ... a lifetime of being used by men and a nasty, pointless death at 36."

"But Lindy, you escaped, you got away. Yes, it's terrible what happened to you, but you escaped, and you are nothing like your mother. You can't compare us, what we have, to what it was like for your mum."

"You don't understand." Lindy's words tumbled, hot and fierce, filling the vast chasm between them. "I gave her a choice, me or them, and she chose them. She chose them! My mother chose those losers, those bastards, over her own daughter. Now, do you see? Now, do you understand?"

Johnny did. With a sinking sense of despair, he saw the problem extended back further than he'd realised, to the very start of Lindy's life. With a flash of clarity, he saw heartache had been her constant companion; how her sense of self-worth had been damaged by the one person who should have taken the most care with it, her mother.

"Lindy," he started, appalled, and scared stiff this was a fight he couldn't win. How could he begin to undo a lifetime of learnt distrust? Where did he start to break down Lindy's perceived notions of her unworthiness to love, and be loved, in return?

"Lindy, I love you..."

"Yeah?" Paranoia snapped into Lindy's eyes, and Johnny's heart almost stopped at her fear and mistrust. "Well, maybe you do now, but what happens then?"

"What do you mean?"

"Okay, say I decide to trust you, put my heart out there. What happens when you get bored and decide to take your love away? What happens then, Johnny? I'll tell you what happens. You leave, but not before you kick my heart around a bit."

"I wouldn't do that, Lindy." Appalled, Johnny tried to defend himself. "I'd never..."

"You're a man!" snarled Lindy. "That's what men do, I've seen it all before, over and over. That's how it happens. Men say they love you, so women give them everything, their heart and soul, everything, and men just take and take!"

"What are you accusing me of?" Johnny asked, alarmed by her rising hysteria. "Of being a man? Well, guilty as charged. Of loving you. Hell, guilty again. Of planning to use and hurt you? No, never Lindy. Of that particular crime, I'm an innocent man."

"I know you think you love me, have no intention of ever hurting me, but you wouldn't be able to help yourself because that's what happens. Love changes people. It turns men into bullies and women into victims, and I won't let that happen to us."

"But that's ridiculous."

Johnny tried to gather her into his arms but was shoved away as Lindy desperately scrabbled into clothes, shaking from her emotional outburst, eyes bright and glittering with unshed tears.

"So instead of taking a chance on me, on us, you'd rather not try at all?"

"That's right," snapped Lindy. "That way neither of us will get hurt!"

"But neither of us will be happy," exclaimed Johnny in exasperation. "Lindy, I love you, I promise to try and never hurt you, but I can't guarantee it. There are no dead certs in life, no sure things. To go through life avoiding every situation where you might get hurt is crazy. You may as well pick out a nice comfortable coffin and climb right in."

"I'm doing this for us," Lindy faced him, expression set and immobile. "I'm sorry Johnny, but unless you're prepared to leave things as they are."

"You mean settle for sex?" Lindy heard the bitterness in his voice, pain, and disillusionment. For a second, a moment, resolve wavered, before she firmly pulled herself back together.

"Yes, why not Johnny? We're so good together, you know we are. Why does it have to be such a big deal? Why does it have to be all or nothing?"

"Oh Lindy," Johnny sighed, sadly shaking his head. "I love you, but I'm afraid I'm an all or nothing kind of guy."

"Okay," Lindy swallowed hard, fighting back the wave of blackness that threatened to engulf at the finality in his reply. "I guess that's it then..."

"I guess it is," he agreed.

She walked to the door. His heart jolted with hope as she paused, hesitated, glanced back, then sighed. She smiled once, a tiny sad smile, and left.

It was hell ... losing her was hell and it was a pain no one could ease or share. None of their friends even suspected, so careful had they been to keep the rest of them from guessing. Johnny had no one to talk to, no one to turn to. His hell was a private one.

Seeing her on such a regular basis made it worse. Johnny began to make excuses not to see the group, anxious to spare himself the bittersweet agony of seeing her; of knowing by the haunted, desperate look on her face, the dark shadows under her eyes, that she suffered too.

Obsessively, he went over their last meeting in his head, analysing every word, look, and nuance in her voice, frantically seeking a way to fix things, to make it all better.

Unused to being denied anything, after his initial devastation Johnny found his natural tenacity beginning to reassert itself. Damn her. She'd find he didn't give up that easily. Just a man, was he? Well, she'd see. He would show her that some men were worth believing in.

Lying awake deep into the still heart of every night, Johnny plotted and planned ways to make Lindy understand. At last, he conceived of a scheme; a wild, reckless, dramatic gesture that might, just might convince her of his innocence.

January reluctantly dragged its cold, grey feet until finally, under lowering, snow-laden storm clouds, the last Friday of the month arrived and with it, Lili's 21st birthday.

Chapter Twenty-Six

"I don't want to end up an old spinster with a lot of cats."

The problem with nobody else knowing your heart has been broken thought Lindy bleakly, is there can be no friendly sympathy; no allowance given for moodiness or uncontrollable fits of depression. However black and twisted life may seem, you must still paint on a happy smile, and act as if you haven't a care in the world.

Sitting opposite Lili in their favourite restaurant in Norwich where the two girls had gone shopping for the day, Lindy listened in smiling detachment as Lili rattled on about the gorgeous dress she'd bought, the lovely one she practically bullied Lindy into buying, and where on earth would they wear such over-the-top, glamorous gowns.

How can she not notice, Lindy desperately thought; why can't she see I'm dying inside, that I've been fading away from real life for weeks?

But Lindy realised, Lili herself had been distracted and out of sorts for months now, only Lindy had been too wrapped up in her unexpectedly passionate affair with Johnny to notice.

Watching closely with attuned vision, Lindy noticed when Lili paused for breath and sipped her wine, there was a flash of something hurting deep within her eyes, and her smile – was it a little too bright? Impulsively, Lindy leant across the table and clasped one of Lili's hands.

"Are you all right, Lili?"

"What?" Lili looked up startled. "Oh, yes, I'm fine, really I'm ... why do you ask?"

"I don't know," Lindy replied slowly. "There's been something not quite right about you for months now, I wondered ..."

She stopped as Lili's eyes slid away from hers in weary denial. It was a look Lindy knew only too well; a look she caught in her own eyes every time she looked in the mirror.

"Who was he?" she asked bluntly. Lili's expression turned to one of alarm.

"How did you ... no one. What do you mean?"

"I know there's someone, or rather, maybe you'd like there to be someone."

"There was," Lili sighed. "There was someone I liked. For a while I thought he liked me too but … it wasn't to be."

"I'm sorry," Lindy squeezed her hand in sympathy. "If there's anything I can do, anyway I can help…"

"Oh, I'm okay," Lili flashed a quick, warm smile, picking up her menu. "So," she began, obviously wanting to change the subject, "what do you fancy to eat?"

Lindy hesitated as Lili diligently studied the menu, then sighed herself, deciding to respect Lili's reluctance to discuss the matter any further.

"Well," she replied, picking up her menu and perusing it again, "I think I'll have the scallops, to begin with, followed by the duck."

"Great choices," declared Lili, folding up her menu. "I think I'll have the same."

Driving home later that afternoon with a boot full of sales bargains, Lindy peered over the steering wheel at the white, dense sky pressing down oppressively.

"Look at that sky," she declared. "It's full of snow."

"Well, the forecast did predict a blizzard over the weekend," replied Lili. "I hope it holds off until after tomorrow night, I want everyone to make it."

Although it was Lili's 21st birthday that day, it had been unanimously decided to book a large table at Lili's favourite restaurant on Saturday night to celebrate.

Lili didn't mind, of course, she didn't, it made perfect sense to delay her celebration by one day so everyone could make it and weren't too tired after work.

But she had been surprised, and yes, she admitted it, a little hurt she hadn't so much as received a single card from her friends on the actual day, and none of them had phoned.

If it hadn't been for Lindy announcing she had a day free and would drive them to Norwich for lunch and shopping, Lili would have spent her birthday alone.

Lindy …

Lili pursed her lips thoughtfully as she stole a sideways glance at her friend. The air of quiet desperation hanging over her friend hadn't gone unnoticed, nor had the dark circles under the eyes, Lili knew Lindy was upset about something but was reluctant to pry or to pressure her into divulging secrets best left uncovered, so simply said, "It'll be nice to go out to dinner with everyone tomorrow."

"Hmm," replied Lindy, casting anxious glances skywards. As they approached Bury, Lindy's new mobile phone rang; Lili fished it out of Lindy's bag and held it to the other woman's ear.

"Hi Kevin, umm, coming up to Bury. What? Oh no, okay, we'll swing by and pick you up. Yeah, sure, no problem. See you soon.

okay, bye." Lindy bobbed her head away and Lili disconnected, dropping the phone back in the bag.

"That was Kevin," Lindy stated unnecessarily. "He's at Felsham Hall. He went to see Lady Felsham about another project and his van's broken down."

"Oh no," exclaimed Lili. "What's wrong with it?"

"Don't know," shrugged Lindy. "It died. So, anyway, I said we'd swing by, pick him up and give him a lift home. Maybe grab a bite to eat or something."

"Oh, okay," Lili perked up at the thought of seeing at least one more of her friends on her birthday. "Maybe we could open a bottle?" she suggested.

"Hmm," agreed Lindy abstractedly. "Maybe."

Night had fallen on the drive home. Lili peered out of her window at the bleak, frozen verges and shivered slightly, thankful for the efficiency of Lindy's car heater as it blasted warm air over her feet and legs.

Soon, they were sweeping through the imposing gates of Felsham Hall, crunching to a halt on the wide gravel driveway. There was no sign of Kevin. Lili assumed he was waiting inside. Climbing out of the car, she shivered. As the sun had fallen, so had the temperature, and she didn't blame him for not wanting to stand outside.

Following Lindy, as she strode towards the door, Lili thought how dark it was. Apart from a lantern in the porch, not a single light shone anywhere. The Hall loomed, uninviting and forbidding. Lindy rang the bell. Moments later the door opened, spilling light and warmth into the night as Lady Felsham hurried them inside.

"Come in, come in," she urged. "I'll go and tell him you're here." She led them down the dimly lit corridor to the large banqueting hall at the end. "He's in here," she exclaimed.

Throwing open the double doors, she somewhat abruptly pushed Lili into the room ahead of her.

"SURPRISE!" yelled thirty-eight voices. Lili jumped back in shock as party poppers exploded, champagne corks popped, and a confusing mass of people rushed towards her.

"Oh, oh!" she gasped in stunned disbelief. "Thank you! Oh, my goodness, I had no idea."

Lady Felsham and Lindy were grinning all over their faces, hustling her further into the room, and Lili's eyes darted in all directions, trying to drink it all in.

The large, normally formal banqueting hall had been turned into a bower of flowers, balloons, and streamers. Happy 21st Birthday banners hung everywhere. Prettily decorated round tables were dotted around a large, cleared area, obviously intended for dancing, and a small bar had been created in one corner.

"Come on," ordered Lindy, taking her hand.

"Where are we going?" Lili asked in a daze.

"Upstairs. We need to get changed and titivate."

"You're going to do what to your tits?" leered Johnny. Everyone except Lindy roared with laughter.

Lili realised all the men were dressed in tuxedos, and all the women wore full-length gowns. Her heart warmed at the thought of how much trouble everyone had gone to.

Twenty minutes later, changed into their new dresses, hair and make-up refreshed and renewed, Lili and Lindy returned to the banqueting hall to join the party, now in full swing.

A cheer went up at their entry, and Lili paused, basking in the moment, as the gang rushed over, warmly hugging and kissing her, thrilled at her amazed delight.

"This is such a surprise," she exclaimed happily to Lindy, as glasses of champagne were pushed into their hands by a beaming Tom.

"Happy birthday, Lili," he exclaimed, kissing her enthusiastically on both cheeks.

"Tom! Is Muriel here too?"

"Over there. She wouldn't have missed it for the world."

Lili followed his gaze and saw Muriel and Richard sitting at a table, smiling warmly in their direction. Seeing her look, they smiled, raising their glasses.

"Lili!"

Lili turned. To her astonished delight, she saw Daisy and Guy pushing their way through the crowd, followed closely by Greg, Conrad, and Matthew, faces wreathed in smiles; an ecstatically happy Sid, and finally, lagging a little behind as if uncertain of his reception ... Jake.

She gasped, the world stilled, and her eyes focused in questioning disbelief on his face, but only had a moment to wonder before she was being warmly embraced by Daisy.

"Happy 21st Lili," Daisy cried, and the others chorused their salutations.

"Daisy," Lili hugged her back in delight. "What are you all doing here?

"You didn't think we'd miss your 21st birthday party, did you?"

"But ... but ... how did you all get here. Where are you all staying? How was this all arranged without me knowing?"

Daisy laughed at the stream of questions. "Conrad and Matthew drove in their car with Greg and Sid, and we drove ourselves down."

"And what about you?" Lili looked at Jake, amazed at how steady her voice was.

"I've got what's probably the world's worst hire car," he stated.

"Jake was a last-minute addition to our party," explained Daisy. "We didn't even know he was in the country until he phoned from Heathrow, said he'd just landed, and could he come and stay. So, of course, we explained it was your 21st and we were all coming down for the weekend, and I persuaded him to come with us. I knew you wouldn't mind, and it works out quite well because he's off to Harwich tomorrow to catch a ferry to Holland."

"Holland?" Lili turned startled eyes up to Jake. "Why are you going to Holland?"

"Oh, research." He seemed uncomfortable, unwilling to look her in the eye.

"So, anyway," Conrad picked up the story. "To answer your questions, Amy phoned months ago to set things in motion, and we've been in secret correspondence ever since. As to where we're staying, well, we're all camped out at yours I'm afraid."

"Oh, okay," Lili blinked in dazed bewilderment. "Is there room for everyone?"

"Don't worry, sweetie," Conrad patted her hand. "It's all sorted, Daisy and Guy have commandeered your gorgeous guest room, Matthew and I have the attic twin with Sid in the other, and the Kolinsky boys are sleeping in Lindy and Amy's rooms."

"What about everyone else?" Lili enquired anxiously. "Where are they all staying?"

"Oh, that rather wonderful friend of yours, Tom, arranged a bus," explained Conrad airily. "It went all around town and the villages picking everyone up, and it's coming back at two to take everybody who's still standing, home. So, everyone except the London contingent will be going back to their own homes."

"So, it's all sorted then," agreed Lili, accepting with good grace all the arrangements that had been made without her knowledge.

"All sorted," laughed Daisy. "All you have to do is have fun."

Later, sitting at a table with Amy, Kevin, and Martin, sipping champagne and nibbling on delicious canapés, Lili looked happily around the room, thinking everyone she knew was there.

Aside from the gang and her London friends, she'd been thrilled to see all her work colleagues and their partners, including Dorothy Evans, who had proudly introduced her to her husband, Jonathon. A tall, warmly handsome man, it was plain to Lili from the way Ms Evans' eyes lingered on his face, his hand firmly clasping hers, that this was a couple still very much in love.

Even Alex and her husband, Simon, were there, Alex gently rounded with their second child, eyes wide at meeting Lili's glamorous friends.

"I still don't know how you managed to arrange it all," she said to Amy, who grinned, exchanging conspiratorial glances with Kevin and Martin.

"We all had our different tasks," explained Amy. "I was in charge of food; Kevin was flowers and decorations; Martin was in charge of the guest list and the bar, and Lindy helped me with the food and was the decoy to get you out of the way for the day; Johnny arranged the band," she paused, exchanging a look with Lili.

"He knows the lead singer from university days."

Lili rolled her eyes, of course, Johnny knew the lead singer, he knew everyone.

"Even Tom helped," continued Amy. "He arranged the bus to pick everyone up."

"Well, it's all amazing," declared Lili, wrinkling her nose as a sudden thought struck her. "And I take it there's no dinner tomorrow night?"

"No," replied Amy. "It was a red herring to throw you off the scent."

Lili nodded, finishing her champagne, eyes roaming over the chattering, laughing crowd, searching, and seeking until she found him. Sitting alone at a table, toying with an empty glass, he seemed apart; separate. Lili came to a sudden decision.

"I'm going to mingle," she murmured, slipping out of her chair, barely noticing as the others smiled and nodded. Detouring via the bar, she purloined a bottle of champagne, and slowly crossed to where Jake sat.

He looked up as she slid into the chair opposite him, carefully poured out the golden, bubbling liquid, pushing his glass across to him, flinching slightly when their fingers brushed, her eyes rising to meet his.

A hint of something flashed in his eyes, and Lili felt that old, familiar tug, which she angrily pushed down.

"Happy birthday, Lili," he said, toasting her with his glass.

"Thank you," she paused, letting the silence stretch out between them. "So," she eventually said. "How's Vivienne?"

"She's ..." he stopped and sighed. "Well, you probably haven't heard, but we separated before Christmas, I'll be filing for divorce when I get back home."

"Oh," replied Lili flatly, tossing back her champagne. She silently pushed her glass forward, watching as he refilled it.

"Why does that sound so familiar," she mused. "Do you know, I could swear I've heard you say that before?"

"I know," Jake paused, flushing slightly, and looking away as if unable to face the accusation in her eyes. "That time in London, I didn't lie to you, Lili. We had separated, but when I left you and went back to the hotel, she called, pleading with me to give her one more chance, swearing she had changed. That she realised how important I was to her, and how important our marriage was," he shrugged, spreading his hands wide.

"What could I do, Lili? You don't give up on a marriage if there's any chance of making it work. Leastways, I don't. So ..." his voice trailed away.

"So, you went back to her," Lili finished the sentence for him, eyes locked on his, needing, demanding answers. He nodded and sipped nervously at his champagne.

"What happened this time, Jake? Why are you here, again? Claiming to be separated, again. How long before you go crawling back to her, again?"

"I'm never going back. It's over this time," he broke off, a hard, steely look coming into his eyes. "Why are you so angry, Lili?" he demanded. "I don't see how it's any of your business."

"No, you're right," snapped Lili. "It's absolutely none of my business. Not anymore."

Jake frowned, as Lili turned away from him, fixing her gaze on the band as they finished belting out their rendition of a popular song. The lead singer, Johnny's old friend, all long legs and spiked blonde hair gestured for silence.

"Thank you," she said. "And now a special song for the birthday girl. It's one of her favourites. This comes to you, Lili, with lots of love from Martin."

Twisting, Lili saw Martin waving at her. She smiled and waved back, hearing, with a sinking sense of inevitability, the intro of the song – that song. Apprehensively, her gaze flicked to Jake, but he seemed oblivious to its significance as he sat, frowning into his glass.

Never had the lyrics seemed so poignant. As Lili felt the first verse pour over her, she couldn't help her lips moving to words that came straight from her own heart.

... the singer begged to know if this was a game, he was playing...

"Dance with me," she demanded. Jake looked up, surprised. "Dance with me," she said again, her voice softer. He smiled and shrugged.

"As the birthday girl commands."

He rose from his chair and gallantly pulled hers back, holding out his hand to her. Nervously, Lili allowed him to lead her onto the dance floor, feeling his hand slip into its usual place on her back. Shocks rippled down her spine as she raised her head to gaze into his eyes.

... whilst the singer crooned of needing him tonight, of wanting to show him a sunset if he'd only stay with her till dawn...

I still love him, she realised in dazed disbelief. I still want him. But I'm tired of it, so tired of it all. The waiting, the hurting, the wondering if he's left her this time, or if she'll crook her little finger and he'll go crawling back to her.

What is this hold she has over him? How can I love him so much? When he feels nothing? It's not fair. I don't want to be in love with him anymore. I want it to stop. I want to move on with my life. Meet someone special who'll love me in return.

Jake's grip tightened, his firm, muscular body pressed against hers. She closed her eyes in despair. It was no good. No matter how logical it was for her to stop loving him she might as well command her lungs to stop taking in air.

Her feelings for him were engrained; etched deep in her soul. His fingers, large and warm, lightly caressed the bare flesh of her back. Lili felt need uncurl in the pit of her stomach.

She knew the sexual attraction so powerfully awakened that day in London was still there as deep and strong as ever. She sighed with the hopeless futility of it all, and Jake's eyes softened as he looked down into hers.

"May I call you, Lili?"

"Well, of course, you can," replied Lili, confused. "Everybody else does."

"No," Jake smiled at the misunderstanding. "I mean, may I phone you? I'm in Amsterdam for a few days. The next book is set there, and I always like to get a feel for where I'm writing about. Then I must return to the States to sort my life out, but I'm coming back for a long holiday..."

"When?" interrupted Lili, heart jogging about in excitement.

"April sometime. So, may I call you when I come back?"

Lili hesitated, unsure how much she could trust him this time, unwilling to peg her heart out again only to have him unthinkingly walk all over it.

The song swept into its powerful instrumental section. Lili knew it was coming to an end. It seemed vitally important to decide before the song reached its climax.

"Okay," she said slowly, considering. "You sort your life out, Jake. When you have, call me."

The song ended. Leisurely, reluctantly, Jake released her and stepped back. In the dimly lit room, Lili could see his eyes, dark and glittering. He smiled; that gorgeous, all-male smile which always turned her legs to water, and her brain to mush. Then pulled her close, pressing a fierce, hungry kiss on her cheek.

"I will call you, Lili." His promise was earnest, and Lili felt herself melt into his arms.

"Now, now, break it up you two."

Greg and Sid were there, laughing, unknowingly rupturing the moment. Lili and Jake stepped hurriedly apart.

"You're not allowed to hog the birthday girl all to yourself," declared Greg, sweeping Lili into his arms. "Hello gorgeous," he twirled Lili round, depositing her, breathless and giddy, back on her feet. "You're going to dance with me now."

"Okay," agreed Lili.

"Who am I supposed to dance with?" Jake scowled.

"Ooh handsome, I'll dance with you," offered Sid, batting his eyelashes.

"Tempting, but no thanks," replied Jake in amusement.

"Oh, go and dance with Daisy," ordered Greg, clutching Lili tightly to his chest as if to defend his prize against all intruders.

"Okay, where is she?" Jake brightened at the thought, peering around hopefully.

"Don't know," Greg shrugged. "Haven't seen her for ages, bye ..." smoothly he manoeuvred Lili away.

From their table, Amy and Martin watched Greg's annexing of Lili, exchanging smiles as Lili threw her head back, laughing at something Greg had said.

"Well," commented Martin with satisfaction. "Lili's certainly enjoying herself."

"Good," replied Amy. "That's good ..." her voice trailed away. Martin peered uncertainly at her, aware through the pleasant fog of too much champagne, that Amy's tone had been a little too bright, a little too strained.

"Is everything all right, Amy?" he asked in friendly concern.

"What? Oh yes, I'm fine, it's ... well, parties make me a little sad, that's all."

"Why?" Martin was puzzled. He always thought the idea of a party was to make people happy.

"Oh, it's nothing. It's probably the champagne talking, but everyone seems to be coupled off, and I can't help wondering if I'll ever meet someone, you know, that someone special. After all, I don't want to end up an old spinster with a lot of cats."

"You, end up alone? Never!" Amy was gratified at the stunned surprise in Martin's voice, feeling a much-needed boost to her sadly deflated ego.

"Really?"

"Of course, really. Jeez, Amy, you're gorgeous. Any bloke would be lucky to have you." Amy flushed with pleasure. Martin, encouraged by this, laid it on a bit thicker. "You know, we should make a pact, you and I."

"What sort of pact?"

"We should agree to be each other's back up. So, if, say, we reach 40 and aren't with anyone, we'll marry each other."

"That's a good idea," Amy blinked owlishly at him, thinking she had never noticed before how attractive Martin was, then thinking perhaps she'd had a little too much champagne.

"Make it 35 though," she insisted. "because I want kids, and 40's a bit late to start having them."

"Ok, 35 it is," agreed Martin, good-naturedly.

"Thanks, mate," Amy carefully clinked glasses with him.

"You're welcome, mate." Equally cautiously, Martin clinked back. Solemnly, they shook hands, then Amy set her glass down and pushed her hair back from her face, the alcohol flushing her cheeks.

"Right," she declared. "Now that's settled, I think I better go and check on things in the kitchen."

Amy had taken on two part-time assistants to temporarily help her over the madness of Christmas. However, in January she decided her business turnover was such, it more than justified making their appointments permanent.

"Right, see you later."

Martin watched, slightly concerned, as Amy lurched out of her chair, weaved her way somewhat unsteadily across the crowded dance floor, and vanished through the door leading towards the kitchen.

"Thank you for the song, Martin." He looked up and smiled as Lili collapsed breathlessly into the chair next to him. "It was sweet of you."

"That's okay," he declared magnanimously. "It's my evening for doing things for friends."

"Huh?"

"Never mind," Martin waved away Lili's enquiry.

"Happy birthday, gorgeous." Tom appeared at their table with a glass of champagne, which Lili accepted with a giggle. "Tell me, Lili," he sat down next to her. "Who's that girl?"

"Which one?"

"The dark-haired one talking to Kevin?" Lili followed Tom's gaze.

"Oh, that's Rose..."

"Rose?"

"Yes, you know my neighbours, Mr and Mrs Jamison? Well, Rose is their daughter."

Tom gazed as Rose threw back her head, laughing at something Kevin had said. Her whole face changed in an instant from average prettiness to stunning vivacity.

Slight, with long dark hair, large hazel eyes and sharply defined cheekbones, Lili considered Rose to be one of those women whose looks are defined by their mood.

When Lili had lived with her grandmother, she envied Rose her open, sunny disposition, her vivacious looks, and circle of close girlfriends, whom she seemed to go out with regularly.

Rose, herself then only 21, had always been kind to the desperately shy and gauche thirteen-year-old girl, but by the time Lili moved back in next door, Rose had moved away from home.

They exchanged pleasantries whenever they met, and Lili did consider Rose to be a friend, there is less of a gap between 21 and 29, yet never felt she knew what was going on behind the friendly smile, and the witty, slightly dry way she had of talking.

"She's beautiful."

Lili smiled at Tom's comment, patting his arm. "Yes, she is," she agreed. "But, unfortunately, do you see that guy sitting at the table behind her? The tall, ugly guy with the sour expression?"

"Yeah."

"Well, that's Paul, Rose's husband."

"She's married?"

"I'm afraid so," Lili shook her head. "And to a complete and utter…"

"Wanker!"

"Martin!" Lili spluttered.

"Well, it's true," he insisted, turning to Tom. "Rose is great. She's attractive, funny and good company, but her husband … complete wanker."

"In what way?" asked Tom, his interest casual.

"He's an arrogant, big-headed, ignorant, rude, egotistical wanker, and he bullies Rose dreadfully."

"He hits her?" Tom's head snapped around, eyes flat and dangerous. Lili felt the jolt she always did when faced with the steely, masculine edge of Tom.

"Oh no, nothing like that," reassured Martin hastily. "At least, I don't think … Lili?"

"No," Lili shook her head. "He doesn't physically bully her, not as far as I know anyway. He intimidates and overpowers her, I mean … uh oh, look. I wondered how long he'd let her talk to Kevin without muscling in."

They watched as Paul, becoming increasingly irate at his wife innocently chatting to another man, finally jerked to his feet, and stalked over to where they stood. Unable to hear what he said, they saw the animation and light in Rose's face switch off as if Paul had reached inside and yanked out her battery. Paul turned and stalked back to his table. Rose mumbled something to Kevin and then trailed dejectedly after him.

"Holy crap," exclaimed Tom in disgust. "What on earth do you think he said to her?"

"I don't know," muttered Lili, waving Kevin over to them. "What was that all about?" she enquired, as he wandered across and dropped into the chair opposite.

"I don't know what that guy's problem is," exclaimed Kevin. "But if I were his wife and he spoke to me that way, I think I'd punch his lights out. Bloke's a complete prick."

"Why is it the complete pricks of this world always seem to have gorgeous wives?" grumbled Martin, to no one in particular.

"Oh, there are Lord and Lady Felsham," exclaimed Lili, rising quickly to her feet. "I must go and thank them for hosting my party."

Kevin watched her cross to the older couple. Clasping their hands and lightly kissing their cheeks, she chatted happily to them.

Johnny appeared beside her, slinging an easy arm around Lili's waist, and drawing her close, holding her far more intimately, Kevin felt, than the occasion called for.

Watching them laughing, Kevin was struck by what a stunningly beautiful couple Lili and Johnny made, with their similar colouring and attractive, finely detailed features. They looked like they belonged together. He swallowed hard to dislodge the lump of jealous bile which arose in his throat.

Amy flopped onto a chair, smiling a greeting at Kevin and Tom. After the cooler air of the kitchen, and the quick glass of water she'd downed, she appeared almost lucid. Her eyes had lost their fixed gaze and she seemed more in control.

"Dinner's going to be announced in about ten minutes," she declared. Kevin dragged his eyes away from Lili, smiling at his nervous, younger sister.

"Relax," he ordered. "Dinner for forty is surely nothing to you now. You've dealt with much higher numbers than that."

"I know," she replied. "But this is for Lili, I want it to be perfect."

"It will be," he reassured her. He stood up, unable to bear another second of watching Johnny with his hands all over Lili. "Back in a moment," he muttered, leaving before the others could ask where he was going.

Heading for the door, Kevin passed Jake sitting at a table with Guy and Greg, staring into the crowd with a fierce scowl on his face. Briefly, he wondered what his problem was, then put it out of his mind as he left the banqueting hall.

Loitering in the dimly lit hall, Kevin decided to sit for a few moments on the dark staircase until dinner, then slip back into the hall. Surely Johnny would have let go of Lili by then?

Quietly, he made his way up the sweeping, double-width staircase, climbing until he passed the first bend and was invisible from the hall below. Sighing, he dropped to sit on the cold marble stair, feeling its chill pass through his trousers, numbing his backside, and making him shift uncomfortably.

A soft sound, a sigh, and the sensation of a presence behind him had Kevin craning his neck uneasily. For a second, the thought of ghosts flashed through his mind, before he firmly pushed it away. Rising to his feet, he softly carried on up the stairs to the top, peering into the dimness. Was that a shape in the corner of the landing?

"Hello?" his voice was hesitant, unsure. There was silence for a second, then the shape stepped forward, revealing itself as human, and female.

"Hello."

The voice was soft and low, yet Kevin had no problem identifying Lili's London friend, Daisy, whom he'd met several times.

"Daisy? What are you doing up here? If you're looking for the cloakroom, it's downstairs."

"Oh, no, I'm fine, thanks. I was ... well, I needed some time alone, that's all."

A shaft of moonlight struck the landing window flooding them with its white, eerie light, cruelly illuminating Daisy's face. Kevin visibly recoiled at the misery and apprehension etched there.

"What is it?" he involuntarily exclaimed. "What's the matter?"

"N-nothing," she stammered. "I'm all right, I ..." As she spoke, her shoulders convulsed in a great sob of despair. Kevin instinctively stepped forward, enfolding her in a brotherly hug. For a moment she was stiff and unyielding in his arms, then disintegrated into a stuttering, damp, bundle.

"Ssh, it's okay," soothed Kevin, feeling a wave of tenderness at her distress. "What's the matter?"

"I thought I was pregnant, I was so sure, I was a week late and I'm never late ..." Daisy's voice trailed away into discomfiture and Kevin hurried to reassure her.

"It's okay, I have a sister, I have female friends. I'm not embarrassed."

"Oh, yes, of course. Well, we've been trying for a baby for ages. Nothing's happened and ... oh it's all my fault, I shouldn't have said anything, but I was so sure, was so desperate, I guess. Now I've got to go down there and tell him it's another false alarm and he'll be so angry with me."

"Why will he be angry with you? It's not your fault."

"But that's just it," Daisy's voice shook.

Kevin stroked a comforting hand down her back, some far off, purely male part of his brain, registering her feminine curves – the softness of the skin at the nape of her neck.

"Before he met me, Guy was in another long-term relationship. She got pregnant and had an abortion against Guy's wishes. He was furious and finished it with her. So, you see, we know he's okay. We know he's not the problem.

"Have you had any tests or anything?"

"Not yet," Daisy sniffed, and snuggled further into the comforting warmth of his chest, liking its broadness, unable to remember the last time Guy had cuddled her without it being a forerunner to another bout of increasingly frantic, baby-making, sex.

"I suppose that's going to have to be the next step, but I'm dreading it. All those invasive examinations, questions into your intimate life," she shuddered at the thought.

Kevin tightened his grip. "But you're so young," he murmured, resisting the sudden urge to kiss her hair. "There's still time, surely."

"For me maybe," cried Daisy. "But Guy's quite a bit older than me, and he's so desperate to have a baby, well, a son really, to carry on the Bellingham name. He wants a big family," Daisy confided. "Always has done. The fact it's taking me so long to get pregnant is stressing him out."

And in turn, he was stressing out his young wife, Kevin thought in quick, hot anger. Accusing and hurting, instead of supporting and understanding. What a bastard.

"I have to get back." Daisy seemed to realise where she was, and what she was doing. Her arms dropped to her side, and she stepped away from him, back into the darkness, and Kevin felt momentarily bereft.

"Thank you," she murmured. "for listening. You've been very kind. I mean, you don't know me and here I am making the front of your shirt all wet."

"That's all right. They say it's easier sometimes to talk to a stranger rather than a friend," he shrugged. "I guess this was one of those times. Come on, I'll take you back downstairs. You've got time to sort out your face before dinner is served."

"Thank you..."

"Oh, and Daisy ... if you want my advice, don't tell him tonight. If you think he'll react that badly to the news, then don't tell him tonight. Wait until you get home."

"You're right, I don't want anything to spoil Lili's birthday. Thank you, Kevin, you've been very kind."

Escorting her down the dimly lit stairs, Kevin was intensely aware of the small, cold hand clasping his arm, and the pretty, tear-drenched face. Martin was right, he thought with sudden, dark humour, the complete and utter pricks of the world always did seem to have gorgeous wives.

Despite Amy's fears, the food was superb, and her face glowed at the compliments and favourable comments, as guests filed past the makeshift serving hatches and were offered a wide range of hot and cold dishes.

Considering the time of year, Amy had opted for hearty comfort food. Great vats full of spicy beef, and a vegetarian chilli gave out enticing aromas, along with platters of individual chicken and mushroom pies with gleaming, golden pastry tops. Mexican rice salad, veggie lasagne, Mediterranean roasted vegetables, and piles of mini jacket potatoes with temptingly crispy skins. There was also fresh green salad.

Even the band took a well-earned break and tucked in with glee, enthusiastically ferrying plates piled high with delicious, homemade fare back to their table. As Lili sat at her table, she couldn't help glancing around the room with an intense feeling of satisfaction at her friends, all together, happy, and well-fed, enjoying the party, the excellent music, and each other's company.

For half an hour the guests relaxed, many paying multiple visits to the serving hatch to have a second, even third, helpings. Amy and her assistants cleared away, then laid out a range of desserts – tropical fruit salad, raspberry cheesecake, sticky toffee pudding, and lemon torte, together with jugs of thick cream and piping hot, vanilla custard, along with an impressive cheese board, and French bread with individual pats of butter.

Finally, when even the heartiest appetites had been satisfied and the plates and cutlery cleared away, a beautiful chocolate and raspberry birthday cake was wheeled out, twenty-one candles burning away merrily. Lili was duly summoned to the stage to blow them all out. Rousing renditions of *Happy Birthday* and *For She's A Jolly Good Fellow* were sung. The singer then informed everyone in ten minutes the music would begin again and would go right through, non-stop, until two am.

Tea and coffee were served. Guests happily chatted amongst themselves, digesting the fabulous food, and looking forward to the rest of the party, agreeing what an amazing night it had been so far.

Lindy was not having a good party. Everywhere she looked, every time she turned around, there was Johnny, his arm around a different woman, laughing and flirting, oozing his trademark charisma.

She forgave him for paying attention to Lili, after all, it was her birthday, and Lindy knew Lili looked upon Johnny as a friend. But, she thought, with gritted teeth, did he have to lavish quite so much charm on every other woman at the party?

Telling herself firmly she shouldn't give a toss whom he flirted with, Lindy watched as he chatted with Rose, his good looks and easy manners causing the older woman to giggle like a schoolgirl, making Lindy's blood boil.

Finally, she'd had enough. Escaping to the cloakroom, running cold water on her wrists, Lindy glanced at her reflection in the mirror, seeing the misery in her eyes. Who was she trying to fool? The truth was she missed Johnny so much it was like someone had taken a cleaver and hacked a hole in her heart. Was it love? Lindy wasn't sure but knew she couldn't take much more of this pain.

Leaving the cloakroom, Lindy decided she would make some excuse and go. After all, her car was parked outside, and she'd only had a glass of champagne. She wanted to go home, craving silence and solitude to lay down her poor, aching head, and to release the tears she could feel pounding at her eyelids and clawing at the back of her throat.

Making her way down the corridor, Lindy heard a familiar voice around the corner ahead and stopped dead. The last thing she wanted was to see Johnny. She hesitated, hoping he'd go the other way. She heard a laugh, a woman's laugh, low and husky. Female curiosity had her silently creeping to the corner and peering round.

Her first thought was what a stunning pair they made; Johnny was leaning against the wall with his back to her, that familiar magnificent body she'd held on countless occasions.

The woman was tall and supple. Raking a hand through her spiky blonde crop, she casually ran her other hand over Johnny's shoulder, smiling up into his face. Lindy's eyes narrowed as she recognised the lead singer of the band, and flattened herself against the wall, ears straining to hear their low, murmured words.

"Don't worry, Johnny, everything's going to be fine."

"Easy for you to say, Carla, you're used to this. It's my first time."

"Oh honey," she drawled huskily. The blonde slipped arms around him and pressed a kiss to his lips. "You're very talented. I'd go as far as saying you could make a living from it."

"Well, I suppose we'd better get on with it. Coming?"

"In a minute, I have to freshen up first."

Horrified at what she'd seen, what she'd heard, what she'd assumed, Lindy watched Johnny give the blonde an affectionate hug, then head back to the hall. Carla turned in her direction; there was nowhere to hide.

Carla rounded the corner and stopped, brows raising when she saw Lindy, eyes sparking with accusation and assumption, fists clenched, her body tense and stiff. The blonde woman stopped, a knowing, understanding smile spread over her face.

"I take it," she drawled, "going on Johnny's description – and the fact you want to rip my heart out and eat it whilst it's still beating – that you're Lindy."

"I don't know what Johnny's said …" began Lindy, words clipped and stilted.

"Oh, Johnny and I are old friends," interrupted the woman. Lindy wanted to scream at the implication she heard in the woman's words.

"I'm not interested," she growled. "Johnny's old lovers are no concern of mine."

"Hold on a minute, honey," Carla held her hand up in sharp denial. "I said we're friends, I never said anything about us being lovers. Trust me, I'm not Johnny's type."

"Every woman is Johnny's type," Lindy replied through gritted teeth.

"Well then, let's just say he's not my type," continued the woman. Her eyes roved suggestively over Lindy's white silk-clad body. "Although … you could be."

Lindy blinked, the woman's words sunk in, and meaning exploded in her jealous brain. She gulped, her posture relaxing slightly, her fists unclenching.

"You know," Carla sauntered past, amusement dancing in her eyes at Lindy's discomfort. "I always assumed the woman who finally won Johnny's heart would be incredibly special, and smart enough to realise how lucky she was." She paused, her eyes becoming sad and thoughtful.

"Guess I was wrong on both counts." She shrugged, leaving Lindy standing, mouth agape, as she leisurely made her way into the cloakroom.

Lindy froze to the spot.

Wild, reckless, thoughts and urges crashed and surged in her fevered brain. She thought of her mother; all those men, the uncles who'd paraded through her childhood. Had any one of them ever made mum a fraction as happy as Johnny made her? Had any uncle ever offered mum his name? Asked her to share his life on anything other than a purely temporary basis?

What have I done, she thought, sudden clarity drenching her, oh fuck, what have I done? Tell him, a small, insistent voice urged, go to him now and tell him. I can't, she almost moaned the words out loud. I can't. I hurt him so badly, how can I tell him I've changed my mind? I wouldn't know what words to use.

Shivering, Lindy crept soundlessly past the open double doors of the banqueting hall. Unable to face other people, she silently slipped up the stairs and perched halfway up, hugging her knees to her chest, laying her cheek on them as she tried to figure out what on earth to do next.

She heard a clack of heels below, and peering through the bannisters, saw Carla sashay past into the hall. A moment later, Lindy heard her voice over the microphone.

"Ladies and gentlemen, could I have your attention, please. First, I'd like to wish Lili a very happy 21st birthday and ask you all to raise your glasses in a toast."

"Happy birthday, Lili," Lindy silently mouthed the words into the chill air.

"I've also got a few thank yous to make from Lili herself," continued Carla. "She would like to thank all of her friends for arranging this marvellous party, especially Amy for providing such an amazing feast, I think we all agree it was fantastic." There was a round of enthusiastic applause and a smattering of cheers.

"She'd also like to thank Martin for arranging the bar, Kevin for decorating the hall so beautifully and providing all the flowers, Lindy for assisting Amy and being such an excellent decoy, Tom for arranging the bus, and an extra special, big thank you, goes to Lord and Lady Felsham for allowing the party to be held in their magnificent home."

"Finally, she'd like to thank everyone for coming tonight. Some of you have travelled from quite a distance, namely London and even America. To you all, Lili has asked me to express her sincere love and appreciation," more cheers and applause. "And now," Carla's voice took on an anticipatory edge, "as a surprise for Lili, we have a special guest singer appearing with us. Ladies and gentlemen, give a big hand please for Mr Johnny Gedding."

The crowd, especially the women, went wild. Lindy's eyes flew open. She nearly fell off her step with shock. Johnny? What on earth? Curiously, she crept downstairs, and stood opposite the open double doors, back pressed firmly against the cold stone wall.

Johnny walked on stage looking devastatingly sexy in his tux. He'd removed his bow tie and undone the top two buttons of his shirt. As he winked at the audience, more than one woman sighed a little to herself. Johnny took the mike from Carla, who saluted him and left the stage.

"Ladies and gentlemen," Johnny held out his hand to calm the wild cheers and yells of encouragement. "Ladies and gentlemen, I would like to dedicate this song to a very special lady, and I don't need to mention any names. She knows who she is."

As one, heads in the crowd swivelled towards Lili standing next to Jake, who laughed with delighted pleasure. Yet, as Lindy watched, disbelievingly, Johnny's eyes scanned the room before, thrillingly, locking onto her face. With a violent thump of her heart, she knew. The song wasn't for Lili, it was for her.

Johnny gestured to the band and soft music began; a piano intro, something bluesy and powerful. It was a song Lindy was unfamiliar with, but, as she listened to the words, she felt something stir deep within her. The song *was* for her.

Kevin, Martin, and Amy sat at a table near the back of the hall, listening with shocked surprise as Johnny began to sing.

"Bloody typical," grumbled Kevin, under his breath. "He would have to be a fantastic singer wouldn't he." Amy smiled, laying a sympathetic hand on his arm.

Johnny's voice was clear and true, a crooner's voice. The crowd swayed, mesmerised by the powerful lyrics, and the sheer emotion that sounded in every word.

"I don't recognise the song," Amy whispered to Martin. "Do you know what it is?"

"It's an old Billy Joel song," he whispered back. "*An Innocent Man*. It's a great song, a classic, and he's singing it well."

"Bit of an odd choice for Lili, though, isn't it?" Kevin mused, listening to the words.

"Umm," began Amy uncertainly, eyes following the direction of Johnny's gaze. "I don't think he is singing it to Lili. Look." She nodded her head towards the back of the hall. Martin and Kevin's heads swivelled obediently.

Lindy. Back to the wall, dress a shimmer of white silk in the moonlight, fists clenched by her side, her face was an anguished story, which told everything to the three watchers, as Johnny sang to her that she could choose to be a martyr, and if she was cruel to him, he'd understand.

Lindy. Who never cried, never showed any weakness at all, face wet with the helpless tears that slid, unchecked, down her face. Three heads turned to stare in consternation at each other.

"Ah," said Amy.

"Oh," said Kevin.

"Shit!" said Martin.

The song finished amongst a crescendo of applause. Johnny modestly accepted his praise, eyes constantly flicking to the back of the hall. They turned as one, expecting, anticipating Lindy to make a move; to do something, say something.

The wall was empty.

She'd gone.

Johnny hadn't known quite what effect his grand gesture would have, but he hadn't expected her to run away and leave without a word, or a goodbye, to anyone. Pushing his way through the chattering, congratulating crowd, by the time he made his way to the doors she was long gone – deep tyre grooves in the snowy driveway a testament to her reckless flight.

He'd lost her.

By running away, she had made it quite plain it was really and truly over, and in the time-honoured tradition of jilted lovers everywhere, Johnny dealt with the situation by getting royally and horribly drunk.

By the time he staggered onto the bus with all the other partied-out guests, Johnny was barely capable of putting one foot in front of the other and had to be helped on by a quietly sympathetic Kevin.

During the party, the threatened snow had begun to fall. Thick and obliterating, it settled over the bleak land casting an eerie, though strangely beautiful, white light.

"Lucky you had the party tonight," Conrad murmured to Lili, as she rested her head wearily on his shoulder. "If this keeps up, you'll be snowed in by tomorrow evening."

"Hmm," she sighed, too tired to talk. "What time will you all leave?"

"Well," Conrad considered, "we'll probably leave soon after breakfast. Much as we love you, sweetie, we don't want to be snowbound in Bury for days on end."

The bus struggled through virgin snow, dropping off exhausted partygoers before heading into town, Johnny was among the first of the village drop-offs. He stumbled up the path, barely registering the frigid air through his alcoholic haze, unaware of three pairs of concerned and anxious eyes watching his drunken attempts to unlock the door.

Snuggled on the back seat, Amy, Martin, and Kevin exchanged worried glances. Martin opened his mouth to comment, but Amy laid a restraining hand on his arm, nodding her head to the seat in front, where Lili and Conrad were sitting.

"We'll talk about it later," she muttered, the others nodding in agreement.

Closing the door, Johnny leant wearily against its solid surface feeling the emotional backlash of the evening. It was over. He had played his last desperate card and failed. Torturing himself, he fumbled in his pocket and brought out the ring box.

Had he thought it would work? That by singing a stupid song to her, no matter how poignant the words; it would miraculously heal decades-old pain? Disgusted with himself, he stuffed the ring in his pocket and staggered into the lounge.

She stood by the window looking into the garden, the unnatural, pale light reflecting off her white silk dress making her appear ethereal; insubstantial. Johnny stopped and blinked, his brain refusing to believe what his dazed eyes were seeing.

"Lindy?"

Shocked, he felt instantly sober. Cautiously, hesitantly, he stepped forward, almost expecting her to vanish like a ghost or a mirage of cool, life-giving water in an arid desert. She turned and looked at him, face unreadable, eyes shuttered.

"Lindy," he said again, at a loss for what to say, what to think. "What are you doing here? You left ... I thought ... well, I thought that was it..."

"I had to go," her voice was low, soft. If he hadn't known better, he'd have thought her on the edge of tears, but Lindy wouldn't ... couldn't ... cry over him. "I had to be alone, had to think, so I went home for a while, then I decided to bring you a present ... here..." She tossed him a plastic bag which he reflexively caught, pursing his lips at the Tesco logo.

"Nice wrapping," he commented dryly and was rewarded with a tiny smile that tugged at the corner of her mouth. Curiously, he opened the bag, brow wrinkling in confusion. "Croissants?"

Lindy shrugged self-consciously. "I thought," she began. Her voice faltered, she took a deep breath, pushing herself to finish the sentence. "I thought we could have them for breakfast."

He stood, puzzled, not understanding, then realisation dawned. A smile of utter and complete relief spread across his face. Dropping the bag, he reached her in one bound and had her in his arms. She gasped, a long, drawn-out sigh of release, arms creeping around his neck as his mouth eagerly sought and claimed hers.

"Thank god," he moaned when they finally came up for air. "Thank god. Oh Lindy, sweetheart, I've missed you so much."

"I've missed you too," she murmured. "So much ... I love you, and I'm so sorry."

"Sorry you love me?"

"No, sorry for being so stupid, for hurting you ..."

"It's all right, you're here now, and you're going to stay?"

"Yes..."

"All night?"

"If you want me to, yes..."

"You have to anyway, it's snowing like mad, too dangerous for you to drive home."

"So, we're snowbound ..." she murmured, nipping at his bottom lip with her teeth.

"Absolutely," he agreed, hands sliding down her silken spine. "You'll have to borrow some of my clothes. Hmm, I like the thought of us being trapped here for days, you dressed only in my shirt."

"Erm, Johnny, I hate to burst your bubble but ..." she kicked her foot at the dark overnight bag at her feet. "I brought my things, just in case..."

"Presumptuous," he muttered affectionately.

"No, organised. Although," she paused, flashing him a coy smile, "If it's a personal fantasy for me to wear nothing but one of your shirts, well, I'm quite happy to oblige." He laughed, dragged her close again, raking his fingers through her immaculate hair, plundering her mouth in a fiercely territorial kiss.

"Bloody hell," she exclaimed when they broke apart. "What have you been drinking?"

"Alcohol, lots of," he admitted sheepishly.

"I love you, Johnny," she gasped. "But if you don't give me my ring now, I may have to hurt you."

Grinning, Johnny fumbled in his pocket, dragged out the ring box, dropping to one knee in front of her.

"Lindy Smith," he said, holding her small warm hands in his. "I love you more than life itself. Please, will you do me the honour of becoming my wife?"

"Yes," she replied, instantly, without hesitation. "Yes please."

With shaking hands, Johnny pulled the ring from its box and slipped it onto Lindy's finger. He bounded to his feet, amazed, and touched beyond belief when he felt the wet tears on her face, enfolding her in his arms, knowing he'd never let her go again.

Why was it, thought Lili, when something wonderful happened it made real life seem dull and ordinary. Standing on the porch the next day, she shivered as she said goodbye to her friends. She understood their reasons for leaving – the forecast threatened a blizzard would descend later that day – but still felt flat, anti-climactic.

"Goodbye Lili, sweetheart." Daisy caught her up in one last hug. "It was an amazing party. Sorry to leave so early."

"That's okay," Lili hugged her back. "You don't want to get trapped here. You all drive carefully and call me when you get home."

Cautiously, cars brushed free of their thick mantles of snow, Conrad, Matthew, Greg and Sid in Matthew's Mondeo, and Guy and Daisy in their car, eased from the kerb and drove away, horns tooting, hands waving out of windows.

Lili waved until they could be seen no more. Standing in the still, white morning, she blinked back emotional tears, until a noise made her turn to find Jake, overnight bag in hand, wrapped in his long, navy-blue wool coat, pulling on thick, leather gloves.

"Ready to go?" she managed to say.

"Yeah," he shifted uneasily as if unsure how to say goodbye.

"Bye Jake," Lili hesitated, planting a quick kiss on his cheek. To her surprise his arms enfolded her. For a brief, miraculous moment he held her tight, chin resting on the top of her head.

"Bye Lili," he said. "It was a great party, and it was good ... seeing you again."

Lili nodded, to overcome with conflicting emotions to reply. She watched as Jake picked up his bag and walked quickly down the path to his hire car. He got in and waved once. Reluctantly, hesitantly, the car growled into life and inched away from the kerb.

She raised her hand to wave, realised he wasn't looking, and gradually, slowly, let it fall to her side, watching him drive away. Lili sighed and turned to go indoors, shivering in the freezing air, feeling its coldness snap in her lungs.

He was gone.

Again, he'd made promises. Lili was more experienced now, was wary of believing them, but she would wait, as he'd asked. She would wait ... until April anyway.

Chapter Twenty-Seven
"Now I get what all the fuss is about."

As promised, by lunchtime a white, whirling blizzard was whipping itself up into a frenzy outside Lili's window. Fat, pristine flakes twirling and twisting, before settling in ever-deepening drifts. Lili wandered around the house feeling depressed and flat, wishing her friends had been able to stay longer, missing company and wondering what to do with the rest of the day.

She stripped and remade the beds, piling it all beside the washing machine ready for laundering. Quickly completing her few other household chores, she struggled out to the shed, lugging in enough logs and buckets of coal to last for several days.

These activities kept her busy until lunchtime – when she ate a solitary sandwich. Then, she phoned her friends to thank them for the previous evening. As expected, they were all in their respective homes battening down the hatches with no plans to go anywhere, or do anything, until the storm passed.

Strangely, Lindy didn't answer her landline, so Lili called her mobile. Sounding flustered, Lindy chatted briefly before abruptly, almost rudely, hanging up.

A little put-out, Lili dialled Johnny's number. After several rings, he finally answered breathless and panting. He had to run for the phone, he explained. They talked, Lili enthusing about the party, thanking him for his part in the preparations, and for the wonderful song he'd sung.

Whilst chatting, Lili couldn't help but feel his attention was elsewhere, surprised when he let out a little gasp, quickly exclaiming he had to go something was boiling over on the stove, then abruptly hung up.

Her London friends phoned to report their safe arrival home. Chatting with them filled another hour, but when she finally put down the phone, silence and solitude pressed oppressively against her eardrums. She found herself roaming up and downstairs, feeling restless and bored. Unused to being by herself, Lili reflected how this would be the first weekend in years she would spend alone.

She curled up on the lounge window seat, peering through the frosty glass at a starkly beautiful white world outside. The snow was falling even harder now. Scarcely a soul was around; only a few hardy pedestrians struggled past, heads bowed against driving flakes, bodies so muffled and wrapped it was impossible to tell man from woman.

Feeling edgy and tense, Lili had the strangest sensation she was waiting for something to happen. Telling herself firmly to not be so ridiculous, this impression of anticipation made her twitchy and jittery, and she was unable to settle to anything.

She tried to read but laid the book aside after only a few minutes, her mind wandering too much to make any sense of the words. She switched on the television but was quickly bored of the mindless sports programmes which formed the staple diet of daytime Saturday TV.

The minutes stretched endlessly into hours, which crept inexorably towards evening. Dusk fell early. By three it was dark enough to switch the lamps on. Lili laid and lit a fire, its crackling, dancing flames a welcome sound in an otherwise silent world; its warmth and colour providing much-needed companionship.

She loaded the stereo with CDs, her mood demanding all be soft, melodious, and romantic. Finally, she wandered into the kitchen, deciding her solitary situation was no reason not to have a special Saturday night dinner.

She opened a bottle of wine, the sound of the cork being pulled, and the glug of ruby liquid splashing into a glass lifting her spirits, taking the edge off her strange, unsettled mood.

Assessing the contents of her fridge, she decided to construct a stupendous pizza from scratch. She pulled out a bowl into which she measured strong white bread flour, yeast, salt, and olive oil, mixing the ingredients with enough tepid water to make the dough.

Gently kneading the dough into a large pliant ball went further towards relaxing her troubled mind, and a generous swig of wine which warmed her throat and settled comfortingly in her empty stomach made her distinctly mellow.

Placing the dough back in the bowl and covering it with a cloth, Lili poked about in the fridge for toppings. She swiftly sautéed leeks, mushrooms, and wine vinegar on a high heat, the pungent cooking aromas making her mouth water.

Putting the vegetables to one side, she mixed peppers with artichokes, and garlic into passata. Finding mozzarella in the fridge she decided to use that, pulling off a generous amount into a bowl.

Wandering into the lounge with the wine, the fire had settled to a comforting red glow, so she tossed on more logs. Placing the bottle and her glass on the coffee table she closed the connecting wooden doors and lit the row of candles in votive glasses arranged along the mantelpiece, smiling at Boris sprawled on his back in front of the fire, a Cheshire cat grin of contentment spread across his face.

Crossing to the bay window, she peered out at a silent, white landscape devoid of all life. It felt like she was the only person left alive on the planet.

But no, as she watched, some foolhardy soul staggered across the road, struggling to walk in drifts by now knee-high. Shivering, Lili drew the heavy damask curtains, shutting the bleak world out, and sighed with pleasure at her beautiful room.

Closing the doors had created a cosy space in which the fire was the instant focal point. Soft music oozed as Clannad sang haunting lyrics in perfect harmony with the rustling and popping of the fire. On the mantelpiece, candles danced, flickering in jewel-coloured glasses, bewitching softly hued shadows onto the ceiling, the only other light cast by a multi-coloured Tiffany lamp.

A sensation of being safe and warm in her burrow arose in Lili. Giving a gusty sigh of satisfaction, she snuggled on the sofa, took a sip of wine, prepared to enjoy her unplanned evening alone.

A moment later the doorbell rang, making her jump and almost spill her wine. Heart hammering with shock, Lili put down her glass and crept almost fearfully into the hall. Through the coloured glass in the door, she could make out a massive presence, looming and menacing. Voice trembling, she called out.

"Who is it?"

There was silence, then...

"It's me, Lili, Jake ... hurry up and let me in, it's freezing out here."

Fingers fumbling in their haste, she hurriedly unbolted and opened the door to reveal Jake, face pinched and blue, dark wool coat wearing an over blanket of heavy, wet snow, overnight bag clutched in bare hands.

"Oh, my goodness," Lili exclaimed, quickly hustling him into the hall and closing the door behind him. "Jake? What on earth are you doing here?"

"Ferries cancelled," he stammered through chattering teeth. "Damn stupid hire car broke down outside Bury. Walked the rest of the way."

"Walked? You must be frozen. Let me take your coat."

He scrabbled at the buttons down the front. Lili's heart contracted with sympathy as his swollen red fingers fumbled uselessly. Gently, she pushed his hands aside, undid them for him, and felt the damp jumper underneath.

"You're soaked to the skin," she cried, dropping to her knees, and struggling to undo the saturated laces of his shoes.

"Yeah, tell me about it." Jake managed a wry grin as he fought his way out of the ruined footwear. "Could I scrounge a shower or something? I've got clean clothes."

"Of course," replied Lili, fighting against the urge to fuss and mother him. "Use the guest room, top of the stairs to the right. There are clean towels and the water's always hot. Come down when you've finished, I've lit a fire and opened a bottle."

"Sounds good," he said, and squelched his way upstairs, leaving Lili – heart beating wildly – painfully aware they were finally alone together, trapped in a snowbound house.

By the time Jake wandered back downstairs warmed through from his hot shower and feeling more comfortable in dry jeans and a shirt, Lili had managed to calm her pounding nerves.

She was waiting for him on the sofa, legs curled beneath her and glass of wine in hand, staring thoughtfully into the heart of the flames.

"Hey," he exclaimed, padding silently into the room with bare feet. "This is lovely."

Sitting down next to Lili with a contented sigh, he stared around the room with pleasure. Lili murmured a non-committal reply, handing him a glass of wine.

"Thanks." His gratitude was heartfelt as he took a big slug of wine, relaxing back into the soft sofa with another sigh of relief. "Let me tell you, Lili, I've never been so pleased to see anything as I was to see you looking out of the window. I worried all the way here you wouldn't be home. I don't know what I'd have done then."

Lili simply smiled, watching with fascination the way the firelight played over the strong, masculine planes of his face. He lifted the glass to his mouth again, slightly tipping his head back as he swallowed, and Lili's mouth went dry with lust.

As if sensing her inner turmoil, Jake turned to look at her. The warm relaxed smile faded into an intense look of consideration. Carefully putting down his wine, he moved closer, taking Lili's hand in his large, capable ones.

"Lili," he began warily, patiently, as though explaining something to a very young child. "I like you. You're a sweet, special person and, who knows, maybe in the future when I've got my life sorted out and things are back to normal, we could see each other again. See if maybe, possibly, there is something between us. But for now, I think it's best if we simply…"

All through his earnest, solemn speech, Lili had sat, head on one side, large eyes fixed unerringly on his. She sighed, placed her wine down, and leant forward pressing her soft, inexperienced lips onto his, stopping his speech mid-flow.

She felt his mouth part with surprise under hers. Emboldened by this, she deepened the kiss, pouring all her need and love into it. His hands hesitantly touched her shoulders, before he was pulling away, face concerned and shocked.

"Lili, I don't think we should, I don't want to take advantage of the situation …" He stopped and gazed into her eyes, their pupils dilated and dark, her lips slightly parted, inviting, urging him to taste further; to explore, touch, take.

Hesitantly, slowly, he lowered his head to hers, unable to resist, unable to fight against her anymore.

Softly, his lips closed over hers.

In a heartbeat, everything changed...

Desire lanced through him, intense and shockingly unexpected – a gut blow. Suddenly, this sweetly unsophisticated young girl whom he felt a mild attraction for was in his arms, and he was kissing her as fervently as she was kissing him.

Hands touched and explored. Mouths plundered and took. Breaking apart, Jake stared at this very different Lili; this flushed and panting woman offering herself to him.

"Lili, I..."

He had no chance to say any more. With a soft moan, she launched herself back into his arms. Small, sharp teeth nibbled their way up his jawline; hands fisted in his hair, and she pulled his head back down to hers. Soft, demanding lips fastened greedily onto his, and Jake was a lost man.

Casting aside all thought of reason, of caution, his hands skimmed across soft shoulders before closing over small, but firm and shapely, breasts. Lili shuddered, groaning with disbelief as strong clever fingers massaged through the thin barrier of her t-shirt. With shaking hands, he grasped the bottom of the shirt, pulling it up and over her head, to reveal a wisp of apricot lace, also quickly disposed of.

Used to Vivienne's more voluptuous curves, Jake found Lili's slender, boyish body immensely arousing. His firm, tender mouth closed enthusiastically over one rosy tipped mound, whilst fingers tantalised and teased the other.

Lili's head fell back, an ecstatic cry choking in her throat as exquisite sensations surged leaving her incapable of speech. She never guessed, never suspected, how it would feel to have Jake's fingers, hands, and mouth on her body.

She'd had no idea. How could she have? Untouched and unaware little virgin, her sexual awareness had been stifled at the age of thirteen, when she spied on her parents having sex and listened to them dismiss her as a retarded nobody.

With trembling hands, she carefully and meticulously began to undo his buttons, concentrating with an almost painful intensity on her task. In her innocence, she was unaware that the feel of small hands softly touching his chest, the sound of her ragged breathing, the smell of her perfume and the sight of those beautiful bare breasts glistening and firm from his mouth, were arousing Jake almost to breaking point.

His hands roved over her satiny skin, feeling, touching, stroking, caressing; enjoying her little gasps of pleasure as he found yet more and more sensitive areas.

Finally, Lili pushed the shirt over his shoulders. Acting purely on instinct, she gently touched the tip of her tongue to his skin, playing with him, tasting him, becoming bolder in her explorations as his groans and pleas not to stop encouraged her on.

Quickly, Jake unzipped her jeans, sliding them with ease down over her slim hips, the matching apricot knickers also speedily pulled down. Laying her back on the sofa, he lifted her legs, hooked them over his shoulders, and ran shaking hands down the inside of her thighs, following their path with his tongue.

Unprepared, Lili's eyes went blind with shock as he feasted on her femininity, cries of abandoned rapture ripped from her soul. Never in her wildest, most intimate dreams of Jake, had she come close to imagining such bliss, such pleasure. Her head thrashed from side to side, fingers clutching at his shoulders as she ascended.

"Jake!" she cried. "Oh, I want … I want…"

Precisely what she wanted Lili wasn't sure, only that she had to have it and it was close, so very, very close, so within her grasp, she just had to…

With a scream of disbelieving elation, Lili's first-ever climax crashed over her. Jake growled with male triumph as he felt her muscles spasm and contract, tasting the salty tang of orgasm on his lips. Dazed and limp, Lili was only dimly aware of the rustle of clothing as Jake hastily pulled off his clothes, shaking with a desperate need to enter her, to be inside her hot, wet depths.

Gladly, Lili accepted the weight of his body, straining up to meet him as his mouth almost savaged hers. Instinctively, her legs parted to make room for him, enjoying the basic, primitive feel of man on woman.

Unsuspectingly, she moaned with pleasure as she felt him, hard and insistent, nudging and rubbing until her swollen, throbbing lips encircled the head of his manhood.

Arms braced to take his weight, savouring the feel of her hot, tight – oh so tight – body, Jake began to push his way inside, groaning with male pleasure, only to come up against the wall of her innocence.

He stopped, cursing in shocked disbelief … a virgin? She was a virgin? Well of course she is you damn fool, he swore at himself, and if you had stopped for one minute to think it through, you'd have known that; would have been prepared for it; would maybe even have thought twice about making love with her.

"Jake?" He looked down into eyes swimming with concerned tears. "What is it? What's the matter? Why have you stopped?"

"You're a virgin."

It was a statement, not a question. Without quite knowing why, Lili found herself flushing, instantly on the defensive.

"Well, yes, does that matter?"

"Does it matter? Of course, it matters."

"Why?"

"Trust me, it matters." With a soft groan, Jake began to pull away from her.

Lili cried out in sharp distress. "No, please," she demanded, wrapping her legs tightly around him, pulling his mouth back to hers. "I want this Jake, I want you, so much ... please, don't stop."

Acting on raw instinct, she wiggled to reposition him, pushed down onto him, moaning with pleasure as she felt his body respond. Encouraged, she rotated her hips, hearing his breathing quicken.

"For pity's sake, Lili, I'm only human. If you keep on doing that, I won't be able to help myself, I'll simply take you..."

"Good," she cried out, glorying in her power over him. "I want you to, please..."

With a final moan of despair, Jake gave in to his body's demands, pushing his way slowly into her. He felt the brief resistance, the give of her virginity, until, with a shout of desperate need, he buried himself deep within her.

Dimly, he was aware of Lili's distress; her soft whimpers, the tears spilling down her cheeks, but unable to stop. He hated himself for hurting her, but it felt so damned good. She was small and tight, the pleasure so keen and intense it was borderline pain, and Jake had never experienced anything like it before.

Bitter tears of disappointment and disillusionment scalded Lili's eyelids. Frantically, she bit her lip to hold back cries of pain. Why had it gone so wrong? What was the matter with her? Why was it hurting so much? Because it was.

It was agony feeling him scrape over her raw, grazed insides, knowing from the hooded, unseeing eyes, and his heavy ragged breathing, it was still pleasurable for him. A wave of self-pitying loneliness swept over her, and she wanted to crawl away into a corner and die.

Lili felt his thrusts quicken, his moans intensify, before he gave a great shout. She felt a hot wetness deep inside, before he collapsed, sweating, and spent.

Lying there, feeling his heart thud through his rib cage onto her squashed breasts, his damp gasps in her ear, Lili gently stroked his hair and felt an incredible sweetness. It would be worth it, she thought, going through all that pain, to experience this moment of intimacy and absolute connection.

Jake eased himself up on his elbows to take some of his weight from her, giving her a sheepish, slightly abashed, smile. He sighed and gently ran a finger down her cheek, frowning at the tears which still clung there. Tenderly he kissed her eyelids, then eased them both around so Lili lay sprawled across his chest.

Gradually, Lili relaxed, feeling him shrink within her, realising to her relief it no longer hurt, although she ached deep inside. Jake's arms encircled, holding her tight, as he softly stroked her hair. Long moments passed before he spoke.

"I'm sorry."

"What for?"

"For hurting you. Once I realised it was your first time I should have stopped. I should have been more careful."

"You tried to stop, but I wouldn't let you, so you can't blame yourself for that, Jake. Besides, it didn't hurt that much," she lied. "I enjoyed what happened before, and this is nice, lying here with you."

"But your first time, Lili. It's meant to be special, romantic."

"It was special because it was with you. Besides, we're laid in front of a roaring log fire, drinking wine. A snowstorm is howling outside, and there's soft music playing. How much more romantic can it get?"

Jake smiled and hugged her tighter, gently dropping a kiss on her head, as Lili snuggled into his embrace, unable to believe only that morning she'd said goodbye to him, not expecting to hear from him again until April.

Now, a few short hours later, she was lying on her sofa with him, naked, having lost her virginity to him.

She sighed, felt him leave her body completely, and squealed with revulsion as a warm stickiness disgorged itself between her legs.

"Oh yuck," she exclaimed, frantically reaching over his head to grab the box of tissues from the table, dragging out a handful and stuffing them between her legs, noticing the streaks of scarlet blood crusting the inside of her thighs.

"Well, that's romantic," Jake remarked dryly, laughing at the outraged look of disgust on her face as she balled up more tissues and wadded them to stem the flow.

"In all the books I've read, which, I admit, is not many," stated Lili firmly, "it's never said anything about the urgent need for tissues when making love."

"Well, authors apply the same rule as they do about characters going to the john. They assume readers know it's a given, so don't waste time writing about it."

"They shouldn't assume any such thing," stated Lili, gathering up the tissues and slithering off Jake to throw them into the fire, where they flared up, bright and hot. Lili sat back on her heels, enjoying the unfamiliar sensation of firelight warming her bare breasts. Relaxed and limber, she arched her back, stretching towards the flames.

Hearing a rustle, she turned to see Jake pull himself up on one elbow, watching her with an intensity she didn't understand but made her feel hot and achy deep inside.

She returned his gaze, firelight sparking off answering flames in her eyes. Wordlessly, he slid off the sofa and began pulling the large cushions down to form a long, comfortable platform in front of the fire.

"Come here," he growled.

Glancing down, Lili saw his manhood for the first time. Thick and swollen, Jake was becoming aroused again, and fear clutched at her throat.

"I don't know ..." she stammered. "Jake, I'm afraid. I don't want it to hurt again."

"It won't," he promised, pulling her down on the bed of cushions with him. "Lili," he whispered, moulding his long, muscular body to her petite, slender curves. "You have my word. Any time you want to stop, we will. If you're scared or unsure, feel any discomfort at all, say the word and we'll stop, because this time it's all about you, okay?"

"Umm, I don't..." Lili faltered under those penetrating blue eyes.

"Do you trust me?"

"Well, I..."

"Do you trust me, Lili?"

Lili took a deep breath. His softly caressing touch was gentle and reassuring. The look in his eyes, whilst it may not have been love, was surely its first cousin.

"Yes," she whispered, placing her well-being entirely in his keeping. Light as a breeze, his kisses fluttered across her eyelids, down her cheeks, across her lips, up her jawline and down her neck. Softly, his tongue dipped and drank from the honeyed hollow at the base of her throat. Lili sighed, as the sweetest of sensations rolled and churned in her stomach.

Tenderly, his large, warm hands trailed over her shoulders, travelling the length of her arms. Bringing her hands to his mouth, he suckled on her fingers, tongue flicking into her palm, his blue eyes turning almost black with desire as he feasted.

Gently, he stretched her hands up above her head, holding them lightly prisoner with one hand, whilst the other skimmed the xylophone of her ribs, pulling her closer to his body, so they lay, skin to skin, face to face.

He bent his head, nipping lightly at her bottom lip with his teeth. Lili strained to reach him, desperate for more, wanting his mouth fully on hers, feeling her breath quicken, her heartbeat skip and race, her breasts heaving with rapidly increasing gasps.

Finally, his mouth closed over hers. She moaned her relief into the kiss. Pulling her hands away from his grasp, she ran trembling fingers through his hair, pulled him closer, until not a flicker of firelight could be seen between their slick, writhing bodies.

A shocked cry burst from her as Jake's fingers unexpectedly trapped a nipple between them, lightly tweaking and twisting, until the peak was pinkly engorged.

"Jake!" Her eyes flew open, hands pushed his head to her breast.

"You want something, honey?" he drawled, enjoying the view as she stared blankly at him, flushed, and aroused.

"Please," she gasped hoarsely, arching her spine upwards, her whole body pleading with him for release. Taking pity on her, Jake bent his head, took the sensitive peak into his mouth, pulling, and suckling as Lili sobbed with relief.

"Harder," she demanded through gritted teeth. "Harder!" she ordered again, as Jake increased the pressure of his mouth, finally resorting to teeth when she begged for more, biting and chewing as her groans grew in intensity.

He slipped one hand between her legs and felt with satisfaction the hot, bubbling spring already welling up there. He gently found the small swollen nub, applied pressure, and heard her choked sobs as her legs instinctively parted, hips rising and falling. She ground herself against the heel of his hand.

Quickly, Jake transferred his attentions to the other breast, biting and twisting the nipple until it was as engorged as its twin. Lili was beyond thought, beyond control, climbing, always climbing, until … until … with a cry of relief the orgasm shuddered through her, the strong muscle contractions pulsing against Jake's hand.

He felt an answering throb in his groin and gently pulled Lili until she lay over him, legs draped either side of his hips, her hot, pulsing centre folded around his painfully erect shaft. Biting his lip from the effort of holding back, Jake grasped her round the hips, urgently moving her up and down, rubbing her sensitive, post-orgasmic clitoris over his own desperately aroused flesh.

Lili felt her orgasm plateau, unbelievably, begin to build again. More urgent, more insistent than before, it swiftly climbed until she was hanging onto Jake's shoulders, grinding herself onto him, aching to reach that place again; to feel that amazing sensation of relief again. So, intent on her own pleasure, she didn't notice that each time she bore down on him, he went a little further into her body.

Finally, the orgasm crested again, dashing waves of ecstasy over her hot, shaking body. As she was sobbing from the intense, knife-edge of pleasure, Jake, with the slightest of pressure, eased all the way in, feeling the vice-like grip of her muscles as they radiated pulses along his shaft. He groaned; eyes fluttering closed as her tight perfect body encased him in bands of soft steel.

"Jake."

He opened his eyes at the whispered awe in her voice. "Hmm," he sighed in reply.

"You're inside me and it doesn't hurt. It's so amazing, so beautiful ... I had no idea..."

Jake's heart constricted at her naivety – her unsophisticated joy at their coupling. Whilst he'd never considered virginity a desirable commodity for a woman, when he made love to Vivienne, he'd always been aware there had been others before him – so many men, even the odd woman. Now, knowing he was the first was strangely exhilarating. It boosted his ego and made him feel like a king.

"You're in charge, honey," he told her. "Do what you want, whatever feels good."

Slowly, almost reluctantly at first, Lili began to move, gaining confidence with each rush of pleasure she felt, with each moan and soft sigh she extracted from Jake. She played with him, experimenting.

What about if she straddled him, sat bolt upright, and slid herself over his slick, solid length? How would it feel if she lay spread-eagled over him and moved her body slowly, tantalisingly slowly, upon his? Would it feel good to lay, side by side, her leg slung over his hip, watching with breathless delight each powerful thrust, touching with fascination their joined flesh, thrilling at the power she had to make him groan with pleasure, to sigh her name as if it were a prayer.

Does that feel good, she whispered. How about this and this and this? Yes, he moaned, yes, yes, all of it, any of it, don't stop, don't ever stop. Finally, she rolled, pulling him on top of her, aching to take his weight, to feel the primitive rightness of her man between her legs, wanting as much as he could give.

"Deeper," she growled, legs bowing around his hips, heels pressing firmly on his buttocks. "I want more," she insisted. "Deeper, go deeper."

"All right," he snarled. "You want more, that's what you'll get."

He jerked himself out of her body, knelt between her legs and yanked her ankles up past his ears. Pausing for a second to admire the pink, glistening folds of her womanhood, he entered her, one swift, deep stroke, his chest pressing against the backs of her knees.

"Oh, yes!" screamed Lili. "Yes, deeper, please Jake, deeper!"

He thrust further into her, right up to the hilt, forcing her legs down until her knees pushed against her breasts, feeling her body buck and arch beneath him, her cries become increasingly frantic, losing all conscious thought as his body raced desperately towards its own, monumentally explosive, orgasm.

"Lili!"

He threw her name into the cosmos, teetering on the precipice, her body racing to ascend the heights with him. Dizzyingly, gloriously, they leapt together, free-falling into the abyss.

"I love you!" he heard her scream. "Jake, oh my Jake, I love you!"

All conscious thought evaporated as the fallout from his orgasm left him quaking and shivering, stunned and awed by its volcanic power, feeling the vicious, almost painful grip of her contractions, her body jerking and thrashing beneath him.

Later, centuries, aeons later, he collapsed beside her, his bones turned to liquid, the blood boiling within his veins. Lili stirred, moaned softly, her breath as ragged and laboured as his own.

"Now I get it," she gasped. "Now I get what all the fuss is about."

"Huh?" As replies went it wasn't much of one but was all he could manage.

"Sex," she continued. "Now I understand why people make such a fuss about it. It's amazing, fantastic, so … so … wonderful."

"Sweetheart," he gasped, raising her hand to his mouth, and planting a kiss in the palm, tasting the salty tang of perspiration. "It's not always like that. I'd say it's hardly ever like that."

"Oh," she raised naive eyes to his, eyes that flashed with knowledge gained and understanding achieved. "Was it good then?" she enquired innocently.

"Honey," Jake groaned, wondering if he'd ever be able to walk again, "if it were any better, I'd be a dead man."

Lili smiled, a smile of pure female triumph, stretching beside him, supple as a cat. Her skin brushed against his, igniting a chain reaction within his weary body, which duly noted the kick of desire it produced but decided it was incapable of doing anything about it.

Seeing the fire was burning low, Lili crawled over and tossed another couple of logs on, sending a shower of sparks up the chimney. Hurriedly scurrying back into the warmth of his arms, she moulded her body perfectly into his, feeling him, damp and warm, nestled into the back of her thighs. She marvelled that it had started so wrong, and, miraculously, wondrously, had become so right.

Jake pulled her closer, the hairs on his chest tickling her back, making her squirm against him as his hand gently caressed her hip and belly. Clannad crooned their last note. There was silence, the stereo clunked, whirled, and the next CD began to play.

Jake frowned as the achingly familiar intro began.

"This song," he began. "I don't know why, but it makes me think of you. Was it the one we danced to last night?" he asked.

"It was," Lili took a deep breath. "We also danced to it at Daisy's wedding, and at her 21st."

Jake gazed at her in silence, as the moment stretched.

"How long?" he asked. Lili blinked in confusion. "How long have you been in love with me?"

Lili's mouth gaped open, unaware of the words ripped from her during that final, earth-shattering orgasm. For a moment, she thought of laughing at the suggestion, of shrugging it off, but something in his eyes stopped her.

"Over two years now," she finally replied.

"So, last year, the night before Daisy's wedding, when you told me there was somebody, but he was unobtainable, that was...?"

"You Jake," she finished softly. "It's always been you, since the first time we met, when you stepped out of the dark, dressed as a cowboy, and saved me from that drunk."

"I had no idea," he sighed, fingers moving up her body, as he dropped a kiss on her gently rounded shoulder.

"Why should you have," Lili shrugged. "It doesn't matter, it doesn't change anything."

"I know," he mused, unable to stop touching her. "But I can't help wishing..."

"What?"

"Wishing I'd met you first."

Warmth spread through her. Smiling, Lili gently kissed him, rested her head on the cushions, her expression thoughtful. Softly, Jake stroked the hair back from her face, noting the way firelight exploded green sparks in her eyes.

"What are you thinking?" he asked.

"I'm thinking," mused Lili. "I'm thinking I'm hungry."

"Hungry?" Jake stopped to consider. "Yeah, me too," he decided. "What did you have in mind?

"What I'd like, is a big, four seasons pizza."

"Well, honey, that sounds great, but I don't think there's much chance of any pizza firm delivering tonight."

"Philistine," Lili glared at him in mock disapproval. "I'm going to cook one."

"You mean you've got a frozen one or something?"

"Double philistine," she laughed. "No, I mean I'm going to cook one. Can I borrow your shirt?"

At his nod, she sat up and pulled it on, doing up the middle button only. She stood up, Jake realising how small she was when his shirt reached almost to her knees. Scrambling to his feet, he pulled on jeans and followed her into the kitchen, bringing the wine with him.

Swiftly, Lili turned on the oven to heat, got tapenade, Parma ham, olives, tomatoes, and the mozzarella out of the fridge. Jake leant against the worktop and took a gulp of wine, watching with interest as she expertly washed and sliced olives and tomatoes.

"Is there any of this you don't like?" Lili asked in concern, pulling the toppings she'd prepared earlier across to join the others.

"No," he shook his head. "It all looks good. Are you really going to make a pizza from scratch? Doesn't that, like, take a long time?" Silently, Lili took the cloth off the mixing bowl, displaying the dough ball which had more than doubled in size, Jake grinned.

"Well, will you look at that," he chuckled. "There's one you prepared earlier."

Smiling, Lili took a sip of her wine. She tipped the dough out onto a lightly floured board, knocked it back, and began to gently knead it. Jake watched, fascinated, as her small, delicate hands sank into the springy white dough.

As she kneaded, Lili became acutely aware of what she was doing, and that Jake was only inches away, watching her every move with intense concentration.

"So," he cleared a throat gone husky. "What are you doing now?"

"Well," Lili nervously swallowed, before continuing, "now I'm kneading the dough."

"Oh," Jake put his wine glass down, moved behind her, hands snaking their way around her waist and up onto her breasts. "Like this?" he casually enquired.

"Umm, yes, that's fine," Lili managed to choke the words out, as his large hands kneaded and caressed. She turned her head to kiss him, but he pulled away, laughing.

"Uh oh, I want to learn how to make pizza. So, what next?"

"Now, we form the dough into a ball and then flatten it into a circle-oh-oh!" Lili gasped as he found her nipples, trapping them between his fingers, rubbing them into erotic peaks against the rough cotton of his shirt.

"Okay, I think my dough has been made into big enough circles," he drawled, pulling her hair to one side, and nibbling on an ear lobe. "What next?"

"Next, we put it onto a well-greased, baking tray," Lili pulled a tray out of the drawer. Using baking parchment to generously smear it with butter, she gently lifted the pizza base onto the tray.

"So, lubricant's important, right?" enquired Jake, innocently.

"Absolutely," she agreed. "Otherwise, it might stick … oh." Her words ended in a soft sigh of pleasure, as Jake sucked his fingers, then ran his hands up and under the shirt, to pluck and massage her still sensitive nipples.

"I think I've got that." He commented wryly. "Next?"

"Next, we put on the toppings. First, passata, which I've mixed with fresh garlic."

"Useful for repelling vampires," he mused, teeth nipping at the base of her neck.

"Then I put the leek and mushroom mixture on one quarter…"

"Uh-huh …" muttered Jake, mouth tantalisingly working its way down her spine.

"Followed by pepper and artichoke mixture on the next…"

"Keep going," he urged, nimble fingers undoing the buttons on the shirt.

"Then the umm … the tapenade and … and … Parma ham…"

"Okay, I think I've got it," Lili heard the rasp of a zipper and felt him press into the small of her back, rampant and ready, as his hands once again paid attention to her breasts.

"So, olives and tomatoes will go on the last quarter, right?"

"What?" Lili groaned, pressing her body into his as his fingers tortured and teased her breasts.

"Pay attention, Lili," he muttered in her ear, enjoying himself vastly. "The pizza, we need to finish the pizza."

"The pizza? Oh yes, pizza." Lili was having problems concentrating as the shirt slipped off her shoulders to puddle in a heap on the floor. "We put olives and tomatoes on the last quarter, then sprinkle cheese all over." Jake snatched up an olive and popped it into her mouth. Catching the finger with her teeth, she nipped it before letting go. "Now we put it in the oven, and let it cook."

"For how long?" he asked, as she opened the oven door and slid the tray inside.

"About twenty minutes," she gasped, slamming the door shut, setting the timer, and turning to press herself eagerly against his waiting, naked body.

"Can you think of anything to do for twenty minutes?" he enquired casually, sweeping all her cooking utensils to one side, and bodily lifting her onto the countertop.

"No, not a thing," she replied breathlessly.

He plunged upwards into her and watched with intense satisfaction as her head fell back, and her mouth opened in a wordless cry of wonder and her legs wrapped themselves around his waist, gripping him, pulling him further in.

"Me neither," he declared.

After every scrap of slightly burnt, but still delicious pizza had been consumed, they went to bed, Lili was thrilled that at last, this man was lying next to her. Between bouts of lovemaking, drifting into sleep, she felt an incredible sense of rightness. He belonged here, with her, moulding so perfectly into her body, the bed creaking companionably as they loved and loved again.

When they awoke late Sunday morning, it seemed the most natural thing in the world to be waking together, making love almost before their eyes were fully opened; a hasty, passionate mating that left them dizzy and breathless. Hunger finally driving them from bed, to exclaim in wonder at the deep drifts of virginal white snow heaped all around the house.

They cooked breakfast together, Jake proving a dab hand at eggs sunny side up. They drank a pot of coffee in front of the fire and talked, Lili eagerly learning more about the man she was desperately, completely, and utterly head over heels in love with.

"You certainly have a lovely home," Jake commented, eyes roaming with pleasure over the room.

"Well, you should thank Conrad for that," laughed Lili.

Instinctively drawn to her bookcase, Jake's eyes widened with surprise as he realised almost every single book on Lili's shelf was one of his.

"Wow," he exclaimed, dryly. "You are my number one fan, aren't you?"

"But of course," replied Lili primly. "I've read everything you've ever written, although I've not quite finished your last one."

Jake frowned. "Wasn't that the one you were reading in London last time we met?"

"Umm, yes, I believe it is," Lili's heart sank, cursing his powers of observation.

"It's not that heavy going, is it?" Jake enquired with a laugh.

"No, no, of course not," Lili rushed to reassure. "It's, well, I'm not much of a reader. I mean, I can read, of course, but the letters move, I have trouble making sense of them ..." her voice trailed away, Jake was looking at her sympathetically and nodding.

"That's tough," he exclaimed. "I went to college with a guy with dyslexia. I know what a struggle it is."

"Dyslexia?" Lili stared at him. "You think I'm dyslexic?" she stammered.

"Well," he frowned, "aren't you? I mean, you described the symptoms of it."

"Yes," she replied, slowly. "I think maybe you're right. It would explain ... everything." She was silent, head bowed. Dyslexic. She was dyslexic, she had no doubt, and flashed Jake a big beaming smile of such radiant relief, he smiled in return.

"I'm dyslexic," she declared happily. "Not stupid."

His smile faded. "Of course, you're not stupid," he replied. "Where did you get that idea from?"

"My parents," she said softly. "They were both so clever, you see. Because I always seemed hopelessly slow and incompetent, I think they wrote me off as being some sort of retard."

"What the hell kind of parents were they then?" he snapped, eyes narrowing in disgust. "Why didn't they get you tested when you were young?"

"I don't know," Lili shrugged. "I guess it never occurred to them."

"One day," replied Jake slowly, putting his arms around her and holding her tight, "you and I are going to have to sit down and have a history lesson; learn about each other's past. But not this weekend. This weekend I want to enjoy being with you."

"Hmm," agreed Lili, snuggling deeper into his embrace, and inhaling his scent, feeling his muscles flex beneath the cotton shirt.

"It's kind of ironic though," he observed with a wry grin. "Here I am – a writer – in love with a woman who's dyslexic. I mean, how perfect is that?" His voice trailed away, as Lili pulled back and stared at him in stupefied amazement. "What?" he asked concerned. "What is it? What did I say?"

"You said …" Lili paused, swallowed hard, and continued. "You said you were in love with me."

"Did I?" Not trusting herself to speak, Lili merely nodded, eyes fixed on his face. "Well then," he bent and rubbed her nose with his, "I guess that must mean I am."

The rest of Sunday passed in a long lazy blur of idle chat, music, and lovemaking. Evening came. They gladly drew the curtains, lighting candles in an unspoken urge to keep real life at bay, afraid this hiatus couldn't last; that something would intrude into the cosy world they'd created and spoil everything.

No more snow fell, and the temperature rose. Slowly, but surely, the isolating drifts began to melt. Lili knew they had no more than a few hours left of their enforced seclusion before decisions would have to be made, and the future spoken about, so she clung with an almost bulldog-like tenacity to each precious minute, second, moment, as they slipped too fast through her fingers.

They cooked pasta, enjoying the experience of eating together. Lili tucked the memory away for future enjoyment – their first proper meal. She discounted the pizza of the evening before, as it had been eaten on the floor in front of the fire, whereas this was consumed in the conservatory, in the flickering, softly romantic light of a dozen candles, music playing quietly in the background, Jake's eyes softening every time he looked at her. He loved her, Lili was sure of it and was starry-eyed with joy.

Going to bed together that night, routines were being established. Each had a side of the bed. She'd learnt that if she let him, he would roll over, taking the covers with him. He knew, deep in the night when she was fast asleep, she'd whimper softly in her sleep, as if reliving unhappy memories.

Waking Monday morning, Lili saw the snow had almost all gone. She wondered how much longer he would stay, hoping definite plans would be made to include her in his future, quietly confident they would be, but still … hoping all the same.

Time was kind to them. They had one more perfect day together before the real world rudely and abruptly intruded.

Jake's mobile rang that evening. Lili was in the kitchen making coffee and he was building up the fire. At first, he was inclined to ignore it, but reflecting there was family who might be concerned, he reluctantly answered. It was Vivienne.

Listening to her drawling, honeyed tones, the annoyance on his face changed to horror, despair, then weary acceptance. When Lili entered, bearing a tray of coffee, it was to find him slumped, phone in hand, with such a look of devastation on his face, she cried out, and almost dropped the tray.

"What is it? What's happened?"

"Vivienne phoned," he said, enunciating every word as if they left a bad taste in his mouth.

"You're going back to her," Lili declared flatly, her heart clutching in fear within her chest.

"No, oh no, no," Jake crossed the room, cupping her face in his hands. "Never, I love you. I'd never go back to her, not now, not after this weekend."

"Then what is it?" she asked, relief and fear mingling in her voice.

"She's pregnant…"

Lili felt the air leave her lungs with a whoosh as she sank onto the sofa, coffee spilling unnoticed onto the floor.

"Pregnant?" Jake nodded, face drawn with concern, eyes never leaving hers. "How … how far along is she?"

"About a month."

"You were still having sex with her a month ago?" Lili felt the bitter sting of betrayal and shot him an accusing glare.

Jake shrugged in despair. "What can I say to you? It must have been the last time we had sex. She made me angry, so angry, we ended up fucking. That's all it was, fucking. Afterwards, I felt so disgusted with myself, I swore it was the last time she'd ever manipulate me that way, using sex to get what she wanted."

"Does she want you back?"

"She says she does, but I told her straight we're over, I'll be filing for divorce as planned."

"But, what about the baby?"

"I guess I'll pay maintenance for it until it's eighteen, and I guess I'll have to see it occasionally."

"It?" Lili's head reared up in shock. "It's a baby, your baby, and it's innocent. This baby didn't ask to be created; it took two people to make it. Whatever you may feel about the situation, Jake, the fact remains you're going to be a father."

"Well, what else can I do Lili?"

"I don't know," cried Lili, despair in her voice. "I don't know!"

They went to bed soon after, coming together in a frenzied, almost violent, coupling of lovers who fear the future. Afterwards, Lili lay awake for hours watching him sleep, worries chasing the very possibility of sleep into the furthest corners of the room. Finally, near dawn, she slipped into a restless and slight slumber in which dreams tormented her.

She saw herself as a child, bullied and tortured by ignorant children, and uncaring parents. Mid-dream, she turned into an unknown child with achingly familiar blue eyes, and Lili suffered in her sleep, watching Jake's child go through the same hell.

Waking unexpectedly, Jake felt for Lili and found her place empty and cold. Confused, he raised himself on his elbow, looking for her, and rubbing at sleep-filled eyes. She sat on the window seat, gazing out at the bleak, empty, pre-dawn world. Fear clutched his heart at the sadness etched onto her face, the quiet determination in her eyes.

"Lili?" he murmured. "What is it? What's wrong?"

"Do you have any idea what it's like growing up knowing your parents don't want you? That you're a mistake? An inconvenience?" Her voice was soft and low in the shadowy room.

"No, but I..."

"I do, and I'm telling you now Jake, you can't do that to this baby. You can't."

"So, what do you suggest then?"

"You have to go back to her. You have to make another go of it with Vivienne?"

"What? Lili, no, are you crazy? You can't possibly want me to go back to that ... that woman?"

"Of course, I don't want you to go back! The thought of you and her, it's ripping my heart out, but there's no other choice."

"What about if I file for joint custody, agree to see lots of the kid, love it, whatever ... hell, Lili, there must be another way."

"No," Lili choked back tears. "For the baby's sake, you have to go back."

"But..."

"No! Do you love me?"

"Hell yes, Lili, more than I realised."

"Then do this for me, please."

"But Lili..."

"If you love me, go back to Vivienne. Be a proper, loving father to this new life you've created."

Jake stared at her for a long silent moment, then slipped from the bed and crossed the room to kneel before her, powerless in the face of her steely resolve.

"Okay," he muttered. "You win. I'll go back to her for you and be a proper father to this child. But no way in hell will I be a husband to Vivienne. If she wants me back, it'll be on my terms. I'm going to insist on a pregnancy test. It's a little convenient she manages to get pregnant at the eleventh hour when she knew our marriage was on the rocks, and that only a miracle would get me to stay."

He stood, lifted her in his arms, feeling her slight body shiver as he laid her gently back down on the bed, sliding in beside her, and pulling the covers back over their chilled naked bodies. Turning to her, he pulled her into his arms, cupping her face in his hand, trying to read the emotions in her eyes.

"I love you," he murmured. "I'm not prepared to let you walk away without a fight. I'll go back to Vivienne, stay with her until the baby's born, then we'll see. I'll want a DNA test, proof it's mine, and I'll be trying to find a way to get back to you. This is too special, too precious to lose. I love you, Lili."

"I know," she sobbed. "I love you too, but I won't be responsible for another person's misery."

"It's the strangest thing," he mused. "That might be the very reason why I love you so much..."

Chapter Twenty-Eight
"Shame you had to bring your wife with you!"

"So, what are we going to do about Lili?" At Amy's question, four pairs of eyes swivelled up from the Chinese food they were busily consuming and exchanged troubled glances. It was two weeks since the party. Two long weeks during which her concerned friends had watched Lili fade away from them.

Not eating, and not sleeping, Lili had stubbornly refused to discuss it with any of them, giving curt, almost rude replies to the anxious questions they had all, singly, and jointly, pressed upon her.

"I'm fine," she snapped, eyes not meeting theirs. "Fine. I'm tired, that's all. Please leave me alone."

But her friends couldn't leave it alone. They continued gently probing with loving concern, until exasperated, Lili announced she was going away that weekend to Guy's 35th birthday party.

Originally, Lili had decided not to go, but with the well-intentioned interrogations of her friends slowly but surely driving her insane, the prospect of a weekend away from it all seemed too good to miss.

She missed Jake. Horribly and constantly.

They'd had only had a weekend together, but Lili felt she had experienced a lifetime of emotion during those days. Had grown up, come of age, fallen deeply and desperately in love.

She could see now, the attraction she had felt for him had simply been a crush; a young, impressionable girl's first innocent infatuation with a glamorous, older man. But now...

Now she loved with a woman's heart; suffered as a woman does; made worse by the fact she had been the one to send him away, that it had been her decision and hers alone.

Sometimes she regretted it and ached to call him, knowing one simple phone call would have him on the next flight back. Several times her hand hovered over the phone, needing, wanting, to hear his voice, if only for a moment.

Were it not for the dreams she may have succumbed and called him, but the nightmares would not let her be. When she finally fell into exhausted sleep it was to plunge into her past.

Over, and over again, she relived her cripplingly lonely childhood – the horror of school – and the torture of being unloved, unwanted, unworthy.

She would awaken, drenched in ice-cold sweat, sheets tangled and knotted around her restless thrashing body, with the relief of knowing it was the past and she'd escaped it, dissolving into the realisation she had done the right thing.

At least Jake's baby wouldn't suffer the same fate. He would be there to love and protect this child.

Whilst thousands of miles away, across an ocean and a continent, Jake sat, head in hands, a piece of paper on the table before him. He had read it three times, each time praying it would say something different. It never changed; the pregnancy test was definite.

He had been granted what had once been his dearest wish. He was to be a father. Be careful what you wish for, the thought resounded through his brain, an ironic grin twisting his handsome face.

Fumbling in his pocket, he dragged out a crumpled pack of cigarettes and hastily lit one, drawing smoke into his lungs with almost pathetic gratitude, before grinding it out into an ashtray. It didn't help, nothing helped.

Lili ... Lili ...

Her name whispered through his brain, his eyes closing briefly in despair. To have realised he loved her; to have shared the most amazing weekend with her and then to have lost her, seemed unbelievably cruel. Jake mourned and blamed in equal proportions.

Perhaps unfairly, he blamed Vivienne, but mostly he blamed himself for being weak. He had known it was over, known the reckless, crazy spell she cast over him had well and truly shattered but had still allowed himself to be angered into screwing her.

A loveless, coldly mechanical act, it had left him filled with self-loathing, and left Vivienne filled with new life.

The phone rang.

Jake glared, considered ignoring it, but decided its endless ringing would be more annoying than answering it. He snatched it up impatiently.

"Yes?"

"Jake?"

Through the crackle of a bad international connection, Jake heard the British accent, his heart leaping through his rib cage.

"Lili?"

"What? Jake? Is that you? Can you hear me?"

"Hi, Daisy."

Resigning himself, Jake leant back, placed his large, booted feet on the coffee table, one heel scrunching up the pregnancy report, listening with half an ear as Daisy chatted about the weather, and how busy she'd been arranging Guy's party.

Giving grunts in appropriate places, Jake wondered if it were too early to have a beer, or if he should try and get some work done when his attention was dragged back by something Daisy had said.

Listening intently, a smile spread across his face for the first time in two weeks, his boots hitting the floor with a decisive thud.

"Daisy!" he abruptly cut her off mid-sentence.

"Yes? What?"

"Is there room for another one at the party?"

"What? Well, yes, I suppose, but ... oh, do you mean you're going to come?"

"If that's okay?"

"Of course, it's okay, we'd love to see you."

"Right, I'll call the airport, book a seat on the next flight, and see you tomorrow."

"Fantastic! Oh, and Jake..."

Jake hung up – his body energised with a new purpose. Lili had told him not to contact her, but if they happened to be at the same party together ... well then, whose fault was that?

Whistling, he went to the bedroom. He'd throw a few things in a bag, head out to the airport. Hell, he'd camp there until the next flight to the UK.

"You sound cheerful?"

Vivienne.

In his adrenalin-fuelled haste, Jake had forgotten about his wife...

Lying alone, grieving, in a bed which was acres too large, Lili hugged the pillow Jake's head had rested on and which still smelt vaguely of him, weeping great uncontrollable sobs of loss and regret. Her friends had only witnessed the tip of the iceberg of her suffering and knew she was in pain.

But without knowing why, they were powerless to help. They could only watch with dismay and incomprehension as Lili vanished before their eyes, becoming pale and insubstantial, a ghost of her former vivid, fun-loving self.

So now, with Amy's question hanging in the air between them, they exchanged uneasy looks, acknowledging that the problem needed to be discussed, but feeling disloyal, as if voicing concerns about Lili whilst she was absent was tantamount to betrayal.

"Well," Martin began, hesitantly and reluctantly, "she's unhappy about something, but I don't know what. I did ask her what was wrong ..." his voice trailed away as he shrugged uncertainly.

"She bit your head off, insisting everything was fine?" queried Amy, Martin nodded. "She did the same thing to me when I tried to talk to her about it."

"So, what do you think is wrong?" asked Kevin in concern.

"A man." Amy and Lindy chorused together.

"It's obviously man trouble," continued Amy. "But I can't see who, or when, I mean, it's not as if Lili's been away on holiday or anywhere to have met someone, and as far as I know she hasn't met anyone new around here."

"There was someone," Lindy broke in, frowning with the memory. "When we had lunch in Norwich, the day of her party, she told me there was someone. She hoped it might become more, but it hadn't worked out."

"So, who is he?" wondered Amy.

"Don't know," Lindy shrugged. "Though she must have spent some time with him soon after her party because that seems to be when it happened. I mean, it's obvious she's not a virgin anymore…"

"Pardon?"

"Huh?"

"What?"

Lindy looked up at Amy, Martin, and Kevin's shocked voices; their wide, disbelieving eyes. Johnny nodded slowly, thoughtfully.

"Yes," he mused. "I did wonder…"

"What makes you say that?" queried Amy.

"How can you possibly know she's not a …"

Kevin's voice trailed away into uncomfortable silence; his face flushed at the thought.

"I don't know for sure how I know," Lindy began slowly. "I guess, maybe, it's in her eyes. A look. Hadn't you noticed she's lost that untouched, innocent air?"

"That's it," agreed Johnny. "I couldn't put my finger on it, but that's it. She's lost her innocence."

"Well," said Amy, after a long pause as the group tried to assimilate the alien idea of Lili with a man. "That would certainly explain her behaviour. If Lili went to bed with someone it's because she's madly in love with him. If, for some reason, they couldn't be together, or he rejected her…"

"Why would any man reject Lili?" demanded Kevin outraged.

He abruptly stopped, appalled at his hasty words which shouted of the depth of his feelings for Lili. Luckily, the others, except for Amy who shot him a glance, took his words at face value.

"Kevin's right," said Martin slowly. "Why would any man reject Lili? No, there must be some other reason why he had to leave her."

"He's married," stated Lindy flatly. "He must be. It's the only thing that makes sense."

"Maybe," conceded Amy. "But I can't see Lili falling for a married man. It's so not Lili."

"The heart wants what the heart wants," concluded Lindy with a shrug, exchanging a sly, knowing look with Johnny.

"Oh, for heaven's sake you two," exclaimed Amy impatiently. "Get a room!"

"What?" Lindy bristled. "I don't know what you're talking..."

"Oh Lindy, Lindy ..." Martin shook his head, amusement dancing in his eyes. "You don't have to pretend, we know everything."

Lindy and Johnny exchanged startled glances, then looked at the smiling faces and knowing expressions of their friends. Johnny shrugged, taking Lindy's hand.

"What the hell," he murmured. "We were planning on telling you soon anyway."

"Telling us what, exactly?" enquired Amy, gently.

"That Lindy and I are engaged to be married..."

The rest of his words were drowned out by a sea of excited voices as they exclaimed, shrieked, and congratulated. Amy rushed to hug Lindy who, cheeks flushed with excitement, pulled a chain out from under her jumper to reveal the beautiful ruby and diamond ring, which Amy examined with oohs and ahhs of envy and admiration.

"Congratulation's mate," Kevin and Martin enthusiastically pumped Johnny's hand.

"Talk about keeping things secret," exclaimed Amy. "If it hadn't been for your little performance at the party, we'd have never suspected in a million years that you two ... oh," she interrupted herself at a sudden thought.

"It might be an idea," she continued slowly, "if you hold off telling Lili, I mean, you know how funny she is about relationships changing people, making them forget their friends, and if she's feeling vulnerable right now..."

"You're right," agreed Lindy. "Now may not be a good time to spring this on her. We'll wait a few weeks and see how she is."

Jake felt the familiar jolt of a plane touching down, tucking the book he had immersed himself in for the entire flight back into his bag. Casting an evil look at the glowingly beautiful woman next to him, he stretched his legs, and an image of Lili looking the way she did after making love, all flushed and tousled, flashed through his mind.

Christ, he missed her ... missed her warmth and gentle humour; missed the way she curled up on his lap when they talked, her large, serious eyes intently watching his.

He sighed, feeling Vivienne's gaze boring into his temple. In the end, he'd had no choice, Vivienne had stated that as his wife and mother of his child she was fully entitled to attend a family party with him, all his attempts to dissuade her making her more determined to accompany him. Jake prayed he would have a chance to see Lili alone...

"So, you went back to her then?" Jake turned from contemplating the wintry landscape through the large picture window at the top of the double staircase. They had reached Hixley Hall in good time, and Vivienne had elected to have a lie-down, one symptom of her pregnancy being extreme tiredness.

Wandering around the Hall, Jake had paused to admire the view, marvelling only a few short hours ago he'd been in bright sunshine. Now all was bleak and grey. At the abrupt sentence he turned, the pleasure in his eyes at seeing Greg fading as he took in his cousin's angry expression.

"Yes," he replied, carefully and slowly. "I went back to her."

"Why?"

"She's pregnant."

"So? Offer her maintenance. You didn't have to go back to her ... for Pete's sake, Jake, what kind of a hold does she have over you?"

"It's ... complicated," Jake turned back to the window, heard Greg's angry steps on the marble as he climbed the last few stairs, and stood beside him.

"Complicated? What the hell is that supposed to mean?"

"It means, it's complicated."

"Cut the bullshit, Jake, this is me you're talking to. What the hell happened? The last time I saw you at Lili's party, you swore to me it was over, you were filing for divorce, nothing would make you go back, yet you did ... why?"

"I made a promise, a promise I intend to keep."

"I hardly think drunken vows exchanged in Vegas constitute an unbreakable promise, not after the way she's behaved."

"No, not that promise," Jake sighed. "I met someone else," he stated, meeting Greg's concerned gaze with a coolly level one of his own. "Someone I care about, hell, someone I love. I made the promise to her to go back to Vivienne and be a good father to this baby."

"Now, I am confused," Greg shook his head, baffled. "Are you telling me you've met somebody else, somebody you love, who loves you, and this somebody made you go back to your wife?"

"She's a pretty amazing person," replied Jake, slowly. "She said she wouldn't be responsible for the misery of another human being, that she knew what it was like to be unwanted and unloved by your parents and couldn't let that happen to my baby. So, she made me promise to go back to Vivienne, and be a good father to this baby. To love it, and make sure it knew it was loved and wanted."

"And so, you went back? You must really love her."

"Yeah," Jake paused, rubbing a hand wearily over his face. "I do. Not being with her, living with Vivienne and hating her more and more every day, it's killing me." Greg placed a brotherly hand on his shoulder, sympathetic understanding on his face. Silently, the cousins looked out across the stark February landscape...

Lili was not having a good day. It had all seemed so simple ... she carefully worked out her route on the road atlas, meticulously noted down the directions on a large sheet of paper which she then taped to her dashboard.

What could possibly go wrong?

Follow the directions precisely and she would reach Hixley Hall by mid-afternoon, giving her plenty of time to settle in and get ready for the party.

What Lili hadn't allowed for was how flustered she would get trying to read signposts and making split-second decisions about which way to go.

Feeling the usual panic welling, Lili desperately tried to calm herself, managing by sheer willpower alone to navigate her way around London on the M25. But she relaxed too soon, misread the signpost, and failed to get off at the right junction.

By the time Lili realised she'd done something wrong, she had gone miles in the wrong direction, all her carefully written notes now next to useless.

A cold sweat of panic breaking out on her forehead, Lili decided to get off the M25 and turned onto the M40, almost crying as she realised, she was well and truly lost.

She stopped at the first services she reached, treating herself to a hot meal and a coffee, gazing at the road atlas with a sinking sense of despair. How on earth had she managed to go so wrong?

Slowly, painstakingly, she traced out the route she needed to take, rewrote all her instructions, and reluctantly climbed back into the car.

When Lili finally, wearily, switched off her engine outside Hixley Hall it was late, and the party was already in full swing. Stretching her cramped and aching back, she lugged her case out of the boot and trudged up the steps.

She rang the bell, waiting long, chilly minutes before the door was thrown open and there was Daisy.

"Lili!" she exclaimed in delight. "We'd about given up on you."

"Sorry," Lili sighed. "I took the wrong turning off the M25, ended up heaven only knows where."

"Never mind, you're here now. I'll show you to your room so you can freshen up."

Twenty minutes later, washed, changed, makeup renewed, Lili made her way downstairs, following the sounds of the party to the room where Daisy and Guy's wedding reception had been held.

Slipping through the double wooden doors, her senses were overwhelmed with sights and sounds. The room was crowded with revellers all determinedly having a good time, and Lili recognised the band which had played at Daisy's 21st and her wedding.

Lili looked around, seeing many familiar faces, but giving herself a moment before making her presence known. The song ended, the crowd applauded and the lead singer, black hair now brushing her shoulders, murmured huskily into the microphone.

"Where's the birthday boy?"

A good-natured cheer went up as Guy stepped forward and raised his hand, Daisy by his side.

"Now, I want everyone to grab hold of your nearest and dearest as I sing a song Daisy has specially requested for her husband, to remind him of their first dance together as a married couple, and to wish him a very happy birthday. This is *Stay with Me till Dawn*, and it comes to you with love from your wife Daisy."

Hot tears pricked the back of Lili's eyelids. Was there no getting away from thoughts and memories of Jake? As the singer crooned the opening bars, Lili couldn't help but remember being with Jake. Loving him, laying in front of the fire, listening to this song two short weeks ago.

She blinked away the tears. She would come back later when the song – with all its painful, bittersweet memories – was over. She half-turned to go and saw him.

He was being dragged reluctantly onto the dance floor by a radiant Vivienne, her lush womanly curves showcased to perfection in a cream, figure-hugging dress.

As Lili watched, open-mouthed with shock, Vivienne slipped into his arms trying to reduce the distance between them, but Jake, tight-lipped with barely concealed loathing, held her at a distance, one large hand holding hers, the other seeming to push her away.

Greg also watched with distaste as Jake fought to hold off his wife. Scarlet mouth curving into an amused cupid's bow, she whispered something which caused his head to snap up, his jaw to tighten. Over Vivienne's shining blonde head, Greg saw a look appear on his cousin's face; an expression of such intense longing and need, Greg caught his breath.

He followed Jake's gaze.

Found Lili.

She stood half-turned, as if contemplating flight, her reed slim body taut and strained, her large, dark eyes locked onto Jake's. As Greg watched, fascinated, he could almost see a line connecting them through the intensity of their stares.

Quickly, he strode over, swept her up in his arms, turning so her back was to Jake and Vivienne. She blinked stupidly at him, weakly struggling to get free.

"It's you, isn't it?" Greg whispered urgently. "Shit, Lili, it's you. You're the one. The one Jake loves. Hold on sweetheart, the song's nearly over. Hold onto me. If Vivienne sees you like this, she'll guess, then she'll make both your lives a misery."

"I can't. Oh Greg, why did it have to be this song? I can't bear it, watching him dance with her to this song, I have to go ... it's too painful..."

She twisted free of his arms, fleeing from the room, face wet with unchecked tears. Looking helplessly round, Greg saw the frown of concern on Jake's face as he unceremoniously shoved Vivienne to one side and rushed by Greg in pursuit of Lili.

"Stall her," he begged.

Greg duly stepped up to intercept Vivienne, sweeping her around in an elaborate dance as the instrumental part of the song crashed over them.

"Lili!"

Jake caught up with her in the hall.

Lili hesitated, torn between her head – demanding she run as fast and far away from him as she could – and her heart – thrilling to see him, wanting to hurl herself bodily into his arms and never let go.

"Please, Lili, I must talk to you!"

Lili wavered, resolve weakening at the desperate look in his eyes. Over his shoulder she saw Vivienne push past Greg, heading towards the doors, grim determination on her face. Desperately, Lili looked around for a hiding place.

"Over here," she insisted, holding out her hand. "Quickly!"

Without pausing to think, Jake placed his hand in hers, allowing her to lead him across to the opposite wall. Hands shaking, Lili pulled aside a corner of the tapestry. Much to his surprise, Jake saw the concealed opening behind.

Barely seconds after he followed Lili through and the tapestry dropped behind them, Vivienne stormed into the hall, followed closely by Greg.

"Where did he go?" she demanded, swinging to fix Greg with a steely glare.

"How the hell should I know?" he shrugged, hiding his elation that Jake and Lili had escaped, to where he couldn't guess. "Perhaps he wasn't feeling well and went up to your room."

Vivienne's eyes narrowed suspiciously. She stared at his innocent expression before turning on her heel, muttering obscenities that made even Greg blink and stormed up the wide sweeping stairs.

Chuckling to himself, he shook his head in amazement at the notion of Jake and Lili, an unlikely couple and yet...

The more Greg thought about it, the more it seemed so obvious, so perfect, so right. He glanced around the hall, wondering where they'd vanished to, silently wished them well, then made his way back to the party.

Hearts pounding, fighting to control their panicked breathing, Jake and Lili froze on the stairs up to the minstrels' gallery, listening to the brief exchange between Greg and Vivienne.

Jake grinned at Greg's blatant misdirection, acknowledging he owed him big time. They heard Vivienne's heels clack up the marble steps, then waited long, agonising moments, before daring to speak.

"What are you doing here?" Lili hissed, retreating up another step away from him. "I asked Daisy, she said you weren't coming."

"I wasn't," Jake replied, hands itching to touch her flushed, indignant face; to stroke her glossy, dark hair. "But Daisy told me yesterday you were coming after all, so I jumped on a plane."

"Oh, you jumped on a plane, did you?" Lili retorted, secretly thrilled to be close to him, but damned if she was going to let him know that. "You jumped on a plane and flew to England to see me. Shame you had to bring your *wife* with you!"

"I'm sorry," Jake's face sobered. "I couldn't stop her from coming," he paused, giving in to the overwhelming urge to touch her. A large hand gently cupped her face.

"Oh, Lili," he murmured. "I've missed you."

A strangled sob burst from Lili's throat as Jake's firm demanding arms claimed her and she stopped fighting, going limp as he enfolded her in his warm, masculine embrace.

A sigh, lighter than a summer's breeze, whispered past her lips, and her arms crept around his shoulders, pulling him closer, her heart pounding a desperate tattoo of love.

"Jake," she murmured. "My Jake."

Her words were an incendiary device. Want, hot and primal, flared uncontrollably between them; bodies strained, hands gripped and held, teeth clashed, mouths met in a savagely demanding kiss.

Up two steps higher than Jake, Lili felt every inch of his lean, strong body pressing violently against hers, could feel his arousal. Instinctively, her legs parted, needing to feel him, hard and ready, moving against her, pushing her over the edge.

"Now," Jake demanded, pulling insistently at her dress. "Lili, I need you now."

She moaned in agreement, hands shaking as she unzipped and pulled him out, so hot and hard, stroking down his velvety steel. Her breath catching in her throat as she caressed his firmness, knowing it was all for her.

Jake groaned as Lili parted her legs, rubbing him between her swollen lips. Clinging to one another, mouth to mouth, muffling each other's cries, he pushed his way straight up and into her.

They paused – muscles contracting and throbbing. Slowly, steadily, Jake began to move, each stroke, each hum of pleasure pushing them further and further into mindless oblivion.

After the first time, sex had always been amazing between them, but this – furtive, desperate, hidden coupling fuelled by adrenalin and frantic desire, combined with the need to remain silent, to go slowly, to not make a sound – this was something else.

Lili felt the pressure building unbearably until it seemed the top of her skull must explode. She gripped Jake's shoulders painfully, whimpering as hot slick flesh rasped over hot slick flesh.

"I love you," she whispered, internal combustion beginning its strong steady climb ever upwards. "Oh Jake, I love you."

"Lili!"

Her name was ripped from his throat. With a choked cry, he emptied himself into her, the shock of it rendering him speechless. Lili felt his explosion. It pushed her, spinning, over the precipice, gasping with disbelief, womb ballooning, intense, orgasmic contractions pulsing upwards, leaving her shaking and drained.

Slowly, their breathing returned to normal. Jake braced one arm against the wall to take his weight, the other supporting Lili as she sagged, boneless and limp, against him. Tenderly, he kissed her eyelids, tasted salt tears on her cheeks, soothed her trembling lips with his own.

"I love you," he whispered, feeling her shudder in his arms.

"I love you too," she replied slowly. "But nothing's changed."

"What?" She heard his disbelief. "How can you say that? Hell, Lili, these last two weeks have been torture. We've tried being apart. It doesn't work. We need to be together. If that means I bankrupt myself with maintenance payments, and we make room in our lives for regular custody of the baby, that's what we'll do, but I can't live apart from you anymore, Lili."

"The pregnancy test…"

"Says she is," Jake confirmed.

"Then, this changes nothing," she repeated, and he felt her begin to pull away.

"No," he whispered hoarsely, trying to pull her back into his arms.

"I'm sorry," she said, stepping back.

There was a stickiness between her thighs from their coupling, and the fresh, ripe odour of sex. Fumbling in her bag, she found a tissue and wadded it between her legs, aware Jake was adjusting himself back into his trousers, the rasp of his zipper shockingly loud in the darkness.

"Please Lili," he caught her as she tried to push by. "Promise me you'll at least think about it, I love you." She heard his despair, her heart nearly dying at the sound.

"All right," she promised. "I'll think about it. Let me go now."

He hesitated, dragged her mouth to his in a fiercely possessive kiss before releasing her and stepping back.

"Lili," his voice, low and insistent, catching her as she lifted the tapestry. "This isn't over," he stated firmly. "One way or another, we will be together."

"Goodbye, Jake," she whispered sadly, and fled up the stairs, along the corridor, heading for the sanctuary of her room, aware of her dishevelled state and needing solitude to think and reflect before she faced the party downstairs.

Sobbing with relief, Lili rounded the corner to her room and ran straight into Vivienne. There was a confusing impression of firm, rounded, perfumed flesh before Lili recoiled in horror, the other woman staggering back on spindly heels, biting off a curse.

"What the …? Oh, it's you."

Vivienne studied Lili closely, frowning as she took in Lili's flustered state, the mussed and tousled hair, the bare, kiss swollen lips, the post-coital flush across Lili's exposed chest, and the slight, but unmistakable, whiff of sex which clung to the younger girl.

"Well, sugar," she drawled. "You certainly look as though you're having a good party. You don't happen to have seen my husband on your travels?"

"J-Jake?" stuttered Lili, a treacherous flush staining her cheeks. "No, no I haven't, sorry."

Vivienne's eyes narrowed to serpentine slits at the lie in Lili's voice. "So," she breathed. "You're the latest little slut Jake's banging. Well, honey, congratulations. He's quite the stud, isn't he?"

"What? I don't know what you mean…"

"Oh, sure you do, sugar," continued Vivienne, voice dripping honey laden venom. "But a word of advice from his wife … enjoy it while it lasts, because it never lasts very long. He gets bored so easily you see."

Vivienne paused, raking her glance dismissively over Lili's trembling form.

"It takes a real woman to hold onto him and sweet thing, well, quite frankly, you haven't got what it takes."

"You're wrong." Lili found the courage to stand her ground, looking Vivienne straight in the eye. "Jake's not like that. He loves me, and I love him. But don't worry, Vivienne, he won't leave you."

"Too right he won't," Vivienne spat, eyes chips of iced fire. "I'm having his baby. That means more to Jake than his little bits of fun. I'm telling you now, honey, if Jake ever leaves me, I'll make damned sure he never sees his kid."

"No!" Lili's shocked cry was instinctive and heartfelt.

Vivienne hesitated, sensing a weakness, a sly smile playing about her lips.

"That's the choice he would have to make – you or his baby. Tough call, huh?"

"You … you wouldn't do that!"

"Try me," Vivienne paused, smiling.

A cold inhuman smile, it chilled the blood in Lili's veins.

"Of course, he might choose you, but you'd forever know you were the reason why he lost his child. Deep inside, you'd wonder whether he blamed you. How long, do you think, could love survive under that kind of pressure?"

Lili staggered back, aghast, as Vivienne sashayed towards her, cream hips swaying. She shrank away as Vivienne stopped, stretched out a perfectly manicured hand, and gripped Lili's chin, tipping her face this way and that as she studied her.

"So young," she murmured. "So very young, but oh, so tempting. All that innocence just waiting to be corrupted."

Scarlet talons sank into Lili's flesh. She cried out in pain as Vivienne pressed her thickly painted lips onto Lili's bare, inexperienced ones, grinding a brief, savage kiss onto them before stepping back, releasing a stunned and shocked Lili.

"Don't suppose you'd consider sharing him, sugar?" she mused, smiling as Lili choked out a horrified gasp and recoiled, clutching a hand to her face where Vivienne's claws had drawn blood.

"No, perhaps not, pity ..."

And she left, walking calmly away from Lili as if she hadn't a care in the world, hips swaying, golden hair flowing down her back, looking every inch the sophisticated woman in control of her life. Yet the snarl of frustrated anger which twisted her mouth, marring her ripe beauty, told another story.

Assuming if he wasn't with Lili, he'd be at the party, Vivienne casually wandered downstairs, gradually regaining control. By the time she located Jake leaning against the bar, talking in a low, urgent voice to Greg, her usual southern belle smile was in place.

Sidling up beside him, she slipped an arm around his waist. "There you are, sugar, I've been looking all over for you."

"Vivienne."

Offering no excuse for his earlier, abrupt departure, Jake smoothly pulled away from her grasp.

"Do you know, whilst I was looking for you, I bumped into Lili. Do you remember her?"

Vivienne noticed with satisfaction the sudden stiffening of his body; the faint, almost imperceptible, drawing in of breath.

"Such a sweet little thing. We had the nicest of chats, you know – girl talk. We learnt so much about each other."

So intent was Vivienne on ladling out spite, she missed the quick, horrified look Jake shot over her head; the silently communicated request, the acknowledgement; the fact that Greg quietly, but speedily, turned on his heel and left the room.

"I'm homesick, honey." Vivienne turned devastatingly blue eyes up to Jake with an expression that would once have turned his bones to mush but now left him cold.

"I think we should go home tomorrow, maybe start thinking about getting the nursery ready for the baby. After all, the next few months will pass so quickly."

She bent her beautiful head, rested it on his shoulder and Jake stared at it in dismay, feeling the prison doors clang shut.

Knocking on the door of the room Greg knew had been assigned to Lili, he waited, hearing no sounds inside, yet sensing her presence. Finally, hesitantly, he turned the handle and let himself in.

"Lili? Lili sweetheart, it's Greg. Are you here?"

There was no reply. Glancing around, he noticed the dress she'd been wearing lying in a puddle of black velvet on the floor. He bent to pick it up and heard the water running in the shower.

"Lili?" he tapped discreetly on the bathroom door. "Are you okay?"

Easing the door open, he heard a noise – an inhuman groan of agony that made his skin creep. Now, seriously worried, he pushed the door open further.

"Lili, if you don't answer me, I'm coming in."

A low, keening howl was his only reply. Greg opened the door fully and entered the steam-filled room. Yanking back the shower curtain he found Lili curled into a small, naked ball in the bath, knees clutched to her chin, rocking in despair as scalding hot needles of water smashed down onto her.

"Oh shit, Lili!"

Quickly, he reached in, soaking his shirt sleeves, struggling to turn off the shower. Grabbing a large towel off the rail, he draped it around Lili's shivering form, bodily lifted her out of the shower and carried her into the bedroom.

Sitting on the bed with Lili on his lap, he rubbed at her with the towel, his large hands surprisingly gentle as he dried her small, still face. He patted the excess water from the hair clinging round her shoulders like fronds of seaweed, making him think of the pictures of mermaids in Daisy's childhood storybooks.

"Lili," he cupped her face in his hands. "Come on, sweetheart, snap out of it."

Relief poured through him as her eyes struggled to focus, and recognition dawned. She looked down at her soaking, naked body, wrapped only in a towel, and a flush warmed her cheeks, her eyes widening with horror.

"G-Greg?" she stammered. "What are you doing here?"

"Jake was worried. He sent me to find you, see if you were okay."

"Vivienne … she … she…"

"I know," Greg interrupted grimly. "She made sure Jake knew she'd had a little 'chat' with you. That's why I came to check you were all right."

Embarrassed, Lili squirmed off his lap holding tightly to her towel. Seeing her discomfort, Greg fetched the towelling robe from the bathroom door.

"Here," he said, handing it to her. "Put this on. I'll be back in a moment."

True to his word, Lili barely had time to finish drying herself, wrap the oversize robe about her, and run a comb through her hair before he was back clutching a bottle and two glasses.

"Brandy," he stated, sloshing a generous amount into a glass, and handing it to Lili before pouring himself one.

"I don't like brandy."

"Drink it down, there's a good girl. It's for medicinal purposes." Dutifully, Lili took a mouthful and pulled a face.

"Now then," Greg settled himself back onto Lili's bed. He took a large mouthful of brandy, raising his brows enquiringly at Lili.

"You and Jake. How long has this been going on?"

"What has Jake told you?" Lili enquired cautiously.

"Not a lot. He told me there was someone, someone he loved. That this person had made him go back to Vivienne to be a good father to the baby. It didn't make sense to me at the time, but when I realised it was you it made perfect sense. Little Lili," his eyes softened. "Always putting others first. Then when I saw the way you and Jake looked at each other, it all clicked."

"I love him," stated Lili quietly. "But we can't be together."

"Now that," remarked Greg, taking another mouthful of brandy, "is where you and I part company. Why can't you be together? It doesn't make sense?"

"She's pregnant."

"So? Jake would see her okay with maintenance, and I know you'd have no problem with seeing the kid regularly."

"That's just it, Vivienne said – threatened – that Jake would have to make a choice, me or the baby."

"Well, hell, Lili, no contest. He'd choose you."

"No, you don't understand. He would have to make a choice, me, or the baby. If he leaves Vivienne and comes to me, she'd make sure he never saw the baby. I can't ask him to make that decision, and I won't do that to an innocent child."

Greg sighed, setting down his empty brandy glass. "I see," he said, and Lili could tell, finally, he did.

"Greg," she asked, hesitantly, unsure whether to voice the quiet nagging concern.

"Uh-huh?"

"Has Jake ... well, is he in the habit of ... what I'm trying to say is, well, does he ... I mean, am I the first, only, Vivienne, she said..."

"Oh sweetheart," said Greg, his stunningly handsome face twisting into an expression of sympathy. "She really did do a number on you, didn't she?"

"It's all right," Lili sighed, looked down at her empty brandy glass. "You don't have to answer. I already know she was lying. She'd have said anything to hurt me."

"Speaking of hurt ..."

Greg moved closer, tilted Lili's face to the light, sucking in his breath at the perfect set of claw marks along her jaw.

"She did this to you?" Lili nodded. His face darkened. "Hope you're up to date with your tetanus jabs," he muttered.

Lili stood, dragging her partially unpacked case up from the floor. With hands that shook, she picked out clean underwear, jeans, a warm jumper, and dropped them on the bed. Carelessly, she stuffed her party dress into the case, tossing makeup and shoes on top.

"Hey, what are you doing?" Greg leapt to his feet in concern.

"Packing," she snapped. "I can't stay here another minute."

"Okay," he frowned. "I understand why you feel that way, but I don't think you're in any condition to drive all that way alone."

"I'll be fine," Lili insisted.

Scooping up her clothes she went into the bathroom, closing the door firmly behind her. Greg hovered indecisively, feeling dismissed, yet reluctant to leave. His eyes fell on the road atlas on the bedside table.

Curiously, he opened it to find a crumpled sheet of paper. Brow creasing in a frown he read the clumsily written, misspelt instructions. When Lili emerged, fully dressed, hair bundled on top of her head, he held out the sheet.

"What's all this?"

Lili froze, face reddening with shame. She snatched the paper away. "It's nothing, my route, that's all," she paused. Taking a deep breath, she decided to tell the truth.

"I'm severely dyslexic," she explained. "I have trouble reading signposts. They flash by so fast unless I'm prepared for them, I miss them and get lost," she sighed. "Which is what happened on the way here."

"That's awful, Lili, I had no idea," Greg felt even more protective "That settles it. You're not driving all that way in the dark on your own."

"Well, what do you suggest?" Lili was close to breaking point. Already drained from the journey up, the evening's events had sapped her energy, leaving her weak and weepy.

"I'll drive your car to mine, and you stay the night. Drive home in the morning, in the light, after you've had some sleep." Lili hesitated. Greg caught her hand in his. "Okay?"

"Why are you being so nice to me?"

"Well," Greg considered, grinning at her. "Three reasons. One, you're a friend, and I like you. Two, Jake is my cousin, he's as close to me as any brother. In helping you I'm helping him."

"And the third reason?" Lili asked, dangerously close to tears.

"Ah yes, the third reason. Well, I'm hoping if I'm your knight in shining armour now when you finally give up on Jake because he's too ugly, you'll remember me, and I'll be in with a chance." He leered so suggestively at Lili that a laugh burst through her tears.

"All right," she agreed slowly, nodding her head. "Thank you."

"Great," enthused Greg. "You finish your packing. I'll grab my stuff and come back for you. I'll make our excuses to Daisy later; I'll say you were taken ill or something and didn't want to cause a fuss at the party."

Lili nodded. When Greg left the room, she sank slowly onto the bed, head sinking into her hands, incredibly weary to the bone, and vastly relieved she wouldn't have to drive anymore.

Total exhaustion claimed Lili soon after the car pulled away from the Hall, and she sank like a stone into a deep, dreamless sleep, which was probably just as well. Greg was an enthusiastic, but inexperienced, driver. If Lili had been awake, the teeth jarring gear changing would have quickly had her demanding he let her drive.

She roused sufficiently to make her way blearily into Greg's studio, shivering with cold, grumbling at the icy bed she was expected to get into. But Greg piled blankets over her and soon she was asleep again, curled up in a tight little ball with barely her nose peeking from under the covers.

Greg sat for a while, sipping the brandy he had purloined from the party, so familiar with the arctic temperatures within the studio he hardly noticed his breath misting before his face. He watched Lili sleep, thinking about the night's events, and wondering.

Soon after two, his phone vibrated. Pulling it from his pocket, he saw Jake's name flash onto the screen. Silently, he let himself out into the corridor not wishing to wake Lili.

"Hi," he murmured.

"Shit, Greg," Jake's voice was low and tense. "I've been going out of my head with worry! That damned woman's been watching me like a hawk. She's only just gone to sleep. Where's Lili? No one's seen her. What the hell's been going on?"

"Relax," Greg soothed. "Lili's here with me at my place. She didn't want to stay any longer, and I didn't think it a good idea for her to drive all that way home, alone."

"Right, okay, she's with you," Greg pulled a wry face at the barely concealed jealousy in Jake's voice. "Is she okay?"

"Not really, Vivienne put the boot in, told her you're a regular screw about town."

"What!"

"Don't worry, Lili didn't believe her."

"Thank heavens for that."

"But Lili was pretty shaken by the whole thing, and Vivienne's claw marks on her face will take a few days to fade, that's for sure."

"Vivienne physically attacked Lili?" Jake's shocked anger echoed down the line, together with his frustration. "Oh hell, I never thought she'd go as far as that."

"Yeah, hell hath no fury and all that," muttered Greg, pacing up and down as the piercing cold finally began to bite. "Thing is, what happens now, Jake? How the fuck is this unholy mess you've got yourself into going to be sorted?"

"I don't know," Jake sighed. Greg heard a world of regret in the sound. "I don't know, Vivienne's demanding we fly back to the States. She even phoned the airline, and managed to change our flights to 2:30pm tomorrow, instead of Tuesday."

"Shit, you going to go?"

"Well, I don't see I have a choice, especially now Vivienne knows about Lili, I want to get her as far away from her as possible."

"Yeah, I can see that."

There was silence, then Jake asked softly.

"Can I speak to her?"

"I don't know that's a good idea. She's wiped and has completely crashed out."

"In your bed?"

"Yeah."

"Well, where are you?"

"Right now?" Greg grinned. "Freezing my nads off talking to a jealous idiot who doesn't appreciate how lucky he is to have Lili so completely nuts about him, that even if I were to smear myself with chocolate, she still wouldn't give me a second glance."

There was another silence.

Then Jake gave a reluctant, low laugh.

"Okay, point taken. It's just, you're there with her, and I'm not. I'm not sure when I'm going to see her again, if ever, and … shit, Greg, you know what I'm trying to say."

"I know," Greg sighed. "It's okay, I know. Look, I'll talk to her when she wakes, see if we can arrange a time when you can call."

"Thanks, I appreciate it."

"That's okay."

"I appreciate everything you've done this evening, Greg, for both of us."

"Hey, she's worth it."

"I think so."

"I wish it was me she was nuts about…"

"Hey!"

"Only kidding," Greg grinned, imagining Jake's face.

"Look," Jake's voice became urgent, "I'd better go. Will you tell her I won't give up? I'm going to keep trying to find a way to make it all right."

"Okay," agreed Greg, good-naturedly.

"Tell her I'll be thinking about her all the time."

"Okay,"

"And that I love her."

"Pushing your luck here now."

"Just give her the damned message, Greg."

"Can I give her anything else from you?" Greg enquired innocently.

"Now who's pushing his luck?" Jake drawled, breaking the connection.

Greg chuckled softly. Stuffing the phone back into his pocket, he let himself back into the slightly warmer studio, checking that Lili hadn't woken during his absence.

In the dim light cast by a battered lamp on the desk, her face was relaxed in slumber, her mouth curved slightly down as if sadness had followed her into her dreams.

It was an unusual face, he thought, his artist's eye noting the sharp angle of high cheekbones in direct contrast to the softness of the rest of her features. A face that seemed young and old – a tantalising blend of innocence and wisdom beyond her years. His fingers itched to sketch it.

Throwing himself down into the chair, he snatched up a pad and pencil from the floor and began to sketch, losing himself and all concept of time as he furiously worked, desperate to finish before she awoke.

When Lili finally stirred late next morning, she was alone, a note from Greg informing her he'd gone to get breakfast. Shivering, Lili scurried into the primitive bathroom, did the best she could with limited resources, before pulling on practically every stitch of clothing she had brought with her.

Still cold, she tugged on an old, paint-splattered jumper she found lying on a chair, muttering about poor starving artists who couldn't afford any bloody heating.

Greg's return bearing hot coffee and bacon butties from the cafe around the corner did much to lighten her mood. They ate breakfast in silence, perched on rickety stools at his old, scratched table, neither mentioning the events of the previous evening until every crumb had been consumed.

"He phoned last night."

Lili froze halfway through clearing away the wrappings, eyes flying to Greg, not needing to ask who he was.

"Did he?" her voice was small and distant as if she doubted the wisdom of enquiring any further. "Was he ... is he, all right?"

"No, he's not all right," replied Greg gently. "He told me to tell you he loves you and will never stop thinking about you. That somehow, he's going to find a way to make everything all right."

"Oh."

Lili folded herself neatly back onto her stool, her eyes downcast, and Greg felt a brief spurt of anger at her calm acceptance of his news.

"Is that all you have to say, oh?" he enquired.

Lili's eyes flashed green sparks. "What else do you expect me to say, Greg?" she demanded waspishly.

"I don't know," Greg shrugged a little sheepishly. "He was worried about you, especially as he's going back today."

"Today?" Lili leapt on his words like a terrier on a rat. "He's going back today?"

"Yeah, Vivienne changed their tickets. Shit that woman's such a manipulative bitch, I don't envy Jake having to live with that day in and day out."

"I know," groaned Lili, raking her fingers through sleep tousled hair. "I wish there was something I could do to help him. I can't bear the thought of him being alone with her. But there's nothing I can do, nothing ... unless..."

Slowly, Lili's head rose, and she fixed shining eyes onto Greg's concerned face. As he watched, confused, a big beaming smile spread across her face. With hands that shook, she leant forward and eagerly clasped his.

"Greg," she began, "do you have any commitments for the foreseeable future?"

"No," he replied slowly, uncertainly. "Not as such, why?"

"Go with him?" she pleaded.

"What? Go to America?"

"Yes, why not? At least he wouldn't be alone. He'd have a friend, he'd have you."

"But ... but ..." Greg shook his head, dumbfounded at the suggestion. "I can't drop everything and go with him."

"Why not?" demanded Lili. "After all, you said you've no commitments and you can draw anywhere, so why not go and stay with your favourite cousin for a while?"

"Because I can't afford it," stated Greg bluntly. "Do you have any idea how much tickets to America cost? And then expenses over there? No, I'm sorry Lili. Much as I want to help, I can't..."

"I'll pay you!"

"What?"

"To go and stay with Jake for a while, I'll pay you. How much will you need?"

"What? No, Lili, that's insane, you can't pay me to go and babysit Jake for you."

"No? Okay," Lili sprang to her feet, grabbed the nearest painting. "How much are you selling this for?"

"I don't see what..."

"How much?"

"Two thousand pounds..."

"I'll give you six thousand, will that leave you enough to go to America on?"

"No, Lili, absolutely not, I won't do it, I'm sorry, I just won't..."

Stretching out his long legs in the cramped space available, Jake heaved a big sigh to himself, wondering what precisely his mad dash to Britain had achieved.

If anything, he had probably made things worse. Vivienne had found out about Lili. Not only that had been given an opportunity to threaten and physically harm her.

Jake cast a considering, sidelong glance at the blonde bombshell flicking through a magazine, happily spending a few moments imagining all sorts of unpleasant endings for her, before shifting uncomfortably in his seat, wondering why the delay in take-off.

Movement at the front of the plane had him rolling his eyes in disgust. A late passenger, how bloody inconsiderate.

Then, his jaw dropped.

Greg sauntered casually down the aisle, flashing his killer smile at the hovering hostess as she nearly fell over herself to show him to his seat, conveniently situated two rows behind theirs.

"Greg?" Vivienne stared in suspicious surprise. "What are you doing here?

"Oh, didn't Jake tell you?" enquired Greg innocently. "I'm coming to stay for a while. Jolly decent of you to invite me, Vivienne, and I promise I'll be no trouble, no trouble at all."

With that, Greg folded himself into his seat, pulled on the headphones, and promptly went to sleep, much to the disappointment of the cabin crew.

Vivienne turned furious eyes onto Jake, who shrugged, an ironically amused smile tugging at his mouth.

"Sorry, must have slipped my mind," he drawled, the smile deepening as Vivienne flounced back into her magazine, furiously flipping pages as the cabin crew went through the usual safety procedures before take-off.

Lili gripped the railings on the observation deck. She watched as the plane screeched its way down the runway, before finally, earth-shatteringly, heaving itself into the steely, cold, blue sky; her eardrums trembling from the roar of its engines. She waited until the plane was a dot in the sky, lost to view, before sighing and turning away, ready to locate her car and begin the long, arduous drive home.

Chapter Twenty-Nine

"It's not fair, and the world's such a cruel place."

Vivienne was not a happy woman. Things were not going according to plan. This was an unpleasant experience for a woman who had elevated getting her own way into an art form. Not only was Jake not falling into line there was the added annoyance of Greg who was there, constantly. Every time she blinked, he popped up out of nowhere with his sarcastic British wit which she didn't quite understand but knew was aimed at her.

If she tried to object, he smiled that devastating, all-male smile, blue eyes daring her to take him on, and she ... Damn it! Vivienne didn't want to admit that Greg still had the power to stir feelings within her. Of all the men, and there had been many – too many to count, too many to think of – Greg was the only one she ever had an emotional response to that could almost have been love.

Outraged he had been the one to leave her, that he was Jake's cousin had played a large part in her decision to snare Jake into marriage. The fact Jake was rich and successful didn't hurt either, and more importantly, came from a solid and respectable background.

The Kolinsky family home on Nob Hill, San Francisco, dazzled even the worldly-wise Vivienne with its antiques and priceless paintings. The fact his family treated the house merely as their home, filling it with family, friends, pets, and noise served to make her bitterly aware of the gap between her background and Jake's.

Yes, Vivienne mused with satisfaction, she had come a long way from Tammy Lou Baker, the third illegitimate child of an amiable slattern, born and raised in a trailer park in deepest Georgia. Tammy Lou learnt from a desperately young age exactly what fools, men were. They thought with their dicks. Given the right motivation could be persuaded to do almost anything.

This knowledge had stood her in good stead, enabling her to claw her way out from under her white trailer trash label. She entered the local beauty pageant, her lush, ripe sexuality prominent even at fourteen, making her the obvious choice for the local mayor who was judging, to pick as the town's homecoming queen.

Later, after the parade and award ceremony were over, they went to his fishing cabin where he took her virginity in a sweaty, hasty coupling, which left Tammy Lou untouched and unmoved and left him promising to help her go places. Especially when she wept crocodile tears at the loss of her innocence, revealing her real age for the first time, and oh so naively whispering that perhaps she should tell her mother, and maybe even his wife.

Desperately thinking of his voters and breaking into a fresh sweat at the thought of a possible prison sentence for statutory rape of a minor, he gave her all the money he could lay his hands on and a bus ticket to anywhere out of there, thankfully putting the thought of her big blue eyes and impossibly knowing smile out of his mind.

Tammy Lou kicked the dust of small-town Georgia off her heels, working her way across the country to her own personal Eldorado – Hollywood. And she made it. It took her six months of slinging hash in greasy diners and hitching lifts with truckers who demanded payment in the back of their cabs, but she made it.

Sixteen years later, she was a star.

She was Vivienne.

Glamorous, beautiful, and married to the famous author, Jack Cole. She'd had it all – wealth, power, and status. So, how had it gone so wrong?

Somewhere along the line, she had played her cards wrong. It had been a mistake to let Jake know about that silly little actress she so effectively got rid of. It had also been difficult keeping up the image she had snared him with – the sweet, misunderstood, small-town girl, who wanted love, and craved stability, a home, and a family.

A smile curved her perfectly painted mouth as she remembered how concerned he had been during the whole baby-making fiasco. Did he think she would allow herself to get pregnant when her career was at such a delicately critical stage?

No, the pill had made sure that didn't happen. It had been amusing though, maybe even a little touching, watching him worry and fret that perhaps he was the problem.

They had that silly little separation last September when he left her and went to England, but he came back. Oh yes, he came crawling back. All it took was a phone call, breathily whispered promises to change, entreaties to forgive, and pleas to give their marriage one last try.

The reconciliation lasted less than a month, then the crack had widened, splitting open into an unbridgeable chasm. He spent Christmas with his family, and she had not been invited, although she tried, oh my how she tried. She telephoned his mother oozing charm and sincerity, only to be spoken to as if she were nothing; was still little Tammy Lou Baker, no good child of a no-account slut.

When he returned home, he had been surprised to find her still there. Then he got angry. Knowing what buttons to push, Vivienne had goaded him, using every trick Tammy Lou knew until finally, she got what she wanted and needed. As he furiously screwed her, spurting unwillingly into her waiting womb, Vivienne played her trump card.

Jake had forgotten about the sperm samples, frozen for future use during the trials to get pregnant. Vivienne hadn't. Being artificially inseminated had been child's play, Jake had already signed the release form. All she had to do was lay back and plot revenge.

It took two attempts to take but finally, the line on the test turned blue, and Vivienne tasted hot, sweet vengeance as she made the phone call to bring him home.

But Vivienne had miscalculated, not thinking beyond getting back her handsome, rich, trophy husband. She had failed to consider the reality of being pregnant, of having an alien entity take root in her unwilling body; the sickness which plagued her, the tiredness, the way her body was changing in unpleasant and unexpected ways.

She hated being pregnant, loathed the baby growing within her. She saw it merely as a weapon to achieve her goal – that it wasn't working made her despise it even more.

And then there was Lili.

It rankled and it burnt that Jake had so quickly replaced her, and with such a mealy-mouthed non-entity who couldn't say boo to a goose and had as much sex appeal as a glass of water. Vivienne's teeth ground together whenever the thought of Lili's pale, scared face crossed her mind, and acid bile bubbled indignantly in her throat.

Small comfort was gained that Jake was with her, not in England with Lili. But it was very cold comfort when Vivienne could feel him slipping further away from her. Desperately, she plotted and schemed, insisting he came with her for check-ups. Still, he was distant, his obvious dislike for her becoming more blatant each day.

And that brought her right back to Greg. Jake's partner in crime, he drew strength from his cousin's presence. The pair of them were always together, and Greg seemed to delight in foiling her plans to lure Jake back.

Vivienne detested him, but at the same time craved him the way a child craves sweets. She considered tempting him into bed but was afraid if the attempt failed – and she had a strong suspicion it would – it would make her situation even more untenable.

No, Vivienne was not a happy woman. Dressing carefully for lunch with her agent, her flawless face settling into lines of discontent, she thought bitterly that life couldn't get any worse.

She was late reaching the restaurant, but then, he wasn't expecting her to be on time. In fact, would have been disappointed if she hadn't gone all out to make an entrance. As he watched her sway alluringly into the room, oozing sex appeal from every pore making even the gay waiters leap to pay homage to her, he couldn't help smiling. His little Vivienne. Because she was his. He'd made her what she was today ... a star in every sense of the word.

Marty Goldman, agent to the best. Possibly one of the slickest, smartest, most unscrupulous men in Hollywood. He not only knew of almost every foul deed and underhand act Vivienne had done – he approved of them. A slim dark weasel of a man, his interest in Vivienne was strictly professional, although he did confess to an almost benign fatherly interest in this client.

She was so glamorous, so beautiful on the outside, but inside – here even Marty shook his head with disbelieving admiration – on the inside Vivienne was hollow. Whatever compassion Tammy Lou Baker had been born with she had lost somewhere on the long, tortuous road to success.

Now, he rose to his feet as Vivienne, after much air-kissing and name dropping, finally reached him, accepting with southern belle grace his restrained peck on both cheeks before allowing herself to be settled comfortably in her chair and accepting a glass of sparkling mineral water.

They chatted in a perfunctory manner; idle gossip about who and what was new in Tinsel Town, both knowing it was merely foreplay to the real reason she was there, and why he had summoned her.

Vivienne waited, not a flicker of emotion showing on her face. She appreciated, perhaps more than any other actress, the adage, 'you're only as good as your last film'. Even though she had three solid films behind her, she needed the next one.

Vivienne adored her career. It seemed to her like getting money for nothing. To be paid for pretending to be someone else, why that was something she did every single day of her life. She not only loved acting she adored the lifestyle that went with it. Let other actresses whinge about having their privacy invaded, Vivienne was always a good sport with the paparazzi, needing that constant buzz of public adoration to reaffirm she'd made it; she was someone; she was a star.

So now she waited, glowing face calm and disinterested, whilst inside she was a churning, seething mess, wondering what role Marty had found for her, hoping that this time it would be the role, and the part, that would catapult her star into the stratosphere.

Primly, she finished her last bite of salad, still hungry, damn that baby, but refusing to give in to temptation and order dessert. She patted at her immaculate lips leaving a perfect crescent of scarlet lip gloss on the snowy white napkin, before folding it neatly back onto the table beside her half-empty plate. Leaning back in her chair, she raised her eyebrows expectantly at Marty.

He drew the moment out slowly, leisurely finishing his steak and Caesar salad, swigging a large swallow of red wine, and fussing with the dessert menu until Vivienne wanted to scream. Finally, he leant his elbows on the table and smiled at her, a smug self-important smile, brimming over with satisfaction at his cleverness.

"I had a call," he began. "From Global Pictures."

He paused for effect. Vivienne felt her pupils dilate and her heart race, the faintest sheen of perspiration breaking out between her breasts. Global Pictures – not the biggest, but arguably the best – they produced quality films almost guaranteed not just box office success, but prestige, critical acclaim, and – Vivienne's pulse spiked, she almost moaned with delight – Oscars.

"They have a role they think you would be perfect for and wondered if you'd care to look at the script. It's all a bit hush-hush still, so you have to keep it to yourself, but it's the big one, honey."

"What's the film?" Vivienne finally found her voice, noting with satisfaction her tone was still calm, still level.

"It's *the* film, Vivienne. They're re-making the biggest film ever produced and they want you for the lead."

"You mean ...?" she paused; swallowed, unable to believe what she was hearing.

"That's right," he stopped, glancing around at the crowded restaurant before lowering his voice and bending further across the table. "They're going to re-make Gone With the Wind, and they want you for..."

"Scarlet O'Hara," she breathed, her composure for once shaken. Her eyes widened, and she gripped at his sleeve. "Oh Marty ..." she murmured. He nodded in agreement.

"This is it, Vivienne, the chance you've been waiting for. Of course, there are a few conditions."

"Like?" she sipped her iced water, struggling to remain calm.

"You'll have to dye your hair. They want to stay true to the novel and Scarlet's a brunette."

"That's fine," Vivienne dismissed her trademark golden locks without a second thought, a smile of complacency slipping onto her perfect mouth.

"You'll have to wear green contact lenses."

"Not a problem." For the chance to play Scarlet, Vivienne would cheerfully sacrifice an eye. "Anything else?"

"And you'll have to lose a few pounds. Don't forget, Scarlet's supposed to have like an eighteen-inch waist or something, but that's easily done. Filming doesn't start until June, so you've got time to get a personal trainer and a dietician."

The smile froze. Marty rattled on, oblivious to her inner turmoil. How could he be? He had no idea her dreams were lying in shattered pieces at her feet. Filming began in June. By June, Vivienne would be six months pregnant, bloated and swollen, with only more weight gain to look forward to.

At last, supreme success was within her grasp, but because of that maggot festering within her belly, it would go to somebody else. Damn Jake. Damn his baby. It was his fault! Rage churned. Vivienne sipped slowly to hide her bitter frustration from Marty, who finally finished talking and was looking at her expectantly.

"Well, Marty," Vivienne smiled a slow languid smile. She was, after all, an actress and a survivor. She would find a way around this. Somehow, she would find a way to have it all.

"When do I get the script?"

Greg, on the other hand, was having nothing but good days. Enjoying the balmy West Coast sunshine, his tan deepened, only adding to his devastatingly male good looks as he cut a swathe through the impossibly beautiful women, who were everywhere he looked.

He was having fun baiting Vivienne; deriving extreme satisfaction from making her life as difficult as he could; goading her with his dry, clever wit before pulling back, innocently wide-eyed on the brink of outright rudeness.

Spending so much time with Jake was also a bonus, and they would sit on the deck drinking beer and talking. True, Jake only wanted to talk about Lili and would desperately pump Greg for every snippet of information he possessed, and Greg realised how little time Jake and Lili had had together; how much they still had to learn about each other.

Jake knew Greg was there at Lili's behest. He knew Greg was in regular contact with her, but Lili refused to speak to Jake feeling it would be unfair on them both, so Jake had to content himself with hearing about her third hand.

Before Greg knew it, three weeks slipped by. He wondered how long he was supposed to stay, and what exactly he was supposed to be doing there. He voiced these concerns to Lili, only to have her beg him to stay a little longer. Unable to say no to her, he capitulated.

During the long sessions when Jake shut himself in his study to write furiously, Greg would take his car and explore. He had been to America before and had even lived in LA for a brief period four years earlier, during which time he'd met, fallen in love with, and then been disillusioned by Vivienne.

Taking his sketchpad and pencil wherever he went, Greg found a wealth of land and seascapes, views, and faces to draw. He discovered a small, family-owned diner, where the coffee was hot and the food home-cooked. He would spend many hours there sketching the owner, her family, and any of the patrons whose faces caught his eye.

The owner, an enormously solid woman named Annie, took him under her wing, attracted by his good looks, his British accent, and quirky, offbeat humour. She mothered him, pouring endless cups of coffee, and saving him pieces of her homemade pies, enjoying watching him put them away with boundless enthusiasm.

Her husband, Walt, a dried-up stick of a man, was an avid chess fan. Upon discovering Greg could play, he pressed him into a game, studying the board with acute concentration as Greg made sketch after sketch of him. Fascinated by the craggy grooves in the man's face, and the gentle, kindly humour that shone in his deep-set eyes.

They had numerous children. By some odd genetic quirk, the girls all took after their mother – large, bovine, and motherly, whilst the two boys were young clones of Walt – slow, patient, and gentle. Together, they ran the diner and food delivery business, their clientele mostly regulars known by name and food preferences, and a family feel permeated the very air of the diner.

Greg ate there regularly, at first due to necessity. Whilst Jake was in the throes of a book he tended to forget about such mundane things as eating. As for Vivienne, well the thought of Vivienne playing a good little housewife in the kitchen was enough to put a grin on Greg's face – acknowledging that with the way she felt about him she'd probably slip rat poison into anything she cooked for him. Gradually he began to eat almost all his meals there, enjoying the easy familiarity and good company.

He got to know the other customers, chatting to them about England and his life there, basking in their admiration of the young artist from London. He'd sketch them, dashing off amusing little caricatures which he'd rip out of his book and present to the bemused subject. Several of his sketches already adorned the walls of the diner in smart wooden frames. Annie had made him sign them, shrewdly deducing they'd be worth something one day.

One particular customer interested him. A young man. There was no regular pattern to his visits, though his order was always the same – coffee to drink and three pieces of pie to go. Annie would pack the pie carefully in a box whilst he drank his coffee, slumped in a booth as if all the cares of the world were on his shoulders. Greg observed him, and one evening asked Annie what his story was.

"Carl?" Annie sighed, watching the slim, sandy-haired man climb into his battered car and reverse out of the parking lot. "He's got a lot on his plate right now. His little girl's not right and needs an operation. Thing is, it's going to cost more than Carl and his wife can afford. So, he's pulling all the shifts he can. He calls here on his way home and takes them some of Annie's homemade pie."

"What's wrong with his daughter?" Greg asked, interested.

"She's ..." Annie pursed her lips, searching for the right word. "Different, I guess that's the best way to describe her. Poor little mite. It's not fair, and the world's such a cruel place."

Greg blinked at the bizarre comment, opened his mouth to enquire further, but Annie had been distracted by a cluster of customers, nimbly manoeuvring her bulk around the counter to serve them, and the subject was dropped.

Greg didn't forget. Whenever Carl came into the diner, he would silently watch him, fingers itching to sketch. But Carl's visits never lasted longer than the time it took him to drain a cup of coffee, so Greg waited, biding his time.

One hot, sticky evening, Jake had gone to some writers' convention he'd agreed to do months before and now couldn't get out of. Watching as he grumbled his way into a black tux, Greg gleefully declined the invitation to accompany him, instead grabbing his sketchpad and driving happily to the diner, looking forward to Annie's famous pot roast and cherry pie.

Leaning back in his seat, rubbing his full stomach in contentment, Greg looked up as the door opened and Carl entered. Dragging himself to a booth, looking even more tired than usual, he rubbed at red-rimmed eyes as Annie hustled to pour him coffee. For once he didn't seem in his customary rush, and when Annie asked if he wanted his usual, he replied wearily.

"Not tonight Annie. Mel and Lisa have gone to stay with Melanie's folks, so I thought I'd have something to eat here. The house seems so empty without them. What can you recommend?"

"The pot roast was pretty special," Greg spoke before Annie could reply. Carl considered, then nodded in exhausted agreement.

"Yeah, sounds good, thanks, Annie."

"Now, you sit down," she ordered. "I'll rustle you up a plateful."

Silence fell over the diner. Due to the late hour, it was practically empty, and Greg's pencil flew over the pad as he sketched the heart-breaking sadness on Carl's face, the weariness present in every line of his body.

"You drawing me?" Carl's comment dragged Greg back to the real world and he hesitated, pencil poised over the paper, as the man looked at him with interest.

"Yeah, sorry, it's a habit," Greg replied eventually. "I'm an artist. I tend to sketch almost in my sleep. Would you like to see it?"

Carl nodded and Greg tossed the pad to him. Catching it with ease, Carl smoothed down the page and silently examined the rough sketch.

"Do I really look that tired?" he murmured, flashing a quick weary smile at Greg, and tossing the pad back. "It's good," he commented. "You're the English artist, right?"

"That's me," replied Greg cheerfully.

"Which part of England are you from?"

"London."

"Oh, right. Mel, my wife, she's got family over there, Shrewsbury, someplace like that?"

"I know it," Greg grinned. "You're not going to ask me if I know them, are you?"

"No, I realise it's quite a way from London." For the first time, Carl smiled a slow, easy grin. It transformed his face, easing the troubled lines and clearly showing Greg how young he was; probably no older than himself, maybe even younger.

"That happen to you a lot?" Carl enquired.

"Oh yes," agreed Greg. "There was one guy, he got quite upset I didn't know his Aunt Betsy, after all, she only lived in Scotland, so why on earth wouldn't I know her?"

Carl's smile deepened, Annie bustled over with his meal and silence fell over the diner as Carl hungrily ate. Greg amused himself with sketching one of Annie's daughters as she leant on the counter, lost in a glossy fashion magazine, a world of wishing on her round, shiny face, as she gazed at the waif models in designer wear.

After that, a casual friendliness sprang up between the two men. Whenever Carl came in for coffee he would sit at Greg's table, talking about whatever subject came up.

Greg was fascinated by the stark contrast between their lives. Whilst he was free from any commitments, Carl was weighed down by obligation. Greg was emotionally unattached. Although women passed through his life regularly, he never considered settling down with any of them. Carl, on the other hand, married his high school sweetheart when he was only twenty, his daughter arriving the following year. Now, nine years later, he worked every shift he could pull as an orderly at a small exclusive clinic to the rich and famous, tucked away in the hills above the city.

"What sort of clinic?" Greg asked with interest. "Plastic surgery?"

"No," Carl's brow wrinkled. "It deals more with gynaecological matters, you know, infertility treatment, stuff like that. It's the place all the top female stars go to when they're pregnant, trying to get pregnant or don't want to be pregnant anymore." Greg nodded in understanding, and the conversation shifted onto other matters.

Another fortnight slipped by and the situation between Jake and Vivienne deteriorated. Resentment brooded and festered like an unwelcome houseguest that wouldn't leave, and Greg observed in alarm as the pressure mounted to almost unbearable levels.

Vivienne seemed to have embarked on new tactics, goading and baiting Jake until the fragile control on his temper came frighteningly close to snapping. He'd snarl with frustrated resentment at her, leave the room, then Vivienne would turn big blue eyes on Greg, tears swimming in their innocent depths.

"Did you see that?" she would cry. "He wanted to hit me. He was that close. Did you see?"

Greg didn't understand what game Vivienne was playing. If she planned to win Jake back, this guerrilla warfare was not the way to do it. He worried the pressure cooker situation was building up to crisis point, yet at the same time he couldn't shake the feeling he was watching a play, something staged, not real.

He wondered what to do for the best. Part of him wanted to catch the next plane home and leave Jake to lie in the bed he'd made. He should go to Lili and tell her he'd done his best and that she should forget about Jake. Forget about Jake and think about him maybe? Greg shook the disloyal seed of thought from his brain before it had a chance to take root.

A brief respite came when Vivienne went away for a few days. Jake seemed to almost revert to his normal self. Almost, but not quite. Staring into his beer, seething with hostile resentment, he barely touched the steak Greg had grilled to perfection.

Greg worried that unless the situation with Vivienne was resolved soon, Jake would go completely off the rails and do something foolish.

Vivienne returned and the atmosphere in the house became oppressively suffocating. Greg escaped to the diner whenever he could – to the familial, undemanding company of Annie and her family; and the casual, easy friendship of Carl. He fretted about leaving Jake alone in the house with Vivienne. He didn't know why, but he couldn't shake the feeling of events being manipulated to a climax.

One evening, Carl commented on how preoccupied Greg seemed and he sighed, making a flip comment on how his cousin and his wife were having marital problems and he was sick of playing referee. His smile didn't quite reach his eyes, and when Carl left the diner his face was thoughtful.

The next evening, he was back carrying a pink envelope with fairies drawn all over it. Slightly embarrassed, he handed it to Greg who studied it with interest.

"It's Lisa's eighth birthday this Saturday. We're having a little family cook-in, and we wondered, Mel and I, if you'd like to come. That's the invite and directions to the house. Lisa made it. She's very excited at the thought of meeting a real artist."

"Hey, thanks," Greg exclaimed with genuine pleasure, opening the envelope to find a sheet of matching pink paper also adorned with gambolling kittens and prancing fairies. He read the handwritten request to attend the eighth birthday celebrations of Miss Lisa Parks, followed by an address and specific instructions on how to get there.

"I'd love to come. Tell your wife thanks and I'll be there."

"The thing is."

Carl hesitated, friendly face worried as he toyed with the salt cellar on the table, almost as if unsure how to continue.

"The thing is ... Lisa ... well, she has a problem..."

"What sort of problem?" Greg enquired gently, and Carl sighed.

"When Lisa was born there were complications, Mel lost a lot of blood and nearly died. They had to operate on her straight away. I was so scared of losing her I didn't pay any attention to the baby until later when I knew Mel was going to be okay. Then, when I wanted to see my daughter, the doctors told me Lisa had problems; there was something seriously wrong with her head. She was deformed." Carl paused and swallowed hard.

"When I finally saw her, I couldn't believe it was my daughter; couldn't believe anything looking like that was human. I feel awful thinking about it now, but at the time, in that split second when I first laid eyes on her, I wished she'd died because the alternative, her living, was too terrible to think about."

Greg nodded his understanding, saying nothing, appreciating that this was, perhaps, the first time Carl had opened-up and talked, really talked, about the complex maelstrom of emotions he'd experienced through that traumatic time.

"The doctors gave some long fancy name for her condition, told me the statistics against it happening, but it didn't mean anything to me because it had happened to us. Against all odds, ours was the baby who was the statistical impossibility."

"What's wrong with Lisa?" Greg finally spoke, his eyes silently flicking up to meet Annie's as she started towards their table with the coffee pot. Almost imperceptibly, he shook his head, and her brows flew up in understanding and she returned to the counter.

"When she was born, the bones forming her face were fused as one solid piece. She's had surgery to enable her to breathe unaided and to allow her jaw to work. Her chances of surviving it were low, but she did survive. She's had six operations since then, and now she's able to breathe and swallow completely unaided. The bone is connected by artificial cartilage, so they'll grow as her face grows. Physically, Lisa's fine and everything works, but..."

"But ...?" prompted Greg when Carl fell silent.

"But her face is still not ... right. Oh, it's a lot better than it was, but it's still not normal, and I'm afraid of what the real world will do to my little girl. Mel didn't go back to work after Lisa was born. She needs around the clock care, and Mel's been teaching Lisa at home, but we can't keep her shut away any longer; she needs so much more. She deserves to have friends, a life, but it worries me. We live in such an appearance-obsessed world and Lisa, well, you'll see on Saturday. That's what I wanted to ask you, well, to tell you ..."

"Don't worry," Greg nodded his understanding. "I'll be careful. I won't hurt her..."

No matter how prepared you are for something, Greg thought following Carl through his small, cheery house and out into the backyard, it's never enough to help you cope with the reality. And the reality of Lisa Parks was enough to make his breath catch in his throat, and his eyes soften with compassionate sympathy.

Later, describing her to Lili, he'd say it was as if her skull was a ball of dough which someone held in their cupped hands, pushing one hand up and dragging the other down. Her face was not right. There were no other words to describe the misshapen, lopsided features of the otherwise elfin child who ran to greet him, cuddling an orange striped kitten, and chased by an enthusiastically barking, white fluffball of a dog.

Laughing, Greg crouched to check her flight as she flew up the deck steps, tripped over the dog, and upended herself into his lap.

"Whoa there, Princess," he exclaimed, his arms full of child, kitten, and dog. "Don't want to hurt yourself on your birthday."

Suddenly shy, Lisa scrambled to her feet and took refuge behind her mother's legs. A trim, petite redhead with merry green eyes, Melanie Parks was one of life's copers. Falling pregnant at nineteen had not been part of the plan but she shrugged her shoulders and dealt with it.

Giving birth to a special-needs child who demanded twenty-four-seven attention, and necessitated Melanie giving up on teacher training had not been part of the plan either. Melanie had put aside her dreams with only a small sigh of regret and instead had devoted her life to her daughter.

Now, Greg found himself being watched by two identical pairs of eyes. Those of the mother were smiling and inviting, but wary, as if waiting for him to say or do something inappropriate which would wound a much loved and protected child. Those of the child...

Greg looked into the solemn, watchful eyes of Lisa Parks, peering at him from behind her mother, her eyes the more beautiful for being set in such a ravaged face, and his heart constricted. Casually, he sat down on the deck steps.

"Well, now," he commented to Carl, gratefully accepting the beer he was offered. "Seems to me I heard it was someone's birthday today, but I can't see a birthday girl anywhere, can you?" Falling in with the ploy, Carl too pretended to look around.

"I can't think where Lisa's got to," he murmured, sitting down beside Greg.

"That's a shame," continued Greg, pulling two gaily wrapped packages and a large pink envelope from his bag. "Oh well, guess I'll have to take these home with me."

There was a subdued squeak, then a silence, during which Greg could almost hear her weighing up the options. Then a little pink pixie squirmed out from behind Mel's legs and tiptoed softly across to him.

"It's my birthday," she whispered, hands behind her back, eyes fixed on those mysterious, oh so inviting presents.

"Is it?" exclaimed Greg in mock surprise. "They have the name Lisa written on them. Is that your name?" Shaking with excitement, Lisa dumbly nodded her head. Greg smiled. "Well then, these must be for you," he said and handed them over.

Taking the presents, Lisa sat on the steps to open them. Wriggling with excitement, she ripped open the envelope to reveal a beautiful card that could be folded to make a fairy castle. Fascinated and delighted, Lisa folded the card into the turreted castle, showing it to the others so they could admire it too.

Next, Lisa dived into the presents, carefully tearing away paper with a restraint Greg thought admirable. Remembering frantic feeding frenzies under the tree on many a Christmas morning, when he and his sisters competed to see who could open their gifts first, he found Lisa's almost reverential unwrapping of her gifts touching.

Leaning back in his chair, he drank his beer, exchanging amused glances with Carl as Lisa finished opening the first present to reveal a pretty, sparkly pink dress, adorned all over with ribbons and sequins. Eyes popping with amazement, Lisa held the dress out to her mother who exclaimed with delight over it. The second present was quickly opened, yielding a sparkly crown, matching wand, and a pair of glittering, pink wings.

Greg grinned, pleased at the rapturous reception his gifts had received, feeling perhaps it wasn't completely honest to take the credit for them. After all, it had been at Lili's command he went shopping for birthday presents, her suggestion as to what to buy, and indeed her money which had paid for them. Still, he reflected, there was no need to bore the Parks with such mundane details, and he basked in the glow of giving.

Insisting on putting on her fairy outfit immediately, Lisa hurried into the house with her mother to change. Other people arrived, and Greg was introduced to Melanie's parents who'd come to stay the weekend, as well as neighbours from either side.

All greeted Greg cordially, yet their eyes remained cautious as if reserving judgement, until Lisa flittered back into the garden, a sparkly pink fairy all lit up with happiness, throwing herself into Greg's arms to thank him.

Gently teasing and tickling her, he glanced up to see expressions relaxing, realising they'd been anxious about how he would react to Lisa. It made him understand how much Lisa's parents had cocooned their child; how right they were to worry about exposing her to the unthinking cruelty of the public.

As the afternoon wore on and turned into evening, Greg relaxed and enjoyed himself. The company was interesting and genial, the beer cold and the food superb. It was a relief to be away from the strained atmosphere between Jake and Vivienne.

Almost unthinkingly, he took out his pad, drawing thumbnail sketches of Mel chatting to her mother, of Carl and his neighbours bonding over the barbecue, and a delightful one of Lisa's kitten, Tinker, which he presented her with, much to her joy.

Finally, inevitably, he found himself sketching Lisa as she lay in a garden chair, sleepily watching the grown-ups who constituted her world, packing up leftovers and chatting amongst themselves.

Engrossed, Greg didn't notice as one by one people observed what he was doing. Gradually, silence fell over the garden, and concerned glances were exchanged.

Mel moved forward opening her mouth to speak, only to be stopped by Carl placing a comforting hand on her arm, and gently, but firmly, shaking his head.

Finishing the sketch, Greg became aware of the quiet and glanced up, understanding dawning as he noted the worried expressions. Flushing slightly, he silently ripped out the sketch and handed it to Carl who looked at it long and hard, before passing it on to Mel, who glanced at it, then sat heavily on the steps, hand to mouth, lips trembling, eyes unblinking with unshed tears.

"I'm sorry." Concerned, Greg slid down to sit on the steps next to her. "I didn't mean to upset you. It's how I see her."

"No, no, you haven't upset me," Mel was quick to reassure, placing a warm hand on his arm, as she looked again at the picture of her daughter, face whole and wonderfully normal.

"It's beautiful," she continued wistfully. "Thank you. It gives us something to aim for, something to hope for."

The others clamoured to see, and the picture was passed around, exclamations and smiles of approval warming Greg's heart as he quietly studied Mel.

Finally, Lisa was whisked off to bed by her grandmother, after first stalling for time by demanding kisses from everyone present, and he was at last able to ask.

"Is there any hope for Lisa? Can any more be done?"

"Yes," Mel sighed. "There are operations which they think could make her face, they think, normal. But it's expensive ... more money than we have. We're saving. Our family and friends have been raising money too, but we still don't have anywhere near enough.

"But I thought you all paid medical insurance?" began Greg, confused. "Won't that pay for it?"

"We do have medical insurance," agreed Mel. "And it did pay for all the other operations, without which Lisa would be unable to breathe or eat unaided, but our insurance company has now decided

Lisa's fine. Any other surgery would be purely for cosmetic reasons and have said they won't pay for anymore."

"How much will the surgery cost?" Carl named a sum which had Greg breathing out a curse, shaking his head sympathetically. "That's a lot of money," he agreed, glancing down at the sketch Mel was still clutching. "But worth it..." he murmured.

Arriving back at Jake's house after midnight, Greg glanced at his phone, saw he had one missed call from Lili but wearily decided to phone her in the morning. He pulled off his clothes and crawled under the covers, falling instantly into a deep sleep, only to be jerked brutally awake again less than an hour later by his phone abruptly shrieking its annoyingly cheerful tune inches away from his head.

Cursing, Greg crawled up from the valley of sleep and fumbled for the phone, blindly stabbing at buttons until he hit the right one.

"Huh?"

"Hi Greg, it's Lili, how did it go? Did she like the presents?"

"Huh, Lili?"

Blearily, he blinked at the bedside clock, the numbers swimming in front of yawning eyes.

"D'ya know what time it is?"

"No, what time is it?"

"1:06am."

"Oh no, I'm so sorry, Greg, I keep forgetting. I'll call back tomorrow."

"No, s'ok, wake now, hold on."

Shaking his head slightly to clear the last remaining shreds of sleep, Greg pulled himself up in bed, swigged some water to relieve a beer dry mouth, knowing Lili wouldn't be satisfied with anything less than a full report of the evening's activities.

When he finished, a long silence fell. For a moment Greg wondered if he'd lost the signal, then Lili drew in a shaky breath, and he realised she was close to tears, if not actually crying.

"That poor girl," she murmured. "Oh Greg, that poor girl. If she doesn't have the operation her life will be a nightmare; bullied and tormented by other children, constantly made to feel different. And as for school ... no, that poor, poor girl."

"I know," Greg murmured, slightly taken aback at the depth of Lili's sympathy.

"I'm sorry," Lili seemed to become aware of the passing of time and the late hour. "I'll let you get some sleep. Sorry I woke you."

"That's okay, I'll call you tomorrow."

"Ok, night Greg."

"Night, Lili."

Greg hung up, snuggling down under the covers to try and get back to sleep, wondering about Lili's reaction to Lisa. Of course, everyone knew Lili was soft-hearted, but it was almost like Lili had personal experience of what Lisa would experience.

He shrugged, dismissing the thought, feeling drowsiness creep over him. As it tugged him under, he realised this had been the first call during which Lili hadn't mentioned Jake.

The phone's shrill tones shocked him awake again in what felt only moments later, dragging him from a dream concerning Mel Parks acting in a play at which he was the only member of the audience.

Confused – where the hell that had come from, true he'd always had a thing for redheads, but still – Greg rubbed at his sleep-encrusted eyes, peering at the clock, and groping for his phone.

"Yeah?"

"Greg, it's Lili again. Listen, I've been thinking and…"

"Lili," he groaned. "Learn how to do the maths."

"What? What do you … oh, sorry, what time is it?"

"5:16am precisely."

"Oh, sorry."

"That's okay," drawled Greg dryly. "Why do I need more than three hours' sleep?"

"Sorry, I'm sorry, but I've been thinking, and there's something I want you to do for me…"

Chapter Thirty
"I didn't do it!"

As he rang the doorbell of the Parks home early next evening, Greg couldn't help hoping Lisa would already be in bed. Not that he didn't want to see her again, he did but felt what he had to say to her parents would be best said when she wasn't present. Mel opened the door, a glad smile lighting up her tired face.

"Greg? Hi! What are you doing here?"

"Hi Mel, I was passing and thought I'd drop in and say thanks for last night. I had a great time. Also, I have something to give you."

"Really? Okay, you better come in."

She stepped back, and Greg followed her to the bright kitchen where he had interrupted her folding laundry.

"Please sit down," she invited.

Greg folded his long frame into one of the ladderback chairs, carefully avoiding Lisa's little white dog sound asleep under the table.

"Do you mind if I finish this," she asked, nimble fingers deftly sorting and folding. "I wanted to thank you," she continued, "for Lisa's present. She loved it. It was so thoughtful of you."

"It was nothing," Greg shifted uneasily. "Although I'd better come clean. The dress was Lili's idea. She was the one who told me a little girl who drew fairies all over her party invitation would probably love to have a fairy outfit."

"Lili?" enquired Mel, curiosity on her pretty face.

"Oh, Lili's a friend of mine. She's amazing. At first, you think there's not much to her; a nice enough girl, very pretty and fun-loving, but shy and reserved. When you get to know her better you realise how special she is; how loving and loyal and kind. She has this knack for collecting friends and surrounding herself with people who love her. In fact," Greg broke off at Mel's gently raised brows.

"You must miss her very much," she commented softly.

"Well, umm, yes ..." began Greg, then realised what she meant. "Oh no," he exclaimed. "You've got it all wrong. I'm not in love with Lili, and she's not in love with me. She loves Jake, my cousin, and he loves her."

"The cousin you're staying with?"

"Yeah."

"The married one?"

"Yes, but it's not like that either. It's ... complicated." Greg sighed. Mel put the last piece of folded laundry into the basket and stood it in the corner of the kitchen.

"Well," she remarked practically, "I'll make coffee and you can tell me all about it."

And because she was so sympathetic, and there seemed no harm to it, Greg did.

When he finished, there was silence. Mel drained her coffee and carefully set her cup back down.

"What a mess," she remarked gently. "I do feel deeply for your cousin and Lili, and although I understand and admire what she did, I'm not sure it was the right choice."

"That's what I thought," Greg shrugged. "But she has this thing about children not having loving parents ... about them being unwanted and unloved. She hasn't said much about it, but I get the feeling she went through something like that when she was a child. Oh, that reminds me of the reason why I came."

Carefully, he withdrew a folded piece of paper from his pocket and slid it across the table to Mel. "Lili wanted me to give you this."

Curiously, Mel unfolded the cheque, and her eyes flew wide.

"Greg, I can't accept this! Why this is ... this is..."

"It's for Lisa, for the operation. I told Lili the amount you said you needed, but she added a little more to it for extra expenses."

"But I can't take it, Greg." Desperately, she pushed it back across the table to him.

"Yes, you can." His large hand closed gently over hers. "Please. Lili can more than afford it and she wants to help. She told me to tell you no child was going to suffer like that, not if a little thing like money could help."

For long minutes Mel stared at the cheque, eyes brimming over with grateful tears. Then she carefully picked it up and tucked it into her jeans pocket.

"Thank you," she murmured. "And please, thank Lili. No, let me have her number and I'll call her myself."

Swiftly, Greg recited Lili's phone numbers, watching as Mel studiously wrote them down. He glanced at his watch, then rose to his feet.

"I must go," he commented.

Mel looked disappointed. "Must you?" she asked. "Carl will be home soon, and I know he'll want to thank you."

"Better not," he replied reluctantly. "Vivienne was going to some studio party this evening, but she never stays late, and things have got so bad between her and Jake, I'm almost afraid to leave them alone together."

"Your cousin's wife is an actress?" Mel asked as she escorted him to the door, the little white fluffball of a dog waking up and prancing along in front of them.

"Yes, Vivienne George. You must have heard of her." Distracted by Lisa's little dog, he bent to fuss over it and didn't see the look of complete and utter shock on Mel's face.

"Anyway, you should be the one to give him the good news. Bye. Tell Carl I'll..."

"Yes, bye Greg," Mel shut the door in his face leaving Greg standing on the doorstep, blinking with surprise.

Inside, Mel sank down at the kitchen table, face blank. She thought over what she had learnt that evening, adding it to what she already knew, and came to an unpleasant conclusion.

Slowly, with trembling fingers, she pulled out the cheque and stared at it, her face crumpling into a mask of indecision.

Back in his car, Greg fished out his phone and dialled Lili's number. It rang for a long time, and Greg drummed his fingers on the steering wheel wondering if she'd gone out, trying to work out the time difference in his head.

"Hello?"

"Hi, Lili, it's Greg, I've given Mel the cheque."

"Oh, good."

Greg stared at the phone, a little put out by Lili's lacklustre response. "Is everything okay, Lili?"

"Yes, everything's fine, I'm tired, that's all," her voice was low and disjointed.

Greg frowned at the change from when he'd spoken to her earlier. "Are you sure? You sound down?"

"No, I'm fine, honestly. I'm glad I could help them, but I need to go now..."

And for the second time in as many minutes, Greg was cut short by a woman.

Lili stood long moments by the window staring at the deserted street. A cold front had arrived the previous day, bringing with it snow that had settled and drifted over cars and pavements. It reminded her of the weekend she had spent with Jake, and a fist clenched around her heart.

Slowly, she wandered over to the sofa and sat, staring into the glowing heart of the fire as it popped and crackled. Boris rolled over and sat up, regarding her unblinkingly with his large, green eyes. She slid bonelessly off the sofa, cupped his head in her hands, and stared into that cool, green regard.

"Oh, Boris," she murmured. "What am I going to do?"

As Greg pulled into the driveway of Jake's split-level home, he saw with a sinking heart Vivienne's white convertible already there. Mentally preparing himself to face more tears and tantrums, or stony, pressure laden silence, he let himself in and wandered through the house in search of Jake, wondering if he was still locked away in his study frantically pounding out the next bestseller.

Passing through the kitchen he snagged himself a beer and ambled into the lounge, only to stop dead in consternation.

A lamp lay smashed to smithereens on the floor, the low table it normally stood on leaning drunkenly against the wall as though it had been tossed to one side.

Alarmed, he crossed over to it and saw the blood.

Carl Parks entered the gloomy house, vaguely anxious at the lack of light. Walking into the kitchen, he flicked the switch – startled to find his wife sitting at the table, staring at nothing in the dark.

"Mel? Is everything okay?" Fear gripped him. "Is Lisa all right?"

"She's fine. Sit down, Carl," Mel ordered. "We need to talk."

Blood, a puddle of it, lying at the foot of the stairs. For long seconds he stared, the hairs on the back of his neck rising. Blood, but whose was it, and how did it get there? Silently he mounted the stairs, heart thudding against his rib cage, eyes straining to see through the gloom. Quietly, he entered Jake's room, jumping forward with a cry of alarm at the body lying slumped beside the bed.

Kneeling beside his cousin, Greg desperately felt for a pulse, relief shooting through him when he found it, strong and steady. Quickly, he looked for any signs of injury, feeling all over his head and down his torso, there were none. As he checked, Jake mumbled something.

"Come on, Jake," Greg ordered, gently shaking him. "Wake up, big fella, up and at 'em," Jake muttered. As Greg bent closer, he smelt whisky. Sour and rank, it encompassed Jake in an alcoholic cloud.

"You're pissed!" Greg exclaimed, almost laughing with shocked relief, then he frowned. There was still the damaged furniture and bloodstains downstairs to explain away. If they weren't Jake's, whose were they? And where was Vivienne?

"Greg?" Jake's eyes fluttered open, pupils dilating as he struggled to focus. "What's going on?"

"You tell me," Greg replied. "What happened here?"

"I don't know." Jake sat up, rubbed an unsteady hand across his face, wincing with pain and clutching at his temples. "Damn this headache," he exclaimed, looking surprised when Greg snorted.

"Try hangover," he suggested mildly. "And as my mother would say, 'you've only yourself to blame. If you will down enough whisky to sink the Titanic'…"

"No, only had one," Jake speech slurred. He stopped and tried again. "Only had one, Vivienne poured it, then we argued…"

"What happened after that?" Greg pressed urgently. "Try to remember Jake."

"Don't know," Jake said again. "We argued," he repeated slowly. "Downstairs, or was it up here, then can't remember anything until I woke up on the floor with you prodding at me."

Greg stared at him in rising alarm, trying desperately to put the pieces together in any way which didn't look so bad for Jake. An excess of alcohol, a violent argument, broken furniture, bloodstains, complete memory loss … he shook his head in concern wondering where the hell Vivienne was, almost jumping out of his skin when the phone began to ring.

Mel finished talking and silence fell between them. Carl looked at the cheque. Finally, he sighed, looking at her with weary resignation.

"You're right," he said. "It has to be done. But if I get caught…"

"I know," she agreed quickly, clasping both his hands in hers. "You'll have to be careful, but we have no choice. It's the right thing to do."

"Greg?" The voice on the phone was low and shaky, almost unrecognisable.

"Vivienne?" he asked, and sensed Jake stiffen beside him. "Where are you? Are you okay?"

"No, I'm not all right," her voice faded, and Greg strained to hear. "I'm in hospital. Are you anywhere near Jake?"

"Yeah, he's right next to me. What's happened? Where…?"

"Well, in that case, I won't tell you which hospital I'm in, Greg, not after…"

"Vivienne! What the hell happened here? Why are you in hospital, are you sick?"

Jake stared at him in befuddled confusion. Greg felt his stomach churn with a sickening premonition he knew what was coming. That sense of unreality he had experienced earlier was back. He remembered his dream and felt again like he was watching something fake and unreal.

"Vivienne …?"

"I didn't go to the party, I went home to talk to Jake, to try and come to some sort of agreement, but we argued," her voice was trembling. Even over a crackly mobile connection, Greg could tell she was crying. "We argued, and he threw me down the stairs."

"What? But that's … he did what?"

"I'm bruised, I have a lump on my head the size of an egg, and I've scraped all the skin off my spine, I guess I'm lucky to be alive."

"I can't believe it. Vivienne, are you telling the truth?"

"Oh Greg," the voice was a distress-laden whisper now. "I lost the baby."

Briefly, Greg's eyes closed with despair.

"He got drunk," her voice continued. "So very drunk. Then he got angry, so angry. We argued. He threw a lamp at me. I ran upstairs to lock myself in my room, but he caught me, hit me, then he ... he threw me downstairs and left me lying there in a pool of my own blood," she exploded into a sob.

"I was in so much pain. I knew I was losing the baby, could feel it leaving my body. I screamed to Jake to call an ambulance, but he didn't answer. I think he'd passed out somewhere. In the end, I had to crawl to the phone and call one myself."

"Oh, shit, Vivienne, I..."

"They had to operate on me, Greg," her voice continued, remorseless, never-ending. "They had to. I was losing so much blood and they couldn't stop it. I ... I lost my baby, and I'll never be able to have another one, all because of Jake."

"I'm sorry, I..."

"You tell him, Greg, you tell him what's happened, what he did. Tell him, I'll be in touch soon to discuss terms."

"Terms? I don't understand. What terms?"

"The terms under which I don't go to the police and press charges." The line went dead. Slowly, Greg's hand dropped to his side, and he looked at Jake in horror.

"What?" he exclaimed. "What is it, Greg?"

"Trouble," replied Greg numbly. "That's what it is. Deep, deep trouble."

Tired of ringing the bell, feeling sure Lili was in, Kevin tramped around the back of the house through ankle-deep snow, letting himself in through the gate, and slipping over the un-swept path to the back door. Surprised to find it unlocked, he silently entered the house and heard music playing loudly from the lounge.

No wonder she didn't hear the bell, he thought in amusement, as Clannad wailed out the eternal question of what were they going to do without love?

Pulling off his boots, he left them dripping on the backdoor mat, then silently padded to the lounge door.

Lili sat on the sofa, one leg pulled up in front of her, a pale, thin cheek resting on her denim-clad knee. She stared, glassy-eyed with grief, into the glowing heart of the fire. Kevin didn't think he had ever seen anyone look so devastated.

He crossed to sit beside her, pulling her into his arms, and felt great shuddering sobs rack her slight body as she cried on his chest, kissing her silky soft hair as the music washed over them.

"I didn't do it!"

"But you can't remember what you did do."

"That's not the point, I'd never hit a woman, much less throw my pregnant wife down the stairs no matter how much I hated her."

"She says you were drunk."

"I only had one. I didn't even want that. She poured it, saying we both needed to relax. I remember her standing there holding out the glass to me. She poured one for herself but didn't drink it."

"What the hell happened then?"

"I think we argued, I can't be sure, it's all hazy. Damn it, why can't I remember? It's like a big chunk of my memory has been carved out."

"Okay, relax, I believe you, but it doesn't make any kind of sense. She can't be lying about the baby, I mean, it's not something she can lie about, so what happened?"

"I don't know … Greg?"

"Hmm?"

"How much trouble do you think I could get into if she did go to the police?"

"It's not going to come to that."

"No, I know, but if she did go?"

"I don't know. A lot, I think."

"Yeah, that's what I thought. Would it be classed as murder?"

"I don't know. Don't think about it, it's not going to come to that. We'll think of something. We'll figure this out."

Slowly, the sobbing abated until Lili lay quietly in his arms, drained and exhausted, a damp, hiccupping heap. Tenderly, he soothed the hair from her face, passed her a tissue, rocking and comforting her as you would a child.

"Oh Lili," he murmured. "Won't you tell me what's wrong?"

"I can't," she whispered.

"I know someone's hurt you. Who was he?"

"I'm sorry, please don't ask me."

"I could kill him for leaving you like this."

"No, you don't understand, it wasn't like that. He had no choice."

"Is he married?"

"Yes…"

"Oh, Lili."

"No, it's not like that either."

"Is there any way I can help? Anything I can do?"

"No," Lili shook her head emphatically, tears sliding down her still damp cheeks. "There's nothing you can do."

"Oh, Lili, I'm so sorry. Time's a great healer, you'll see. You'll forget about him."

"I won't, I can't."

"You feel that way now, but give it some time and..."

"I'm pregnant."

"Pregnant?"

Lili's eyes fixed on his face. "That's right. I'm going to have a baby, and I don't know what to do."

Kevin took a deep steadying breath as every constant in his life came crashing down about his ears.

For a moment he considered going, simply getting up and walking away from her, then he saw the fear and pain in her eyes and knew nothing had changed.

This was still Lili.

He still loved her.

"Well, there's one thing you could do."

"What's that?"

"You could marry me."

It had been almost twenty-four hours and still, Vivienne left them to stew. As they waited, Greg wondered and worried what this latest turn of events would mean for Jake and Lili. If Vivienne was to be believed, the baby was gone, and with it, Lili's reason why Jake should remain with his wife. But Greg had a bad feeling about what exactly Vivienne's 'terms' would entail, convinced she would rather see him rot in jail than fly off into the sunset to spend the rest of his life with another woman.

He was worried about Jake. Withdrawn and brooding, he moped about the house refusing to eat, barely sleeping, and jumping at every sound. Finally, when Greg was reaching the point where the thought of going to the police themselves was preferable to sitting and waiting, she rang – her call brief and to the point.

"I'm coming this evening, eight-thirty. Oh, and Greg. If I don't see you standing at the door, I'll simply drive away. I will not put myself at risk by being in the same house as that man." She broke the connection. Greg gestured helplessly at Jake.

"Eight-thirty, tonight."

"Okay," Jake frowned. "I don't care what she says, Greg, I didn't do anything to her, I swear it."

"I know, I know you didn't, but this evening when she gets here, you must try and hold your temper. Don't give her any ammunition." Jake nodded as Greg's phone once more began to ring, the number flashing up as unknown. Hastily, Greg answered, wondering if Vivienne was calling back with a change of plan.

"Hello, Greg? It's Carl."

"Hi, Carl. I'm sorry, now's not a good time..."

"Can we meet? There's something I need to tell you, something you should know."

"Umm, I don't know if I can right now. As I said, it's not a good time."

"Please Greg, it won't take long. It's very important. I could meet you at the diner, in say, twenty minutes?"

"Okay," Greg replied slowly, struck by the urgency in Carl's voice. "I'll see you there." He disconnected and looked at Jake, who raised his head to stare blankly back. "I'm going out for a while to pick us up some dinner," he commented. "I won't be long, okay?"

But Jake merely shrugged, his face drawn and worried.

It was snowing – fat, fluffy flakes – as it had been snowing that other day. Silently, Lili walked up the stairs of her parent's old house. She looked down at herself, knowing it was a dream, expecting to see herself as she had been then; plump and frumpy, but realised with a distant twinge of surprise she was still herself.

Stealthily, she reached the top of the stairs, peered through the door, knowing what she would find ... her parents making love on the sofa. She heard the swish of her mother's silk dressing gown; the soft, throaty cries as they reached climax.

She watched, dispassionately, with the eyes of an adult; her mother's blonde head thrown back in ecstasy, her father bending to take her breasts in his mouth.

All was as she remembered, and she wondered why she was dreaming of this moment in time. Surely it was in the past. Perhaps finding out she was pregnant was the trigger.

Maybe that was why she was revisiting the precise moment when she stopped hoping for love from her parents, or perhaps it was Kevin's surprise proposal.

In her dream, Lili felt herself frown ... Kevin. She had told him she needed time to think before she could give him an answer. He went away disappointed, but hopeful. Suddenly, the dream deviated from real life. Her mother's head turned, and she looked at Lili with a mocking smile on her beautiful face.

"You're too late," she smirked, and before Lili's horrified eyes her mother's face changed into Vivienne's sultry, pouting beauty.

"You're too late," echoed her father's voice. When she looked, he too had changed, into Jake, his face twisted in a sardonic smile.

"Didn't you know?" Vivienne asked, throwing her head back in a gale of mocking laughter. "Didn't you realise?"

Lili sat bolt upright in bed, heart racing, a sticky sheen of perspiration slicking her body, its dampness making her nightgown cling. With shaking hands, she switched on the lamp, its warm glow throwing light into the darkest shadows of her mind.

Yet still, the dream haunted her...

Carl was already there when Greg arrived, sitting in his normal booth, glancing towards the door nervously. His relief at seeing Greg was palpable.

Greg sat opposite, and Carl slowly slid a large white envelope across the table towards him.

"First of all," he began. "I want you to know this has nothing to do with the amazing thing you and your friend Lili have done for Lisa. I like to think I would still have done this even if you hadn't given us the cheque." Confused, Greg nodded.

"We didn't make the connection, you see. We didn't realise who your cousin's wife was, not until you told Mel last night. When we realised, when we understood what had happened, well, I went into work today and made copies of this."

He tapped the envelope, drawing Greg's eyes towards it. Carl stood up, held out his hand, which Greg shook, still confused as to what exactly Carl had given him.

"Good luck," Carl said, pulling on his jacket. "Oh, and Greg, I'd appreciate it if you kept it to yourself where you got this from. I risk more than losing my job if anyone found out."

"Sure," agreed Greg.

"See you around, Greg."

"Okay, bye Carl. Say hi to Mel and Lisa for me." Greg watched as Carl made his way to the door, saying goodbye to Annie as he passed the counter, the swing door banging shut behind him.

Slowly, he opened the envelope, sliding out the wedge of papers it contained and started to read. A minute later he straightened in disbelief, and a smile spread across his face.

Lili moved through the day as if still asleep. She puzzled over the dream, wondering why her subconscious had connected her parents to Jake and Vivienne. She also knew Kevin was waiting for an answer yet felt incapable of making such a momentous decision.

On the one hand, she knew and trusted Kevin. He was a dear friend and she loved him. If she married him, her baby would want for nothing.

Instinctively, she knew he would be the very best of fathers; kind and loving. A part of her craved for the family they could be...

But ... he wasn't Jake, and she wasn't in love with him.

She drifted through her work, unfocused and distracted. Her colleagues noticed her preoccupied manner and wondered. After work she wandered home, hesitating outside; unwilling to go in, not wanting to be alone.

On a whim, she climbed into her car and headed out of town, seeking something, not sure what. Realising she was headed towards Johnny's, decided to visit for a while. Perhaps his easy company would relieve her troubled mood.

Lili parked her car outside the cottage and knocked on the door. There was no answer, and she shivered in the chill March breeze, wondering if he was in his workshop in the garden.

Carefully, she picked her way over the churned-up ground and let herself through the gate, grateful to reach the firmer footing of the patio. A movement through the full-length windows had her glancing into the lounge, where she saw them.

She froze in place, the scene burning into her eyelids. The couple entwined on the rug in front of the fire, completely oblivious to her presence; the scattered remnants of a picnic and the overturned empty bottle of wine told the story of fireside late lunch interrupted by a spontaneous burst of passion.

From where she was standing, she could see their faces locked together in a deeply intimate kiss. She watched in stunned, voyeuristic fascination as Johnny moved slowly between her thighs, his powerful, bare shoulders braced above her, dark hair falling forwards as he tenderly cupped her head in his hand.

Lili couldn't see much of her, long tanned legs revealed by her rucked-up skirt, a slim arm curving possessively around his back.

She turned to go, embarrassed to be spying on Johnny and his latest conquest when some nagging sense of recognition made her turn back.

The woman arched her spine, long black hair falling away, face tipping up until Lili could see her features. She felt the breath catch in her throat. It was Lindy.

She ran, the image was too painfully close to her dream to deal with, slipping across the icy ground and desperate to get away, the bitter taste of betrayal in the back of her throat.

Johnny and Lindy?

When had this happened?

How had it happened? Lili didn't understand, and fresh hurt punched at her heart.

Greg watched through the window in silence as the cab pulled up in front of the house. It was exactly eight-thirty. He saw Vivienne's shining blonde head leaning forward to pay the driver. He walked to the door and opened it, standing so she could see him. She looked at him through oversize sunglasses which didn't quite manage to hide the bruising on her right cheek. Her mouth tightened.

He turned to cast a glance towards Jake sitting at the table, his eyes glittering with anticipation.

"She's here," he murmured, and Jake's expression hardened.

"Good," he replied, a wolfish smile spreading slowly across his face. "It's showtime…"

The train jolted, pulling away from the station, and Lili let out the breath she hadn't realised she was holding. Racing away from Johnny's, the image of them branded into her vision, a desperate urge for flight had gripped her. When she reached home, she phoned Conrad, pleading to come and stay for a few days.

Startled by the stark despair in her voice he agreed immediately, asking what was wrong. But Lili had brushed away his concerns, merely saying they'd talk when she arrived.

As the train gathered speed, hurtling through the familiar countryside, Lili felt an overwhelming sensation of escape; of putting space between herself and her friends.

She wondered if she would ever be able to face Johnny and Lindy again after seeing them together like that. As for Kevin, Lili shifted uncomfortably on her seat.

Part of her was grateful to him for offering her and her baby his name, but a small part of her was angry; angry at him for wanting to change the dynamics of their friendship, and for daring to say he loved her and forcing her into this situation.

They sat at the table, the three of them – Vivienne on one end, Greg and Jake opposing her on the other. She sensed their united hostility towards her, and a small smile teased her painted mouth. She'd show them.

This time she was the one with all the power.

She would have it all.

"We need to talk," she began, voice thin and wavering, as befits a woman who's been to hell and back.

"Okay," agreed Jake smoothly. "Talk."

"Because of you, I lost my baby. Not only that, but I can never have any more children. I think that entitles me to some kind of … consideration, don't you?"

"Cut the bullshit, Vivienne."

Jake's snarled command made her jump. She glanced nervously at Greg's blank dispassionate face, afraid of the raw anger she saw in Jake's eyes.

"All right," she sobbed, fingers flying to her face to gently touch the livid bruise marring her ripe beauty. "There's no need to be so hostile towards me, Jake. This is your fault. You're the one who lost your temper and violently abused me in my own home. I'll never forget it as long as I live. You picked me up and threw me down the stairs, I'm lucky to be alive, but I lost my baby … our baby…"

She paused for effect, sobbing desperately into her hands. Disconcerted by the stony, detached expressions on their faces, she pushed on with her prepared speech regardless.

"If you only knew what it felt like, lying there, feeling our baby drain away from me," she shuddered delicately, allowing a tinge of anger to touch her voice.

"But how could you know? You're only men. You have no idea what it's like to carry a child in your womb. To love it more than life itself, then to lose it. I lay in my blood, Jake, begging for you to help, but you didn't, I had to crawl to the phone myself and call for an ambulance, all the time knowing it was too late. And then ... and then ..." she gulped for air, tears pouring down her face.

"To be told by the doctors that I will never be able to conceive again, how can you possibly know what that feels like? How can you even begin to make it up to me?"

She dropped her head into her hands and waited, heart beating, knowing she'd given the performance of a lifetime, and waiting for her audience's reaction. When it came, it wasn't quite what she'd been expecting.

They clapped, slowly and together.

Vivienne raised her head to stare at them in disbelief as they applauded her, their faces twisting into almost identical expressions of amused disdain.

"Congratulations, Vivienne," drawled Jake. "I always knew you were one hell of an actress, but I must admit, I had no idea how good you really are."

"What ... what are you talking about?" stammered Vivienne uneasily.

"I'm talking about this," snapped Jake, sliding a wedge of photocopied papers across the table towards her. Instinctively, Vivienne caught them. She glanced at the top page, heart almost stopping as she realised what they were – her gynaecological notes.

"They make interesting reading," mused Jake mildly, enjoying watching his wife's dawning horror as she flicked the pages.

"I especially like the repeat prescriptions for the contraceptive pill you were taking the whole time we were allegedly trying for a baby. Not very fair, Vivienne, making me think I was the one with the problem."

"Nah," drawled Greg, idly examining his nails. "I like best the bit where she got herself artificially inseminated. The thought of you lying on your back with a turkey baster between your thighs, Vivienne, what an image!"

"And then, we get to the interesting bit," Jake leant forward, eyes narrowed to murderous slits. "The fact you had an abortion and were sterilised two weeks ago. So, if you had already murdered our baby, how is it possible for you to have lost it when I allegedly threw you down the stairs?"

"I ... I ... these notes are forgeries, it's made up ..." Vivienne was floundering on treacherous ground as she watched all her clever fabrications unravel.

"Shall I tell you what I think happened here that night, Vivienne?" Not waiting for her answer, Jake pressed on regardless.

"You came home with the deliberate intention of picking a fight with me. You insisted I have a glass of whisky which you'd already doctored, I'm not sure which drug you used, but I'm guessing it was something like Rohypnol, the date rape drug. As the drug was taking effect, you lured me upstairs where I passed out in the bedroom. You then sprinkled whisky over me to make it appear I'd passed out drunk."

"I don't know what you're talking about." Vivienne's eyes darted between their steely stares, heart hammering with fear.

"Shut up, Vivienne," Jake commanded mildly. "Now, where was I? Oh yes, you smashed the lamp and smeared blood on the floor. That was a nice touch, by the way, really added a layer of authenticity. You then called a cab and drove away, knowing Greg would be home soon and would find your little stage set, assuming the worst."

"No, no, you threw me down the stairs," Vivienne insisted, throwing her head up to face them both bravely. "Where the hell, did I get this from then?" she demanded, indicating the colourful bruise on her temple.

"Oh, yes, the bruising. Again, a nice touch. Greg," Jake turned to his cousin, who grinned with anticipation, "would you do the honours, please?"

"It would be my pleasure," replied Greg, and pulled a small pack of make-up remover wipes out from under the table. With one stride he was on her, pushing her head to one side, swiping at the bruise with a wipe.

"Take your hands off me!" ordered Vivienne, struggling futilely in his strong grasp. Greg grunted with satisfaction and held up the wipe onto which the bruise had transferred.

"Excellent makeup job, Vivienne," he commented, strolling back to his seat. "Very convincing, but I knew there was no way Jake would ever raise his fist to a woman, even one as evil as you."

"You bastard!" she spat, eyes flashing blue fire at them both. "You're jealous because I was with him. Maybe it's time your dear cousin learnt the truth about you..."

"Vivienne..."

"How we were lovers before I married him. How you tried to get me into bed whilst we were married. It's true!" she shrieked, as Jake raised an eyebrow, exchanging an amused glance with Greg.

"I know it is," he commented, and Greg smiled as Vivienne's mouth dropped open. "Well," he continued lazily. "I know the bit about you being lovers before you met me is true, as for the other, I know Greg well enough to know that's a lie."

"I told Jake about us ages ago, Vivienne," explained Greg scornfully. "I wasn't comfortable keeping secrets from him, so came clean about it last year."

Vivienne slumped in her seat, defeated. Every weapon in her arsenal had been deployed. She sat, alone and vulnerable, as Jake lazily got to his feet and planted both palms on the table. Leaning forward, he faced her with a smile of satisfaction.

"Now then, Vivienne, what would your adoring public think if this sordid little tale was leaked to the press?"

"You wouldn't!" she gasped, already imagining the headlines.

"Wouldn't I?"

Jake's smile widened.

Suddenly, Vivienne was very afraid he would. Shaken, she paled as she saw her perfect image being tarnished; her perfect life crumbling to dust.

"I might be persuaded not to contact the press..."

Jake paused, and Vivienne's head slowly raised, resignation in her eyes.

"Now," Jake smiled, "why don't we discuss terms. My terms..."

Kevin leant against Lili's fridge, watching as Boris tucked into his dinner with relish, confused and worried by Lili's text saying she was on her way to London for a few days to think about things and would he mind feeding Boris.

He didn't mind, of course, he didn't, but wished Lili had given him some indication of what her answer to his proposal was going to be. She needed time, he could appreciate that, but couldn't help feeling if you needed time to think about something, probably the answer was going to be no.

He looked up as her phone began to ring, a wild hope clutching his heart that it was Lili calling to speak to him. After all, she knew he'd be here now, feeding her cat for her. Quickly, he picked it up.

"Hello?"

"Hi, is Lili there please?"

Not Lili, a man's voice. American, and vaguely familiar.

"No, sorry, she's gone up to London for a few days. Can I take a message?"

"London?" the man ignored his offer, again recognition of his voice nagged at Kevin. "Has she gone to stay with Conrad?"

"Umm yes, I'm sorry, who is this?"

But whoever it was, had gone, and Kevin slowly hung up the phone, wondering why the call had left him with a vague sense of foreboding.

"She's not there." Jake hung up, turning to face Greg who was watching him with anticipation. "She's in London, staying with Conrad."

"I have Conrad's number," offered Greg eagerly.

"No, I'm not going to call her." Jake seemed to decide.

"What? Why not?"

"How can I explain all this over the phone?"

Jake gestured helplessly with his hands, and Greg's face twisted with consternation.

"So, what are you going to do?"

"I'm not going to call her," repeated Jake, a grin splitting his face. "Hell, I'm going to jump on a plane, fly to London and get the girl. Are you coming?"

Greg grinned in reply. "You bet!"

Chapter Thirty-One
"There's something else I have to tell you..."

What am I going to do? The question burnt in Lili's mind, and she was struck by the awful irony of her situation. She sent the man she loved back to his wife so his child wouldn't grow up without a father. Now she was pregnant and facing the prospect of her child being fatherless. Lili's mouth twisted in a wry grin of black humour.

Concerned about the pale, quiet little ghost who arrived on their doorstep, Conrad, and Matthew hurriedly cancelled plans to take her to dinner, instead deciding to eat at home. Conrad desperately wanted to press her for answers but was reined in by Matthew's insistence they let Lili talk in her own time.

Gradually, the tranquillity of their luxurious apartment and their undemanding, easy company began to relax Lili, and she felt her defences start to crumble.

Finally, Matthew judged the moment was right and sat quietly beside her, placing a comforting arm around her shoulders, and pulling her close for a fatherly hug.

Lili glanced up, flashing him a small, scared smile. Hearing Conrad banging around in the kitchen, and seeing Matthew's kindly concerned face turned towards hers, she felt it was time to talk to someone. She had to let all it all out before she went mad.

"There was someone ..." she began hesitantly. "Someone I loved, but it couldn't be. I had to send him away. It hurts ... so much ... that we can't be together, even though I know what I did was right."

"The right thing is often the most painful," Matthew agreed.

"I know Conrad has told you about my childhood, about Phyllis, my parents ... Well, I went to see Johnny and found him with Lindy. They were – I saw them like my parents were that time."

"You saw Johnny and Lindy making love?"

"Yes, through the window, I didn't mean to spy on them. It was an accident."

"Did you overhear them talking about you?"

"No, of course not, but ... it brought it all back. Especially following the dream..."

"What dream?"

"I had a dream," Lili paused, anxiously gnawing at her lip. "I dreamt about the day I saw my parents having sex on the sofa, only they turned into ... other people."

"What people?"

"My lover ... and his wife."

"He's married then?"

"Yes. But when we were together, he was separated from her."

"I see," Matthew hesitated and considered going into the whole issue of dreams, their subconscious meanings, but decided against it. "So, you feel somehow betrayed by your friends?"

"Yes. It's silly of me, they've done nothing wrong. If they are a couple I should be pleased, because now I've thought about it, I realise how perfect they'd be together."

"I think, given time, you will come to terms with your friends' relationship and will be able to wish them well. As for this man, if he has gone back to his wife, perhaps it would be best if you tried to forget him."

"It's not that simple."

"Oh?"

"I'm pregnant."

"Oh," Matthew paused, taking a deep breath. He squeezed Lili's hand. "I see."

"And I'm scared, Matthew, of being alone. Of raising this baby by myself. It terrifies me," Lili faced him, her eyes steady and determined. "A child needs two parents and that's why I think I'm going to accept Kevin's offer."

"What offer is that?" Matthew asked, his heart sinking.

"He's asked me to marry him."

"That's a very big step, Lili. Are you sure? Do you think you could love him?"

"I don't know," Lili shook her head sadly. "He's one of my best friends, I love him very much, but he's not ... my baby's father. I don't think I could ever love anyone the way I do him."

"If you feel that way, Lili, you need to ask yourself whether it would be fair, on yourself, the baby, or Kevin, to enter knowingly into a loveless marriage."

"He says he loves me. I know he would love the baby ... I don't know, maybe it will be enough. But I can't do it alone, I can't."

"But you wouldn't be alone, Lili. You are blessed with many wonderful friends who all love you very much. You wouldn't be raising this child alone. We'd all help."

"I suppose," Lili paused, shaking her head in confusion. "I don't know what to do for the best, I need to think about it some more."

"I'm confident you'll make the right decision, Lili," Matthew gave her hand another squeeze. "Now, why don't we go and tell Conrad he's going to be an auntie?"

The next morning Lili overslept and awoke to find herself alone in the apartment, Conrad and Matthew having already left for work. She sighed and stretched, thinking over the previous evening.

After his initial shock, Conrad had been ecstatic at the thought of being an uncle. As he enthused about colour schemes for nurseries, baby clothes and names, Lili felt a small thrill of excitement as it finally struck home that she was going to have a baby.

Wonderingly, her hand touched her still flat stomach, amazed that growing inside her was a new life. Slowly, she rolled over in bed, trying to sort out her jumbled emotions.

Did she want it?

Yes, the answer came back instantly.

Yes, she wanted the baby with an intensity that almost made her weep. This baby had been created by love; the love she bore for Jake, and the love he had for her. Even if she never saw him again, she would at least have his child.

Feeling more positive Lili got out of bed, wondering what to do with the day. First, breakfast. Since falling pregnant she had discovered skipping meals was no longer an option. The baby wanted, demanded, she start each day with a big, healthy breakfast. Lili quickly showered and wandered into the kitchen to raid the fridge.

As she was finishing the last slice of strawberry and yoghurt topped waffle, her phone rang. Lili hastily swallowed her mouthful and picked up the phone, frowning at the unfamiliar number.

"Hello?" she began cautiously.

"Hello, Phyllis?"

"Umm, yes."

The voice was familiar, Lili could hardly believe...

"It's Lionel, your father."

Shock rendering her incoherent, she gaped futilely at the phone.

"Hello? Are you still there, Phyllis?"

"Yes, I'm still here. How did you get this number?"

"From your answerphone message. Phyllis, I'm in London for a few days and wondered if I could come down to see you?"

"I'm in London too," she mumbled, thoughts in a whirl.

"You are? Well, that's even better. I was wondering, Phyllis, hoping, that I could take you to lunch?"

"To lunch?"

"Yes, but only if you want to," he added hastily.

Somehow, the doubt and hopeful uncertainty in her father's voice made her realise she did want to see him.

"I'd like that," she replied quietly.

"Splendid," his response seemed genuinely enthusiastic. "Give me your address, and I'll come and collect you."

In the three years since Lili last saw her father, he had changed drastically. Still a handsome man, his bookish good looks now seemed faded, washed out, as if life had taken a walk across his face, leaving him defeated and beaten.

When Lili opened the door to him, he saw a beautiful, confident young woman, glowing with health and vitality. For a second felt a jolt of pride that this was his daughter.

Wonderingly, his eyes roamed over the lavish apartment, appreciating its classic dignity. Unable to resist, his fingers brushed wistfully over the stunning pieces of sculpture Matthew collected.

"This is a lovely apartment," he commented. "Is it yours?"

"Mine?" Lili turned startled eyes onto him and laughed. "Good heavens no, it belongs to friends, I'm staying for the weekend."

"Oh, I see."

Gallantly, her father helped her into a warm coat. Although the snow had now all but faded, a bitingly chill wind was blasting at the windows, reminding all that winter had not quite relinquished its grip yet.

"I suppose you're not used to the cold anymore," Lili commented as they left the apartment, locking the door behind them. "It's quite warm over there in New Zealand, isn't it?"

"It's very changeable. The locals say you can have all four seasons in one day, and I must confess it does sometimes seem like that."

Lili smiled as her father escorted her into the waiting taxi. She could handle this, she decided. It was going to be fine.

An hour later, she was not so sure.

They had journeyed to the restaurant in almost total silence, her father making a few desultory comments about the changes in London, before lapsing into his thoughts. Lili desperately racked her brains to think of a topic other than the weather but could think of nothing to say to him.

In the restaurant, the busyness of being seen to their table, ordering drinks, and looking at menus filled some time, but then the waiter left, and they were alone, looking at each other with fixed smiles.

"I must say," her father remarked, "it's lovely to see you looking so well, Phyllis."

"Could I ask you a favour, Dad?" Lili decided to take the bull by the horns.

"Of course, anything," her father paused, looking concerned. "What is it?"

"Well, nobody calls me Phyllis anymore. Everyone calls me Lili."

"Lili. That's very pretty, it suits you. Yes, yes of course, if that's what you prefer."

"It is."

"Then, of course. I must confess, I never did like the name Phyllis, but your mother insisted it was your grandmother's wish," he broke off, looking thoughtful. "I'm not sure she got that right, though," he murmured, almost to himself.

"Where is mother?" Lili didn't care but thought it polite to ask.

"She's here, in London, with me, of course."

"Is she well?"

"She's ..." her father paused, and a look of sadness swept over him. "No, Phy ... umm, Lili. No, she's not well at all, I'm afraid."

Lili looked at him in consternation. "What's wrong with her?"

"She's in the early stages of Alzheimer's. It was a terrible shock when she was diagnosed. She's always been so healthy, and then this, it was a dreadful blow."

"Yes, I can see it would be," Lili murmured, confused at the maelstrom of emotions she was experiencing. They were talking about the woman who made her childhood a living hell; who bullied and mentally tortured her; but ... Alzheimer's? That was a fate Lili would not wish on anyone. Gazing with sympathy into her father's heartbroken eyes, she realised it had more than one victim.

"I'm sorry," she said, touching his hand with genuine compassion. "I'm so sorry, for both of you."

"Yes, well, that's why we're in London," he continued, taking his glasses off and rubbing at his eyes. "We're here to see a specialist. Certain drugs can ease the symptoms, but of course, there's no cure, no cure at all." He paused, clearing his throat.

"Anyway, why don't you tell me about yourself? Are you well? Happy?"

"I'm very well, thank you. I'm up for a promotion at work."

"Really? What is it you do, exactly?"

"I work in an employment agency. I'm the receptionist, but one of the seniors is leaving and Ms Evans, that's my boss, has asked me if I'd like to take on the position. Of course, it will be a little difficult for me ..." Lili let her voice trail away, staring pointedly at her father.

"Difficult? Why's that? Why will it be difficult for you?"

"Because of my dyslexia."

"Your ... dyslexia?"

Her father stared in consternation as the waiter bustled over with their starters. He waited, eyes fixed on her face, as the man fussed about with pepper, napkins and topping up glasses, before finally getting the hint they were waiting for him to leave and waltzed off back to the kitchen.

"Yes, that's right, Dad. Dyslexia. Turns out I'm not stupid or special needs. I'm severely dyslexic. Something which should have been realised when I was a child."

"Dyslexic! Oh, my word, but that's ... are you sure?"

"Yes, I'm sure. When my boss talked to me about taking on a more responsible position, I told her I thought I might be, and she arranged for me to be tested. It's definite, I have severe dyslexia."

"I see." Her father picked up his knife and fork then put them back down again, not seeming to know what to say. "I'm sorry," he said eventually.

Lili shrugged. "It's all right, I'm coping with it. It was a relief to find out what the problem was. You see, I spent my whole childhood believing I was some sort of abnormal retard. It would have helped if I'd known I'm not, but better late than never I suppose."

"I'm sorry," her father said again, gesturing helplessly with his cutlery.

"There's something else you should perhaps know ... I'm pregnant."

This time her father was speechless, and a tiny part of Lili enjoyed watching him gape like a landed trout.

"That's right," she continued calmly. "You're going to be a grandfather."

"I see," he managed finally as he took a large gulp of wine. "And the father?"

"Is married, so can't be with me," Lili replied, surprised at her cool, level tone.

"Right, umm, yes, I see."

"Although, a friend has asked me to marry him and has offered to adopt the baby. I think, on reflection, it might be the best solution all round."

"Maybe," he looked at her with a worried expression. "But do you love him, Lili?"

"He's one of my best friends," Lili replied, completely wrong-footed by his question. "I care for him very much, and we have similar interests…"

"Are you in love with him, Lili?"

Her father leant across the table – his eyes earnest.

"Marriage is one of the hardest things in the world to get right. There has to be love, deep and abiding love, otherwise, it's doomed to failure."

"He says he loves me. Maybe, in time, I could learn to love him."

"And maybe not," retorted her father. "If you have any feelings at all for this man, Lili, you know you can't short-change him with marriage to a woman who doesn't return his love. It wouldn't be fair to do that to a friend."

"I know," whispered Lili, miserably. "But I'm afraid of raising this child alone."

"I don't see why," replied her father, offhandedly.

"After all, you raised yourself, and you turned out all right…"

After lunch, Lili and her father lingered over coffee, both feeling a bond, albeit tenuous, had been formed; that a new understanding had been reached between them. As Lili watched her father pay the bill, she realised at least her child would have a grandfather, even if he did live on the other side of the world.

He insisted on escorting her back to the apartment. If she was honest, Lili had rather enjoyed the experience of being with her father, having lunch with him. It seemed so ... normal.

"Would you like some more coffee?" she asked at the front door.

"I better not," he frowned at his watch. "I promised your mother I wouldn't be late."

"Does she know you were meeting me?" Lili asked curiously.

"No," he shook his head regretfully. "The illness has made her a little irrational about a lot of things; I didn't want to risk upsetting her." He patted Lili's arm apologetically, and she smiled to show she understood.

"Well, bye Dad, thanks for lunch. It was ... nice," she hesitated, pressing a quick kiss to her father's cheek.

"So, isn't this a pretty picture?"

Lili and her father looked up in alarm as her mother sauntered around the corner, her body language hostile, and her expression accusing. Lili stared in dismay.

Her memory of her mother was of an immaculately turned-out woman, hair always sleek, make-up flawless, nails perfectly painted talons. But now ...

Was this her mother?

This wild-eyed, wild-haired woman, whose ripped and bitten nails had not seen varnish for a very long time? True, she was wearing make-up, but it was smeared and inexpertly applied as if a child had been given free rein with the cosmetics box.

"Now, Elizabeth ..." her father began, stepping forward, his hand held out.

"Don't you, 'now Elizabeth me'," her mother snapped. "I had my suspicions you were carrying on with someone. Meeting an old colleague, hah! You think you can fool me, but I knew what you were up to, creeping out to meet some little tart."

"Elizabeth, please."

Her father sounded weary, rather than upset. Lili wondered how often he had to deal with this, and her heart ached for him. Instinctively, she stepped forward to shield him, and her mother's accusatory gaze swung onto her.

"And as for you," she started. "You cheap little whore. He's a married man, old enough to be your father. Have you no shame?"

"Mother?"

Elizabeth Goodwin stopped dead in her tracks, confusion crowding into her eyes. She shrank back.

"Mother ..."

Lili took a step forward and her mother cringed away, shooting a terrified, pleading glance towards her husband.

"Mother, it's me, Phyllis."

"Lionel?"

The voice was the whine of a bewildered and terrified child, and her husband hurried to her side, gathering her up in his arms.

"Ssh," he soothed. "It's all right. You don't have to worry about anything."

"She said she's Phyllis, but she can't be, can she?"

Her mother peered at her over her father's shoulder, and Lili saw there was no spark of recognition at all.

"She can't be Phyllis. Because Phyllis is dead. Isn't she?"

Lili gasped in shock, and her father shot her an apologetic look.

"I'm sorry. She has good days, bad days, and occasionally very bad days. This is one of them. I need to take her back to the hotel."

"Of course," murmured Lili, trying to reconcile the monster from her memory with the pathetic, plainly ill woman rocking gently in her husband's arms. She was looking at Lili as if she were the monster; the one to be feared.

"Thank you for lunch," she added, as he gently began to steer his wife away.

"Take care of yourself, Lili."

He stopped at the corner, readjusting his wife in his arms, shooting Lili a meaningful glance.

"Take care of both of you. If ever you need me, you have my number."

"Lionel? Who is she? Where are we?"

"No one, Elizabeth, we're on our way back to the hotel."

"I want to go home."

"We are. Soon, very soon."

When Conrad and Matthew returned, they found Lili packed and waiting, a fiercely determined look in her eyes and a newly acquired air of resolve settling around her shoulders like a cloak.

"I have to go home," she explained, her chin lifting with determination.

"I have to stop running away and expecting everybody else to fix things for me. I'm a grown woman. It's time I started acting like one. I have a responsibility to myself and my baby, and I will do what's right. What I must do to ensure the best life possible, not only for my baby but for myself as well."

"Sweetie," Conrad exclaimed, almost silenced by the quiet maturity in her voice. "Are you sure? You know you're welcome to stay as long as you like."

"I know," replied Lili, gently kissing him on the cheek. "Dearest Conrad, if the definition of a mother is someone who prepares their child for life, you've been more like a mother to me than my real one. I thank you from the bottom of my heart, for all you've done for me. Both of you," she broke off to hug them. "I love you both. Don't worry about me, I'll be fine."

"What time is your train?" Matthew gently enquired, seeing Conrad was unable to speak. "We'll drive you to the station."

Later, driving back after seeing Lili safely onto her train with more hugs and promises extracted to take care, Matthew flashed a glance at Conrad.

"There are tissues in the glove compartment," he commented mildly, and Conrad sniffed disdainfully.

"I am not welling up!" he snapped, fumbling for the tissues, blowing his nose loudly and shooting Matthew a furious look.

"Well, even if I am," he continued. "It's a very emotional moment, our little girl all grown up and having a baby of her own."

"You're right, it is" agreed Matthew gently, bestowing such a look of tenderness upon him that Conrad buried his nose in the tissue again.

"Oh, Matthew," he exclaimed. "Do you think she'll be all right?"

Matthew was silent for a long while as if solemnly considering the question from every angle. Conrad peered curiously at him over the top of his tissue. Finally, Matthew nodded and smiled.

"Yes," he said slowly. "I rather think she will be."

Having splurged on a first-class ticket, Lili found herself alone in the compartment, so determined to make the most of it. Taking out her phone, she decided to make the easiest call first and dialled Lindy's number.

"Hi, it's Lili."

"Hey Lili, how's London?"

"Fine, I'm actually on my way back."

"That was a quick visit."

"Yes, it was. Umm, Lindy ... do you have something to tell me?"

There was a long, long silence. Lili waited, a small smile playing over her lips as she sensed her friend's consternation.

"You know about...?"

"About you and Johnny? Yes, I know."

"But how...?"

"It doesn't matter how I know, I wanted to tell you how happy I am for you both. To tell you I love you and that I think you two are perfect for each other."

"Oh, Lili! I'm so relieved you know. We wanted to tell you, but you seemed so down we thought it might upset you."

"Yes, I have been sad, but I'm not going to be anymore, and the one thing that has cheered me up is the thought of my two best friends together."

"It's not just a relationship," Lindy confided, obvious relief in her voice at finally being able to tell Lili the truth. "He's asked me to marry him."

"No!" shrieked Lili in delight.

"Yes!" Lindy shrieked back. "Wait until you see my ring. It's awesome."

"Oh, my word, Lindy, that's so amazing!"

A sudden thought struck Lili and her eyes went wide.

"Oh, oh, Lindy. You're going to be the future Lady Felsham."

"Yeah, I know," commented Lindy dryly. "Not too shabby for an Essex girl, hey?"

"No," agreed Lili happily. "Not too shabby at all."

They parked the car and rode the elevator to the apartment in silence. Matthew, knowing Conrad was feeling emotional, wisely left him with his thoughts.

He merely opened a bottle of wine and poured them both a glass, smiling as Conrad sipped distractedly from his, plainly still thinking about Lili.

The door entry phone buzzed, and they glanced at each other, startled, the same thought flashing through their minds ...

Was it Lili? Had she come back for some reason?

"Yes?" Matthew spoke into the intercom.

"Hi, Matthew, it's Jake..."

"And Greg..." piped up a familiar voice.

"Can we come up please?"

Matthew looked at Conrad who shrugged, his perplexed expression mirroring Matthew's own as he pressed the door release button.

"I didn't even know they were back from America," Conrad murmured. "What on earth do you think they want?"

"I don't know," Matthew replied, eyes thoughtful. "But I have a feeling..."

"What?" interrupted Conrad eagerly. "What is it?"

"I think," Matthew continued, "we may be about to get the last piece of the puzzle."

Conrad stared at him, but before he could enquire any further, they were there. Immediately, the tranquil, peaceful atmosphere of the apartment was shattered.

They crowded into the spacious room making it feel small, their bulky overnight bags, red-rimmed eyes and spiky chins telling of a long journey and no sleep.

"Where is she?"

Conrad frowned at the blunt opening question.

"Where's who?"

"Lili, where is she?"

"Well, she's gone..."

"Gone? Gone where?"

The urgency in Jake's voice lit fires of alarm in Conrad. He leapt to his feet, hands fluttering with consternation.

"She's gone home. We just put her on the train..."

"Shit!"

"Jake, what is it? What's the matter? Why are you looking for Lili?"

"Where's your wife, Jake?"

Matthew spoke for the first time.

Jake glared at him, meeting Matthew's calm, slightly accusing gaze with a guilty defensive one of his own.

"She's in Mexico," he replied. "Getting a divorce."

"I see," Matthew nodded as if everything had become clear. "So, you'll soon be a free man."

"That's right," drawled Jake almost fiercely.

Conrad's eyes practically popped out of his skull, as the penny suddenly and resoundingly dropped.

"Oh, my God!" he cried. "It's you, isn't it!"

He pointed a quivering finger at Jake.

"You're the mystery man. You're the father of Lili's baby."

"What?"

"What?"

Conrad stopped, aghast, at the twin expressions of shock which exploded from Greg and Jake. The cousins exchanged glances, then Jake stepped up to Conrad almost seizing the smaller man by the collar.

"What did you say?"

Conrad shrugged apologetically, shooting a frantic look at Matthew who smoothly placed a gentle, though firm, hand on Jake's shoulder.

"Why don't you sit down, Jake," he suggested.

Jake sank obediently onto the cream-coloured leather, his face a mask of stunned disbelief.

"Lili's pregnant?" he turned almost pleadingly to Matthew. "It's not true, is it?"

"Yes, it's true," the older man confirmed. "Lili's pregnant, and you're the father."

His expression softened as Jake raked a shaking hand through his hair.

"The question now, Jake, is what are you going to do about it?"

He didn't answer his landline so Lili phoned his mobile, almost hoping he wouldn't answer, even though she had an overpowering desire to sort everything out before she got home. It was irrational, she knew but was maybe part of her new resolve to take control of her destiny.

Seeing her mother, finally confronting her past, and realising it no longer had the power to hurt her, had had a profound effect on Lili. She felt energised, empowered, mistress of her destiny – her own and her baby's.

There was a click, and he was there. Lili's heart skipped a beat.

"Hello, it's me," she replied in answer to his greeting. "I've been thinking a lot about you and about me, and I wanted to talk to you."

Lili felt the expectant silence emanating down the line and took a deep breath before continuing.

"First of all, I want to say thank you for being my friend. For always being there for me and for always being so supportive and understanding. And now, when I needed a friend more than ever, for once more coming through for me. You are truly an amazing man, Kevin."

Lili paused, took another deep breath, and continued.

"I think you're going to be a wonderful husband, and I know you'll be the best father ever…"

Parked on the roadside where he'd pulled over to take the call, Kevin rested his head on the steering wheel, tears of relief in his eyes.

"What am I going to do?" Jake gazed at the three waiting, expectant men and his mouth twisted into a go-to-hell grin. "I'm going to go get her, that's what I'm going to do." He snapped his fingers at Greg. "Car keys," he demanded.

"You haven't slept in over forty-eight hours," protested Greg. "Do you think it's a good idea to drive now? Why don't you get some sleep and go tomorrow?"

"I'm going!" Jake insisted. "You going to stop me?"

"Hell no," replied Greg, tossing him the keys, and stifling a yawn. "I hope you're not expecting me to come. Gooseberry is so not my colour."

"Call us," demanded Conrad as Jake headed towards the door, new purpose in his stride. "Tomorrow. Call us and let us know what happened. You!" He turned on Greg, who looked alarmed. "You're staying to dinner and are going to tell us everything, and I mean everything."

Matthew followed Jake to the door and placed a hand on his shoulder. "Drive carefully," he ordered. Jake gave a sharp nod. Matthew's grip tightened and Jake looked at him, brow raised in enquiry.

"I think you should know," Matthew began, lowering his voice to avoid being overheard. "Lili told me that her friend Kevin asked her to marry him and that he wants to adopt the baby."

"The hell he did!" Jake's jaw tightened. "And what was her answer?"

"She was seriously considering it."

"Well, she can just un-consider it then, can't she?" replied Jake, with a rakish grin.

When Lili finally reached Bury St Edmunds night had fallen, and a fine, misty drizzle was shimmering in the streetlamps. She was late. She'd missed her connection and had to sit, fretting and fuming, over a cup of hot chocolate at Cambridge station until she could catch the next train an hour later.

Now, she was tired and hungry. She wanted to go home, have a shower, and an enormous plate of dinner. To be alone and think over the life-changing consequences of the answer she had given Kevin.

She walked out of the station. As usual, there were no taxis.

"Hey, pretty lady," Lili froze at the familiar drawl, her heart thudding. "Need a lift?"

He was leaning nonchalantly against a car, arms crossed, blue eyes intently watching her. There was a long, heavy stillness as she studied him, shock buzzing through her system.

He was here, but he should be thousands of miles away with Vivienne. His clothes were rumpled, his hair tousled. He looked tired, his eyes were bloodshot, and dark shadows lurked beneath the brilliant blue gaze. At least a day's growth darkened his face. Lili had never seen anything so beautiful in her life.

"Hi," he murmured.

Lili shook her head in confusion. "You're here, but you shouldn't be. Where's Vivienne?"

"In Mexico, getting a divorce," he replied, and Lili stepped forward in shock.

"A divorce? But, what about the baby?"

Jake's face darkened. She saw something flash across his face and settle in his eyes – a profound sadness and regret. Unconsciously, she took another step towards him.

"Jake?"

He sighed and briefly shook his head. "There is no baby, not anymore," he paused, looking her straight in the eye. "Vivienne had an abortion," he stated flatly.

Lili gasped, hands flying instinctively to her stomach. "An abortion?" she echoed in horror and gently touched his shoulder. "Oh, Jake, that's awful, I'm so sorry."

"You know, even though I never wanted the baby because it was the one thing stopping us from being together if I'd known what she was planning ... If there had been any way I could have stopped her, I would have. You must believe me, Lili."

"I do," she murmured, hand gently stroking his rough cheek. "I'm sorry," she said again.

"Oh, Lili," Jake sighed, a world of wanting in his voice. Lili's hand fell to her side.

"There's something you need to know," she said.

Jake's face split into a grin. "No, there isn't," his large hand tenderly rested on her stomach.

"I didn't do it on purpose," Lili cried desperately. "To trap you, I mean, I didn't..."

"Ssh," Jake's fingers pressed lightly to her lips. "I know you didn't. Hell, you're nothing like Vivienne. There are no lies or secrets between us. You're my Lili. I know exactly what you are."

"No lies?" Lili repeated, taking a small step back. "But there is, Jake, I'm not who you think I am."

"Well, who are you then?" laughed Jake.

"Lili's not my name. I was born Phyllis. Plain, stupid, frumpy Phyllis. I changed my image and my name when I was eighteen. That's when I became Lili, so everything you think I am, is a lie."

"That so?" enquired Jake casually, his mouth twitching into a smile at her earnest nod. "Lili, I don't care what your name was or what you changed it to. You're still you. Besides, changing your name is something we understand a lot in my family, Daisy's real name is Margret, mine is Jakob and as for Greg ... Gregory's only his middle name. His real name is Viktor..."

Lili's brows shot up. "Viktor?" she murmured.

Jake's eyes warmed with the shared joke. "Yeah, don't tell him I told you. So, you see, Lili, it doesn't matter what you call yourself. It's who you are inside that counts. As far as I'm concerned, you're Lili. The most beautiful, sweetest, kindest woman I've ever known. The woman I intend to spend the rest of my life with."

Lili's bottom lip trembled, tears welling in her eyes as she realised for the first time that Jake was right. It didn't matter what label someone gave themselves. After all, would she love her friends any less if she discovered their names were not the ones they were born with? Would she feel any differently about Amy, Lindy, Martin, or Kevin ... Kevin...?

Her heart stopped, remembering a decision reached on the train, a vow made, a promise given. She looked at Jake with trepidation.

"There's something else I have to tell you..."

Chapter Thirty-Two
"You look awfully pale, as if you'd seen a ghost."

The small country church was dressed for a Spring wedding, its pews crowded with smiling people dressed in their finest awaiting the arrival of the bride and admiring the stunning arrangements of Spring blooms the bride had insisted on. No showy, hothouse flowers for this wedding, instead, the pew ends, and the altar glowed with the bright, smiling faces of daffodils, tulips, irises, and crocuses.

At the front of the church, both traditionally handsome in morning suits with pale blue waistcoats and cravats, Kevin and Johnny surveyed each other nervously.

Kevin tugged at his cravat, sure no matter how much Amy had fussed with it, it still wasn't right.

A sudden swell of organ music and the rustle of the congregation rising to its feet – all necks craning excitedly towards the back – brought lumps of anticipation to the throats of both men.

Johnny clapped Kevin encouragingly on the shoulder.

"Sounds like we're off," he murmured.

"Yeah," Kevin replied, giving up his cravat as a bad job.

"It's okay," stated Johnny firmly. "We can do this."

"We can do this," agreed Kevin. "We've got the rings?"

"We've got the rings," agreed Johnny.

"Okay," breathed Kevin. "Let's do it."

Both men stepped into the aisle, turning to watch the wedding party as it made its way towards them.

The bride was stunningly beautiful in a rustling swirl of ivory taffeta which Lili had joked made her look like a giant meringue.

Her dark hair was swept into a complicated knot on the top of her head, where a delicate crystal tiara shimmered and twinkled, holding an antique lace veil that frothed and foamed almost to the floor.

Besides the bride, beaming with pride, walked Martin, still not quite believing he had been asked to give her away. His eyes constantly slid sideways as if to reassure himself she was still there, and that he was doing his job correctly.

Behind the bride glided a pair of bridesmaids, both slim and petite, both gorgeous in lilac silk, their bouquets of spring flowers matching pretty circlets of flowers encircling one dark head and one fair.

Amy flashed a smile at her fellow maid as they slowly paced down the aisle, following their best friend to her wedding.

Lili looked around the crowded church, carefully measuring her paces, not too fast, not too slow, heart swelling with happiness at the thought that every single person she loved in the world was there.

She passed a pew containing Tom and Muriel; Tom's rugged maleness looking strangely at home in a well-cut morning suit; Muriel resplendent in a large peach hat.

Beside them sat Richard, very frail now, yet still sprightly and upright. His eyes caught hers, and a beaming smile of encouragement broke out over his face.

Daisy and Guy were sitting together, yet seeming strangely apart, and Lili frowned slightly to herself. She was worried about Daisy, knowing the couple's attempts to have a baby had met with one failure after another, and that Guy was now pressurising Daisy to go for tests. Daisy was uncertain and fearful. Lili hoped they would find a way to get what they both craved so much.

Conrad and Matthew were next wearing smart morning suits. Sharing smiles of pleasure, they watched the wedding party proceed down the aisle.

Next to them was Sid, anxiously chewing on a nail as he watched the bride gliding to her wedding, in the dress he designed for her.

The bride reached the top of the aisle. The music swelled to a crescendo then stopped.

Absolute silence fell on the church.

The famous photographer, Daniel Craven, a friend of Johnny's, was poised to take the perfect picture as the groom tenderly lifted the veil away to reveal his bride's glowing face.

"Dearly beloved…" began the vicar.

The congregation settled down to enjoy the glory and quiet solemnity of a traditional, English church wedding.

Lindy placed her hand in Johnny's.

Facing the vicar, they pledged their hearts and souls to one another forever.

Feeling her feet pinch in new satin shoes dyed lilac to match her bridesmaid's dress, Lili resisted the urge to fidget, lips twitching into a smile as Kevin, Johnny's best man, caught her eye and flashed a mock disapproving frown.

Kevin…

Lili could still remember as if it were yesterday, the conversation they had on that fateful day when her life had changed forever.

"You are truly an amazing man," she said. "I think you're going to be a wonderful husband, and I know you will be the best father ever ... one day."

"Lili, please ..." he breathed, and she winced at the pain she was causing him.

"I'm sorry, Kevin, so sorry," she said. "But I love you too much to make you second best because you deserve so much more than that. You deserve to be with someone who will love you unconditionally in return and will give you children of your own."

"But I want to take care of you, Lili," he pleaded desperately. "Of you, and the baby..."

"And you can," exclaimed Lili. "Because, I'll admit it, Kevin, I'm scared stiff of having this baby on my own. I'm going to be counting on my friends, all of my friends, to help me through this."

After a long silence, Kevin sighed. "I love you, Lili."

"I know," she replied, gently. "And I love you too."

Now, Lili watched him, blond and handsome in his morning suit which strained to fit across broad shoulders, as he rummaged in his waistcoat pocket to produce the rings.

She hoped he'd soon meet someone special to love him; take away the tinge of sadness that lingered in his eyes, especially as Amy had finally bought a house of her own and moved out, leaving Kevin alone in the cottage.

Lindy and Johnny were exchanging rings now, eyes meeting in private vows of their own. It reminded Lili of her wedding to Jake the previous June when she had simply and quietly, walked into the registry office in a column of cream silk Sid had designed for her. It's clever draping over the waist concealing a slight, four-month pregnant bump and made her vows to love and cherish and protect.

Conrad had given her away, Lili feeling it would be insensitive to ask Kevin. As they shared a glass of champagne, waiting for the car, Conrad had fussed gently over her dress and hair, eyes suspiciously bright, and Lili realised she was having an emotional mother and daughter pre-wedding moment after all.

Her eyes met and locked with Jake's, a look passing between them as if he were aware of her thoughts and shared them.

She remembered how worried he had been that evening outside the train station, when he'd asked her to share his life and she hesitated, afraid to confess another promise she had made – a vow to herself that her child would be raised in her grandmother's house.

The house, which was now so much a part of Lili, the thought of leaving it was inconceivable.

He laughed with quiet relief at her worry that he would want to uproot her, take her away from the life she'd created for herself, and try to replant her in America.

No, he insisted, a writer could write anywhere. He'd live anywhere, so long as she was there too, and they could make frequent visits to America to see his family.

So, they married without fuss and ceremony, a simple and stylish occasion which suited the pair.

The reception had been held at home. Lili's happiness at having their home bulging at the seams with family, friends, and loved ones, had known no bounds.

Five months later, Jake had hastily flown halfway around the world from a book signing tour in the States to be with his wife, when she went into labour three weeks early and gave birth to their first child.

And there she was, sitting on her doting father's knee; five-month-old Phoebe Kolinsky surveying her surroundings with wide, brilliantly blue eyes, a legacy from her father.

Lili's face softened into a maternal beam of pride, smiling as her precious baby clutched hold of her father's blue cravat in damp, sticky fingers and stuffed it into a gummy mouth, where she managed to inflict quite a lot of dribble damage before it was rescued by Jake.

He frowned at the stained cravat, shooting a fierce look at the amused Greg sitting beside him.

Lili turned a smiling face forward.

Yes, life was sweet.

Watching her best friend Lindy marry her best friend Johnny, the future Lord and Lady Felsham, she thought it couldn't get any better.

Two weeks later, Lili was a woman on a mission. As she shot into a space in the car park and glanced at her watch, she realised she was also a woman who was running an hour late and silently cursed her husband and his libido.

He had walked into their bedroom after putting Phoebe down for her nap, silently watching in brow-raised admiration as his wife pulled on new lacy red underwear, which he then persuaded her to take off.

Her mouth curved into a smile.

Oh, but it had been fine.

Frantically, she snatched a trolley and dashed into Waitrose, pulling Amy's crumpled list from her pocket as she checked the time on her watch.

She realised, with a sinking heart, that in one hour the newlyweds would be arriving at Johnny's cottage to find a surprise welcome home from honeymoon party in full swing, and that Amy would even now be wondering where the last-minute shopping was.

Tugging self-consciously at her new, chocolate brown jeans, Lili began to toss things into the trolley, knowing Amy was probably waiting to create some fabulous salads and cursing Lili's tardiness.

Lili and Jake had spent five days in London last week to celebrate the release of Jake's latest book. To commemorate Lili finally regaining her pre-Phoebe weight, Conrad and Sid had whisked her off clothes shopping, leaving Jake and an indulgent Uncle Matthew to look after the baby.

They had fun, and Lili had been talked into buying several pairs of the latest, hipster, bootcut trousers. Being petite and slim they suited her, making her appear taller, but she'd learnt to be cautious of bending down or stretching up as several inches of underwear appeared if she did.

Everything on the list was now in the trolley, except the olive oil Amy needed to create her famous salad dressing.

Desperately, Lili's eyes ran along the shelves of oil above the freezers, knowing how fussy Amy was about olive oil. She searched each bottle and label with a growing sense of panic.

Finally, she gave in and called her.

"Hi honey, it's Lili! Yes, I'm in Waitrose now, I know, sorry, running a little late, but I've collected the wine and champagne and picked up the cream, baguettes, pate, brie, nibbles, and fresh fruit. Was there anything else you needed? Right, okay, thing is, they don't have the olive oil you needed to make the dressing."

Lili listened as Amy gave a suitable alternative, tucking the phone under her ear as she searched along the shelf.

"Okay, yep, they've got that one, shall I get it instead? Okay."

She plucked the desired bottle from the shelf.

"Anything else? No, okay, I'm on my way back now. Has everyone arrived? Oh, they're going to be so surprised, I can't wait to see their faces. okay, bye, see you soon, love you."

Lili disconnected, slid the phone into her bag, right, that was it. Now all she had to do was hit the checkout and then…

She froze as emotion swept over her. An intense wave of longing, pain, despair, and need. It rooted her to the spot, unable to move, struggling against its negativity.

Slowly, cautiously, she turned, tears starting to her eyes at the raw anguish she was suffering, feeling instinctively it was not her pain affecting her, rather it was somebody else's that was somehow being projected onto her.

There was no one there.

Disbelievingly, Lili stared up and down the aisle, not sure what she was looking for. Everything seemed normal except for an abandoned trolley practically touching her own.

Frowning, she gazed at its contents, shuddering slightly at the heap of salt, sugar, and fat-laden articles it contained. Who on earth would want to eat such rubbish?

She reached to push the trolley away and a spark of static electricity shot through her fingertips triggering a thought, a memory, and her frown deepened.

"Are you all right?"

Lili started. A motherly looking woman wearing the store's uniform was gazing at her with concern.

"I'm sorry?" Lili dragged her attention to the woman with difficulty.

"Are you all right?" the woman repeated. "You look awfully pale as if you'd seen a ghost."

"Perhaps I have," murmured Lili, wonderingly. "Perhaps I have…"

Chapter Thirty-Three
"She's going to be fine, just fine."

First day of term. A new school year. The playground bulged with excited, noisy throngs of children all busily renewing old ties and old resentments, except for one group – those children for whom this really was the first day. They hung back, huddling against the shelter of their parents' legs, watching the older children racing and shouting with wide-eyed envy, coming together in tightly knit little cliques, shrieking holiday news to each other.

She was short and silent. Her long, dark hair moulded itself to her small, neat head as she peered anxiously through a too-long fringe trailing in bespectacled eyes, her shy anxiety and nervousness apparent in the constant chewing of her bottom lip, and the way she clutched her shiny new school bag protectively to her thin chest.

"Hello."

She looked up in silent wonder at the bright and beautiful apparition that danced across to stand in front of her. She gazed with wistful longing at the stranger's strawberry-blonde curls caught up in pink ribbons, that should have clashed but somehow didn't, and up at the other girl's freckled-faced, open confidence.

"Hello," the pink princess said again, smiling. "It's my first day today, is it yours?"

Dumbly, she nodded, wondering if she could persuade her parents to buy her pink ribbons and tie her hair up that way.

"Good. I hope we'll be in the same class."

The princess waved her arm towards a small knot of children standing behind her, also staring at the shimmering, bright light that was the strawberry-blonde princess.

"That's Harry, Daniel, Mariah, and Laura. We've made a gang. We're all going to sit next to each other in class. Do you want to be in our gang too?"

The dark-haired girl nodded shyly, a sudden, happy smile spreading across her face, lightening her features, and sprinkling prettiness where before there'd only been anxiety.

"Okay," agreed the princess happily.

She took the hand of her newly acquired comrade and led her over to the others, where they shuffled shoes and surveyed each other, bonding as only five-year-olds can.

On the edge of the playground, anxious mothers, and a few fathers, equally anxious but hiding it behind a blasé façade, watched as their precious little ones took their first steps towards independence in the real world.

"Do you think she'll be okay?" Jake asked, worry tugging at his voice, and Lili smiled.

"I hope so," she murmured, watching as Phoebe ran off with her newly found friends to examine the play equipment.

Silently, she looked around, it felt strange to be back in a school environment; odd to be standing here, watchful, hopeful that her daughter would fare better than she did and wouldn't suffer at the hands of other children the way her mother had.

Here, Lili's jaw tightened, Phoebe wouldn't be bullied because she, her mother, wouldn't allow it.

Unthinkingly, she rubbed at her eight-month swollen abdomen, and Jake slipped a supportive arm around her shoulders.

"Is he kicking again?" he enquired.

Lili nodded ruefully, leaning back for a moment into the solid support of her husband.

"You've been doing too much," he murmured in concern. "Maybe you shouldn't go and see your mother this afternoon."

"No, it's okay, I'll be fine. I haven't been for several days, and Dad looks forward to me coming. It gives him a break."

"Want me to come with you?"

"Would you?"

"Sure."

Lili smiled her thanks at her husband and rubbed again at her stomach, thinking of her mother and how her condition had drastically deteriorated over the past four years.

So much so, her father had been forced to give up his job in New Zealand and had moved back to Bury to be closer to Lili and the support of his family.

Jake had been reluctant to let Lili have much to do with her mother. Tales of her childhood chilled him to the bone, arousing fierce indignation that she should help such a woman.

Then he realised how much Lili wanted to do it; how in some strange way it was cathartic.

Gradually, he relaxed his guard around her parents, to the extent he and her father often enjoyed a game of chess or a debate about literature.

Lili couldn't explain why she felt the need to visit her mother, only that it was something she had to do, almost feeling that by returning her mother's cold cruelty with kindness, she was somehow cleansing away the past.

She sighed as she watched her daughter interacting with the other children, remembering her last visit. As usual, her mother had been completely oblivious to her identity, relaxing around her purely because of the familiarity induced by Lili's frequent visits.

Lili had gently washed her face and brushed her mother's thinning hair, all the while murmuring small talk about the weather and what Phoebe had been up to lately.

Listening to the antics of her small granddaughter always seemed to relax her mother, even if she didn't comprehend the relationship between them.

"Thank you."

Lili had knelt to slip on her mother's shoes. At the sound of her voice, low and quivering, she glanced up, startled, to find her mother looking at her almost as if she knew her.

"Phyllis?" she murmured.

Lili started to shake.

"Mother? Yes, it's me, Phyllis..."

Her mother studied her for a moment, then smiled, a sad apologetic little smile.

"I'm sorry," she murmured. "So, sorry, Phyllis..."

Her eyes closed wearily, and then she was gone again, vanished into the jumbled maelstrom of her mind.

Thinking of that moment, Lili felt again the sensation of peace and acceptance which had swept over her, in that instant knowing she had fully forgiven her mother for the past.

It was over.

Lili could finally, completely, let it go and move on with her life.

Phoebe dashed up to them, face glowing with excitement, trailing her small band of disciples behind.

"Mummy, Daddy," she exclaimed, full of self-importance. "This is Harry and Daniel and Mariah, and Laura, and this ..."

She pulled forward a slight child with long dark hair, bemused large brown eyes blinking through oversize glasses with obvious signs of hero-worship of Phoebe's confident vivaciousness.

"This," she continued, "is Mathilda, but we're going to call her Tilly. We're all friends and we're going to be in a gang together, like you and Uncle Johnny and Auntie Lindy and Auntie Amy and Uncle Martin and Uncle Kevin."

"That's wonderful, darling," exclaimed Lili, hugging her glowing child, and straightening one of the bows in her strawberry-blonde hair.

"Come on," ordered Phoebe and dashed off, her devoted little band of followers rushing dutifully after her.

"Do you think we need to stay?" asked Jake, pulling his wife close, watching the small group of children rush across to the chalked hopscotch to noisily begin a game.

"No," Lili shook her head, smiling with relief. "I think we can go now. She's going to be fine, just fine."

Together they walked to the gate, pausing for a moment to look at their bright daughter with her new friends.

Lili wondered if it was another gang in the making, pressing a quick, thankful kiss to her handsome husband's cheek.

"What was that for?" he enquired, eyes crinkling with love.

"Just because," she replied. "Because I love you."

"My Lili," he murmured, as she leaned against him.

They watched the next generation at play, and then, after a while, they went home.

~The End~

If you have enjoyed this book,
then why not continue the adventure with
Lili, Jake, and all the gang?

Chaining Daisy

Volume Two
of the
Perennials Trilogy

Now available as an eBook, paperback,
and free to read on Kindle Unlimited

Keep reading for a sneak preview
of the opening few pages

Prologue

She should be happy. Why wasn't she happy? She was young, healthy, and married to a fabulous man who adored her. They were comfortably off so had no money worries, all their family were well and happy, and she had lovely friends. She was currently sitting in a pretty country church, surrounded by people she liked, attending the wedding of two of those friends. To top it all off, she had a nice dog. So, why wasn't she happy?

Daisy shifted on the hard pew and felt, rather than saw, the look Guy flicked her way. Instinctively flinching from him, she straightened. Arching her spine into the firm wooden back of the ancient, uncomfortable wood, she reflected on how they were designed to keep sinners' backs erect, rather than comfort unhappy women in their mid-twenties.

Yes, she was unhappy. You might as well admit it she thought fiercely, and a sudden urge to cry, to bury her face in her hands and bawl her eyes out like a toddler denied, swept over her. Blinking rapidly, she swallowed it down, burying the rising tide of panic – something she had been getting good at lately.

Concentrate, she told herself and forced her attention to the front of the church. Ah, a sudden surge in music and the Wedding March crashed out from the enthusiastic organist's fingers. There was a combined rustle as the congregation collectively rose to their feet, and the bridal party progressed slowly down the aisle.

Lindy was being given away by Martin. The grin that split his youthful, handsome face, and the careful way he led the glowing, ivory silk-clad bride to be married, managed to bring a small smile to Daisy's face. She remembered Lili telling her how stunned and proud he had been when Lindy asked him, in the absence of any other father figure in her life to give her away.

Lindy ... beautiful, exotic Lindy, her black hair coiled elaborately around her head, a veil of finest gossamer shimmering over her shoulders. Never had Daisy seen her look so radiant. Her eyes met those of her handsome, soon to be husband, waiting for her at the top of the aisle.

Then came the bridesmaids, gorgeous in pale lilac silk, flower circlets on one blonde and one brunette head, their young faces glowing with happiness for their friend. Lili briefly glanced her way, and for a second Daisy thought she saw a flicker of concern cross her best friend's expression before she turned back to the job at hand and the moment had passed.

The bridal party reached the top of the aisle, the music subsided, and there was another scramble as the congregation sank back down. Daisy looked at Johnny and Kevin, magnificent in morning suits, their faces solemn with the importance of the occasion.

Kevin fumbled awkwardly at his waistcoat pocket and Daisy hoped he had remembered the rings, feeling a rush of warmth towards him. She had never forgotten how kind he had been to her the night of Lili's 21st; the night she discovered her hopes of being a mother were yet another false alarm.

How he had comforted her and advised her not to tell Guy that evening – but to wait until they were back in London so as not to spoil Lili's party. Recalling the scene that had followed her confession to Guy, Daisy shuddered slightly, thankful she had done as Kevin advised and delayed telling her husband until they were home.

Kevin flexed his toes in his new shoes, lord how they pinched, longing for the comfort of his old gardening boots. He glanced over at Johnny and Lindy holding hands, exchanging vows, their young faces alive with so much love and hope.

Kevin swallowed, a sudden yearning to be looked at that way by someone, anyone, searing through him. Pathetic loser he thought bitterly, not allowing his glance to even think about flicking backwards to where she stood.

Lili.

The woman he loved more than anything else in the world. There had been a moment – a brief glorious instant last year – when he thought, maybe, there was a way she could be his.

True, she was pregnant with another man's child, but it seemed impossible for her to ever be with that man, so Kevin had stepped forward and offered her his name and his heart, wanting to look after her and the baby and make them both his. Then he would have the family, and the woman, he had been dreaming of for years.

It wasn't to be.

Life had turned so that Lili got her Jake, the man of her dreams. They married last year, and Kevin had stood there with the others, watching her accept his ring, his pledge, his hand, and his heart.

Should have been me, he had thought then. Should have been me, he thought now, knowing if she glanced at anyone it would be at Jake and their baby daughter, Phoebe. He was happy for her though. No, really, he was. It was obvious to anyone who had eyes how totally in love she and Jake were. They were the golden couple, the perfect match. And he was happy for her. He was. It was just...

Lindy and Johnny had exchanged vows and were moving away to sign the register. The congregation burst into a rousing chorus of All Things Bright and Beautiful, the only hymn the bride had known so that was the one she had picked.

The photographer, that Daniel Craven chap, followed them, fussing about, moving the vicar to a more suitable spot, and flirting with the bride. He was world-famous, apparently, but Kevin had never heard of him and didn't much care for him either.

He had watched the way he chatted up the ladies, all warm, blue eyes and rugged, bearded good looks – arrogant prick. Still, he was a friend of Johnny's and was doing the wedding for free, so that was something.

Finally, the service was over. They moved down the aisle, Kevin escorting Lili as head bridesmaid, heart stumbling at the feel of her small hand on his arm, her laughing presence by his side. Pacing behind the newlyweds – trying not to stand on the bride's veil – his eyes found those of Daisy, Lili's London friend.

For an instant, he remembered a shared moment on a dark staircase – the tears of an unhappy, scared girl soaking the front of his shirt, and her whispered confession. He smiled at her, but her attention was already gone, back to that bastard husband of hers – another arrogant prick.

The congregation spilt into the sunshine, heels sinking into the grass between crookedly aligned headstones, manicured hands clutching at hats and fascinators as a light breeze ruffled veils and plastered feathers onto lipstick. The men gathered, hands in pockets, exchanging bluff pleasantries.

All watched as the photographer positioned and fussed, bossing people into groups, squinting into his lens until he was happy, and another perfect picture was snapped.

Kevin stood with Amy, his sister, and Martin, patiently waiting his turn to be grist for the photographer's mill. He watched as Lili held out her arms to her pretty baby who gurgled and waved her arms in response, and saw Jake enfold his little family in a big, all-encompassing hug, his chin resting on Lili's head.

Pain shafted Kevin's heart and he turned away. He saw Daisy again across the crowd of morning suits and pastel, the look on her face making him pause, reconsider. She and her husband had been trying for children for as long as he had known her, but still nothing. He remembered how scared she had been of telling Guy it was a false alarm and wondered if he was still giving her a tough time about her failure to conceive.

Then, he was ushered forward by the photographer to clench his teeth in a forced smile, stand for endless photos, all the while praying for it to be over so he could get through the horror of the best man's speech and finally relax.

It was unfair, so unfair. Lili was her best friend. She loved her, knew how hard her life had been and was happy she now had everything she had ever dreamt of, but still ... in that instant when her baby wrapped her pudgy arms about Lili's neck, and her handsome, besotted husband pulled them into an embrace of obvious devoted love, Daisy hated Lili.

Hated her with an intense, brief passion that scared her with its violence. She didn't hate Lili, of course, she didn't, but she was jealous of her baby – her perfect, beautiful baby.

Glancing up at Guy, Daisy saw the look on his face and knew he had seen the proud father holding his tiny daughter in his arms. His mouth briefly twisted into a frustrated snarl and Daisy's heart sank.

Because they were away because it was a wedding and Guy adored weddings, just because, really ... she had hoped this weekend would be a break from the endless pressure of trying to conceive. She wondered if the ovulation kit were in his bag, knew without a doubt it would be, and her smile became brittle.

Thinking ahead to what would happen when they got back to their hotel suite, she decided to get horribly drunk at the reception, hoping the alcohol would numb the reality of enforced, loveless, meaningless, baby-making, sex.

Intrigued?
Chaining Daisy is available on Amazon
in paperback, eBook format, and is free to
read on Kindle Unlimited

About the Author

The multi-genre author Julia Blake lives in the beautiful historical town of Bury St. Edmunds, deep in the heart of the county of Suffolk in the UK, with her daughter, one crazy cat and a succession of even crazier lodgers.

Her first novel, The Book of Eve, met with worldwide critical acclaim, and since then, Julia has released ten other books which have delighted her growing number of readers with their strong plots and instantly relatable characters. Details of all Julia's novels can be found on the next page.

Julia leads a busy life, juggling working and family commitments with her writing, and has a strong internet presence, loving the close-knit and supportive community of fellow authors she has found on social media and promises there are plenty more books in the pipeline.

Julia says: "I write the kind of books I like to read myself, warm and engaging novels, with strong, three-dimensional characters you can connect with."

A Note from Julia

If you have enjoyed this book, why not take a few moments to leave a review on Amazon or Goodreads?

It needn't be much, just a few lines saying you liked the book and why, yet it can make a world of difference.

Reviews are the readers' way of letting the author know they enjoyed their book, and of letting other readers know the book is an enjoyable read and why. It also informs Amazon that this is a book worth promoting, and the more reviews a book receives, the more Amazon will recommend it to other readers.

I would be very grateful and would like to say thank you for reading my book and if you spare a few minutes of your time to review it, I do see, read, and appreciate every single review left for me.

Best Regards
Julia Blake

Other Books by the Author

The Perennials Series

Chaining Daisy – the shocking and gripping sequel to Becoming Lili
Rambling Rose – the sweeping conclusion

The Blackwood Family Saga

Fast-paced and heart-warming, this exciting series tells the story of the Blackwood Family and their search for love and happiness

The Book of Eve

A story of love, betrayal, and bitter secrets that threaten to rip a young woman's life apart

Black Ice

A magical steampunk retelling of the
Snow White story

The Forest
~ a tale of old magic ~

Myth, folklore, and magic combine in this engrossing tale
of a forgotten village and an ancient curse

Erinsmore

A wonderful tale of an enchanted land of sword and sorcery,
myth and magic, dragons, and prophecy

Eclairs for Tea
And Other Stories

A wonderful collection of short stories and quirky poems
that reflect the author's multi-genre versatility
Includes the award-winning novella – Lifesong

Printed in Great Britain
by Amazon